TEXAS HEAT

Fern Michaels

BALLANTINE BOOKS • NEW YORK

Library of Congress Catalog Card Number: 86-90841

ISBN 0-345-33100-1

Manufactured in the United States of America

First Edition: June 1986

In memory of Lucy Baker Koval, mother, grandmother, and friend.

ACKNOWLEDGMENT

It's true what they say about Texans; their hearts are as big as their wonderful state.

You invited me into your homes; you shared your lives, your families, your victories, and your secrets with me. Your warm hospitality, delightful humor, and unending assistance was greatly appreciated. My special time with you will always be remembered.

My sincere thanks to Eve and Houston Daniels; Helen and Rufus Abrams, Sharon and Mike Glazer and all those Texans who said, "Howdy, ma'am, welcome to Texas." Without all of you *Texas Rich* and *Texas Heat* would still be in outline form. I couldn't have done it without your inspiration.

Fern Michaels

The Coleman Family Tree

Seth Coleman
Born Jan. 22, 1892
Died July 30, 1970

Married
Sept. 9, 1915

Jessica Helen Connors Riley
Born May 9, 1896
Died Nov. 1, 1943

Amelia Edna Coleman
Born May 27, 1920

Married
July 5, 1941

Geoffrey Nelson
Born Sept. 7, 1917

Rand Nelson
Born Dec. 31, 1939
(Geoffrey's natural son)
(Amelia's adopted son)

Moss Seth Coleman
Born April 9, 1918
Died Jan. 12, 1974

Married
June 17, 1942

Willa (Billie) Ames Coleman
Born June 10, 1925

Margaret Jessica
Coleman
Born Feb. 4, 1943

Married
June 1, 1968

Cranston Tanner

Susan Amelia
Coleman
Born Feb. 6, 1944

Married
July 9, 1966

Jerome de Moray

Riley Seth Coleman
Born Sept. 2, 1945
Died Oct. 19, 1969

Married
June 8, 1967

Otami Hasegawa
Born Nov. 21, 1949
Died April 11, 1983

Sawyer Coleman
Born March 6, 1956

Coleman Peter Tanner
Born April 2, 1969

Jessica Margaret de Moray
Born Feb. 14, 1985

Riley Shadaharu Coleman
Born Sept. 18, 1969

{{{{{{{{ PROLOGUE }}}}}}}}

Sawyer Coleman watched the patterns the lazy California sun created on her cluttered desk. It had been weeks now since she'd seen the shiny cherrywood surface. Papers were strewn into haphazard piles, pencils with broken points, pens with chewed tops, all signs of overwork and frustration. She really should hire an assistant, someone to help with the load, but no one had ever satisfied her and she loathed having to check and recheck someone else's work. She had admitted to herself a long time ago that she was a workaholic, but lately she seemed to meet herself coming and going.

Heaving a sigh, Sawyer ran her long, manicured fingers through her wealth of golden-blond hair. There was no getting away from it; the work had to be done, and she was the best one for the job. Coleman Aviation was a family-held enterprise, a leader in manufacturing and designing small private jet planes, and she was the only one with the background and education to handle the growing company.

There were those about her, in the outer offices, who said Sawyer was too dedicated, too persnickety. She'd just heard that one the other day. Persnickety, for God's sake. The only thing she was certain of was that it wasn't complimentary.

Sawyer rummaged in her top drawer for cigarettes and lit one. She rarely smoked, usually only in tense situations

1

or as a ploy to stall for time. She was doing both now.
Stalling because she didn't want to look at the invitation
a second time, and tense because she hadn't heard from
Rand in over two weeks. That alone was enough to make
her itchy. Add that to Maggie's invitation and she could
become a basket case within the hour.

Mother Maggie. Maggie, mistress of Sunbridge.
Maggie the man-eater. Maggie, her own mother. Sawyer
grimaced.

She was up and out of her chair, smoothing the soft
gray flannel skirt over her trim hips. At the window she
fixed her gaze on the bright ball in the sky. Aztec gold,
she thought inanely as she puffed furiously on the cigarette she didn't want. The invitation was for a command
appearance, a return to Sunbridge to watch Maggie preen.
But there was more to it. Maggie needed the family's
approval to take the helm. Bad girl Maggie returns to the
scene of her crime but is forgiven. Sawyer laughed and
choked on the cigarette smoke, sputtering until tears came
to her eyes.

Grand would probably call soon, by tomorrow the
latest. Then the others. And Rand, she thought with sudden hope, yes, Rand would call. Long-distance relationships were hell, overseas relationships even worse.

Damn, now her whole day was ruined. Why couldn't
Maggie have sent the invitation and her chatty little bull-
crap letter to the apartment instead of the office? Com-
munication with Maggie shouldn't be so upsetting after
all these years, but it was. She wished she had a hide too
thick for Maggie to penetrate. What she did have was a
sore, bruised heart that would never heal.

Family reunions should be outlawed. There was no
way she could escape the invitation. She'd just have to
put a good face on it. Seeing young Riley again would be
worth a confrontation with Maggie. And to see Rand and
spend time with him, she'd travel to Africa if necessary.

Rand. Her life, her love. Without Rand in her life, there
would be nothing but endless days of work and endless

nights alone. It was time to think about settling down, time to think seriously about marriage. Just the thought excited her and made her feel warm all over. Her work could be done just as well in London.

Quickly, before she could change her mind, she scrawled a note of acceptance to the July fourth bash. Later, when it was all over, the family would all say what a good sport Sawyer was. Good old Sawyer. Sawyer didn't bleed red blood like everyone else. Sawyer just hurt and ached inside, but the wounds didn't show.

Having Rand to herself would make up for everything. Just his smile would drive Maggie from her thoughts. Rand was all she needed, now and forever.

{{{{{{{{ CHAPTER ONE }}}}}}}}

Today would be one of Sunbridge's finest hours. Tomorrow's newspapers would carry each detail, right down to what the waitresses were wearing. When Sunbridge had a party, it was news, but when Sunbridge hosted a Texas-style barbecue, it was even bigger news. The family would come, and an impressive showing of some of Texas's most influential people. Maggie Coleman Tanner's smile widened. Funny the way she always personified Sunbridge, as though it were a living entity. In some ways it was. Sunbridge had been her past, and now it would be her future.

Maggie's eyes, blue as the winter sky, took in the flurry of activity below the bedroom balcony. Servants, caterers, waitresses—a whole passel of them, as old Seth would say—were getting *her* first barbecue under way. The fatted calf, the return of the prodigal child, Maggie thought. She herself was the prodigal, but could a prize longhorn steer qualify as a fatted calf?

She had ordered red-and-white checkered picnic cloths and matching napkins from Neiman Marcus by the dozens. She also vaguely recalled ordering two hundred wicker bread baskets that went for forty bucks a shot. Lobster flown in from Maine, shrimp, crab, and beef, all the accoutrements of a successful bash. The theme might be "country," but there wasn't anything provincial about her guests' tastes. It would be her way of showing them all that she was one of them, that the years she'd lived in New York hadn't been spent under a rock. She'd traveled in sophisticated circles where conversations centered on the theater, the stock market, and the new exhibit at the Guggenheim—conversations in the abstract. Here in Texas, the topics were more to the point—money, oil, beef, and more money, and not necessarily in that order. The crystal wineglasses winked up at her in the bright sunlight, reminding her that while Texans liked to pretend a "down-home" style of living, they were all smart enough and rich enough to know Baccarat from Cristal d'Arques.

Old Grandpap was probably turning over in his grave. His idea of a barbecue was beer on tap and red beans and rice, his patronizing attempt at being a "common man who made good." No one would have dared criticize if he'd chosen to serve good bourbon in paper cups; Seth Coleman was too important and influential to offend. On a whim, he could make or break a man and his fortunes, and there was no telling when the old codger would take it into his head to lead you to ruin just for the hell of it.

Things were different now. Old Seth was dead and buried and Maggie was mistress of Sunbridge. This party was just a way of driving that point home. Home. God, it felt wonderful to be back at Sunbridge. No, that was wrong. It felt wonderful to finally *belong* at Sunbridge.

All her invitations had been accepted; everyone would be here—half of Texas, not that she gave a damn about them, and the family.

Maggie leaned over the railing. This party was costing a fortune and she wasn't even truly certain why she was throwing it. What was she trying to prove, and to whom? Living here, holding the deed, that was the real proof of who was the owner of Sunbridge. Why did she feel this need to flaunt her ownership? Or was it really because she needed to show the world that she'd finally won her father's approval, that Pap had thought enough of her in the end to leave his beloved Sunbridge to her, and to no one else? By God, Sunbridge was her birthright! Sawyer had taken it away from her. Her daughter had lived at Sunbridge almost her entire life, while she, Maggie, had been banished. Now Sawyer would be returning as a guest in Maggie's home. That had to be some kind of divine justice.

Maggie stared off into the distance at the softly rising knoll overlooking the front of the house. All the white cross-fencing and rich golden meadows belonged to Sunbridge. A possessive heat blazed in her. This was Coleman land, her land, and it was alive again because she was home again. She could feel the power of this place. Two hundred and fifty thousand acres of prime land, Coleman land, and she would make it grow and prosper and flourish. She could almost understand what had kept old Seth going all those years. It was Sunbridge, the vigor of the land beating through his veins. His authority had gone unchallenged; he'd been supreme ruler, the invincible force that had built it and loved it and mastered it. Seth, meanest old man who ever took a breath, mean enough to depose his own grandchild. Sunbridge had been meant to go from Seth to his son Moss and then to his grandson Riley. Her sister Susan and she were insignificant females, worthless to him. "Do you see me now, old man?" she said, focusing on the gently sloping knoll where he was buried. "I'm here now, where I belong, where I've always belonged."

Coleman Tanner, Maggie's son, walked on cat's feet to stand behind his mother. He knew he could wait there for an hour and she wouldn't be aware of him until she turned and actually saw him. It was only Sunbridge, this place, that interested her. All her talk of his belonging, of hanging his Stetson on the peg near the front door beside those of his great-grandfather, grandfather, and uncle, was just bullshit. The hat was dumb, just like everything else in Texas. When he did wear it, it was only to humor her. Half the time he didn't know where it was, but somehow his mother always managed to find it and hang it on its appropriate peg.

Coleman was never certain if he should intrude upon his mother when she was alone like this. "Alone" wasn't quite the word to describe these moods of hers, when she seemed to close herself in with her thoughts. Insulated would be closer to the truth—insulated against everything outside herself, including her own son. When he was younger, it used to hurt and wound him; now it only made him mad. At school, the other boys would comment on how beautiful she was—gleaming dark hair worn just above her shoulders, falling softly around her face to contrast sharply with her crystal blue eyes. He'd even seen some of his instructors watching her slim figure when they thought no one was looking. And there was no smile like his mother's smile—open, bright, and genuine. When she laughed, her eyes would sparkle and the corners of her mouth would turn up and crinkle. She was beautiful —Coleman had always thought her so—but none of that beauty belonged to him. She was a stranger, and it had been so long since she'd smiled for him, really for him.

Coleman wasn't certain what Maggie was thinking about, but he did know her thoughts weren't on him. She hadn't even been available to pick him up from the airport when he'd returned from school three days ago. Some anonymous chauffeur had met him promptly upon his arrival, instead. She'd explained by saying she'd lost all track of time, what with planning the party and everything. On and on she'd explained, and he'd let her. He liked it when she got flustered and tried to apologize for something she thought she'd done wrong. That meant he could usually get what he wanted out of her without hardly trying.

Cole was growing and, in time, promised to be taller than any of the Colemans, thanks to his father. His eyes and nose were Cranston Tanner's, the father he rarely saw, but his strong chin and square white teeth and wide, generous smile came from his mother's side of the family. Maybe his feet, too, but no one seemed certain. A size-thirteen shoe at the age of sixteen was something no one wanted to discuss. He wore his light brown hair close to the head, in a military butch, and he thought it made him look like a boiled owl. But his mother said he looked just like the pictures of her father when he had finished boot camp.

Cole wondered when he'd gain weight. Lean instead of slim, they'd put him on a bodybuilding regimen at school, but so far it didn't seem to be working, no matter how much he busted his hump. He did it because it was required of him, just like he did everything at that rotten school. He hated it, hated the regimentation, the other boys, the uniform, the instructors, and the pomp and circumstance, yet he excelled in everything. Once, the major had told his mother he was the nearest to a perfect student he'd ever seen.

Maggie had done her motherly duty and smiled and sort of hugged him. But she didn't really give a damn, Cole thought. She was just concerned with appearances. Get rid of the kid, pay the duty calls and the bills, and then turn on the mother act for vacations. Like now. Fourth of July. Barbecue time. A real Sunbridge shindig, she was calling it. He'd heard about them for years, but he'd never attended one. He wasn't sure he wanted to be here now. He felt like an intruder. This would never be his.

He was expected to dress Western; that's what Maggie

called it. Western-cut jeans and shirts and boots that pinched his toes. That pissed him off. Wearing a military uniform ten months of the year was bad enough, and now he had to wear another costume. Nothing made him feel like himself, not the uniform or this dude ranch crap. He wanted to pick out his own clothes, like his Brooks Brothers tassled loafers and the other designer things that hung in his closet, things he seldom got to wear.

"For someone who's about to throw the biggest party in Texas, you look worried, Mother," Coleman said suddenly.

Maggie whirled. "Coleman! You startled me. . . . And how many times have I asked you to call me Mam? You used to, when you were a little boy."

She was jabbing at him. It was always like this; he saw it as her way of keeping him at a distance. Never answer a question directly; never say what you were thinking. Instead, launch the attack. But why was he the enemy?

"It's probably hereditary. You insist on calling me Coleman, when you know that Cole is the name I prefer. I've told you enough times." Coleman's voice was deep, and always shocked Maggie these days. Somehow it didn't go with his gangling youth.

"Touché. It's just that you *are* a Coleman, and I don't want either of us, or anyone else for that matter, to forget it."

"How could *you* forget? It's all you ever talk about or think about. I know you'll take back the Coleman name when the divorce becomes final. Don't worry about it, Mother. Everyone knows who we are; changing your name isn't going to prove a thing." Coleman's voice was accusing; a smirk twitched at the corner of his mouth.

Maggie appraised her son. He was a Coleman—not in looks, but certainly in his ability to cut straight through to the quick. She knew he was reminding her of her alcohol dependency, of her failures as a mother, and saying that nothing, neither Sunbridge nor changing her name, would ever erase those facts. He was a boy, she reminded herself. What did he know? She grimaced. At his age she'd been older than Methuselah and more knowing. At his age she'd already given birth to Sawyer, who had reaped all the benefits she and her son had been denied. Until now. Things were going to be very different with her in charge. Somehow she had to make Coleman understand, make him see that this was where his roots were.

"This is where I belong, son, and so do you. Sunbridge was built for the Colemans."

"Maybe for you, Mother, but not for me. My name is Tanner and it always will be. This is just a place, not a way of life—not my life, anyway." There was anger in his gray eyes, carefully restrained bitterness in his tone. "I don't like Texas and this hokey cowboy crap. I don't like the clothes you make me wear and that stupid hat. I don't want to be here; I want to go to Europe."

"You want to do *what*?" Maggie shrilled.

Cole snorted, his fine brows arching upward. "I thought as much. Don't you *ever* read the notices they send from school? My French class is going to Europe till the end of August. I signed up and even paid the deposit."

Maggie turned back to the balcony to hide her confusion. For a long moment she watched the activity taking place below. Vaguely, she remembered something about a trip. But she hadn't given her permission; of that she was certain. Why did he have to bring this up now, when she was preoccupied with her family and herself? Her eyes narrowed. Was it possible there was more of Pap in her son than she realized? This sudden announcement in the midst of an argument was like something her father would have pulled. If she gave Coleman her permission to go to Europe, he'd be perfectly behaved at her party, showing family and friends their close, loving relationship. He'd be the perfect son and grandson, warm to Amelia and charming to Susan. He'd pretend to be Sawyer's adoring half brother. But if she didn't play his game, this cranky, selfish son of hers would show his true colors.

It wasn't fair! Why couldn't she make him see that all

this was for him, too, to make him a part of the family, to lay his birthright at his feet? This was her party—she'd chosen the Fourth of July weekend for the barbecue to symbolize her freedom from the past, her own independence. She couldn't allow a sixteen-year-old boy to spoil it for her. She turned to face Coleman, watching him, knowing he was waiting her out, confident he would win, as always. Not this time, she thought. There were new rules now. "Why don't I take this matter under consideration and let you know my decision *after* the party?"

Coleman bristled. He hadn't expected this, and he understood perfectly. Behave, act the perfect son, and maybe, just maybe, she'd give him permission for the trip. He didn't like it, but he was caught, trapped, and he would have to play the game by her rules. He nodded, giving his agreement, and knew he was dismissed when his mother's eyes returned to the scene below.

Coleman left the room, closing the door behind him. She'd have her way—for the time being, at least. But if she thought she'd keep him here at Sunbridge, trapped under her thumb and exchanging the excitement of a trip to Europe for "down-home" living, sweating horses, and ignorant Texans, she had another think coming.

She wanted him to belong to Sunbridge. He'd never belonged anywhere except military school. He used to feel ashamed that his parents had no time for him, that they didn't want him around, until he'd realized the other boys had almost identical problems. Once his adviser had convinced him he could become a man, a real soldier, without his parents, he'd felt better. "Be independent; heft that gun, soldier. You're ten years old now. Act like a man."

After that, Coleman didn't cry into his pillow at night when his shoulder hurt from carrying the heavy rifle. He'd suffered the black-and-blue marks from the rifle's kick during target practice without a whimper. He'd worked himself up in rank, becoming one of the youngest platoon leaders, forcing himself and his men to do extra marches, score higher marks, achieve more awards.

By the time he was twelve, he'd been promoted twice. Rank, he discovered early on, carried untold privileges, and he'd learned to use each and every one to his own advantage. He knew how to wheel and deal, to hustle the lower classmen and strike fear into the skinny little boys with their glasses and protruding teeth. Coleman liked power. At the end of the term he was acknowledged as the undisputed head of E Wing, Zone five. Now, how was it going to look if he didn't go on this European trip because his mommy said no?

When Cole closed the door behind him, Maggie's shoulders slumped. She couldn't allow him to ruin things for her, but she couldn't give in to him, either. He was still a child, looking to her for direction and challenging her at the same time. Coleman was so different from her younger brother, Riley. At sixteen, Riley had been warm and caring, his gentle, unspoiled nature and charismatic charm attracting people to him. Anyone who knew Riley loved him. He'd been all the things her son wasn't and probably never would be.

Maggie didn't need anyone to tell her where she'd failed Coleman. Caught up in her own life, her own despairs, she'd never really been there for him. How could she have handled a small boy's problems when she hadn't been able to cope with her own? And her marriage to Cranston had been on a downhill slide for the past seven years. She'd hung on, telling herself that she had to keep the family together for Coleman's sake. In truth, she'd hung on so long because there was nowhere else to go, no one else to go to. *That* Maggie Coleman Tanner hadn't liked herself very much, and her low self-esteem had only added to her fears of being alone. As long as Cranston hadn't made any moves to end their marriage, neither had she. But at last her self-loathing had spilled over onto Cranston, and after she'd started drinking too much as well, he'd left her.

Maggie shook her head as though to clear it. She didn't

want to think about all that now, not today. She'd come
a long way from that desperate, unhappy woman. She
was still uncertain about this new person she wanted to
become, but she'd taken long strides. Pap leaving Sunbridge to her had done that—given her a kind of assurance
that she did belong somewhere, that she was loved, that
she hadn't been overlooked by the one person who'd been
more important to her than any other. Pap. All her life
she'd wanted his approval, his love. She'd been such a
mixed-up kid and then such a hostile, mixed-up woman.
But she was determined to change all that, and now, for
the first time, she felt success was within her grasp. No,
she wouldn't think about Coleman now; she wouldn't let
anything spoil this day.

The colorful Japanese lanterns strung around the front
yard were perfect. They wound in and out of Grandmam
Jessica's rose garden and down toward the long, winding
drive. They'd be lighted at dusk; just as the guests began
to arrive. That's when the orchestra would begin to play,
and later on, when the food was served, the piano player
would pound out Scott Joplin tunes in accompaniment to
a banjo. Billie would probably choke when she saw the
ice sculpture of a rearing stallion where champagne would
cascade through transparent tubes. Maggie shrugged.
Tacky, of course, but expected. It would keep Austin
buzzing for weeks.

The hot July sun beat down with merciless intensity,
and she was glad she'd chosen the colorful striped tent
awnings that sprawled across the lawns. It all looked so
gay. Funny how something as banal as acres of yellow-
and-white canvas could make her feel so good. The surprise of the evening would be the special fireworks that
would be displayed over the pond behind the house. Even
Coleman would approve of the millions of starbursts that
would light up Sunbridge at midnight.

A stray breeze caressed Maggie's shoulder. Soon it
would be time to dress for the family's arrival. She planned
to wear one of her mother's original designs, a Christmas

gift. She loved the filmy rainbow creation and had been saving it for a special occasion. Wait till Mam saw her. Billie's eyes would light and she'd smile that warm, loving smile.

When Maggie had first gotten the idea for this party, she'd never realized it would become so important to her. For weeks now she'd lived with only one thought—the reunion. Even Coleman's homecoming had taken second place to the business of preparing Sunbridge for today. She'd had to send a chauffeur to the airport to meet Coleman instead of driving in herself; then she'd been late getting home from town and had missed his arrival. When she had at last returned home, he'd waved lazily in her general direction and gone back to reading his book. She did go up and hug him, but he'd been stiff and unyielding, punishing her for her oversight. She'd made a mental note to work harder at her relationship with Coleman, but he resisted her so, and rejection still came hard to Maggie.

Perhaps young Riley would be a steadying influence on Coleman. She was eager to see her brother's son. Not long ago she would have had to admit that she wanted him here to assuage the guilt she felt over her brother's death. But now she knew she wanted to share some part of Sunbridge with Riley. He was her nephew and a member of the family.

She remembered the day Billie had called to tell her Otami had been killed in an automobile accident in Tokyo. All the old guilt had come rushing back then, until she'd literally been sick to her stomach. First Riley and then his lovely Japanese wife. Only young Riley was left. His Japanese grandparents had taught Maggie something about unselfishness and generosity. Immersed as they were in their grief, it would have been understandable for them to keep Riley all to themselves. Instead, they wanted him to come to America to take his place as a Coleman, to become a part of his heritage. Wisely, they realized they wouldn't live forever. What would become of their precious grandson after they'd gone? "For as long as he needs to be there," Billie had said. It was more than all right with Maggie. The last time she'd seen the boy, she'd seen how much he resembled his father. And she'd been terribly flattered that Billie would trust her to care for Riley, the only child of her only son.

A sudden breeze, stronger and different in character from before, chilled Maggie. Nothing, not even an act of God or nature, was going to spoil this party. She looked to the sky, still crystal-blue, only a rare puffy white cloud scudding across the horizon.

Maggie was feeling restless; and the confrontation with Coleman hadn't helped. She glanced at her watch; it was still too early to dress. On a sudden impulse, she kicked off her high-heeled sandals and ran through the house and outside, heading for the stables in search of Lotus, her favorite mare.

Lotus nickered in anticipation of a run when she recognized Maggie. Maggie bridled the roan and led her to the mounting post. She hiked up her skirt, straddled Lotus's satiny back, dug her bare heels into the mare's flanks, and was off. A startled groom stared after her, then shrugged. Lotus needed a run.

Maggie took Lotus at a fast canter, following the white cross-fencing circumventing the back corrals and pastures, taking the full circuit until they approached the knoll overlooking the front acres of Sunbridge. Lotus knew her way, head held erect with confidence, obeying the urgings of her mistress.

Once upon the knoll, Maggie slid from Lotus's back. First it was her grandmother Jessica she visited. Then it was Seth, and then Agnes. Pap was always last. The best was always saved for last.

While Lotus cropped the fresh green grass, Maggie went to Jessica's headstone, reaching out to follow the deeply chiseled letters of her name. She'd never really known her grandmother; Jessica had died when Maggie was only an infant, but Billie had often mentioned what a kind and gentle soul she'd been. Seth would grumpily agree with Billie, then add his own interpretation. "Timid is what she was, no grit!" Seth, cantankerous old man who'd ruled Sunbridge with an iron hand. Dead now, but never forgotten. Maggie grimaced when she looked to the left of his tombstone. Nessie, Seth's first horse, and then Nessie II and then Nessie III. It was obscene that three horses should rest in the family cemetery, but Seth would have it no other way, and no one else seemed to mind. Maggie had no fond memories of any of them—not Jessica, whom she'd never known; not Seth, who had condemned and banished her; not Agnes, who'd been a flesh-and-blood buzz saw with no one else's interests at heart but her own. Yet each of them had shaped Sunbridge, Maggie knew; each had left an indelible mark.

Pap. Tears pricked her eyes as she dropped to her knees. Idly, she picked at a weed and tossed it onto Seth's grave. Her father, her own Pap, was the real reason she came here. Here she talked and visited and felt more welcome in his presence than she ever had when he was alive. There were times when she'd spend hours here talking to her father, working things through in her mind. It was Pap's last act that had turned her life around; he'd given Sunbridge to her.

"Listen, Pap," she said, "this is my day. I think I'm finally going to make it. Giving me Sunbridge made me back up and take a second look at Maggie Coleman Tanner. Did I tell you I'm taking our name back when my divorce comes through? Well, I am. And about this shindig today, I don't know where the idea came from, but I think it's one of my best. The whole family is coming and I'm sure they'll all be trooping by here, so keep an eye out for them.

"And I'd appreciate it if you'd accept young Riley. He is one of us, you know, and I think you also know by now that life's too short to waste on old grudges and stupid prejudice. Riley loved Otami and together they had this wonderful boy. You cheated us all, especially Mam, when

you didn't tell us you knew Riley had a wife and son.
Wherever you are, be kind and gentle in your thoughts
of all of us, especially Riley. You know I'm still carrying
this guilt around with me. I could have stopped my brother
from running off to join the navy, but I encouraged him
because I knew it would hurt you. I should have stopped
him, but I didn't. You didn't do a lot of things, either.
Maybe I can make up for it now, just the way you tried
to do by leaving me Sunbridge. I know, you always thought
I was a rebel, freethinking and independent. Well, I'm
not. I'm so damned insecure I get sick inside. How come
you never knew that?

"Hey, Pap, do me a favor, will you? Tell my brother
I'm going to make things right for his son. The way you
did for me. I love you, Pap. Tell Riley I love him, too."

Maggie, her eyes glistening, brought her hand to her
lips and then gently touched the tombstone.

{{{{{{{{{ CHAPTER TWO }}}}}}}}}

Home to Sunbridge. Billie rested her head against the
back of the seat, her soft hazel eyes half closed against
the sun's glare. She watched Thad at the wheel as he
handled a bend in the road. Driving an automobile was
as natural to him as flying a plane; both were done with
an economy of movement and the same enjoyment. She
could see the sharp bridge of his nose and his gentle gray
eyes, eyes that were always ready to brighten with laughter or reveal the depths of his love. The first time she'd

met him, so long ago in Philadelphia, she'd thought his eyes were his nicest feature, softening his chiseled, craggy features and echoing his smile.

Thad Kingsley hadn't changed much over the years. His mellow gold hair was paled with gray now, but he still had that same burnished tan. He carried his height with dignity and he was still military fit and trim. Despite the fact that he was a world traveler, his voice still carried the hint of a crisp New England accent, the vowels slightly flat. Now that he was again living in his home state of Vermont, his accent had deepened, become more a part of him.

When she'd first told Thad of Maggie's phone call inviting them to this Fourth of July party, he'd grinned and said, "When do we leave?" Just like that. No matter what he was doing, Thad would stop on a dime to do something that was important to her. Dear Thad. God, what if she hadn't opened her eyes in time and listened to her heart? What would have become of her?

A rolling tumbleweed skittered across the road. Billie noticed Thad didn't bother to brake. The weed was out of sight by the time the rental car sailed down the road.

Texas. Land of the rich and powerful. She realized now she'd never liked it, not really. She'd never belonged. It was too vast, too high-powered for her. She liked living in Vermont in the two-hundred-year-old farmhouse they'd modernized with a hot tub, a spanking new kitchen, and a greenhouse. The guest cottage had been converted into a studio for her, but she found she was using it less and less these days. Licensing out her trademark name of *Billie* had brought her all the money she could ever hope to need. She enjoyed being sought after to design a special pattern or fabric for one of her rich, famous clients. Sometimes she obliged and sometimes she didn't. It all depended upon what Thad was doing and how much free time he had. They were a unit, a twosome. She loved her life and wouldn't change it for all the Sunbridges in the world. Billie Coleman Kingsley had found her place in this world and the one person she wanted to share it with, Thad.

"We're almost there," he said softly, breaking the silence. He removed his hand from the wheel and placed it on her silken leg. "You can handle it, can't you, Billie?"

She heard the anxiety in her husband's voice. "Thad, I can handle anything, even those nine puppies of Duchess's we left behind. This is a visit. Of course there are memories here for me, but that's exactly what they are—memories—and they belong to the past. Promise me you won't worry about me."

"I promise." He patted her leg reassuringly, then put his hand back on the wheel. "Are you worried that Maggie is up to something?" he asked.

"I admit it crossed my mind, but it's not fair to Maggie, is it? Why do we always expect people to remain the same and never change? We all change, don't we, Thad?"

He took his eyes off the road for a moment to grin at her. "Not you, Billie. You're still the same girl I met at the USO dance in Philadelphia. You're still the angel on my Christmas tree."

Billie flushed beneath the intimacy of his voice. "Life changes all of us, and that includes Maggie. I think she just wants to see us all under the same roof and wants us all to know she's happy at last. How could I deny her this visit? I'm her mother. Even if—and I don't believe it's the case—even if Maggie had an ulterior motive and I knew about it, I'd still have come. She asked us. She didn't manipulate or demand; it was a hopeful invitation. I wanted to come for Maggie. It's been a long while since I've seen her. We talk on the phone, but that's hardly the same thing."

"The gathering of the clan. I like the idea. Families are important," Thad said quietly.

"My one regret, darling, is that I couldn't give you children. If only I'd been stronger, reached out for what I knew I wanted sooner, there might have been time for us."

"And I've told you a hundred times, having children

was never important to me." He reached for her hand
and squeezed. "You've always shared your children with
me, and in a large way, I feel Sawyer belongs to us. As
long as I have you, that's what's important. You promised
you weren't going to mention that ever again."

"And I meant it. If this invitation hadn't come up, I'd
have stuck to my word. This is quite a family, the Colemans. Of course there will be outsiders, like Amelia's
husband—" Billie threw her hands into her lap. "You see
what I'm doing? I'm just like these Texans; I guess it's
become ingrained after living with Seth for all those years.
I'm decreeing who belongs and who doesn't. Old Seth
always called you that 'Yankee cracker,' warning Moss
to 'Watch out, boy, or that Yankee'll get the better of
you.'

"I worry about young Riley, Thad. I know how Sunbridge can devour a life. I know how it can suck out the
fine things like loyalty and courage and devotion. This is
a demanding place, taking the best and spitting out anything that doesn't measure up."

"Don't forget Sawyer. She was born and raised at Sunbridge, and it hasn't done her any harm."

"That's because I was older and wiser then with my
own children when I took Sawyer into my care. I was
strong for her; I protected her and saw to it that her values
weren't confused."

Thad was silent for a moment. They'd had this conversation before, and Billie had mentioned that she was
nervous about Sawyer coming to Sunbridge. Maggie and
her daughter had been apart for too many years; the hurts
and wounds ran too deep, Billie said. He wondered if
Sawyer would have accepted the invitation if she weren't
bringing young Riley in from Japan.

As if reading his mind, Billie said, "In many ways
Sawyer and Riley are alike. Two little orphans coming
home to Sunbridge. Sawyer was terribly shaken by Otami's death. They'd become very good friends, you know.
There was no time to prepare for what happened, if it's

ever possible to prepare for a death. One second Otami was alive and the next she was gone. A drunk driver and a life is gone, one we all treasured." Billie wiped her eyes.

Thad could feel a lump in his own throat. When the news of Otami's death reached them in Vermont, Billie had wanted to fly to Japan immediately. But when he'd called the Hasegawas, they'd urged him to stay in Vermont and to allow them to handle their grief in private. Thad had understood and tried to make Billie understand.

"I wouldn't worry too much about Sawyer, Billie. That young woman is doing just fine. She's successful, charming, and beautiful, and your granddaughter. And she's in love."

Billie was silent for a long time, her thoughts on the family. She *was* worried about Sawyer. Thad was wrong. For all her sophistication and intelligence, Sawyer was as vulnerable as a child, still believing that everyone was going to live happily ever after. There had been very few disappointments and little unhappiness in Sawyer's life.

"Billie? Did you hear me?" Thad broke into her thoughts. "I said not to worry about Sawyer."

"I heard. And I'm not worried about her business capabilities; she more than proved herself as an aeronautical engineer. I don't know what's actually bothering me. Perhaps I'm being foolish, but I can't help it."

Thad laughed. "Hey, listen, I'll never ignore your intuition again. When you said Duchess was going to have her puppies on Monday night and then woke me at three in the morning to tell me mother and all nine daughters were doing fine, you made a believer out of me! If things look like they might turn sticky between Sawyer and Maggie, I'll just remind them who I am."

"And who's that?"

"Fleet Admiral Thaddeus Kingsley, Retired, now farmer and horse breeder."

Billie giggled. "That should certainly impress them. Aren't you going to tell them that the politicals in Vermont want you to run for Congress next time around?"

"Naah, that sounds too much like bragging. People who live in Texas don't care about Vermont, unless of course their maple syrup is slow in arriving. Let's not mention it."

"I won't, but I think it's wonderful. The United States Congress!" Not for the world would Billie let Thad know the idea scared the daylights out of her. She didn't want to live in a Washington fishbowl. And she didn't want her husband compromising his principles, as she knew most politicians were forced to do eventually. But if it was what Thad wanted, she'd back him all the way.

Thad was saved from replying. "We're here."

Billie raised her eyes. There it was, the high wooden arch with the name Sunbridge emblazoned on it. Miles of white fencing stretched into the distance; tall oak trees arched over the winding drive; and behind them was an expanse of bright green lawn dotted with sprinklers pulsing rhythmically.

Billie always felt as though she were traveling through a tunnel of dappled green. The drive ahead of them sparkled with reflected sunshine, and when they made the final turn, the house came into view.

Thad braked the car, as much for himself as for Billie. Both of them sat for a moment, still captivated, still awed after all these years, at the sight of Sunbridge.

Sitting upon a gently sloping rise, the great house basked beneath the blue Texas sky and was caressed by the sun. Billie had once thought that only here, in this place, could the sun seem so warm and golden. In Vermont, she'd learned the same sun was warmer, even more golden

The house was a three-story brick of the palest pink, flanked by two wings that were also three stories, but set back from the main body. This expanse of prairie rose was accented by white columns that supported the roof of a sweeping veranda. A multipaned fan light crested the huge double front door, and the design was replicated in miniature over each window on the top floor. Ornamental topiary trees and crape myrtle hugged the foundation, and surrounding the house was a magnificent rose garden complete with trellises and statuary.

"In the old days, Thad, this was called 'a spread'—at least that's what Seth called it. I can still hear him boasting, 'Two hundred and fifty thousand acres of prime land!'"

Thad laughed. "I can almost hear the old bastard. And to think that he built this all himself—the son of an itinerant sharecropper, a boy with no education, only good sense and a talent for ruthlessness."

"Sunbridge," Billie said softly. "It's the perfect name for it. Even Jessica told me she was amazed by Seth's poetic turn of thought when he named it. He always said he felt as though he could reach up and touch the sun from here. I never felt that way, but I'm sure Maggie does."

Thad reached over and slid the back of his hand down Billie's silky cheek. "What say we get this show on the road, Mrs. Kingsley?"

"Sounds good to me!" Thad could always make the darkest moment bright again. God, she loved him.

Maggie stood beneath the portico, waiting. She'd felt lightheaded from the moment she'd heard the sound of a car coming up the drive. Who would arrive first? She strained to make out the passengers. Mam! And Thad! Thank God.

The car had almost come to a stop when she realized Coleman wasn't beside her. She'd called out to him on her way down the stairs, but he hadn't followed her. No matter—there'd be time for Coleman later. Mam was here! Mam had come to visit her at Sunbridge.

Billie was out of the car and up the steps, her arms outstretched. Thad watched from his position inside the car. He reached for one of their bags. It was all right; everything was going to be all right.

"Mam, you're stunning! The most beautiful mother in all Texas. Did you design that silk dress yourself?"

Billie nodded shyly as she noticed Maggie's silk lounging outfit. "Didn't I give that to you for Christmas? Let's see . . . how many years ago?"

Maggie laughed. "I don't deal in those kinds of numbers anymore. You're right, though; this is one of yours. I'd bet the rent that everyone in the family will be wearing a Billie Original today."

"You look wonderful, Maggie. You look happy."

"I am, Mam, really happy. Come inside. Coleman— he wants to be called Cole—will be down in a minute. Thad, come along. You must be thirsty."

Billie approached the door. Everything was the same. The ethereal grace of Jessica's rose garden and the feminine sweep of the pink clematis vine softened the heavy, masculine-looking oak doors, made them seem more welcoming. Inside would be the same, Billie suspected; Maggie wouldn't have changed a thing. Shining oaken floors, massive beams studding the first-floor ceilings, thick dark Oriental carpets, and man-sized leather furniture. It all bore Seth's stamp; Jessica's influence was nowhere apparent on the first floor of the house. Only outside and in the bedrooms could her whimsical and very feminine hand be felt. Billie imagined for a second that she could smell Seth's cigar smoke. The great house of Sunbridge, Coleman domain. No, nothing had changed, and she doubted it ever would.

Maggie embraced Thad affectionately. The tall man smiled down at her. Amazing how coming home to a pile of stone and brick could affect a person, he thought, how a true sense of belonging could bring out the best. "Just point me in the right direction," he said, indicating the piece of luggage, "and I'll be back before you know it."

"Top of the stairs, second door to the left," Maggie said easily. "And if you see Cole up there, tell him it's time for him to come downstairs. Someone will see to bringing the rest of your things upstairs and parking the car down by the garages."

Billie felt her breath explode in a loud sigh. She turned to look at her daughter.

Maggie flinched. "Mam, you didn't think I'd put you and Thad in your and Pap's old bedroom, did you?"

"I . . . I wasn't sure," Billie answered hesitantly. It was exactly what she'd thought.

As though reading her mind, Maggie tilted her head and smiled shyly. "Friends, Mam?"

Billie wrapped her arms around her daughter. "Always and forever, darling."

"We've had some rough times, and some things can never be fixed. Someday I want to sit down and talk. Maybe to apologize, maybe to try and explain . . ."

"It isn't necessary, Maggie. All I've ever wanted was for you to be happy. That's all any mother really wants for her children. Sometimes we make mistakes along the way, but if the intentions are good, somehow they right themselves in the end."

Maggie's eyes were bright with unshed tears. "I'm being selfish; you've had a long trip and must want to freshen up, too. I'll be out on the patio. I hope that scamp Cole didn't run off on me. He says he doesn't like parties."

Billie laughed. "I can remember a party or two that his mother managed to wriggle out of."

Maggie grimaced after Billie left the room. Where the hell was Cole, anyway? She wanted to show him off, but she was still worried that he'd do something to embarrass her. Billie's reminder of how often she'd refused to attend family events was grim. She crossed her fingers. The boy would behave; she'd see to it. She decided the kitchen with its array of tempting food was the logical place to look for him.

"Martha, have you seen Cole?" she asked the buxom cook, who looked up from chopping vegetables.

"No, Mrs. Tanner, he hasn't been in here."

"I thought he might be in here filching a Coke or something."

It was on the tip of Martha's tongue to suggest that Cole might be found outside filching beer, but it wasn't her place.

"Well, if he comes in here, please tell him I want to see him."

"I'll do that, Mrs. Tanner."

A worm of apprehension crawled around in Maggie's innards. What was Cole up to? He knew how important this party was to her.

When Maggie finally found her son on the rear patio, she had to stifle a laugh. She had to admit he looked a bit ridiculous in his Western outfit. The jeans Cole had purchased were too crisp, too new, and the bright plaid shirt, which should have had a pointed spread-wing collar, instead had a typical Ivy League button-down over the black string tie. "Cole, your grandmother and Thad are here. They went upstairs to freshen up. I'd like it if you came into the living room to welcome them."

Cole looked up from his magazine and stared for a moment at his mother. "Righty-o, Mam," he drawled.

"And don't be a wise-ass. I know you can behave like a gentleman. I pay that school enough to teach you manners, so practice them."

"It's a bit hard to act a gentleman in this getup," Cole retorted. "You think I'll fit in with all the other cowpokes?"

"Stop it, Cole. Get into the house; Mam'll be down in a minute. Don't screw up. I mean it."

Cole threw down his magazine, obeying his mother. He liked it when she used slang to get her point across. That meant he was getting to her.

Billie felt a sense of exhilaration as she linked her arm in Thad's to walk down the long, winding staircase. This was someone else's house now; she and Thad were visitors. They could leave anytime they wanted.

"You aren't sweating this at all, are you?" Thad grinned.

"Not in the least. I'm looking forward to seeing my children. I was just thinking that Sunbridge has no hold over us anymore. I'm all right, really."

"I can see that. I hope you're looking forward to our trip when this visit ends."

Billie's eyes brimmed and Thad was immediately sorry he'd brought up the subject of Japan. "I am looking forward to seeing the Hasegawas again. Otami is with Riley now, and that's all she ever wanted. As for young Riley coming here to Sunbridge, the Hasegawas' unselfishness amazes me."

"It didn't surprise me. Shadaharu was wise to give Riley the choice."

"Feel better?" Maggie called from the bottom of the stairs.

"Much better." Cole was standing beside Maggie, and Billie swallowed a giggle at the vision her grandson presented. A cartoon cowboy all decked out for a Saturday night. She knew Thad was reacting the same way—she could feel the tremble of laughter in his arm.

"You've grown, Cole, and you're so handsome! But then, I suppose all grandparents say things like that." Billie wrapped the boy in her embrace. She kissed him and leaned back, her hands on his shoulders. "Yes, very handsome." She beamed. "So much like your father."

Cole laughed, but the humor never reached his eyes. "What you're saying, Grand, is you have to look to find the Coleman in me."

"There's better than Colemans in this world, dear. But you *do* have your grandfather's smile and jaw."

"The world isn't big on jaws. It's the rest that counts," the boy joked.

"You're home, and that's what matters," Thad interjected. "Besides, a fella can get a bit overwhelmed by all these Colemans. At least you can keep your grandmother and me company. You know our veins don't pump Coleman oil. It takes good old Yankee blood to crank our machinery."

"Home to Sunbridge," said Maggie. "This is the first time Cole has been here for more than a long weekend. Remember, Mam, how hard you said it was when you first came here?"

"I certainly do. Your mother's right, Cole. It's overpowering at first, but you won't let it get the better of you."

"I'm sure you're right, Grand."

"Say, why don't you and I go find something cool to drink?" Thad said to Cole. "Perhaps your mother and Grand would like to talk before the others arrive."

"I'm with you." Cole clumped out behind Thad, his stiff new Western boots creaking.

Billie couldn't help herself and began to giggle. Maggie frowned and then laughed, too. "Mam, he hates dressing like that, and he just doesn't know how to put it all together. I'm the first to admit he makes himself look ridiculous."

"Then why?"

"When in Rome, right?"

"But the boy looks so unhappy."

"For a few hours it won't hurt him. If he'd let me help him select his clothes and had taken the time to break in his boots, he wouldn't look like a sore thumb."

"Poor Coleman." Billie sighed. "Perhaps when Riley gets here, they can commiserate with each other. Being half-Japanese in Texas is being another sore thumb."

"Don't worry about him, Mam," Maggie said. "I'll be backing that kid up all the way. And don't underestimate the people here in Texas. Attitudes have come a long way in the forty years since you first arrived. Besides, Riley's last name is Coleman. If that doesn't turn the trick, nothing will."

"I'm sure you're right, Maggie. But I can't help worrying about the boy. He's leaving everything he knows." Her hazel eyes were touched with grief. "When a boy is sixteen years old, he should know where he belongs."

"He will," said Maggie. "He'll know he belongs here in his father's house. I've had Riley's old room made up. I even went up to the attic and got down all of his stuff— you know, his camera and books and all those little treasures from when we were kids. They belong to Riley's son, don't they, Mam?"

"Maggie, it's wonderful of you to do that for your nephew."

Maggie flushed. "Can you believe I found those old Flash Gordon sheets and the Lone Ranger blankets? I made up the bed myself."

"I think of our Riley almost every day," Billie said quietly.

"So do I. Especially since I'm back here at Sunbridge. Mam, why wasn't a grave marker put up on the knoll for Riley? I know his body was never recovered from the plane crash, but why not a memorial stone?"

"That was your father's doing. He couldn't bear it."

"When the time is right, I'm going to talk to young Riley about it. Something should be done, don't you think?"

"I think that when the time's right, you'll know what to do. Whatever you decide, you can count on me."

"Otami, too? A memorial stone, I mean."

Billie's brows shot upward. This certainly was a new Maggie, with this sense of family. "Perhaps. But Riley might not want to stay at Sunbridge. You must prepare yourself for that, Maggie."

"As sure as I'm standing here, the boy will stay. I feel it in my bones."

"Perhaps. Come along, dear. Let's go find Cole and Thad. I could use something cool to drink myself. What time do you expect the others?"

"Within the hour. Isn't it wonderful? All of us under the same roof; all of us back at Sunbridge after so long."

The sound of a car pulling up the drive and a blaring horn saved Billie from further reply. Who else could it be but Amelia, returning to Sunbridge with fanfare. Billie stood back as Maggie raced for the door and out to the portico.

"Auntie Amelia! And this must be Cary! Welcome, welcome to Sunbridge."

Billie, standing in the shadow of the doorway, registered shock that she immediately concealed. Cary Assante, Amelia's new husband, was young, quite young in fact—

at least twenty years younger than Amelia. . . . Billie disliked what she was thinking and stepped out the door, her arms open.

"Billie! How wonderful to see you again. I really snagged a winner, didn't I? Admit it!" Amelia whispered in Billie's ear as the women embraced.

"He has my vote." Billie laughed to see her sister-in-law and best friend so animated with happiness. When Amelia had become widowed during the Second World War, she'd only been a few years older than Billie. Amelia had spent a good portion of her life alone, but now she had Cary. "I'm happy for you, Amelia," Billie murmured sincerely. "And you look wonderful!"

"I should!" Amelia said with her usual candor. "I've had everything lifted that could be lifted. I've more tucks than the good friar himself!"

Billie thought of her own wrinkles. The laugh lines around her eyes, the tiny brackets at the sides of her mouth, the deeper grooves in her forehead. For a time she'd toyed with the idea of a nip and a tuck herself, but as long as Thad loved her the way she was and pink light bulbs in the bedroom could work their magic, all was right with the world.

Amelia squared her shoulders imperceptibly, something she found herself doing whenever a younger woman was in Cary's presence. Maggie looked gorgeous, alive and vital. Just like Cary.

Cary Assante was movie star material. Slightly taller than medium height, lean and chiseled; something animal and hungry in those sparkling dark eyes. He was magnetic, handsome in a rough, virile way. His shoulders broad, like those of a boxer, back straight, light gray trousers hugging muscular thighs. His Italian heritage was visible in his sable-black hair and in his skin, which accepted a healthy tan. He had the look of a hawk, hungry and alert, but when he smiled, his expression was genuine and friendly, and it was obvious that he was quite comfortable with his good looks.

When they all moved to the shady back patio, Billie

found herself observing Cary while introductions were being made to Thad and Cole. He was carefully put together, she decided. His thick dark hair was meticulously barbered and windblown to exactly the right degree. His tan—earned no doubt, on the tennis courts beneath the California sun—was also exactly right, neither too leathery nor too blushingly pink. Everything about him seemed carefully designed for natural elegance—his Lauren shirt, Cerruti jacket, Italian shoes, and the solid gold Rolex winking on his furred arm from beneath his sleeve. Everything he wore had obviously been selected for him by Amelia; at least it was obvious to Billie, who was so familiar with Amelia's tastes.

The introductions completed, Cary approached Billie. His voice was a light baritone with shades of a New York accent, easy to listen to. He smelled awfully good, too. "I've been eager to meet you and your family. Amelia speaks of you all so often, especially you, Billie. I have to admit, I'm jealous, since I've no family of my own."

"None at all?"

"Not that I know of. I was raised on the charity of New York City in a Catholic orphanage. But," he added lightly, holding up a finger, "don't feel sorry for me. I survived, and some of my friends from those days did, too. In fact, they're still with me in business."

"What do you think of Texas? Have you ever been here before?" Billie asked. She really had to buy some of his cologne for Thad.

"I like it. And no, I've never been before, except for a week or so a few months back. I've been considering a parcel of land this side of Austin for a housing development. No, actually, it's much more than that. It's kind of an inner city outside the city." He laughed. "Townhouses, condominiums, and single-family homes, complete with shopping center and some light industry."

"Here in Texas?" asked Maggie, who had overheard.

"Yes, outside of Austin," Cary repeated. Maggie relaxed instantly: no city lights would be seen from Sunbridge. "Amelia agrees it could be a good idea. I'm going to look into it. This party will give me an opportunity to talk to some of the locals and see what they think of the idea."

Billie tried not to show her dismay. Something as large as what Cary was talking about would require a great deal of money and expertise, not to mention luck.

"You wouldn't believe this man," said Amelia. "He reminds me of Moss; he has a finger in lots of pies, all of them exciting!" There was an uneasy silence as Amelia looked from one face to the other. "Cary, perhaps you'd better tell them, right now, that you didn't marry me for my money."

Amelia had caught everyone off guard, but it was so typical of her that Billie almost laughed. "Amelia, no one—" Her eyes were drawn to Cary, who had moved closer to his wife.

"That's what I call letting it all hang out." He put his arm around Amelia's slim shoulders. "No, I didn't marry Amelia for her money; in fact, I'm not certain this lady isn't a gold digger herself. But I took my chances because I love her." He sighed dramatically. "So if there's anyone to be concerned about here, I guess it's me."

"What he means," Amelia said, smiling mischievously, "is that he's worth about ten times more than any of us here. At least at last count."

Billie sighed with relief and Amelia felt better immediately. It was important to her that Billie like Cary. "There's a difference in our ages, but Cary says it isn't important. What's important is the here and now, and the devil take the rest."

"Amelia makes *me* feel young," Cary said, grinning, as if that explained everything. "And now that we've gotten that out of the way, what do you say about something cold for a parched throat? It's a throwback to the old days when I didn't have two nickels to rub together. I talk about money and my mouth goes dry."

They were all on the back patio sipping drinks, and none of them heard the car come up the drive. "Well, hello, everyone!"

"Susan!" Maggie cried exuberantly, jumping up to embrace her sister. "Suse, I'm so glad to see you. Almost everyone is here now."

Cary, who had never met Suse or her husband, Jerome, was standing now and walking toward them, his hand outstretched. Amelia followed quickly behind her husband. Susan, who had lived with her in London as a girl was like a daughter to her, was only a year or two younger than Cary. Amelia felt it in every step she took. Yet she embraced her niece with genuine affection, her laughter real, her blue eyes sparkling. The introductions were made, and Amelia felt herself stiffen when Cary kissed Susan. But he immediately turned back to her and slipped an arm around her shoulder. He kissed her teasingly, lightly, below her ear. "I think I can detect a faint resemblance."

Amelia let out her breath in a sigh. With Cary's arms around her, everything was all right. He was behaving the loving, dutiful husband. Now, why had she thought such a thing? she wondered. Cary was always affectionate, always demonstratively loving. She mustn't allow herself to bristle like that. He was so in tune with her, he noticed any change almost immediately. But she could have been mother to all of them...including Cary, the man she adored.

{{{{{{{{ CHAPTER THREE }}}}}}}}

Billie had recently visited with Susan in New York, so there was no urgency to push through the rush of kisses and hugs and fond hellos, promises to meet more often, and latest travel gossip.

When they'd all settled down again, Maggie said, "You look weary, Suse." Her tone was fond and caring. It was true; Susan's normally fair, blond prettiness now seemed wan and pale, and her light eyes were rimmed with circles not even Estée Lauder could hide.

"She always looks that way after a tour." Jerome's voice sounded slightly harsh, as if he were annoyed at Susan's fragility.

Billie frowned and Maggie could feel something building inside herself. Susan looked more than tired; she appeared ill. "Well, I have just the remedy, Suse," said Maggie. "You sit between Mam and Amelia, and they'll pamper and pet you, and I'll get you whatever your heart desires. Name it—cold drink, something to eat?"

"Anything, as long as it's cold. Do you mind if I kick off my shoes?" Susan felt like crying.

"This is home, Suse," Maggie called over her shoulder. Then all the women gasped when they saw how swollen Susan's feet were.

"It's flying," Jerome interjected quickly. "Lots of people's feet swell from sitting too long."

"You should never take your shoes off on the plane," Amelia advised. "You'll never get them on again."

"You fly first-class," Billie said with concern. "Can't you reserve a bulkhead seat? Ask the stewardess for several pillows and prop your feet up."

As Jerome spoke with Thad and Cary, it seemed to Maggie that he was forcing his smile, pretending a joviality he didn't feel. In the past few years Jerome de Moray had lost his robust, youthful appearance to a kind of overfed middle age. He wasn't fat, only threatening to become so. His clothing seemed one size too small, and his once boyishly pink cheeks now seemed florid. His sherry colored eyes had kept their intelligence, but his easy smile now seemed pinched and forced, as though his shoes were too tight.

Amelia reached out and patted Susan's knee. "Darling, don't you think it's time to cut back on these grueling tours?"

Jerome, standing across the patio, answered for his wife. "Not at all, Amelia. Susan always gets tired, but she recovers soon enough. She's such a perfectionist, you know. Every detail, every reservation, is arranged by her. Do you know she personally irons my shirts when we're on the road?"

Amelia snorted. She'd never cared for Jerome, and now that his early promise had faded—if one was to believe the critics—he was hanging on to Susan for dear life. Susan was the talent; Susan was the box office draw. Cary quickly moved to Amelia's side and pulled her up from the chaise. "They're playing our song." He laughed lightly. "Let's show everyone that fancy dance step we learned in New York." Cary led her to the open floor and whispered, "You were about to put your foot in it, my darling."

As Amelia fell into step beside her husband, Coleman raised the volume on the stereo. The music blared as they took center stage on the patio amid hoots of approval and applause.

After five minutes, Amelia collapsed onto the chair

beside Billie, her face flushed. Cole wanted Cary to teach him the step and began to ape his movements. Amelia laughed as she watched them. "I hope you're the only one to see how frazzled that left me, Billie. I'm not as young as I used to be. My heart's going like a trip-hammer."

"Cary relieved a bad moment. I saw it coming but didn't know what to do."

"The man can read my mind. Jerome and I have had several arguments in the past about Susan. Cary was avoiding a scene. He never fails me." Amelia lowered her eyes, then looked back up at Billie. "You see, I'm doing it again, trying to justify my marriage to Cary, always pointing out how wonderful he is. I don't know why I do it! Or is it myself I'm defending?"

"Why don't you just be you and let Cary be himself? I like him, Amelia. The man's in love with you; any fool can see it. Enjoy it; don't let old ghosts ruin this for you."

"We do make our own hell, don't we. We make so many mistakes along the way. But I'm not wrong about Susan. She looks ill, doesn't she, Billie? It's not my imagination."

Billie glanced at her younger daughter, seeing again the tired dark circles under her eyes, the yellow pallor, the puffiness around her ankles and fingers. "No, I'm afraid you're not. We should have a talk with her later on."

"Easier said than done. Jerome isn't about to let his bird out of her cage. Over the years he's become an absolute dictator. I thought I liked him once, but that was when he was a young, blossoming virtuoso. I put down his temper and eccentricities to his being a genius. Now I think he's just spoiled and selfish. Oh, how I wish I'd been able to convince Susan that Peter Gillette was the man she needed, and not Jerome. But Susan and her 'tidy' life couldn't bear up under the scandal of Peter leaving his wife and children for her. I tried to tell her it'd blow over in a matter of time, but she was so afraid, she jumped for Jerome as though he were a lifeline." Amelia sighed, a frown creasing her brow. "I worry about her, Billie."

"I know you do, but let's not worry now and spoil Maggie's wonderful party. It's getting late, isn't it?" She glanced at her watch. "Sawyer and Riley should have been here by now. Rand, too."

"The plane was probably delayed. Rand was going to wait for them at the airport so they could all drive out together."

The tall, wheat-blond-haired man lounged in his chair at the airport bar, drawing appreciative glances from passing females. Unabashed, he stared back at them, making his own assessments: too short, too tall, too skinny or fat, too much makeup. He disliked the kind of frizzled hair that seemed to be all the rage these days, or hair that was cut boyishly short. By the time he'd finished his second Bombay gin, he'd warded off one flagrant flirtation and had taken two more subtle ones under consideration before smiling his gleaming white smile that echoed in his coffee-brown eyes.

Rand Nelson hated airports and train stations almost as much as he hated to be kept waiting. He'd been waiting nearly three hours now for the flight from Japan via San Francisco. Even from this distance, his keen gaze could read the green-screened monitor declaring the two-hour delay from San Francisco. In two hours he could consume four more drinks and probably smoke an entire pack of cigarettes. He considered calling Sunbridge to alert them of the delay.

In some ways he was already regretting this trip. At the age of forty-three, he was old enough to know what he wanted and didn't want in his life. Mostly, he realized, he wanted life to go smoothly. Perhaps he'd remained a bachelor too long; perhaps he was too set in his ways. Rand wished he could pinpoint the time and place when he'd realized he'd achieved all of his major goals. He enjoyed his successes, savored each of them, but some instinct told him it was time to start winding down, time to stop and smell the roses. Bulging bank accounts, fingers in pies that didn't require his personal involvement, had allowed him to think about the pursuit of pleasure, doing something creative or having the choice of doing nothing at all.

The Bombay gin slid down his throat, crisp and icy. He'd learned to like his drinks American, that is, with ice and served in frosted glasses. There wasn't much of the Englishman in him. He supposed having Amelia for a mother and almost constant world travel had erased his tastes for warm beer and warmer liquor and endless days of London weather. Lord Randolph Jamison Nelson, Earl of Wickham, was a name and title that had little to do with the man; it was a name listed in the peerage and would be as long as there was an England, but it said nothing about himself.

Sawyer. Her name brought a vision of sunshine and energy and the sound of a girlish voice softened with a Texan accent. Slim, lovely, bright, intelligent, and only twenty-six years old. She was on the brink of discovering her abilities, of putting her education and her unique position as head of Coleman Aviation into effect. Her instincts for business were as sharp as her grandfather's and great-grandfather's had been before her; with little more than legal advice, she'd been successful in licensing the most innovative, lightweight personal aircraft in aviation history—and keeping the copyrights intact for Coleman Aviation to boot. Sawyer was hooked on achievement, and nothing would keep her from testing her abilities. The trouble had nothing to do with Sawyer's ambitions and success, in fact, he admired her for making the most of her talents. But he'd had enough of high-powered business deals. What would become of Sawyer and him if they married? He wanted to wind down, and she was just coming into her prime. Age was just a number, but they were two people at opposite ends of a rope.

Sawyer had been in Japan and it had been almost two months since he'd seen her, time enough for Rand to think, to really face the fact that while he loved Sawyer Coleman, he was not in love with her. He hated to think of himself as capricious, and in his heart he knew he wasn't, but time had a way of changing people, often against their will. His time with Sawyer had been wonderful. They'd had so much in common, working on designs and specifications for her grandfather's aircraft. Common goals, loving the same people, seeing things the same way. But the goals had been won, and loving the same people and being involved in the same family wasn't enough. Now Sawyer had new goals to conquer, and she would embrace them the way she embraced all of life—with humor and gusto and a sense of adventure.

Rand ordered a fresh drink and lit the last cigarette in the pack. The minutes on the clock over the bar ticked away. Soon the plane from San Francisco would arrive. Soon he'd have to look into Sawyer's crystal-gray eyes. What would she see in his own?

Perhaps Sawyer would argue that he was "dropping out," but Rand knew he wasn't. He simply wanted time to himself, to reap the rewards of his hard work. There were things he'd always dreamed about but could never find the time to indulge: fishing, hunting, and yes, even planting that garden and watching it come to fruit. Books, pleasure trips, refurbishing the four antique automobiles he'd collected. But most of all he wanted time for the people he loved, those involving relationships he'd been unable to develop as he'd run from one airport to the other.

Rand stubbed out his cigarette and paid his bar tab. His tip was overgenerous. If Sawyer had been here, she would have computed the bill and stuck the overage in his breast pocket. Sawyer did things by the book. Rebelliously, Rand placed another dollar on the table. A weary waitress working a dull shift on the Fourth of July needed a little extra. She'd probably missed her family barbecue in order to work today. All Texans went to a barbecue on the Fourth.

Crossing the terminal, he passed a monitor. The blinking words "at the gate" meant Sawyer's plane was in and she and Riley would be deplaning. His step quickened and he straightened his tie. Then he smoothed his tousled thatch of wheat-gold hair. If only he were happy to see her again, if only he didn't feel like a first-class rat. Worse, a coward.

She was beautiful, tall and slim as a fashion model. Men turned for a second appreciative glance; women envied her graceful, long-legged stride. Those incredibly long, shapely legs were bringing her closer and closer. Rand hardly noticed the tall young man beside her. This was Sawyer: brilliant gray eyes, clear pink skin, and generous smile that lit her surroundings. Bright and fresh, her skirt barely wrinkled, every sleek blond hair in place despite the intolerably long trip from Tokyo.

Sawyer stepped into his arms; her soft lips found his. He responded lightly, wishing his heart would stop its furious pounding, wishing she wouldn't look at him with such open-hearted love.

"I missed you, Rand. We have a lot of time to make up," she whispered, then drew back and looked into his eyes. Whatever she saw there seemed to satisfy her. "Riley!" she said. "We're almost forgetting you!"

"You must have grown a foot since I saw you last, Riley," Rand said, stretching out his hand.

"He's cropping out at six feet and still growing; what do you think of that?" Sawyer beamed like a proud mother.

"It's uncanny how much like your father you are. You're even built like him."

"I could hardly believe it myself." Sawyer laughed. "He was just a little twerp when we saw him last, and now look at him! There's a picture at Sunbridge of Grandpap and Riley when he was this age. I'm going to hang a picture of you right beside them. I'm embarrassing you, Riley. I'm sorry."

"It's okay." Riley smiled. "I'm used to you by now. I weigh in at one sixty; she usually mentions that next," he said to Rand. "How are you, sir? It's been a while."

"Too long." Rand clasped the boy's hand. "I was awfully sorry to hear about your mother, Riley. This must be a difficult time for you."

"Thank you, sir." The grief was there, clouding the clear nutmeg-colored eyes, but the chin was firm, the voice steady.

Sawyer took a playful swipe at her cousin. "I can't wait till Grand sees you! She's going to flip out. You were a plump little sushi roll when she saw you last!"

"Come on, let's get your baggage," Rand said. "Have you been embarrassing this lad all the way from Tokyo?"

"I don't mind." Riley smiled. "Which way to the baggage area?"

Riley followed behind Sawyer and Rand, glad to be in the company of people as tall as himself. It had been getting difficult in Japan. Towering over almost everyone else brought attention to himself, and at the age of sixteen going on seventeen, being conspicuous was the last thing Riley wanted. He was tall like his father, and had become the butt of much good-natured ribbing. It always pleased him when comparisons were made to his father, and he took pride in the resemblance. He'd inherited his strong profile and well-defined nose from his great-grandfather Seth; and he knew his smile and thick crop of fine black hair, which bore a tendency to wave, also came from his American background. Only his eyes revealed his Oriental heritage. Because of his height and build, people often mistook him for Hawaiian. Sawyer told him not to fight it when his ancestry was mistaken. "Eventually, people accept you for *who* you are, not *what* you are," she'd said. "People who matter, anyway."

On the ride to Sunbridge, Sawyer carried much of the conversation, telling Rand about the business meetings she'd had in Tokyo and their fruitful outcome. There was a tenseness in Rand's shoulders; Riley could see that his eyes never left the road to smile at Sawyer's jokes. And even though he laughed, there was something hollow in the sound. Sawyer was trying too hard to be amusing, reaching over too frequently to smooth Rand's hand or rub her palm against his cheek.

By the time they reached the turnoff for Sunbridge, Riley could feel the tension in his own shoulders. Sunbridge, an ancestral home. His father's roots were here. But were his? He hoped it hadn't been a mistake to come here. What if he was viewed as a burden? Perhaps Maggie had just been doing what she thought was her duty. Maybe resembling his father as he did would make everyone uncomfortable. He wished he knew. Traveling halfway around the world to come to Sunbridge had been difficult, especially since it meant leaving his mother's family. His Japanese grandfather would be terribly disappointed in him if his stay in America wasn't a success. "Knowing only one side of your ancestors is knowing only one-half of yourself," the old one had counseled.

The "old one." Riley smiled to himself. It was the name Grandpa Hasegawa preferred. It denoted wisdom and respect in the traditional Japanese manner. Japanese... American... who was he?

He looked American, from the top of his billed baseball cap to his scuffed Adidas. Sawyer had assured him it was all right to travel in jeans. The button-down plaid shirt was his own attempt at dressing up. The cap had belonged to his father, and it was never off his head, except when he ate and slept.

Riley couldn't wait to meet his cousin Cole. They'd eat American pizza, hot dogs, tacos, and burritos. For starters. Listening to rock music was his second-favorite pastime. Maybe he and Cole could go to a rock concert together. He could almost picture them walking through the crowd looking for chicks. All American boys were after chicks. Riley frowned. Girls shouldn't be called "chicks," but he was going to have to adapt. A girl was a girl in any language, and the universal response was always a smile. Sawyer told him he had a smile that would knock girls dead. He grinned to himself.

Sunbridge land. Rolling green hills, crisp and clean and

sharp, as though painted on canvas. He particularly liked the tumbleweeds and remembered the way he'd chased them across the lawn on his last visit.

He wasn't visiting now. He was to make this his home, the old one had said. He'd always known he'd come back here someday, but he hadn't expected it so soon. If his mother hadn't been killed, he'd still be in Japan attending the university. This is what she would have wanted for him, the old one had said. The old man had cried at the airport, his stoic Japanese resolve abandoning him. Riley had shed tears of his own, but not until he'd gone to the restroom on the plane. He missed Tokyo already; he missed the old one.

Sawyer leaned over the back seat. "So, what do you think? Has Texas changed?"

"It looks the same to me, just as beautiful. I always expect to see men on horseback come galloping along."

Sawyer laughed. "They only do that in the movies. Another mile or so and we'll be there. A bit anxious, eh?"

"A little," Riley admitted.

"The one thing you can count on, Riley, is that Sunbridge will never change. Perhaps some new paint, the trees get bigger, the animals get fatter, but aside from that, everything stays the same. I feel as though I'm coming home. For such a long time this was my home. I can't imagine how you must feel."

"I want to belong," Riley said simply.

"You do. This was your father's home. If he hadn't died, this place would have gone to him and to you as his son. We talked about that on the plane. Just because Maggie holds the deed doesn't mean a thing. Sunbridge is as much yours as it is Maggie's and Cole's. Maggie herself will tell you the same thing, I'm sure."

"They may consider me an intruder."

"I'm sure that will never happen, but if it does, Grand will make it right. You belong here. Accept it, Riley."

"Yes, ma'am," Riley said, saluting smartly.

"How do you feel about coming to Sunbridge, Rand?" Sawyer asked a trifle anxiously.

"I've always loved Sunbridge, ever since I was a tad and Amelia brought me here for the first time, during the war. It's a grand place."

"I know. . . ."

"I can see the arch," Riley said, breaking the awkward moment.

"That means we're home," Sawyer said airily. Home-comings were so important to everyone, for different reasons.

When they climbed from the car in the wide, circular driveway, Sawyer found herself brushing shoulders with Rand. He was so silent—the kind of silence that trembles. How absurd! she thought. Rand was the most together person she knew. He didn't have a nerve in his body. But she did give him a second look before she threw her arm around Riley's shoulder.

This was her mother's house now. Not Sunbridge, not their home. Maggie's home. Sawyer couldn't help but wonder how Riley was going to fit in. For all her brave, reassuring talk, she wasn't certain. Maggie had loved her brother, and if things went right, she would love young Riley, too. For Maggie's own reasons.

Riley's smile and dark good looks were certainly charming everyone else. The baseball cap was clutched fiercely between his hands. A pity the boy didn't know he had nothing to fear. At least from the Coleman women. The envy and dislike in young Cole's eyes might give the boy a spot of trouble later on, but that was to be expected. Boys were always rivals in one way or another.

Maggie took center stage, calling for quiet. "I think we're all here now. I'm so happy you could come here today. It's kind of a momentous holiday. Freedom and independence, that kind of thing. It's been such a long time since we were all gathered under the same roof. If we can, let's put the past behind us and move closer to making this the kind of family we should be. It's what I want, and I think all of you want the same thing. For any of you who don't know, Riley is going to be staying with us here at Sunbridge for as long as he wants. This is his home as well as mine. Sunbridge belongs to all of us. This is home."

Cole stood up and clapped his hands. "Bravo, Mother. Very well said." Maggie flushed with embarrassment. "Cole," she said apologetically, "doesn't understand what Sunbridge is all about. He's going to learn, though. This summer he's going to ride the range and do all the things Pap and my brother used to do. He's going to learn what Sunbridge is all about. Riley, too."

Cole sputtered. "You promised. . . . You lied to me . . ."

"That's enough, Cole," Maggie said quietly.

"Why? So you can pretend to all these people, this wonderful family of yours, that you're the grande dame of Sunbridge? You had no intention of considering my trip to Europe! You had this summer all planned out for me. For him, too," Cole said, jerking his head in Riley's direction.

"I said that's enough, Cole," Maggie said, coldly this time.

"Stuff this party, Mother. I'll be in my room," Cole said, stalking off and turning his ankle just as he walked through the doorway.

Maggie's eyes spun around the assembled guests. To apologize for her son or not . . . Everyone had family problems. Her gaze locked with Rand's. The rosy circles on her cheeks stood out starkly.

Billie let her breath out in a soft sigh. She was standing beside Riley. Her hand went protectively to his arm. She wanted to say something comforting but couldn't find the words. It was Riley himself who saved the moment.

"Aunt Maggie, which horse will I have? And if I'm to ride the range, how many days will it take for my blisters to heal?"

Maggie laughed, a light sound of relief. "About a good two weeks. For starters, I think you can ride Lotus. She's fairly gentle and she likes an apple for any ride over thirty minutes. Later, you can ride Stormy. Your father's riding gear is in his closet. From the looks of you, it'll just fit."

Rand glanced over at Sawyer, who was still staring at

the doorway through which Cole had stumbled. He knew her feelings for Maggie were unresolved. It was never easy being abandoned. Sawyer was quite sensitive on the subject of her mother. He found himself gulping his drink. Knowing this, how could he be such a heel? How could he add to her hurt?

There was a knock on Cole's door and Riley was standing in the open doorway. "They sent me up to find you," he explained. "I'm glad to meet you. I wanted to see you the last time I was here, but it just wasn't possible."

"I lived with it," Cole said sarcastically. His cousin stood head and shoulders above him had made him feel all of four years old. "I could live with it if you left right now. I don't understand why you're here to begin with."

Riley took a step backward as though he'd been dealt a physical blow. He'd never encountered such rudeness; it would never have been allowed in his grandfather's house. But the old man had cautioned him not to bring shame on their family, and the boy answered quietly, "This was my father's home. I never knew him; Sunbridge is as close to him as I can get. I'd like to know how he grew up here in Texas. I'd like to experience it for myself."

"Well, I don't want to be here, and I sure as hell don't want to live with some Japanese orphan. Don't go getting any ideas we're going to be buddies and that I'm going to ride the old south forty to help you chase down your father's ghost."

Riley bristled. "I won't ask you for anything. I didn't come here to freeload, if that's what you're thinking. I can earn my keep."

"Oh, yeah, and what're you going to do? Ride the range, herd cattle, mend fences, muck the barn?"

"If I have to," Riley said sharply. "You don't have to like me, Cole"—there was an inner core of strength in his voice—"but I'm not going to let you walk all over me just because I'm a guest in your mother's house. I can handle myself."

"Look how impressed I am. I was on the boxing team

at school. You're just what we need around here, a smart-
ass with a black belt in karate."

Riley laughed. "Is that the same thing as being a wise-
ass?"

Cole didn't laugh; he knew Riley was mocking him.
Cole turned his back and took two steps away, the hackles
on the back of his neck warning him that Riley could
pound him to a pulp. He was ready for anything, ready
to fight if Riley made a move. "Dumb Jap prick!"

Cole turned suddenly, expecting Riley's onslaught, but
he found himself alone and facing an empty doorway. Cole
swept his arm over the top of his dresser, finding small
satisfaction in the tinkle of broken glass.

{{{{{{{{{ CHAPTER FOUR }}}}}}}}}

Maggie presided over the long, linen-draped table. If she
noticed the vacant place beside hers, she gave no indi-
cation. Coleman's presence, she decided, was almost inci-
dental to this gathering. Smiling, she rose to offer a
welcoming toast. "To our family, each one of us!"

The chorus of enthusiastic responses pleased Maggie.
"Wait," she said, holding up her hand. "We have another
toast. To Sunbridge!" This time the responses were more
subdued. Only Riley beamed from ear to ear, and it was
his echoing toast that could be clearly heard.

In deference to the huge Texas-style barbecue that
would be offered later that evening when the other guests
arrived, Maggie's luncheon menu was purposely light:
salad in aspic, which she noticed the men refused, baked

lemon sole fillets, and asparagus tips. For the heartier appetite, a rich fish chowder was served, complete with thick slices of French bread and crumbled bacon. And, for dessert, coffee, pie and ice cream.

"Still watching your weight, Susan?" Maggie asked as she dug into her apple pie.

"In a way. At our age it's difficult to take it off. Besides, I'm looking forward to those barbecued ribs."

Jerome, mining his way through a second piece of pie with double ice cream, glanced at his wife. "I don't want you to overdo tonight. Remember your diet." Then, looking around at the others, he said, "Susan has to be careful. It's critically important how she looks onstage. She's been admired for her angelic, ethereal appearance when she sits before the piano. One bulge and it's all ruined."

"Susan has always been a disciplined person," Billie said. "I quite admire you, darling. And as for your figure, you have nothing to worry about. Whatever do you do when you want to binge? What's your secret?"

"I look at Jerome, Mam," Susan said coolly. An uneasy silence shrouded the table.

"I think you need a good, long rest, Susan," said Amelia. "You're looking a bit peaked," she added bluntly.

"There's nothing wrong with Susan," Jerome said sharply. "It was the trip, coming off the tour and getting ready for the next one. Susan is fine."

Thad whispered to Billie, "Methinks he doth protest too much. Follow your instincts, darling. She's your daughter."

"I'll talk with her later, Thad. She looks miserable enough now; I don't want to add to it."

There was a lump growing in Susan's throat. All her family was here, and if there was ever a time to make an announcement, this was it. Damn Jerome and his career. Damn the tour and damn the critics. First she looked at Amelia, and then at Billie, who nodded slightly to show she understood. Susan had something to say, and this was as good a time as any to say it.

The knife was in Susan's hand before she could think, and she was tapping lightly on her water glass. "Listen, everybody, I have an announcement." She carefully avoided looking at her husband.

"Susan! We've discussed this," Jerome hissed at her across the table. "Not now, for God's sake!"

"Now!" she said. "Everybody..." She took a deep breath. "Everybody, I'm pregnant! Isn't it wonderful?"

Maggie was off her chair and took her sister into her embrace. "Suse! How wonderful! I'm so happy for you! This calls for another toast!"

"There hasn't been a baby in the family since Coleman." Billie laughed. "When is this wonderful new addition to arrive?"

"In time for my birthday. February." Susan was brightening before Billie's eyes. Already there was more color in her cheeks, and her eyes were glowing.

"That's if all goes well," Jerome said.

"Why shouldn't it?" Amelia asked. "Our Susan's a strong, healthy woman. Or is there something you're not telling us, Jerome?"

He was saved from having to reply by Sawyer, who had left her place at the table and stood behind Susan's chair. "If you're in the market for a godmother, I volunteer. How lucky you are, Susan! So very lucky." She squeezed Susan in a hug.

Rand's pulses were pounding. The naked want on Sawyer's face saddened him and terrified him at the same time. They'd talked of this, of marriage and children. Sawyer should have children, lots of them. She'd be a wonderful mother. But what of himself? He just couldn't see himself at fifty with toddlers climbing on his knee. He knew Sawyer was looking at him, willing him to share her secret smile, to give her some sign that one day the two of them would achieve this miracle. When Rand refused to meet her eyes, Sawyer dropped her head, silky blond hair hiding her face.

Susan patted Sawyer's hand and looked directly at Jerome. "Don't say another word, but I'm going to have another scoop of ice cream." There was a challenge in her eyes, determination in the set of her mouth. There, it was out in the open. She'd told her family and they were delighted. Until this very moment, with Jerome's badgering, she hadn't been certain herself that she wanted this baby. But now her family knew, and they were happy for her.

Servants were clearing the table, bringing out an array of cordials: Courvoisier for the men, Grand Marnier for the women. Bowls of fruits and boards of cheeses replaced pie plates and ice cream salvers.

Billie followed Riley's gaze as it rested first on one face, then another. It hurt to look at the boy. Her heart ached for her dead son. Seeing Riley, now a young man, recalled so many old torments. It was uncanny how much he resembled his father, her son who had died so young. Hardly fifteen, but already he was as tall as his father had been at twenty. Maggie was right: the worn jeans and favorite shirts and perhaps even the boots that had been stored away because no one could bear to dispose of them would fit the boy now. If Riley chose to wear them. And Billie knew what his decision would be. She hoped she'd be gone from here before then. Grief, it seemed, held to no time clock.

Maggie clutched Billie's hand as they walked back to the house to rest for a while and change before the guests began to arrive. "I'm scared as hell about tonight, Mam. I don't know if I can pull this off."

"You'll do fine, Maggie. Stop worrying and just enjoy your guests. Everything's under control, and you have your entire family here to back you up."

Maggie slipped her arm around Billie's shoulder and squeezed. The deep sable tones in her hair contrasted with Billie's blondness. "I know, and I appreciate it, believe me. It's just that I'm afraid to make a fool of myself. Sunbridge is home now; it's important to me to be accepted by my neighbors."

Billie laughed merrily. "I'd hardly call the governor

and his wife neighbors, but I know what you mean. As we were driving out today, I saw how developed Crystal City has become. I remember when it was Crystal Crossroads, with nothing but a general store and a gas station. Now, it seems, culture has arrived. Boutiques and bookshops, and didn't I see an art gallery and gift shop?"

"You did. And a hair salon and haberdashers. You name it, we've got it. Most of the shops and businesses have been opened by bored matrons from the country club. Their clientele consists mainly of one another, but I'd say they're thriving, giving Neiman-Marcus a run for its money."

"It's been almost a year since you're out here, Maggie. Have you joined the club and made friends?"

"I've joined the country club, but I don't know if I've made friends. Oh, I play tennis and even some golf, and I'm a member of the Cattleman's Association, but I don't really know if they accept me."

"I felt the same way when I lived here with your father. They're a closed unit, and while they smile on the outside, I guess you have to be one of them to know what's going on inside. I wasn't born here, Maggie; you were. You're more like them than you know—you belong here. Besides, you're not lacking in social skills. I remember some of the clippings from the social columns describing the parties you threw when you lived in New York with Cranston. And even before that, you were director of Sandor Locke's art gallery as well as his unofficial hostess. I should think that New York crowd would be much more critical than people here in Texas. You've always been a success, Maggie; things won't change now."

"I hope you're right, Mam. This is a first for me." Maggie opened the door to the house and allowed Billie to step through. "I didn't get one refusal, but I can't fool myself. I know why they're coming and so do you. They want another look at all of us, Amelia, Susan, you."

"Perhaps you're right, but we'll present the united front you want. Stop worrying. As you said, no one refused your invitation, not even the governor!"

"They want to eat my food and drink my liquor! They're all freeloaders who live from one party to the next!"

Billie giggled. "Seth used to say almost the same thing. ... And Maggie, I noticed that you aren't drinking at all. I'm proud of you, believe me."

"I do, Mam. I need a clear head for my future, and I won't clutter it up with booze and pills. I don't want to be dependent on anything except my own resources. I have Cole and Riley to think of now. It's a new Maggie."

"And I like her," Billie said. "I always liked the old Maggie, too."

"For a while I didn't know that, Mam. I wasn't certain anyone liked the old Maggie, not even myself."

"Maggie, Sawyer doesn't—"

"Not now, Mam. Not today. I'm not so sure this new me is strong enough to tackle that old skeleton. Let me take it one step at a time."

"All right, Maggie. But it won't go away, you know. Sooner or later you and Sawyer will have to resolve your feelings."

"I know. I'm doing my best. I'll try, really."

"You know, just for a minute you looked like Moss," Billie said quietly. "That same haunted expression used to come into his eyes when he was forced to make a promise he had no intention of keeping. I'm sorry, Maggie. I don't want to press you."

Billie shivered and a sudden prickle of goose bumps broke out on her arms. "Come away from the door, Mam; we're standing in a draft." Then, in a lighter tone, "Guess what I'm wearing tonight."

Billie laughed. "The honeysuckle-patterned beaded gown?"

"Exactly. It'll knock everyone's eyes out. Everyone will know you designed the fabric especially for me. Amelia said she bought a new Adolfo, and Susan told me she's wearing the two-piece watered silk you sent her for Christmas. I didn't get a chance to ask Sawyer."

"Whatever she wears, she'll be stunning. Are you planning on a receiving line, Maggie?"

"Absolutely. All the Coleman women will be lined up to let 'em get a first-crack look at us. What're you planning to wear?"

"Well, since you insist they're coming to gawk, I just might wear my birthday suit! That should set them back on their heels!"

Cary stepped out of the shower and into the thickly carpeted bedroom, a scanty towel wrapped around his hard, lean middle. With another towel he was drying his obstinately wavy black hair.

"Are you finished with the bathroom?" asked Amelia. "How come you always get to use the shower first?"

"Because I don't stay in there for two hours and you do." Cary quipped, moving closer to plant a kiss on the side of her neck. Lovingly he took his wife's hand and held it, oblivious to the network of blue veins and the faint brown splotches. He only felt the softness and the affectionate pressure she returned.

"Mmmm. You smell so good." Amelia relished the feel of his lips against her skin and his fresh soapy scent. Beads of water clung to his shoulders and glistened in the thick mat of his chest hair.

Cary recognized the expression in Amelia's eyes and the heated quality of her voice. "I'll give you a nickel if you yank off this towel," he murmured intimately. "And two bits if you follow through."

Amelia resisted the intoxicating invitation and quelled her pulse-thumping reaction with a laugh. "Make it a dollar and you might have a deal." She moved away from him, carrying the impression of his touch with her. She didn't want him to see how much his overtures pleased her, how hungry she was for him. "But first I'll have my shower, and it's going to take me time to redo my makeup...." She paused thoughtfully. "On second thought, make that ten bucks."

"Sweetheart, you could appear at this shindig wearing a J.C. Penney towel, and you'd still be the best-looking broad here."

"No, thank you, I'd rather wear the dress I brought especially for this occasion." She stepped over to him and presented her back for him to undo her zipper. "Cary darling, what did you think of the clan?" His answer was important to her and Cary knew it, too, so he chose his words carefully.

"It's a family I'd like to belong to."

"You do. You married me."

"I mean, I'd like to have been born into it."

"No, you wouldn't. Trust me. You think we were always like we are now. Well, you're wrong." Her tone lowered, old regrets coloring her voice. "Cary, people did awful things to one another in this house." Then, wanting to be on firmer ground, she asked, "What did you think of Billie?"

"She's terrific. Her admiral is an okay guy, too."

Cary's streetwise vernacular never bothered Amelia. In fact, she enjoyed being called a "good-looking broad." She'd known others with more refined speech and manners who hadn't half the honesty and character of Cary. She sucked in her breath when he dropped the skimpy towel around his middle and stepped into silky bikini briefs. She blinked and looked at her watch meaningfully.

Cary grinned. "You had your chance."

Amelia escaped temptation by flying into the bathroom. Chances. Maybe that's what her life really was, just one chance after another. Susan's announcement had come as a shock. Cary was only a few years older than Susan. Did he compare ages? If it hadn't occurred to him already, it soon would that she, Amelia, was almost like a grandmother to Susan's baby. Grandmothers, those little shrunken women with rosy cheeks and sparkling white aprons to match their hair. She didn't fill the bill and neither did Billie. But there was a new breed of grandmother these days: taller, slimmer women who hid their age with the help of Clairol, belly suctions, and face lifts.

Stepping up to the bathroom mirror, Amelia studied herself. She was a network of fine scar lines almost invisible to the naked eye. But she knew where each and every line was. Time and gravity, those two ancient enemies to be warded off at all cost. Especially now, especially since Cary.

A rigid regimen of diet and exercise, torment and torture, was worth every deprivation, every sore muscle, if it meant having Cary. She lifted her arm and looked into the mirror over her shoulder. No trace of a wrinkle or loose, crinkly skin. She could wear a sleeveless dress without a worry. For the time being, at least. Sooner or later it was going to catch up with her, and then what? Cary wouldn't want her then. Amelia peered closer into the glass. Behind the visage of a smooth-skinned, wide-eyed, almost beautiful woman, she saw a Disney version of an old hag crooning in a cracked and wicked voice, "Mirror, mirror on the wall..."

Upon reentering the bedroom after her shower, Amelia found Cary struggling with the string tie he was attempting to thread through a silver clasp. "Damn it, I'm going to look as stupid in this getup as that kid did this afternoon. What's his name, Cole?"

After Amelia came to his rescue and fastened the tie, he stepped back and struck a pose by shoving his thumbs into his belt. "What d'you think? Will I pass muster?" His Western-cut pants fit him like a glove, hugging his thighs and falling to exactly the correct spot over his boots.

Amelia pretended to ponder. Would he pass muster! Every female with a hormone left in her body would be after him tonight, and some of these Texan ladies were like barracuda in open water. "You'll do," she said off-handedly. "I only hope I won't have to defend your honor later on tonight."

Cary's brows rose slightly. There was an angry, feral glitter in his dark eyes. "What's that supposed to mean?

You make me sound like a fox in a chicken coop!" It annoyed him when Amelia said things like this. Christ, didn't she know he loved her? She was everything he wanted in a woman: smart, classy, affectionate, and open-hearted. Women were strange. Why couldn't they just accept things, accept the truth and go on from there? Why did they always have to look for problems? He knew exactly what he wanted and that's why he'd married her.

It hadn't been easy kicking and clawing his way to where he was now. Growing up in an orphanage, barely making it through high school and having no way of going on to college. He'd been street-bred and street-raised. Life had been tough, but he'd never forgotten his debts. He'd started out driving rich people's cars cross-country, making contacts and eventually going into the limousine and rental car business. By the age of twenty-nine he'd made his first million in real estate, but long before that he'd been sending monthly checks to St. Anthony's Orphanage in downtown Chicago. He was a hustler and didn't have a lot of class or polish like these Colemans, but he could hold his head up. Self-made. From what Amelia had told him, her old man had been self-made. That said a lot for a man and his character. Class could be bought and the polish would come later.

Having a seven-figure bank balance and another ten million on paper didn't make Cary feel rich, compared to these Colemans. He couldn't imagine, considering his humble beginnings, what it would be like to live like this, to be so damned important that a governor would drop everything to attend a Fourth of July picnic. Strange, this life of the Texas rich—but something he could take to like a duck to water. Cary's financial success had come from making the right deals, being in the right place at the right time. Luck. Relationships and friendships had never entered into it. Cold, impersonal phone calls, listening to the advice of brokers, and having a nose for money had been the extent of his involvement. Now Cary found himself wanting to belong in Texas, and that feeling

was strong. Amelia could guide him, introduce him, set
him on the right course. He'd mingle with people who
weren't overwhelmed by his wealth, play a friendly game
of golf, and be welcomed for himself, not just because
someone wanted to talk a deal.

"You're deep in thought." Amelia glanced at her husband's reflection in the vanity mirror. "I didn't mean to
offend you, really I didn't. You're a city boy; you've no
idea how little chance a fox actually has if there are enough
chickens in the coop. And there'll be enough chickens
here tonight. I can't blame you because you're so damned
attractive, so don't blame me if I'm a little jealous and
insecure. I worry that you might regret marrying me. But
if I were ten years younger, darling, the shoe would be
on the other foot." She meant to convey teasing humor;
instead her tone came across as bitter.

"If I ever regret marrying you, you'll be the first to
know. I don't like it when you talk like this. I thought we
agreed you weren't going to keep harping on this damned
age business."

Amelia blew him a kiss and returned to her mascara.

"And there's something I don't understand. How come
men wear plaid shirts and sport coats and the women
wear gowns and jewels?"

"Because you're in Texas; that's the way we do things.
The way the women dress is how the men are measured.
Get it?"

Cary digested the information and nodded. "Makes
sense, if you're a Texan. How much did that gown you're
wearing cost?"

"You don't want to know. Besides, it was before I
married you."

"I'm serious, Amelia. How much?"

"You are serious, aren't you? . . . Four thousand."

"For one dress!"

"For one itty-bitty dress," Amelia drawled. "You don't
want me looking tacky, do you?"

"God forbid!"

"I know how you can spend your evening. Get together with Rand. He has quite an eye for jewelry. Between the two of you, you can calculate the cost of what the women are wearing. It'll blow your mind."

"You have five minutes, Amelia," he told her, looking at his watch.

"God! I'll never be ready in time! Hurry—help me with these snaps and hooks." When he'd finished his struggle with the tiny hooks and even tinier eyes, she turned to face him. "Well, what do you think?"

"I think you're going to outshine everyone else," he said, approval lighting his eyes. Her cocktail-length dress was made of some silky sapphire-blue material that rustled softly and shone like satin. Cut high in the front with bell-shaped sleeves, it was nearly backless, revealing the graceful sweep of her back and flawless light olive skin. Cary realized it was the cut and fabric, rather than any ornamentation, that lent the dress its elegance. He especially approved of the way it revealed Amelia's shapely legs and trim ankles, showcasing her sexy high-heeled sandals. "Honey, you're a knockout." He whistled. "Wear that perfume that drives me nuts."

Amelia promptly spritzed herself with Van Cleef & Arpels' "First." Sapphire and diamond earrings and a simple matching brooch worn high on the left shoulder was all the jewelry this dress demanded. Cary sniffed with delight and put his arms around her from behind. She loved it when he groaned with pleasure and nibbled behind her ear. It was a good thing he didn't ask how much the perfume cost.

{{{{{{{{ CHAPTER FIVE }}}}}}}}

Austin society arrived in Mercedes-Benzes, Rolls Royces, stretch limos, Ford Rangers, and pickup trucks. They came to see the Coleman women and weren't disappointed. An hour into the party and Maggie's eyes were sparkling.

She'd been accepted. Oh, she'd seen the little huddles, could imagine what all the whispering was about, but she didn't care. She'd pulled it off—with the help of her family. On her own it would have taken years. But with this one magnificent master stroke, Austin was hers. You didn't offend a Coleman.

Maggie beamed and bustled about. In December when the society reporters rehashed the year's social events, Maggie knew this affair would be number one on the list. She felt wonderful—until she saw Cole draped over a chair on the back patio. He'd been drinking. God, if he threw up, it could ruin everything. For a moment she panicked; then she saw Rand walking toward her. If she could get his assistance, she just might be able to avoid a scene. But before she could wind her way through the knots of people, Rand was out of sight. As she neared Cole she saw that Riley was already there. His left arm was braced against the stone wall while his right arm held her son up. He was laughing and Cole was snarling.

"Darlings," Maggie cooed, coming up quickly behind Riley, "I think both of you should go indoors and get something to eat or some coffee."

"I'll second that," Rand said firmly. Maggie whirled, relief shining from her eyes. "If you can do some fancy footwork and a little chitchat, I think I can get Cole into the house without too much of a stir. Riley will help me."

"I don't need any help from you or any slant-eyed Jap," said Cole.

"If there's one thing I can't stand, it's a drunk. A nasty drunk is worse," Maggie said coldly. "This is unforgivable, Coleman." To Riley she added, "He didn't mean what he said. You can see he's not himself."

"It's all right, Aunt Maggie. I think I got to him before anyone saw what was happening."

Maggie was rainbow bright as she danced her way around the clusters of guests, stopping to chat first with one group, then another. Out of the corner of her eye she watched Rand's progress. As soon as it was possible, she darted through the wide French doors and headed for the kitchen to join them. She was disgusted and ashamed of her son, doubly ashamed of his cruel remark to Riley.

"Cole's a bit young to be hitting the sauce," Rand said coolly.

"It's my fault. I should have kept an eye on him. He was angry . . . is angry with me. . . . I was so busy. . . ."

"Don't defend him, Maggie. He's old enough to know better. There's nothing worse than a mean drunk. A mean sixteen-year-old drunk is something I don't even want to discuss. I think it's time to get him into the bathroom. Grab him, Riley."

Maggie watched in dismay as Rand and Riley literally dragged her son into the bathroom. The familiar sounds that filtered through the door made her wince. She'd been on that end more times than she cared to remember.

She paced the kitchen uncertainly, feeling down. Her son needed her, yet she should also be with her guests, circulating. Her hand was on the doorknob when Rand opened it.

"Go back to the party, Maggie. I'll get him to bed. I'll let you know when he's tucked in."

"I should be . . . How could this . . . I feel . . ."

"Guilty? Look, the kid is drunk. He's sick. It's not the end of the world. We'll get him to bed and tomorrow will be soon enough to deal with it. Trust me, Maggie."

"Go ahead, Aunt Maggie. We can handle it," Riley said.

"If you're sure... Thank you, Rand," Maggie said, standing on tiptoe to kiss his cheek. For one startled moment she stared deeply into his eyes. It was Maggie who looked away first.

Forty minutes later, Rand sought her out as she stood in a family group. "We stuck him under the shower and put him to bed; he's sound asleep. He's going to have a big head tomorrow, but he'll survive."

"I'm grateful, Rand. It could have been disastrous. What can I do to thank you?"

Riley didn't flinch when Sawyer's nails bit into his arm. He could feel the trembling in her body. There was something wrong. "Dance with me," he said abruptly.

"Nice try, Riley. I'm not in the mood to dance. What I need is a drink, maybe two or even three."

"Make it one. I've had enough drunks for one night."

"That's what I like, an opinionated male," Sawyer said bitterly as she headed for the bar. Riley came up behind her in time to hear her order a double Scotch straight up. Damn Cole Tanner.

When the last shower of fireworks lit the heavens and the final strain of "Deep in the Heart of Texas" filled the air, Maggie loosed a sigh of relief. It was three-forty-five in the morning, and as far as she could tell, not a single guest had left. This, then, was the closing signal. Unless, of course, she wanted to serve a champagne breakfast at dawn. Tiredly, she toyed with the idea. It would be a massive undertaking.

"Don't even think it," Amelia whispered, coming up behind her. "I've danced my feet off and it's time for bed. Just start saying good night and they'll leave. Pap used to stand up and say, 'That's it folks, party's over!' It was a real smash, Maggie; you did yourself proud."

Maggie turned eagerly to Amelia, warming to her aunt's affection. "I couldn't have done it without all of you. I know that now. Hell, I knew it from the beginning." She smiled wearily. "By the way, that's some guy you got there. I like him, Aunt Amelia."

"So do I, and I thought we were going to dispense with that aunt routine."

"Habit. I'll try and remember. So, how does your husband like all of us?"

"What's not to like? He adores us, all of us. If you want the truth, I think this little shindig blew his socks off. To him a barbecue is hot dogs and hamburgers on a grill in the backyard. Six guests, tops. He'll get used to us Texans. I think he's serious about wanting to buy that property he was talking about. High middle-income housing. Something like that."

"If he is serious and wants to look into it, why don't you both stay on here until he makes up his mind. God knows there's plenty of room. You could see more of the boys, and Cary might be a good influence on them. Think about it. Uh-oh, they're getting ready to leave. Once Orwell Snyder puts on his Stetson, that means he's going home. Come, we have to smile and play the game."

That's exactly what it was—a game. Winners and losers. And tonight, for the first time, Maggie was a winner.

When the massive oak doors closed for the last time, the weary Coleman family followed one another up the long, circular staircase.

"This house needs an elevator," Susan complained. Her husband shot her an angry look and leaped up the steps two at a time. Susan held on to the rail, each step torture for her aching, swollen feet.

Billie, walking behind her, kept silent. She knew Jerome wouldn't appreciate interference from her or anyone else. Then, as she waited for Thad to open the bedroom door, she pretended not to see the hunger in Sawyer's eyes as Rand said good night and left her standing outside his bedroom door.

Come home to Sunbridge and all its problems, Billie thought wearily. Welcome home.

Maggie stopped to chat a moment with Sawyer, then looked in on Riley. She let the boy hug her and kiss her soundly on the cheek. "It was a great party, Aunt Maggie. I'm glad I was here to help celebrate."

"This is your home, Riley, for as long as you want. Remember that."

"Thank you, Aunt Maggie. Get some rest; you look tired."

"I am, but I don't think I'll be able to sleep. I think I'll have a cup of tea and maybe unwind all by myself. Sleep well."

Maggie had had no intention of having a cup of tea, but once she mentioned it, the idea sounded good. She fussed with the kettle and found the tea bags in the canister on the kitchen counter.

She carried her cup outside to the front lawn, glad of the cool, early-morning air and the silence. Carefully she picked her way through the party debris. Tomorrow the caterers would clean up, but now there was just quiet and solitude. She was sitting with her feet propped, heels kicked off, when she realized she wasn't alone.

"Too much party?"

"Rand! I thought you'd be sound asleep by now."

"I never sleep when I have things on my mind."

"I'm like that, too. This party was so important to me, and now that it's over I have to unwind. I thought tea would help. I don't drink anymore."

"I noticed. Maybe one of these days I'll go on the wagon myself."

"How long are you staying?" Maggie asked quickly. She had no desire to discuss her abstinence from alcohol; it was a private thing.

Rand shrugged. Maggie shrugged back. Colemans didn't limit their invitations; he knew he could stay a month and be welcome. She settled back in her chair.

"I don't know which I like best, the sound of the crickets at night or the early-morning chirping of the birds," she said, sipping her tea. "The birds, I suppose, because their chirping means the beginning of a new day. I'm into new beginnings."

Maggie's words startled Rand. This soft-spoken, almost humble person wasn't the Maggie he had avoided in the past. "I can understand that," he replied, so softly Maggie had to strain to hear him. "I'm more or less in a winding-down process myself. So, I suppose that's a new beginning of sorts. I'll have to adjust my life and go on from there."

"Sort of getting your house in order, that kind of thing?"

Rand laughed. "I guess you could say that. Tonight convinced me that I want to sit back now and enjoy my life. I'm not getting any younger—that's for certain."

"None of us are. It's amazing where life has taken us. Good things, bad things, things that are so meaningless in the end and yet so crucial at the time. Do you suppose this is a time to mend fences, to ride into the future without regard for the past?"

"For some of us. But there are always fences that are impossible to mend, words said that can't be taken back, only be forgiven." Guiltily he thought of Sawyer. He should be upstairs right now, this minute, making love to her. She had expected it—he read it in her eyes. "That's what hurts, that's when you have to be strong—do what must be done, say what must be said, and suffer the consequences...." Rand smiled. "Early-morning philosophies always sound so profound," he mused. "I wonder why. Perhaps because the early hour simply lends an air of profoundness to very ordinary observations."

Maggie leaned her head back, eyes closed, thinking about what he'd said.

"You should go to bed, Maggie. In an hour or so the sun will be completely up."

"That's okay by me. The dark and I don't get along. I sleep with a night-light, and if you ever tell anyone, I'll deny it."

Rand laughed, a genuine sound of amusement; it made him realize that he hadn't laughed in some time. "I can top that. I have this raggedy old cat that goes everywhere with me. It has a permanent niche in my suitcase, and I can tell you I've gotten some pretty curious looks when I go through customs. Still, where I go, she goes."

"Sally Dearest?" Maggie asked in amazement.

"You remembered?"

"Remember? When we were little I would have killed to get that cat away from you. It was so broken in, so ugly, so incredibly..."

"Dirty and mended. It was my security blanket. I guess in some ways we never give those things up; we only trade them in for other things. Still, old Sally Dearest was a comfort."

"I wouldn't know about comfort. I was never permitted to take anything to bed with me. I wasn't allowed to suck my thumb or anything children do to settle themselves down. We went to bed cold turkey, and we slept or we didn't, but we went to bed. Nurse was a bitch."

"You survived," Rand said softly. He lifted his glass to get the last ice cube and started crunching on it. Maggie liked the sound.

"If you want to call it surviving," she said. "God! I'd never want to go through that again. Youth isn't all it's cracked up to be."

"It's good you understand that, Maggie. I think you're due for a round of battles. Cole is a very unhappy young man."

"I know. What I don't know is how much of his unhappiness is my responsibility, or what I can do about it. We'll work it out," Maggie said confidently. "We have to."

"I hope so."

"You're doubtful?"

"I am. Perhaps Riley being here isn't such a good idea. Cole already resents him. Riley will do his part; family and friendships are important to him. But Cole feels intruded upon; that's evident. That kind of bitterness is personal, Maggie, and has nothing to do with prejudice. I have the feeling your guts are going to be churning from time to time. But if you listen to your heart, if you're fair with both boys, I think you'll be able to handle it. That's the key word, Maggie. Fair."

"You're probably right, Rand," Maggie said quietly. Already, she knew she preferred Riley, although she loved Coleman because he was her child. A finger of guilt touched her. No, she thought, shaking her head, that was just being honest. Who wouldn't prefer the open genuineness and affection of Riley to the darker, troubled, guarded Cole?

Rand turned to look over his shoulder toward the east. "It's been a long time since I've seen the sun come up," he said softly.

"Well, you're in the right place. There's nothing to compare to sunrise in Texas, unless, of course, it's the sunset."

Rand laughed again, turning to Maggie, finding the reflection of his own amusement in her eyes. "Spoken like a true Texan," he said. "Let's enjoy the peace and quiet, Maggie. It won't be long before everyone is up and about and the circus begins again."

While Rand slid down in the chair to rest his head against its back, Maggie craned her neck in the direction of the house. Her eyes widened when she scanned the upper windows. Most glowed with light. Sawyer was outlined against the sheer curtains. Maggie's heart thumped in her chest at the realization of having been observed without her knowing. A shadow passed before Riley's window. He, too, was awake.

Rand, questioning Maggie's silence, opened his eyes and followed her gaze. He recognized Sawyer's slim form at the window. He could feel her staring at him, could feel her confusion and her silent accusation. It was his fault she was up there alone. They hadn't seen each other in over two months—he should be there with her, not out here sharing this sunrise with her mother.

Billie lay restlessly beside Thad in the big, oversize bed. Overtired, she told herself. But she knew it was this house, Sunbridge, that was making her restless. She wished now Maggie had put Thad and her in the studio behind the house. Even with the dust and the mildew, the studio would have been preferable to sleeping here. She'd spent more than half her life beneath this roof, had known her greatest happinesses and greatest sorrows here. But she'd never belonged here.

Her hand reached out to smooth the flatness of Thad's belly. Softly curling hairs grazed her palm and she felt him move beside her. He wasn't sleeping, either. He'd seen how nervous she'd been when they were getting ready for bed and had sensitively known that she feared he would want to make love to her, here, in this house, where she'd spent so many years with Moss.

"We're both tired, darling," he'd murmured as she'd nestled her head onto his shoulder. "Let me hold you until you fall asleep." His lips had brushed her temple as he'd taken her into his arms.

Until that moment she hadn't known how anxious she'd been about sharing a bed with Thad in this house. Thad was too special, their love too cherished, to taint with memories of Sunbridge.

Billie snuggled down further, wrapping her arm around him. If she just lay here, quietly, and tried to relax, surely sleep would come.

The voice was intimate and cunning when she heard it whispering in her ear. "You fell asleep first," Amelia replied playfully.

"But I'm not sleeping now," Cary said, sliding closer to her, his warm, knowing hands gliding the length of her body.

Amelia wrapped her arms around his neck, pulling him down to her to find the warmth of his mouth. "I love making love at dawn," she murmured, her voice languid with desire.

"I love it any time of the day or night." Cary nibbled her lower lip, teasing the tip of his tongue along the sensitive inner flesh.

"Don't talk about it; do it!" Amelia slid her hands over

the muscular smoothness of his back, squeezing her fingers between their bodies, searching for him, knowing that his arousal would come hard and swift from the pressure that was already throbbing against her thigh.

He felt her touch and she was satisfied by the sound of his indrawn breath. His kisses grew heated; his hands searched the hollows of her offered body.

"How much time do we have before this house starts jumping?" he asked, smiling at the familiar response of her arching back as his fingers slipped softly between her legs.

"Never enough," came her breathless answer as she surrendered to the sweet abandon to which only Cary could bring her.

Billie snapped the latch of her Gucci carry-on bag and tried not to listen to Susan and Jerome squabbling in the room across the hall—the room she had shared with Moss. It had heard many such arguments and seen much unhappiness.

Thad was stuffing his shaving gear into his bag as quickly as he could so he and Billie could escape this place. No way were they going to stay for four days! One night and he'd had enough of Sunbridge for a year. Anxiously he watched Billie out of the corner of his eye, knowing she couldn't help but hear Susan and Jerome.

Billie saw Thad watching her, and their eyes met. "Perhaps if I knock on the door and tell them we're leaving, they'll stop." Suddenly, she dropped onto the bed, her head lowered, hands over her ears. "Oh, Thad, I thought I'd never have to hear the word abortion in connection with one of my children again. I only hope no one else can hear them."

"If you knock on the door, they'll stop—but only pick up where they left off once we're gone. You know, Billie, I never really had an opinion about Jerome until yesterday. The guy's an out-and-out bastard."

Billie shook her head. "I didn't know. All this time I thought Susan and Jerome were so well suited for each

other. They seemed to share so much. But if they can't
agree on becoming parents...there must be chasms of
differences between them. Now I know why Susan blurted
out the news of her pregnancy yesterday. She thought
once it was out in the open, Jerome would never dare
push the issue. But it seems he has it all figured out. Thad,
I have to talk to her."

"Darling, play it by ear. If we miss this plane, we'll
catch another. Don't worry about time schedules; you
and Susan are more important."

Billie flashed him a smile of gratitude. There were times
she thought it would be enough just to have Thad love
her; his understanding her was a bonus not many women
enjoyed.

The sounds of the argument continued, and as Thad
and Billie finished their packing, they couldn't help but
listen.

"Damn you, Susan, you agreed you wouldn't tell anyone! You said you'd think about an abortion. We can't
have a baby ruin our lives. Why weren't you more careful?
I can't forgive you for this."

"Then don't. I never agreed to an abortion. You did
all the talking, Jerome. You made all the decisions. This
is my life, my body, my child."

"It's my child, too, and I don't want it. What about
the tour? Do you just expect me to cancel because you're
pregnant and aren't supposed to fly so often? It isn't done
that way and you know it. Copenhagen is very important
to me. I wouldn't put it past you to have done this deliberately."

"Copenhagen is important to *you*, not me! What's
important to me is this baby. But I'll compromise. I'll tour
for another three months; I'll be in my fifth month then.
Take it or leave it."

"Three months doesn't cover Copenhagen," Jerome
said angrily. "If you're going to do it, do all of it or nothing."

"If that's the way you feel, then it's nothing. You can
leave today if you want. I can stay here with Maggie, I'm
sure."

"We don't need a baby; we don't want one. What's going to happen when it arrives? Are you planning to retire? What about me?"

"You always want to know how something affects you. What about *me*? You may not want this baby, but I do. I'm getting older. I never thought I'd become pregnant. I didn't plan this; it just happened—and I'm *glad* it happened! It's not the end of the world."

"I've heard enough, Thad," Billie said. "It's time to leave."

"Are you certain?"

"Certain." She smiled weakly. "From what I've heard, Susan is handling herself admirably. She knows what she wants and she'll fight for it. I'm proud of her."

Thad was relieved. "Okay. Just give me a chance to get these bags downstairs and then say good-bye to Susan. We can work on the hugs and kisses with the others downstairs."

Billie walked across the hall and knocked softly on the door, calling her daughter's name. Susan swung the door open, her eyes filled with tears, and fell into her mother's arms sobbing. Billie cradled the blond head to her breast. "Do what's best for yourself, Susan. Make your decision and stick with it. I gave you our itinerary for the next month; after that, you can get in touch with me in Vermont. Our home is yours if you ever need it."

"Mam..." Susan gulped. "I never meant for you to know. I didn't want anyone to know. I never thought Jerome could be so selfish...so cruel."

"Darling, all our idols topple from time to time. We just learn to live with it and to forgive them. Now, dry your eyes. Thad and I are ready to leave."

Maggie stood on the front portico, a lump in her throat. It was hard to have her mother leave her. Always before, she had done the leaving...or the running away. She felt a stab of regret for all that had been forever lost—until Billie stopped in midstride and ran back to her, throwing her arms around her daughter.

"This is what you've always wanted, Maggie; now work to keep it. I know it's going to be all right; if I wasn't certain, I wouldn't leave." It was a lie, but a small one. If Maggie could take comfort from it, she could be forgiven. "Seth used to say this is the time to fish or cut bait. Last night was a magnificent beginning for you. Use it."

"I'll make it, Mam," Maggie whispered fiercely.

"I know you will. Take care of yourself and the boys."

"Tell the Hasegawas I'll take care of Riley, not to worry. And Mam. Tell them thank you, for me."

Maggie's eyes lingered on the winding driveway long after the car had disappeared.

"I never did care for good-byes myself." Rand's voice was loud in the quiet morning.

Maggie whirled around, annoyed that someone had seen her at such a private moment. "Haven't you been to bed yet?"

"No, and from the looks of you, I don't think you have, either."

"Since I'm still wearing my dress from last night, I wouldn't exactly call your observation astute. I'm going up now to shower and change. Do you think you're up to riding with the boys? I heard you make plans yesterday afternoon."

"Yes. But I don't know if Cole will remember. By the way, I looked in on him and he's still sleeping."

Maggie winced. "Don't wait for him, Rand. Go with Riley. Cole will be a wet hornet when he does haul himself out of his bed. Did you have anything to eat?"

"No, not yet. I noticed the buffet in the dining room. Very English." He smiled in approval. "All that's missing is the kippers and kidney pie. I'll shower first and then get something. Maybe by that time Riley will be down."

"He's already in the barn. He said his good-byes to Mam and Thad and ran off. I think he was afraid he'd cry if he stayed to watch them leave."

Rand climbed the stairs to his room. He knew Sawyer was up. She'd never have missed kissing her grandmother good-bye. He found himself lightening his step as he passed her room and then hating himself for it. Damn it, what kind of coward was he?

Once in his own room, he stripped and turned on the shower full blast. The steam rose and misted invitingly. He was already behind the frosted glass shower door when Sawyer opened his bedroom door and closed it softly behind her.

She waited a moment, feeling the strength seep slowly out of her. Nervously she touched the door latch, about to step back into the hall. Then, before she could change her mind, she pressed it, locking the door securely.

Whatever was wrong with Rand was going to be settled now. She'd waited long enough. It was difficult to ignore what she was thinking, what Rand was making her think by avoiding her, by his indifference. It would be so easy just to step beneath the needle-sharp spray and press herself into his arms. She loved the feel of his body against hers, loved it when they showered together, wet and slick with water and soap, touching, kissing, yielding. It had been so long, too long, and she *needed* him. Last night he'd begged off, saying he was tired. But he hadn't been too tired to stay with Maggie, and he'd still been with her when Grand and Thad had pulled out of the drive.

Sawyer didn't like what she was thinking. And she feared what she was feeling. Don't think, she told herself. Act!

Trembling fingers fumbled with the belt of her terry robe. Prickles rose on her skin in the warm room when her nightie dropped to the floor. If he just holds me, it'll be all right, she thought nervously. Rand will make it right. Over and over she whispered the words to herself, working up the confidence to open the bathroom door and step into the clouds of steam.

She could just make out his form behind the clouded glass. The sound of rushing water filled her ears, echoing the desperate rush of her need for him.

Rand stood beneath the invigorating spray, trying to purge the effects of a night without sleep and the haunting image of Sawyer's face. The water was hot, almost too hot; he could feel the slope of his shoulders and his buttocks reddening from the heat. Punishing, but good; one kind of pain to mask another.

Silently, the shower door opened, and he felt her before he saw her. She stood almost as tall as he did, long-legged, slim, water beading on her shoulders and the fullness of her breasts. Venus dawning from the sea. It was the expression on her face, her hopeful smile, the deep yearning in her eyes, that paralyzed him.

Her movements were slow and fluid when she reached for him, pressing herself against him, drawing him into her embrace and searching for his kiss. Her body was impatient in its demands; her pelvis danced a sensuous rhythm; her thighs clung to his. His skin was clean, fresh; rivulets of water entered her mouth as her tongue licked near the base of his throat. She enticed him closer with the firm press of her fingers on his haunches, pulling him closer, inviting him with almost imperceptible gyrations of her hips. If she was aware that his arms did not hold her, that his lips did not return her kiss, she did not show it.

Sawyer felt the panic swell in her throat. There was an emptiness within her that only he could fill; yet his arms hung limply at his sides, his mouth did not respond to pressure. Boldly, she clutched at him, demanding he answer her caresses, appealing to his senses, refusing to accept his denial. She found herself falling to her knees, wrapping her arms around his legs, finding him with her mouth, almost crying with frustration when she realized that her urgings were futile. He was hardly aroused; he did not want her; she could not make him want her.

Rand's hands were clutched at his side. He wanted so much to reach for her, to soothe her, to explain; but how could he without encouraging her? If he released his rigid control for even one instant, he would lose his resolve. To use her, to make love to her when he did not love her, would be more unkind.

A low groan of misery escaped him. He raised his head,

unable to look down into her face. Even squeezing his eyes shut could not prevent the tears that ran down his cheeks to mingle with the shower spray.

Blindly Sawyer struggled with the shower door, throwing her weight against it, forcing it open. With an almost frenzied desperation she fought against the scream that was building in her as she skidded across the slick bathroom tiles. She needed to get away from him, to hide, to find oblivion.

Stumbling, stopping only long enough to jam her arms into her robe and wrap the thick terry cloth tightly around her body, she flew back to the privacy of her room.

Water that hadn't been absorbed by her robe ran in rivulets down her legs and puddled at her feet. Her hair was wet, dripping onto her shoulders and face, but she was oblivious to it all.

Rand, Rand! she cried to herself. Why? What has changed? What changed you? It can't be over between us. I won't let it be over.

Sawyer sank onto the bench in front of the old-fashioned dressing table, unable to meet her eyes in the mirror, afraid of what she would see. She'd sensed this change in Rand, had refused to admit it. She'd closed her eyes to his indifference, shut her ears to his excuses. But no longer.

Premonitions. Dread. Fear of losing someone you love, someone you want to love you. It was a familiar story to Sawyer. It was being a child again, writing letters to Maggie and waiting days by the mailbox for answers that never arrived. It was always feeling sore and bruised and heartsick.

She looked up, and a bitter smile met her reflection in the mirror. Well, she'd been forced to accept the situation as a child, but she wasn't a child anymore. This was one situation she refused to accept! If nothing else, she would find out why Rand had changed.

Sawyer glanced around the room. This wasn't hers; she'd grown up in the studio out behind the house. There she'd had a room that was her own. All her things were there, her childhood things. That was where she wanted to be. This impersonal room Maggie had assigned her made her feel like a guest, as though Sunbridge hadn't been her home, her past, almost her entire life.

She made up her mind in an instant, shedding her damp robe to change into a worn pair of jeans and a blue denim shirt. In scuffed riding boots, comfortable as a pair of old slippers, and with her hair pulled back into a ponytail, she felt more like her old self, the self that hadn't been humiliated in a shower with Rand. The self that still believed Rand loved her.

{{{{{{{{ CHAPTER SIX }}}}}}}}

Amelia tripped into the dining room, Cary behind her. Her eyes sparkled and her cheeks were rosy. It was obvious to everyone that she had just made love, very satisfactory love. She smiled warmly at Susan and Jerome. Riley was already seated at the table, digging into a plate of ham and eggs and sipping from a monstrous glass of orange juice. Cole was nowhere in sight.

"Good morning, everyone," Cary said genially as he filled his plate. "Are Texas mornings always this beautiful?"

Susan shrugged. Jerome merely burrowed deeper into himself. "I think so," Riley responded shyly. "When I was here before, it was springtime, but it was gorgeous."

"You could have asked me, Cary," Amelia said with a pout.

"And listen to a dissertation on Texas weather? Don't

forget we have things to do this morning."

Susan's head shot up. "Are you going out, Aunt Amelia?" she asked anxiously.

"As a matter of fact, I am. I think we'll be gone till later in the day."

"Could we talk after you get back?"

Amelia hesitated. She was not in the mood to be a mother hen to Susan today; she wanted to concentrate on Cary. "I'll see, sweetie. Perhaps before dinner, okay?"

"Sure...."

As Susan went back to toying listlessly with the scrambled eggs on her plate, Cary stared at her sympathetically. She looked awful—tired, bloated, and unhappy. Apparently, pregnancy did not agree with her.

Jerome got up from the table, his plate empty, and finished off the last of his coffee. "Ready, Susan?" he asked.

"No, I'm not. I think I'll have another cup of coffee."

"No, you won't. Caffeine makes you nervous and you won't be able to practice later."

"I wasn't going to practice later. I'm on vacation—or did you forget? Besides, I don't feel well."

"You'll feel better if you practice," Jerome said.

Cary stopped with his fork halfway to his mouth. He didn't like Jerome, he decided. The man was a bully, he'd always hated bullies. If he didn't watch it, Jerome could ruin his entire day. Then, out of the corner of his eye, he could see Amelia warning him to stay out of their argument.

Jerome saw the silent exchange between Amelia and Cary, and sensed his argument with Susan could result in a family confrontation. Without another word, he turned on his heel and stomped from the room.

"Susan," Amelia chuckled, "you never told me Jerome was so testy in the mornings."

Susan's eyes brimmed. "Aunt Amelia, there are a lot of things I haven't told you about Jerome. I do need to talk to you."

"Yes, yes, of course you do. I promise we'll be back

before dinner." With a bright smile, Amelia patted Cary's hand and stood up. "No time for another cup, darling. We're late as it is."

Hurriedly she bent down and kissed Susan's cheek. "Cheer up, darling. All men are bears when they wake up in the morning. This, too, shall pass," she said lightly, and left the room clinging happily to her husband's arm.

A wayward tear splashed into Susan's coffee cup and she rose in disgust. Mam was gone, Amelia was off with her new husband, and she was alone. She supposed she could talk to Maggie or Sawyer...or she could try to solve her problems herself. Sighing, she stood up and headed back to her room. Whoever would have thought having a baby could destroy a marriage and a career?

How forceful could she be? she wondered. She'd never really been tested. As long as she'd done what Jerome wanted, things had gone smoothly. But for the first time in her life, she was tired of doing what Jerome wanted. Tired of traveling, tired of playing the same music over and over, tired of doing laundry in hotel rooms. She wanted a home. And a child. What was wrong with wanting to take a year or so off to have a baby? It was time to feel life, to nurture it, to have someone to love and love her unconditionally.

Susan entered their bedroom and slammed the door behind her, looking at her husband in surprise. "What are you doing, Jerome?"

"What you should be doing. We're leaving. We have commitments, and I won't allow you to cancel them on a whim."

"A baby isn't a whim, Jerome. We have a week. You promised. I need this week. Why are you being so awful about this? I don't like it!"

"You know I never liked this place. You told me you didn't like it, either. I don't understand why all of a sudden you want to stay here. Music and I, we're your life. Aren't we?"

Susan stared at her husband until he looked away. "It's

the only home there is, for now. I can rest here. I'm very run-down."

"It's not my fault you don't take your vitamins," Jerome snapped.

"It's not just a question of vitamins. We're always eating on the run; the food is either overcooked or underdone. And I don't get enough sleep. All we do is travel and work. I can't keep it up. You have to understand."

"What I understand is you should have gone for an abortion the first thing. That's what I wanted. That's what's *best for us.*"

"For you, maybe, but not for me! I told you I don't want any part of an abortion. I couldn't live with myself. Listen to me, Jerome—I will never, ever get an abortion!"

Jerome's stomach tightened into a knot. He was so angry he could barely force out the words. "You're ruining me! Deliberately! You're putting an unborn baby before me. You don't love me. You never loved me!"

Susan sank onto the edge of the bed. Maybe he was right. Maybe she never really loved him. She felt confused. Then suddenly she realized Jerome always did this to her—made her feel guilty just to get his way. Well, not this time. She was a Coleman, by God, and all the Colemans had grit! "Exactly what is it you want from me, Jerome?" she asked, an edge of steel in her voice.

"Get an abortion. We'll finish the tour. We'll take it easy next year. I promise you we'll take that trip to the Greek islands you've always wanted. I don't think that's too much to ask."

"Are you interested in hearing what I want? Or what I feel is good for me and our baby? Let me tell you. I'll finish off the tour, and if Maggie will have me, I'm coming back to Sunbridge to have our baby. I'm going to take two years off. You can continue on your own. You can go back to England or you can come home here to Sunbridge. That, Jerome, is my one and only offer. And whether we leave today or at the end of the week is not going to change my mind. Either you take it or you leave it."

Jerome's brain was clicking away like an overworked computer. Once he had Susan away from here, he was sure he could get her to do whatever he wanted. And he wanted Copenhagen. "It's a deal. But I want to leave today. This evening. We can take the Concorde back. What do you say?"

What difference did it make, really? Susan thought tiredly. She'd be back in three months anyway. Pray God, Maggie would agree.

Cole swung his legs over the side of the bed and immediately fell backward. His head throbbed, his heart pounded, and bile rose in his throat. He knew he had to make it to the bathroom but couldn't move. He rolled over and retched on the dark brown carpet. He groaned. Why in the hell had he messed with beer? He could have gotten high on a joint without a hangover. One thing he knew, he'd never make a drunk.

Had he made an ass of himself last night? Evidently, or he wouldn't be feeling this way now. Memories of Rand and Riley floated around his buzzing head. He remembered Rand sticking him in the shower after he'd puked his guts up, while Riley had looked on. Goody-two-shoes Riley. Already he hated the little Jap and he'd only been here a day.

Cole's head continued to throb. There was something he'd planned on doing this morning. If only he could think. He wondered why his mother hadn't come in to check on him. She'd probably had a flying fit last night. Maybe she'd peeked in while he was asleep. He didn't really care one way or the other.

A quiet knock sounded on the door. Cole ignored it. The knock sounded a second time. It wasn't his mother; she'd have walked right in. When the knock sounded a third time, Cole rolled over and yelled, "Come in!" wincing at the sound of his own voice.

Riley poked his head in the door. "Are you going riding, Cole?"

"Not today I'm not. And don't count on me for future days. I hate horses."

Riley blinked. How could a Texan not like to ride? "Can I get you some aspirin or a glass of water?"

"No, thanks. Get out of here. I've got things I have to do today."

"Cole, your mother sent me up here to get you. I wouldn't have bothered you because I—"

"Knew I was drunk last night. Well, this morning I'm sick. I don't care if my mother wants me or not. Tell her I'm still sleeping. That way you can be the conquering hero just like your old man."

Riley bristled. "What's that supposed to mean?"

"It means whatever you want it to mean. Why are you here, anyway? How long are you staying? Who invited you?"

"My grandfather and our grandmother talked it over, and Aunt Maggie sent the official invitation. I'm to stay here as long as I want. This was my father's home, too." He wanted to say more, but decided against it; Cole was sick and angry enough without a fight.

"And I'll just bet you can't wait to get your share, right?"

"My share of what?"

"Don't play dumb, little Jap boy. This place. Sunbridge. Well, the deed is in my mother's name, and when she buys it, I get this place. The first thing I'll do is sell it."

"Cole, I don't need a share of anything. I'm here because I never got a chance to know my father. That's the only reason."

"Sure, sure," Cole muttered as he struggled to his feet. Immediately, he grabbed hold of the bedpost. "I thought I told you to get out of here!"

"I'm going. I hope you feel better later on," Riley said, closing the door behind him.

What was he going to tell Aunt Maggie? Riley asked himself as he walked quietly down the hall. A lie was a lie no matter how you looked at it. Maybe he could stall by going back to his room for a while. He grinned. It would be worth it just to look in the floor-length mirror again. Every stitch of clothing he had on was his father's, right down to the Jockey shorts. Everything had been preserved in plastic bags and cardboard boxes—he'd seen the cartons in his closet, all bearing his grandmother's handwriting—then they'd been taken out, laundered, and placed in sweet-smelling drawers. He'd repacked his own things and piled his suitcases on top of the shelf. From now on he was going to wear only his father's things.

Riley returned to his room and sat down at his father's desk, rubbing his cheek on his shoulder. The checkered shirt gave off an aroma of cleanliness...and something. The same scent that lingered on the baseball hat his grandmother had brought to Japan on her first trip.

This room that had belonged to his father was so different from his room back in Tokyo. There the furniture had been Eastern, light and airy. Here the furniture was heavy Western style. He could see traces of the boy in the man's room. The shelves in the closet held treasures he would go through when he felt the time was right. He could envision himself sitting here at the desk, using the same gooosenecked lamp, poring over the same books, maybe even using some of his father's pencils; there were enough of them in the drawer.

He wanted to charge outside and explore and investigate. On the long plane trip with Sawyer he'd fantasized about doing all kinds of things with Cole; they'd be friends, inseparable buddies. Sixteen was almost grown-up. There would be girls and they'd date, and then in the confines of their rooms they'd talk about those dates.

It wasn't going to happen. Fantasies? Not really. The reality of his situation had hit him the moment he'd been introduced to Cole. Cole Tanner was his cousin, but he was pure trouble. And right now, trouble was something he didn't want to deal with.

Sighing, Riley stood up and took a last look at himself

in the mirror. He couldn't delay going downstairs any longer. Aunt Maggie had sent him to get Cole, and he'd have to tell her something. He was relieved to see Cole when he rounded the corner of the hallway. He didn't hurry his step and wasn't surprised when his cousin didn't wait for him.

Riley knew his aunt Maggie thought they were together when she appeared at the foot of the stairs and watched them come down. Neither boy did anything to make her think differently.

"There you are. I was beginning to think you were going to sleep all day." She was talking to Cole, but she turned to Riley. "Ken has your horse ready to be saddled. You might as well learn from scratch. Cole will join you soon. I want to have a cup of coffee with him first.

"Feeling a bit under the weather, are we?" Maggie said indulgently after Riley had left.

"Come off it, Mother. I'm suffering from a hangover and we both know it. Cheerfulness isn't going to help my pounding head or my sour stomach. And let's set the record straight right now: I'm not going riding, with or without my cousin. I'd appreciate it if you wouldn't keep shoving him at me."

Maggie took a deep breath. Obviously it was going to be one of those mornings. "Look, Cole, you and I have quite a few things to discuss, and now is as good a time as any. That's an order."

The minute Martha had poured Cole's orange juice and left, Maggie started in. "I'm very disappointed in you, Cole. I expected more from you last night. You knew how important that party was to me. How could you do that? You're only a child!"

"I seem to recall someone saying you'd already had a baby at my age, Mother," Cole drawled insolently.

Maggie flinched but refused to take the bait. "Cole, we have to talk. I don't like what's happening here. I want us to be a family. We have things that need discussing."

"Like the way you said you'd think about allowing me

to make the trip? That was just lip service, wasn't it. You never had any intention of letting me go. Admit it!"

"I admit it," Maggie said through clenched teeth. "I want you here at Sunbridge. You aren't going back to military school, either. In the fall you'll go to school right here. I'm sorry to hit you with all this when you aren't feeling up to par, but it's necessary."

"No it isn't. You like jabbing me and you know it. Why is Riley here? You never did give me a straight answer to that. Don't get any ideas that we're going to be best buddies, because it won't work."

Maggie set her coffee cup precisely in the center of her saucer. "I was hoping it would work. I was hoping you'd try because it's important to me. Are you jealous of Riley, Cole?"

Cole snorted. "Me? Jealous of a Jap? Come on, Mother."

"I can't force you to like him, but I can insist you be civil. And I do insist," she added sharply.

"Or what? You already said I can't go on the trip. You said I'm going to the local schoolhouse, so what's left?"

"Why are you being so difficult? Why can't you meet me halfway? Why do we always end up at each other's throats?"

"Why is it always *my* fault? *You're* the one who seems to have problems with relationships," he snapped.

"I'm getting very tired of you throwing up my past. I'm trying to get along with you. I've made my mistakes and I'm living with them. I don't want the same thing to happen to you."

"The nut doesn't fall far from the tree. Is that what you're saying?"

"No, that's what you're saying. I'm trying to prevent you from making my mistakes, and your attitude isn't helping."

"If you'd leveled with me from the beginning, we wouldn't be having this discussion."

"Would you have listened? Would you?" When Cole shrugged, Maggie continued, "As for Riley, he has as much right to be here as you and I. If his father had lived, *he* would have inherited Sunbridge."

"Second best, eh, Mater?"

"Stop it, Cole! You're not funny. Right now, you could take a few lessons in manners from your cousin."

"I knew that was coming. He's tall and handsome! I'm a head shorter and skinny. He looks good in his father's clothes, and I look like a clown dressed up for Halloween. Well, you can't make me into something I'm not, Mother."

"I'm not trying to make you into anything. I'm trying to give you a decent home so you can put down roots. It's important, Cole. Before, you were at school during the year and a guest in an apartment in New York for holidays. That wasn't home. *This* is home!"

"*Your* home, Mother. It's just a house to me. The apartment was fine. I liked New York."

"Well, I didn't."

"That's the bottom line, isn't it. It's what you want. It's always what you want. You and Dad didn't even tell me you were getting a divorce. I had to hear it from my counselor at school."

"I wanted to tell you. Your father did, too. But your counselor thought it would be best coming from him. And unfortunately, we listened to bad advice. I'm sorry about that, but I can't undo it."

"I called Dad this morning."

"You *what*?"

Cole laughed. "I thought that would get a rise out of you. I called Dad this morning. He'll be here this weekend. He said he was planning on coming next week as a surprise, but he'd move it up to this weekend because he's free." Cole savored the look on his mother's face, for a moment, then moved in for the kill. "He said I could come and live with him in New York if I wanted."

Maggie managed to gather her composure. She reached for her coffee cup with trembling hands, gripping it around the middle, but she didn't drink. "I have sole custody of you, Cole," she said evenly. "You cannot go to New York unless I agree. I do not agree. Do you understand?"

"Dad's a lawyer. He said he'd work it out with you."

"There's nothing to work out. You're staying here."

Cole jumped up from the table. "You can't make me into your brother or your father! That's what you're trying to do. You wanted to see me in a military school so I'd wear a uniform like Grandpap did. You constantly try to find a resemblance to him in me. Now you want me to play cowpoke like your brother. You want to use me to make yourself feel better."

"That's not true!"

"Isn't it? Then why is Riley here? You could have said no when Grand asked you if he could come. You're using him, too."

Maggie brought the coffee cup to her lips. The boy's words bothered her.

"No, Cole, you're wrong."

"No, Mother, I'm right."

"I won't argue the point. Now that you've told me of your father's visit, we'll wait till he gets here to discuss it. Meantime, you will do as I say—when I say it. I know you don't feel up to riding, but they can use some help in the barn; so if I were you," Maggie said, her voice firm but not unkind, "I'd get moving and get your chores done."

Cole stared at her, mouth agape. He was about to protest, then thought better of it. He'd keep a list to present to his father. His father would understand; his father would take care of everything.

When Cole had stomped angrily out of the dining room, Maggie crumpled. Suddenly a firm hand was placed on her shoulder, and she started in surprise. "Rand!"

"I thought you handled all that very well. I'm sorry I eavesdropped, but when I heard the discussion, I didn't want to come in and interrupt."

"That's all right. I guess you can see I have a problem on my hands."

"Yes, you do. Perhaps when the boy's father arrives, you can work something out."

Maggie laughed bitterly. "That's not likely to happen.

Cranston didn't give me an argument over Cole. He simply wanted nothing to do with him. He was happy to give me sole custody of the boy. We're in the middle of divorce proceedings. For Cole to go to him . . . It did upset me."

"He's no different from most kids. He'll play both ends against the middle if he can get away with it."

"I don't understand. I've given him everything. The finest schools, the best clothes, an adequate allowance. Wonderful vacations. What more does he want?"

"That's not exactly the question here. What he did want before—what he needed—was a family, but he was sent off to school. Admit it, Maggie. You weren't the most attentive mother. I'm not trying to be insulting; believe me. Now you suddenly want a family. Cole is confused and he's angry. He sees Riley as an intruder, an interloper. Somehow you're going to have to work it out. Hopefully, Cranston will help. Parents always want what's best for their children."

Maggie let loose another sardonic laugh. "Time was I would have called that a bold-faced lie. I have a lot to learn, Rand. I'm still deep in the woods, but I see a patch of light."

"That patch will get bigger and brighter. Just keep your eyes open."

Maggie laughed. "I always do."

Rand bit into a piece of toast. She was beautiful when she laughed.

Sawyer loved the sweet smell of hay and the pungent odor coming from the barn. Of everything on Sunbridge, this was her favorite spot. It was a large milk-white barn with apple-red trim. From here she could see the studio with its southern exposure and vast skylights. It looked so neat and tidy, so empty, its inhabitants long gone. Even some of the memories were gone. If only time could stand still, just for a little while. Time to capture the memories and make them a part of oneself, so that just by closing one's eyes they could be relived.

Her eyes traveled lovingly to the gentle slope she had rolled down so many times to the house called Sunbridge. It was beautiful in the late-morning sunshine. Prairie pink, with the golden globe casting it in shades of light mauve and dusty rose. The windows winked at her like diamonds. There were secrets behind those panes of glass, secrets both joyful and painful, even shameful. Rand was behind one of those windows. What was he thinking?

She was startled by a noise behind her. "Cole, I didn't know you were here."

"I'm not here because I want to be, that's for sure," he said sourly. "Our mother seems to think I need the discipline of cleaning out this smelly place. Riley is going riding with Rand, if you're looking for him."

Sawyer studied her half brother for a few moments, wondering how much, if anything, they had in common. She hardly knew him, but so far there'd been nothing to indicate he could be even remotely likable. "I used to do exactly what you're doing, almost every day, as a matter of fact." She smiled. "It's necessary for their comfort and health, and in time you get used to it. I love horses."

"I don't. I don't like to ride, and we have stablehands. Mother is just being nasty this morning."

"Oh, why is that?" Sawyer asked nonchalantly; she couldn't help herself.

"I disgraced myself last night. I drank too much beer and it went to my head. Rand and Riley rescued me and Mother observed and is meting out the punishment. She's also more than a little ticked that I called my father in New York."

"Isn't that permitted?" Sawyer asked curiously.

Cole squinted into the bright sunlight. "Under normal conditions she usually doesn't care, but this time I asked him if I could live with him in New York. He's coming here this weekend. Mother was a tad upset," Cole said, smiling viciously.

"I had the feeling you liked it here. I know that we don't know each other very well, but it isn't because I didn't try. I want you to know that."

Cole looked at his sister. He liked her, he decided. He'd always liked her short, on-the-mark letters—and she always sent the keenest presents. "I know," he replied slowly. "I never had the opportunity to either like or dislike this place. This land was taboo when I was growing up. I wanted to come here, but Mother always wanted to go someplace else. You know what I'm talking about."

Sawyer grinned. "Poor little rich boy. The kids used to call us poor little rich girls; Maggie, too. I had my share of cruelty. I was illegitimate. The names used to hurt. . . . I know how you feel, Cole, if that's any help."

Cole didn't answer, but Sawyer decided he wasn't being difficult or remote; it was just that he was a boy, and he was hurting. "Listen, I have some hostility I have to work off," she said. "If you get another pitchfork, I'll help. I was going riding, but I can do that anytime. We can bitch to each other about what a hellish job this is. What d'ya say?"

Cole smiled. "Wait here. I'll get the other fork."

It was Cole's intention to let his sister do the bulk of the work, but when he saw her attack the job as if she meant business, he couldn't do less. They worked, sweating and grunting with exertion, in a companionable silence. When Sawyer declared it was time to take a break, they both fell back into a mound of straw.

"I'm out of shape," Sawyer gasped.

"I'm hung over," Cole grunted.

Sawyer burst out laughing. "I bet that really threw Maggie into a fit."

"It sure did. She's got herself convinced that I'm into drugs, booze, and whatever else is out there. It was the only way I knew to handle that damn party. She wanted to show me off as one of the Colemans. But I'm not really a Coleman; I'm a Tanner. Then Riley showed up," Cole blurted, surprising himself. He rarely confided in anyone like this.

"Ah, that must have been a little hard to take."

Cole leaned on his elbow, a piece of straw stuck between his teeth. "About as hard for me to take as it is for you to see Rand cozying up to my mother."

"Among other things, you're a smart-ass, too," Sawyer said coolly.

"They're having breakfast together this morning."

"Are you deliberately trying to hurt me?" Sawyer asked.

"Probably," Cole replied. "She's your mother, too. Whatever she's done to you, she's doing to me in a different way. Our mother is a bitch."

"And you and I are the good children, and she's out to destroy us. Is that what you're thinking?"

Cole flushed. "I didn't say that. But she falls a little short of being the perfect mother. Surely you noticed."

"I've noticed. I didn't know that it carried over to you, though. I'm sorry about that. You see, I had Grand. You didn't even have that."

Cole jumped up. "Don't feel sorry for me."

Sawyer noticed Cole's white-knuckled grip on the pitchfork. "No way, kid," she said lightly. "You're going to have to grow up the way the rest of us did and make the best of it. Let me give you one little piece of advice, though. Colemans don't snivel, and they don't buckle under. In public, that is. Since you're half Tanner, you're going to have to make your own decisions." Sawyer stood up. "Let's get back to work before I cool down and have to work up another sweat." Sawyer put her arm around her brother and then clapped him on his thin shoulder. Cole responded by leaning into her a little. Sawyer felt pleased.

An hour later Cole leaned on his pitchfork and said, "Hey, I'm sorry about that crack I made about Mother and Rand."

Sawyer turned, but didn't break her rhythm. "Was what you said true?"

"Yeah."

"Then there's no reason to be sorry. I'll handle it."

She would, too, Cole thought. He was sorry now that he'd missed getting to know her all these years. He sensed that she would work double time at being his sister. But he also knew she would make him meet her halfway. And she would be a friend, too. The thought pleased him.

"So tell me, what do you think of Riley?"

Cole shrugged noncommittally.

Sawyer paused in her work. "He's a nice kid, Cole. You could make all the difference to him on his visit here."

Cole shrugged again.

{{{{{{{{ CHAPTER SEVEN }}}}}}}}

Cary was glad of Amelia's company. He enjoyed doing things with his wife. She made everything sound interesting and somehow or other managed to find a challenge in whatever she did. Right now, she was better than any tour guide, pointing out landmarks and property lines, quoting the cost of fencing, and estimating the manpower hours needed to run a ranch, even a small one.

The fields were rolling pastureland. It was a beautiful Texas day, clear skies with only a cottonball or two dotting the porcelain blue that matched Amelia's dress. "Have you ever seen clearer skies or breathed cleaner air?" Amelia asked, drawing deeply into her lungs.

"I can't say that I have. This is country. I expected to see more houses. How big would you say this ... spread is?"

"This is Santo land on the right. Mr. Santo is a Tex-Mex who started out when Pap did. I'd say he's got around seventy thousand acres. One of his sons has a house back in there. You just can't see it from the road."

"The main house looks big," Cary said, craning his neck.

"Oh, it is. It's a Mexican villa type. All one floor. It's gorgeous."

"As beautiful as Sunbridge?"

"In its own way, yes. The Santos are nice people. I think you'll find most Texans are nice. Shrewd business-men, though."

"There you go, reading my mind again."

Amelia shrugged. It was true. She always seemed to be able to anticipate his next question, especially if she was really paying attention and it was a one-on-one con-versation. She squirmed around in her seat so she could study Cary's profile. Strong, chiseled. Firm. She liked that. She sighed deeply, and Cary glanced at her.

"What's on for this evening, or are we just staying home with the family?" he asked.

"What do you say to a night in Crystal City? A little wining, a little dining—we have to watch our waistlines—a little dancing, and then a great deal of lovemaking later on."

"I'd be a fool to turn down an offer like that. Crystal City it is. Would you like to invite the others, or is this strictly a twosome?"

There it was. Amelia knew Cary was just being gen-erous; he was like that. But she only wanted to be with him. She certainly didn't want to share him with her fam-ily. "If you think I'll bore you for a long evening, then we can invite the entire household," she said lightly.

Cary cursed inwardly. He'd screwed up again. Now she was going to sulk all night unless he could cajole her out of it. It occurred to him suddenly that he had been doing a lot of that lately.

"Well, here we are. This is the tract I was telling you about."

Looking at it, Amelia estimated the parcel to be just under two square miles. Out here, with Austin's skyline visible in the distance, the land was flat and uninterrupted.

"You see," Cary was saying, "the highway leads right into the city, so there'll be no difficulty with access. Of course, we're hoping that the offices and light industry space, as well as the shopping mall, will take care of jobs for those living right here."

Amelia raised her eyebrows. "You'll need more than a few square miles for that."

"That's what's so beautiful about the plan. We begin construction at the heart of the project and spread outward. There are fifteen available square miles here, on both sides of the highway and out there"—he pointed— "beyond that slight ridge. We'll be buying out several homeowners. Many of them, in fact. But then we're also thinking of incorporating the existing homes and small ranches into the project. That'll give us an even wider scope in the future."

"Then it's decided you're going to throw in with the developers?"

"I'd like to. Of course, I wouldn't decide anything without you. We'd have to live here, at least until things got under way. That's a decision for the two of us to make."

"You know, I believe some of this land belongs to Jake Baker. It hasn't seen a plow or a steer in a good number of years. Good drainage, though. Pap always said look at the ditch first." She laughed. "Jake's an old horse trader. His land won't come cheap."

"Let's take a walk over to the ridge. We can get a better perspective from there."

She looked down at her four-hundred-dollar Ralph Lauren crocodile shoes and winced as he took her arm and led her into the field. The thorny bush and dried grasses snagged her nylons and she kept a wary eye out for snakes and prairie dog holes. Being from the city, Cary assumed that empty land was just that—devoid of life. He never considered the insect and other life that dwelt on any open stretch of country land.

"You realize I don't know a hell of a lot about building and architecture. In fact, it's safe to say I know nothing. I can learn, though," he said positively. "Sewers, electricity, building permits, union workers, the whole bag. But I have a feeling about this, Amelia. The minute Johnston and Alphin brought me out here, I knew this dream could become a reality. I knew I wanted to be a part of it, more than an investor. And long after I'm gone, it'll still be here, some part of me."

"Can you afford it?"

"If I can't, there's always the bank. I think I could swing it; I know how to deal."

"Cary, I can always throw in with you."

"No, you can't. This is our project, but my money. We've gone all through this, babe. All I want is for you to point me in the right direction. Alphin says a deal like this has to be finessed, and it doesn't hurt having a wife who comes from around these parts. He knows what he's talking about, honey. He's a good ol' boy from North Carolina and he understands people. He says this is too near the heart of the farmland; ranchers might think they're being crowded. No one likes change, not when it affects them personally."

"Your man seems to know how people think, all right. Even though most of our neighbors are well-to-do and like to think of themselves as progressive, they have roots planted in this country. You just might meet up with some opposition. What about Johnston? What does he say?"

Cary grinned. "He takes Alphin's word to heart, just like I do. But if there's one thing Johnston knows about, it's building. He's creative, knows the best materials, the top-of-the-grade contractors. He was the one who came up with the idea of this 'inner city outside the city' idea. He nixed the idea for tract houses, saying that a certain amount of exclusiveness would be more acceptable to the local powers."

"He's right, you know. But first you have to get the land, and that's going to be tricky. Texans don't part with land if they can help it; they might lease it, but they won't sell."

"Hell, Amelia, that isn't going to do me any good."

"You'd quibble over a ninety-nine-year lease with an option to buy?"

A slow smile lifted the corners of his mouth. To Amelia he looked just like a cat who'd swallowed a canary—she could almost imagine him smacking his lips. "Of course, things could get a little sticky, me being an outsider, I mean."

"And that's where I can do you the most good. Amelia Coleman Assante, returned to the heartland!" she said. "We'll entertain, join clubs, become a part of the local politics. And you can do it, darling. You love a challenge. You'll have them eating out of your hand."

Cary was becoming more excited about the project; his dark eyes shone with the thrill of the challenge. "Johnston says customization is the key. Everything tailored and first-quality. He says there's money out here and Alphin agrees. 'Don't judge a man by the age of his truck or the green of his grass,'" Cary drawled, doing his impersonation of Alphin's soft Carolinian accent. "'That ol' boy'll be sittin' on more than he wants you or Uncle Sam to know about.'"

Amelia laughed. "Stick with them, darling, and you won't go wrong."

"And you're right about joining clubs and making friends. I know what it means to be an outsider. I know all about closed shops and being the only dago in a school full of Irish. You have to earn the right to belong. And by God, Amelia, I want to belong to this place."

"Okay, then let's go talk to Jake Baker and see what he says. Let's see if he remembers Seth Coleman's little black-haired girl and the fact that Pap bought my first pony from him."

"Sounds good." He was already leading her back to the car.

"Customized, eh?" Amelia mused. "Ask me what I'd

want in a house, Cary. I've got hundreds of ideas."

"Okay, I'm asking."

"A gorgeous kitchen. Out-of-this-world bathrooms. I'm big on bathrooms. Room-size dressing rooms. Hot tub, Jacuzzi. Fireplaces. Solid oak floors. Curving stairways. One in the front of the house and one off the kitchen. Adequate servants' quarters. Swimming pool built like a grotto. Designer landscaping so the house looks as if it's been there for years. Ironwork, grills, that sort of thing; decorative, of course. But Cary, I have to admit it's such a colossal undertaking that it frightens me. Building houses is one thing, but planning a city and all the things you were talking about last night makes me nervous. It's going to take millions!"

"Amelia, look at me. Do you believe I can do it?"

"Of course I do. But remember, though I might come from money, I wasn't one of the ones who did the making. I think it's natural for me to be a little nervous."

Cary sighed. He wanted Amelia to have faith in him. He'd been doing a little worrying last night himself. The contacts he'd made at Maggie's barbecue would come in handy later, but it was going to take more than just contacts, and he knew it. "Financing, I think, isn't going to be too much of a problem. Banks love the building industry."

"What you're saying is every man has a selling price."

"That's right. With some men it's harder to find than with others. Everyone has a price."

Without stopping to think, she said, "My father and brother didn't have a price."

"Yes they did. You just don't know what it was. Or if you do know, you don't want to think about it."

Amelia didn't like the conversation and was sorry she'd blurted out her opinion. She'd never really argued with Cary before. Hesitantly, she asked, "And what's your price?"

"It's there. It never pays to let a woman know all a man's secrets."

"That's my line—or I should say that's a woman's line.

Women are supposed to be mysterious, never letting their lover know everything."

"What don't I know about you, Amelia?" Cary asked, his voice serious.

"Not a damn thing. I've been an open book with you. Unfortunately or fortunately, as the case may be, I am neither mysterious nor secretive. What you see is what you got. Now you're going to get me in a snit until I figure out what your price is."

"I wouldn't lose any sleep over it, darling. It may never show up till I'm eighty years old."

God! If he were eighty, she'd be . . . "My shoes are getting ruined, Cary. I can wait in the car if you want to explore a little more."

"I think I've seen enough. I know what I want, and the next thing to do is see about getting it. After we see Jake Baker, we'll go back to Sunbridge and I'll start setting up my appointments."

"I could do that for you," Amelia said. If he was going to spend hours on the phone, what was she going to do?

"This is man's work, baby. You did your share at the party when you paved the way for me. I can handle it from here."

"Don't need me anymore, eh?"

Cary turned the key in the ignition. "I'll always need you, Amelia. I can't imagine what my life would be without you. I was serious when I said until death do us part. Don't you know how much meaning you give to my life? Hell, I was only a rich drifter when we met. A hustler. You turned me around. I'll never forget that. We're a team, we belong together, and don't you ever forget it."

Amelia beamed. She forgot about the mud caked on her shoes. She forgot about the phone calls that would take Cary away from her for a little while.

After working in the stables cleaning stalls, Sawyer and Cole rewarded their efforts by taking a long ride through the back hills. They purloined a picnic lunch from a kitchen in amazingly good order, considering the amount of activity that had taken place there the night before.

Sawyer led Cole along her favorite riding paths, skirting the scrupulously fed and watered lawn, taking him into the low-rising hills far out of sight of the house and sound of occasional trucks on the highway. Off in the distance, they'd seen Rand and Riley returning from their morning's ride, and Sawyer watched them until they were out of sight. She felt the distance between Rand and herself was much greater than the mile or more of Sunbridge acreage that separated them now. She flushed when she remembered how she'd tried to seduce him earlier that morning. Why wouldn't he talk to her, tell her what was wrong?

When Sawyer and Cole returned to the house, they turned their mounts over to a groom. "I'm for a shower," she said, "and you don't smell so hot yourself. C'mon, I'll race you!"

Cole ran close on her heels. He had the slim, loosely jointed body of a natural athlete, and he moved with grace.

"Nice going!" she called over her shoulder. "C'mon, don't stop now!"

Rand, sitting on the back patio, heard Sawyer's familiar laugh, and when he turned, he saw her running ahead of Cole toward the house. The sun shot her hair full of golden lights, and her long, slim legs ate up the distance. He'd never thought there was much resemblance between Sawyer and her half brother, but now he noticed the same agility, the same loose stride, slim hips, and coltish legs. He found himself smiling.

When they'd rounded the side of the house and were no longer in view, Rand laid his head against the back of his redwood armchair. Seeing Sawyer running across the lawn with Cole was another reminder of how young she was. So wonderfully young. But he knew her youth wouldn't protect her from the pain he was inflicting. He must talk to her, explain. But what explanation could a man offer a woman who loved him and thought she was loved in return?

He laughed, a bitter, tight sound. That was just the trouble: he did love Sawyer. He simply did not love her enough.

She was young, resilient; she'd forget him. She deserved the best life had to offer—a family, children to mother, the right to fulfill her ambitions and build her career without a disenchanted husband who wanted a quieter, simpler life. She should not have to sacrifice anything for him.

Rand sat lost in his thoughts for a very long time, grateful that no one came out to the patio to interrupt the silence. He liked it out here amid the huge redwood tubs, which held shrubs and bright red and yellow flowers. Maggie had seen to every comfort. Intimate groupings of brightly cushioned furnishings invited leisure and conversation. Less than a step away on the dull gray flagstones was a portable bar, well stocked with cold drinks and snacks, with a television and telephone on top. The pool nearby was perfect for cooling off, although he'd been too lazy to indulge when he'd returned from his ride with Riley.

There were stirrings in the house now—voices, footsteps. Rand glanced at his watch: almost the cocktail hour. His stomach churned in rejection of the idea, anticipating the inevitable confrontation with Sawyer. Suddenly memories of their times together, their shared experiences, came flooding back. He pushed them away, refusing to be drawn into the intimacy they created.

"Hello, I thought I'd find you out here," Sawyer said lightly as she leaned over to kiss his cheek. "Can I get you something to drink?"

"If you're buying, I could use a Coke."

"And what kind of day did you have?" Sawyer asked cheerfully as she walked over to the portable bar.

"Lazy. What did you do?"

"I got to know Cole a little. I helped him clean the barn and we went riding. He seems to be a nice enough kid who has a few problems, but then don't we all?" She handed Rand his soda in a frosty glass and sat down in the chair opposite his. "What did you think of my step-brother?"

"I'm the last person you should be asking. He managed to tie one on last night, and Riley and I had to dry him out. He's a bit young for that sort of thing. Other than that, I can't say I know the boy at all. Riley, now, is something different. I spent quite a lot of time with him last year when we were in Japan, and he's what a young man is all about."

Sawyer could hear the clipped British formality in Rand's voice, a sure sign of his disapproval. Defensively, she replied, "It was probably the only way Cole could get through Maggie's party. You have to admit it was over-whelming."

"The boy could have caused quite a scene, and this party was very important to Maggie. He should have had enough consideration for his mother to behave."

"You sound like a stern father."

"God forbid! That's the one role in life I'm not cut out for. I suppose it is easy to preach about other people's children."

"Yes, I guess so. Isn't it exciting, though, that Susan is going to have a baby?" Sawyer said dreamily. "A baby at Sunbridge again. I was the last one."

"That's right. Cole wasn't born here, was he?"

"No, in New York. I don't think he regards Sunbridge the way the rest of us do. Sometimes I think we're all obsessed with this pile of bricks."

"It's a beautiful place. I can't deny that," Rand said, bringing his glass to his lips.

Sawyer noticed, not for the first time, that he was having trouble meeting her gaze. "What's wrong, Rand? Did I do or say something that offended you? You've been avoiding me since we got here. Even as far back as Easter I sensed something was wrong. Have you had a change of heart?" There, the dreaded question was out. She held her breath, locking her gaze with Rand's.

"Sawyer, there's no easy way to say this. It won't work for us. We're worlds apart in just about everything. You're young and you have your whole career ahead of you. I'm so much older than you. You deserve children. I don't want children. I . . . I don't think I even want to get married."

Sawyer could feel the heat on her face. The sick feeling in her stomach was crawling up to her chest and throat. She wanted to cry, could feel the tears welling up in her eyes. She should be saying something, but she couldn't seem to think straight. "Don't I have anything to say about all of this?" Sawyer whispered in a choked voice. "The children, marriage, our ages?"

"No."

That one word, so dreaded, so quietly said, destroyed her. This was final; she could read it in the pain in his eyes, in the set of his jaw. Sawyer stood up, her glass shattering on the flagstones unnoticed. She jammed her hands into her pockets so he wouldn't see how they trembled. "I love you, Rand. I thought you loved me."

"And you had every right to think so." He stood to face her; his hands reached to steady her, to soothe her. "I love you, Sawyer. You're a beautiful, wonderful person. But I'm not in love with you. It . . . it just wouldn't work for us. Believe me, I never wanted to hurt you—"

"Is there anyone else?" she blurted, unable to stop herself.

He seemed startled that she should ask, even offended. "No, of course there isn't. I'm so sorry. You know I wouldn't hurt you for the world."

Sawyer clapped her hands over her ears and squeezed her eyes shut. She wanted to kick, to scream, No, I don't know any such thing! You just ripped my heart out and you say you wouldn't hurt me for the world. You're my world, Rand, you! But she bit back the words, swallowed the screams. Colemans don't snivel and they don't buckle under. Isn't that what she'd said to Cole only hours ago? Well, she was a Coleman . . . and right now she wanted to throw herself at this man who had just crushed her world, beg him to take back the words.

Cole stood in the doorway. He'd heard part of the

conversation, and now he saw the expression on Sawyer's face, in her eyes. Without thinking, he ran out to the patio, seized Sawyer by the arm, and dragged her into the house. The first open door led into Seth's old study, a small room occupied by a large desk and several worn leather arm-chairs.

"You can cry now," he told her. "I'll never tell."

Sawyer sank down behind the huge oak desk beside Coleman. She hid her great heaving sobs from the world, accepting only the solace Cole offered with his presence and hesitant comforting pats. He dug in his pocket to offer her his handkerchief.

A long time later she blew her nose lustily. Look-alike eyes met in understanding. "He'll change his mind," she said. "He loves me. You'll see. He loves me."

{{{{{{{{ CHAPTER EIGHT }}}}}}}}

The Texas sky was dark, the usual puffy white clouds now a dark blue blanket shrouding Sunbridge. Rand stood on the wide front portico overlooking the old rose garden and tree-lined drive, his hands jammed tightly in his pock-ets. There was a storm brewing; winds from the southeast were churning tree limbs and rattling the shutters. He should have left Sunbridge by now, but he'd wanted to stay because of Sawyer. Once he'd told her it was over between them, he felt it only fair to be around in case she needed to talk. He'd had enough of avoiding, of running away, and he'd wanted to see for himself that Sawyer would be all right.

Instead, it had been Sawyer who had avoided him, occupying herself with Cole and Riley; but Rand had often felt her watching him, listening to his conversations with others. He'd known she was waiting for him to approach her, to say something crazy had gotten into him and beg her to forgive him. Yesterday she'd left Sunbridge, her eyes dark with questions and hurt. He knew all it would take was one phone call from him and Sawyer would return. He could make her world right again. . . . But no, this was best, for both of them.

A sudden driving wind buffeted through the portico, forcing him backward into the shelter of the doorway. The air was thick with humidity, strong with the smell of oncoming rain. The slender stalks in the rose garden bent before the wind; petals swirled upward like confetti. The storm was welcome; it gave him something to think about besides Sawyer and what he'd done. He could find shelter from the rain inside the fortress walls of Sunbridge, but what he really needed was safety from his own emotions.

It was darker now; the arthritic old trees bent beneath the onslaught. He searched the slate-gray sky, having heard tales of the merciless twisters that could plague this part of Texas.

He turned around and looked up at the house. No lamplight shone from the front windows. Susan and Jerome had left Sunbridge days ago, but Amelia and Cary were still here, out promoting their land deal. Riley and Cole were probably in the barn, which left only Maggie and the servants in the house.

Rand went inside and pushed the door closed against the wind. It was darker in the foyer than it was outside. Not a single light shone, and the bleakness increased his anxiety. "Maggie! Maggie!" he called, moving to the interior of the house, switching on lamps as he went.

At the bottom of the stairs he called upward, "Maggie, you up there? It's really blowing up out there; we're in for a real Texas storm!"

He fumbled for the wall switch, and the magnificent center mahogany staircase appeared. The thick Navajopatterned carpet runner silenced his footfalls as he mounted the steps. Maybe it was the oncoming storm, but something had him thinking too much, remembering too much. He tried to shrug off all his thoughts, thoughts of Sawyer, Cole, Maggie. . . . He'd been concerned about Maggie since she'd told him Cole had invited Cranston to Sunbridge. He wondered how she'd handle seeing Cranston again here, in her own home. He liked Maggie—probably more than he should.

Suddenly he decided to finish his packing and leave, storm or no storm, right away. He wanted out of Sunbridge, away from Maggie and her son, now, before Cranston arrived. He didn't belong here.

"Can't wait to leave, is that it?" Maggie queried as she swept down the hallway, only to back up at the sound of Rand's suitcase snapping shut. "By the way, thanks for lighting the house."

"No problem, I assure you," he said, his voice gruff.

"Is anything wrong, Rand?" she asked uneasily.

"Not at all. I just thought I'd leave a bit early. Who knows what'll happen to the flights or how long this storm will last."

Maggie's face showed alarm. "Surely you aren't thinking of driving to the airport now. Have you ever seen one of our storms?"

"Yes, I was thinking of leaving now, and no, I've never had the pleasure. Don't tell me you're concerned for my safety." He'd said it sarcastically, yet he realized that her answer was important to him. Right now, he needed someone to care about him.

"Of course I'm concerned," she answered seriously, searching his face with her eyes. "Rand, it's raining now, the proverbial buckets. I doubt if you'd get as far as Crystal City before the road washed out. I was going to suggest you call the airline and reschedule your flight till tomorrow or even next week. You aren't in a hurry to get back to England, are you?"

"Won't it be a little awkward when your husband arrives?" he said stiffly. "Amelia and Cary are hardly ever here. I'd just be in the way."

"In whose way? Certainly not mine. I don't care if Cranston never comes. Once he gets here it'll be one problem after another. Unfortunately, I have to deal with it this time: Cole's future is at stake." She gave him a tight little smile. "Cranston doesn't want Cole to come and live with him, not really, except for the fact that it would hurt me. He's just using the boy. Your being here might even ease the situation a little."

"No, thank you, Maggie. I don't like playing middle-man in a domestic situation."

"I wasn't trying to use you for that, Rand, really I wasn't. It's just that . . . that . . ." Maggie looked down at her shoes, and Rand almost expected her to scuff them in the carpet. "You see," she began again, "Cranston has always been able to intimidate me. Everything that happened between us has always been my fault, according to him. Most of it was, I suppose, but not all of it. Maybe it's just the way I react around some men. My father and grandfather always intimidated me, and now when I look back, I think it was one of the reasons I was drawn to Cranston. I thought I had something to prove. If Cranston could accept me, love me even, then it might mean that my father and grandfather could respect and love me, too."

"And what about me, Maggie? Do I intimidate you?"

She laughed. "Not at all. I'm quite comfortable with you. I'm sorry you're leaving; I could have used a friend while Cranston is here. And I'm even sorrier that you seem unhappy."

"You know something went wrong between Sawyer and me, don't you? You're just too polite and well-mannered to ask."

"I wasn't prying, Rand. Sawyer is your business."

"In a way, she's yours, too."

"No, not really. We may be mother and daughter, but we're two very different people."

"It might have helped her to talk to another woman."

Maggie flinched at Rand's words. She'd tried to

approach Sawyer but hadn't been able to face her daughter's hostility. How was she to explain that to Rand when she couldn't explain it to herself? "A—a friendship has to be earned. It's never been that way between Sawyer and me.... Well, I have things to do. Let me know if you'll be here for dinner, won't you?"

She was gone, down the hall and around the corner to the stairs. She'd caught him off guard with her candor. It was something he'd never been led to expect from Maggie. The *old* Maggie, he corrected himself. He decided he liked this Maggie. And he especially liked the scent of her perfume. Hell, maybe he would stay until after dinner.

Rand managed to kill time by reading seventy-seven pages of a novel whose title he later couldn't remember. He hoped no one ever quizzed him on the contents.

A drumroll sounded overhead, followed by a second, a third, and then a loud crash. Jagged streaks of lightning tore across the sky, piercing his room with a blaze of light. Another ominous collision in the sky and the room went dark. The power was out. Faintly, he could hear Maggie's voice calling from downstairs for everyone to stay still and she would be up with candles.

"Sort of like Halloween, isn't it?" Maggie smiled as she entered his room, a candle in one hand and a hurricane lamp in the other. "The boys are downstairs. We have a generator, but I don't know the first thing about it. Would you mind taking a look? We could be without power until tomorrow. This is a bad one." Maggie nodded toward the window. "We should have dressed for the occasion. I wish I'd thought of it earlier. The boys might have had some fun. They look so glum. No television, no stereo, just plain old conversation or reading by lamplight."

"I imagine we'll all survive," Rand said. He was standing too close to Maggie, drinking in the scent of her, seeing the softness of her hands and wanting to touch them. He backed up until she was bathed in pale yellow light. It was true; a woman looked beautiful in candlelight. At least this woman did.

"There are so many shadows here, so many dark corners. Susan and I used to hide and play games up here. I always found Susan."

"Susan couldn't find you. Is that it? You must have been aces at the game."

"Susan didn't like to play games," Maggie said thoughtfully. "She preferred to read or color in her books."

"I remember Susan as a child," Rand smiled. "She was like a little sister to me, too. She was always more interested in her studies than in games. I think of those days often."

"I never think about them," Maggie said firmly.

"Maybe you should. Maybe it would help you understand your own son a little better."

They were standing at the top of the stairs. Everywhere there were candles in decorative holders, hurricane lamps, and a flashlight or two casting light upward.

Maggie turned around until she was just inches from Rand. "Why do I get the feeling you can't make up your mind if you like me or not? Does it have something to do with Sawyer?"

"Maggie, you're wrong. I do like you. Too much. I know exactly where you've been and where it is you want to go. I've been down that road myself a time or two." He paused, then added almost brusquely, "Don't analyze. One thing has nothing to do with the other."

Maggie searched his eyes for a long moment, then smiled and turned away, starting down the stairs. Rand followed close behind. "Dinner is by candlelight," she said cheerfully. "I suppose the boys will think it's eerie and will complain about not being able to see their food, but I think it's romantic."

"What time do you expect Cranston?"

"He should have been here by now. It's possible his plane didn't land," Maggie said blithely. "We're certainly not waiting dinner for him."

"I don't mind waiting."

Maggie smiled. "But I do. The boys are hungry and so am I. The cook can fix a plate for Cranston if he arrives.

... You notice I said 'if.' He's notorious for saying one thing and then doing another. He used to promise to take Cole to ball games and then wouldn't show up. Once he was supposed to take him to the circus, and Cole was so excited he threw up. Cranston didn't show up that time, either." Maggie turned and actually bumped into Rand. "My husband was and probably still is the consummate bastard. He was cruel in lots of little ways. But I was no better. I baited him, and I think we fed off each other's hatred. I know where mine came from, but I never knew what ate at Cranston. The only thing I truly regret is that he wasn't a better father to Cole."

"Were you a good mother to the boy?"

Maggie hesitated. "I could have been better. I made my share of mistakes, but I love Cole. I'm not sure Cranston ever did. He has our pictures on his desk at the office. Isn't that funny? A picture of the little woman holding her son's hand is supposed to instill comfort and confidence in clients. What that client doesn't see or know about are all the other women, the ones who make him feel young again. If I sound bitter, it's probably because I am, a little. Cranston used me and I can't even hate him because I used him, too.... End of true confessions. I hope you're hungry. Prime rib and roast potatoes."

Rand laughed. "It's always prime rib. Don't you Texans ever make lamb chops?"

"Bite your tongue. This is a cattle ranch. Lamb and pork are dirty words out here. When we want pork or lamb, we go to Crystal City."

Maggie did her best to keep the conversation lively during dinner. Occasionally Riley lifted his eyes and contributed. Cole was sullen as usual, chewing his food noisily and slurping his water.

"Did you call the airport?" Cole asked suddenly.

"The lines are down. You know the phones are the first to go during a storm like this. Rand is going to look at the generator after dinner, so we'll have television, at least. We can see just how bad things are. It's more than possible your father's plane didn't land."

Cole scowled and stuffed an entire buttered roll into his mouth. Maggie tried not to notice and concentrated instead on Riley, who was eating quietly but steadily.

"Did you have a good day, Riley?" she asked. "Aside from a sore bottom, I mean."

"Very good, Aunt Maggie. When I was here before, I was too young to go riding alone. I've always wanted to see just how far Sunbridge goes. So far I've only covered about half of it."

"Are you homesick?" Rand asked. He noticed that Cole stopped chewing long enough to hear Riley's answer.

"Not at all. I do miss Sawyer, though. She's been a good friend to me." His voice was quiet, but his eyes bored into Rand. "She promised to write to me."

His sister said she'd write to *him*, thought Cole.

Maggie looked up, first at Rand and then at Cole. She could feel her heart start to pound. There was going to be trouble here in a minute. "Tomorrow," she said quickly, "if this storm is over, there's going to be tons of work to do. We might even have to hire on some extra help to clean up."

"When do you think the power will be back on?" Riley asked.

"A day, two at the most." In the awkward silence that followed, Maggie willed Cole to say something, anything, to show he was part of the group, that he belonged. Riley was trying, at least; so was Rand. Her son, on the other hand, had chosen to maintain a stubborn silence. Why? She sighed wearily.

"What's for dessert?" Rand asked heartily.

"Apple pie, I think. Martha made some this morning. Ice cream. She makes that, too."

Rand laughed. "Top that off with some good Colombian coffee and you have an order."

"Me, too," Riley seconded.

"None for me," Cole said as he tossed his napkin on

the table. He didn't excuse himself, merely pushed back his chair and left the room as dessert was being served. Riley's eyes fell to his plate. Rand wanted to run after the boy and shake him till his teeth rattled. He half expected Maggie to go after her son, but she didn't. Instead, she looked at Riley and smiled.

"You're certainly going to have a long letter to write home," she said, watching as Riley made short work of his pie. "The party, the storm, seeing Billie and Thad and all the others. Where did Sawyer go? Do you know?"

Riley flushed. He'd promised Sawyer not to tell Rand, but how was he to lie to Aunt Maggie? He was searching for the words when Rand himself came to the rescue.

"She said something earlier about going back to California to finish up some business. Are you concerned, Maggie?"

"No, just curious. . . . Another piece of pie, Riley?" she asked cheerfully.

"No thanks, Aunt Maggie. I want to go out for baseball in September, so I have to watch my weight. If you don't mind, though, I'd like to take a look at the generator." He pushed his chair back and stood up. "I know where it is. Finish your dessert."

"He's such a nice boy," Maggie said after a moment's pause. "I hope some of him rubs off on Cole, but I'm not expecting miracles." She smiled brightly. "So, what did you think of the pie?"

"Probably the best I've had since I was here last. That's a beautiful dress you're wearing. What do you call the color?"

"Wineberry. It's a Billie Original."

"There's no reason to sound defensive."

"Was I? Sounding defensive, I mean. I didn't mean to. For a long time I wouldn't wear the things Mam designed for me. Now I wear what I have to death. By the way, what do you think of Thad going into politics?"

"My personal opinion is he's too honest for it. The leeches and parasites who'll make it possible will chew him up and spit him out. Billie's the one I pity."

"But do you think he could make it?" Maggie asked.

"With his record, chances are he will. But I'm not sure, from talking to him, that it's what he wants. Billie mentioned the word governor to me in a very shaky voice. I think she's worried."

"Just how deep will the opposition dig into Thad and Mam's background?" Maggie asked sharply.

Rand hesitated. "To the bare bone."

"That's what I thought."

In that instant, the lights came back on and Rand was able to see the anguish in Maggie's eyes. "It's something else for you to worry about now, isn't it?" he asked, his voice soft.

"Yes. My life can't stand up to a microscopic examination. A bare bones investigation will harm Thad. Mam, too. They don't deserve that. Thad's a great guy, the greatest in my opinion. I'd put him right up there with Pap. They were best buddies, you know." Maggie leaned her elbows on the table and cupped her chin in her hands. Rand thought her skin looked like satin in the bright light. "Isn't it funny how we go through life never thinking our past is going to catch up to us? When it does, it usually cripples us. God! I don't want to be the reason Thad doesn't make it if he decides to run for office. I couldn't bear it if Mam had to defend me in public."

"Did you talk to her about it?" Rand asked gently, seeing Maggie's eyes glisten with unshed tears.

"How could I? This place was like a madhouse, and then they left so quickly. I'm sure they must have discussed it. What will I do if Thad's career in politics is ruined because of me?"

"Vermont is far away, Maggie, and that was so long ago."

She laughed, a bitter sound. "He could be in Guam and they'd still sling mud. That's what politics is all about. Mam is news and so are the Colemans. And my drinking and outrageous behavior wasn't that long ago. Enemies have long memories."

"The elections aren't until next year. I wouldn't start

losing sleep over it now. A lot can happen in a year and a half. The best advice I can give you is to wait."

"What else can I do? I can't turn back the clock."

Suddenly Rand tilted his head to one side, listening. "Has the rain let up? Let's take a look at the telly and see how much damage has been done. I just might be able to make the airport after all." Rand couldn't have said why, but he was pleased to see the look of disappointment on Maggie's face as they left the dining room.

Riley called to them from the hallway. "It works!"

"And there was light!" Maggie called gaily.

"Did you have any trouble?" Rand asked.

"No. I simply turned the switch. Anyone could have done it."

"Easy or not, we have power and that's what's important. Now, let's see what the weathermen have to say. Rand is eager to leave us."

Every TV station they tuned in had preempted regular programming to give a report on the storm. According to one, the airport in Austin had been closed down for four hours. It was open now, but all flights were delayed. Disgruntled passengers were shown mumbling and muttering about their time schedules. Flooding on the roads was lessening. Rain was needed, "but this is ridiculous," chortled a weatherman from his dry control room. Trees were down, blocking the highways, but maintenance and power workers were out in full force. Electricity would be restored by noon tomorrow.

Maggie looked at Rand expectantly. "You're leaving." It was a statement.

Rand nodded. "Riley, would you give me a hand?" The boy nodded without enthusiasm.

"I'll have your car brought around front. I'm sorry you're leaving, Rand. I hope you'll come back over the holidays. Consider this your invitation."

"I'll think about it. It'll be nice to see the boys again and to spend the holidays with my mother and Cary."

"I'll get your bags," Riley said. "Is your jacket upstairs?"

"No, it's in the hallway. Thanks, Riley."

"Do you suppose he thinks I'm getting infirm, or has he been counting my gray hairs?" Rand asked lightly.

"Truthfully, I think he just wants to be rid of you. He's confused right now. He adores Sawyer, has from the first moment. So in a way you're his enemy now. There's a lot about Riley I don't know. There was a righteous streak in my brother—perhaps I should say it was a keen sense of justice. I think Riley's the same." She reached up to kiss his cheek lightly, then smiled. "Keep in touch, Rand."

{{{{{{{{ CHAPTER NINE }}}}}}}}

As Cole was looking out the parlor window to watch Rand leave, he noticed a white Cadillac powering up the drive. It could only be his father!

He rushed past the dining room, where he could hear Riley and Maggie talking, and stole out of the house to greet Cranston beneath the shelter of the portico. He waited for the car's engine to stop before rushing around the front of the car to greet his father. "Hi, Dad. I was afraid you wouldn't make it because of the storm."

Cranston climbed from the car. He was a tall man, lean as a reed and tanned from his recent trip to Florida. "I almost didn't make it," he said offhandedly, leaning once again into the Eldorado to retrieve a garment bag, which he unceremoniously handed to his son. "Goddamned power lines are down. I thought we'd have to reroute back to Atlanta." Casually he tossed Cole the keys. "Get my luggage out of the trunk and bring it into the house."

Cole's face mirrored his disappointment. This was hardly the greeting he'd been expecting. He took a deep breath. "Dad, I told Mother I want to live with you in New York."

"Oh, you did, did you? I believe I told you not to say anything until I'd had a chance to talk with her. What did she say?"

"She wants me to stay here. She'll probably raise a stink, but you can handle her, can't you, Dad?"

"Like I said, Coleman, this is between your mother and me. Where is she? Did you have dinner yet? I'm hungry as a bear."

Coleman watched him go into the house before retrieving the luggage from the trunk. He didn't like the way his father had said, "This is between your mother and me." That meant only one thing—his father was going to use him as leverage to get something else he wanted. Still, he had come all the way from New York. That meant something, didn't it?

Maggie was midway up the stairs when the front door opened behind her. She turned to find Cranston standing there, looking up at her. "So, you made it after all. I'll call Cole."

"I've seen him. He's outside getting my luggage." Cranston Tanner found himself looking at his soon-to-be ex-wife with incredulity. Surely this wasn't Maggie—not this healthy, vital woman staring down at him? "You look wonderful, Maggie."

She laughed. "You expected otherwise?" Damn right he'd expected otherwise. She knew him so well, this husband of hers. He'd hoped to find a broken-down old sot, an unfit mother unable to concentrate on anything but the next drink. That would have completed his fantasy.

"You always were a beautiful woman," he said. "Sunbridge obviously agrees with you. I haven't seen you looking this lovely in years."

"Thank you, Cranston. Now I'll show you to your

room so you can freshen up. Then you can have dinner if you haven't already eaten. Cook is keeping a plate warm for you."

For a tall man, Cranston moved with quickness and grace. With only a few steps he was on a level with Maggie. Close up, he decided she looked even better. He was about to lean over and kiss her when she moved slightly to avoid him. For a moment his eyes, the color of an overcast sky, narrowed. Then he caught the light, drifting scent of her perfume, one he'd always liked and usually purchased for her at Christmas. Maggie. His wife. His soon-to-be ex-wife.

"You really are stunning, Maggie. I approve."

Maggie murmured her thanks for his compliments, but she found herself resenting his mellow, intimate tone and decided not to compliment him in return. He was well aware of the elegant picture he created in his custom-made summer suit and his handmade Italian shoes. Flawless. Handsome. Brilliant.

Cranston knew he'd been rebuffed and smarted as he walked alongside his wife up the long, curving staircase. "How's Cole been?" he asked for want of anything else to say.

"He sulks, something he does very well these days. I think we should have a talk before we bring Cole into this. That is, if you're interested in his welfare, Cranston, truly interested. But if this is just another of your triyearly visits..."

"Still haven't lost your capacity for cruelty, I see," Cranston snapped. "Besides, it hasn't been three years since I've seen the boy, it's only been—"

"Two years and eight months if you're counting," Maggie said sweetly. "Cole has been counting. What you call cruelty, I call concern for Cole. And another thing, Cranston, spare me any of your courtroom melodramatics. It won't work any longer."

Cranston's eyebrows shot upward. Apparently things were very different here. After a moment, as he followed her down the long second-floor hallway, he remarked on how much Cole had grown.

"Did you tell him that?" Maggie asked pointedly. She stopped in front of one of the closed doors. "I'm putting you in Grandmother Jessica's old room. I think you'll find it comfortable."

Cranston paced the large bedroom that had once been Jessica's. He found it too feminine for his taste, but it would do for now. Taking off his jacket, he threw himself across the bed, unmindful of the smudges his shoes made on the white bedspread. If Maggie noticed, she said nothing. "I don't think I've ever been in this room before," he told her.

"That's right, but then you've only been to Sunbridge twice before. Once for a day and a half and once for six hours."

"I didn't know you were counting, Maggie." He grinned, a studied, charming gesture. Maggie knew it for what it was but felt a pang in her chest in spite of herself.

"How long are you staying this time?" she asked.

"As long as it takes to make a decision about what's best for Cole. At least through Sunday."

Maggie laughed, a bitter, sardonic sound. "I see *you* haven't changed. Time limits, conditions, you name it. We're talking about our son, Cranston. What if we don't resolve this by Sunday? Will you still leave?"

"Of course. I have pretrial arrangements and appointments for Monday."

"Of course." He was better-looking than the last time she'd seen him. Perhaps it was the deep, golden tan. She surprised herself by blurting, "Are you seeing anyone in particular these days?"

Cranston's mouth tightened imperceptibly. "Not really. Dinner, the theater, that sort of thing."

"Does that mean you're celibate?"

"Well, well, some things never change, do they, Maggie? Go right for the throat."

"Wrong," Maggie said breezily. "Actually, Cranston, I couldn't care less what you do or who you see. But your life-style has a direct bearing on Cole. Besides, I want to be sure nothing stands in the way of our divorce. All the agreements still hold, right?"

"There is one difference. Cole said he wants to come and live with me. I know you have custody of the boy, but we have to do what's best for him. Why the hell you took him out of that military school is beyond me. You didn't even consult me."

"Why should I?" Maggie flared. "You weren't intersted. You're his father, but all you've really done for him is send a support check every six months. And you don't even see to that personally—someone from the accounting department at the firm does it."

"The school was doing wonders for Cole," Cranston said as if he hadn't heard her. "He's an expert marksman. His grades are way above average. His deportment is excellent. He's under close supervision. He's not on drugs. Face it, Maggie: you made a mistake by taking him out. He wants to go back to the academy or to a private school in New York."

Maggie's heart fluttered. She could feel the first stirrings of panic. "Cole needs a home, a sense of family. He doesn't need strict rules and regimentation. I'm sorry I ever listened to you and enrolled him in the first place."

"Come off it, Maggie! You didn't want to be bothered, either. He was cramping our style. Every chance you got you sent him off somewhere. Now all of a sudden you have motherhood running in your veins, and you think you're going to make him live in this godforsaken shrine to your father. I think that's sick!"

Maggie flinched. "It's what's important for Cole *now*!" She took a deep breath. "And I refuse to let you draw me into some discussion only a lawyer can win. If you want to talk about Cole, fine. If not, I'll leave you to whatever it is you want to do.

"By the way," she added, "my nephew, Riley, is here. Please be civil and don't allow your prejudices to get in the way."

Cranston blinked in surprise. This definitely was not

the Maggie he once knew. Something about her reminded him of Billie—the same iron fist in a velvet glove. He got up from the bed and began to prowl the room.

"Okay, let's talk. Cole called me and asked me to come here. He told me that he wanted to live with me in New York. I told him I'd think about it and would discuss it with you. I didn't promise him anything. But what are you going to do, Maggie—force him to stay here? He said he hates this place."

Maggie sat on a soft green slipper chair and crossed her legs. "Cole is just angry because I took him out of school. He wanted to go off this summer on a trip to Europe with his friends, with little or no supervision. I said no. I think it's time he put down roots, and Sunbridge is as good a place as any. It's my home now, and it's his home. Trust me when I tell you this is what's best for him."

"Best for him or best for you?"

"For him, of course! A sixteen-year-old doesn't belong in a New York City apartment with no supervision. Cole has some problems, and I think this is the place to work them out. No child likes upheaval, but he'll come around if you back me up. Right now, Cole doesn't like either of us, Cranston, and if we let him, he'll play us against each other. I don't want that to happen—and I'm going to need your help to prevent it."

"I have to talk to Cole. I'll make my decision after I hear what he has to say."

"I'll fight you, Cranston. All the way. You gave me sole custody. You can't rip him away from me now. You don't want Cole; admit it. What you want is to get back at me."

"Now you're talking like a child. Why would I want to get back at you?"

"Because I left you before you left me. I walked out on you and took Cole with me. You didn't care about us. All you cared about was how it was going to look to your partners and friends. You had to make explanations, tell lies. And you cooked up some pretty wild stories—I know because they filtered back to me. I didn't bother to defend myself at the time because I was afraid of you. But I'm not afraid of you any longer."

"The Coleman grit. It's awesome, I have to agree. You're on your own turf here. I can see how you'd get cocky."

"Damn you, Cranston! I'm doing my best to turn my life around and make something of it. I also want to help Cole, and I won't stand by and see you ruin him. Now, that's all I'm going to say about it. I don't think I'll join you in the dining room after all. I'll send Cole in my place. I think it's time you saw your son."

"I do, too. I guess I'll see you at breakfast."

"Only if you're downstairs at seven sharp. Otherwise, you'll have to wait till lunch. I have things to do."

"Mistress of Sunbridge." Cranston laughed.

Maggie pretended not to hear as she left the room, but she could feel her cheeks grow warm. He made it sound like a dirty title from a grade B movie.

When she reached her own room, the first thing she did was lock the door. Then she let the tears come. Lonesome tears, which rolled down her cheeks and onto the wineberry dress, spotting the delicate fabric. She should have worn a suit of armor for her meeting with Cranston, she reflected bitterly. Battles always left the wounded and bloodied.

She began to pace restlessly, trying to think. Cranston could do her in with legal mumbo jumbo. He was the boy's father. He could say he was busy trying to earn a living to support his wife in the style to which she'd become accustomed. Juries loved to sink their teeth into anything even remotely scandalous or sensational. Her past was going to rear up and slap her smack in the face—not once, but twice, when Thad's opponents got a crack at her.

It occurred to Maggie suddenly that she had no close friend, no confidant. If ever there was a time to confide in someone . . . Without thinking, she picked up the phone, dialed the airport, and had Rand paged. Ten minutes later she heard his anxious voice on the phone.

"Rand, it's Maggie. I need a friend."

"I'm all yours. I've another two hours before my plane leaves, and even then it's doubtful I'll get off before morning."

Rand smiled as he listened to Maggie talk. Suddenly, the airport seemed less lonely. They spoke for nearly the entire two hours, and he never once looked at his watch. He doubted he would have heard if they'd announced his departure. But it really didn't matter: there would be other planes.

It was Maggie who reminded him the two hours were nearly up. "Lord, Rand, I don't know what got into me."

"You said you needed a friend. We're friends. Don't make it complicated."

"I feel as though I've gone through my entire life without someone I could turn to. Thanks, Rand. Perhaps I can return the favor one day. See you over the holidays."

Rand listened to the dial tone for a few moments, then, very gently, replaced the receiver.

{{{{{{{{ CHAPTER TEN }}}}}}}}

Maggie sat in her favorite lounge chair on Sunbridge's back patio soaking up the late-August sun. It felt good, warming her to the core. It wasn't often she felt warm these days; Cole's hostility had been arctic since Cranston's visit just after the Fourth of July.

Nothing had been settled by the time he left, and he'd returned to New York alone. Maggie knew then that he hadn't really wanted the boy; if he had, neither heaven nor hell would have prevented him. But Cole could not be convinced. Meanwhile, she had to suffer their son's petulant antagonisms.

Aside from that, however, things had progressed nicely for Maggie. The Fourth of July bash had given her entrée into several social circles, mainly the country club set in and around Crystal City. Her calendar was filled with tennis and luncheon dates, and she often reciprocated with informal picnics at Sunbridge. Last week she'd held a cocktail hour and sit-down dinner for twenty in honor of Jamison Royce, an artist of acclaim whom she'd known back in New York. Her ability to bring new and interesting people to the Crystal City set guaranteed her success.

Amelia and Cary were busy with Cary's project, but not too busy to decorate most of Maggie's shindigs with their special kind of West Coast glamour. Maggie's new-found status also brought another benefit—Riley was making friends with the younger set. Cole, of course, was an entirely different matter. Maggie felt a frown wrinkling her brow when she thought of her son and purposefully smoothed the lines with her fingertips. She felt drowsy sitting here frying in her own fat, and she didn't want to think about anything unpleasant, including Cranston's impending return visit to Sunbridge sometime tomorrow.

Cole appeared out of nowhere, a talent he seemed intent on developing; obviously he enjoyed the way it unnerved his mother. He plopped down at the foot of her chaise, the all-too-familiar scowl on his young face. Maggie squinted through the sunlight at him, noting he was dressed in snowy white ducks and a striped jersey that seemed to accentuate his slimness.

"So, Mother, did you hear from my father? Have you two come to a decision?"

"You already know my decision, Cole." Wearily

Maggie laid her head back and closed her eyes again. "Your dad will be here sometime tomorrow. Monday is the last day for school registration; I'd like to settle this once and for all before then. . . . Cole, why aren't you down at the corral with the others? Don't tell me Riley didn't invite you, because I heard him myself. There's at least a dozen kids down there setting up for tonight's barn dance and they're having the time of their lives. Don't you like to have fun?"

"Not that kind of fun. Riley's a fag."

"The others don't seem to think so. I think he's adapted very nicely, and he certainly has gone out of his way to make friends. You're the one who refuses to get involved, Cole. Personally, I think you're a glutton for punishment. Or is it that you want to embarrass me and Riley?"

"If you say so, Mother," he replied insolently. "Are they all staying for dinner?"

"They're having an afternoon cookout. Then they'll go home and be back for the dance tonight. I told Martha not to fuss with my lunch; a sandwich will do me. I thought you'd be with the others. . . . I'm really sorry you've been so unhappy this summer, Cole. I was hoping you'd meet me halfway."

"Look, Mother, I don't want to go to this yokel school. Did you get a look at those kids? The girls especially!"

"Of course I did. They look like kids anywhere, and that includes your fancy military academy."

"They're all a bunch of faggots. I don't like them; can't you understand that? I don't fit in with them, and I don't want to. I don't belong here."

Maggie sighed. "At least make an appearance down at the barn. Sunbridge is your home, Cole, and you're the host. Do the proper thing."

"Riley's doing it for me. He's the one they like, not me. And don't tell me it's my fault, 'cause I don't want to hear it. Besides, I don't care. I got one over on old Riley this morning, didn't I?"

"How?"

"With that letter I got from Sawyer, that's how. Riley hasn't heard from her in weeks, but I have. He pretends it doesn't bother him, but I know it does and I'm glad."

Maggie hadn't realized Cole was hearing from Sawyer, and she was instantly curious. There were questions she wanted to ask about her daughter, things she wanted to know, but when she saw the look of smug satisfaction on Cole's face, she decided not to play into his hands. "Are you or aren't you going down to the corral?"

"All right, have it your way. But I don't understand why you're doing this to me. I hate it here. I hate everything about Sunbridge. Why are you making me stay?" His voice had risen to an agonized pitch somewhere between the frustration of a boy and the rage of a man.

Maggie's face drained of all color; she was speechless. She'd once cried those words—but in reverse. Light years ago she'd howled, *"Why are you sending me away? I belong here. Don't make me go! Why are you doing this to me?"*

Cole stared at his mother. He'd never seen that look on her face before and it frightened him. She seemed about to shatter into a thousand pieces. "I'm going, I'm going! Forget I said anything. Just forget it." He turned and began to run toward the corral, where Riley and the other kids were cooking hot dogs. He knew he'd hit a nerve, a very sensitive and painful nerve. It exhilarated him to have such power over her, and at the same time it frightened him to realize that his mother could be so easily destroyed.

"Hey! There's Cole! Just in time for lunch!" called one of the boys, enjoying the titters of laughter from the others.

"Where've you been, Cole?" one of the girls demanded, brushing her hands off on the seat of her jeans. "We've just hung the last paper streamer in the barn, everything's ready for tonight, and you didn't do a thing to help us." She giggled. "Maybe you shouldn't come to the dance tonight, even if it is your party."

"Cole had something to do for Aunt Maggie," Riley said quickly. "Otherwise he'd've been hanging from the rafters like the rest of us. Who gets the first hot dog?"

Cole bristled; he didn't need Riley to defend him and lie for him. "I didn't have—"

"Hey!" someone shouted from the barn. "Look what I found! Let's have a tug-o'-war! Guys against the girls!"

"No fair! No fair!" the girls complained. "It's even-steven or nothing!"

Sides were chosen, weight estimated and evenly distributed on both sides. Cole was encouraged to join and instinctively chose to pull opposite Riley. Riley was the tallest of the boys and he also had the prettiest girl beside him—if you didn't care about her braces, that was.

Cole grabbed his end of the rope and dug his heels into the soft ground. He felt the hardness of his muscles in his thighs, the tension and rigidity across his shoulders. This wasn't a game; it was personal. He clenched his teeth and pulled, surprising himself with his strength. Sawyer had been right; all the work he'd been doing this summer was the same as bodybuilding.

"Pull, Cole, pull! I think we've got 'em," the yell went up.

"That's what—you think," came from the other side, grunting. "C'mon, Riley, pull! Use those—muscles. You're—the anchorman."

"And his anchor's in his ass!" Cole shouted. He gave the rope a vicious yank, straining so hard he thought he tasted blood. His leg muscles shivered, his hands grew slick with sweat and threatened to slip, a pain tormented the back of his neck, and there was a freight train pounding through his head. But he kept his eyes focused on Riley, groaned and grunted and held his ground. He was the first man on his side of the rope, Riley the last on his. Inch by inch Cole's grip closed the distance between them; step by step Riley's team fought defeat. They were giving way; they were losing. If it killed him, Cole was determined to see Riley go down.

Cole's hands were still frozen around the rope when his teammates were laughing and clapping him on the back. "We did it! We won!" A tiny girl named Marcy kissed Cole on the cheek. "That's for winning." Cole blushed.

Riley dusted himself off and grinned as he held out his hand. "That was great, Cole. I guess you're right about where my muscles are. Hefting that pitchfork all summer really built you up!"

Cole looked pointedly at his cousin's outstretched hand. Then he smirked and walked away.

Embarrassed, Riley flushed and jammed his hands into his pockets. "Hey, Riley, lean down here," Marcy said.

"Why?"

"'Cause I want to kiss a loser. Don't pay any attention to Cole. He ruined Grace's party, too, by being a jerk. Ignore him," she said, planting a wet kiss on Riley's cheek.

Riley shrugged. Cole wasn't a jerk. He wasn't sure what Cole really was, but he wasn't a jerk.

Feeling cocky and smug, Cole sauntered back to the house. His mother was nowhere in sight. He flopped down on the chaise she'd been in and pulled Sawyer's letter from his hip pocket.

It was a long letter, but only a single sheet of paper. Typed. Cole grinned. Sawyer would never make it in the office pool: the letter was full of typos and crossouts. But what mattered was that she'd taken the time out of her busy schedule to drop *him* a note. He'd already rehearsed several versions of his response, but he wouldn't actually write till he heard his parents' decision regarding school.

Hello, little brother,

Bet this surprises you. Surprises me, since letter writing isn't one of the things I do best. I meant to write sooner, but work is keeping me pretty busy and I had some other things to take care of, too— you know, wounded pride, sore heart, tearful recriminations... If you're interested, and I know you are, I'm not any better but I'm not any worse.

Right now, I'm staying with an old college buddy, Adam Jarvis. He's a great guy—kind, gentle, considerate, and he wipes my tears when they get out of hand. He's a cartoonist. I think he's a genius.

We live on the upper east side. His apartment is a mess, but I pretend not to notice. What it needs is a good dose of Billie to fix it up.

I hope things are going well for you. How's your back? Not broken yet, I bet. Try not to be bitter, and take some advice from me; anger only eats you alive. I don't want to have to worry about you.

Christmas isn't that far away. Perhaps Maggie will invite me for the holidays. Or, if possible, you might want to wangle an invitation out of me to come to New York after Christmas. Riley's welcome, too, if you can tear him away from the ranch. You guys would have a ball.

Well, it's time for me to get to work. I got up early this morning to write this and I have an 8 A.M. appointment with an eye doctor. Guess I need new reading glasses. Things get blurry every so often. Adam says my tear ducts have dried up. He's probably right.

I know you must be very busy, but if you get a chance, drop me a line—and remember what I said about Christmas.

Say hi to Maggie and tell Riley I'll probably write him tomorrow. I'm giving you my phone number in case you ever want to call me.

Take care,
Sawyer.

Cole stared at the scrawled signature for a long time. Up till now it hadn't mattered that he had a sister. Now it was different. He had to remember to tell her about the tug-of-war. She'd laugh. He could almost see her eyes crinkle up and then the thick fringe of her lashes would glisten.

He read the letter a second time. Christmas in New York sounded great. Better than here. Maybe he could make a deal with his parents. If they decided he'd have to stay here, and he was sure that was the way it was going to be, then he'd simply make the deal for Christmas. Or he'd threaten to run away. That always put the fear of God into a parent.

Maggie slithered into a cornflower-blue lounging gown shot through with silver threads. The high mandarin collar brought the color close to her gently tanned face and cloud of dark hair, while the short capped shoulders exposed her gracefully rounded arms. Two side slits from the ankle to above the knee softened the line of an otherwise severely straight skirt. The outfit looked as though it had been made for her, and it had.

She knew Cranston would approve of the way she looked tonight. Glamour, that's what he expected and demanded, glitter and glitz, all the things that had nothing to do with reality and living.

Cranston didn't know Maggie Coleman Tanner anymore, she reflected wryly. He didn't know that she was different now, inside as well as outside. But tonight was her chance to show him that he wasn't dealing with the old Maggie, that Cole was important to her and that she'd fight for him if she had to. With all the Coleman money and the Coleman legal firm behind her, she could put up a pretty impressive fight. She hoped it wouldn't come to that.

She patted a stray strand of hair into place. Pearls? Why not. Her grandmother Agnes's matched strand would be perfect. She put them on and admired her reflection in the mirror. Yes, Cranston would be impressed. He knew real from imitation—and this time, she was real. More real than he was.

She twirled around until she was dizzy. "Hey, look at me now!" she cried to the empty room. Then, just for a moment, she felt foolish. She didn't have to prove anything to anyone. She didn't have to impress anyone, either.

The old Maggie did things like that.

Still, she didn't remove the pearls or the cornflower-blue dress. They were part of her. They, too, were Maggie Coleman Tanner.

As Cranston maneuvered his car down the long, tree-lined drive to Sunbridge, he was thinking about Maggie. Since his last visit, he'd done little but think of Maggie. She'd blossomed somehow, grown beautiful, more mature and elegant, more confident; desirable traits in a woman, definite assets in a wife. Even her attitudes seemed different, so different, in fact, that he'd been forced to reassess his decision to divorce her. At first he'd thought that she'd somehow manufactured all the changes. But in the weeks since his last visit, he'd decided that Maggie Coleman Tanner of Sunbridge might be a valuable asset indeed. With the Coleman money behind him, Maggie to perk up his dinner parties, and Sunbridge at his disposal for holiday weekend entertaining, he should have no trouble succeeding in his plan to buy out the other partners in his firm and reign as undisputed head of a law dynasty. He smiled at the image of himself playing lord of the manor—on a part-time basis, of course.

Cranston dug around in his briefcase for his tobacco pouch, then stuck a pipe, a gift from a grateful client, in his mouth and proceeded to puff thoughtfully. Just how hard would it be to get Maggie back? he wondered. Probably not too hard—you simply had to know your adversary. And Maggie was his adversary . . . for the moment.

Two weeks at Sunbridge ought to just about do it. Yes, he thought, amused, Greece could wait. It was time he got to know his wife and son. And by tonight, if he played his cards right, he wouldn't be sleeping alone.

Martha, the Mexican housekeeper, opened the door wide for him. She beamed a smile and ushered him into the wide foyer. His eyes went immediately to the Stetsons lined up on the hall hat rack. He grinned at the baseball

cap on the last peg. He knew it didn't belong to his son.
The Japanese kid—Japs were big on baseball.

"You finally made it."

Maggie walked into the foyer, looking beautiful and
smelling wonderful. Cranston opened his arms in welcome, ready for her to step into his embrace and curl
herself against him. Instead, she kept a formal distance
between them, looking just a bit smug as she ushered him
into the library. It annoyed him.

"Steven will take your bags upstairs later," she said
graciously. "You look well, Cranston. Winning your case
agreed with you, I take it."

"It's important to win," Cranston replied, his voice
brittle. "I was prepared."

Maggie smiled again. "So, it isn't true, then, that old
adage: it doesn't matter if you win or lose, it's how you
play the game that counts?"

"I told you I was prepared. I knew I would win. You
can't go off half-cocked in the courtroom. Substantiated
facts and a sympathetic judge. It's a winning combination."

Maggie grimaced. "Can I get you a drink?"

"What are you having?"

"Ginger ale."

"Then I'll have the same. It must have been hard for
you to give up liquor."

Maggie looked at her husband. "Yes, it was hard. I'm
getting my life in order, Cranston, slowly but surely. I'm
proud of myself because I did it on my own. Every day
I tell myself I'm an alcoholic. I'll make it."

Maggie's smile or little speech somehow irritated Cranston. "I'm sure you will," he said curtly. "How's Cole?"

"Antsy. He really believes you're going to take him
back to New York. Now that Sawyer is there, there's
more incentive for him to want to go. I'd like you to talk
to him as soon as possible. Tomorrow is the last day for
registration at Crystal City High. I had to make a concession, too. Private school for both boys at this point is

something I feel won't work. I want them to relate to all kids, not the chosen few who can afford expensive private schools. What do you think?"

"I'm willing to go along with you on the public school. For a semester. If it doesn't work out, we'll go on from there." Always concede a little, he reminded himself, so that when the time comes, they'll remember you were fair. He'd won more than one case that way.

Maggie felt relieved but somehow suspicious. "What happens after the first semester?" she asked. "Are you going to take him? Fight me for custody?"

"That's a long way off. Why worry about something that may never come to pass? We can deal with it when the time comes."

"In the meantime you'll find a way to get an edge on me. I know you, Cranston. Let's spell it out now. I don't want any surprises later on. Cole thinks you'd be willing to take him. Now we both know that's wishful thinking. I'm willing to give up child support but still allow you fair visitation rights."

"Mother Maggie. Whoever would have thought you'd become a lioness defending her cub."

"I just want what's best for him."

"That's what you say."

"Stop talking like a lawyer. If you want legalese, I'll call Dudley Abramson and you two can go at it. In the meantime, the boy stays here till it's settled. I mean it, Cranston."

"I know you do," Cranston said, holding out his glass for a refill. "This time add a little whiskey. How's Cole getting on with your nephew?" he asked.

"They aren't. And it's Cole's fault. He's sulky, insolent, disrespectful, and a general pain in the butt."

"Why haven't you done something about it?"

"I'm trying. But he needs a father—and he needs to know we're united where he's concerned. I really need your help, Cranston."

"I'll talk to him. Where is he?"

"He's probably lurking somewhere trying to figure a way to devil Riley. He's jealous, and I don't know what to do about it."

"Send the kid back to Japan."

"I can't do that. I won't do it. Riley has every right to be here. Besides, Riley isn't the source of Cole's problem. We are his problem."

"All right, so we'll work on it." Cranston saw Maggie watching him speculatively and he knew she was trying to figure out if he had an ulterior motive. Or was she thinking of the good days in the early part of their marriage?

"Are you seeing anyone?" he asked abruptly.

Maggie laughed, a delightful sound that sent shivers up Cranston's arms. "No. I don't have the time right now to get involved in any kind of a relationship. Besides, I like things the way they are, for the present."

"What about Rand? Now, don't jump down my throat," he said when Maggie opened her mouth to protest. "Cole mentioned it to me and he was upset."

"Upset about what? That Rand and Riley had to dry him out? Your son got drunk at the barbecue and made an ass out of himself. He just likes to twist the truth and the blame. That's the kind of thing I'm talking about, Cranston."

"Cole said Rand broke off his long-standing relationship with Sawyer. He also said Rand was cozying up to you."

"I hate that expression. We just talked, about everything and nothing. I didn't know about Sawyer until after Rand left. I had nothing to do with Rand's decision—and I was not the reason they broke up."

"If you were, it'd be damn shameful. Mother steals daughter's boyfriend. There's probably cause for a suit there somewhere."

"Stuff it, Cranston. Rand and Sawyer are adults."

"I told Cole you were probably trying to patch things up between them rather than break them up. Of course the boy didn't buy my explanation. He said Sawyer left early, and that you didn't try to stop her. Still jealous of her, eh?"

"No! Cole sees what he wants to see. He had no right to make assumptions and then run to you with them. You're doing the same thing. Admit it, Cranston. You think I'm having an affair with Rand."

"I never admit to anything."

"Well, that's your problem; it always was a thorn for me. . . . Don't get up," Maggie said coolly. "I'll see where Cole is."

Cranston watched his wife's retreating back. So, tonight he would sleep alone. He'd been a little premature in his estimate. It would take a few days. At the most.

In the falling dusk Cole and Riley faced each other at opposite sides of the tennis court. Cole thwacked the ball viciously, sending Riley running for it out of bounds. He'd seen his father arrive and now felt as if he were going into an emotional tailspin. One moment, he was certain his father would put his mother in her place and take him back to New York. The next, he saw his father for what he was and knew he'd be left behind with his mother. At Sunbridge.

The tennis ball sailed back over the net, but instead of hitting it with the racket, Cole caught it and pitched it back to Riley with a snap of his arm.

"You've got a wicked curve ball," Riley panted after leaping up to catch it. "If you'd been on the mound, that would've been a strike."

Cole hunched over and positioned himself for Riley's serve.

"Are you going out for the baseball team? You should. The competition will be stiff, but I bet you could make varsity if you wanted."

"You make it sound like it's definite that I'm not going to New York," Cole snapped. "Do you know something I don't know?"

"No. I just thought . . . even if you go to a new school, you should consider going out for baseball if they have a team. You're good," Riley said sincerely.

"Sports aren't my thing."

"What is your thing? You have to start somewhere. You're a natural."

"Look, why don't you mind your own business?" Cole said angrily. "You must know by now that you and I aren't going to make it as friends or cousins. So why don't you just buzz on out of here and let me alone?" He watched Riley's retreating back, then called out, "I got a letter from Sawyer yesterday."

"I got one today," Riley called back over his shoulder.

"I got one today," Cole mimicked. "Well, she's *my* sister!" Angrily he threw a tennis ball in Riley's direction—and almost hit his father.

"I've been looking all over for you," Cranston said, neatly catching the ball. "Hey, good throw. Who knows, you might be Yankee material."

"Not good enough for your Orioles, huh?" Cole shot back. "Mother told me that you always had a secret desire to play for them. I'm a Mets fan myself."

"They're losers. Never align yourself with losers or you might become one." He noticed Cole was getting taller, broader across the shoulders. The suntan seemed to take some of the narrowness from his face, Cranston thought. There was an improvement here, a noticeable one. Maybe Maggie was right—maybe Sunbridge was best for Cole right now.

"They've come from behind before. They did win the pennant once. They aren't going to do it this year, but they might get a shot at it next time."

"Nope, they're losers," Cranston said coolly. "Take my word for it."

"That's your opinion. It doesn't necessarily have to be mine." Cole paused, then asked belligerently, "Did you and Mother decide?"

Cranston's eyes narrowed at his son's tone of voice.

"Yes. You're going to Crystal City High the first semester. We'll evaluate the situation again in February. Be ready at nine tomorrow. I'll be taking you to the school to register."

Watching the expression on Cole's face, Cranston softened a little. He found himself searching for just the right thing to say to his son. "This was not a rash decision on our part, Cole. Your mother has been to the school and talked to the principal. There are some very qualified teachers there if you're interested in learning. Their sports program is enviable, too. Your mother has taken the trouble to arrange a car pool so you won't have to take the bus. I know this doesn't fit in with the plans you had, but you have a lot of years to make plans.

"Your mother said Riley registered himself several weeks ago. He wanted to sign up for several extracurricular activities. It wouldn't have hurt you to sign up at the same time."

Cole snorted. "I'm not Riley and I'm not interested in computers and baseball."

"Just what the hell are you interested in, Cole?" Cranston asked, exasperated.

"Nothing around here, that's for sure. I'll go to Crystal City High, but don't expect any great things from me. I'll put in my time."

"Your grades had better reflect that time, young man."

"Aren't you a little late with this parental concern?"

"Look, I don't have to take any of your bullshit, Cole. I demand your respect and I'll settle for nothing less."

Cole turned till he was facing his father, fixing him with a level stare. "Mother always taught me that respect has to be earned." He turned away and walked toward the house.

By the time Cranston rejoined Maggie, he was scowling. He felt as though he'd just lost the most important case of his career.

"Maggie, if you don't mind, I have a few notes to go over and some letters to sign. I tried to clear the decks before I left, but ended up filling my briefcase. Can you have the cook send me up a pot of coffee, and then I'm going to make it an early night. Have Cole ready by eight-thirty tomorrow morning."

"All right," she said, feeling strangely disappointed; she'd been looking forward to spending the evening with Cranston now that they'd agreed about Cole. "Would you like a sandwich, some cookies or fruit?"

"No, coffee's fine. See you in the morning, Maggie."

"Good night, Cranston."

Maggie spent the rest of the evening curled in a chair, sipping tea and reading a mystery novel. At ten-thirty she was just closing her book when Riley walked in, looking flushed and happy. "Did you have a nice evening?"

"Yes, I did. I'm not late, am I? I asked Cole to come along, but he didn't want to go. I guess he was waiting for his father."

"Cole will be going to Crystal City High with you. His father told him this evening."

Riley rolled his baseball cap in his hands, his short black hair standing up in little spikes on his head. "I hope he goes out for baseball. Aunt Maggie, he has a curve ball that'll knock your eye out."

"Really! I didn't know that. Cole never seemed inter-ested in sports. I know he played tennis and golf at the military academy, but that was mandatory. He did some canoeing too, but I didn't—"

"He's good. Better than me. I don't mean that I'm that good, but I think I might make the team. Cole wouldn't have any competition at all. All the kids asked about him tonight. I explained about his father arriving. . . ."

"Riley, you don't have to make excuses for my son. And don't ever for one minute think you don't belong here. You do." She smiled at him. "I saw that you got a letter from your grandfather today. How is he? Are things all right back home?"

"They miss me. The old one writes short letters, but he says what he has to say. Two of my cousins had girl babies. He grumbled. He asked me if I was going to come home over your Christmas holiday. We'll be off for three weeks. I don't know what to do."

"You don't have to make a decision right away. What I can do is make a reservation for you to make sure you have a flight. It can always be canceled later on if you decide not to go. The holidays are bad for travel from here to any foreign country. Christmas, unfortunately, is the worst. I have the school calendar, and I can do it tomorrow if you want."

"Yes, please. I will explain all that to my grandfather. He has never been to America."

Maggie laughed. "Then why don't we invite him? Mam and Thad would surely come for the holidays if they knew your grandfather would be here."

"I don't think he would come. It's such a long trip. It would be nice, though."

"We'll give it a try. Everyone likes to be invited, even if they have to turn down the invitation. I'll do it first thing tomorrow."

"Thanks, Aunt Maggie," Riley said, and gave her a bone-crushing hug. He kissed her soundly on the cheek before he took the hall steps three at a time. Such long legs, thought Maggie, just like his father. She touched her cheek gently with the tips of her fingers. Her own son had never kissed her or hugged her like that. Never, not even when he was little. How much she'd missed in her life! She sighed. How much she could never recapture.

Impulsively, Maggie looked at the phone and calculated the time difference in England; it would be four-thirty in the morning there. She frowned. Perhaps she could pretend she'd miscalculated . . . Before she could think about what she was doing, she dialed the operator and placed a call to Rand.

A sleep-filled voice came alive when the nasal twang of the operator announced an overseas call from Texas.

"Maggie! Good Lord, what's wrong?"

"I woke you. I'm sorry. I confused the time. There's

nothing wrong. I simply wanted to talk to a friend."

"Well, I am that—a friend, I mean. You're sure nothing is wrong?" Rand asked anxiously.

"Absolutely nothing is wrong," Maggie assured him. "I lost track of time. I'm sorry I woke you. How are you, Rand?" How stupid that sounded! "I enjoyed that funny little card you sent. It made me smile all day."

"That was my intention. I didn't mean it.... What I mean is, you didn't have to feel ... your letter, I enjoyed it, too." No reason to tell her he'd read it at least a dozen times.

"One of these days I'll write you another one," Maggie said, feeling shy. "Have you seen Susan lately?"

"Two weeks ago, and she looked terrible. Ill, very ill. Jerome said it was the heat, but I think it's more than that. I was thinking of calling you and telling you to get in touch with her. If Amelia were here, she'd have her in bed.... Sorry I don't have better news."

"That's all right. Overseas calls are usually sad or full of news— I don't know why I said that, Rand. Possibly something from when I was a child and a call came in from overseas and Mam always got upset.... Cranston is here," she blurted.

So, Rand thought, that was the problem. "Will he be taking Cole back with him?" he asked in what he hoped was a neutral tone.

"No. We agreed that Cole will go with Riley to Crystal City High for at least one semester. Cole, of course, isn't happy about it, but it's settled. Cranston will be here for two weeks. It's his vacation and he plans to spend some time with Cole."

"Does Cole plan on spending any time with him?"

"Very funny. We're all going to try.... How are things in England?" Maggie asked.

"Very merry as usual. That's a joke. Listen, I'm glad you called. I've been thinking of you the past few days. I didn't know if I should answer your letter or not. There were no questions to answer and I didn't want to presume.

I'll be leaving this afternoon on a business trip. I'll drop you a line."

"I'd like that. You know, Riley mentioned tonight that his grandfather would like him to return to Japan for Christmas. I suggested inviting him to Sunbridge, and Riley seemed to like the idea. I thought I'd invite the whole family again. Please try and make it."

"I'll do my best."

"I'll look forward to it and the letter you're going to write to me." She laughed. "I'd better hang up now so you can get back to sleep."

Rand wanted to tell her not to hang up. There was so much he wanted to tell her. So much. He took a deep breath—and said, "Thanks for calling. I'll write. Take care of yourself, and if you do call Susan, make it sound like it was your idea."

"I'll do that. Have a safe trip."

Maggie replaced the receiver. Neither of them had actually said good-bye, she realized.

"Boyfriend?" Cranston asked, coming up behind her.

"Friend." Maggie smiled.

"That's not what your eyes say."

"It really doesn't make a difference, does it? We're being divorced. What are you doing down here, anyway? You said you were turning in for the night."

"Huffy, aren't we? I brought the coffeepot back to the kitchen. I'm an excellent guest. I like to be invited back."

"Good night, Cranston," Maggie snapped as she set about turning off the lights. "I'm going up now myself. Sleep well."

"I'd sleep better if you joined me," he said boldly.

"If that's an invitation, I'm afraid I'll have to decline. You see, the only thing we have left in common now is our son."

"We could try."

"Not tonight we couldn't."

Cranston laughed, a sound that was deep and hoarse. It made Maggie shiver.

Back in her room, she looked at the shiny brass lock on the door. Without hesitation, she turned the latch.

Rand's voice had sounded so clear, she thought as she hung the cornflower-blue silk on a padded, scented hanger. Almost as though he were talking from the next town. And so . . . so warm. Was Rand the reason she'd locked her bedroom door? she wondered. Earlier, she'd looked forward to spending the evening with Cranston. If she hadn't called Rand, she might have accepted Cranston's invitation. It had been a long time since she'd had sex. And years since she'd made love. For a while she hadn't known the difference.

Maggie looked at the tiny bedside clock. It was still early; she rarely fell asleep before two or three. She could write some letters, maybe drop a note to Sawyer. Tomorrow she could get her New York address from the boys. Or Susan—should she write or call? Rand had made her illness sound serious. Maybe she should wait and talk to Amelia. There was still time; she and Cary weren't home yet.

Quickly, Maggie penned off a short note asking Amelia to stop by if she wasn't too tired. Then she stood by her door, listening, before she opened it. She felt sneaky and ridiculous. This was her house! Boldly, she walked down the hallway past Cranston's door. No trace of light showed on the hall carpet. Riley's and Cole's rooms were dark, too. When she reached Amelia and Cary's room, she stuffed the small piece of paper between the door handle and the jamb.

Then, on an impulse, Maggie crossed the hall to the darkened nursery. She switched on the light and looked around.

Nothing had changed. The crib, the cradle, and the single bed were still there, all freshly made-up. The rocking horse with the plumed tail stood in the corner, its black eyes staring at the wall. She had the crazy urge to get on it and rock till she was dizzy. The padded rocking chair with its scarlet cushions looked so inviting. She should have sat in that chair and rocked Sawyer. Someone else had done that—Mam and the nurse. Angrily, Maggie marched over to the chair and sat down. Her arms were empty. It was too late.

The toy box with its hand-painted clowns drew her like a magnet. She propped up the lid and stared down at the contents. There was her own Raggedy Ann doll, well worn, well loved. She looked up; Nancy Drew, the Hardy boys, and Cherry Ames marched across the bookshelves, old favorites she'd read over and over again. Maggie's eyes filled with tears. So long ago! Roots. Beginnings. Memories. Most of them were good, especially the ones from this room. Only when she'd moved down the hall had the memories turned sour.

It was several minutes before Maggie realized she wasn't going to find what she was looking for in this room. There had been another child here once, but there was no trace of her now. Sawyer's childhood possessions were locked away in Mam's studio, inaccessible and remote. Just like Sawyer herself.

))))))))) CHAPTER ELEVEN)))))))))

As Maggie approached her room, she noticed Amelia still in her evening clothes with her arm raised to knock on the door. Maggie wondered how a woman her age could look so vital at midnight.

"What's wrong? I read your note. Cary is asleep on

his feet. Dancing in pointed shoes isn't the treat for him it is for me. Poor dear, what he puts up with. Tell me, what is it?"

"Rand called earlier," Maggie lied, unwilling to admit to something that might be misinterpreted and cause trouble. "He said he saw Susan and she was very ill. He said if you were there, you'd have her in bed. You don't seem the type, or at least you never did, to overreact. I take it Susan is very sick but continuing with the tour."

"Jerome will drive that girl into the ground to get what he wants. He's a nothing without her. I think he knows it, too. He's trying to get as much mileage out of her as he can on this tour." Amelia sighed. "I don't know what we can do, if anything. Certainly we can call. Jerome will get on the phone and say Susan is resting or Susan is sleeping or Susan is shopping. She never gets my messages. I think he even screens her mail. She called me once so upset she could hardly talk—said everyone was ignoring her and so on. I tried explaining, but she wouldn't believe me. She said Jerome would never do anything like that because he loved her. Well, my dear, if *that's* love, it's sick."

"I didn't know that," Maggie said softly.

"There's a lot you don't know. About all of us. I don't mean that to be unkind, but there was a time when you—"

"I know, Aunt Amelia. Things are different now. I was going to wait up a little longer and call around seven or eight Susan's time. What do you think?"

"I think it's a good idea, but if Jerome answers, I don't know how far you'll get. I'll be glad to wait it out with you. Why don't I go down and get us some tea and crackers or something."

"I have a better idea. That's a Galanos you're wearing. Why don't you change and I'll get the tea and crackers."

"A hen party, I love it." Amelia giggled.

"Chicks, Aunt Amelia," Maggie said, smiling. "We're not old enough to be hens."

"Chicks it is. By the way, is the big C here? I saw the rental car in the driveway."

"Yes, Cranston is here. He arrived this evening. He's going to be here for two weeks. At least that's what he says now. Go change. We can talk later."

First Amelia checked on Cary, who was tucked between the satin sheets on their bed, snoring lightly. How handsome he looked! And he was all hers, every goddamn inch of him. Then she removed her gown, draped it over the back of a chair, and quickly changed into a frothy creation of champagne-colored silk with a matching robe. Later, she would remove the carefully applied makeup. No point in frightening Maggie if she didn't have to.

"I'd kill for that creation," Maggie said in awe when the two women had settled in for a cozy talk.

"I almost did." Amelia laughed. "I had to fight this buxom woman from Austin who was six sizes bigger. She said she would diet to get into it. It's a six."

Maggie smiled. This was so nice—she and Amelia, sitting here late at night, sipping tea and talking like equals. Family. "You know, Aunt Amelia, I was always jealous of you and Susan and your close relationship."

"I'm sorry about that. Listen, could we forgo that aunt business? It makes me feel old."

How like Amelia not to go into some long song and dance about it being the best thing at the time, Maggie thought. "How are things going in the building business?" she asked.

"The building hasn't started yet. Cary is such a stickler about everything. Then there's the financing. We're talking millions here. He bit off a good-size chunk and he's doing a lot of chewing. I think we might turn him into a Texan yet."

"You really love him, don't you?"

"Heart and soul, Maggie. Not too long ago I was thinking to myself that all the little affairs, the relationships, the one-night stands—and we've all had them—they were nothing more than exercises for this one grand love. They

always say you'll know when you're in love. I remember
the way I used to ask my mother, and all she'd do was
smile and say, 'You'll know.' She was right. I take it the
grand moment hasn't yet arrived for you."

Maggie grimaced. "Not yet, and time is really flying
by."

"Tell me about it. I just had my last face-lift. No more
nips and tucks. This is it. I don't think I really mind
growing old; it's just that I have this miserable skin that
tends to wrinkle. When I was twenty-nine I must have
looked like I was forty. It's hereditary."

"Don't tell me that," Maggie said, fingering her cheek.

"Not to worry. You got your skin from Billie. We're
talking flawless here."

"I know. There are so many things I'm grateful to her
for. One of these days I'm going to sit down and tell her.
The time just never seems right."

"What do you hear from Sawyer?" Amelia asked pointedly.

"Nothing. Both boys have heard from her. I know she's
in New York, but that's about it."

"She must have been devastated when Rand broke it
off. She was so in love with him, it made me want to cry.
At the time I thought to myself, no woman should ever
allow herself to love a man that way. And look at me—
I'm worse than she is. But Sawyer does have youth on
her side. I'm sure she'll bounce back. On the other hand,
I'd just shrivel up and die if Cary left me. This is between
you and me, Maggie. If you ever say a word, I'll deny
it."

Maggie replenished her tea. "What we talk about is
between us. It will never go any further. Tell me, what
are you doing while Cary is out there beating the bushes?
You're never home."

"I run interference for him. He really respects my opinion. I'm the idea person. So far, it's working out great.
Don't get the notion that Cary can't make a decision or
that he needs my ideas because he doesn't have any of

his own. It's just that we really share everything. A duo, a matched set, a union—call it what you like. I never thought I could be so happy." She leaned back and took a sip of her tea. "Now, enough about me. I've hardly seen you these past weeks."

"I've been busy, too," Maggie said. "If I'm not on this committee, I'm on the next one. I try to get in a set of tennis every day and play golf once a week at least. I've been doing the standard volunteer work that Mam did for a while and sort of carved my own niche. I'm pretty interested right now in a gallery that's set to open soon in Crystal City. The curator is a friend of a friend. He even offered me a job. I said I might be interested on a part-time basis. I want to be here when the boys get home from school. It's all busy work, Amelia, but I'm content."

"You look content, and that's what matters. This is none of my business, but I'm asking anyway. Is there any chance you and Cranston might get together again?"

"I don't think so. Cranston and I have drifted apart. We aren't enemies or anything like that. In fact, right now, we're both working to cement some kind of relationship with Cole."

"Your mother?"

"We're friends. I couldn't want or ask for more."

"Rand?"

Maggie hesitated. "He's a friend."

"And none of my business, right?"

"For now," Maggie said quietly.

"He's my son."

"I know."

"I wouldn't want to see him hurt. I think he's hurting right now."

"I know that," Maggie said, bringing the teacup to her lips. "Are you telling me you're one of those people with long memories?"

"Not at all. I know how precious love—real love—can be. More so when one has the nerve to reach out for it. All I'm saying is each of us does what we have to do for our own personal happiness. Because we're the ones who have to live with that happiness. If it's at someone else's expense, we have to live with that, too."

"Gotcha. That was a nice little sermonette. I enjoyed it." Maggie smiled.

"I rather thought you would. I should have spiked this tea. I'm wide awake. How much longer before we can call Susan?"

Maggie looked at her watch. "At least another twenty minutes. Something's bothering you, isn't it? I've noticed you've been squirming in that chair since you sat down. Do you want to talk about it?"

"Yes. No. Oh, I don't know. I haven't even said anything to Cary yet."

"Come on, Amelia, what you say here isn't going any further. We settled that a while ago."

Amelia paused for a long moment, then took a deep breath and blurted, "My mother's house is for sale!"

"Really!"

"I want to buy it."

"Why? Are you going to settle back here?"

Amelia set her teacup down and leaned toward Maggie. "I don't know if you can understand this, but my father sold that house from under my mother. She wanted to keep it so she could take Moss and me there to learn about her side of the family, the way her family did things. My father wouldn't permit it. He said she didn't need anything but Sunbridge, especially not another house. It was his way of making sure she stayed under his thumb. It almost broke her heart. We used to talk about it. I probably know that house as well as you know this one. I know where every stick of furniture was. Of course, everything was sold off long ago, but I remember it all. In fact, Mam and I made drawings of the whole house. I think they're probably still up in the attic with my old school things. I could redo it."

"Why?" Maggie asked. "Will you live there?"

"Why? Why did you want to come back here? I know

it sounds silly, since I grew up here at Sunbridge. If Mam couldn't have it, maybe I can. Who knows what I would do with it? Look at it, walk through it. Maybe Cary would want to live in it. I didn't say I was definitely going to buy it," Amelia said defensively. "I just said it was for sale. Cary won't be needing me as much once the building gets under way. They don't like women hanging around construction sites. It would give me something to do. Something Mam would have wanted."

"Then you should do it," Maggie said. "I'm for whatever makes you happy. How much is it?"

"I called," Amelia said in a hushed voice.

"How much?" Maggie whispered.

"One million six in an area that's not exactly what it used to be. The surrounding acres are what's driving the price up."

"God! Are you prepared to..."

"Yeah.... I'd liquidate everything to get that house."

"Are you telling me that's all you have?"

"I'm talking about liquidity. Don't forget I'd have to refurbish. It would cost a fortune. I have it; that's no problem."

"The way I see it, Amelia, you have to ask yourself what it's worth to you. Look, if you need some—"

"Maggie! I have more than enough. Cary could buy it for me if I didn't have it, which I do. It's just ... What I mean is, I don't ... Hell, I don't know what I mean."

Maggie remained silent. This was a side of Amelia she'd never seen. Now she could understand the deep friendship between her mother and this woman.

"What would you do, Maggie?"

"I'd go for it. Life's too short. If it's going to make you happy, then that's the way to go."

"But I don't know if it will. That's a lot of money. What if I can't handle it?"

"Amelia, I don't think there's anything in this life you can't handle. If it doesn't work, bail out. Resell it. It's that simple."

"I'm not going to rush into it, but on the other hand,

what if someone snatches it out from under me?"

"Take an option. Put down some money till you've thought it through and talked it over with Cary. That's what you're really worried about, right?"

"A little. He's a wonderful person, and sentimental in his own way. But I don't think he'll understand the price tag or what it will cost to refurbish."

"If it's what you want, I think he'll agree."

"Maybe you're right. I'll talk to him about it tomorrow. God, it must be time to call Susan by now."

Maggie tossed and turned all night long. The telephone conversation with Susan had done nothing to reassure her. Jerome had been reluctant to call his wife to the phone, but Amelia had insisted. Susan had sounded weary, as if even a telephone conversation was too much for her, although she'd tried to reassure Amelia and her sister that she was feeling fine.

"Someone's not telling the truth here, and I know it isn't Rand," Amelia had said bitterly after they'd hung up. "I'm worried, Maggie, really worried. I know Susan, and I didn't like the way she sounded. And Jerome saying she was just tired doesn't make sense. It's first thing in the morning over there, for God's sake; she's just had a night's sleep! Another thing—Susan was always a chirpy little bird in the morning; she said it was the best part of the day for her. I don't like it, not at all."

Maggie hadn't liked it, either. She worried over her sister all night long and still felt uneasy the next morning, as the lacy lavender shadows of a pale pink dawn followed her over the footpath to the cemetery on the knoll. When her feet grew wet and slippery from the dew, she bent down to remove her sandals and noticed for the first time that someone had walked the path earlier.

She stopped and looked around, slightly irritated that someone was intruding on what she considered to be her private place. Who from Sunbridge would be out this early? And why the cemetery? She walked softly on her bare feet, not afraid, only curious; she couldn't imagine anything bad happening in this peaceful, tranquil place.

As she came closer to the knoll where the Coleman family rested, her sense of unease increased. She could hear a voice, indistinct and hurried. She crept even closer, careful to make no sound. Something seemed to warn her to remain out of sight. A splash of color, vibrant purple in the pale light, drew her eyes like a magnet. Amelia!

Maggie felt an enormous sense of relief. Of course it would be Amelia; who else would care enough to come to this place? As she debated whether to wait or leave, her aunt's voice carried clearly to her on the fresh, clean air of a beautiful new day. . . .

"I think it's a wise move on my part, Mam. I suppose I'm not being exactly honest with everyone when I tell them I'm buying your old homestead because of you. It's too late for you. Maybe it isn't too late for me. Maybe, maybe, maybe. I'm going to buy that damn house, and I'm going to fix it up just the way it was when you lived in it. Hell, Mam, maybe I'll even live in it myself with Cary. God, I wish you were here. There's so many things I'd like to talk over with you. This awful insecurity. Who would ever believe I live in mortal fear that Cary will leave me?"

"I would," Maggie whispered to the quiet around her.

"You know, Mam, I'm so much older than he is. One of these days he's going to take a good hard look at me and realize just how old I am. If you only knew how much I love this man. I think I could kill for him. . . .

"Did you ever have the feeling that when things are so good, something bad is going to happen? That's exactly how I feel right now. I know something is going to go wrong. It's too perfect. I'm too happy. I wouldn't want to live if Cary left me. I couldn't face the emptiness. Is that how you felt? Is that why you curled up inside yourself? But it wouldn't take me twenty-five years to die, Mam," Amelia whispered. "I know quicker ways."

Maggie turned away, blinded by her tears. She had no right to stand here and listen. She felt like a criminal as she tried to back up the narrow footpath. A sudden purple movement made her dart into the bushes and crouch down. From her position in the shrubbery she had a clear view of Amelia standing by the gravestones. She didn't know whether to laugh or cry when she saw Amelia thumb her nose in the direction of Seth's grave.

Moments later, Amelia's pedicured feet passed by. Maggie waited for what seemed like a long time before she stood up. She made sure there was no sign of Amelia in her purple dress, then stepped onto the footpath.

Cary was just emerging from the shower when Amelia walked into the room. "So, you weren't kidnapped after all. Watching the sun come up?"

"More or less. I was at the cemetery. It seemed like the thing to do when I woke up." Amelia smiled warily.

"You don't have to be defensive with me, Amelia. You don't even have to explain. I thought you were downstairs on the patio watching the sun come up.... Is there anything bothering you, hon?"

Amelia sat on the edge of the bed watching her husband dress. She loved the way he kind of took a little hop and then zipped his pants. He grinned, and she grinned back, then took a deep breath. "I want to talk to you about something. I want your opinion and your advice. I suppose that's what I was looking for at the cemetery, but it was kind of a one-sided conversation. I guess I wanted to talk it out in my mind first.... Am I making sense?"

"Absolutely. What is it?" Cary asked, sitting down on the bed next to his wife.

"I want to buy a house."

Cary threw his hands up in the air. "So what's the problem?"

"It's not just any house. It's the house that my mother grew up in. I told you how Pap sold it out from under her. I found out it's for sale and I want to buy it. I want to be sure I'm buying it for the right reasons."

"Seems to me that if it was your mother's house, that's reason enough. Buy it."

"You don't mind?"

"Amelia, whatever makes you happy makes me happy. If you don't know that by now, you never will."

"I'll have to renovate. There's probably a lot of work to be done. The price is high, but then all real estate these days is high. I have the money; that's not the problem."

"Then what is the problem?"

"I'm not sure. I don't know anything about real estate. Maybe you won't even like the house. I have diagrams and a picture up in the attic. If I do decide to buy it, I want it to be exactly the way it was when Mam lived there. I thought it would give me something to do when you're out on the construction site."

"I like the idea. Home is wherever you are, babe. You know that. And don't worry about what you know and don't know. Who the hell ever thought I'd go into the building business? Go for it."

"The price is one million six."

"Steep. If you want it, get it."

"No. Do you still think I can do it?"

"Hell, yes. Just don't pay cash. Take as big a mortgage as you can get. It'll be one hell of a tax write-off."

"Mortgage? I was going to pay cash."

"Never pay cash. Always use someone else's money. How do you think I got where I am? You're going to have to palaver a little."

"Oh, yeah." Amelia grinned. "Seems like I just said that to you not too long ago."

"I took your advice. Now it's your turn. Go to whoever owns the house now, make an offer, then go to the bank. I wish I could go with you, but you know my schedule today. If you need me, call."

"I will. . . . You know, Amelia, I feel as though I belong. Almost. Thanks to you, everyone has taken a real interest and no one has screwed me. I don't expect they will, either. A handshake is good enough. You did all that for me."

"That's what I'm here for."

"Oh, lady, you are so wrong. This is what you're here for."

Amelia giggled as Cary's busy hands fumbled with the ties of her dress. "You're going to be late," she warned.

"Who cares? I'm the boss, remember? This is more important. You come first, honey. Remember that."

Amelia sighed, growing languid now in his embrace.

"Now let's do what we do best."

When he held her like this, close against him, his hands urgent and demanding, taking possession of her before warming and slowing to tender caresses, Amelia's heart pounded with an answering passion. She could be young again in Cary's embrace, young and breathless and just a touch innocent. There was nothing to think about except his need, nothing to fill her world except this man. She loved him, needed him more than she wanted him to know. She wanted to satisfy him, to pleasure him, for only in his pleasure would she find her own.

Cary felt his wife yield to his embrace and offer herself to his hands and lips. He wondered at the miracle of her, at the way she instinctively knew what caress would heighten his desire, at the way she was always accessible to him, never holding back her favors. She was an experienced lover, knowledgeable of her own body, of what would make her respond and bring her satisfaction. Yet there was something fragile and innocent about her, too, and she always brought a freshness to their lovemaking that excited him and made him anticipate being locked in her embrace the next time. She imbued him with a sense of his own manhood, made him know and feel his own power; but most of all, Amelia made him know that he was loved, unconditionally, forever. That, more than anything, coming from a background where love, if given at all, was given in very small measures, made him completely hers.

Cary rolled onto his back, bringing her with him, putting her in the female-superior position they both enjoyed. Her knees gripped his hips as she rode him, her hands braced against his broad chest to push herself backward and take him deep inside herself. He steadied her movements by gripping her buttocks, supporting her with his pelvis, and measuring his movements to hers. Soon he felt the initial tremblings that told him she was near her climax. He watched her face, saw her close her eyes and throw her head back, an expression of sheer joy illuminating her features. That he could bring this woman such rapture, this woman he loved so well, brought him a special kind of satisfaction, a certain desire and passion. Just as he was aware of her body closing tightly around his, as her undulations deepened and a kittenish sound began to rise in her throat, he rolled her to the side, following after, his hips still imprisoned between her thighs, He buried himself deep within her, mimicking the rhythmical movements she had made while astride.

Amelia clung to Cary, following him with her body, answering him with her soul. That she could satisfy this man was a joy beyond joy, and at the moment they shared their climax she laughed—a soft, deep sound of triumph.

Maggie was uneasy about several things this morning as she sipped her coffee at the breakfast table. First of all, there'd been that ludicrous conversation with Jerome and Susan; and secondly there was Amelia. Each time she pondered one, the other seemed to break into her thoughts.

Amelia. . . . Maggie knew her aunt dearly loved Cary Assante, but she was also aware of the difference in their ages. At the moment, it seemed Carry was also very much in love with his wife; but how long would that last? Forever? Was anything forever?

Cranston was the first one down, looking fit in a striped blue cotton knit pullover and casual white duck pants that hugged the lean length of his thighs. He helped himself to breakfast from an array of food laid out on the sideboard, then took a seat across from Maggie and poured himself coffee from the electric percolator.

"Nothing like life in the country, is there?" he asked enthusiastically. "Maggie, darling, why don't we all go on a picnic today? We can leave as soon as Coleman and I get back from registering him at the high school."

Maggie looked across the table, hardly believing her ears. "A picnic? I didn't know you liked picnics. I don't believe we ever went on one together. Or did we?"

"No, we didn't. We should have. There's a lot of things we should have done, Maggie. Maybe it's not too late to start. I'm here now; I have all the time in the world. Why don't we try getting to know each other again? It might make things easier between us. For Cole's sake," he added casually.

"Thank you for not throwing blame on me, Cranston," Maggie said softly. "I wasn't much of a wife, I know." She hesitated. "I'm not sure about the picnic, though. I have two meetings and a luncheon scheduled for today. I gave my word. People expect me. I can't just—"

Cranston leaned across the table. "Cancel them, Maggie," he said, his voice husky.

Again Maggie hesitated. A picnic might be fun. There was no denying Cranston could be pretty persuasive when he wanted to be. Right now, his handsomeness, the tone of his voice, the vulnerability he was displaying, made it hard to believe they'd been so unhappy together. All the past hurts, the destruction they'd heaped upon one another, seemed so far away. . . .

"Okay, you've got yourself a date," she said, getting up from the table. "Just let me make a few phone calls and have Martha arrange a picnic basket for us. It should all be done by the time you come back with Cole."

Cranston rewarded her with a boyish smile, one she hadn't seen in what seemed like a hundred years.

When Cranston returned from Crystal City he found Maggie waiting for him, dressed in hip-hugging jeans and a loose-fitting sky-blue shirt, which she'd tied in a knot at her slender waist to expose a small patch of sun-darkened belly. Cranston drew in his breath. In a pair of scuffed sneakers with rolled-down socks and a bouncy ponytail, she looked about sixteen.

"Where's Cole?" Maggie asked, looking behind Cranston for their son.

"He said picnics didn't exactly turn him on, so I dropped him off at some kid's house to go swimming."

"Whose house?" Maggie demanded. "Don't you know who it was?"

"Mike something or other. Hey, don't get so worked up," Cranston said soothingly. "I'd like to think I was the main attraction at this picnic."

Maggie forced herself to relax. There could be other picnics with the three of them and after all, if she and Cranston got to know each other better this time, wouldn't that eventually benefit Cole? "You won't be the main attraction once you smell Martha's fried chicken," she laughed gaily.

Cranston felt the tension leave his shoulders. Not for anything did he want Maggie to know that he'd lied to Cole about this picnic in order to have her all to himself. "Do you have a spot in mind?" he asked as he led Maggie out the door and relieved her of the picnic basket.

"I know a beautiful spot. Susan, Riley, and I used to play there when we were little. We'd carry out play dishes and Riley would carry the picnic basket, and we'd stay there for hours."

"So, you did have some good times here, after all," Cranston said smoothly.

"Of course I had some good times," she said defensively. "It just so happens that the bad outweighed the good." She smiled. "You should have seen Riley trying to carry the basket. We had to tie a string on it so he could pull it. . . . I miss him, and there are times when I feel so guilty." The moment the words were out Maggie regretted them. Cranston was not someone she wanted to confide in.

"Why in the world should you feel guilty about Riley?" he asked. "He was killed during wartime. Is that why you brought young Riley here?"

Maggie shrugged evasively. "I'm alive. I'm going on a picnic with a handsome man. Riley won't even be able to go on a picnic or play ball with his son. I feel bad about that. And no, that's not why I brought Riley here. The boy has every right, Cranston. All of this," she said, waving her hand, "would be his if his father hadn't died. I can't forget that and I won't. I thought Cole and Riley would become friends since they're cousins and the same age. Unfortunately, Cole is prejudiced, much like you, Cranston. But Riley is doing well on his own. He's got all sorts of friends and"—she grinned—"he's already beating the girls off with a stick. The children have accepted him more readily than they've accepted Cole. But it's Cole's fault. He simply isn't interested. He doesn't even seem interested in girls. Academically, though, I think they're going to be neck and neck." Maggie pointed down a small incline. "So, what do you think?"

Cranston peered over the small ridge to gaze down where his wife was pointing. "Looks like a glade of some sort."

"It is. There's a small spring-fed pond that makes the ferns and bushes grow. There're some pines on the other side. It smells so good. All pungent and woodsy. Susan used to fall asleep on the fern fronds. We'd make little pallets. First the pine needles, then the ferns. Do you want to?" Maggie asked eagerly with a peculiar light in her eyes.

"Why the hell not!" Cranston shouted as he slid down the embankment, Maggie right behind.

They worked in companionable silence arranging their fragrant pallets. Maggie knew Cranston was having fun in spite of himself. It was probably the first time he'd actually put his penknife to use. She felt like a kid herself.

"I think mine's a little neater," she said when they'd finished, "and I didn't have a knife. But I'm experienced.

You have to be careful the way you break off a fern frond. Yours will do, but you left too much end on the frond; it's going to prick you. I'll spread the cloth and you can take out the goodies. Martha always outdoes herself for picnics."

"She must have; this basket was a bastard to carry. I have a crick in my neck."

"Don't complain, Cranston; just enjoy. I think both of us have forgotten how to do that. I'm getting on track now, and you should, too."

"What's that supposed to mean?" Cranston demanded.

"It means whatever you want it to mean. For me it meant time to stop and relax, take stock of myself. The only person who can make you miserable is yourself. The only person who can make you a workaholic or an alcoholic is yourself. In the end we all have to pay our dues. I'm lucky—I woke up in time to realize I didn't like my life. I was existing. I wasn't living."

Cranston bit into a crisp chicken leg and chewed thoughtfully as he listened to his wife. An hour later he'd learned more about her than he'd known in all the years they'd been married.

"And another thing," Maggie said, pointing her chicken leg in his direction. "I know why you're here. I know why you came the first time, too. Even if Cole hadn't called, you'd have found a way to get to me. There was a lot of hatred there, on both sides, when I left. You were going to try and get custody of Cole so it would look good on the divorce decree. And Cole played right into your hands. I also know that you have the opportunity right now to buy out the other partners in your firm, and that you're considering it. It'd be a real coup for you. . . . Ah, I was right. I can see it in your face." Maggie shook her head. "What happened to your courtroom poker face?"

"I left it in New York," Cranston said shortly.

"I left a lot of things in New York, too. This is a new life for me. As I said, I'm on track now. There's a lot I still have to do. I know now there are some things I can never make right again and I—I'll have to live with that."

Cranston leaned back with his head cupped in his clasped hands. "Neither of us worked at the marriage. I'm willing to take my share of the blame. How in the hell did we ever manage to have a child?"

"If you want the details, I can give them to you." Maggie laughed, then busied herself repacking the hamper. "Between the two of us we almost destroyed Cole, you know. The fact that we can talk now and actually be civil to each other is a big step." She stopped for a moment. "I can't even believe you're here. When was the last time you actually took a vacation?"

"Maybe ten years. I can't even remember."

"Was it all worth it?"

"Right now I'd have to say yes. Yesterday I probably would have said no. I am what I am, Maggie. The firm is my life. Maybe it shouldn't be, but it is."

"And if you do buy out the others and the firm becomes yours, what then?"

Cranston shrugged. "King of the heap. Come here and lie next to me."

Despite herself and her better intentions, Maggie allowed Cranston to pull her down beside him and cradle her head against his shoulder. And even though it felt so right, so easy, to be here beside him this way, she still felt uneasy, as if she were being taken in somehow. "I'm not sure this is such a good idea, Cranston," she forced herself to say, her voice light, a shade breathless. "We're being divorced, remember? By the way, when is the court date?"

"The first week in January sometime. I forget the exact date. Are you telling me," Cranston asked as he propped himself up on one arm, "that you don't feel anything, anything at all?"

"I won't let you manipulate me. If and when I want to go to bed with you, it'll be because it's what I want, not what you manipulated me into doing." She moved away from him a little. "Now, about the divorce. We have to discuss Cole. I don't want you just walking in here and snatching him away from me."

Instantly Cranston lost all his amorous thoughts. "Cole is old enough to make his own decisions," he said sourly. "A judge will talk to him, and it'll pretty much be what the boy wants."

"Damn you, Cranston, that's not good enough! You gave up custody. What'll it take for you to keep it that way?"

"Absolutely nothing. Cole is the one who is unhappy. Look, Maggie, I don't like to take potshots at you, but you were an unfit mother. A drunken, unfit mother. Judges pay attention to things like that."

"And what does that say for you? You wanted out so bad, you signed away your rights to your son to a drunken, unfit mother."

"What that would mean in a courtroom is Coleman money intimidated and paid off. Next question?"

"You son of a bitch! Tell me you wouldn't do that to Cole and me."

"We all do what we have to do. Those are your words, Maggie. I'm just repeating them."

"Money, that's it, isn't it?" Maggie cried. "You need money to buy the firm. Using all of yours, paying bank loans, will strap you. Now, let's see, where can you get money at no interest? Who'd be sucker enough to go for a deal like that?"

"There's probably one or two people walking around who might go for a deal like that," Cranston said smoothly. "Your mother, for instance. Isn't Thad going to run for office? I know some very influential people. You could come out smelling like a lily. On the other hand..."

"You bastard!"

"Is that the same as son of a bitch?" Cranston laughed.

"And to think I almost made love to you. You're vile and disgusting."

"You're wonderful, exciting, and I feel as if there's an electric current running through me. Forget all this bullshit and make love with me," Cranston said, pulling her back into his arms.

Maggie struggled. Cranston's heart was beating so fast, she thought he would collapse—or was it her own heart? It had been so long since she'd been with a man. Her struggles increased, then grew weaker as Cranston's arms pinned her to him.

She knew exactly what she was responding to—this was passion, not love. This was frustration, even desire, but it was not love. Over and over she repeated this to herself, issuing warnings that were overridden by the feel of his body pressing into hers, by the heat of his hands as he fumbled with the buttons on her blouse.

"Don't fight me, Maggie. You know you want it as much as I do. We were always good together; we can be good again." He was breathing into her ear; there was a desperate edge to his voice.

Maggie's fingers dug into the flesh of Cranston's back. What he was saying wasn't true. They weren't always good together. There had been times when he'd rejected her, refused her, played nasty little games to punish her. But there had been times when he'd deemed her "worthy," times when her self-esteem had almost equalled his; those times had been good, very, very good. "Don't do this, Cranston," she pleaded. "I don't want it; I don't want you!"

"Yes, you do. You know you do." Suddenly he ripped her shirt apart, popping the buttons, revealing her breasts. "Look at yourself. Look at the way your body wants me to touch it, to kiss it, like this..." He lowered his head and took one pouting nipple into his mouth, running his tongue over the hard nub, biting it lightly. "I can feel the heat coming off you, Maggie." His hand slipped between her legs, rising upward along the inside of her thigh. "You're already wet for me, aren't you? You were always wet for me, Maggie, and it always drove me crazy." He was gasping the words against her mouth, claiming her lips, invading the soft recesses with his tongue. "Show me how wet you are, Maggs. Show me," he demanded, working the zipper of her jeans, exposing her flesh to the filtered sunlight dappling through the trees.

Fireworks shot off inside Maggie's brain. Her mind was telling her one thing while her body demanded another. Against her will she was helping him, kicking her legs free of jeans and underpants. He laughed with satisfaction to find her wet and ready for him.

"You're no good, Cranston," she breathed, "no damn good. But I want you, good God, I want you!"

"What do you want, Maggie?" he teased. "Show me. Tell me!"

"This!" She wriggled beneath him, finding him with her hand, touching the hardness of him. "Don't tease me. Don't do this to me," she nearly cried, her voice a choked sob. "Take me now, for God's sake, take me now!"

When it was over, Maggie lay in Cranston's arms. He could be gentle now; the first chaotic rush of passion was over; they had both gotten what they wanted. Tears blurred Maggie's eyes. It shouldn't have happened; she never should have placed herself in this situation. She was ashamed of herself, ashamed of the need she had revealed to him. Another weapon, another triumph for Cranston.

"Why so quiet, Maggs?" he asked, nuzzling her ear. "Wasn't it good for you? It was wonderful for me."

Maggie remained silent.

"Don't be sorry, Maggs," he whispered, as though reading her thoughts. "It was inevitable. We haven't gotten over each other. You know it and so do I. This is the way it should have been all along. I can't tell you how sorry I am for the bastard I was to you. To you and to Cole. I don't know how you'll ever forgive me, but I'm begging you to try. Please try, Maggs, please."

A rush of emotions rebounded through Maggie. How long she had waited to hear those words. How much she needed to hear them. Cranston continued to purr in her ear. She listened, she dreamed . . . *Family!*

{{{{{{{{ CHAPTER TWELVE }}}}}}}}

The loft in midtown Manhattan was a work of art, thanks to its renovator, Adam Jarvis. He was a political cartoonist whose biting satire caused Washington to gasp as often as it cackled in glee. He was successful, semisatisfied with his life, and in love with his loft. When he'd purchased it years ago for an outrageous sum of money, he'd spent weekends renovating, and it was now pretty much what he wanted—open space, skylights, lush green plants, colorful furniture with brilliant cushions, shiny oak floors that were almost like mirrors. Probably the only thing it lacked was a woman's touch, and at times he wasn't sure even a woman could improve it, except to lend her presence to the vast openness. Four thousand square feet of space was a lot for one person. His only companion until Sawyer had arrived was a female cat with a ferocious appetite, named Marble. Probably, he was the only political cartoonist in the United States to walk a cat on a leash and carry a poop scoop.

Work wasn't going well today. It hadn't been going really well since Sawyer moved in. It wasn't that she bothered him; it was that she was so desperately unhappy and there was nothing he could do to ease her pain.

She arrived, this old high school chum and college buddy, in the middle of the night, tear streaks on her cheeks and lips quivering. She'd cried a lot that night and he'd held her like a father holding a daughter, but there were no words, no comfort he could give her.

He'd suggested she move in, and she'd agreed. Room-mates only, though, she'd said. She'd insisted on paying her share of the expenses. And she did, to the penny. She didn't tidy up after him and he liked that. She didn't interfere in any way with his work schedule. Once she'd transferred to the Coleman New York office, she was up and out of the loft by seven in the morning; most times she didn't come home till eight or nine in the evening, taking her meals in restaurants if she ate at all. He noticed a weight loss and debated whether or not to speak to her about it. He personally liked to see a little meat on a woman's bones. Probably because he himself was so tall and rangy. He ate like a horse and never gained an ounce. Sawyer always said he looked like a string bean with curly red hair.

Sawyer. He'd adored her when he'd first met her and had fallen shamelessly in love with her soon after. Friends, she'd said. She had things to do and places to go. Rela-tionships only got in the way of her goals. The years had gone by, and Adam remained a bachelor—by choice. He'd never been able to get Sawyer out of his thoughts. Time and distance had dimmed his memory a little, but he'd continued to love her. He loved her now. It was that simple. Only he couldn't tell her. She needed a friend, not some lovesick cartoonist.

The blank paper on the drawing board stared at him. For a moment he felt frightened. What if he was losing it? What if Sawyer and her pain consumed him to the point where he couldn't work? He stirred uneasily. Maybe he should water his plants or make something to eat. Hell, he could even put the dishes in the dishwasher. That's exactly what he should do, since the sink was filled to overflowing.

He got up and headed for the kitchen, his cat-green eyes peering across the dim space to where Sawyer was sitting writing a letter. She wrote a lot of letters these days. The only personal mail she received was from the boys in Texas and her grandmother in Vermont.

The Coleman clan was something he didn't like to think about. He was from Texas himself; he knew a thing or two about clans. His own family was so goddamn normal, it was disgusting. When he'd first met Sawyer, he used to wish the Jarvis family had a scandal, too, so he and Sawyer could be branded together. He'd been a staunch, feisty defender of Sawyer's parentage; he'd even squired her to dance recitals and plays, generally making an ass of himself. Oh, how he'd suffered at Sawyer's hands. God, how he loved her.

When the last glass had been added to the dishwasher, Adam filled the soap dispenser and turned it on. Jesus, the thing sounded like a jet cutting back on its engine power.

Sawyer came up behind him and tweaked his ear. "Susy homemaker," she said fondly. "You got any apples?"

"Do I have any apples? Do I have any apples? Do I look like a supermarket? The answer is no. I have some oranges, though. Good, juicy ones. Real orange. No pits. I'll peel it for you." Christ, how could he not have apples? Sawyer loved apples. "Wait a minute. I have some apple juice. No good, huh? Shit!"

"I'll take the orange. For God's sake, what's wrong with you?" Sawyer asked, noticing his agitation.

"Wrong? Nothing." His hands were busily peeling the orange. He offered it to her as though it were a prize. "It's not a good orange unless the juice trickles down your chin," he said inanely.

"I know. If the pulp doesn't stick in your front teeth, it's worth shit, right? That's what you always used to tell me at school. Remember the time Mrs. Snyder sent you out of class for picking your teeth?"

"You remember that?"

"I remember everything. Sometimes I feel as though my head is so full it'll burst. . . . I don't want you looking like that at me. I'm not worth it," Sawyer said flatly. "Forget it, Adam."

Adam's heart pounded. Christ, was he that transparent? "Nick Deitrick was right. You are ugly. I wasn't sure until now."

"You aren't exactly a prince, you know," Sawyer said lightly. "Nick never knew which end was up."

Adam grinned. "You always were a bitch."

"That's true. But you were never a bastard." She shook her head and turned away. "I'm sorry. I am grateful, Adam. I had no right coming to you with my problems and just moving in. I can leave if you—"

"Did I complain? You aren't bothering me. I'm worried about you, Sawyer. Listen, I'm ahead on the strip," he lied. "Why don't we take off a few days and get some sun. Florida, California, wherever. You could use a break. You're killing yourself. Take a look in the mirror."

"I can't take the time off. Besides, work is the best thing for me right now. I mean it, Adam, if I'm cramping your style—"

"You're not. I told you I was between ladies at the moment. A hiatus, if you will."

"Okay." Sawyer noticed the relief in his eyes. "You having trouble with the strip today?"

"Sort of. I have days when nothing I do seems right. I must have gone through a ream of paper already."

"When all else fails, take a potshot at Reagan. Your fans'll love it. By the way, did I tell you Cole is now a fan of yours? He said you're sharp." She yawned. "I think I'll turn in now. I'll wash the towels tomorrow; it's my turn."

"Damn right it's your turn. I had to call Bloomie's to order more this morning."

"Tell me you didn't do that!"

"Have I ever lied to you? I had thirty-six towels when you moved in here. There are thirty-six towels in the laundry room. All of them dirty. You're the one who uses a towel for her hair, one for her body, and one for her face."

"You went into the laundry room and counted the dirty towels and didn't wash them? You didn't wash them, but you counted them! That's disgusting!"

"It's your turn," Adam said loftily.

"How many did you order?"

"Three dozen."

"You're nuts."

"I know. Go to bed. I just got an idea."

"Thanks for the orange and the conversation."

"Anytime. Sleep well."

In her room, Sawyer threw the letter she'd written to her grandmother into her handbag; she'd mail it on the way to the office in the morning. Then she undressed, throwing her clothes on a chair, and sat down wearily.

It was time for bed. Time for sleep. She was so tired; always so tired. It seemed a lifetime since she'd left Sunbridge like a thief in the night. For so long afterward she'd hoped, even prayed, that Rand would come after her. But he hadn't, and now nothing seemed worthwhile. Not even her job, which she loved. She was just going through the motions of living, unable to take pleasure in anything. Rand was all she thought about.

Humiliation and rejection. She fed on humiliation and rejection, knowing she would never be able to help herself: the need she felt could never be filled. But it didn't really matter now. Nothing mattered.

Tears of self-pity rolled down her cheeks. She made no move to stop them or wipe them away. Crying always made her sleep. Tomorrow she would simply wear her dark glasses. There wouldn't be anyone at the office to notice except the janitor. If only there were some way she could fill this aching void inside her. Would the time ever come when she could put all of this behind her and start a new life? Would she ever be whole again?

The satiny quilt caressed her bare shoulders as she snuggled beneath it. The loft creaked and then settled into quietness.

Two hours later, Adam checked on Sawyer. She was sleeping soundly, her hand cupped on her cheek. He went into the laundry room and started the washing machine filled with towels. He waited through the cycle, then tossed the load into the dryer. He drank three cups of coffee while he waited for the towels to dry. He folded three fluffy yellow towels and laid them gently at the foot of Sawyer's bed. The last thing he did before going to bed was write a note to himself to call Gristedes and order apples.

Maggie lay beside Cranston in Jessica's high bed. He was breathing lightly and felt warm beside her. She marveled at how quietly he slept while she tossed and turned restlessly. In the mornings, Cranston's side of the bed was smooth and unruffled, while hers looked as though a flock of chickens had been scratching and nesting.

Cranston's vacation was almost over. Day after tomorrow he would leave. She'd heard him speaking on the telephone, making arrangements with the office to ready his caseload and begin making appointments. Two weeks. A time of renewal, Maggie had tried to convince herself. A time to make a fresh start with Cranston, for them to get to know each other again; hopefully, to like each other. And it had almost worked.

Cranston had been saying all the right things at all the right times. She had responded to his mesmerizing eyes and his softly spoken words. Wanting and needing to believe, to trust. Oh, yes, she had to admit to herself that her needs for husband and family were very real. Husband, security, identity—they all meant the same thing. The divorce proceedings could be stopped at any time, or so Cranston said. He'd made it sound so tempting.

She looked over at him, resisting an impulse to brush the lock of hair off his forehead. She'd come so close to falling in love with him all over again. He'd as much as told her she could have it all—dutiful husband, full-time son, the entire ball of wax—if only she agreed to move back to New York with him, give up living at Sunbridge, turn her back on everything she loved, everything she'd fought for her entire life. Oh, and one thing more. Cranston's law firm. For a cool three million dollars it could be all his. All she had to do was supply the three million.

Maggie was a big girl now; she'd learned the rules of the game. The money didn't bother her. But Cranston did. If she went back to New York with him, she would soon become just another of his possessions, like his town car and his sailboat. There was every danger he would devour her again, as he had once before—telling her how to dress, what to say, how to behave, making her doubt herself, always feeling his disapproving eye. He would use her, and he'd use Cole if she allowed it.

Reaching across the pillow, Maggie gentled the stray lock of hair that gave Cranston such a boyish look. She supposed that all along, despite her bravado and heroic attempts to straighten out her life, she had secretly wanted the security of being Cranston's wife, to erase the rejection, to have a second chance at having a family, of belonging to her own little family. Yet despite his smooth words and heated passions these past two weeks, he had made no mention of love, of growing old together, of sharing. Things Maggie wanted, things Billie had found with Thad. With Cranston, Maggie would have an agreement, a contract. This for that. Whatever he wanted.

The mattress shifted slightly as Maggie swung her legs over the side. This wasn't what *she* wanted. She didn't want to be an extension of her husband; she wanted to belong to herself, to be admired for herself and loved for herself. It might even be exciting to see what else might be in store for Maggie Coleman Tanner on her own terms. If Cranston wanted her, he'd have to take her on those terms.

Maggie bent over slightly as her foot traced a pattern on the floor, searching for her slippers. When she felt herself drawn backward into Cranston's arms, she didn't struggle against it. It would be a very nice way to say good-bye.

{{{{{{{{{ CHAPTER THIRTEEN }}}}}}}}}

There was a true October chill in the air as Amelia made her way to the lawyer's office. She stood outside the old building, in deep thought. Was she doing the right thing? She hoped so. It felt right.

She took a look around at the brilliant foliage. Everything was so lush, so radiant; it reminded her of autumns she'd spent in the North Country of England. Texas wasn't usually this blessed in October. More often, the long, hot, dry summers forced the trees and grasses to suffer a premature death. But this year summer seemed to have vanished quickly, bringing warm sunny days and brisk, cool evenings. It was going to be so nice lingering in the house with a fire blazing merrily in the hearth. Maybe once in a while Cary could take time off from his project to join her for a picnic-style lunch in front of the fireplace. And in the winter evenings, they could curl up there together and sip sherry, talking quietly, sharing ideas and business decisions. She could almost see him sitting there with her, the glow from the fire highlighting his classic Roman features and throwing shots of gold into his wavy dark hair. He'd look at her with those falcon's eyes, and she would read his desire there, hear him laugh softly as she went into his arms to be crushed against his chest. The daydream was so strong, so forceful, Amelia's heart began thumping. Determinedly, she pushed open the door to the Abramson building. The old house would be hers.

An hour and twenty minutes later, Amelia pulled her silver Porsche into the driveway of her new house. Hers. Signed, sealed, and delivered. She tried to swallow past the lump in her throat. Mam's house.

"This is for you, Mam," she said, fitting the key into the old lock. She wondered if it was a lie.

It was an incredibly old house, well over a hundred years old. Nearly thirty acres surrounded it, a major reason the price had been so steep. The structure itself looked incongruous out here in the hill country of Texas; it would have seemed much more at home in a small seaport in Maine overlooking the harbor. Three stories high, with a widow's walk cresting the sloping mansard roof... Amelia had always thought it looked like something out of *Peter Pan*. Clapboard walls and brick walks and drive. Sixteen rooms in all, every one of them holding a hundred layers of paint, even the beautiful chestnut woodwork. Only the front door and the staircase spiraling through the center of the house seemed to have escaped the painters' merciless brushes. Amelia had already decided she would save what she could of the original structure and decor, and remodel what she couldn't. Her efforts would be a tribute to Jessica and would ultimately create a home for Cary and herself.

The briefcase she'd brought with her contained drawings and diagrams of what she planned to bring to life here. What a celebration she and Cary would have when it was all finished! Dinner by candlelight in front of a fire. Champagne, pheasant under glass—Cary had always said he wanted to eat pheasant under glass—the works. Cary would smile in awe over the miracle she created and then they'd make love and live happily ever after.

For a moment she felt frightened. Was it possible she'd bitten off more than she could chew. She opened her briefcase and took out a yellow pad, fresh and unwrinkled, and a pencil with a sharp point. Ready to make notes, she chewed thoughtfully on the end of the eraser. She decided to make a list of everything to be done, beginning with the kitchen, then the library, front parlor, and so on through the house. Purposefully she made her way to the door behind the stairs.

Hours later, when she'd finished her inspection, Amelia felt depressed. This was supposed to be fun, a lark of sorts. Her list was monstrously long. The previous owners had done a lot of work, modernizing most of the house. Thank God they'd at least left the wainscoting in the library and front parlor. And the chestnut staircase— that, too, was beautiful. Hand-carved. She knew from her mother that the post at the bottom end of the landing unscrewed. Jessica had often told her she hid things in the little hidey-hole

Amelia caressed the antique wood, wondering if the previous owners had been aware of the secret. Her touch was gentle as she twisted the carved pineapple. She didn't expect to find anything and sure enough, the little cavity was empty. Yielding to her curiosity, she walked up thirteen steps to the landing and twisted the second pineapple, then hesitated a moment before putting her hand into the small space. Her eyes widened when she withdrew a brass ring, tarnished and black, and a small piece of yellowed paper with brown edges, obviously ripped from a notebook. Little shavings of the paper fell away as Amelia carefully unfolded the note and read its contents.

Her eyes filled with tears that slowly rolled down her cheeks. Her father had written this little note to her mother over sixty years ago. It was short and to the point, just like Seth himself.

To the prettiest girl in all Texas,

Some day, Jess, I'll give you a ring full of diamonds. I'll build you the biggest, fanciest house in all of Texas. I ain't much for writing but you can take these words for true. If your finger gets green from this ring, keep it in your pocket to remind you of me and my promise.

Seth Coleman

So much for promises. Amelia swiped at her tears with the back of her dusty hand, leaving streaks down her cheeks. He'd made good on his promise to her mother. He had given her a ring full of diamonds. And Sunbridge was the biggest, fanciest house in this part of Texas. It might have its equal in size, but she knew there was none better. The only problem was, Sunbridge hadn't been built for Jessica; it had been built for Seth himself. Jessica had just resided in it. But she'd saved the ring and the note in her secret place.

Angry now at what she'd found, Amelia whirled about. There was no one to scream or yell at. Her mouth was grim, her teeth clenched, when she returned the brass ring and note to the empty cavity. Not for the world would she ever open it again.

She turned to the light switch on the landing, then peered over the banister railing at the chandelier. Most of the crystals were gone. It must have been magnificent in its day, she thought.

Jessica had once told her it had been installed when she'd been about seven, during the Christmas holidays. When it was turned on, she'd said, she gasped in awe because it looked as if someone had taken a big blanket full of diamonds and flung them into the air. Amelia decided this was one project she personally would undertake. She made a note on her yellow pad: cleaning the crystals.

She looked at her watch. It was getting late. The house would be dark soon, and there was no power. Tomorrow the electric company, the phone company, and the furnace company were coming to turn everything on.

Tomorrow she would go up into the attic. Who knew what treasures she would find? She loved attics. Susan and Rand used to play in the attic back in England. God, that was so many years ago. Numbers made her itchy. Always numbers.

Halloween arrived. Maggie scurried between the new art gallery, her Red Cross work, and all her various meetings. Having an eye for detail and decoration had put her at the top of the list of volunteers. Somehow—she wasn't sure how—she'd ended up being the chairperson for Crystal City High's October dance festival committee. Both boys had dates for the dance. As far as she knew, it was the first boy-girl date for either of them. In a way she was pleased about being on the committee, since it was Cole who'd asked her to help out. He certainly seemed different these days, almost as though he were coming around.

The day before the dance, Maggie sat at the dining room table in front of a pile of papers and lists stacked next to boxes of paper pumpkins and crinkly witches, all of which had to be organized, folded up, and then tied. As she worked, she reflected that she should have recruited some of the girls from the boys' classes; but they were always so busy with after-school activities. She really could use some help.

"Could you use some help?"

Maggie looked up in stunned surprise. Cole stood watching her from the dining room doorway. "As a matter of fact, I could. Actually, I could use about six pairs of hands."

"All I have are two, but they're all yours," Cole said, sitting down next to his mother. "Just tell me what to do."

Mother and son worked together amicably for a while. Maggie noticed that Cole had a good eye for color, and his nimble fingers sorted through the piles and stacks of papers. Within minutes, it seemed, things were organized.

"Who's going to decorate the gym tomorrow?" Cole asked.

Maggie laughed. "You're looking at her. When I was put on this committee I had three helpers. I'm what's left."

Cole was silent for a few seconds. "I'll help you. Standing on a ladder isn't one of the things you do best. I'll see about getting out of my first class. I'm carrying an A average so far, so I don't think it'll be a problem." His voice was gruff, as if he were afraid she might reject his offering.

"I'd like that if you can manage it," Maggie said softly. "And you're right; hanging streamers from a ladder isn't one of the things I do best." She waited for him to make some sort of snide remark. When he didn't, she smiled at him. He grimaced and she laughed.

It wasn't togetherness, but it would do for now.

Susan's eyes popped open the moment the alarm sounded. She felt awful. Why did she have to get up? This baby she carried in her was taking its toll—in more ways than one. It seemed that all she and Jerome did these days was fight and bicker. She knew she was beginning to hate him; she certainly hated the music he insisted they play. Wincing, she shifted her position, quietly, so as not to wake Jerome. She didn't want to have to talk to him if she could help it.

Oh, how she wished she were back in Sunbridge with her family! The brief visit in July had fortified her somehow, enabled her to continue with Jerome and this damnable tour a little while longer. But she should have stayed behind. Maggie would have let her stay till she was feeling better.

Susan dangled her legs from the bed, wanting to cry at the sight of her swollen ankles. She dreaded looking at her hands, knowing she might not be able to play the piano if they were puffy and pink. Jerome would get the ice water immediately. Good old Jerome, he would get the last ounce out of her if it killed her.

She decided to take a shower, then eat some crackers and take her medication. Maybe after that she'd place a call to Rand. Let Jerome squawk.

She hobbled to the bathroom, her swollen feet protesting at every step. The pipes groaned as she turned on the water, yielding little more than a trickle, which irritated her. She didn't need this. A towel wrapped around her, she made her way to the dresser. The cellophane crackled as she removed it. For some reason crackers always settled her stomach in the morning. She took her vitamin and three other pills, and was sitting with the phone in her lap when Jerome woke.

"What are you doing, Susan?" His voice was light, almost indifferent. But he had to fight with himself not to get up and rip the phone from her hands.

"I'm going to call Rand. Do you have any objections?" Susan asked coldly.

"Why don't you wait till later, until you're more awake and things are settled."

"I'm settled and I'm awake. I've taken my shower, eaten my crackers, and taken my pills. What I haven't done and what I have no intention of doing is polishing your shoes, packing your bags, or going to the store for fresh rolls for you. I'm not even going to practice today. I'm going to sit right here with my feet up. I might even read a trashy magazine instead of music scores. I'm fed up. Do you hear me? Fed up!"

"You can't give in to these little aches and pains. You have to keep going."

"No, Jerome, *you* have to keep going. I don't! I'm quitting right now. I can't bear the thought of sitting at a piano for five or six hours. Even the doctor said I should be resting with my feet up. Now I suppose you're going to tell me he doesn't know what he's talking about, that you know more than he does."

"I know *you*. That's what's important. You can't do this to us. We've come too far, worked too hard—"

"I've certainly worked too hard—and I've had it! If you don't have the guts to cancel the rest of the tour, I'll do it. Or, go it alone."

"Susan, look at me. We only have five more performances. You can do it. I know you can. We'll cut out practice today. I can see that your legs and feet are swollen." Jerome's insides churned. He had to find a way to keep Susan going. He took a deep breath and fished around the tiny refrigerator for some milk to soothe his stomach. When there was none to be had, he waved his hands about like a maniac. "You know I need milk! You were supposed to get it yesterday. A lousy container of milk and you couldn't even do that for me."

"Yesterday my physical condition was worse than it is today," she replied tightly. "You had me practicing for five hours. The concert lasted three. You had me laced into a maternity corset that almost suffocated me. All because you didn't want people saying I looked like a cow." Her voice grew shrill. "That's what you said, Jerome, a *cow*! I had hardly anything to eat because you said it would fog up my head. If the stage manager hadn't given me a banana, I would have fainted on stage. And when we got back here, all the shops were closed. Where was I supposed to get your milk? It's *your* stomach—*you* get the goddamn milk!"

"Calm down or they'll throw us out of here," Jerome said, hugging his stomach.

"That's the best thing that could happen to us. To me especially. No more, Jerome. This is it. I'm calling Rand."

"And what's Rand going to do for you?"

"Something. I don't know. Just shut up, Jerome, and leave me alone. Don't get any funny ideas about trying to stop me, either. Because if you do, I'll go to the lobby and make the call from there."

"Please, Susan, don't do this," Jerome begged. "You know how important this tour is to me. I'm just as sick as you. We can't cancel out now. People are depending on us."

"If you're as ill as you say, then you shouldn't be continuing this tour, either. I have a baby to think of. I'm sorry now I let you talk me into leaving Sunbridge."

Jerome wept, but Susan ignored him as she placed her call to England. The moment Rand's voice came over the wire, she felt better. "I need your help, Rand. Jerome and I are in Germany at the moment.... Yes, but I want to go home, back to Texas.... Yes, now. Will you call Maggie and ask her if I can stay at Sunbridge? I haven't heard from her or Amelia for so long I don't think they remember who I am. Will you do that for me, Rand?" Susan listened to Rand for a few moments. Her eyes narrowed as she stared at her husband. "I really don't know if I can make it to the airport.... Well, I suppose it wouldn't matter if I left my luggage. . . . Right. I'll wait for your call."

Jerome stared at his wife. For the first time in his life he was afraid.

"You bastard," she hissed. "You black-hearted bastard. Why didn't you tell me my sister and Aunt Amelia called me? I didn't believe Amelia that one time when she tried to explain—I couldn't believe it of you! Where are my letters? Rand called, too. He wrote *three* letters. I want them. They're from *my* family. You had no right to keep them from me! It would have made all the difference in the world. I needed their support. You took that away from me and didn't give anything back. Don't come near me, Jerome, because I'll smash this phone in your face. How could you! How dare you! You would have worked me to death just to finish this tour so you would look good. You don't care about me or the baby. You know what, Jerome? We don't care about you, either."

Jerome's helplessness exploded in rage. He slammed about the tiny hotel efficiency suite, sending hairbrushes, perfume bottles, and sheet music crashing into furniture and walls. He cursed in every language he knew, and still she sat passively on the edge of the bed, the hard, black telephone receiver clenched in her fist.

His fists clenched, he stared at her, eyes brimming with fury. She was ruining him, this bitch. Ruining his career, ruining his future. And for what? A squalling brat that would interfere in their lives, suck the energy out of their work. He hovered over her, arm raised. He wanted to hit her, destroy her the way she was destroying him.

"Don't do it, Jerome," she warned in an icy tone. "If there's breath left in my body, I'll see to it you enjoy the comforts of a German jail. And how will that look in the press releases?"

Jerome's fist fell to his side.

"On second thought, Jerome," Susan was saying, no hint of remorse or even of pity in her eyes, "I'll help you pack." Jerome stormed out of the suite, the door shuddering on its hinges behind him.

* * *

The transatlantic calls came in one after the other. First Billie, then Maggie and Amelia. Of course she could come to Sunbridge, Maggie cried happily. The nursery was there and waiting. She could stay as long as she liked, forever if she wanted.

"Are you sure you're well enough to make the trip?"

"Rand is going to meet me in England and bring me home. He's got it all planned. I'll stay on a few days and get a good checkup and then we'll head for Sunbridge. Maggie, I am so grateful, I don't know what to say."

"Then don't say anything," Maggie said in a choked voice. "This place needs a baby. This place needs you, Susan. You've been gone too long. Everything will be ready. I'll make an appointment with a good g-y-n man for you the day after you get here. I can't wait to see you!"

"Sure you don't mind that Rand is coming along?"

"Of course not. He was coming for Christmas anyway. The more the merrier. I'm worried, though. Is Jerome going to cause you any trouble? He'll let you go, won't he?"

"I'd like to see him try and stop me. I'm not bothering with luggage. Rand said something about a wing and a prayer."

"I can shop for you. I know your size. That's the least of your problems. You're sure you're okay?"

"Now I am. I may have regrets later, but I have to think about the baby. Today I just blew up."

"Take care of yourself, Suse. We'll be waiting. We love you."

"I know, and I love all of you," Susan said softly. "I'll see you in a few days. Thanks, Maggie."

She was just checking her purse to be sure she had her passport when the phone rang. It was Rand.

"If you get to the airport in the next forty-five minutes, there's a reservation in your name."

"I can make it. I'm dressed. I'm not sure if I have

enough money on me, though. Enough for taxi fare, but that's about it. Jerome handles the money."

"Just get to the damn airport. The ticket is prepaid. Once you get here, everything'll be fine. Hurry now."

"I will. Thanks, Rand. I'll see you in a few hours."

Suddenly Susan felt guilty. It didn't seem right to just walk out on Jerome like this. Everything had happened so quickly. She laid his passport and the tour schedule on the dresser next to his keys. Quickly she penned off a small note.

Jerome,
    I'm sorry it's ending this way, but I must think of the life we both created. I'll be at Sunbridge if you want to get in touch. Take care of yourself and don't lose your passport.

                              Susan.

Ninety minutes later Susan was airborne. When she landed in England hours later, Rand's was the first face she saw. She literally fell into his arms.

Rand sat with his arm around Susan's shoulders on the ride to his house. He had to do something for her before he took her to Sunbridge. Amelia and Maggie would worry themselves sick over her. It was all he could do to keep the shock from his own face. Rest, some good food, some fresh air, and maybe, just maybe, she'd be ready to travel in ten days or so.

Then it would be back to Sunbridge. Back to Maggie. And Amelia and Cary and the boys. His heart soared.

Cole stood beside the empty bleachers watching the Crystal City High School in practice, their short skirts swinging about their slim thighs, their sweaters bouncing with each leap and jump. Kelly Jensen was one classy chick. Captain of the freshman squad, she was one of the most popular girls in school. All the boys had the hots for her, including him. Even Riley lost his cool when Kelly was around.

Watching Kelly was only a side benefit. Cole's real purpose in coming to the athletic field was to watch Riley being put through his paces as right guard for the junior varsity team. He squinted into the sun, looking for the familiar number sixty-four, bold green numbers on a white jersey. Even from here Riley looked intimidating: tall, broad, long powerful legs pumping him across the distance as he took down the opposing tackle to enable the quarterback to get off a clean pass. The coach blew his whistle; the play was ended. Saturday was a big game for Crystal City and excitement was running high.

"Good play, Coleman!" Some of the other boys jostled Riley's shoulder pads. Ass slapping was for the pro teams.

"All right! Hit the showers! Practice tomorrow after school, films tomorrow night! Show you guys what you'll be up against when you play Edison. Who's number one?" the coach shouted.

"Mustangs! Mustangs!" came the hoarse, masculine cries of the team.

"Who's number one?"

"Mustangs!"

Cole's eyes narrowed as he watched Riley walk off the field, Coach Hamrah's arm on his shoulder, heads close together. Then he returned his attention to Kelly, who was waiting near the gate for Riley. Cole spat the bitter taste from his mouth. If Riley's last name weren't Coleman and if he weren't a part of Sunbridge, no girl would even give him a second look. Especially not Kelly, a bluenose who probably didn't even know the last name of her family's Mexican housekeeper. Cole spat again; still the bitter taste lingered. Just went to show what the right name and the right contacts could do for a guy, he thought contemptuously.

That Cole had recourse to the same name and contacts was a reality he ignored.

At the gate leading onto the field, just within earshot,

Kelly was playing up to Riley. "A bunch of kids are going over to Patti's house tonight. Her father got a copy of *E. T.* from the film studio. Did you ever see it?"

Riley shook his head, a faint blush staining his cheeks.

"Want to come with me? They're going to show it right after dinner; it'll be an early night, I promise."

"I don't know, Kelly. I've got that English paper to do by next Tuesday and I'm behind."

"What if I said I'd help you with it on Sunday?" Kelly coaxed. "Mine's done; I've got plenty of time. I could even go to the library for you while you're at films tomorrow. That would save some time, wouldn't it?"

"Yeah"—Riley grinned—"it would. But I can't ask you to do that for me."

"You're not asking; I'm offering. My mom and I can come by Sunbridge right after dinner, say about six-thirty? You'll be home before ten. I promise. Say you'll come, Riley, please?"

Cole thought he was going to throw up. Kelly Jensen begging up to nobody Riley Coleman. Couldn't she see that he wasn't one of them? Cole didn't even want to wait around to hear Riley agree to go to the film. Patti hadn't asked him to come, and she was supposed to be his friend.

Walking beneath the bleachers so Riley wouldn't see him, Cole went back to his moped. His mother had bought one for each of the boys, since taking the school bus wasn't always practical when there were after-school activities. He was astride and backing up when Gina Higgins hopped on behind him. "Take me home, Cole. I've got a date tonight."

"I've got better things to do than drive you around. Where's your bike?"

"Got a flat and it'll be dark soon. C'mon, Cole, don't be a pain."

"Get off, Gina. I'm not taking you anywhere." He knew where Gina would be tonight—at Patti's, probably with Dan Carroll, another hotshot football player. "I told you I've got something to do."

Reluctantly Gina climbed off the back of the moped, her pretty face in a pout. "What have you got to do? Watch your soon-to-be all-star cousin? I saw you watching him. He'll make all-star, you know, just like Danny. Next year, Riley will probably make squad captain. Must make you feel like shit."

Cole burned rubber as he throttled down.

"It shows, you know!" she yelled as he made a U-turn. "Everybody knows you're jealous, Cole. Why don't you just cool it and give us all a break?"

He heard what she said. Everything true. He hated her. He hated all of them!

Thirty minutes later with still a mile to go, Riley slowed his moped beside Gina. "What are you doing walking this road in the dark?"

"Your cousin refused to give me a ride. He's a jerk."

"Just like that? For no reason? Put the helmet on or you don't ride with me," he ordered.

Gina snapped the chin strap. "It was my own fault. I told him he was jealous of you and that you were going to be captain of the squad next year. Guess he didn't want to hear that. I think I may have mentioned you were going to be all-star."

Riley groaned. "Please, Gina, I have enough problems with him as it is. I wish you hadn't said that."

"I'm sorry, Riley. He gets my goat, though. He's always hanging around—sneaking, really. I think he likes Kelly. You know something else? I think Kelly likes you. We were talking at practice yesterday about the homecoming dance. She doesn't have a date, in case you're interested. I'm not sure, but I think she's waiting for you to ask her."

"Me! Do you think she would go with me?" Riley asked incredulously.

"I think so. Why don't you ask her? Look, I'm sorry about Cole. I was niggling him. I'll apologize tomorrow. But I still think he's a smart-ass. How can you stand him?"

"He's different; you have to know him," Riley said

defensively as they pulled into Gina's driveway.

"Sure, sure." Gina grinned as she handed back the helmet. "Don't forget to ask Kelly. Promise?"

"Okay, I promise, but if she turns me down, it's your hide I'm coming after."

"Danny will protect me." Gina giggled. "See you, Riley."

When Riley entered Sunbridge by the back door, Cole was just finishing his warmed-up dinner. Maggie was perched on a stool trying to make conversation.

"Sorry I'm late, Aunt Maggie."

"I was getting worried. Did you stop off somewhere? Your dinner is in the oven. Martha had prayer meeting this evening, so I'm chief cook and bottle washer."

Riley glanced at Cole. He quickly averted his eyes, but Maggie saw the look. "I had to drop Gina off. She missed the bus and her bike had a flat." He knew he sounded defensive. He always did when he was around Cole.

"Gina's a nice girl. I know her parents well. What in the world happened to her hair?"

"She was on the summer swim team and the chlorine in the pool turned it all colors," Riley said as he removed his dinner from the oven. "Boy, am I hungry.

Maggie didn't bother pouring Riley a glass of milk. She set the pitcher in front of him and knew he would drink it all. His father always had an enormous appetite. She noticed that Cole stayed on his stool staring at Riley as he wolfed down his chicken and pan-fried potatoes.

"Is either of you going to the homecoming dance?" Maggie asked lightly, trying to draw her son into the conversation. Cole shrugged. Riley grinned as he attacked his blackberry pie.

"I'm going to ask someone to the dance tonight," he said. "Maybe she'll go and maybe not. I thought I'd try. If she says no, I'll go stag. This is real good pie, Aunt Maggie."

"Martha will be glad to hear that. I think she cooks

just for you two boys. Don't keep us in suspense, Riley. Who are you going to ask?" Maggie asked, leaning over the counter to smile at her nephew.

Riley wiped his mouth and laid down his fork. "Kelly Jensen," he said firmly, his eyes on his cousin.

"Ha!" Cole laughed. "Fat chance."

"The way I look at it"—Riley grinned—"is I'll know firsthand what rejection from a girl feels like. It'll be an experience for me. I know what rejection is, but this is different. Who are you going to ask, Cole?"

"I'm not going, and they don't allow stags at homecoming."

For a moment Riley's face fell. Cole was doing it again. Trying to make him feel unwanted, like an outsider. The boy's spine straightened. He'd had about enough of Cole Tanner. "I guess going stag is okay if you're on the football team," he said firmly. "The only reason you aren't going is because you can't get a date. You've made an ass of yourself with every girl in school. Tell Aunt Maggie why I was late. Go ahead—tell her!"

"Shut up!" Cole said, jumping off the chair.

"I don't have to shut up. I live here, too." Riley looked directly at his aunt. "Gina asked Cole for a ride and he refused. I had to take her home."

Maggie's eyes widened. She'd never heard the boys go at it before. Riley was usually quiet, defensive, and, if anything, inclined to stick up for Cole no matter what. She wasn't sure she liked this openness. Where would it lead—to fights, punching, downright war?

"How could you do such a thing, Cole?" she asked. "Gina's parents are my friends. What happened to good manners?"

"You just take his word for it, just like that! You don't bother to ask me if it's true or not. Some mother!" Cole slammed from the kitchen, the door banging against his heels.

Maggie was off the chair in a second. She sprinted through the door and grabbed Cole by the ear, literally dragging him back into the kitchen. "Now, we can settle this one of two ways. Either you tell me the truth—or I will call Gina's parents and get the truth."

Riley wanted to fall through the floor. Cole's face flushed crimson, but he stood defiantly trying to jerk free of his mother. Maggie waited.

"I lied, Aunt Maggie. I thought you would be angry if I was late for dinner again."

Maggie's heart turned over. She knew Riley was lying and she knew Cole expected him to lie. Cole said nothing, just stood there smiling impudently. With a sigh, Maggie let go of him and turned away.

"Go to your room, Cole."

"Yes, ma'am," Cole said with a sneer.

When the door closed behind him, Maggie placed a gentle hand on Riley's shoulder. "I wish you hadn't lied for him. You don't have to, Riley. He has to make it on his own or he'll never be a worthwhile human being. You must have been particularly fed up with him this evening to say what you did."

"I was and I'm sorry. I'm nervous about asking Kelly. What will I say if she turns me down? I never asked a girl for a date before."

"It's not easy for a girl, either. Most times, girls have to sit and wait for a guy to call. They get all frazzled that the wrong one will call, and then there are excuses to make—and girls do make excuses. Not out of meanness or anything like that. It's more like trying to save the boy embarrassment. Girls are sensitive, for the most part."

"I'm going to see her tonight. We're going over to Patti's house to watch a movie." Riley's cheeks reddened. "I don't know if I'll have the courage."

"Then why don't you call her? It'll be easier over the phone. Trust me," Maggie urged.

"Then I'd better call her now, before she leaves to come pick me up. Jeez, I hope I'm doing the right thing. Kelly's one of the most popular girls in school. She's captain of the freshman cheerleaders and she's on the honor roll. She'll probably make National Honor Society in her junior year."

"I know." Maggie grinned. "But she's still a girl. Those are things she does. It's not who she is, Riley. Go ahead—call her from here. Do you want me to leave?"

"Heck no. Stay here. I need all the support I can get. If I get tongue-tied, just take the phone from me and tell her it's a wrong number."

Maggie's heart pumped furiously as she watched her nephew dial Kelly Jensen's number. A movement at the door made her turn. Cole, standing outside listening.

"This is Riley Coleman. Can I speak to Kelly, please?" Riley took a deep breath and rolled his eyes back in his head.

"Kelly? . . . Hi, it's Riley. I'm calling because I . . . I was wondering if you would like to go to—to the homecoming dance with me. Of course, if you're busy or have a date . . ." Out of the corner of his eye he could see Maggie shake her head no. He groaned inside, then his eyes widened as he listened to Kelly's reply. "You will?! That's yes? Yes, you'll go with me? It was just hard to hear for a second. My aunt is rattling the dishes . . . Okay! Great! Yeah, see you later. . . . Yeah."

Maggie laughed. "See! It wasn't all that bad." She rattled dishes to make her point. "Do you like this girl, Riley?"

"Me and every guy in school. She's nice, but she hasn't dated one particular guy. She goes to all the parties and . . . Aunt Maggie, I'm sorry about Cole."

"I'll talk to Cole after I clean up here. You'd better get ready if you're going out tonight."

Riley hugged his aunt and grabbed an apple and a bag of potato chips off the kitchen counter. He was almost to the swinging kitchen door when he returned for two bottles of Coke.

"Bottomless pit." Maggie sighed as she attacked the dishwasher. When she finished in the kitchen, she made a phone call.

"Gina, this is Mrs. Tanner." The silence on the other

end warned her to be careful. "Gina, I want to apologize for Cole. I'm sorry he left you to get home on your own." She felt awful taking such an approach to the situation, but she had to know for sure what had happened.

"It's okay, Mrs. Tanner. Riley picked me up and brought me home. I guess Cole was a little mad at me. I was needling him."

"That's still no excuse. I'm sure Cole will apologize tomorrow."

"It's no big thing, Mrs. Tanner. Don't make a big deal out of it for Cole. We all have bad days."

"It's nice of you to be so forgiving. Give my regards to yours parents."

"I'll do that. Good night, Mrs. Tanner."

Maggie marched upstairs, tromped down the hall, and entered Cole's room without knocking. "I want to talk to you."

"About what?"

"I want to know why you let Riley lie for you this evening. Why couldn't you be man enough to stand up and tell the truth. I called Gina myself and she confirmed it.

"Gina is a big mouth. What difference does it make. She made me mad. If I was going to go out of my way to take her home, the least she could do was to be appreciative. All she did was needle me."

"About what? What could she needle you about that would make you leave her by herself when it was getting dark?"

Cole could feel the blood rush to his head. He actually felt lightheaded. Through tight lips he snarled, "She was giving me the business about being a gun-toting, military snot. Stand straight, aim, fire, that kind of crap. She made me mad."

Maggie listened to her son. She felt he was lying, but what could she do? She couldn't force him to tell her the truth. All she could do was try to understand and be there for him if and when he decided to confide in her. She sighed. "All right. Good night, Cole. Lights out by eleven."

Cole pounded his fist into his pillow. He was enraged that his mother had called Gina, humiliated that Riley should have tried to cover for him, and even a little scared by the tone of his mother's voice when she'd said good night. It was as though she'd dismissed him, didn't care about him, maybe even wished he weren't her son.

"Damn it!" he exploded. "Why can't anyone ever take *my* side? She's supposed to be *my* mother, not his!"

{{{{{{{{ CHAPTER FOURTEEN }}}}}}}}

"Texas! I never thought I'd be this glad to be here," Susan sighed wearily as she dropped down onto a banquette in the baggage area. "I feel about a hundred pounds lighter. I'm very grateful to you for bringing me home, Rand."

"My pleasure. I have a perfectly good reason to visit Sunbridge and see Amelia again. I miss her. You're very fortunate to have a place to come home to, Susan."

"Yes, I know." Susan smiled at her cousin. "I loved living in England with you and Aunt Amelia. I never could have pursued my music in Texas the way I did there. But I suppose, in many ways, Sunbridge is home. And I'm looking forward to putting myself under Aunt Amelia's wing."

Rand laughed. "In a few weeks' time I'll remind you you said that. After you've had enough coddling and pampering and you begin to complain the way you always did when you were a child."

"Aren't we all children? Even you, Rand, all grown-up and terribly capable. You've lived an exciting life, successful in business, heir to a fortune and huge estate; you were even an officer in the RAF. Quite diversified, quite accomplished. Tell me that you don't become a small boy again around your mother. It's almost impossible not to. When I was here in July with Mam and Aunt Amelia, I felt as though I were twelve years old again."

"And now there's even Maggie to pet and watch over you. Spoiled thing," Rand teased.

"Maggie's been wonderful about all this. She made me feel so wanted. You know, we weren't always close, but we managed to keep in touch. She's had more than her share to cope with over the years. All of us have, in one way or another."

"And now Maggie is a part of Sunbridge. Or is it the other way 'round?" Rand said quietly.

"Maggie is right where she wants to be. I think—and this is my personal opinion—that it would take an act of God to get Maggie away from Sunbridge. Don't you?"

"Yes. It's as though she were meant for it."

"She was. Is. When you and I closed up the flat in London yesterday, I didn't feel anything. It was just five small rooms and an overworked piano. Half the furniture wasn't mine. Just walls. Perhaps it was my fault. Maybe I should have tried to make the place homier. But Jerome and I were rarely there, and it seemed such a terrible effort. We did get all my things, didn't we?"

"Every last stitch. All that's left belongs to Jerome."

"He'll go back eventually. If for no other reason than to auction the piano. But my point is, Maggie could never pack up and leave Sunbridge the way I left my apartment. I think it would kill her. She had to leave once. It must have ripped her heart out. But she's happy now, and that's what matters."

"Our baggage is here," Rand said abruptly. "I'll have a porter take it to the curb. You wait with it till I pick up the rental car. Are you certain you'll be all right? Are you warm enough?"

"I'm fine, Rand. Really. I can manage. Stop hovering. You're reminding me of how awful I must look."

"Little mother, you're a beauty." Rand winked and offered her a dashing smile.

"And you're a pretty liar." She giggled. As they followed the porter, with Susan straggling behind, she was amused by the admiring glances Rand received. His height and imposing good looks always caught feminine eyes. And Susan knew Rand's attractiveness was more than skin deep. He was a genuinely nice person, kind and considerate; she knew how bad he must have felt to break it off with Sawyer. The breakup of a relationship could be devastating. She knew.

"This way, Susan." Rand came back and took her arm. "We'll have you home in no time."

"Does it look good to you?" Rand asked as he pulled the car beneath the shelter of the portico.

Susan sighed. "It looks beautiful!"

"Then let's get a move on and make you part of that wonderful household. Maggie's probably chewing her nails and Amelia is wearing out her shoes pacing the hallway. Go ahead. I'll bring in the baggage and park the car."

Susan's steps were light when she climbed the stairs leading to the portico. Maggie burst through the door and hugged her sister while her eyes searched the car for Rand.

"Come inside," she said. "It's chilly out here. You look exhausted. Tea. Some good sugar cookies and an afghan. Soft music and a nap."

"Maggie! I'm not an invalid. I'm pregnant. But I'll take all those things for now because I am tired. Tomorrow, though, will be different."

"One day at a time. I made a doctor's appointment for you on Friday."

Maggie was readying the tea tray under Martha's supervision when Rand walked into the kitchen. The spoon clattered against the sugar bowl Maggie was holding. How handsome he was! "Rand, it's good to see you. Thank you so much for bringing Suse home. What did the doctor say?"

"That she's to stay off her feet, get plenty of rest, fresh air, and good food, nothing fattening. She's dangerously close to miscarrying" Rand stepped closer to her. "I'm so glad to see you, Maggie."

"I . . . I . . . wasn't expecting . . . I thought I would have . . . Christmas is when you were coming back. What I mean . . ."

"I'm confusing things for you is what you're trying to say?"

"In a way." Maggie could feel herself drifting toward him, the sugar bowl still clasped in her hands. Her pulses were hammering so loud she was sure he could hear them. "We had this humongous pumpkin for Halloween," she said inanely.

"Really."

"Martha and I carved it. We toasted the pits."

"Amazing."

"This is difficult for me. . . . You see . . ."

"It isn't easy for me, either."

"This wasn't supposed to happen."

"It usually works that way."

"Mam wouldn't . . . approve."

"I know."

"There's Sawyer. I don't know if I can handle that."

"I don't know if I can, either."

"I missed you after you left."

"I thought of little else but you," Rand said, taking the sugar bowl from Maggie's hands. He set it on the tray and picked the tray up. "Our patient's tea is getting cold. We have three whole days to discuss what we have to discuss."

"Three days? That's not very long."

"A lot can happen in three days. In some cases it's almost an eternity. It's seventy-two hours."

"Seventy-two hours sounds better than three days,"

Maggie mumbled as she followed Rand into the study, where Susan lay propped up on the sofa.

"I'm letting you wait on me today, but that's it," Susan said, reaching for her teacup. "Oh, Maggie, it feels so good to be home. I know you're anxious to hear what happened, but I can't go through that right now. I don't know if I'll ever be able to talk about it."

"You're home now, Susan. There are no demands, no restrictions, no orders to be followed. All you have to do is take care of yourself and your baby. I'll do the rest."

"What did Mam say?"

"She wants you to call her, and if you need her, she'll be glad to fly down."

"I don't think that's necessary. Christmas will be soon enough. She's so happy up there with Thad. I don't want her worrying about me."

"That's exactly what I told her, but you know Mam. Later, after you nap, you can call and reassure her."

"Where's Aunt Amelia? I thought she'd be waiting for me."

Maggie met Rand's glance. How was she to tell her sister that Amelia was never home, that she had other things now to occupy her time? This was going to present a problem, one *she'd* have to deal with.

"When do you think Aunt Amelia will be home?" This time there was an edge to Susan's voice.

"Probably around dinnertime," Rand said soothingly. "This is a good chance for you to nap so you'll be fresh when she gets here. She's been working long days, or so Maggie tells me."

Rand added another log to the fire while Maggie covered Susan with the afghan. "Sleep, little Susie," Maggie whispered as she bent to kiss the wan cheek. Then she and Rand quietly left the study.

"Would you like some lunch, Rand?" Maggie said when they were in the foyer.

"No. I would like to take a walk to clear my head and maybe get rid of a little of this jet lag. Want to join me?"

"I should stay here with.... All right. I guess I owe you the treat of showing off our Texas foliage. Most of it is gone now and—" Maggie stopped, realizing that if she didn't watch it she'd soon be babbling like an idiot. "I need a jacket, though. Wait."

Wait. As though he had anything else to do. As though there might be anything else he'd *rather* do than wait and take a walk with Maggie.

"I'm ready," Maggie said, buttoning a dove-gray suede jacket. A brilliant scarlet scarf that boasted the name Billie at the end was thrown carelessly around her neck. Rand thought she was beautiful.

"How are the boys?" he asked as they left the house.

"At each other's throats most of the time."

"What happened with Cranston?"

"We agreed to agree. I have Cole until the next semester. Then Cranston will reevaluate the situation."

"What about your divorce?"

"January. Nothing has changed. We both tried to . . . oh, patch it up, I suppose, but it was for all the wrong reasons. Once you realize that, things go forward. I think Cranston and I can be friends now."

"Is that what you want?"

"For a while I didn't think so. I thought a lot about family and the commitment we both have to Cole, but now . . . yes, it's what I want. It's such a relief to say those words out loud."

"How's Amelia doing, and the great inner city?"

Maggie laughed. "The great inner city is coming along beautifully. Everything is under control. Cary is happy and tired when he gets home at night. I think that annoys Amelia a little. There isn't much time for partying during the week, but they make up for it on the weekend. To be honest, I rarely see them. I stopped by the house Amelia is renovating; you heard about that, didn't you?"

"Her mother's old house. Yes, she seemed quite excited about it."

"She's doing a wonderful job and spending a fortune. She's doing most of the work on the inside herself and contractors are working outside. I think they finished up this week. She wanted all outside work done before the bad weather set in. It's amazing, Rand. She gets up at five in the morning, has breakfast with Cary, and then goes straight to the house. I don't know if I could be that dedicated."

"Look, there's an old log," she said, striding ahead. "Why don't we sit down for a while. The sun is warm."

Rand stared after her, watching her long-legged stride in low-heeled boots beneath a wide, circular skirt. Fashionable, he thought. Always fashionable.

Maggie patted the space next to her on the old tree. "Tell me what you've been doing since you left."

"Getting along. Marking time. Waiting for Christmas."

"You just said the same thing three different ways." Maggie laughed.

"I did, didn't I?"

"What will you do when you go back?"

"Get along. Mark time. Wait for Christmas."

"Why go back?"

"That was the deal."

"What if I said the deal could be changed?" Maggie said hesitantly.

"I'd still go back. I think we both need more time."

Maggie picked at a piece of loose bark with her fingernail. "I suppose that is best. The family..."

"Will that make a difference to you?"

"Of course it will make a difference. Mam will... Mam won't approve. Cole... God only knows what he will think, do, or say. He's become very close to Sawyer. Which brings us to my daughter. I haven't heard from her since she left. Have you?"

"No, I haven't."

"Why are we talking like this?" Maggie asked in a hushed voice.

"Because we're two people who are drawn to each other. We're also adults and know that other people can get hurt by our actions."

"There was a time in my life when I would have plunged

in regardless of the consequences. I don't think I can do that now," Maggie whispered.

"It's Sawyer, isn't it?"

"Of course, it's Sawyer. It's Mam, too. And myself most of all."

"It's over between Sawyer and me."

"You know that and I know that, but I'm sure Sawyer still has feelings for you. Very strong feelings. She loved you, Rand, heart and soul. I know it hasn't been easy for her. Once in a while Cole will drop something. Mam is worried about her."

"Sawyer is twenty-six years old. People do live when a relationship ends. First they grieve, then they get angry, then they accept it."

"You sound very knowledgeable. Have you been through it yourself?"

"In my own way. Only I was doing my grieving before the relationship with Sawyer was over. While I was coming to terms with the fact that I didn't want the same things Sawyer wanted. There was anger and finally acceptance."

"I think that's the way it was with Mam and Pap."

"So what do we do?"

"I don't know. I do know I'm very attracted to you. When Cranston was here I found myself comparing him to you. When you said you'd write, I started watching the mail. I had to fight with myself to keep from calling you. I don't want anyone to be hurt. I know that sounds strange coming from me, but it's the way I feel."

"What about us?"

"It would be kind of hard to have a secret affair. That's what you're talking about, isn't it? I've lived in the shade too long, Rand. I want everything out in the bright light. I want the sun to smile down on me. I want to be happy with my choices. . . . I think we should both think about this some more."

Rand laughed. "Ever practical Maggie. If that's what you want, so be it."

Maggie smiled, then stood up and stretched. "I think

we should be getting back. Why don't you take the car and see the house Amelia is working on? I know she'd be pleased to show it off to you."

"Sounds like a good idea. What will you do?"

"Watch Suse sleep so she sees me first thing when she wakes up."

"Mother Maggie,"

Maggie laughed. "Sometimes I surprise even myself. As soon as I knew she was coming, I had all her things brought down from the attic. The old canopy bed and her little dressing table. I thought she'd like that."

"Home. There's no place like it."

"You make it sound like you never had one."

"Not like here. During the war we were shuffled from pillar to post, and half the time we lost most of our things. There was no permanence to anything then. The house I live in now is just a house. It has no character. There are no memories. It's a place to sleep."

Maggie's eyes twinkled. "There's always room for one more at Sunbridge. You can call this home."

"You'd run like hell if I moved in bag and baggage."

"Right now I would. Who knows what I'll do later? It's something for both of us to think about."

On the walk back to Sunbridge, Rand held Maggie's hand. When they were almost to the back garden, he stopped. "I think I'm falling in love with you, Maggie. I want you to be aware of that."

Maggie raised her eyes. They brimmed with tears. "I'm aware."

"And?" It was a tortured question.

Maggie shook her head. "Not now. I need time. Please understand."

"I have all the time in the world. I can wait. And I will."

"No one ever said that to me before." Maggie's smile was as golden as the last rays of the sun.

"I left the keys in the car, so if you give me directions, I'll go on over to Amelia's and see how she's doing."

*   *   *

Maggie took off her boots outside the study door, then walked softly inside and had a peek at Susan's peacefully sleeping face. The tea in the pot was still lukewarm, but she barely tasted it as she watched Susan sleep and thought about what had just happened.

It was out in the open now. She'd known it would be— from the moment she'd first heard his voice on the phone telling her he was bringing Susan back. How was she to handle this? The woman in her wanted to wait until everyone slept, to go to him in a froth of lace and silk, to stand in the moonlight in his room. The mother in her told her she would regret such actions. The daughter in her insisted it was her life to do as she pleased.

This would be no brief fling, no casual affair.

Rand, following Maggie's directions, turned onto the road leading to Amelia's new project. My, my, he found himself thinking, the Assantes are certainly hot for real estate. He wondered at Amelia's sudden need for a project, an interest. She'd always been keen on people, had forever been surrounded by interesting personalities. Now, married to Cary and supposedly still enthralled with newly wedded bliss, she'd adopted some sort of massive undertaking. Why?

The dark gray slate tiled mansard roof came into sight in the distance. The house stood alone, a sentinel guarding the expanse of surrounding land. Scaffolding climbed the clapboard exterior; men crawled about, scraping and painting what had been a dull yellow to a soft dove gray. The gingerbread fretwork was coming alive with a fresh coat of white.

Rand gave a low whistle as he looked through the windshield. This place must have cost a pretty penny, and obviously the restorations involved were mind-boggling. The house did have character, though; he'd give it that much.

"Rand! You devil! How good it is to see you," Amelia cried as she wrapped her arms around him. "When did you get in? How was the trip? Is Susan all right? Lord, you get more handsome each time I see you, or is it only a mother's pride? . . . Well, say something."

"Susan is fine—or will be, I'm sure. We got in a few hours ago. We had a smooth trip. And I'm no devil, but you're right; I'm handsome. How's it going?"

"Look around you and tell me what you think."

"I see one hell of a big mess. Why didn't you just buy a new house?"

"Oh, Rand, I thought you'd understand," Amelia said, disappointed. "I used to talk about this house to you when you were little. Don't you remember?"

"Of course I do. It's just that it looks like such a monstrous job. You must be spending a fortune. Are you planning on living here, or are you fixing it up as a shrine?"

Amelia's eyes clouded. Rand somehow had an uncanny knack of zeroing in on things. "I like shrines. I might live here, and then I might not. Does it make a difference?"

"Not to me it doesn't, but I should think it would to you. What's the bottom line?"

"It keeps me busy. It was Mam's house, and I think it should be preserved."

"Let me ask you something, Mother. If you lived out-of-state and you came back to Texas, and this house and Sunbridge were both available to you, which would you choose to live in?"

"I don't feel like playing games, Rand. Come along. I want to show you what I've done. It's marvelous what the right people can do."

Rand followed Amelia from room to room, listening while she droned on about what had been done to date and what still was in the works.

"It'll be fit for a king when I'm finished."

"What about the queen?" Rand asked seriously.

Amelia laughed. "Wait till you see the chandelier. The crystals are coming from Bavaria. They promised delivery in December. Mam was always partial to this particular chandelier. She said it was like a fairyland when it was lighted."

"What's your target date for completion?"

"Spring of next year, I think. I'm not rushing it."

In that one instant Rand felt sorry for Amelia. In all the years since she'd taken him under her wing, he'd never pitied her. He felt confused and saddened. "If Cary doesn't want to live here," he said, his voice purposely light, "you have a tenant waiting and ready to move in."

"I think Cary will like it. When I first started the project, I would call him and he'd come by and we'd have a picnic lunch, but he's too busy now. He's out on the site and I can't bother him."

"You must get lonely all day here by yourself."

"Not at all. The workmen are here and we chat and have lunch around the same time. We're a congenial group." Amelia laughed.

"I understand Cary's project is quite an undertaking. You must be very proud of him."

"I am. You can't imagine how well he's doing. He loves it. The men like and respect him, even the *real* Texans— you know, the older ones."

"Cary's a nice chap. What's not to like?"

"I was worried in the beginning that you two might not hit it off. I mean, he is younger than I."

"Mother, if you're happy, then I'm happy." He hesitated. "I would hope you'd feel the same about me."

Amelia looked away. "Have you heard from Sawyer?" she asked pointedly.

"No. I didn't expect to. Have you?"

"No. Rand, you never told me what happened, and I never asked. I'd like to know so I don't say the wrong thing at the wrong time."

He sighed. "It wasn't working. Sawyer deserves to have a family; she's young and full of life. I'm winding down and she should be revving up. So I had to let her go."

"That sounds like the flipside of my situation with Cary," Amelia said thoughtfully.

"You're wrong. Cary loves you madly and you love him. Sawyer and I never had that, not really. It just wouldn't have worked. Believe me, Mother, I wish it could have."

"Enough. I'm sorry I brought up the subject. It's just that everyone is so sorry for Sawyer, and they think you dumped her." Amelia grimaced. "I hate that word."

"When it comes right down to it, Mother, it's no one's business but Sawyer's and mine."

"I understand you're returning for Christmas. Sawyer won't come if you do."

"Is that your way of telling me to stay away?" Rand asked.

"No. It's my way of telling you you've deprived Sawyer of her home. Everyone wants to go home for the holidays. Think about that."

Rand nodded his head slightly. Then he kissed her and left without another word. Amelia watched him from the window. The moment his car turned at the corner, her shoulders slumped. She sat down on the window seat and brought her knees up to her chin.

She didn't need another problem right now. And Rand and Maggie would be the worst kind of problem. Did he think she was blind? Wanting and denial were worse, in her book, than all the sins in the world.

Trying to shake off Rand's visit wouldn't be easy. Tonight was going to be an at-home evening. When Cary had finally returned her calls, he'd told her not to expect him till after ten. She had two choices: she could either stay here and read a book or go home and pretend it didn't matter that Cary would be late.

Pretend. That's what her life was all about these days. If she hadn't asked her husband, she wouldn't have known his plans, would have spent the entire evening anticipating his arrival.

The lights were on now. The place looked messy, as if the job would never get done. But it would. She'd see to it, even if she had to spend money like a madwoman. Often the workmen looked at her as if she were crazy when she gave an order to rip something out that had twenty or thirty years of life left to it. Cary said he understood, but she also knew he looked in her ledger almost every day, keeping a running account of the money she spent.

The workers began to troop out one after another, calling good night over their shoulders. Home to families who waited for them. It was dinnertime, and here she was, all alone, in an empty house.

Damn it, she was lonely! What she wanted to do more than anything in the world right now was drive to Cary's construction site. She'd hoped that her husband would ask her to work in the trailer office answering the phone and ordering supplies. But he'd said it wouldn't look good if his wife worked on the site. As if she cared what anyone thought! But she didn't dare oppose Cary. He was happy having her here, puttering around, where he could find her at a moment's notice.

She'd felt restless these past few days, not in tune with herself. She wondered if it had anything to do with Susan's and Rand's return. Reminders of her age. She didn't want to have to stay cooped up at Sunbridge and hover over Susan, even though she loved her dearly. Fussing and fretting over Susan and worrying about Rand's possible affair with Maggie was simply not what she had in mind for herself. God, why did she feel so depressed?

Maybe she should lock up and go home. By the time she reached Sunbridge, dinner would be over and the kitchen cleaned up. The boys would be studying in their rooms. Rand, Maggie, and Susan would probably be in the study talking over after-dinner coffee. She'd say her hellos, give the proper hugs, then go upstairs. A long warm bath, a sexy gown, a drink, and she'd be ready for Cary. She could even call Billie; that always gave her a lift. And if Susan was still up afterward, she would visit with her.

When Amelia walked through the wide front doors of Sunbridge, her eyes, as always, went to the hat rack in the foyer. The sight of Riley's baseball cap always seemed so incongruous beside the Stetsons. But it brought a smile to her lips. Change.

The sound of subdued conversation and the soft clink of silver echoed out to the wide center hall. Taking a deep breath, she headed for the study. Susan lay propped up on the couch with an afghan covering her stomach and legs.

Immediately Amelia's heart went out to this girl who was like a daughter to her. She dropped to her knees, one hand fondly patting Susan's stomach as she pretended not to see the tears in Susan's eyes. Always before she'd been able to make things better for her niece. Not this time.

"Darling, how nice it is to see you. Under the weather, are we?" she said cheerfully. "Well, we'll have you right as rain in a week or so. All this Texas air has to be good for something. I'm glad you're here, sweetie. Imagine, a baby at Sunbridge," she said, turning to face Maggie. "It's been years since a child's footsteps echoed in this old place. Since Sawyer. What a dear child she was! So good and yet so mischievous. Billie did try to keep her to the studio, but she liked to come here and run about, especially up and down the steps. To look at her now, you'd find it hard to believe she was such a precocious toddler. Smart! My dear, that child has brains she hasn't used yet." When she saw Maggie flinch, she stood up, planted a kiss on Susan's brow, and said, "Well, I'm off to my avocado bath and thirty minutes in the Jacuzzi. Rand, tell Susan about my house. I'll fill you in on the details later. I'm going to call Billie. Does anyone want me to deliver any messages?"

Maggie felt as though a stone had lodged in her throat. She shook her head. Rand managed to mutter something about sending his regards, and Susan said to send her love. Amelia smiled at everyone and bustled out.

For a few moments, all was silence. Damn you, Mother, Rand seethed, seeing the stricken look on Maggie's face.

Susan, who was oblivious of the drama being played

out before her, spoke first. "If you don't mind," she said, sighing wearily, "I think I'll turn in."

Rand held out a stiff arm. "Grab hold."

Susan bounced to her feet and laughed. "This baby has had one tough life so far. A jolt or two now isn't going to matter. Good night to both of you." She kissed Maggie soundly and held on to her a moment longer than necessary. "Thanks for having me, Maggie. I don't know what I would have done without you. And Rand, thanks again. I know I'm repeating myself, but I am so grateful. I actually feel safe. Now isn't that a sad state of affairs?"

"Sleep well, Susan. I'm going to be right behind you. I have some letters to get out. Rand, why don't you lock up and turn off the lights?" Maggie said, averting her eyes as she hurried to follow Susan up the stairs.

Rand sat downstairs for a long time. Amelia's words echoed in his brain . . . and he knew he could never find it in himself to forgive her.

The ritual Amelia went through after her bath was long and tedious. First, she applied scented lotion to her entire body, then she powdered it with the same feathery scent. She creamed her face, oiled her eyelids and earlobes, and waited ten minutes. She applied light makeup, knowing the peach-colored light bulbs she'd placed in all the lamps would make her look dewy and fresh. She blow-dried her hair, gave it a few twirls with the curling iron, and then fluffed it out with her fingers. She added tiny gold-and-diamond earrings to her ears, a gift from Cary on her last birthday. The turquoise silk nightgown slithered over her body, making light swishing sounds. The side slit in the gown showed off a generous expanse of satiny leg as she fished around in the closet for matching high-heeled mules.

The bedside clock read 9:45; time to call Billie.

"Is anything wrong?" were Billie's first words.

"Wrong? At Sunbridge? Surely you jest! I just thought I'd call and see how the sap is running in Vermont."

"Thad says it's fine. How are you? How's the house

going? You said you were going to write and tell me all the things you did. I've been waiting for a letter."

"You shouldn't believe a promise like that. It's so much easier to pick up the phone and call. I think I'll be done by spring. I want your promise that you and Thad will come to my housewarming."

"Complete with gift." Billic laughed.

"How's Thad? Any more news on whether he's going to run for office?"

"The committee is doing its best to talk him into it. I don't say anything. It has to be Thad's decision."

"Susan is here, you know. She looks ghastly, Billie."

"I spoke to her today. She sounded tired. Maggie said she thought rest and fresh air would do it. We'll see what the doctor says. I feel better about her being in the States, but I am sorry about Jerome. Coleman marriages certainly seem volatile. I'm so glad you're staying at Sunbridge."

"I'm not here much of the time, but I'll do what I can. I tend to think Susan and Maggie will draw closer now."

Billie listened to her old friend. There was something different about Amelia's voice. It sounded strained, and the vibrancy she'd always associated with Amelia was missing. Her heart fluttered wildly. Something had happened and no one was telling her. "How's Cary doing with his project?"

"Wonderfully. I hardly ever see him, but then, I'm busy myself. We seem to meet up in the bedroom, which is all right with me. He's working seven days a week, poor darling."

"I'm eager to see it. Thad was asking me about it just the other day. He's very interested. Men love that sort of thing."

"*It*, as you put it, isn't much to see at this stage. The land's been cleared and there's a bunch of trailers used as on-site offices. Some slabs and foundations have been installed. And oh, yes, I mustn't forget about sewer and water, gas and electricity lines. Everything is underground, you know. There are even provisions for a cable

TV system. It's all very exciting," Amelia said listlessly. "We're just praying the weather holds."

"Amelia, is anything wrong? You sound funny."

Amelia closed her eyes, clutching the receiver. How could she admit, even to Billie, that she was afraid her young husband was losing interest? Suddenly she blurted, "I think something's going on between Rand and Maggie. He's here now; he brought Susan home. I'm beginning to understand why Sawyer left the way she did after the breakup, poor dear."

Billie settled back in her chair, concerned. She'd never heard this vein of bitterness in Amelia's voice before, and certainly not in connection with Rand.

"Billie? Are you there?" Amelia asked shrilly. "Didn't you hear what I said? I think there's something going on between Maggie and Rand!"

"I heard you, Amelia. Perhaps there is something between Rand and Maggie; perhaps it goes even deeper than friendship. Now I'll tell you what I said to Sawyer when she confided her suspicions. Knowing Rand, I'm pretty sure his relationship with Sawyer was already over before the Fourth of July. Second, she has nothing to base those suspicions on except seeing Rand and Maggie talking on the lawn after the party. And finally," Billie said sternly, "I think her bitterness toward Maggie is childish and unfounded."

Amelia bristled. "Perhaps you approve, but I don't. Something like this could tear the family apart, and we've had enough of that already. I more or less let Rand know how I feel. If he wants to end his relationship with Sawyer, that's certainly his prerogative. But he doesn't have to throw Maggie in her face." She sighed. "Oh, I don't know what to think, Billie. I don't know how far it's gone or if it's just getting off the ground. I am staying here in Maggie's house, so unless I'm prepared to leave, I have to be careful what I say."

"Good thinking, Amelia."

Amelia gasped. "You seem quite approving."

"I really don't know what to think. I'm terribly confused, and my better sense tells me to keep out of it. I don't know the reasons Rand and Sawyer ended their relationship. I thought they would marry. It must have been more one-sided than we thought. But I do know Maggie well enough to say she wouldn't deliberately set out to hurt Sawyer. I can't believe that."

"Rand is my son, but he's a man and he goes after what he wants. And I can't hold my feelings in; I'd hate it if it was done to me. I can feel Sawyer's pain. I can feel it!"

"I know," Billie whispered. "I was in that same place once myself."

"What should we do?"

"Nothing. They have to work it out for themselves. I've had a few letters from Sawyer since July. None of them really said anything, but I can read between the lines. I'm worried sick. She's such a child, really. Her life has been ... well, charmed, one might say."

"*Charmed?* How could you say that?" Amelia asked hotly. "She was a child born of a child and rejected by her child-mother. It would have been better if she'd never been born. You never should have insisted Maggie go through with that pregnancy. Why did you?"

"Why? Because of you, Amelia. Because of that terrible botched-up abortion that left you unable to have another child. I believed abortion was wrong then and I still do. And if Maggie had had an abortion, we wouldn't have Sawyer today, would we? And perhaps we wouldn't have Cole, either." Silence on the other end of the line. Suddenly Billie was ashamed of herself. "Amelia, forgive me. I had no right. What's wrong? It isn't just Sawyer and Rand. I don't believe I've ever known you to be bitter, and yet that's what I'm hearing in your voice. What is it?"

"Nothing. I'm just edgy these days. And there's nothing to forgive, really. I shouldn't have said what I did." Amelia swallowed against the tears that always seemed so close to the surface these days. "Isn't there something we can do for Sawyer?"

"Thad suggested I go to New York on one pretense or another. But Sawyer would see right through my motives. She knows I'm here for her if she needs me. I have to think of Maggie, too. What do you suppose she's feeling?"

"Maggie's fighting it. I know she is," Amelia said. "But she isn't strong, Billie. She's looking for something in her life. For a while there, I thought she and Cranston were going to patch things up, but I guess it didn't work out...." She sighed. "You're right, Billie. Let's leave it alone for now. Besides, Rand will be gone in a few days. I know he has to get back to England. He's selling out the estate, or most of it. Did you know that? He leaves day after tomorrow."

Days, Billie was thinking. So much could happen in three days. She reflected on her time in Hong Kong with Thad years ago. You could fall in love in minutes; you could commit your entire life to that love in days. Other people could be destroyed by that love and commitment in an instant. Where had she and Thad found the strength to deny themselves? Tears glistened in Billie's eyes at the knowledge of all the time wasted, time they could have had loving each other, being there for each other. Was that really what she wanted for Maggie? And in the end, would it really make any difference to Sawyer? It wouldn't make Rand love her again.

"Billie?... Billie, are you there? Can you hear me?"

"I hear you, dear. Keep an eye on Susan for me. You're so good at that. I'll never forget the way you took care of me when I was pregnant with Suse. If it weren't for you, Susan might never have been born. Thad and I want to know when you and Cary are going to come visit us here in Vermont."

"One of these days. Probably when I'm old and gray. It's so cold in Vermont, and it's all I can do to anticipate a Texas winter. I'm not looking forward to it."

Billie laughed. "Our winters are bitter, but then it's a

matter of who you spend them with. Thad's back is a wonderful place to warm cold feet."

"Bless you, Billie, for even admitting your feet get cold. I thought I was the only one."

It was eleven-ten when Cary walked into the bedroom. He grinned at Amelia and then groaned. "You're the best thing I've seen all day. And you smell good, too."

Amelia's heart soared. "Are you hungry? Can I get you a drink?"

Cary leered at her, his dark, expressive brows lowering over that hawklike gaze. "What I want from you doesn't come from the kitchen or the bar. This is going to be the shortest shower on record. Strip down, baby. I'll be right back."

Amelia found herself laughing happily. "That's the best offer you've made since yesterday." She did as he'd told her. The silky sheets felt cool against her naked skin. But that was only temporary.

Amelia rolled over onto her side, her face buried in her pillow, Cary sleeping soundly beside her. She didn't care that the pillowcase was making creases in her face or that if she didn't make herself sleep she'd be a wreck in the morning. All she cared about at the moment was that Cary had fallen asleep almost in the middle of their lovemaking. Her brain told her how exhausted he was; demon Vanity was telling her that she wasn't exciting enough to keep him awake.

Before anyone had come down to the breakfast table, Maggie sat there in her usual place addressing an envelope. She hummed as she picked up her engagement book and leafed through it. Lord, she was spreading herself thin. An accident about to happen, Riley liked to tease. She was keeping the three weekdays before Thanksgiving free in order to oversee preparations for the big day. The football game, the family dinner, the homecoming dance for the boys the following night. The expected letdown when it was all over. Then the official beginning of the Christmas shopping season.

A thrill ran through her at just the thought of Christmas. Presents, family, belonging. She wanted this year to be the most festive ever, even outdoing Billie's efforts when she'd lived here.

Her eyes dropped to the envelope she was addressing to Sawyer. She'd tried several times to call Sawyer at her office. Each time she'd been put on hold, then was told Sawyer was out of the office and wouldn't return until late: was there a message? Well, Sawyer couldn't ignore a letter.

Dear Sawyer,

I tried calling your office today, but your secretary said you wouldn't be back till quite late. As you know, I'm not much of a letter writer, but I thought I'd take a crack at it since you didn't return any of my other phone calls.

Obviously, you're upset with me—more so than any time in the past. I think we should have talked this out months ago. I'm sorry now we didn't.

The boys tell me you're staying with Adam Jarvis. I'm glad. I know what a good friend he's always been. Why don't you bring him home with you for Thanksgiving? (I don't want to make this an official invitation because this is your home and I want you to come anytime you feel like it. The door is always open to you.)

Christmas this year promises to be a huge success. Everyone will be here. I'm sure the boys have told you Susan is already here. She's looking much better these days. We're all sort of hoping for a boy, but no one's saying it aloud!

I've told both Riley and Cole they can return to New York with you the day after Christmas, assuming you come. At first Riley was going to go back to Japan, then he decided against it. I wrote his grandfather inviting him here, but he said he was too old and too set in his ways to make the trip. He also said he understood Riley's vacation was too short for a trip of that length.

I want you to know how grateful I am for the interest you've taken in Cole. It's made all the difference in the world to him. I wish he and Riley got on better, but they don't. I'm working on it!

I'm enclosing my Thanksgiving menu to entice you and Adam. Please try to make it. My Christmas menu is also enclosed. I only added one thing to it from our old traditional menu—plum pudding. Rand said he's partial to it.

I hope you aren't working too hard, Sawyer. New York is the place to be at this time of year. Enjoy yourself and get in touch even if it's just to say hello.

Love,
Maggie

Maggie carried the letter out to the mailbox. The air was cold and damp, and the thin sweater she'd wrapped around her shoulders for the walk down the drive wasn't much protection. But there was also a chill inside her. She felt awful about mentioning Rand to Sawyer in her letter. But she'd had to let her know he was going to be here. Sawyer had to make up her own mind.

Maggie leaned against the mailbox, unconscious of the cold, biting wind. How alone Sawyer must be feeling! How empty. Her heart went out to her daughter; she didn't want to see her hurt. Perhaps in time she'd forget about Rand, find someone else to love. What hope was there for Rand and herself otherwise? Any relationship between them would tear this family apart.

Abruptly Maggie turned and began to run back to the house as though a demon were at her heels. The cold air filled her lungs; her heart pounded. But she couldn't escape the words ricocheting in her head. *What about me? What about me?*

* * *

"Hey, I'm home! Anyone here?" Sawyer called as she bolted the door behind her. "Guess what. I took off early to cook dinner. Spaghetti and meatballs. I hope you're hungry. I bought all the stuff on my way home.... Anyone here?" she called a second time.

Adam groaned. Not ten minutes ago he'd finished a triple-decker sandwich with a side bowl of Franco American something or other. He looked down at the dimples and crevices on the House Speaker's face. The man just wasn't coming alive. Maybe it was the nose, or the hair. ... The hell with it. "I'm here. Did I hear you say you were going to cook? The peanut butter and jelly princess of Austin, Texas?!"

"Come see for yourself." Sawyer sailed her hat in the general direction of a chair. She flung her coat over another chair and sent her shoes and handbag in different directions.

Adam poked around the mesh bag. "Ahhh, jarred spaghetti sauce! Is this the one with savory herbs and spices that I'll recognize as being better than my grandmother's?"

"Same one. Of course, I'm going to add a few things to it to make it even better. I do know how to cook. It's just not one of my favorite pastimes."

"What is your favorite pastime?"

"Making love."

Adam stared at her. "What happened to you today?"

"I don't know. It started this morning when I put on my funky watermelon-colored hat. People stared at me. It was one of those contagious things. They smiled and I smiled. Strange for New York, eh?"

"Very strange. You should wear it every day if it has this effect on you. How long till dinner?" he asked, trying to look hungry.

"An hour, hour and a half at the most. I know you must be starved. I'll hurry."

"No, don't hurry. Why don't we have a drink while

the sauce bubbles, or doesn't it have to bubble since it's from a jar?"

Sawyer peered at Adam's face. "You've eaten, haven't you?"

"A little of this and a little of that. Mostly I picked and nibbled. By ten o'clock I could probably eat a nine-course meal. You could put that time to good use by cleaning the bathroom. It's your turn."

"I was going to do it tomorrow."

"That's what you said last week. Once you do the meatballs, you know the rest takes care of itself. I'll do the tub and shower if you do the sink and the floor. I'll flip you for the john."

"No, you won't. I can handle all of it. Go back to your drawing board. Dinner will be at ten and I get to take the first shower in the clean bathroom."

"Wipe down the damn walls, will you?"

"Go, go, go." Sawyer made shooing motions out of the kitchen.

Adam settled himself in front of the drawing board, and within seconds the paper sprang to life. As he worked, his characters took on distinct personalities, and the little quote he finally thought up to give to the House Speaker in the bubble made him chortle. A few more bold strokes, his name scrawled at the bottom, and he'd finished for the day.

"Bathroom's done!" Sawyer called. "I'm going to take a shower. Drain the spaghetti when the timer goes off. We can dine when you pour the wine."

Adam's stomach rumbled. He wasn't hungry. But he would do justice to this culinary endeavor if it killed him.

Sawyer joined him later wearing a flowing tangerine-colored caftan and high-heeled slipers with fluffy pom-poms. She'd applied a light dusting of powder to her face and added some perfume. Adam approved—oh, yes, he approved.

She played the perfect hostess that evening—waited on Adam as if he were the love of her life, inquired if the food was done properly, saw that his wineglass was filled, and kept her dinner conversation lively. He tried to ignore the strain he saw in her blue eyes.

"The least I can do is clean up. Take the wine bottle into the den and put on some good music. I'm too stuffed to do anything but crash out. You outdid yourself tonight, my dear," Adam said in his best W. C. Fields voice.

"What rest of the wine? We drank it all. You drank most of it."

"Guilty as charged. We'll simply have to crack open another bottle. Get out of my way while I clean up." In sixty seconds Adam had the dishes in the sink, the condiments back in the cabinet, and the lid on the spaghetti pot. He whisked the bread crumbs onto the floor, explaining that Marble would clean them up later. By the time he'd placed the bowl of fruit back in the center of the table, Sawyer had uncorked a second bottle of wine.

"Ah, if only this was Dom Perignon." Adam sighed.

"You're half-buzzed now. Riunite will be just fine. You're lucky it isn't Ripple."

"I cut my teeth on Ripple. So did you. Don't go getting fancy on me." Adam grinned.

"We did have fun in those days, didn't we?"

"Things haven't changed all that much," Adam said as he put his arm around her shoulder. "You're you and I'm me. We grew up a little. Supposedly, we're responsible adults now. Know what? Sometimes I want to be a kid again."

Sawyer turned. "What you want, what we all want at some point in our lives, is yesterday. To go back and relive the important times. That's what I'd like to do."

Adam grew serious. "You're talking about Rand, aren't you? Why do you keep torturing yourself? You said it was over."

"I didn't say that. I did, actually.... What I mean is that's what Rand said. I know he doesn't mean it. It's the age difference. When I see him at Christmas, I think we can patch it up. I know I'm going to try. Whatever I did

to upset him will have faded and we'll be able to talk and
straighten it out."

"What if it doesn't work?" Adam asked quietly.

"It has to work! I can't see myself going on without
him. He loves me; I know he does. We ... we just have
a problem, and we're going to work it out."

"Maggie?"

Sawyer's face colored. "I'm ashamed of myself, Adam.
How could I have thought such a thing just because I saw
Rand and Maggie talking? *Talking*, for God's sake! I know
I've always said Maggie was a man-eater, but I was just
blowing off steam. Sometimes she made me so mad I
couldn't think of anything horrible enough to say about
her. I must've been crazy to think she set out to snatch
Rand from me. Maggie just wouldn't do anything like
that!"

"Well said, well said."

"For God's sake, she's my mother! Besides, Rand is
too decent, too much of a gentleman, to do anything so
... so ... "

"Shitful?"

"Yes, damn it, yes!"

"Hey! Cool down. I'm agreeing with you." He poured
from the bottle a second time. By now his eyes were
glassy and he had to keep blinking in order to focus.

"I have it all planned. I know exactly what I'm going
to say," Sawyer told him, her voice slurring a bit. "I'll
make sure it's at just the right time. I've rehearsed it a
hundred different times. It really is true, that old saying
... if you want something bad enough, you can get it if
you keep trying."

"Sawyer, I don't want to see you set yourself up for
another disappointment."

"Don't look at me that way! There's pity in your eyes!"
Suddenly, she covered her face with her hands; her sobs
came in great choking heaves.

"No, no, there's not," Adam said, alarmed. He crept
closer to her, taking her into his arms. "My heart is break-

ing for you, Sawyer, but that's not the same thing as pity, is it?"

She buried her face in the crook of his neck. He could feel her body shuddering, shaking with the force of her sobs racking through her delicate bones and heating her flesh. Too much wine, too little control, and Sawyer was fragmenting into tiny shards, each of them stabbing his heart.

He held her for a long time. When at last it seemed her tears were exhausted, he carried her to bed as though she were a child. She felt so light, almost weightless; he wondered how many meals she'd skipped, how much weight she'd lost. Could a person truly die of a broken heart?

He placed her gently on her bed and pulled the comforter up around her shoulders. She was so still, so silent, he thought she was asleep. Just as he was about to leave, she reached for his hand. "Don't leave me, Adam. Please. I don't think I can bear to be alone. Hold me. Just hold me."

Adam lay down beside her, cradling her in his arms. She pressed her face into his shoulder; he could feel her warm breath on his neck. "I'll hold you, honey. Forever, if I have to. Sleep, try to sleep."

"You're good, Adam, so good."

Through the night he held her, calming her night tortures when she stirred and soothing the little sobs that erupted without warning.

He loved her. And if she couldn't love him in return, then it would have to be enough that she needed him.

{{{{{{{{ CHAPTER FIFTEEN }}}}}}}}

When Adam awoke in Sawyer's bed next morning, she was already up and moving around. He cracked an eyelid open and followed her progress across the loft to the bathroom. He heard the rush of water and the now familiar rattle of the aspirin bottle.

Adam lay quietly, trying not to think of the interminable night through which he'd held her, soothed her, his own heart breaking with the futility of it all. He'd calmed tears shed for another man when all the while he wanted her for himself.

When the shower stopped, he burrowed a little deeper into the covers. Sawyer came back into her room and selected several items from her closet. Back in the bathroom the blow-dryer whined. He could get up, he thought, see to it that she had some breakfast—but he wasn't certain what kind of reception he'd receive. The last thing he wanted was for Sawyer to be shy and ashamed of having needed his comfort during the night. Would she be embarrassed that she'd bared her soul to him? That the bravado she'd been trying to exhibit had crumbled into a thousand pieces, leaving her so vulnerable?

Adam's eyes snapped shut. Sawyer was on the move again. The scent of her perfume trailed behind her, seeming to settle near the bed. When the scent localized, he knew she was staring down at him; he could hear her breathing. "Sleep well, dragon slayer," she whispered as she kissed him on the mouth. "Thank you."

When the door to the loft closed, he brought his finger to his lips.

Today was a work day, Adam tried to convince himself, not that he had any ideas. He didn't feel like working. He didn't want to work. What he wanted to do was impose on an old friend who was a practicing psychiatrist and talk to him about Sawyer. Six-thirty in the morning wasn't too early. Nick would grumble and complain, but he'd come through. That's what friends were for.

"What do you mean you're still sleeping?" Adam asked with mock indignation. "You told me and everyone else you know that you run through Central Park at six in the morning. Five miles!"

"So I lied. I run around the apartment at seven o'clock. Same thing." The sleepy voice groaned. "It's a sin to call someone this early."

"I need to talk to you, Nick. It's important. How about stopping by before the office and I'll make us some breakfast."

Nick's voice was suddenly brisk, almost professional. "What's wrong? You sound okay. This won't be for free, you know."

"It's Sawyer. She needs some help."

"If she needs help, why isn't she calling me instead of you? She'd at least have the decency to wait till seven thirty. You can't save the world and everyone in it, Adam. When are you going to get that through your head?"

"The same time you do. Who do you think you're kidding? I know how you spend your free time. You're the biggest savior of all. We have to try."

"You're a pain in my butt, Jarvis. I want eggs Benedict, fresh-squeezed orange juice, and a side order of home fries. Real ones."

"If I do that, I don't want a bill."

"Fine. Swear to me you'll send a hundred fifty dollars to the YMCA Children's Camp Fund."

"You son of a bitch, is that how much you get an hour?" Adam squawked.

"Someone has to pay for my Park Avenue address. I'll see you in forty-five minutes."

"Eggs Benedict and home fries, my ass!" Adam fumed as he stormed around the kitchen. He was just rinsing the last vestiges of shaving cream from his face when Nick Deitrick banged on his door.

Nick was round, a one-size-fits-all type body type. He had a trusting, compassionate gaze, pink cheeks, and a winsome smile that endeared him to his patients. No one who wanted to remain his friend ever referred to his encroaching male pattern baldness.

"At least you could have put out the ketchup to kill the taste," he grumbled. "What did you fry these eggs in, and why are they brown like this? I never saw eggs this color."

"The butter burned. I never said I was a cook. How are the fries?"

"Don't ask. Talk while I eat. I can do two things at the same time, unlike some people I know."

Nick studied his friend as he talked. The man looked terrible, like the life was being drained out of him. And Nick knew why.

"Sawyer's been here since July, as you know," Adam said, running his fingers distractedly through his hair. "She was pretty heavy into a relationship with this English dude. He used to be an RAF jet pilot and he tested the Coleman Aviation plane. You remember that?" Nick nodded. "She had herself convinced they were going to get married. Over the Fourth this guy, Rand, broke it off with her and she came here. There's another problem. It's possible that Sawyer's mother, Maggie, and this guy Rand might have something going. When Sawyer first came here, that's what she thought; now she's convinced it's not true, or at least she *says* she is. I'm worried about her. She looks like a ghost. She's lost weight; she works sixteen hours a day; she gets these headaches all the time.

She doesn't seem able to throw off her depression. Last night she told me that she's going back to Texas for Christmas and Rand will be there. She's convinced she's going to make things right between them."

Nick chewed his toast and swallowed his coffee. "Aside from playing big brother in all of this, what's your interest?"

"I love her, Nick. You've always known that."

Nick nodded. "What Sawyer is going through is normal and natural. Everyone has a time clock for grief, and she is grieving, you know. Depression is usually triggered by a loss of some kind: a mate, a lover, a job. When you have to face a loss, you feel lost. Sawyer was pulled up short, stopped in her tracks. The thread of continuity in her life snapped. Are you following me? Sawyer's life wasn't ever smooth to begin with; you've told me the story."

"But this isn't like Sawyer," Adam protested. "She should be coming out of it a little. Instead, she's planning and scheming ways to get Rand back. She won't let go."

"And of course you want her to let go so you can step in," Nick said quietly.

Adam leaned across the table. "Yes, that would be nice, but I don't bank on it. Sawyer had plenty of opportunities to have me if she wanted me; she didn't, and I'd be a fool to think she would now."

"But you're hoping."

Adam stood up abruptly, toppling his chair backward. "Yes, dammit, I'm hoping!" he cried, slamming his fist on the table in an uncharacteristic display of rage. "But I'm afraid for her. I know she's on the ragged edge, and she's basing everything on Christmas. What if it doesn't work out? What happens to her then? What if she wasn't off base about something going on between this dude and her mother?"

"I could reel off a lot of medical jargon, but I won't. Sawyer's loss is challenged. It was forceful, unexpected, and right now she probably can't imagine her life without Rand. In her depression she's mourning the loss of that someone who gave meaning to her life. She should be searching for a replacement so she can build on her loss. But before she can do that, she has to accept the end of the relationship.... I should be talking to her, not you," Nick grumbled.

"Are you saying it's okay for her to go back home over Christmas and try again? That maybe it'll show her the relationship is really over so she can go on from there?"

Nick shrugged. "Like I said, I should be talking to her, not you."

Adam raked his fingers through his hair. "Look, Nick, I need to understand. I might be able to get through to her and even get her to go see you."

"Fine, but I suspect it won't be easy. It's hard to come to terms with a loss. Sawyer is probably thinking that to go on without Rand is being disloyal to her own ideals as well as to him. Silly? Incongruous?" Nick smiled. "Yeah, I know, but that's the way it is. Some people take longer than others. You can't measure love with a yardstick."

"What can I do to help?"

"Be her friend. Be there for her. Try to get her to seek professional help. It can shorten the grieving. Many of us need to be given permission to let go of the past."

"I appreciate this, Nick. I should have made you a decent breakfast."

"Forget it. Nick wiped his chin and swallowed the cold dregs of his coffee. He reached out with pudgy pink hands to grip Adam's long, slender fingers. "Sawyer is a survivor. Remember that."

"I'll try. Christmas is looming like a monster for me now. I was going to Vermont to ski, but now   "

"Go!" Nick was as concerned about Adam as Adam was about Sawyer. If his friend wasn't careful, he might end up in Sawyer's shoes, suffering the same kind of loss. He sighed. "And call me if there's anything I can do, will you?"

Adam smiled. "Thanks, Nick."

"Anytime. Don't forget about the YMCA."

"It's done."

* * *

Sawyer sat at her desk rubbing her eyes, trying to massage away her headache. It was only eight-ten and most of the staff was just straggling in. She'd made the coffee, picked up the Danish on her way to work, and was contemplating the rest of the day. In order to face it, she had to look back at the long, long night.

She had used Adam. Eagerly taken the comfort he'd offered and given nothing in return. But in truth, she'd do it all over again if it meant she could get through another long, lonely night. It was the nights that were impossible to bear, when memories and dreams chased sleep like the demons they were. She'd slept more last night than she had in months. And when she'd stirred, Adam was there to comfort her.

Adam. She loved him—in a special way. Was that what Rand meant when he'd said he loved her but wasn't in love with her? No, no, it was different with Rand. They'd been lovers; they'd shared something she had never shared with Adam. Maybe she *was* being selfish, using Adam this way, but she couldn't help it. Anything was better than this madness; anything was better than being alone with the emptiness and broken dreams.

Sawyer shuffled some papers on her desk, and a red-and-blue TWA ticket holder slid across her desk. She was supposed to go to Hong Kong at the end of the week! How could she have forgotten such an important trip?

Grandpap's fuel-efficient, small-scale jet plane, christened the *Coleman Condor* by Billie, was slowly but surely creeping toward full-scale production. It was an important project, one that could secure the Coleman family fortunes. So, even though Sawyer was primarily an aeronautical engineer, she had undertaken to see personally to every detail of its completion. In Hong Kong she would be supervising the purchase of quality fabric and the manufacture of the *Condor*'s luxury-detailed seats and overhead liners.

One glance at her appointment book told her she was going to be on the run up until it was time to board the plane. Three-and-a-half weeks in Hong Kong was a long time. Perhaps she should write the boys before she left—or, better yet, call them.

Sawyer asked for an outside line, and in seconds she heard Martha's voice telling her to hold on. When Cole's voice boomed over the wire, she slid the phone away from her ear. She'd forgotten how deep and loud the boy's voice was. "It's Sawyer, Cole. I'm sorry about calling so early, but I wanted you to know I'm going to Hong Kong in a few days. I'm behind on my letter writing. I didn't want you worrying about me or trying to call."

"Hong Kong! I wish I could go. Grandmam Billie said it's a wonderful place to visit."

"It is, but this is business. How about next summer? I can probably arrange my vacation to coincide with whenever you're free. Work on it. It'll give us both something to look forward to.

"What's going on at Sunbridge? How's school? Keeping your marks up? How's the football team doing?"

"School's okay. My grades are A's and the football team is undefeated. It's because of Riley," he said grudgingly. "I think he's going to make the all-stars."

"Does that bother you? The truth now."

"Sure it bothers me. He does everything great. The coach says he's a natural for football and any other sport, for that matter. I can't hack sports. He even snagged the best-looking girl, and she's captain of the cheerleading squad, for his date at the dance. Every guy in school has the hots for her. I don't know how he did it."

"By being nice, probably. He is a nice kid, and so are you. You guys could have made a great team. I wish you'd work on it, Cole. Jealousy is an awful thing to have to deal with."

"Mother is on my back all the time about it. By the way, Rand is here." He heard the deadly stillness come over the wire and wished he could cut his tongue out. "He brought Aunt Susan here. She's sick, or it's something about the baby. Mother says she looks awful," Cole babbled. "He's not staying. In fact, I think he's leaving tomorrow."

"It's okay, Cole. You don't have to make explanations to me. And you're right; it does hurt. I haven't heard from him at all."

"He's a bastard, if you want my opinion. He's on mother's tail no matter where she goes. I watch them. Aunt Amelia chewed him out the other day. I heard him tell that to Mother. Aunt Susan keeps watching them, too. Riley . . . well, it's hard to tell with Riley, but I think he stares at the two of them a lot." Another deadly silence.

"Listen, do you want me to say anything to him? Cole said desperately. "Give him a message or tell him about your trip?"

Sawyer could feel a sob building in her throat. She had to get off the phone. "No, no, don't say anything. I—I have to get back to work now, Cole. And you better get off to school before you're late. I'll send you a postcard from Hong Kong," she said hoarsely. "Take care of yourself."

"You, too. Goody-bye."

Cole looked at the telephone for a long time. His eyes spewed anger as he made his way to the dining room and saw his mother and Rand at the table, laughing and eating together like an old married couple.

"Cole! You're going to be late!" Maggie warned.

"I've got a study hall first period. Don't you care if I eat or not?"

"Of course I care. I thought you ate with Riley. He's gone."

"My plate is next to yours. Does it look like I ate?" Cole asked snidely as he filled his plate with scrambled eggs. He jerked his head in Rand's direction. "What's he still doing here?" It pleased him to see Rand's lips tighten.

"What do you mean, what's he doing here? Rand brought Susan home."

"She's been home for two days and he's still here. Don't tell me—he's holding her hand. Oops, wrong again.

It's your hand he's holding," Cole said coldly. "Isn't that right, Mother?"

"That's enough! Apologize."

"To who for what?" Cole asked with his mouth full.

"To Rand."

"He doesn't deserve an apology. I don't think he belongs here. A few other people don't think he belongs here, either." He stood up abruptly. "Well, I have to get going so I don't miss my second class." At the doorway he turned and asked, "Just when *are* you leaving, Rand?"

Goddamn little monster, Rand thought. Sawyer's champion. But how could he blame Cole for trying to protect his sister?

"Soon," he said.

"How soon?" Cole shot back.

"Will tonight be quick enough for you?"

"No, but if that's the best you can do, then do it. We don't need you here, none of us."

Maggie got up from her chair, her face drained of all color. "I don't want to hear another word out of you, Cole. We'll discuss this tonight."

"Before or after the Earl of Wickham leaves?" Cole said before stamping from the room.

Maggie stood silent for a long time, her arms crossed over her chest, her chin raised in defiance. "Goddamn you, Rand. Why didn't you break it off with Sawyer when she was in California? Why here, where for some reason everyone believes it's my fault? My God, I can't even defend myself. Cole believes we're having an affair. He probably told Sawyer and Mam and anyone else who would listen. He's absolutely right; you have to leave—the sooner the better."

"I do want to have an affair with you. It's all I've been thinking about. Admit it—you've been thinking the same thing!" Accusation met accusation; Maggie stormed from the room and Rand felt like a dog.

Susan was holding on to the banister as she descended the stairs. She looked a little better; at least there was some life in her eyes. Rand met her halfway up.

"Late for breakfast again," she said. "I'm ravenous. And I'm going to eat."

"Good girl. You'll be feeling better in no time at all. Well, you better get along before Martha clears the sideboard. I've got some packing to do."

"Are you leaving so soon?"

"There are those among us who think I've overstayed my welcome. Just out of curiosity, what do you think?"

Susan stared at this man she'd known practically all her life. He was like a big brother, an uncle, almost a father image. She loved him and was grateful for the many kindnesses he'd done her over the years. She tried to choose her words carefully. "I think, Rand, that you should return to England, not because of what anyone thinks or feels, but because this isn't the right time. Sawyer's one of us. It always comes down to that in one way or another, us versus them. Right now, you're one of them. We Colemans have a tendency to close ranks. You saw it happen with Jerome. Maggie is vulnerable right now."

"And you think I'd take advantage of that, do you?"

"Not deliberately. Maggie can't keep her eyes off you. I noticed you have trouble in that department yourself. There's a ghost between you. For God's sake, Rand, Sawyer is Maggie's daughter! You understand that, don't you?"

"Only too well. What would happen, Susan, if I told you I loved Maggie and she loved me? What would all you Colemans do then?"

Susan shook her head slowly. "I don't know. I suppose we'd have to wait and see. I know what Sawyer must be going through. She loved you, Rand. She thought you were going to marry her. Now, Sawyer is not a stupid woman. She must have gotten that impression somehow. You've hurt her terribly, Rand. Her Coleman pride prevents her from letting you know just how much."

"Would you want me to marry Sawyer if I wasn't in love with her?"

Susan's puffy eyes were cold now, heartless. "You made the decision. You didn't give her a chance. You just ripped out her guts and walked away." She brushed past him, then turned abruptly, almost losing her balance. "Can I ask you something, Rand?" He nodded. "Did Sawyer ever say the age difference bothered her?"

"No."

"Did she ever say she wanted children?"

"Not in so many words. All women want children."

"Did she ever say she could be just as happy with you without children?"

"In words to that effect," Rand said harshly. "If you're trying to make me feel guilty, you don't have to bother. I feel terrible."

"It wasn't a mutual ending. She didn't have anything to say about it. She didn't deserve that kind of treatment."

"You're right; she didn't. I'm not disagreeing with you. But I'm not apologizing, either."

"Maybe you should," Susan said softly, and turned away.

Up in his room, Rand flopped miserably on the bed. He lay for a long time with his hands laced behind his head, his thoughts racing. Right? Wrong? If he had it to do over again, would he do it any differently?

There had been a time in his life when people's opinions hadn't bothered him. Now that he was older, it was important to him what other people thought. Billie and Thad were at the top of the list. And Amelia. He didn't want them thinking he was a bastard. If something wasn't right, it wasn't right. Did he have to be miserable to make someone else happy? But then again, did he have the right to make someone else miserable?

Poor Sawyer, what had he done to her? The answer was so terrible, he rolled over on the bed. One clenched fist pounded the pillow. He'd destroyed her. He knew it as sure as he knew he had to take another breath. Beautiful, wonderful Sawyer. And he was itching and lusting for Maggie. Jesus.

Rand rolled back over and stared at the ceiling. There was no way he could make things right. What was done was done. He, Sawyer, and Maggie were going to have to live with it.

Her scent arrived before she did. Rand opened his eyes in surprise to see Maggie in front of the closed door.

"Are you leaving?" she asked in a strange voice.

"I didn't hear anyone asking me to stay. I'm some kind of bloody pariah now. Susan just laced into me coming up the stairs. Cole hates me and does his best to make it known. Riley can barely tolerate me. My own mother told me where to get off. You've pushed me away. And you want to know if I'm leaving? I'm sorry I came."

"I'm not. I felt so happy with you here. It's almost as though you belong."

"I don't belong here. Sawyer's ghost lives here."

Maggie's eyes spewed fire. Her lips trembled and she clenched her hands into white-knuckled fists. "It's always Sawyer. No matter what I do, no matter where I go, she's between me and whatever it is I want. I can't get away from her. I've always been jealous of her. She was given what should have been mine. If it had been mine from the beginning, I never would have become a roadside whore at the age of fourteen and she never would've been born!"

"Maggie, Maggie, you don't know what you're saying."

"Oh, don't I? Don't I?" She crossed the room and loomed over him. He was sitting on the edge of the bed now, alarmed at her sudden intrusion, overwhelmed by her fury. "She even had you, damn her, she even had you!" Enraged and provoked by his feeble attempt to soothe her, Maggie attacked, pummeling him with the heels of her hands, beating him in her madness; all the while, hot tears streamed down her face, heaving sobs erupted in her throat.

Rand caught her against him, throwing her onto the bed beside him, attempting to control her struggles with his weight. Bit by bit her fury passed, leaving her exhausted and miserable. He smoothed the silky dark hair back from her forehead, crooning to her, comforting her. "Cry, Maggie. Cry for the both of us."

She looked up at him, a curious little expression in her eyes, as though she were seeing him there for the first time. "I don't want to cry! I want to make love to you!" At the edge of her tone was a trace of desperation.

Rand covered her mouth with his own, pulling her body against his. Yes, yes, Maggie was thinking. Yes, make love to me now, while I'm still angry enough to go through with it, while I don't give a damn about anyone or anything except what I want.

As Maggie surrendered herself to Rand's loving, her wild thoughts scurried like mice in a maze. She told herself she wanted Rand; she even believed she loved him. She was Maggie; not Billie, who had made a career of self-sacrifice until her commitment to her family was completed. Life was too short to be so good and noble. Life was too empty and it was hard to be alone.

Alone. Alone. The word echoed in her brain. She focused on it, allowing all the rage, jealousy, and resentment to fall aside. Only the guilt remained. But it's only for now, Maggie told herself, only for this little while. She'd come into Rand's room blind with rage. She was maddened with herself that she was sending Rand away and out of her life, and yet, ridiculously, she was angry with him that he'd hurt Sawyer. Absurd, ludicrous, and even lunatic, but that's the way it was.

Rand was reveling in the feel of Maggie's arms clinging to him. This was what he'd been dreaming of for months. This was what had kept him awake and miserable all those long, lonely nights. To be with her, to hold her in his arms this way, to know she felt the same way about him. All the notes and letters, the telephone conversations, ways to get to know her. Seeing her here at Sunbridge, knowing her concern for family, all these things brought her closer to him. Even Cole, who never missed an opportunity to be difficult and unloving; Maggie loved the boy. Her devotion to Riley, her understanding with Susan, even the rage with which she'd first entered his room. All these things were a part of Maggie and he loved her.

In his arms he held a woman who had tested life and had come to know herself. She wasn't a child who believed love could overcome any obstacle. Experience and maturity, those were a part of Maggie, too. And now he wanted to become a part of her, to share with her, be understood by her and, in turn, to understand her. This Maggie, his Maggie.

His lips seemed to devour her, nipping gently at her throat and falling lower between her breasts. Eager fingers, greedy for the feel of his skin, lifted the bottom of his sweater, exploring the expanse of his back, the solidness of his muscles, the width of his shoulders. Fury still pounded through her blood. She wanted Rand in spite of herself, in spite of Sawyer's pain and what might be ahead of them.

Maggie became immersed in Rand's kisses, allowing his gentle, unhurried touch to calm her roiling emotions. Again and again his mouth came down on hers, sometimes softly and at other times with a sense of desperation, as though he believed she might slip through his arms like a vaporous dream. He seemed to sense that she wanted him to take her quickly, because he murmured, "Slow, Maggie, slow. I want it to last. Make it last."

His movements were unhurried and controlled, arousing her, allowing her to put everything behind her and to concentrate only on him. Her heart was beating randomly; all her senses awakened, responding to him, becoming acutely aware of his touch on the fullness of her breasts and of the heat that was generating at her center. He undressed her—slowly—unwrapping her as though she were a long-awaited gift, discovering her inch by inch and always smoothing or kissing her newly exposed skin.

When she lay naked upon his bed, he undressed himself beneath her heated gaze. Her eyes were drawn to the masculine slope of his shoulders, the flat of his belly, and the firm globes of his buttocks. Fine golden hairs furred his chest, and when he stepped closer, the light from the window revealed the integration of silver among the gold.

He lay down beside her and she moved easily into his arms, pressing herself against him. She nuzzled the delicate skin at the base of his neck, tickled her lips against his crisp chest fur, inhaled the spicy clean scent of his shower soap, aware of the presence of his own male scent beneath.

Rand's hands were in Maggie's hair, lifting the glossy black strands to his lips, stroking the nape of her neck and tracing patterns along her jaw. It was as though he were committing her to memory, as if his lips and fingers were branding her image in his brain. The kisses he traced along the curve of her neck sent little shivers of delight up her spine. Anticipation throbbed through her veins and warmed her center. It seemed an eternity that she wanted to know him this way, but it had only been a matter of months. Months, weeks, a lifetime. She'd tried to rid him from her thoughts and, failing that, had attempted to place him within the confines of friendship. She'd failed. Only now could she admit to herself that during Cranston's visit and their most intimate moments together, it had been Rand she'd wanted and needed. She'd tried to substitute, but nothing she'd dreamed or fantasized could have prepared her for this moment.

His hands traveled her body, lightly skimming her tingling flesh from the hollows beneath her breasts to her smooth haunches. He explored the curve of her hips and the softness of her belly to the firmness of her bottom. She shuddered beneath his hand when he leaned up on one elbow to follow this newly discovered path with moist kisses and gentle teasings of his tongue. It was as though she were rediscovering herself through this journey of hand and mouth. She reveled in his delight and in the growing, hungry need that burned through her loins.

Maggie was unable to lie still beneath his touch. His

caresses had inspired something in her, a need to share, a desire to give. In tender, sensuous patterns she stroked his flesh, beginning at the definition of his chest to the plane of his belly. She traced his hair patterns, following the lines that swirled upward over his breasts and downward over his middle to a darker, thicker patch surrounding his sex. He quivered when she kneaded the muscle of his inner thigh and moved upward to his groin. Her movements were teasing, enticing, affecting her as well as Rand until the throbbing in her veins became a roaring demand to have him for her own, to become a part of him and him a part of her. His mouth moved over her body with exquisite care, nipping, nibbling, heating her flesh.

"Now, Rand, now?" she whispered. It was a question; it was a demand.

"Now, Maggie, my Maggie." His voice was husky, filled with emotion. He wanted her, had wanted her these many months, but the emotion was deeper than being with her this way. He didn't merely want to couple with her; he wanted to fulfill her, to know her and become a part of her. When he placed himself between her open thighs, he looked down into her face, seeing there her kiss-bruised mouth, moist and pouting, the flush of passion staining her cheeks and spreading over her throat. But it was her eyes that held him, the color of a summer sky and glistening with tears. His heart reached out for hers as he kissed the crystal droplets that had fallen onto her cheeks. Her own heart, Maggie's heart, was only a breath away. And when she cried his name, it seemed their souls broke through an eternity of desolation to reach out, to touch. Loneliness and emptiness were banished, and it was with a boundless joy that she drew him inside her, the passage hot and wet, stroking with long, slow undulations.

He arched his back, holding himself above her, his loins pressed hard against hers, forcing himself to be still, struggling for control as he had not since his first sexual experience. That same boyish impatience flooded through him, but the man he had become knew the wisdom of waiting and relishing each sensation and sharing it with his partner. But Maggie refused to be still beneath him. Her hands raked his chest, teasing his nipples and pulling at the hair. Her hips moved, rocking her body beneath his, locking him against her, her sheath stroking and rippling around him until he yielded to her passions and her driving needs.

He thrust himself into her, seeking to relieve this pulsing ache she had created in him, unable to go deep enough or hard enough, until the fire spread from his loins to touch every part of him, and he surrendered to the blinding rapture and joyful knowledge that Maggie was just behind him, following closely, sharing in this glory.

Maggie became a part of him, suffering the same agony, seeking the same release. She followed the route he charted, heard the cries from his throat and reveled in the deep thrusts that filled her completely. She held herself to him, matching his movements, feeling herself floating beyond these delicious physical sensations to a place that was quiet and still, a place where he waited for her to touch her soul with his own. Her fingers dug into his flanks as she penetrated the last barrier before finding her own satisfaction, giving herself over to the warm waves of pleasure ebbing and flowing with each beat of her heart.

They held each other for a very long time, like two children hiding in the dark while they waited for the danger to pass. He rested his chin on the top of her head, smoothing the round of her shoulder and stroking the tender skin near her temples. She was crying. There were tears in his own eyes and a lump in his throat. He didn't need to ask why she was crying; words were unnecessary when two souls touched. They had done it, committed the very sin of which they were accused.

"Now, more than ever, I have to leave, Maggie." His voice was deep, ragged.

She nodded. "Yes, you must leave." She choked back the tears, swallowing hard, working her throat muscles until she could ask, "Will you come back, Rand? Will you?"

"That's up to you, Maggie, my Maggie," he said when he could speak. "Will you want me to come back? We've found something together, darling, something very, very precious. The question you must ask yourself is do we have any right to keep it?"

{{{{{{{{ CHAPTER SIXTEEN }}}}}}}}

The kaleidoscope of autumn's colors gave way to the drab browns of encroaching winter. Halloween passed with a lone jack-o'-lantern dotting the portico of Sunbridge. The early weeks of November rushed past accompanied by, according to the weather forecasters, the most severe weather in years.

The last football game of the season was played and won by Crystal City High, thanks to Riley's defending tackle and interception. The dance ended on a high note of frivolity. Maggie herself was one of the chaperones. Cole did not attend.

December found Maggie meeting herself coming and going. Texas, it seemed, went all out for Christmas. She was forever chasing from one meeting to another, freely lending her name and her expertise. She used her lunch hours to run to the Crystal City Post Office, where she rented a mailbox. At least every other day box 771 held an airmail letter from England. She sat in the parking lot, nibbling on crackers, while she read Rand's latest offering. She herself wrote almost every day—light, chatty, newsy letters full of the happenings of her life. Always she ended each letter with the hope that he would join all of them for the holidays. She said she counted the days, the hours, and sometimes the minutes.

Today she had to Christmas shop. She'd put it off too long already. She wanted mountains of gifts for everyone, and the biggest Christmas tree in all of Texas. And she meant to have it. This was a special Christmas.

Another few days and the boys would be out of school for the holidays. She'd made no definite plans yet. She didn't even know for sure who was coming for the holidays. Billie and Thad had agreed to come, subject to last-minute events at the farm. She'd been unable to reach Sawyer for confirmation. Cole and Riley claimed to be uncertain of Sawyer's plans. Rand hadn't definitely committed, either, but she was certain he would come because she wished for it every night.

She was so busy planning parties, luncheons, and tree trimmings, not to mention a private church service, she hardly had time to remember that her divorce from Cranston would become final soon after the New Year. She would deal with that on the second day of January, she told herself.

Maggie sat for a few moments holding Rand's letter to her breast, oblivious to the mink-clad woman who walked past the car. Amelia was tempted to tap on the window, but didn't. There was something clandestine about the way Maggie was sitting in the parking lot of the post office holding a paper close to her breast. Obviously she had a secret. It didn't surprise Amelia. And it didn't take any brains at all to figure out who the secret was.

Amelia completed her business at the post office and was leaving the building when she saw Maggie pull out of the parking lot. It was probably a good thing Maggie hadn't noticed her, she thought as she got into her car. She might have said something that could be taken wrong.

Amelia sighed as she pulled out of the parking lot. Life at Sunbridge was not what she'd thought it would be. There were so many undercurrents these days! Cole and

Riley were at each other's throats hourly. Susan wandered
around the house with a vague, lost look in her eyes.
Maggie was always flitting from this place to that. Even
Cary seemed out of it. Business was consuming him; their
lovemaking had dwindled to once a week on a Sunday
morning—and even then only if she initiated it.

Every day this week she'd called and invited Cary to
lunch. Every day he'd refused, nicely of course, saying
he had to be on the site. She'd offered to bring a picnic
basket in the car, but he'd vetoed that, saying the other
workmen wouldn't appreciate it. They ate together, all
the hard hats, with the bosses.

She was almost at the site now. Maybe she could stop
and at least say hello. She could go into the trailer office,
have a cup of coffee, and leave a note for her husband
on his clipboard. He'd get a kick out of that. Or would
he feel she was chasing him, not giving him breathing
room? The hell with what he felt. This was what she
wanted to do and she was going to do it.

The road leading to the construction site was a series
of deep potholes, all of them filled with water. For miles
all she could see was acres of mud and slabs of concrete.
Here and there were trailers with wires hooked up to
generators. Bulldozers, all manner of heavy-duty equip-
ment, were at work.

She sat for a minute before she turned off the ignition,
wondering if it all was going to work. Was Texas ready
for Cary's dream? God, it was going to take ten years to
complete. She could be dead by then. Cary would just be
coming into his own, a handsome fiftyish widower. The
thought was so terrible Amelia almost leaped from the
car. Mud splashed up on the silvery mink. She cursed
loudly and strongly. Then she laughed. She'd wear hip
boots and slog through mud up to her waist if she could
be near Cary. She'd eat out of a metal lunch box and wear
a bright yellow hard hat. She might even give up her false
eyelashes and fingernails if they got in the way.

Amelia drew in her breath when she opened the door

to the trailer office. The last time she'd seen it, it was dirty and messy. Clutter everywhere. Some magical fairy must have been at work, she decided. Now there were tailored drapes on windows that just last month were practically solid grime. Green plants rested in wicker baskets on the tables. The floor was clean and the lamps dusted. There were piles of incoming and outgoing mail in wire baskets on Cary's desk, next to a new computer/printer. Amelia frowned. Cary hadn't said anything about a computer. The old black telephone was gone, too, replaced by one of AT&T's newest consoles.

Amelia looked completely around her. She didn't remember the walls being paneled. Or the aluminum-framed pictures of different sections of the state of Texas. Four chocolatey-colored chairs were scattered about the long room, with not a trace of fuzz or dust on the deep-welted corduroy. The bar, another new addition, was stocked with expensive brands of liquor. She knew there'd be a refrigerator behind it, filled with beer and soft drinks. Clients? Hardly. Probably Cary and his partners. The union men wouldn't be permitted to tramp in and out of this office.

The last thing she checked was the tiny bathroom. It had been newly carpeted in pink—pink!—and a wicker basket with yellow-and-white daisies sat on the back of the toilet. She peered into the bowl. It was clean. So was the sink. Pretty paper towels in a stack. Hand towels? A bottle of Avon hand lotion and little squares of what looked like Cashmere Bouquet soap were piled neatly next to the paper towels. Even the mirror and overhead light were different.

Who had done all this? She wondered. Cary hadn't said a word about it. For some reason, she felt annoyed—and vaguely uneasy. She also felt hot.

She was turning down the portable heater when the door opened and a pair of trim ankles in outrageously high heels came into Amelia's view. She turned and stood erect. "I thought this was set too high. Fires can happen with these things," she said coolly.

"I suppose you're right. It gets very cold in here. Drafts from the door. Can I help you? First I have to take off my coat and scoot to the bathroom. I had to get lunch for the men. Chinese," she called over her shoulder.

Amelia blinked. Whoever she was, she had the closest thing to a perfect figure Amelia had ever seen. She also had good skin, and she was young. Very young. Twenty-five, tops. Perfection? Confection? The men must love coming in here, Amelia thought.

"I'm sorry to keep you waiting, but nature calls every so often," the young woman said blithely. She settled herself behind the desk, hiked up her clinging blue jersey skirt, and looked directly at Amelia. "Now, what can I do for you?"

"Perhaps you could tell me where my husband is."

"If you tell me his name, maybe I can. My name is Eileen Farrell."

"Cary Assante. I'm *Mrs*. Assante."

Eileen's deep brown eyes widened. "*You're* Mrs. Assante?"

"In the flesh," Amelia said coldly.

"Uh . . . hi! Cary didn't say you'd be stopping by. He's out on the site somewhere. We're supposed to have lunch at one o'clock, but they're late now. We'll probably have to put it in the microwave."

"There's a microwave here?" Amelia asked in surprise.

"I insisted. What with the cold weather and all. The men need something warm when they come in. It's over there behind the cartons. It was the only place to hook it up. Cary said it's a wonderful idea. Everyone seemed pleased."

Microwaves, bars, green plants, pink carpets in the bathroom, and this . . . this ball of fluff. Amelia wanted to gag.

"Tell Cary I was here," Amelia said, bringing the mink close to her neck. It tickled her chin. Any other time she would have smiled.

"I'll do that, Mrs. Assante. I love your coat. It must have cost a fortune. Someday I plan to get one."

"Make sure it's a Fischer if you do. If someone else is paying for it, that is."

Eileen giggled. "Oh, you mean if I get a rich husband or lover."

"Whatever. It was nice meeting you, Miss Farrell. By the way, how long have you been here?"

"Exactly a month tomorrow. You wouldn't believe what this place looked like when I took the job. The first thing I said to Mr. Assante was I couldn't work in such a messy place. He gave me some money and told me to fix it up. Everyone loves it. It's a pleasure to come to work now."

"I just bet you're worth every penny of your salary."

"Mr. Assante says I am. The others seem to agree. I finally got the hang of this computer. I'm the only one who knows how to work it. The Wang Company sent someone out here to train me."

"How much are you earning?"

"I guess it's okay to tell you, being you're Mrs. Assante and all. Four fifty a week."

"Dollars?" Amelia asked in amazement.

"Plus benefits," Eileen chirped. "Dental, eyeglass plan, major medical, as well as three weeks' vacation and twelve sick days. I snapped this right up."

"I would, too," Amelia snorted as the door closed behind her. So, nothing was new on the construction site. Well, Eileen Farrell was new, like a bright, shiny penny. Even her eyelashes were real, heavy-fringed and perfectly mascaraed. Soft brown naturally curly hair that she'd kill for. And she was young.

Amelia returned to her mother's house. She wasn't in the mood now for carpenters or paperhangers. She didn't want to see the workmen goof off and she didn't want to remind them that she was paying them by the hour.

A whole afternoon to get through. She knew she wouldn't accomplish anything—she'd just be waiting for the phone to ring. Cary would call her; that much she knew. He'd think something had happened. She never visited the trailer anymore—not since he'd told her it didn't look good to the other men. She didn't want to embarrass him, did she? Oh, no. She'd *never* do anything to cause Cary trouble.

Eileen Farrell. Who was she? The intricate wooden sign on her desk had read Design Consultant. Eileen Farrell, Design Consultant. But just what the hell did that mean? What did she design . . . and who did she consult with?

Amelia felt like smashing something—preferably a mirror, any mirror.

It was three o'clock when the phone rang. Amelia let it ring seven times before she answered. She made her voice sound breathless and impatient. "Yes?"

"Hi, babe, how's it going?"

"You really don't want to know. I'm handling it. How are things at the site?"

"Fouled up as usual. I'm sorry I wasn't here when you stopped by. You could have joined us for some Chinese. You didn't miss anything, though; it wasn't all that good."

"Poor baby," Amelia cooed. "I didn't know you had a microwave."

"Oh, sure. We got one when we fixed up this place. How'd you like it?"

"I thought you did a pretty good job."

"Hell, I didn't do it. The little gal Eileen did it. I just gave her the bucks and told her to go to town. It was a smart move the day Jacobsen brought her here and we hired her. Things sure are running smooth. We even got a computer with a printer. Damn fool thing scares me, but Eileen is a whiz with it."

"What does she design?" Amelia asked airily.

"Elevators. Best one in the business according to Jacobsen. And he's the best architect in Texas."

"Elevators are important," Amelia said stupidly.

"Damn right. You can't do anything without elevators." Amelia thought she could hear a giggle in the background.

"Gotta go, darling," she said with false lightness. "One

of the workmen is calling me. I'm glad you're getting hot meals for lunch these days; I do worry about you. See you tonight."

Cary hung up the phone and grinned at Eileen. "She's something, my wife."

"She sure is. I loved her coat."

"She must have twenty. All different colors and lengths. She's one classy lady."

"I could tell," Eileen said sweetly.

"Listen, Eileen, if Sherm Alphin calls, tell him I'll be in around six-thirty and not to leave till he hears from me."

"Mr. Assante, why don't you get a beeper? Each of you men should have one. It would make things so much simpler for you. I could have the phone company come out here and hook up a phone in the middle of the site and you guys could just call to your heart's content."

"Do you really think we should get those things?"

"I certainly do. I can make the arrangements and have them ready for you by the middle of next week."

"Do it," Cary said, clamping his hard hat on his head. "It occurs to me that you're doing the work of a secretary instead of what you're supposed to be doing."

"Mr. Jacobsen pays me extra for design work. I don't mind doing all of this. Besides, design consultants don't get benefits. Your package was what I needed. I'm only too glad to help out. The pay's good, too." Eileen grinned. "How else do you think I could get a mink coat like your wife's?"

"You could get some guy to guy it for you," Cary laughed as he closed the door behind him. Cute kid. Lots of savvy. He wondered if Jacobsen had a thing going with her.

Cary grinned as he made his way through the mud holes back to the work area. He understood the Eileen Farrells of this world; he, too, had had to claw his way off the bottom. It had to be harder for a woman. Inside of a month Eileen Farrell had taken over, and she was fast proving herself an indispensable member of his team. With right clothes and the right connections, it would be clear sailing for the little girl who'd come from a small town under the *x* in Texas.

The really funny part of the whole thing was, she was smart as a whip, and she had a brain like a calculator. Beauty and brains. In a year probably she'd be asking for a slice of the pie; he could almost guarantee it. And if she got that far, he'd vote in her favor.

He had to remember to ask Amelia what she thought of Eileen. Amelia knew women almost as well as he knew men. He really respected her opinions. They'd compare notes and then make a wager like they usually did. Half the time Amelia won and half the time he won. Good odds.

A week before Christmas a festive air settled over Sunbridge. Garlands of balsam decorated the stairway and mantels. Mistletoe hung in open doorways. A monstrous twelve-foot blue spruce waited in the corner for its branches to settle in preparation of tree-trimming night. Aromas of baked cookies and spice cake drifted about, greeting each person who entered the house. Gaily wrapped packages were propped on chairs and in corners waiting to go under the tree. Fragrant pinecones burned in the fireplace. At last, Christmas was about to arrive.

Sunbridge's guest list would be identical to the one for Maggie's Fourth of July bash. She was pleased. Just this morning she'd received a letter from Rand saying he would definitely arrive Christmas Eve.

Since that morning in Rand's room, letters had gone back and forth between England and the States on a daily basis. Long letters, pouring out doubts, reaffirming affections, but always excluding the word "love" except in closing. "Love, Maggie," she would write, or sometimes "Love, your Maggie," remembering the way he had said to her that morning, "Maggie, my Maggie."

Their favorite topics were each other—how one felt about this, the other about that—and questions about the way the family would either accept what they had come to mean to each other or not. The "not" always caused the greatest alarm, the deepest distress.

The past few letters had broached the subject of Cranston and Cole and the wisdom of not allowing anything to interfere with Maggie's divorce. As a result, they'd decided they would have to remain "discreet." Logically—and because they both wanted it so desperately—discreet meant sacrifice. And since they'd promised each other to discreetly sacrifice their desires, there was no reason Rand shouldn't come to Sunbridge at Christmas. Logical, reasonable, adult—and so very, very dangerous. The day Maggie received Rand's confirming letter, the smile stayed on her lips all day.

Everyone would be home for dinner this evening. It seemed as though the Christmas spirit was drawing the family closer together, although in Cary and Amelia's case, the weather probably had more to do with it. As far as Maggie knew, the site was closed for a few days because of the last storm. Susan, pounds heavier but looking wonderful, was taking her meals downstairs now, along with the boys, who chatted and bantered. Even Cole was making an effort to be civil. He obviously wanted to very much be allowed to go to New York with his cousin the day after Christmas.

It was a heavy, cold-weather Texas meal. Beef stew cooked in the old iron pot for seven hours, savory and incomparable. There was corn bread and sourdough biscuits, along with asparagus and a green salad. Three meringue pies dotted the sideboard: banana cream, coconut custard, and lemon.

As Martha ladled out the stew, Maggie asked everyone at the table, "Have you finished your Christmas shopping?" The diners responded with sheepish looks, nods of agreement, and hoots of displeasure for the reminder.

"I finished yesterday. Now all I have to do is wrap." Maggie smiled victoriously. "I think I bought out the stores."

"I ordered through the catalogues," said Susan, "and everything arrived except one item. I plan to finish wrapping this evening." She sighed. "If I don't eat too much and fall asleep, that is."

"I'm done," Cary boasted. "Finished last week, as a matter of fact." No need to tell anyone he'd slipped Eileen his charge cards to do his shopping.

Amelia groaned. "I've been so busy with the house and all, I lost track of time. I've got the major portion to go. I'm hitting the stores tomorrow as soon as they open."

"I'm almost finished," Riley volunteered. "I'm waiting for something from home."

Cole looked up and around the table. "I didn't start yet."

"I hope everyone remembers everyone. Rand will be here, Mam and Thad, and Sawyer, although she hasn't said definitely that she's coming."

"Maggie, would you mind if we invited someone from the outside?" Cary asked.

"For dinner? The more the merrier. Who do you have in mind? Your friends, Sherm and Clara Alphin?"

"No, they'll be in North Carolina with their grand-children. Not just for dinner, either. I was thinking of Christmas Eve and Christmas Day. The girl in our office, Eileen Farrell. She'll be alone in an empty condo with a plastic tree. This family is so informal, I thought it would be nice for her to be with a big family."

Maggie could feel Amelia's stillness and was afraid to look at her. The request surprised her, and there was no way she could refuse. "Of course. Sharing is what Christ-mas is all about. That means, of course, that I'm not done shopping. You said her name is Eileen? I'll pick up a few things, cologne, a scarf, a book, so she has presents to open. Shall I send her an invitation, or will you take care of it?"

"I've already asked her. I knew you'd say yes. You'll like her. Amelia thinks she's great. We'd be lost without her at the site, I can tell you that."

Riley looked from Cary to his aunt Amelia, who was sitting beside him. He could hear her grinding her teeth.

He went back to the asparagus he hated. Adults sure had a funny way of showing approval.

"She designs elevators and acts as a major domo of sorts," Amelia said breezily. "She's even gotten Cary and the others to wear a beeper. Now he can be paged anytime of the day or night."

"I'm impressed." Maggie laughed. "Where's she from, Cary?"

"Under the x in Texas," He laughed. "She went to some design school in New York. She knows her business, all right. Let me tell you what that little filly did."

Amelia sucked in her breath. She could feel Riley watching her. Filly? Is that what they said under the x?

There was a chorus of "What?" from around the table.

"She asked for a contract. I told you she's no fool. She knows this project is going to take almost ten years to completion. She wants to be sure she gets her share."

"Does she want a percentage, too?" Amelia asked, her voice cool and controlled.

"It came up in the discussion," Cary said vaguely.

"How much?" This time she didn't try to control her tone of voice.

"One percent, a half. No one decided. I'm not sure it's a good idea. I don't mind the contract."

"I thought all of the investors had to put in a certain amount of money. You did say that, didn't you?"

"Hell, yes."

"It would seem to me that if she's going to be given a percentage, you should take her off salary. You're paying her handsomely now. What was it you started out with, four fifty? It's up to seven hundred now, I believe. Elevator design pays extra."

Maggie met Susan's concerned glance across the table. Striving to keep her voice casual, she said carefully, "I thought the first thing you learned in business is you never, ever, under any circumstance, *give* anything away."

"Maggie's right," Susan said tightly. "Running an office and designing elevators hardly seems enough of a reason to give the woman a percentage. You ought to fire her and let Amelia run the office. She'd be a whiz."

"I offered," Amelia said coolly.

"I told you, Amelia, I didn't want you working out there. You have your own thing going with the house. You wouldn't have the time. It's not good for a husband and wife to work together. Look, since you all seem opposed to the percentage business, I'll vote it down. Maybe it wouldn't be a good idea for her to come for Christmas."

Amelia looked around the table. No one said anything. Maggie didn't reinforce the invitation. Susan looked glum, and the boys had no opinions. It was up to her, and she would have to be careful. "On the contrary, Cary, I think Eileen should come. She should get to know us. I'll buy her something special from both of us."

Maggie sighed with relief. Cary looked at his plate. Amelia had just bailed him out of a touchy situation, and he knew it. He'd never make that mistake again.

"Billie, I'm not sure we're going to make it to the airport," Thad said in a worried tone. "The Bronco will make it if the plows have been out, but I'm not sure the planes will be taking off. Call again."

Billie called and repeated the message. "United is still flying the friendly skies. Look, Thad, I'm not going to be upset if we can't get to Austin. I'd kind of like to have Christmas here with just you and the dogs. It seems we're always somewhere else at Christmastime. I can open my present here as well as there. You did get me a present, didn't you?" Billie teased.

"I thought you wanted to see Sawyer. And to see how Susan is progressing. And to check on the Maggie and Rand thing. Not to mention Riley and Cole."

"I do, I do, but I can do that after Christmas. After all, our safety is the most important thing. What d'ya say, let's stay home."

"Lady, did I ever tell you how happy you make me?"

Billie laughed. "I know now. Why didn't you just come out and say you didn't want to go? I'd've understood."

"It's not that I don't want to go; it's that I'd rather stay here. Our tree is up and I want both of us to enjoy it. *Us*, Billie."

"I only said I wanted to go because I thought you wanted to get away from all the politics and pressure up here. We could pretend we're gone, though. Let's just snuggle in. We have plenty of food; leave the Bronco in the garage. There won't be anyone driving by to see our lights, so we're safe. They all think we're going since we've been talking about it for the past month. Better yet, let's disconnect the phone."

"After you call your family."

"Let's do that right now."

"While you do that, I'm going up in the attic to get down my old sled. It's a Flexible Flyer, you know. I'm going to wax the runners tonight and pull you all over the farm tomorrow."

"Really, Thad!" Billie hugged her husband, love shining in her eyes.

"Well, maybe not all over the farm. You have put on a few pounds. We could take turns."

"Already you're wimping out. When you get tired pulling me, we can take a spin on the snowmobiles. I'm so glad we aren't going."

The relief on Billie's face was almost comical. Thad grimaced. "We must be getting out of sync here. Usually, I know what you're thinking and visa versa."

"It's the family, Thad. You know, you feel guilty. But I'm sure they won't even miss us. They'll toast us and then go on about their holiday activities."

"Aren't you being a little hard on them?"

"Not at all. That's the way it is. Go get your sled while I try to call Sawyer. I know she's avoiding me, but I'm going to try."

Adam Jarvis answered the phone. "Merry Christmas, Mrs. Kingsley."

"The same to you, Adam. Is Sawyer there?"

Adam's brief hesitation told Billie the girl was there but wasn't taking any calls. She couldn't call Adam a liar, and she wanted to thrash Sawyer within an inch of her life. Why was she being so stubborn? "Will you give her a message, Adam? Tell her Thad and I won't be going to Sunbridge for the holidays. We're having an awful storm here and we expect the planes will be grounded momentarily. Ask her if she'll call me back so I can wish her a Merry Christmas. Oh, and tell her I sent her gifts ahead to Sunbridge so I wouldn't have to carry them on the plane. Have a happy holiday, Adam."

"You too, Mrs. Kingsley."

Maggie was next on Billie's list. She had just explained the situation and heard Maggie squeal, "Oh, no, Mam, I was so counting on you and Thad! I understand—" when the phone went dead. Billie looked at the receiver in her hand and burst out laughing.

"We're cut off from the world," Billie yelled to Thad, who was up in the attic. "The phone just went dead."

"My God, do you mean it's really just you and me and the old Flex and the dogs?"

"You got it," Billie chortled. "Do you want me to make some popcorn?"

"Hell, no. Go put that lacy green thing on. We'll sit in front of the fire and I'll wax the runners on the sled."

"What are you going to put on?"

"Not my long johns, that's for sure. We haven't made love in front of the fire for a long time."

Billie sprinted up the stairs like a young girl. Life was so good, so wonderful! "Thank you, God," she whispered.

"You really put me on the spot, Sawyer. Your grandmother knew I was lying. I could tell by her voice. Why won't you talk to her?

"You know, I hate going off and leaving you here by yourself. Swear to me that you really are going to Sunbridge so I don't drive myself nuts worrying about you."

"I am going to Sunbridge. For Christmas Eve and Christmas Day. I plan on bringing the boys back with me for a few days. Rand, too, if he can make it."

Adam's heart turned over. Her eyes were too bright, her cheeks too flushed. She really believed what she was saying. "You didn't answer my question about your grandmother," he said gently.

"I didn't want to have to go into the whole thing. Grand understands. It won't be the same without her, but I'm glad she's with Thad. Now, there's a marriage made in heaven."

"She's concerned about you, Sawyer. It's cruel, what you're doing. Does Maggie know you're coming?"

"Of course. I was invited, remember?"

"Sawyer, what if things don't . . . what if . . ."

"You worry too much, Adam. Everything'g going to work out. I've played the game by the book. I didn't call, write, or pester. When Rand sees me and realizes what a mistake he's made, things'll be just fine. We're in love."

You mean *you're* in love! Adam wanted to shout. He knew what was going to happen to her, and it made his guts churn. But this time Sawyer would have to deal with it herself. He wasn't going to be there.

"I can't believe you're taking all that stuff!" Sawyer said in awe. "A man could go to war with less. Didn't you say you were staying only five days?"

"That's what I said, but that was before . . ."

"Before you invited Paula Zachary to join you. I took the call, remember?" She laughed.

"See this little thing? This is what I'm taking to Sunbridge. I know how to pack."

"Know-it-all." Adam sniffed. Secretly, he wondered if he'd packed too much, but he absolutely refused to do laundry while he was on vacation.

Sawyer grinned. "Who's picking you up? A taxi or a truck?"

"Actually, I hired a limo. Paula has quite a bit of stuff herself. Stop being so nosy. I've gotta go. The limo should be here any second now and I said I'd be downstairs."

"I'll carry your skis and your boots. Do you think you can manage the rest?"

"I'm gonna have to, since I'm not about to make two trips. You always were a big help—a pain in the ass, but a help nonetheless," Adam said fondly.

"I hope you have a good time. Think of me when you toast in the New Year."

"I always think of you. New Year's Eve isn't going to make a difference. Make sure you think of me. And I hope it goes the way you want. Say hello to your family. Merry Christmas, Sawyer," Adam said as he kissed her lightly on the cheek. "I left your gift under the tree."

"Yours is in the duffel bag. Don't break a leg now."

The limo pulled up to the curb, and there was the usual confusion as to what went where and Adam telling the driver the best way to go to pick up Paula. Sawyer rolled her eyes at him and grinned.

Then he was gone.

Sawyer walked around the loft, picking up one thing and laying it down, only to pick up something else. Adam's work area was clear, especially neat. The kitchen, too, was neat and tidy, the dishwasher emptied. No crumbs littered the floor. Marble, the cat, lay contentedly under the table.

There was nothing to do. The laundry had been done earlier, washed, dried, and folded. it would be dark soon; maybe she should turn on the tree lights. It was a gorgeous tree. Adam had trekked out to Long Island in a borrowed pickup and lugged the tree all the way back. It was beautiful when it came to life with hundreds of tiny lights. The decorations, Adam said, had been sent to him from Germany by a friend. Adam had so many friends. Thoughtful friends, who never forgot him. She thought about it for a while and decided Adam had a lot of friends because he was a friend. She couldn't even begin to imagine what she would do without him.

Gift. He'd said he left her gift under the tree. Actually,

there were two gifts bearing her name. One would be frivolous and the other, she knew, would be serious. She poked, rattled, and shook the gaily wrapped boxes. She could tell by the puckered Scotch tape that Adam had wrapped them both himself. Store gift wrap never puckered.

Adam hadn't said she couldn't open the gifts. After all, she would be leaving tomorrow and wouldn't be here for Christmas. She really should open them just in case he called while she was at Sunbridge.

Sawyer played a game with herself as darkness invaded the loft. First, with only the twinkling tree miniatures for light, she poured herself a glass of wine and toasted the holiday. Then she made a toast to her future happiness with Rand. She walked all around the tree, admiring it, sipping from her long-stemmed wineglass. There were a lot of gifts underneath. Two days ago the tree skirt had held nothing but a few pine needles. It smelled so good— Scotch pine was her favorite. Rand said he loved Scotch pine best, too. They always had blue spruce at Sunbridge.

Sawyer kept staring at the gifts. She turned on the small brass lamp atop the desk, then dropped to her knees and sorted through the presents: To Adam from Nick. To Adam from Blake. To Adam from George and Hugh. To Adam from the gang. To Adam from Mom and Dad. To Adam from Joan. To Adam from Steve, Bill, and Carmen. To Adam from Alice and Ed.

So many friends who thought enough of him to drop by with presents! Sawyer wondered if he'd bought presents for all these people. Her gifts, she noticed, were a little to the side. She finished her wine and poured another glass. On hands and knees she scrambled to the bookshelf in the corner, selected a Christmassy-sounding audio cassette and popped it into the player. Now it seemed like Christmas.

The oddly shaped box that didn't rattle was her first choice. Even as a kid she'd always gone for the biggest first, knowing full well the best was in the smallest package. Carefully she opened the box and stared down at her present. Her very own Cabbage Patch doll! The adoption papers read, Willow Carmena. Wait till Adam opened his duffel and found Willow Carmena's twin, Cornell Damian. She shrieked with laughter.

Spent, she leaned against the sofa and opened her other gift, the small one, the serious one. It was a book of poetry simply titled *New Beginning*. Sawyer turned the pages, pleased to see that the poetry was Adam's; she'd recognize it anywhere. Dear God, all the poems were for her. How much time and effort must have gone into this book! It was bound beautifully in rich Moroccan leather with her name embossed on the inside. As she leafed through the slim volume, a small card slipped out.

Merry Christmas, Sawyer,
    I didn't know what to get you for Christmas, but I wanted it to be special from me to you. I wanted to give you part of myself because you won't accept the whole of me. Enjoy my humble effort, and if you ever tell anyone I gave you this, I'll deny it.

All my love
Adam.

Sawyer wept, tears of sorrow, of anger, of remorse. If only they could be tears of happiness. "Oh, Adam," she sobbed, "I do love you, but not the way you want!"

{{{{{{{{ CHAPTER SEVENTEEN }}}}}}}}

Riley woke suddenly from a horrible dream. Sweat soaked the sheet he'd wrapped tightly about him in sleep. His arms and legs flailed as he came to grips with the reality of a new day. The dream had been so real. He'd awakened from surgery; a nurse handed him a mirror. Heart pounding, he'd looked for the tiny sutures around his eyes that would make him as American as his father. There were no sutures and no Westernized eyes. If anything, his eyes were more lidded, more oblique than ever. He rolled over, burrowing deeper into the covers. Having his eyes Americanized was his dream and his nightmare.

Christmas Eve. One of the happiest days of the year in America. His room looked dim, grayish and dull. It had to be mid-morning. He leaped out of bed and whipped open the lacy curtains. Snow! Aunt Maggie said it always snowed at Sunbridge for Christmas. The overhead light went on and both lamps were lit. Riley dived into his clothes, gave his face a skimpy wash and his perfect white teeth an even skimpier cleaning. The fine stubble could wait till later. He wasn't hairy like Cole, and it made him self-conscious. Cole, he knew, *had* to shave every day, whereas Riley could do it once a week, and even then it wasn't necessary. His legs and chest were also free of the fine curly furring that bloomed on Cole. The girls teased him in the summer, but he'd accepted it good-naturedly, saying he'd just been waxed. And at least he had a delicious—according to Kelly Jensen—full head of wavy black hair. He grinned as he brushed it into place.

Sawyer was supposed to be here by noon. Rand was to have arrived before breakfast, Aunt Maggie had said. Tree trimming was set for late afternoon, fiveish or so with cocktails, and then there was to be a six-course dinner followed by carols in the huge drawing room. Midnight service in Crystal City and then gift opening. He could hardly wait.

The breakfast table was full. He took his place amid smiles and light teasing about being a sleepyhead and slugabed. He grinned as he piled his plate with sausage and eggs, then crunched on toast as he looked around the table. Rand, fresh from an early flight, was busy buttering a piece of toast. Aunt Amelia and Cary were bickering about whether she should go out in the snow or not. Cole had just finished gulping the rest of his orange juice and now stood up, throwing his napkin onto the table. Riley was relieved to hear his cousin say he was going into Crystal City to finish up his last-minute shopping.

Suddenly, everyone was talking at once, and all the conversation was directed at him. Everyone laughed and he flushed.

"We'll back that all up and start over," Cary said kindly, noting the boy's flushed face. "Amelia?"

"I was wondering, Riley, if you don't have plans for the rest of the morning, would you come over to the house and shovel the driveway? The weathermen are predicting sleet later, and I'd like to salt down the steps and the walkway. Cary has to go over to the site and check on the gas lines and then pick up Miss Farrell."

"Sure I'll do it. I love the snow."

"Good, that's settled. Amelia is like a bee with one wing this morning," Cary said fondly as he patted her on the shoulder. "Susan, you're next."

"It's no big deal. I just wanted to know if you'd carry my gifts downstairs. Some of them are rather large and awkward. I'm not too graceful these days. Would you mind?"

"I'll do it when I finish breakfast," Riley said cheerfully.

"I just wanted to remind you to call your grandfather later on, and I'd like to wish him a happy holiday," Maggie said. "I know it's not a holiday for him, but he is so aware of ours, I thought it would be nice."

"I won't forget. I was going to wait till about eight o'clock this evening. It'll be Christmas morning in Japan and the old one will just be rising. Did he send presents?" Riley asked anxiously.

Maggie laughed. "A truckload. It took United Parcel an hour just to unload. It took Steven another hour to carry the packages indoors. I'd say he didn't forget you or anyone at Sunbridge." There was an odd tremor in Maggie's voice. Riley suspected it had something to do with the fact that Rand was sitting next to her.

"The old one always played Santa Claus at his newspaper for Christmas," he said. "A lot of the employees were American. He got a kick out of it. He likes to exchange presents."

"Rand, how was—the weather in England when you left?" Susan asked nervously.

"Nasty." He hesitated. "I tried to call Jerome before I left, but the phone was disconnected."

Susan's heart thumped. Disconnected? Why? Despite the resentment she felt, regardless of his rejection of their child, Susan's feeling toward her husband were ambiguous. More than ever, she wanted someone to share this experience with—Maggie and Amelia simply weren't enough. A child should know its own father, and that father should provide a home for his family. Even if that father was Jerome, damn him.

"Well, I have to be going," Cary said, standing up and bending over to kiss Amelia on the cheek. "I should be back by mid-afternoon. Nice to see you again, Rand. Maggie, is there anything I can bring back from Crystal City for you?"

"No, it's all under control. Thanks for asking, though. Please, drive carefully; the roads are bad."

"'Bye, darling, see you later," Amelia called gaily.

"You be careful driving, too. Don't forget, Eileen will be with me."

"Darling, how could any of us forget?" Amelia said coolly. "You've mentioned it at least a dozen times."

"Who's Eileen?" Rand asked after the door closed behind Cary.

"The girl who works in Cary's office," replied Maggie, glancing apprehensively at Amelia. "It seems she'll be alone for the holiday and Cary asked if she could spend Christmas with us."

"Excuse me, all," Amelia said stiffly. "I want to call down to the barn and have them bring up some rock salt. Riley, dress warmly and see if you can't find the snow shovel. It used to hang inside the cellarway. Is it still there, Maggie?"

"As far as I know. Drive slowly. We'll keep the fires burning and have a toddy ready for you when you get back. Is there any last-minute wrapping you want me to do?"

"No, I've got it all covered. You'll be busy enough entertaining Sawyer when she arrives." Amelia looked at her pointedly. "She's due soon, isn't she?"

"Around noon, I believe." Maggie smiled and hoped her breezy tone would drive the disapproving look from Amelia's face. "Have fun, you two! See you later."

Susan excused herself right after Amelia and Riley left. There was an awkward silence, and then Rand spoke.

"It appears we're alone," he said quietly. "You're acting like a cat on a hot griddle. In other words, sweet, you're feeling guilty."

"Am I?" Maggie whispered. "I guess it's because I am."

"For God's sake, Maggie. We went through all this. You told me just last week on the phone you were your own person and you were going to do what you wanted, and that included me. Have you changed your mind?"

"No . . . yes . . . oh, I don't know. I so wanted this

Christmas to be perfect. First, Mam can't make it. Amelia disapproves of us and is acting as though I stole her jewels. Susan is avoiding me. Cole refuses to do more than look at me, and when our eyes do meet, his are full of disgust. Riley is torn. Sawyer will be here soon. My God, I feel like a thief. Please, you have to try and understand."

"I do understand. I shouldn't have come. It was a mistake, Maggie. I don't like playing games."

"Neither do I," Maggie said, so quietly Rand had to strain to hear her.

"I think I'm in love with you, Maggie."

"Don't say that. Not now."

"It's Sawyer, isn't it? The rest you can handle."

"I'm not sure. You know how I feel. My God, yes, I want you. I've caused so much hurt in this family I can't cause any more. You have to understand my position."

"No thumbing your nose at them and happy ever after?" Rand asked quietly.

"Maybe I could come to England.... We ... could ..."

"Goddammit, Maggie, I'm not talking about some cheap affair. I'm talking about you and me. Us. Our lives."

"The others ... they'll think ..."

"Who the devil cares what they think? We have to think about what's best for us. They'll all come to accept it. Don't make this more difficult than it is now."

"I do care about the others. My son, Mam, Riley ..."

"What about Sawyer?" Rand asked coldly. "That's what this is all about, you know. Admit it. Mother versus daughter. I'm in the middle."

Maggie's face closed. "That must make you feel pretty powerful. Two women in love with you."

"Sawyer is in love with an image. I wasn't sure till now that you care for me. Is the word love so hard to say?"

"For me it is. I never had any. I'm not even sure I know what love is. The concept of love, maybe. I do feel something for you I've never felt for anyone else. But you're wrong about Sawyer. Sawyer loves you with her whole heart. For Sawyer it was now and forever. That kind of love. How could you not have seen that?" Maggie asked angrily.

"I did see it, damn it. Don't jam home the guilt, Maggie. I was Sawyer's first love. That will always be special to her. I didn't love her enough. It has to be mutual or it doesn't work. You have to realize that I was a father image to Sawyer. I believe that in my heart. You have to believe it, too. You had the same kind of problem with your own father."

Tears burned Maggie's eyes. Sawyer, always Sawyer. "Could we just put all this on hold, get through Christmas, and then work it out?" she asked, swallowing hard. "I really can't deal with it today."

"Right now I feel if I don't take you in my arms, I won't be able to take another breath," Rand said hoarsely.

"Right now if I don't get up from this table, I will let you do exactly that, and then I'll end up hating both of us. This is the way it has to be ... for now. Forgive me," Maggie whispered as she ran from the room.

Only in her own room with the door closed behind her did she let go. Why me? Why is it always me? I didn't lead him on. I didn't set out to snatch him from Sawyer. It just happened. I'm sorry. I can't change feelings. Why do I have to be the one who has to give everything up? Why does Sawyer get it all?

Maggie watched as the snow swirled about the tree-tops. She'd seen enough Texas storms to know this one was just about over. The snow was fine, powdery, perfect for skiing. There must be at least six inches on the ground. The drifts on the north end of the house were up to the windows on the first floor. As a child she and Susan had jumped and played snow angel in them. How long ago that was!

Something churned inside Maggie. A need to confide, to talk, to seek answers to her problems. Susan was besieged with her own worries right now, and Amelia, while loving, was disapproving. Mam? She could give it a try.

Quickly, she dialed the familiar number in Vermont, only to be told the power and telephone lines were out due to the storm. Service would most likely be restored by late afternoon. But that was too late. She needed to talk *now*.

In the blink of an eye, Maggie had on wool slacks and her heavy parka. She found her boots by the kitchen door in the boot tray.

"If anyone asks where I am, you don't know," Maggie told Martha as she pulled on her boots over heavy socks. She almost laughed at the startled expression in the woman's eyes. "It's uphill most of the way. The drifts are on this side. Look, it's almost stopped snowing." Before leaving the kitchen, she plucked a bright red poinsettia from a plant on the kitchen counter.

The gravestones looked desolate with their mantles of snow. Mittened hands dug a hole in the snow. Already the poinsettia was frozen; she propped it up with scoops of snow. It looked like blood—her blood. "Merry Christmas, Pap," she said softly. "I think I'm just going to wing this one."

Maggie returned the way she'd come. She placed her boots neatly in the back door tray, hung her parka on the wooden coatrack near the back door. Martha held out a cup of coffee for her, which she accepted gratefully as she made her way up the back stairway to the nursery. She felt better. At least she was in control of her emotions now. Fresh air had a way of clearing the head.

She didn't see him at first simply because she didn't expect anyone to be in the room.

"That was a damn fool thing to do," Rand said coolly.

"Yes, I suppose it was," Maggie replied just as coolly. "However, it was something I needed to do. I usually do what I want. I'm all grown-up now."

"Being grown-up doesn't necessarily mean you always make the right decisions. We need to talk, Maggie."

"No. Not now."

"When? Tomorrow, next week, next month, a year from now? When? Give me a time and a date."

"I can't do that. Don't pressure me, Rand. This isn't any easier for me than it is for you. I'm going to have to handle it my way, and you're going to have to handle it my way, too."

"You really mean it, don't you?" Rand asked incredulously.

"Yes, I do." Maggie's gaze was level, defying Rand to pursue the matter. When the door closed behind him, her shoulders slumped.

Her cheeks were as rosy as if she'd dusted them with crimson rouge. Biting wind or . . . Rand?

Rand marched downstairs to the beat of a drummer he'd never heard before. He headed straight for the study and the portable bar.

Susan looked up from the magazine she was reading. "A bit early, isn't it?" she asked gently.

"Early, late. What the hell difference does it make?"

"A lot, if you really care about Maggie. If she sees you hitting the sauce because you can't handle . . . whatever, she might—I'm not saying she will but she *might*—decide to take a drink herself."

Rand was a straight-up two-finger whiskey man. His hold on the bottle was tight, the knuckles stretched taut. He put the bottle back in the rack and picked up the newspaper.

Susan sighed. "Don't worry," she said. "I'm not going to lecture and preach. That's the one thing I don't do. I really believe I've become a fatalist."

Rand nodded absently. His innards were roiling. He glanced at his watch. Allowing two hours for bad weather, road conditions, and other acts of God, Sawyer should be arriving within the hour. He almost wished he were back in England.

"So, what did you get everyone for Christmas?" Susan asked.

Rand's teeth dug into his lower lip. "What you really want to know is what I got Maggie and Sawyer."

"You must have had a tough time selecting the gifts that would say something, yet say nothing. Men are always so conscientious that way. One gift for commitment and one for. . . . What's the word for discarded?"

"Knock it off, Susan. I've had about enough."

"I'm sorry. I don't know why I . . .Forget it.

"It's almost Christmas Eve. Peace on earth, goodwill to men, right?"

"If you say so." Rand sat down in the chair opposite Susan and picked up one of the newspapers from a nearby coffee table. "Have you decided on a name for the baby yet?" he asked idly.

"As a matter of fact, I have. If it's a boy, it's going to be called Moss. If it's a girl, it will be Jessica. What's the news in the paper?"

"It's full of peace on earth, goodwill to men. What else do you want to know?"

"Not a thing," Susan said, going back to her magazine.

It was three o'clock when Cole returned to the house, his arms laden with red-ribboned boxes. Amelia and Riley arrived fifteen minutes later, each going their separate way. Maggie was halfway down the stairs when the doorbell rang. Susan entered the foyer from the dining room, opened the door, and immediately squealed with delight.

"Sawyer!"

Maggie's stomach heaved as she forced a smile to her lips and continued down the stairs.

Mother and daughter locked glances for just an instant "Merry Christmas, Sawyer.

"Merry Christmas, Maggie. Where shall I put all these?" Sawyer asked, indicating two huge shopping bags. "The other packages arrived, didn't they?"

"Yesterday. I took off the wrapping paper and string. They're in the hall closet."

"That was nice of you. Thanks. Where is everyone?"

Maggie waved her hands about. "We're having eggnog

shortly and then tree trimming. Come along into the study. Susan, where are you going?"

"Where I go every ten minutes, the bathroom. Merry Christmas, Sawyer."

As Sawyer hugged Susan, her eyes met Maggie's for the second time.

"I guess you know your grandmother won't be here for Christmas," Maggie said, leading the way into the study.

"I know. Christmas won't be the same without her."

"We're going to make the best of it. Rand's here. He got in early this morning. And Cary will be bringing his office girl." Maggie looked at her watch. "About now, as a matter of fact. We're a houseful."

Rand. In just a few seconds she would see him. Sawyer's mind suddenly went blank. All the rehearsed phrases, all the practiced smiles in the mirror, deserted her. She ached. Maggie looked so confident, so self-assured, that Sawyer's heart started to pound. If it was a fight Maggie wanted, a fight was what she would get. She set her jaw determinedly.

Out of the corner of her eye Maggie assessed her daughter, calculating the cost of her outfit with a practiced eye. Oscar de la Renta slacks fitted into knee-high Bally boots, both in the same shade of taupe. Autumn haze mink coat, styled with wide shoulders and wide leather belt. A matching hat that swallowed Sawyer's golden-blond hair. And at her neck a blazing red-orange silk scarf for that right touch of pizzazz. Chic and fashionable were the only words to describe her.

"Rand, darling!" Sawyer cried breathlessly. She ran to him, throwing her arms around him. She drew back immediately and stared into his eyes, frightened by what she saw. She kissed him lightly on the lips and linked her arm through his. "Come, sit here by me and tell me everything that's happened since July. I should strangle you for ignoring me these past . . ." There was a slight pause. "Weeks. Don't tell me you're still angry with me."

"I could never be angry with you, Sawyer," Rand said gently.

"Tell me I look lovely. You always tell me that," Sawyer teased. "I spent a fortune on this outfit and one for tomorrow. I want to dazzle you. Maggie always said when you're in love with a man, you have to dazzle him. Isn't that right, Maggie?"

Maggie forced a laugh. "I do seem to recall saying something like that. I think Mam was the one who said it to me, or maybe it was Aunt Amelia." She was too gorgeous for words, this daughter of hers. And somewhere between July and now, she'd learned how to fight. Maggie literally backed up a step. "What would you like to drink?"

"Same as Rand, two fingers of whiskey straight up. The things this man taught me, you wouldn't believe. Oh, darling, I'm so happy to see you! I have such wonderful plans for us. By the way, I'm taking the boys back to New York the day after Christmas. Please say you'll join us. I've arranged to take a week's vacation. We can celebrate the New Year together."

Rand glanced at Maggie, then turned away at the look in her eyes. Fortunately, he was saved from replying by the arrival of Cary and Eileen Farrell. Their entrance, directly behind Susan's, was exuberant and filled with Christmas cheer. He could feel Sawyer stiffen at his side as Maggie made the introductions.

"English nobility!" Eileen gushed. "What a Christmas this has turned out to be." Maggie watched with interest as Eileen settled herself beside Rand and immediately began conversing. Sawyer on one side, Eileen on the other; Susan and she directly opposite. Opposing generations.

"Where's my wife?" Cary asked enthusiastically.

"Upstairs. She just got in a few minutes before Sawyer. You have exactly thirty minutes to get back down here for drinks before tree trimming."

"Yes, ma'am." Cary grinned. "Take care of my girl here."

"You can count on it," Maggie said, and settled her gaze on Miss Farrell. She decided the woman was a man-chaser. It was obvious in the way she gushed over Rand, the familiarity with which she conducted the conversation, and the fact that she was all but ignoring her hostess. Eileen's attention automatically homed in on the male species, while her treatment of other women was apparently offhand and damn near condescending. Maggie bristled. Just what Sunbridge needed for the holidays, as if there weren't enough going on already.

Cary and Amelia made their entrance. Cary had changed from a business suit to casual light tan slacks, which fit with tailored perfection, and a White Stag ski sweater of softest mohair. But it was Amelia who came under Eileen's scrutiny, and Amelia knew it, had expected it. She'd deliberately elected to wear an understated little number by Nippon—a bright red silk shot through with silver threads, whose skirt swung easily with every step. The newly fashionable wide shoulders were emphasized in a long-sleeved shirt jacket that flattered her neck and hipline; its short skirt revealed one of Amelia's best assets, her long, gracefully turned legs.

Immediately, Eileen rose to her feet to cross the room, offering her hand in greeting. "Mrs. Assante, how nice to see you again."

"You remember Eileen, Amelia," Cary prompted.

"Of course." Amelia smiled congenially. "How could I forget? Merry Christmas, Eileen." She linked her arm once again through Cary's for much-needed moral support. Her dress and shoes cost more than half of Eileen's wardrobe, but it couldn't substitute for thick shoulder-length natural blond hair and a dewy complexion. Damn! She wished Billie were here. It was far from flattering to be an entire generation older than some of the women in the room and two generations older than the rest. "Cary, I'm going to offer your services as bartender. You don't mind, do you, Maggie? Cary makes the best hot toddies. Order up, everyone," she said with forced gaiety. "Cary is a specialist."

It seemed to Rand that Sawyer was at his heels for the entire afternoon. She was there when he lit the fire and again when he added more logs. It was to him that she handed each ornament to be hung on the tree, all the time chatting vivaciously, sharing memories of past Christmases. Susan and Rand also had memories in common: living in the townhouse on Halston Square, vacations in the country, the petty fights and arguments that all young people have. Amelia and Rand reminisced about wartime England and one particular Christmas when their pet dog had had puppies.

It seemed to Maggie that she was the only one without memories to share.

Cole and Riley joined in for the tree trimming, and together with Sawyer they made a happy threesome, joking and laughing and singing Christmas carols to records. Maggie couldn't remember ever seeing her son quite so happy. It was Sawyer who made the difference. Sawyer could give Cole something she couldn't. Was it that way with Rand, too?

They all shared a late dinner, carrying their plates into the living room to eat near the tree. Susan sat at the grand piano, striking familiar chords from Handel's "Messiah." They all chanted the "Hallelujah" chorus—Eileen, surprisingly, taking the high octave soprano. Cary divided his attention between Eileen and his wife, seemingly oblivious to the look in Amelia's eyes or the grim line of her mouth.

"Perhaps you'd like to go up and lie down for an hour or so, Mrs. Assante. You look tired," Eileen was heard to say.

"Do I?" Amelia challenged, her eyes burning coals of defiance. Eileen smiled and turned away quickly.

Maggie, witnessing this exchange, deftly interrupted when she saw Amelia's arm reach out to grasp the younger woman's shoulder. "We should all be thinking about getting into town for the midnight service, don't you think, Amelia? There's quite a few of us, so we'll have to arrange the cars. Why don't you and Cary take Riley and Susan in your car? Cole and I can take Rand and Sawyer, Eileen, and Martha in the station wagon."

She saw the relief in Amelia's eyes and realized her aunt was near the breaking point. However, Eileen was right: she did look tired; exhausted, as a matter of fact. Her sleek brunette hair had flopped forward onto her brow. She was pale, and the bright red of her silk dress made her skin look sallow. And Maggie knew Amelia's feet had to be killing her in those four-inch heels.

"The station wagon is behind all the others, Maggie," Sawyer said sweetly. "Why don't Rand and I take the boys, and you can use your own car to take Eileen and Martha."

"That sounds like a fine idea," Amelia said hurriedly. "I'll just run upstairs for my coat. Cary, why don't you come with me? I want you to wear something warmer." She could hear the edge of panic in her voice. If Maggie hadn't interrupted, she would have clawed Eileen's face to shreds. She had to get control of herself. She'd had too much to drink and too little to eat. Fear and jealousy had knotted her innards. Get control, she repeated over and over.

All the way to the church Maggie was silent. With one deft stroke Sawyer had succeeded in keeping Rand and both boys to herself while she, Maggie, rode to church with a housekeeper and a stranger.

Maggie's mood was much uplifted by the time she returned to Sunbridge. The church service had been lovely, the choir heavenly. Meeting and greeting friends and acquaintances; Rand maneuvering to sit beside her in church. The candlelight, the music, the whisper of softly falling snow outside the stained glass windows, peace on earth and goodwill.

She shed tears for those who were not there this Christmas and held Riley's hand tight, knowing his thoughts were on the father he'd never known and his beautiful mother, Otami.

Maggie tried not to think of Sawyer, who was sitting

on the far side of Rand, sharing a hymn book and helpfully turning the pages. When all their voices were uplifted in song, Maggie caught a glimpse of Sawyer's lovely face, radiant with the moment and with being so near to Rand. Her daughter, her own child. They'd been so far apart for so many years, but now there was Cole and Rand and Riley. How could two women share their men?

Maggie's eyes closed, a crystal tear shining on her cheek. What kind of woman was she to do this to Sawyer, to even entertain the thought of being in love with Rand? She'd had her chance at happiness when she'd married Cranston; shouldn't Sawyer have her chance? And Rand, what this must be doing to him. . . . Or was she allowing herself to be taken in again? Perhaps Rand had been a bachelor for so long that the idea of marriage was frightening to him. Perhaps he really loved Sawyer but was unable to commit himself. What if he was simply using her—Maggie—to drive a wedge between himself and Sawyer?

Maggie looked up at Rand, saw his finely chiseled profile, the gentle sweep of his brow, the soft blond hair that fell over his forehead. And then he turned, his chocolate-brown eyes meeting hers, and they were filled with a longing that told her of his love. For an instant she allowed herself to be filled with the meaning of his gaze, feeling her own emotions brim. No, Rand would never use her; he'd never use anyone to suit his own purposes. Not this man who had taken her in his arms and made love to her. The man who had whispered, "Maggie, my Maggie," and had touched her soul with his own. She could feel Rand still looking at her when she herself had turned away.

The Christmas mood prevailed during the drive back to Sunbridge. This time Riley and Cole had squeezed into the car with Maggie, Eileen, and Martha. Maggie knew it was a kind of conspiracy to leave Rand and Sawyer alone, but she didn't care. She trusted Rand, even if it meant she might be hurt. Her voice carried with the others as they sang all the way home.

* * *

"We draw lots to see who hands out the gifts," Maggie said gaily when they were once again around the Christmas tree at Sunbridge, warming themselves with hot chocolate and rum toddies. "Whoever gets the blank paper plays Santa."

Cary won the honor and beamed with pride. Amelia, Santa's helper, glowed beneath her husband's attention as he teased that she shouldn't look only for the presents labeled with her own name.

Eileen's eyes burned as she watched gift after gift happily bestowed. She was pleased but stunned that there were so many gifts for her. The Coleman family wasn't only rich; it was generous.

By the time the last present had been opened and admired by all, it was almost dawn. Eileen felt as if she were in the bargain basement of a huge department store. Stereos for the boys; someone had received a hand-tooled saddle—the Amerasian boy, she thought. Adidas sneakers replete with little calculators that measured distance, speed, calories burned. Jewelry galore. Cary had given his wife an expensive serpentine gold chain from which dangled an eye-bruising diamond. Perfume, designer clothes, silk scarves, and Gucci bags. Golf clubs and riding crops; Maggie's son got his own full-scale video game. Even Susan's unborn child received toys and cute little shirts and baby booties that made the momma-to-be squeal in delight.

"It always seems like such a letdown when all the presents are opened." Maggie smiled wearily. "Such wonderful presents."

"And now there's this mess to clean up." Riley yawned.

Eileen laughed. "All that fancy gift wrap and ribbon cost more than all my Christmases put together. I'll clean it up; it's the least I can do to thank you all for your lovely gifts. I never expected anything; being here was more than enough."

"It was our pleasure," Amelia said generously. "The vase you gave Cary and me is exquisite."

Eileen dropped to her knees and began to roll the papers together. Rand joined her. "Go on to bed, everyone. Eileen and I will have this mess cleaned in a minute."

"Rand!" Sawyer exclaimed. "Eileen is our guest; we can't have her doing chores. I'll do it. You go along to bed, Eileen," she said in a no-nonsense voice, actually grabbing Eileen's arm and lifting her to her feet.

"Yes, come along," Amelia said sweetly. "Leave it to the *family*. You, too, Maggie, you've had an exhausting day."

Maggie found herself with the rest of the clan as they climbed the stairs to their respective rooms. She knew what Amelia was doing, and there wasn't a damn thing she could do about it . . . or wanted to do.

When they were alone in the living room, with only the light from the Christmas tree twinkling against the darkness, Sawyer turned to Rand and said softly, "I thought I'd never get you to myself. I've been waiting all day for this moment."

Rand wished her tone weren't so intimate, so seductive. He knew where this conversation was going to lead. On the way home from church Sawyer had tried to fill him with memories of things they'd done together, of what they'd been to each other. In the car he'd been able to head her off by inducing her to sing Christmas carols and talk about Riley and Cole. Now he was trapped . . . and perhaps it was just as well.

"Thank you for the wonderful gift," she was saying. "I'm so pleased you remembered my passion for bracelets, but really, you were too extravagant. Do you know I wear the one you gave me for my birthday all the time? I love the earrings you gave Maggie. Do you think she'll wear four-leaf clovers? Are they significant somehow?"

Rand was tired; it had been a long and difficult day. His nerves were stretched to the breaking point, and he felt like a criminal, guilty and condemned. But where was the crime in loving Maggie? "Sawyer, you must listen to what I have to say. We're going to talk, and this time you're going to listen and *hear*. I don't want to seem cruel, but somewhere you've gotten the idea that we can just pick up where we left off before the July holiday. It's not that way and I'm sorry."

Sawyer rocked back on her heels, a tangle of ribbon threaded between her still fingers. She tried to focus on his face, saw the way the tree lights reflected in his hair.

"I care for you, Sawyer, very much, but what I feel isn't love, at least not the kind of love your looking for. I don't love you enough. I regret that."

"Stop!" Sawyer clamped her hands over her ears. "I don't want to listen!"

He grasped her hands, pulling them away from her ears, holding them tightly against his chest. "You've got to listen! You're becoming obsessed with the idea that I'll come around and find that I've loved you all along and that I'll always love you. Don't do this to yourself, Sawyer, and for God's sake, don't do it to the rest of us!"

She seemed frozen in time, hearing but not believing, incapable of believing. "You loved me once..." she began.

"Yes, and I still love you, but not the way you want." He gentled his voice, loving her and pitying her at the same time. She had to set him free, him and Maggie.

"Last time you said we were at opposite ends of life. That you didn't want a family. You wanted to settle down to a simpler life. All right, then, no children, no work, just each other. I want only you, Rand. Nothing else means anything, only you."

Rand was shaking his head, lost in the futility of it all. "No, Sawyer. What I told you then was the truth; that's how I feel about where I am in my life. But a simpler truth is that I can't love you the way you need to be loved. The way you *deserve* to be loved. Can you understand? It's not enough for you and it's not enough for me."

She raised her eyes, holding him with her gaze. It was as if she were delving into his head, demanding answers for questions she couldn't ask. "It's not supposed to be this way. I was so sure, so certain—" Her voice broke; a shuddering sob, silent and terrifying, shook her.

Rand wanted to reach out for her, to hold her against him, to give comfort where none could be found. "Don't do this, Sawyer; please don't do this."

"You said that before. Only you said not to do it to the rest of you. Who's that, Rand? Who else am I hurting besides myself?"

"I only meant that something like this could break the family in two. I know you don't want that."

"You know what I want. I guess I made a fool of myself again. I thought time and distance would've changed your mind. I know now I was wrong. But I need you to tell me something first." Sawyer choked back a sob. "I need to hear you say there's nothing between you and Maggie. Tell me you aren't having an affair with my mother." When there was no answer to her entreaty, her eyes filled with tears. "I think I could take anything but that. I can't believe you'd betray me like this."

"Sawyer, it's not a betrayal. Why won't you accept that what we had wasn't strong enough?"

There was a wild thing beating in Sawyer's breast. Words, all the wrong words. Adam had known. Even she had known. Hearing it again was like a death sentence, one she could not accept. "Apparently it wasn't, since you couldn't wait to jump into my mother's bed," she cried hoarsely. "My God! Doesn't she have any decency?"

"Sawyer, it wasn't like that. What can I say to make you understand?"

"Why don't you ask what will make me forgive you, because I understand all right, damn right I understand! I know what she is even if you don't. I'm sorry for you, Rand, terribly sorry." She fought her way to her feet, hampered by the empty boxes and cartons, the snarls of ribbons and acres of shredded paper. Only in the privacy of her room did she let the tears flow; quiet, hateful tears.

Rand sat with his head in his hands for a very long time. When the daylight, bright from the reflection of the snow, penetrated the draperies, he hefted himself to his feet and began to clear away the litter. He made four trips to the back service porch, where he piled the hefty sacks of trash neatly one on top of the other. He was hurting and he wanted to be comforted.

He wanted Maggie.

{{{{{{{{ CHAPTER EIGHTEEN }}}}}}}}

Christmas Day was the horror Rand dreaded. He thanked God untold times for the boys and for Eileen, who kept things going. Neighbors visited with traditional good cheer, and Riley and Cole's friends livened things up with a spontaneous party, dancing to records and making a pleasant din amid the silence. Sawyer joined the young people, her laughter strained and her face a bit too pink from Cary's hot toddies. Maggie, ever watchful, knew what must have happened. Amelia, knowing nothing but her jealousy of Eileen Farrell, stuck close to her husband. Susan lay down for a long afternoon nap and finally asked to have her dinner sent to her room. Only Cary, oblivious to everything except the holiday fun and the exuberance of the youngsters, enjoyed himself.

It was four o'clock in the morning the day after Christmas when Cole found Sawyer downstairs in the living room, her head buried in her arms as she lay facedown on one of the sofas. On the floor within reach was an empty decanter of Scotch and a toppled glass.

Cole knew an overwhelming sense of helplessness. What could he do to help her? All day she'd been too bright, like a bulb just before it burns out. She hadn't told him what was wrong, but it hadn't been hard to guess, seeing the distance she'd suddenly put between herself and Rand when she'd been falling all over him on Christmas Eve.

Right now he had to get her upstairs and into the shower. Somehow she had to be sober and fit to travel by seven in the morning. But he couldn't do it alone.

Riley woke at Cole's touch and sat up groggily. His first thought was something had happened to his grandfather. "Say again?"

"I said I need your help. Sawyer's downstairs and she's dead drunk. If we don't do something, neither one of us will be going to New York. Hustle your ass, Riley, and get downstairs. Do you know how to make coffee?"

"No, do you?"

"No, but she needs it to sober up."

"Hey, Cole, you know what you learned in school. Nothing sobers you up, not coffee or food or anything, only time!"

"That's exactly what we don't have. We've got to be leaving here in three hours! Now hustle!" he hissed. "We don't have to get her sober enough to drive, only to get her on her feet and moving."

Riley grabbed his terry robe and followed Cole down the stairs.

"Let's get her into the kitchen. You take one arm and I'll take the other. Between us we'll figure out how to work the percolator. She's so drunk it won't matter how it tastes."

"It might make her sick. That's what happened to you."

"Yeah, at least she'll puke up the booze in her stomach before it hits her bloodstream. I learned *that* in school, too. Meanwhile, you got any better ideas?" Cole snapped as he gently took Sawyer under the arm in a firm grip.

Sawyer was roused enough by the manhandling to mutter, "Let me alone. Let me sleep." Determinedly, they dragged her into the kitchen.

"It might help if you'd tell me what's going on," Riley said as he tried to hold Sawyer erect on the chair. "I've got a right to know."

"Yeah, I guess you do," Cole said grudgingly as he filled the electric percolator and dumped coffee into the strainer basket. "I think Rand's got something going with my mother. I'm pretty sure of it. The bottom line is he dumped Sawyer."

"That was in July. Why'd she get drunk now?"

"I think she thought they could patch it up. I just found her like this a little while ago. And if we both want to go to New York, we better fix her up quick."

For the next two hours both boys badgered, cajoled, and walked Sawyer around the kitchen. When her insides ripped loose, Cole held her head over the sink and Riley steadied her.

"I'm going to kill both of you for this," Sawyer sputtered as Cole doused her entire head in lukewarm water.

"You told me if I made an ass out of myself, I damn well better be ready to take the consequences. This is your consequence. We're gonna get you upstairs and you can change your clothes. You've got exactly forty-five minutes to get ready and be downstairs. You got that?"

"Miserable, rotten cretins. I'll lose you in New York. I'll starve you!"

"He's not worth it!" Cole cried vehemently.

"Just shut the hell up. I'm all right now. I can walk by myself. It wasn't necessary to wet my head."

"Wear a hat," Riley suggested.

"Riley, get your gear and stow it by the front door," Cole ordered. "The car will be out front by seven. I'm packed. Once we get her in her room, I'm going back to clean up the kitchen. Watch her."

"Who put you in charge?" Sawyer demanded. "You sound like a goddamn drill sergeant."

"When the first in command falters, the second in command takes over. So move it! And be quiet."

Riley opened Sawyer's door and shoved her inside. "I have to get my bags and get dressed. I'll be right back. Can you manage?"

"I can manage. I'll be ready. What are we doing about saying good-bye to my hostess?"

"I thought you said good-bye last night. I did. Aunt Maggie said she was sleeping in. I guess Cole did the same thing."

"You're right. I'm just a bit foggy. Do what you have to do."

Sawyer snapped the latch on her bag and looked around to see if she'd forgotten anything. She was bundling her damp hair into a knot on top of her head when the door opened. Maggie stood in the doorway.

"If you're here to gloat, do it quickly. It's almost time to leave," Sawyer said flatly. "I want you to know something before I leave because I won't ever be coming back. All those years when you were so rotten, I found excuses for you. I used to cry myself to sleep saying over and over, 'Tomorrow she'll write,' or 'Tomorrow she'll call.' You never did. You simply didn't give a damn. I feel sorry for Cole. At least I had Grand to care. And you know what, Maggie? You deserve to see all your chickens come home to roost. I hope I never have to see you again."

Maggie's insides crumbled. She listened and knew she deserved everything Sawyer said. But it didn't make it any more bearable. "I thought you had more guts, Sawyer," she said. "I'd hoped you were a fighter, a survivor like me. I was wrong. Good-bye."

Sawyer stared at the closed door. Guts. Be a fighter, a survivor like her. No thanks, Mother, not if it means being like you.

Cole raced up the stairs, taking them three at a time. As he rounded the corner of the wide upper hallway, he met Riley. "Where's Sawyer?"

"She's almost ready. She told me to get lost," Riley muttered.

"That's probably the best advice you'll ever get," Cole answered coldly.

"I've had enough of you, Cole! Get off my back. You want to start something, now's as good a time as any."

"I'm not afraid of you. I'll take you on, but some other time. First, I want to get away from this place."

Both boys eyeballed each other. Their day of reckoning was coming and they both knew it.

Maggie stood by her bedroom window watching the limo roar down the drive. She sank against the window, her brow cooled by the glass. How could things have gotten so messed up? She hadn't wanted an open confrontation with Sawyer; she had gone to her daughter's room to check on the boys and say her good-byes. It had been Sawyer who'd lashed out first. Maggie's hands formed into fists, the knuckles whitening. Why did she have to fight for everything she wanted? And why was she always the one to wear the black hat?

"They've gone, have they?"

Maggie swung around to see Rand standing in the open doorway. He looked terrible.

"Yes, they've gone," she replied. "And as usual I've made a mess of things. I got up to say good-bye to the boys and came face-to-face with Sawyer. She let me have it with both barrels."

"Were you surprised?"

"No, but I regret it. I've never had much of a relationship with Sawyer, but when she said she never wanted to see me again, that she'd never ever come back here to Sunbridge, it was like being hit over the head." She laughed, a bitter sound in the quiet room. "I've got a lousy track record, Rand, and it doesn't seem to be improving."

"What will you do?"

"I was just thinking about that. I was remembering the way they sent me to Vermont after Sawyer was born, and how I cried and cried and told Mam that I hated her and that I'd never love her again."

"And what did Billie do?"

"She said it wasn't important that her children love her. That she hadn't brought us into the world to fill a gap in her life. She brought us into the world because she loved us and that love carried a responsibility. And that's why she was sending me away from Sunbridge, because she loved me and it was for my own good."

"Do you believe that now?"

"Yes, without a doubt. But I can't seem to get over the hurt that I wasn't wanted here in the first place. That I could never seem to find my own niche here."

"You do belong at Sunbridge, Maggie. And you also belong here." He opened his arms to her and she walked into his embrace. He held her close, burying his face in the fragrance of her neck. "And I do love you, Maggie. Without doubt."

The ski lodge was toasty warm. Adam leaned back in his swivel chair by the fire. How was he going to tell Paula he had to leave? Just up and tell her, or take the coward's way out and fake a virus? She'd be fine on her own, and since everything was paid for, she could stay on. The hot coffee mug warmed his hands. His breakfast was lying heavily on his stomach. He was brooding, fighting off a feeling of impending doom. All was not right with his beloved Sawyer. He had to get back to New York.

"Paula," he said lazily, "how upset would you be if I cut out and returned to New York?"

"Work, stomach virus, or the truth? . . . You're worried about Sawyer. I'm sure I can manage. I am staying on here, right?"

Paula was a great girl. Fun, understanding, and no strings attached. Bedroom eyes smiled at him. "Go, you big goof. You'll only make both of us miserable if you stay. The shuttle leaves"—Paula looked down at the slim square on her wrist—"in forty-five minutes."

"You're a sport. I can be packed in five minutes."

"You never really unpacked, did you, Adam? Just pay

the bill, honey, and leave my airline ticket on the dresser."

"I should marry you is what I should do." Adam grinned.

"No way. You'd be drawing cartoons of me and hanging them in the bathroom after the first month. Why spoil a good thing? Enjoy yourself, because I'm going to have a ball."

"See you." Adam waved airily. Paula waved back. She *would* have a good time, the witch.

Sawyer herded the boys into the dingy freight elevator. "I know this looks rather weird, but when you see the loft, you're going to be surprised."

As soon as they walked through the front door, a horn blared. Confetti streamed from the top of the door sill. "Welcome home, gang!" Adam yelled at the top of his lungs.

"Adam! What are you doing here?"

"I got tired of sitting by the fire and drinking toddies. You must be Cole, and of course you're Riley," Adam said, extending his hands to both boys. "Are we going to have a ball. I've been dying to see New York ever since I moved here. I mean really see it. This slug"—he indicated Sawyer—"is just along for the ride. Come on, I'll show you where you're bunking. Then I'll show you some of my better work; we'll catch some news on TV—that's a must, because I make my living spoofing the politicos—and then we'll take off for one of my favorite eating places, the Back Porch. There's no place like New York for eating out. You guys are gonna beg to come back here."

The Texans took on the Big Apple with verve and determination. The hectic week started off with a visit to the most famous lady in the world, the Statue of Liberty, followed by Wall Street, the Twin Towers, the Village, and Chinatown's Mott Street. They breakfasted at Samantha's, lunched at the Four Seasons, dined at the Sign of the Dove, and managed to fit in Sloppy Louie's for the best fish in the world. Cole, who'd lived in New York most of his life, discovered places he had never known. Bloomingdale's, Saks Fifth Avenue, and St. Patrick's

Cathedral were followed by a trip to the Seventh Avenue garment district. The Museum of Natural History and the Modern Art Museum vied with a matinee of the Broadway show *Cats* and a screening of the latest Chuck Norris adventure.

"Someday I'm going to write a book about this town," Adam said during the hair-raising ride to Kennedy Airport in a cab being driven by a Lebanese camel jockey.

There were manly handshakes, boyish kisses and hugs. The memories of New York were something none of them would forget.

"By God, that was one of the best weeks I've ever had," Adam said happily on the ride back to the apartment.

"Adam, I don't think I can ever thank you for what you did this past week."

"Thank me? Hell, I should be thanking you. I really saw New York. I lived it; I loved it. I'll probably never do it again. I think the boys had a ball."

"They did. They really liked you, Adam. Texas is going to seem tame after this glorious visit." She paused thoughtfully. "I was surprised that Cole went to see his father yesterday. For some reason I thought Cole had scratched him off his list of people to know and love."

"New Year's Day, what do you expect? He probably felt it was something he had to do. He did seem a little subdued afterward, but he snapped out of it."

"Subdued? I thought he was like the cat that ate the canary. I know him. Something went on yesterday, and we probably won't know what it is until he's ready to tell us."

Back in the loft in front of the fire, Adam poured generously from the wine bottle. "Now, tell me, how are you? We've danced around it all week. It's time to talk."

Sawyer's voice was flat, almost a monotone. "I feel like I'm in a holding pattern over hell. Does that explain it?"

"It explains the way you feel; it doesn't tell me what happened," Adam said gently.

"There's not much to tell. Rand's having an affair with

Maggie. I asked him point-blank and he didn't deny it."
She laughed bitterly. "Then I got drunk, very drunk. Cole
found me early in the morning. That kid's okay, Adam,
he really is. Maggie screwed him up just like she screwed
me up. If there was a way I could take him away from
her, I would," Sawyer said grimly. "I've been thinking all
week of having a talk with Cranston. Maybe we could
strike up a deal."

"You'd go that far to get back at Maggie?" Adam asked
in awe.

"I'd go that far. Don't judge, Adam. Not until you've
walked in my shoes."

Marble, tired of warming herself by the fire, leaped
onto Sawyer's lap, knocking the wineglass out of her hand.
The cat immediately began licking the wine.

"Don't worry about it; she's been drunk before," Adam
laughed, and the tense moment was over.

"I'm not worried about the cat," Sawyer grumbled good-
naturedly. "What about my skirt?"

"Sponge it off. It's no big deal. That's the secret to
life, you know. You have to know what's important and
what isn't."

"You really can be a nag, Adam. However, I love you
dearly. I don't know how I could have made it through
the week without you."

"No thanks are necessary. Have some more wine. Do
you think Marble's whiskers are turning gray?"

"Probably. She's old, or hadn't you noticed? Speaking
of old, you should have seen the show Ms. Eileen Farrell
put on for my aunt Amelia. She had her hooks out for
Cary, but when she found out Rand was what she called
'nobility,' she homed in on him. Aunt Amelia is so jealous,
it oozes out of her pores. I had a few moments of feeling
sorry for her, but I was so wrapped up in my own problems, I forgot about it till this minute. Cary is such a good-
looking man. You know, I really believe he loves my aunt.
She adores him, but she's playing the same game we all
play, making her own hell. She's just waiting for the day
he wants firm flesh and nubile breasts."

"Did you ever think about talking to her? Maybe she needs an ear. We all do at one time or another."

"Not my ear. I'm young. I'm the enemy. Grand is the one she'll talk to if she ever needs a confidante. I think we should eat something; I'm getting woozy from all this wine."

"I'll cook if you clean up. I'm just as woozy, so you're taking a chance letting me cook. Of course, you don't know how to cook, so maybe you aren't taking a chance after all."

"You're not woozy; you're blitzed."

"So are you."

Sawyer giggled. "I know. Just make sandwiches."

"Fluffernutters okay with you? Those boys ate us out of house and home, and that's all that's left."

"Sounds good to me. Put a dab of jelly on mine."

"You got it," Adam muttered as he went into the kitchen.

Sawyer watched him for a moment, then rubbed her eyes. She could hardly focus. Wine never did this to her before, and she was getting another one of her headaches. Too much excitement. She'd rest up tomorrow or go into the office and think about taking a vacation.

The New Year began for Maggie with a mixture of joy and sadness. Joy because Rand was staying on at Sunbridge, sadness because of Sawyer.

They played a little game, Rand and Maggie. By day, they enjoyed riding in the frosty winter air and made the rounds of holiday parties with Susan or Amelia and Cary. By night, they made love and slept in each other's arms.

It had been decided that Rand should remain at Sunbridge until Cole and Riley returned from New York. If there was to be any flak, Rand wanted to be there for his share instead of leaving Maggie to face it alone. When they did return, the day after New Year's, neither of the boys seemed to have much to say, but their sympathies clearly lay with Sawyer.

For once the two boys seemed to be in agreement about something. At times Maggie thought they were engaged in a conspiracy against her, although she knew they still didn't get along. Even Riley had changed toward her. Before the trip he'd always asked her how her day had gone, was interested in the daily workings of Sunbridge. In return, he'd share his day with her, air his views, and discuss his plans. Now he had nothing to share and little to say. Cole was so openly hostile, Maggie avoided his company altogether. Something about his bearing, in the way he looked at her, told her he'd found a way to strike back. Only in her darkest hours did she think of Sawyer, and when she did, Cole was always there in her thoughts. The two of them allies, children against their mother.

Aside from Rand, the only bright spot on Maggie's horizon was her divorce from Cranston. She could hardly wait to put it behind her. Once she was a free woman, she and Rand could bring their feelings for each other out in the open. Then, and only then, would they be able to face the family together, firm in their right to be together. Disapproval for other reasons, such as loyalty to Sawyer, would simply have to be ignored. Besides, they loved each other and didn't need anyone else's approval.

Just after New Year's the phone at Sunbridge shrilled to life. Maggie caught it on the fourth ring, taking her coat and hat off at the same time. A cheerful voice told her Cranston Tanner was calling long distance. When he came on the line, Maggie took a deep breath and said cheerfully, "Happy New Year, Cranston." Then she waited.

"I've decided to sue for custody of Cole," he said abruptly, not bothering to return her greeting. "You can fight me, Maggie, but it won't do you any good. Of course, that puts the divorce on hold for now. You'll want time to see your lawyers and time to speak to Cole. In the end it will be what Cole wants, and he wants his father."

She'd been expecting it; she'd known Cole had been up to something when he'd returned from New York. "Why?" was all she said, all she could say.

"Because I'm getting married again and the boy deserves a family."

"You said you weren't seeing anyone," Maggie said hoarsely.

"That was in September. This is now. You could say I've found the love of my life. Cole will fit in nicely."

"You don't want him; you're just trying to get back at me for rejecting you. I thought we came to an understanding. You said the divorce would come off on schedule and we'd do what was best for Cole for the second semester."

"That's exactly what I'm doing. Cole can finish out the school year, then come here in June. This way he can spend as much time with Sawyer as he wants. I've spoken to Sawyer and she thinks it's a good idea."

"Sawyer! What right do you have to...Damn you, Cranston! Sawyer has nothing to do with this."

"Sawyer has everything to do with this. She's Cole's sister and probably the only person he really cares about. He came to visit me while he was in New York. He didn't tell you, did he?"

"No, he didn't, but I suspected. What did he tell you?"

"Enough so you'll never keep the boy. I'll win, Maggie. I always win. Look, I admire the fact that you've gotten your life together and stopped drinking. I'm glad that you're happy at Sunbridge. But you're no good for Cole. You never were. You weren't any good for Sawyer, either. You're not a mother. That about sums it up. Now, we can do it the easy way or the hard way."

"You can go to hell, Cranston."

"I expect I will someday. I'll probably see you there," Cranston replied smoothly. "Nice talking to you, Maggie. Give my love to Cole."

"You bastard!" Maggie screamed into the mouthpiece as she hung up.

"Who's a bastard?" Amelia asked. "God, I need a drink. Tonic water," she added hastily.

"Have what you want. Other people drinking doesn't bother me. That was Cranston. He's going to try to take

Cole away from me. He's getting married and he wants Cole to be able to see Sawyer as much as he wants. That girl has ruined my life. I can't even stand to hear her name anymore."

"You don't mean that. You're upset."

"Of course I'm upset, and you're right; I don't mean it. My bottom line is always Sawyer. I don't know how much more I can handle."

"You'll handle whatever is dished out. That's how you survive. According to Cary, God never gives us more than we can handle. Personally, I sometimes have trouble believing it, but there must be truth in it because we're both here kicking and scratching. Was going to bed with Rand worth all of this? That's what it's all about and you know it."

"Who I go to bed with is none of Cranston's business. If he's getting married, he's gone to bed with someone, too."

"What are you going to do?" Amelia asked curiously.

"Spend a sleepless night and call Dudley Abramson first thing in the morning. I can't believe Cranston could be this cruel. I'm going to call Sawyer and give her a piece of my mind, and then I'm going to talk to Cole."

Amelia finished her tonic water. She couldn't wait to get to her room so she could have a real drink. And think about the Christmas present Cary had given her. It had been delivered today, a gorgeous Persian rug, almost identical to the one her mother had said was in the library. The owner of the small store had delivered it himself, thrilled that it was going into such a beautiful house. She'd spent an hour with the little man, showing off her renovations. Then, something the carpet dealer had said burned in her brain till she couldn't take it anymore. "The young lady was very pleased with the carpet. She had the specifications all written down." Amelia had sent the workmen home early and locked up.

My God, how she'd gushed and trilled to Cary about his wonderful gift! And that damn Eileen had just sat there looking smug while she'd made a fool of herself. What angered Amelia more than anything else was Cary's play-acting, pretending that he'd trudged into the city and roamed and searched till he'd found the "perfect gift" for his beloved wife.

"I guess you'll want privacy for your call, so I'll toddle along upstairs," Amelia said, shaking off her thoughts. "I expect Cary early this evening. Hopefully, in time for dinner. What's on the menu? That's the first thing he asks."

"Beef stew and corn bread. Cherry pie. Martha made ice cream today. The boys seem to love it."

"Great." Cary would love it. "I'll see you at dinner-time." As as afterthought she called over her shoulder, "I wouldn't worry too much, Maggie. Things will work out for the best, or at least the way they're meant to. I'll see you in a little while."

Maggie waved absently, her mind already on the call to New York she was about to make. She dialed the oper-ator, gave her Sawyer's business number, and made the call person-to-person from Coleman Tanner. The moment Sawyer's voice came on the wire, Maggie cried, "How could you go behind my back to conspire with Cranston? That wasn't what I meant by guts. I won't have a chance in hell of keeping Cole now. My God, how could you?"

Sawyer tried to listen, but her head was pounding so, she could barely make out Maggie's words.

"I really don't want to get involved with you and Cran-ston, Maggie," she said. "Handle your own affairs. I thought I made that clear to you before I left."

"Well, let me make this clear to you right now. Cole is off-limits to you. Don't call him and don't write to him."

For several moments Sawyer stood there and listened to the dial tone, feeling as if she were going to be ill. If only she could get rid of this damn headache! Suddenly she gripped the edge of the desk and swayed.

Peter Andrews, on his way back from the water cooler, saw Sawyer sway. He quickened his step when he saw her loosen her grip on the desk. An instant later her knees buckled and she slid to the floor. He shouted for help. In twenty minutes Sawyer was on her way to the hospital. Peter personally undertook to notify Adam Jarvis and Sawyer's grandmother.

Amelia was on her way down to the library and the evening paper when the phone rang. Cary, of course. She'd known it even before she picked up the phone.

"Darling, I'm not going to make dinner. Keep something warm for me, will you? There're some things here I want to clean up tonight. Eileen's going to help me. I know we agreed to catch some television and lounge around this evening, but . . . Amelia? You aren't angry, are you? I'll try to get out of here as soon as I can."

"No, of course I'm not angry. You're missing a good dinner, but I'll keep yours warm. Beef stew gets better the longer it sits. We have homemade ice cream and cherry pie."

"Oh, God, I can taste it now. Keep a light in the window. Love you."

"I love you, too," Amelia cried passionately. "The light will always be there for you. Drive carefully; the roads are slick." The connection was broken; Amelia looked at the receiver for a long time before she replaced it.

"The temperature must have dropped outside," Eileen complained. "I have all four heaters on, even the one in the bathroom. Are you sure you want to stay and finish this up, Cary?"

"You were the one who offered to stay."

"That was before the temperature dropped. I'm afraid my car is never going to start."

"So, I'll give you a jump. You should be wearing warmer clothes," Cary said, eyeing the thin jersey material of Eileen's dress. "This trailer is like a wind tunnel. Wool slacks and a heavy sweater would be more practical."

"Well, bring your chair around by me, then. We can

at least huddle. An hour, Cary, that's it. I've got the bids all sorted. I have three proposals on hand. Sherman looked at them today and made comments in the margins. Let's get to it so we can get out of here."

"You sound like you have a heavy date."

"I do, but not with the man I'd like to have a date with. I've been wanting to ask you since Christmas if Rand is still here. Is he involved with anyone?"

"I really don't know. For sure, I mean," Cary said truthfully.

"Maybe I'll give him a call tomorrow and see what his reaction is."

"By the way, that really was nice of you to get the carpet for me. I made six trips to Austin and made a dozen or so calls to Houston and Dallas looking for that damn thing. You really saved my hide and I appreciate it. How in the hell did you find it, anyway?"

"I started off with the yellow pages and went on from there. It was such an expensive item that all the shops I called were more than willing to help. Of course, when I told them who it was for, they were even more helpful. The Coleman name is very powerful in Texas."

"So I've found out. I wouldn't be where I am now, nor would you, if it wasn't for Amelia's help."

"You'd have found a way. You're a very talented man, Cary."

Cary's eyes were only inches from Eileen's. "No, I wouldn't. I couldn't have done any of this without Amelia. She believed in me and made me believe in myself. The most you can say for me is that I know what a hammer is." He paused, then said pointedly, "We're a team, Amelia and me." Imperceptibly Eileen moved her swivel chair. Her eyes were the first to lower. She understood.

They worked for over an hour without a break. Cary smiled when he closed the folders. "Done! Tomorrow you can zero in on the other stuff, and from there it's smooth sailing. At least now I can see some daylight. Thanks for staying, Eileen. Get your things and I'll turn off all the

heaters and get the lights and lock up. I'll wait to see if
your car starts."

Thirty minutes later Eileen's old Ford was still dead.
"You probably need a new battery. Where the hell did
you get this clunker anyway?"

"From a used car lot. I can't afford anything else."

"Jesus Christ, with what we pay you, how can you
stand there and tell me you can't afford anything better?"

"Would you like to see my rent receipts? You know,
it isn't easy being single and living alone. I barely make
ends meet. I like to take a vacation at least once a year,
so I have to save for that. I'm not a Coleman," she said
coldly. "I'm just a working girl."

"Okay, okay. Maybe we can find a way to get you a
company car. I suppose we could lease it, or I could cosign
a loan. Get in the car. I'll drive you home."

"I can't afford the payments. I'll have to take a taxi
tomorrow morning and that's going to cost me at least
twenty dollars. I can't seem to win these days. Thanks
for wanting to help, though."

"It's going to take at least ten minutes for the heater
to warm up the truck. Damn, I should have called Amelia
to tell her I was going to be late."

"I'll call her tomorrow and apologize. I'll tell her it's
my fault and explain the situation."

Cary's heart raced. "For Christ's sake, don't do that!
I'll handle it." He calculated the time it would take him
to drop Eileen off and return to Sunbridge. He'd be lucky
if he got in by ten-thirty. For the first time it occurred to
him to wonder if Amelia was jealous of Eileen. He knew
she had no cause, but even so. . . .

"How bad are the roads?" Eileen shivered inside her
cashmere coat.

"Icy. They'll be worse by morning. I'll pick you up.
Have someone come to look at your car tomorrow. Tell
them to bring a battery just in case. I'll talk to Sherman
and Clara about you using one of their cars, at least until
most of this bad weather is over. Then we'll see about

getting you a loan. Maybe we can work something out with the company. But if it can't be written off, we can't do it. That's Sherman's rule of thumb."

"It's a good rule. Companies like yours need tax breaks. If getting me a car helps, I'm all for it."

It was half an hour's ride into the city of Austin. Eileen and Cary kept up a cheerful banter of office gossip and business all the way.

"Thanks, Cary."

"No problem. Spiffy building," Cary said, eyeing the doorman.

"A girl has to be safe. We have an elevator operator, too. It's a good security building. That's why I moved here. Most of my salary goes to pay for rent."

"How much?"

"Thirteen hundred a month. It's going co-op in six months. I'll have to move, since I can't afford to buy. Drive carefully."

"I'll pick you up at seven-thirty," he called before driving off.

Eileen let herself into the luxury apartment. It was like a layout in Bloomingdale's catalogue. Right down to the porcelain figurines. Soft gray and peach, easy on the eye and elegant. Amelia Assante would be hard-pressed to find anything wrong with this apartment.

Borrowing that old clunker of a car from a friend was going to pay off. Everything would pay off, sooner than she'd hoped. The company car would lead to a BMW, and soon the apartment would be picked up, too, as a corporation property. But she'd hold the title, of course. They needed her. That was the bottom line. Just like she needed their money. A trade-off. She'd certainly learned a lot since she'd started to work for the company.

Eileen's slender fingers plucked at the row of cassettes. She selected a Lionel Richie tape and popped it into the stereo. She stripped down and headed for the shower. She'd order dinner to be catered. One way or another she would find a way to put it on one of the men's expense accounts. She might have to put out a little tonight, but she'd get it back when it came time to buy the BMW. The man she was seeing tonight was a BMW dealer. Cost? Perhaps below cost.

You scratch my hand and I'll tickle yours. She giggled.

{{{{{{{{{ CHAPTER NINETEEN }}}}}}}}}

It was almost midnight before the duty station nurse would allow Adam into Sawyer's room. She seemed to be sleeping, but the squeak of the door alerted her to a presence in the dimly lit room. "Adam, is that you?" she asked wanly.

"Who else? I've been sitting outside for hours. Look at me; I'm a wreck—and you're the one who's in bed. How do you feel?" he asked anxiously.

"That holding pattern I'm in seems to have shifted a little, dropping me closer over the hellhole. Exhaustion, I guess. Don't worry, Adam. I'll be fine in a day or so. I can't believe they brought me to the hospital. All I need is a couple of days of rest and some of your greasy cooking."

Adam tried for a smile but failed. "The nurse said something about tests."

"I don't know. Standard hospital procedure, I'm sure. There's nothing wrong with me. I'm planning on leaving here tomorrow. They already did some tests."

"What kind of tests? For what?"

"Blood tests. They X-rayed my shoulder, my neck,

and my head. Seems I hit it when I fell. My mouth is so dry. Could you get me a drink?"

"Sure." Adam poured from a carafe and handed the glass to Sawyer, then watched as she reached out for the glass and missed, spilling the water over the sheet. "It was my fault. I'm sorry," he said soothingly.

"I guess I'm still groggy. They gave me a shot of something. It seems to be wearing off now a little. What time is it?"

"After midnight. I didn't want to leave until I was sure you were all right."

"What time did they bring me here?"

"This afternoon. Late, I think. I'm glad they did. Now they can check you out and put you on some good vitamins. I'll be back in the morning."

"You don't have to do that, Adam," Sawyer said sleepily. "I'll be leaving and can take a taxi back to the apartment."

"I'll call you, then. How's that?"

"That's fine..." Sawyer's voice trailed off. Adam stayed for a long time watching her. Her breathing was easy and she seemed to be in a deep sleep. A drugged sleep. He knew she'd sleep through the night, but still he didn't leave. It wasn't until the night nurse poked her head in the door and suggested he go home that he moved. She was right, of course. He couldn't do anything here.

At the nurse's station he stopped to talk. "Miss Coleman told me that she was scheduled for more tests tomorrow. What kind of tests?"

"Are you a member of the family?"

"She lives with me." At the nurse's blank look, Adam explained, "We cohabit. As in live together. I am the closest thing to a relative she has here in New York."

"We don't give out information to anyone but family. You aren't family," the charge nurse said in a no-nonsense voice.

"Look," he said, deciding to try another tack, "I'm the one who is going to be paying the bill. That makes me responsible. So, if I'm responsible, you can tell me what I want to know." He leaned over the desk and lowered his voice. "My mother doesn't approve of us living together, either, but it's the only thing I could think of to get her to marry me. I'm monogamous. But she's afraid because her parents didn't have a happy marriage." The nurse seemed to be relenting, so Adam drove home his advantage. "You look like you have a good head on your shoulders. Wouldn't you do the same thing if you were me? I'm in love with her. I can't lose her."

The nurse's stiffly starched uniform crackled as she moved back a step, closer to the rack that held the patients' charts. Adam watched in relief as she flipped through the charts arranged according to room number.

"Neurological testing," she said through tight lips. "Another urinalysis and additional blood tests."

"She already had a blood test. What are they looking for?"

"This is not a question-and-answer period, young man. I shouldn't have told you what I did. Now, if you want more information, you'll have to speak to doctor. I'm simply not at liberty to say anything else. It's late and your voice carries. We can't have you waking our patients. Call doctor tomorrow."

Adam looked at the plump starched nurse. Her iron-gray hair was like tiny corkscrews sticking out every which way from her white cap. Her eyes were round and serious, but oh, so wary. She was on the defensive now that she'd done something she knew was wrong. Probably she had never broken a rule in her life, until now. "You take good care of her, for me. I'll be back in the morning."

"I won't be here," the woman blurted.

"I'll be back in the evening, too. Thank you."

"Young man . . ."

"Yes?"

"It's routine when a patient has a blow to the head. Get a good night's sleep."

* * *

Marble hissed nastily when Adam sat down on the sofa and pulled the phone to his lap. She continued to hiss and spit, her claws digging at the sofa cushions. Adam swatted her on the rump and pushed her off the couch. "The other lady in my life is first right now. Eat that popcorn if you're so hungry," Adam muttered as he tossed fat fluffies on the carpet. Marble hissed again and walked away, her plumed tail straight in the air.

"Nick, it's Adam. Sorry about the late hour, but I have to talk to you."

"Late, early, what difference does it make when you're here to serve the masses? My time is yours as long as you pay for it. What's wrong?"

"Sawyer's in the hospital. She fainted and they're scheduling neurological tests for tomorrow. They took a blood test today and more are scheduled for tomorrow. I...That's all I know."

Nick's voice was suddenly professional, clipped and cool. "Was she hurt when she passed out? Did they take any X-rays?"

"Shoulder, neck, skull. She gets these blinding headaches. I thought it was because of the stress and strain. Remember how I used to tell you she had the eye of an eagle? Well, she just got glasses. She really has to wear them. She complained one day that her vision blurs every so often. Put the migraine headaches, the glasses, and the fainting spell together, and there's room for worry."

"It's possible they found some abnormality and are doing more testing to be sure. On the other hand, it could be nothing. Both of us could speculate all night, but I'm not the attending physician. Be glad she's in the hospital where they can take care of her. If you like, I can stop in and see her tomorrow."

"Do that. Call me and let me know what you think, okay?"

"Will do. Take two aspirins and go to bed."

Sawyer didn't leave the hospital that day or the next. She made threatening noises to the doctor but in the end realized she was too weak and drained to do more than make a token effort. The results of her tests would take another day.

"I hate airports, Thad. They have such bad connotations for me. I have this feeling that something is terribly wrong. Adam didn't know anything really. I guess that's what's worrying me more than anything. Young girls don't land in the hospital for four days for a fainting spell. Sawyer is going to be angry with Adam for calling me, and she's going to be angry with me for calling Maggie."

"What I can't understand," Thad said as he packed down the tobacco in his pipe, "is why Maggie won't go to New York and meet you. She is Sawyer's mother, after all. I'm sorry, Billie, but that's something I will never understand if I live to be a hundred. Maggie has come so far, made so many changes in her life. Why can't she and Sawyer come to some kind of terms?"

"Who are we to say Maggie must do this and Maggie mustn't do that? Maggie and Sawyer have to work things out themselves. From what Amelia has told me, Christmas was a total disaster. Now I'm really glad we were snowbound."

"They're calling your flight, darling. Call me when you land and again after you see Sawyer. If you need me, call, any time of the day or night. Promise now."

"I promise." Billie kissed him soundly. "Say a little prayer on the way home that Sawyer is all right."

"I will, darling. Have a safe trip."

Billie was uneasy during the plane trip. The feeling stayed with her while she claimed her luggage and called Thad. It was still with her on the cab ride to Adam's loft. When there was no answer to her repeated ringing, she left her suitcase beside the door and hailed a cab for the hospital.

Billie's stomach churned as she made her way down the corridor to Sawyer's room.

Outside the door, she stood quietly for a moment trying

to compose herself. Sawyer was going to be upset that she'd made the trip, but she could talk her way out of that easily enough. What was going to be hard to explain was Adam's frantic phone call to her. And if Sawyer should ask, she would have to admit that she'd called Maggie. Of course, she wouldn't have to tell her how Maggie had reacted. Billie suspected there was more to the situation than met the eye. With a smile on her face, she pushed open the door to Sawyer's room.

"Grand, what are you doing here? . . . Adam called you, didn't he? I can see it in his face. He worries too much. We're waiting for the doctor to come in and discharge me; he's supposed to have all the reports from my tests. I've been burning the candle at both ends, and it finally caught up with me. I'm run-down, anemic probably. They'll give me megavitamins and send me home. You shouldn't have made the trip."

"I wanted to. It's nice to see you again, Adam. You haven't changed at all."

"Still as good-looking as ever, right?"

"I said you haven't changed." Billie forced a laugh. Something *was* wrong here; she could feel it.

"Perhaps I should go on to the loft. I did go there first and left my bag. You'll want privacy with the doctor."

"That's silly, Grand. Wait. You can certainly hear what the doctor has to say. We'll all go back to the loft together."

"Makes sense to me. I always said this chick had a head on her shoulders," Adam quipped.

"Beautiful head." Sawyer grinned. "Oh, here's the doctor." Sawyer made the necessary introductions. "Now tell me, Dr. Finley, how many vitamins do I have to take a day? I'm anemic, aren't I? Do I need B-twelve shots? . . . You look so serious. Don't tell me I have an inner ear problem; I used to get that when I was little."

Billie hadn't realized she was holding her breath until it escaped in a tortured sigh. Adam was squeezing and releasing his fists. He could feel it, too.

*   *   *

There was little in Susan's imagination that could compare with the dreariness of early January in Texas. All the life seemed to drain out of the land, leaving a poor imitation painted in indistinguishable shades of gray upon gray. And she fit perfectly into the landscape, gray and lifeless like an aging slug whose middle is too swollen for movement. She longed for a warm climate, blue skies, sunshine.

For as long as she could remember, she'd never been this lonely. First, it had been Mam and Pap and the rest of the family here at Sunbridge, and then Amelia and Rand, and finally Jerome. She'd never lived on her own or had the responsibility of making a life for herself. Even now she was under the protective umbrella of Sunbridge and the family. But it didn't relieve the loneliness.

Every day she wondered where Jerome was and what he was doing. She'd sent letters to the flat and to their agent, Theodore Lewis. All of them had been returned unopened. It was as though Jerome had dropped off the face of the earth. When she'd called Theodore, he'd been unwilling to give any information, although he'd expressed confidence that Jerome would soon come to his senses. "He'll turn up," Theodore had said. "Perhaps he just needs a little time to get accustomed to being a father." Eight months wasn't enough time?

Yes, sooner or later he'd turn up. Of that Susan was sure. He'd appear suddenly, like an apparition, after the baby was born and she was able to go back to work. He'd be filled with plans and schemes and probably have a tour schedule in his pocket.

She worked at her fingers, massaging them gently. How puffy they were. She'd tried just the other day to play the piano, but the finely tuned instrument hadn't responded. In the end she'd slammed down the lid. Maybe she'd never play again. Maybe she'd never do a lot of things again. Right now her top priority was staying well so she could play out her own private miracle of giving birth.

Susan patted her belly, pleased with the little ripples

that made her fingers jump. She wondered if her child would be a boy or a girl. It didn't matter. She would love it. And the child would love her back, unconditionally.

A walk on the portico would feel good now. She'd seen the workmen clear the snow away earlier; there would be no danger of her slipping and falling. Before she could change her mind and snuggle down into the comfortable chair, Susan slipped her arms into a down coat and added a woolen hat to her golden head.

"Suse, where are you going?" Maggie asked in alarm as she watched her sister maneuver awkwardly down the stairs.

"I need some fresh air. I thought I'd walk up and down the portico."

"Wait, I'll go with you. I don't want you falling. They always manage to leave little patches of ice."

"I'm dressed, so I'll wait for you outside." Already she could feel the perspiration beading her forehead.

Maggie joined her sister and they began to stroll, arm in arm. "I wonder what the temperature is today," Susan said. "Remember how we used to cup our hands to our mouths and blow out clouds of what we called venom?"

"I remember. I think I remember everything about our childhood. I went for analysis and the things I remembered shocked the psychologist so much, he suspended my visits till he could get a handle on it. I never went back. I learned that you have to help yourself first, and if you need someone for the rocky spots, then you consult a professional. How are you doing with your rocky spots?"

"I was thinking upstairs that I'm going to have to make a life for myself very soon. I'm going to have to find an apartment and a job. I screwed up, Maggie. Before I came here I didn't take my share from our bank accounts. There's nothing left except the trust fund Mam set up for me here."

"For God's sake, Suse, is that what's been making you look so glum? I have enough for both of us. That should be the least of your worries. You can stay here forever if you want. I love having you here. I can't wait for you to have the baby. Please, I want you to stay. I'll switch over some monies tomorrow. I can even do it today."

"Maggie, I can't. . . . It isn't right . . ."

"Of course it is. Don't even think about paying me back. I'm glad to help. Whatever's mine is yours. This is your home. Pap said I should fill it with sunshine. I don't want you to even think of leaving. Listen to me. Jerome might have cleaned out the bank accounts, but you can stop any further monies from Coleman Enterprises being sent to England. I'll do that for you. It will be funneled here to your bank account once we open it. It's not the end of the world. Your baby is going to be well provided for. That's what you're really worried about, isn't it?"

Susan nodded miserably. "I really thought she or he would be born a pauper dependent on your generosity."

"My God, Suse, why didn't you say something? We should have done some serious talking a while ago. I didn't want to intrude, because you seemed so out of it. Many nights I got as far as your door and then turned around and went back to my room because I thought you wouldn't want to be bothered."

"I thought you were too busy with Rand and the kids and everything. I didn't want to be an added burden." Susan dabbed at her eyes and sniffed. "I feel so alone."

"Well, you're not alone, so stop thinking like that. We both fouled up. We Colemans are good at that. For some reason we never get around to talking till it's too late. If we hadn't met like this this afternoon, you probably would've driven off one day and left me standing here wondering what I did to make you leave. We're going inside right now and talk. I have a lot I want to get off my chest, just like you do."

"What about Rand?"

"What about him? You're important to me, Suse. Rand will just have to manage to entertain himself while we do what we do best. Lord, how we used to jabber for hours on end. We're going to have a pot of tea and some cake, just you and me." Maggie squirmed under Susan's grateful gaze. How could she have been so insensitive to her sister? That was all going to change now.

Much later, the sisters walked hand in hand to dinner down the long stairway. Rand stood at the bottom. He was so handsome, Susan thought, but she was now seeing something she'd never seen in him before. A new awareness, a certain vitality that seemed to form a nimbus around him. It was a silly thought and she smiled. Rand didn't notice; he had eyes only for Maggie. She exerted a little pressure to her sister's hand, her seal of approval. Let them be happy if this is what they both want. Maggie responded with a tight squeeze of her own. It would be all right, she realized. Maggie had a grip on things.

Rand noticed the imperceptible change in Susan and smiled warmly. "I'm starved," he said, "but may I say the wait was worth it? You both look lovely."

"We know." Maggie grinned. "May we say you look quite dashing?"

"You may."

It was a wonderful dinner. Riley and Cole were drawn into the conversation when the talk switched to ice hockey. Maggie was stunned by her son's knowledge of the dangerous sport. She hadn't known he'd played goalie on his old school team.

When the boys returned to their rooms to study, the trio had coffee in front of the fire. Rand regaled Maggie with tales of Susan's young life in England. It was one of the most enjoyable evenings of Maggie's life.

It was after ten when Susan excused herself, saying her eyes would no longer stay open. At almost the same moment, the telephone rang. As Maggie went to answer it, Amelia and Cary opened the front door, a blast of cold air swirling about them. Susan wished everyone a good night and was halfway up the stairs before she heard Maggie's voice change.

Rand watched in alarm as the color drained from Maggie's face. Her grip on the telephone receiver was so tight, her knuckles looked iridescent.

"Thanks for calling me, Mam. I'll . . . What I'll do is . . .

I'll. . . . Yes, of course. . . . This is unreal. . . . I'll . . . call you tomorrow. No, no messages."

Amelia's voice was just short of shrill. "What's wrong? Did something happen to Thad? For God's sake, Maggie, *what is it*?"

Susan echoed Amelia's words. "Are you sure Mam is all right? *Maggieeeeee*!"

Maggie turned till she was facing the small group. She was trembling so badly, Rand jumped up and put his arms around her shoulders. She leaned gratefully into his hard body. "I . . . don't know quite how . . . how to say this except . . . except . . . Sawyer has an inoperable brain tumor." The silence around her brought tears to Maggie's eyes. "Sawyer is still in the hospital. They're calling in another team of neurosurgeons." Suddenly overwhelmed by guilt, she drew away from Rand and walked to the liquor cabinet. She gripped the gin bottle tightly. "I was going to go, you know, when Mam said Sawyer was in the hospital, but when . . . but when she left here, she said she never . . . never wanted to see me again."

The sight of Susan gripping her stomach brought Maggie to her senses. "We're . . . we're all going to handle this. Right now, I don't know how, but we will. Susan, go to bed. You need the rest. We're all in shock right now, so why don't we wait till tomorrow to . . . to talk about it."

"You're right, of course," Amelia said as she reached for Cary's hand. "It's my opinion that all doctors are quacks. They probably made a misdiagnosis and we're all . . . Billie wouldn't have called unless it was . . . Good night, everybody," she said in a small voice.

Maggie sat down on the love seat across from Rand. They watched each other for a long time.

"I think I know what you're thinking," Maggie said gently.

"I *know* what you're thinking," Rand said just as gently. "It's too late.

"We have to try. My God, Maggie, what kind of people would we be if we didn't try?"

"I didn't say I didn't want to. Sawyer is the one who won't let us exorcise our guilt. That's what it is. Pity is an awful thing. I could never go to Sawyer out of pity. She'd see through it in a minute."

"She's alone," Rand said in a choked voice. "She has to go through this alone."

"She's not alone. Mam will always be there for her. Sawyer's staying with an old friend of hers. Adam has loved her since they were little kids. Rand, I feel so helpless. I can't even comfort you and you can't comfort me."

"Maggie, I'm in love with you. This is . . ."

"Going to change things. I understand that. I have to think, Rand. I'm going upstairs. The boys have to be told, but I think that can wait till tomorrow."

"Maggie!"

"Yes?"

"Did your mother say . . . did she say how long Sawyer has?"

"A year, possibly. They're not certain . . . less. Doctors tend to shy away from. . . . What they do is they won't commit. . . . A year. A goddamn lousy year."

The bolt shot home on Maggie's door. Long fingers raked through her hair. She felt itchy all over. The tears had stopped. Had she cried? She couldn't remember. She rummaged in the drawer for a cigarette. She lit it, puffed on it, crushed it out, only to light another. She paced the room with the cigarette clamped between her teeth.

When she was younger, when Pap was still alive, she'd prayed to God and the devil that Sawyer would die. The memory was so vivid, she raced for the bathroom and upchucked her dinner. Her hand trembled so badly, she could barely brush her teeth. "God, I didn't mean it!" She knew it for the lie it was.

Maggie dropped to her knees, her head resting on the edge of the tub. "I need your help. Please, show me what to do," she prayed.

A long time later, Maggie dragged herself from the bathroom. She dialed New York information for Adam's number, then called him without a thought as to the time.

Neither Adam nor Mam would be sleeping. Would any of them ever sleep again?

"Mam. Help me."

"Maggie, I wish I could. This is something you'll have to handle by yourself. I think I'm still in shock. Adam is." There was a little pause. "Adam is praying. I did that, too. I imagine you did the same."

"I did, but I tend to think He ignores me. Just like that, no warning. I can't accept that."

"It wasn't quite like that. Those migraine headaches Sawyer's had for the past few years, that was the onset." She recounted other maladies that Adam had repeated to her. "We mustn't come to any fast conclusions, Maggie. The doctors don't believe the tumor is malignant, but it is in a vital area which they usually consider inoperable. I told you, there's another team of neurosurgeons coming to see Sawyer. We'll have a better picture then. Go to bed, Maggie, and try to rest."

"Mam, how did you get through Riley's death?"

"One day at a time. Listen to me. Sawyer isn't dead. She's very much alive. Remember that. She still has time."

It was three o'clock in the morning when Maggie descended the attic stairs, a cardboard box in her hands. Her old diaries. Journals, Mam always called them. Little leather-bound books that covered five years of one's life. From her closet she removed the corrugated box she'd brought with her from New York. These were one-year journals, filled out in more detail. Only here in these pages had she been honest.

Maggie Coleman Tanner's life. In two cardboard boxes. It was going to take a lot of guts to read these. The first diary started on her eighth birthday. She smiled when she looked at the childish scrawl. She remembered sending Sawyer a diary on her tenth birthday—a handsome leather-bound journal with her initials embossed in gold.

Maggie sorted through the diaries, placing them in chronological order. She stared at them for a long time.

A person's life shouldn't look so neat. She shook her head and went downstairs to perk a pot of coffee. She carried the percolator and a fresh pack of cigarettes upstairs. The last thing she did was put a note on her door telling everyone she was sleeping and not to waken her. Then she slid the bolt home and settled herself down to read.

Maggie's life exploded before her very eyes, one page at a time.

{{{{{{{{ CHAPTER TWENTY }}}}}}}}

When Maggie heard the sound of the garage door closing, she steeled herself. Telling Riley and Cole about Sawyer was going to be the hardest thing she'd ever done. Riley, she knew, would remain calm on the surface. But she couldn't even begin to imagine what Cole's reaction would be. Should she wait till they got upstairs and talk to them in their rooms, or should she call them into the study?

"I'll wait till they settle in," she decided aloud, unconsciously wringing her hands.

Rand watched her as she paced the study. He knew she was exhausted; she'd told him how she'd spent her night and morning. Her eyes looked hollow and bruised, her face pale and drawn. But there was beauty in her, and an inner strength that would allow her to stand tall and accept last night's phone call. He ached for her, wanted to comfort her in some way, but he hurt so bad himself, he couldn't make the effort.

"If it were me, I think I'd tell them in private," he said quietly. He watched her a short while later as she climbed the steps to the second floor.

Voices from the corridor outside the kitchen made him turn. Amelia must have come through the kitchen, Susan in her wake. Both women had cups of tea in their hands. If he drank one more cup of tea, Rand thought, he would float out the door. He greeted both women with a kiss on the cheek, then poured himself a triple Scotch.

"I couldn't stay at the house another minute," Amelia said. "Nothing went right today. I thought I was going to crawl out of my skin. I tried to call Cary nine times, but he was out on the site and couldn't be reached. I *needed* to talk to him," Amelia said in a brittle voice. "I have to call Billie. Maybe I should go to New York. Sawyer would understand. She'd know I was making the trip for Billie. But . . . I'm not sure now. I don't know how to . . . How in the name of God are we supposed to act? Do we rally 'round, offer . . . what? Sympathy? Pity?"

"I think you should do whatever feels right to you," Rand said, staring at the amber fluid in his glass.

"What are *you* going to do?" Amelia demanded. "How are you handling this?"

"Very carefully. I'm taking it hour by hour. Look, I did the right thing and I did it for the right reasons. You're both going to have to accept that. Maggie wasn't in my life when I broke it off with Sawyer. I'm sorry you've all chosen up sides. I'm the bad guy now. I'd cut off my right arm if it would help Sawyer."

Amelia leaned her head back wearily. "I know, Rand. In a lot of ways Sawyer had more than most, but she also had less of the things that really count. Billie isn't going to be able to make this right for her. And she shouldn't have to," Amelia said angrily. "From here on out it's Maggie's job."

"Sawyer was supposed to be godmother to my baby," Susan said tearfully.

"What do you mean *was*?" Amelia asked. "She isn't dead, you know. Of course she's going to be the godmother if she's up to it. How could you even think of anything else?"

"It's such a shock. I guess I haven't fully accepted it yet," Susan said softly.

"And that's another thing. Stop whining, Susan. Other women have babies. Other women's husbands leave them. Face up to your responsibilities. Grow up!"

"Aren't you being a little hard on her?" Rand asked, his eyes wide.

"You're another one. Sometimes you make me so angry. You're sitting here riddled with guilt, not knowing what to do. You already did it. Now stand up to it and handle that guilt. Do what's best for Sawyer. And what's going to be best for Sawyer is that you not be here when Susan's baby is born. Go back to England."

"I'm not a kid anymore that you can order around. Why do I have to go back to England? What's done is done. I intend to work my tail off making Maggie see that I care for her. If that means I have to stay here, then I will. We will all deal with this situation the best way each of us knows how. I'm sorry you feel this way, Mother."

Tears pricked at Amelia's eyes. "Sawyer's needs will be different now. She needs the warmth, the caring, of a man who loves her. If only you hadn't been so rash. You could have put your life on hold for a year to see her through this. This betrayal, this blatant carrying on with Maggie. Just imagine what Sawyer must be going through, how she must be feeling."

"There isn't a day that goes by that I don't think about it; no one will let me forget! But I still wouldn't have done things differently. I don't love Sawyer. Would you stay with Cary if he didn't love you?"

Amelia flinched. "Of course not," she cried.

"Susan, would you stay with a man who didn't love you?"

Susan sniffed. "That's a strange question to ask me. I'm here for just that reason. I don't think any of us should say any more. We're all uptight and liable to say things we're going to regret later. Where's Maggie?"

"She went upstairs to tell the boys. If there was a way I could do it for her, I would. She's really hurting, Mother. You saw it at lunchtime, didn't you, Susan?"

"Yes. I wanted to cry for her, but it wouldn't have done any good. We'll talk when the time is right for Maggie. I think I'll go up to my room now and watch the news. It's time I took an interest in what's going on in the world. I'll see you at dinner."

"Now, what's really bothering you, Mother?"

Amelia sighed. "Aside from Sawyer, it's Cary. I told you I called him nine times and he didn't return my calls. He wears a beeper and there's a portable phone in the Bronco." She looked up at him defiantly. "Don't get the idea that I call and pester just for the sake of hearing his voice. In fact, I make it a practice not to bother him. But I really needed him today."

"So, what are you trying to say?"

"I don't think Eileen gave him my messages."

"I think you're off base, Mother. Surely, if that was her intention, she knows you would mention it to Cary this evening and ask him directly. What could she gain?"

"My husband. One of the other investors. She made a play for you over Christmas. Have you been in touch with her?"

"She called me one day and invited me for dinner, but I begged off. I don't need any Eileen Farrells in my life."

"I don't need an Eileen Farrell in my life, either," Amelia cried passionately. "God, she's so young. Sawyer is so young. I'm sorry, Rand. It's been a bad day. I think I'm going to go up and soak in a hot tub. If I'm not down by seven, check to see if I drowned."

"I'll do that. Do you want a copy of the evening paper?"

"No, thanks. I have enough problems without taking on the world. Relax, Rand, and don't let this string you out to the point where you do something foolish."

"I'll bear that in mind." Rand poured himself another drink. Then he settled down, his eyes fastened on the stairway, to await Maggie's return.

Both boys stared at Maggie in disbelief. "Is there anything you want to ask me? I don't pretend to have all the answers, but I can call Mam and find out."

There were tears in Riley's eyes. "It isn't fair!" he cried.

"No, it isn't fair at all. We all have to make the most of the time we have."

"Can we call her?" Riley asked in a quivering voice.

"Of course, but I'd give it a week or so. Why don't you write a letter first. What you put in that letter is going to be up to you, so be careful."

"I will. I'm going to write my grandfather. He's very fond of Sawyer. Excuse me, Aunt Maggie."

Maggie was left alone with her son. There had been no show of emotion on his face when she'd told him about Sawyer. There was none now. "Cole, I . . . wish I wasn't the one who had to tell you this. I know how much you've come to love Sawyer. I'm so sorry."

"Sorry, Mother? I find that a little hard to swallow. You've always hated Sawyer. Why should you be sorry now? Won't you dance on her grave when they bury her?"

Maggie's hand shot out. The bright red mark on the boy's face didn't make her apologize. Cole backed off a step. "This should fit right into your plans. You and Rand live happily ever after. Grand won't have Sawyer to fuss over anymore, only you and Aunt Susan. You'll be the queen bee, the great matriarch of Sunbridge. She'll haunt you, Mommy dearest, until the day you die. You fucked up," he said cruelly.

Maggie's hand shot out a second time. "If you ever— I repeat, ever—talk to me like that again, you'll wish you hadn't. We don't use words like that here. Remember that. I suggest you sit down and think about the coming year and what you can do to make it better for your sister. Dinner is at seven."

"I'm not hungry." Cole's hand was on his cheek.

"I don't care if you're hungry or not. Be at the table and be civil. If not, you'll get more of the same, only next time I won't hold back. Do we understand each other?"

"Perfectly," he sneered.

Outside in the hallway Maggie leaned against the wall. She was trembling so badly, she had to wrap her arms around her chest. She wouldn't cry. She couldn't lose control now.

As she stood there trying to gather herself together before going downstairs, the blinding whiteness from the second-floor landing drew her. She looked out at the mounds of snow extending into the distance as far as the eye could see. She'd been happy here for such a short while. Her heart told her that happiness would never return. Mam's phone call had changed everything. Or was it the hours she'd spent reading her diaries, looking into her soul? What was that elusive thing called happiness? Did it really exist? Was it waking up with a smile in a place you loved, ready to take on the world? Was it titillating bits and pieces of time that made the adrenaline flow? Did it come from within or from outside? Was it insulating yourself from everything and anything so you didn't feel? She shook her head. If you didn't feel, you'd be safe from pain, but then you wouldn't know happiness, either. It was a package deal.

Tears rolled down Maggie's cheeks as she made her way downstairs. She made no move to wipe them away. Let the world see, for all she cared. The phoenix had risen from the ashes; so would she. She'd fight.

Cole Tanner stood in the center of his room. He felt disoriented. He should do something. Pound the walls, stamp his feet, bellow out his rage. He jammed his shaking hands into his jeans pockets.

Sawyer was going to die.

Not Maggie, not his father, not his aunts or Riley, but

Sawyer. How could that be? She was so healthy, always taking vitamins and exercising. She'd worked like a dog with him this summer in the barn. If you were sick, you couldn't work like that. She'd been fine in New York. She'd eaten as much as the rest of them, had trekked along for hours and never seemed to be the worse for it. She'd laughed and had a good time. He knew you could do all those things with a broken heart, but when you were sick you slowed down. You didn't laugh when you were sick. Not Sawyer. Anybody but Sawyer.

He was going to be alone again.

Anger rushed through him. It wasn't fair! Not to Sawyer and not to him. He didn't care about the others: his mother, his grandmother, or his father. What did they know about loneliness, not belonging?

He didn't care what his mother said. He picked up the phone and called Adam Jarvis. Adam's voice came on the line, the same voice he remembered, only stronger somehow. "Can I speak to Sawyer?"

"She went for a walk with your grandmother. I'm not sure when they'll be back. Cole, she's all right for now. She's trying to come to grips. She knows what the doctors told her, but she can't quite believe it. Do you know what I mean?"

"I suppose so. I wanted her to know that she could count on me if she needs me. I could drop out of this next semester and come to New York. My father would agree to that. My mother would have a fit, but I don't much care."

"Sawyer knows she can count on you, Cole. Right now, though, I think she has to learn to count on herself. I'll tell her you called and give her the message. Don't be hurt or surprised if she doesn't call you back for a while. And Cole?"

"Yes?"

"I'll take care of her. Trust me."

"Shit, I know that. Tell her . . . tell her that . . .Oh, shit."

"Kid, the word love isn't so hard to say. You have to

practice it and use it. I'll tell her for you."

"No, don't do that. I'll do it myself when she calls me. Just tell her I called."

"Cole, how did Riley take the news?"

"It was a blow. He loves her, too. He said he was going to his room to write to his grandfather. I think Sawyer and his grandfather were very close. Sawyer was good friends with his mother, too."

"Maggie?"

Cole's voice was cold, so brittle Adam thought he could hear the wire crackle in his ear. "Business as usual. Dinner's at seven. Nothing upsets the routine here. If you want to know if she's upset, I can't tell you."

Adam hesitated. "Rand?"

"That's one cool dude. It's in his eyes. I'd say—and this is only my opinion—he feels bad. He should for hurting Sawyer."

"Don't place blame, Cole. People do what they have to do even if we don't understand their reasons. Don't hate him; Sawyer doesn't. Take care of yourself. I'll tell Sawyer you called."

"Call me, Adam, even if Sawyer doesn't. Promise."

"I promise, kid. Hang tough."

Riley opened the door at the sound of a knock. He was stunned to see Cole standing in the doorway. "C'mon in." He made no move to wipe away the tears streaming down his cheeks. Both boys stared at each other. "I don't care if you see me crying. I don't care if you tell anyone, either," Riley said belligerently. "Here." He handed his cousin a wadded-up ball of toilet paper.

"Who'm I gonna tell? She's my sister. She's the only one who ever cared about me." Cole gulped. "What gets me is she didn't look sick to me. We had such a good time in New York. Now she's gonna die. I don't understand."

"I don't understand, either. I was talking to my mother fifteen minutes before she was killed. I feel like you do. I don't have anyone, either, but my grandfather, and he's very old. Here in the United States I have no one but the

Coleman family. I've been thinking about going back to Japan. That should make you happy."

"Finally realized you don't belong," Cole said coolly. "About time."

"That's not why. I'd never let you drive me out."

"I'd never stay someplace I wasn't wanted."

"When it's you doing the wanting, it doesn't bother me. *If* I do decide to go home," Riley said defiantly, "it won't be because of you."

"I didn't come in here to discuss that. I came to talk about Sawyer. We get out of school the end of May. I thought maybe she'd like to go on a trip or take a vacation. We could go for the whole summer. I don't know anything about brain tumors, how she'll feel or anything. Do you?"

"No. We could call up a doctor and ask. Your mother would probably know."

"I'm not asking my mother anything. Adam will know. He'll want to go, too. It'll be like Christmas. We could make all the plans and sort of spring it on her and Adam."

"Who's this supposed to help? Them or us?"

"Us, you jerk. Nothing can help Sawyer. We're just gonna be her support system. But we're gonna need a lot of money. How much do you have?"

"In the bank or on me?"

"You are a jerk. In the bank. We'll need money for tickets and money to rent some place. I've never been to Hawaii. Have you?"

"Only on a layover on the way here from Japan. I think I have thirty-three hundred in the bank, maybe less. The statement didn't come yet and I took out a lot for Christmas. I can get some money from my grandfather if you tell me how much we need. How much do you have?"

"You must be kidding. I have fifty-six dollars and no place to get any more. It's up to you if we pull this off."

"I knew there was a reason you came in here. I'm writing to my grandfather now. How much should I ask for?"

Cole sat down at Riley's desk and pulled out the calculator. "I've seen commercials on TV for flights to

Hawaii. They quoted a $599 ticket, so that's $2,396 for the four of us. Maybe we can rent a condo. That's the off season for tourism in Hawaii, so let's say $1,500 a week. If we stay a month, it will be $6,000. We have to eat and see the sights, take in the other islands. Probably $5,000 on top of that. Figure a total of $25,396. My mother will give me some money, and I can squeeze some from the old man. Not a lot, though, so don't count on it." Cole looked up anxiously. "Do you think your grandfather will send it?"

"When I tell the old one what it's for, he won't ask questions. What if we run short?"

"Then ask for a little more. If we don't use it all, you can send it back. Look, I'm sorry I can't contribute, but I can't draw on my trust fund till I'm twenty-one. You know how hard it is for me to get money out of my mother. If you don't want to go along with this, say so now."

"I think it's a good idea. Sawyer will approve of what she calls our ingenuity. Adam'll probably be glad we took care of the details. The money isn't the problem. It's me and you that's the problem."

"We'll call a truce. I don't get in your way and you don't get in mine. We managed at Christmas and we can do it again."

"Okay. Truce." Riley sighed. "Someday I hope you tell me what it is you have against me. I came here prepared to like you."

Cole snorted. "Fat chance."

"Right. And now that I've made you feel better, you can toddle off to your room and act like a man instead of a sixteen-year-old who thinks it's shameful to cry. When I hear from my grandfather, I'll let you know."

"You aren't throwing me out. I'm leaving on my own." Cole turned at the door. "By the way, I . . . I called Adam. He said Sawyer went for a walk with Grand. He'll call us and keep in touch. I thought you might want to know."

"Thanks for telling me."

"Drop dead," Cole muttered as he closed the door.

Riley sat with his chin cupped in his hand, staring at

the door for a long time. It was really the first time Cole
had come into his room and stayed to talk. Maybe they
were making progress of a sort. He wished there was
something he could do for Cole. How lonely he must be.

It was late; the bedroom lamps cast dim shadows into
the corners of Maggie's bedroom. The house was asleep
except for the two of them.

Maggie lay in the crook of Rand's arm, wide awake.
He, too, was awake, staring at the ceiling. He liked the
pressure of Maggie's dark head on his shoulder, liked the
feel of her body pressing against his. If this was wrong,
why did it feel so right, so good? It was crazy, but he felt
like he'd finally come home after a long, long journey.
They nurtured each other, loved each other, and he didn't
want to lose what they'd found together. But it wasn't
going to be up to him. He knew Maggie was sending him
away. This was their last night together; he'd return to
England tomorrow.

He'd tried to explain to Maggie that what happened to
Sawyer wasn't their fault. The tumor had been there,
growing, long before last July. Their loving each other
hadn't caused it.

"But our loving each other is causing this pain!" she'd
cried.

She'd listened to his arguments but hadn't heard a word
he'd said. When he'd finished baring his soul, she'd looked
at him with tears in her eyes and told him she'd miss him
terribly. That she felt as though she were giving up a part
of herself.

Now she lay in his embrace, her fingers tracing patterns
down the length of Rand's arm. "I know you don't understand. I don't understand, either. It feels right to me, so
I have to do it. I'm an expert at giving up things; it comes
easy to me. I learned at an early age that it was expected
of me. They all expect me to give you up now. I don't
have any choice. Maybe someday..." Her voice trailed
off.

"Someday isn't good enough. What's been done is done.

I'm not sorry. Maggie, we can't let the past rule our lives. We have to deal with the future and with today the best we can. My going back to England isn't going to change things. I know Sawyer. She'll never come back here."

"I have to try. Somehow I—"

"It's too late, Maggie."

"We have to go on from here. It's something I have to do alone. If you're here, I won't be able to do what I have to do."

"What exactly are you going to do? What miracle are you going to perform to make things right? Tell me, Maggie, so I can understand."

"I don't know, Rand. When I returned to Sunbridge, I thought my fighting days were over. I know now those little skirmishes were only preliminaries for the biggest fight of my life. And I have to win this one, not just for me but for Sawyer as well."

Rand turned so he was facing Maggie, his face just inches from hers. "There are some things that can't be fixed, Maggie, things that are better left alone. You're going into a very volatile situation. You'll need me here for support."

"It's true; I do need you, my darling, and that's the reason I'm sending you away. I can't allow myself the luxury of depending on you when the going gets tough. I have to start off like Sawyer—alone. Please, Rand, don't make this any harder on me than it already is. Pap told me once that you have to take responsibility for your own actions. That's what I'm trying to do. We'll talk to each other from time to time. I'll write; hopefully, you'll write back. I want us to be friends."

"Maggie, I want to marry you."

Maggie turned away. How she'd longed to hear those words! For the first time in her life she was loved with an intensity she could return . . . and she had to give it up. What irony.

"I'll drive you to the airport in the morning."

"That's your answer—I'll drive you to the airport?" Rand asked incredulously.

"It's the only answer for now."

There were no arguments left. Rand gathered Maggie into his arms again and held her close. Memory after memory flashed before him. He tried to lock them in his mind for all the long, lonely months ahead. He knew Maggie was doing the same thing.

They slept in each other's arms, a light sleep full of dreams and promises.

Rand sat in the airport bar, an empty beer glass in his hand. He hadn't wanted the beer—any kind of drink, for that matter—but he couldn't sit and take up space without ordering.

He didn't like Kennedy Airport. It was too big. There were too many travelers, none of them smiling. And he'd never known it to fail yet: every damn time he hit Kennedy, his flight was delayed. This time, he had an hour to kill. An hour to think. If only he could forget.

A familiar scent teased Rand's nostrils. Sawyer's perfume. He looked around anxiously. He could almost feel her presence, yet he couldn't see her. He sniffed again. He wasn't imagining things—there she was! He'd been so deep in thought, he'd almost missed her. Billie was with her; they were walking from the lounge, their arms linked together. He left crumpled bills on the table and rushed out.

"Sawyer! Billie!"

Sawyer turned, her face alive and bright for a split second before it closed to blankness. Billie wore a startled expression. Neither spoke; neither greeted him.

"Hello," he said warmly. "What are you doing here?"

"I'm going back to Vermont," Billie replied. "Sawyer decided to wait with me. What are you doing here?"

"Going back to England. I'm sorry you couldn't make Christmas. We all missed you."

"We were snowed in." Billie lowered her eyes, made a show of rummaging through her purse, looking for something she knew wasn't there. Why didn't he go away and leave them alone? Surely he knew. Maggie would have told him.

"What time is your flight? Can I buy you both a drink? I have an hour to kill." He cringed at the casual use of the word kill. He wanted to bite his tongue.

"No, thanks. Grand has only a few minutes till boarding. Have a nice flight, Rand."

"It was nice seeing you, Rand," Billie said quietly.

Rand watched their backs as they walked away from him. Well, what in the hell had he expected?

He waited until Sawyer returned from the security gate. When she saw him, she tried to avoid him, but he blocked her path.

"I want to talk to you."

"I don't know why. You said everything there was to say at Christmastime. What makes today any different? I have to get home, Rand."

"That's a lie and we both know it. Come into the lounge and sit with me for a few minutes."

"Why?"

"Because I want to talk to you."

"I'm sorry, I have to go. I don't want a scene, but if you persist, I'll make one."

"Sawyer, don't hate me. Please."

"Hate? That word is probably right up there with love. Hand in hand, you know, like salt and pepper. When you're going to die—and don't pretend you don't know— that word takes on new meaning. There's only one person in this world I hate. And it isn't you."

"That's what I want to talk to you about. You have it all wrong. Why won't you listen?"

"Because I don't care. That means I'm not interested. Why won't *you* listen to me?"

She turned her back and started to walk away. This time he didn't stop her.

As Rand was flying toward the shores of England, Sawyer lay on her bed, collapsed in tears. She was glad to be alone, glad Adam wasn't there to comfort her. She cried not for herself but for what she'd done to Rand. She'd left without giving him a shred of understanding, taking victory in the fact that he'd left Sunbridge and wasn't with Maggie. She'd deliberately hurt him, wanted to stun him and force him to carry her bitterness away with him. She wanted to punish him because he didn't love her. Was what she had done to him loving?

Hours later she awoke with a nagging headache and tried to sit up. The loft was too quiet. Adam was probably out running, she decided. He'd stayed pretty close these past days trying to bolster her. Steady-as-a-rock Adam. Who could blame him if he had cabin fever? She'd been just as steady, accepting the doctor's prognosis like a real trooper. She knew she was still in shock—half believing, half disbelieving. Other people got brain tumors. Other people died. But God, she was only twenty-six. A year wasn't enough time!

If it was all you had, it had to be long enough.

She fluffed up the pillows behind her head, picked up the notepad and pencil on her night table. Resign her job at the office. Money? Her bank account was healthy enough, no worry on that score. Her insurance was paid up. She had to change the beneficiary now; Cole, of course. Billie would understand. She'd make a will. Her stock to Cole and Riley. Little by little she'd dispose of her things so that when the time came and Adam had to clean out her part of the loft, he'd only have to deal with her clothes. Neat and tidy. Now it was down to basics.

What did she want? To be loved. To be wanted and needed. She wanted to share and laugh and possibly cry, but for the right reasons.

The biggest challenge of her life. Late into the night, when Adam thought she was asleep, she'd lain thinking about her grandfather Moss. He hadn't whimpered and whined when he was told he had leukemia. He'd had a time limit, too, and had used that time to work toward his dream. She herself had carried out that dream with her grandmother's help. How could she do less? She was, after all, a Coleman.

Since there was nothing she could do about her own condition, she had to start thinking about Cole. He would be her number-one priority. Maggie had forbidden contact with her son, but at this point in time, what Maggie wanted or didn't want was of no interest to her. Like Moss, she would have to leave something behind, something Cole could sink his teeth into. Her dream. The only problem was, she didn't have a dream of her own. She made a note to make an appointment with Cranston. They would be allies. She, for the betterment of Cole; he, for his own reasons.

Now the pen flew over the yellow paper. She had to write Cole—Riley, too. She would put both letters in one envelope addressed to Riley; he'd see that his cousin got her letter.

All things considered, she felt she had a handle on everything. She'd make it if the others gave her space. Adam was trying. So was Grand. Poor Grand. First Riley and then Moss. There'd been such love and worry in her eyes at the airport, but she'd carried it off.

The day Sawyer mailed her letters to Riley, one arrived from Cole. She read it several times and then showed it to Adam, who laughed in delight. "By God, those kids are something. I say we should go for it."

"Me, too. Did you notice, Adam, that although Cole makes a point of saying it was all his idea, he gives financial credit to Riley? I told you the way the two of them sobered me up over Christmas. That was a joint effort, too. I'm pleased."

"And well you should be. I'll send the money back to Riley's grandfather," Adam said generously. "The kids will never have to know."

"No, no, no, you can't do that! Mr. Hasegawa would lose face. You can't ever return a gift to a Japanese. Besides, he'd give the world to Riley if he could. Money means nothing to them. If his generosity could make Riley and me happy, he'd clean out his bank accounts. He gave blank checks to my mother for my grandfather's plane. Blank checks! No, we're going to accept, but I think three months is too long. Let's go for six weeks and play the rest by ear. Agreed?"

"Sounds good to me. That means I have to get my work in ahead of schedule. I'm not going to have too much time to spend with you. What will you do?"

"Do? Do, you ask? Shop. As in shop. I'm going to run my credit cards to the limit. From here on in it's plastic all the way. Do you need anything? As long as I'm shopping, I can pick up whatever you want. Listen, Adam, we agreed, business as usual. Don't start pampering me now. Get your work done. Get it in so we can leave with free minds. Promise?"

"You got it. You want to rustle up something to eat while I shower? You didn't do the towels, did you?"

"Nope, but I will. It won't kill you to use the one you used yesterday."

"And the day before that and the day before that," Adam muttered on the way to the bathroom.

He stood under the shower spray, letting the water beat on his head. In the oblivion offered by the steam collecting on the shower door, he sank back against the tiles. Dry, heaving sobs racked him, the sound stifled by the pounding spray. Where would he find the strength to continue this charade? To go along with Sawyer as if everything were normal, as though they hadn't told him he was losing her forever? He was already grieving, already denying what he knew to be true. Even though she would never say the words he so desperately wanted to hear, he loved her. He couldn't think of a life without Sawyer. In the isolation of the shower he cried his grief, and for long after he remained there, struggling to regain his composure in order to face her again. He mustn't let his emotions show; he mustn't let her see his anguish. If he did, she would send him away, and he intended to share every waking moment with her for as long as they had.

* * *

Over breakfast Sawyer asked Adam's advice. "Grand told me about this place high in the hills in Hawaii that Seth arranged for her and Moss when he was on leave. A lady, Ester Kamali, owns it but doesn't live there. I wonder if she could somehow get in touch with the lady and ask if we could stay there. There's a caretaker and housekeeper, or at least there was. Grand said it was the nicest place in the world and one of the happiest times of her life. Once she told me in secret that she thought that was where she fell in love with Thad, only she didn't know it at the time. That's where I want to go. I'll call this morning and write to the boys so they can cancel any condos the travel agency wants to rent them. Grand has pictures. I'll tell her to send them so you can see what I'm talking about."

"I don't like to bring this up, but I have to." Adam bit into a piece of crunch toast. "Is it possible that Maggie can stop this trip? She does have sole custody of Cole now."

"I suppose anything is possible. Riley already has his grandfather's permission. I'm going to talk to Cranston. I don't think we have anything to worry about. Maggie won't interfere. If she does, we'll have to switch to plan B."

"Which is . . ."

"Whatever the boys come up with. You and I are only along for the ride."

"Then I won't worry about it. . . . This toast is good. I kind of thought you were going to cook something. You know, something I could sink my teeth into, like eggs or pancakes. Food."

"I don't have time. I have to do the laundry and go shopping. Maybe I'll stop by Cranston's office instead of waiting for an appointment. He'll see me because he'll think it has something to do with Maggie and Cole. As soon as those towels are in the wash, I'm calling Grand. Get to work, Jarvis. I don't want anything spoiling this trip, even if it is months away."

Sawyer called her grandmother. Billie's heart soared when she heard her granddaughter's request. "I'll get on it right away. I can't promise anything, Sawyer. It was so long ago. I'll call you back this evening."

When Billie hung up, she dug out her address book and scanned the numbers. At Sunbridge there were ledgers, journals, notebooks, all dusty now, full of names. Surely Ester Kamali would be listed there somewhere. She called Amelia.

Amelia said she'd drop everything and return to Sunbridge to get the information, then call back as soon as she had news. When Amelia hung up, she called Maggie, who agreed to go to the basement and search out old telephone bills. Thank God, nothing at Sunbridge was ever thrown away.

When Thad returned to the house at lunchtime, Billie told him what was going on. Thad looked at her in amazement and then laughed. "Billie, why didn't you call the house in Hawaii and ask to speak to whoever is there? It's possible Phillip and Rosa aren't there anymore, but someone should be. There's also the possibility that the place has been sold."

"Don't you remember, the telephone number was unlisted."

"Ah, now that you mention it, I do seem to recall having to carry the number in my hip pocket. That's one for your side. What will you do if you can't get the house?"

"Shhh," Billie said, placing a finger on his lips. "One way or another, we'll get that house for Sawyer. Trust me."

"I do. I do. Personally, I think what those two young boys are trying to do is just as wonderful."

Billie smiled wanly. "Not trying, Thad. They're doing it. By tonight, it will be a fact."

And so Ma Bell worked her magic, from New York City to Vermont to Texas, from the Pentagon to the Miramar Naval Air Station in San Diego, then on to Pearl Harbor and ending up in Hong Kong.

Amelia was on one extension and Maggie on the other

as they called Billie to give her the news. "We got it for you, Mam," Maggie said breathlessly. "I tried the number in Hawaii and it's been disconnected." There was awe in her voice when she said, "I had no idea Seth traveled in such high places. Amelia did some razzle-dazzling that would knock you off your feet."

"Billie, we have the number for you. Everything sounded positive. The house is empty, has been for years. Rosa and Phillip passed away. There's a grandson who looks in on things. Miss Kamali is living in Hong Kong and has never returned to the island." She repeated the number twice to be sure Billie had it right. "You should be able to place your call. It's tomorrow over there. Take a shot at it—and good luck."

"Mam, if there's anything I can do, call me," Maggie said.

"I'll do that, Maggie. Thanks again."

"I got it, I got it!" Billie said, dancing around Thad's chair. "Cross your fingers that Miss Kamali gives her okay. I'm going upstairs to make the call. This is going to be woman talk."

"Go ahead, darling. I'll sit here and smoke my pipe and remember the time we spent in Hawaii."

"Just don't fall asleep till I get back."

"What do you have in mind?" Thad leered.

"The same thing you do. Stay alert!"

Thad watched his wife run up the stairs, seeing the young girl he fell in love with. He thanked God again, as he did every day, for his good fortune. He packed his pipe, struck a match, and waited. He would always wait for Billie. Till the end of time, if necessary, and in eternity he'd be there with his hand in hers.

Billie's heart pounded furiously as she placed her call. She crossed her fingers and waited. Six rings, seven, and then a soft voice came on the line.

Billie introduced herself and waited to see if the woman would remember her.

"But of course I remember you. My housekeeper did

nothing but talk of you for months after you left. What can I do for you, Mrs. Coleman?"

"It's not Mrs. Coleman anymore. It's Mrs. Kingsley. My husband died several years ago." Billie quickly explained her problem. "Whatever the cost, I'll pay it. Please, Miss Kamali, whatever it takes, I'll do it."

"My hesitation has nothing to do with money, Mrs. Kingsley. The house has been closed up for many years. I don't know if it's fit to live in. One of the caretaker's grandsons is supposedly looking after it, but they get lazy, if you know what I mean."

"That's not important, Miss Kamali. I'd be glad to pay for repairs and to get it ready."

"Please, call me Ester. I feel as though I know you. May I call you Billie?"

"But of course." Suddenly Billie blurted out that she had worn the rainbow silk dress that had been packed in the chest.

Ester laughed. "Rosa told me. She said you looked beautiful in it. It made me happy knowing someone got to wear it. My beloved never got to see me in it."

"You've never been back to that beautiful house since you left?" Billie asked in awe.

"Never. My soul is there. I'll go there when it's time for me to die. For now, my heart is here in Hong Kong. I have a pleasant life with a man who loves me very much."

"And do you love him very much?" She had no right to ask, but she wanted to know about this faceless woman who could fill Sawyer's life with sunshine for a little while.

"There are some loves that are for yesterday and others forever. My love belongs to yesterday and so do I. For now, what I have is pleasant. I'm able to live quite happily, but there are too many shadows in my life for me to move on. But to give you an answer, of course you may have the use of my house. Your father-in-law was very kind to some members of my family years ago. I could never forget that. If you can manage to send someone to Hawaii to look things over and have the house opened, you have my blessing. There will be no discussion of monies. It will be my gift to your granddaughter, and I will pray for her and for you. I'll send you a set of keys tomorrow."

Tears streamed down Billie's cheeks. "I don't know what to say. You're the second-kindest person I've ever known. I can accept your generosity only if you allow my family to make any repairs the house may require. It would break my heart to see that lovely place fall into ruin. Please, say it's all right."

"I accept, but you must tell me who the *first*-kindest person in your life is." There was a smile in Ester's voice and Billie played to it.

"The person whose love for me is forever, my husband. Thank you, Ester. I'll stay in touch. Perhaps one day we'll meet."

"I'll look forward to that time. Good-bye, Billie. My prayers are with you and your granddaughter."

Now she had to call Sawyer and tell her everything was set. Then a quick call to Sunbridge.

Sawyer was delighted. "I'll tell the boys I know of a place. I know they'll be thrilled. Thanks, Grand."

"For what?"

"For coming through for me."

"All I did was make a few phone calls for you. Good night, darling. I'll talk to you later in the week."

The call to Sunbridge left Billie stunned. "Let me do it, Mam," Maggie pleaded. "Let me go to Hawaii and get the house ready. Sawyer doesn't need to know I'm the one who's doing it. Let her think the place is ready to move into. I'll make up some story about where I'm going for the boys. I *need* to do this, Mam. Please say yes."

"You're sure you can handle it? Sawyer and the boys are not to know; is that right?"

"I think it would be best, don't you?"

"For now, anyway. Maggie, what about your divorce and Susan and the new baby? When will you go?"

"The end of April, beginning of May. That would give

me plenty of time. There's not much I can do about the divorce. The lawyers are handling that for me. Cole is old enough to speak for himself. I'm hoping this time he's going to spend with Sawyer will open him up to life. What I do from here on in is going to have a direct bearing on his decision. I'm hoping for the best, but I'll be able to handle the worst. I'll be here for Suse when she has the baby and the christening. It'll all work out."

"I'm sure it will. Maggie..."

"Don't say it, Mam. Let me do this my way."

"Maggie, please, listen to me. I was going to ask you about Rand."

"I sent him home. I thought you knew."

"Yes, I knew he went back to England, but I didn't know you sent him back. Why? I thought you loved him. I thought he loved you."

"Yes. Yes. He does. I do. We do. Oh, Mam.... It was for the best."

"Who? For God's sake, Maggie, for whom is it best?"

"Everyone. Sawyer, Amelia. The boys. Suse, too."

"What about you?"

Maggie snorted. "Since when does it matter what I want?"

"It matters to me. Fight, Maggie. If Rand is what you want, then fight for him. Don't let Sawyer or anyone else take that from you. If it's right in your heart, then it's right for you."

Maggie's voice was suddenly lighter, buoyant. "Mam, do you know what you just said to me?"

"Of course I know. You deserve to be happy, Maggie. So does Rand; so does Sawyer. Each of you has to find the way to make that happen. It isn't too late for you and Rand. What was the last thing your father wrote to you, Maggie?"

Maggie recited the short, last letter Moss had written her. "Be happy. Those were his exact words. Mam, he said to be happy. Oh, my God, I sent Rand away. I was afraid to be happy. I'm still afraid. I love you, Mam,"

Maggie cried before she hung up the phone.

"And I love you, too, Maggie," Billie said softly as she replaced the phone. How important those words were! Everyone should say them at least once a day. Well, she was going to say them right now to the person who deserved them the most.

"Is this what you call staying alert?" Billie laughed at the sight of Thad dozing in the chair with three of Duchess's puppies snuggled against him. She dropped to her knees. "Are you going to tell me happiness is snuggling with a warm puppy?"

"They were just standing in till you got here. Did everything go all right?"

"Everything's fine. Come along, darling. I have plans for you, but first I want to tell you I love you with all my heart."

Thad stared down at his wife, at the invitation and promise in her eyes. "And I love you for now and forever."

"We make a good team, don't we?"

"The best," Thad said as he snuggled the puppies next to Duchess in her bed by the fire. "The very best."

Maggie lay propped up with a stack of lace-edged pillows behind her dark head, paper and pen in hand. Rand would think she was out of her mind. Maybe she was.

Dear Rand,
     When you receive this letter, you will probably think me out of my mind. I feel like a yo-yo and so must you.
     I made a mistake when I told you to go back to England. You made a mistake by doing what I asked. I thought I was sending you away for all the right reasons, but I was wrong. Mam made me see it. She said if we love each other, we should be together and happy. The rest will take care of itself.
     I'll be here till the end of April, but I know you

may need some time to think. And I understand. I just want you to know that I love you, for all the *right* reasons.

Forgive my fear and my weakness. Be happy with me.

All my love,
Maggie

{{{{{{{{ CHAPTER TWENTY-ONE }}}}}}}}

Jessica Margaret de Moray made her entrance into the world on February 14, Valentine's Day. She was golden-haired and pink-skinned, weighed six pounds, two ounces, and measured eighteen inches long. For Susan it was love at first sight. Maggie and Amelia crowed with delight when the pink bundle was held at the viewing window for their pleasure and first introduction. Cary beamed and cooed through the nursery window.

"A woman shouldn't have to go through this alone," Cary muttered to Amelia and Maggie on the ride back to Sunbridge.

"You're right; she shouldn't. But who the hell knows where that dog Jerome is? And he wouldn't have wanted to be here, anyway. Susan didn't ask for him once, but I knew what she was thinking. She felt deserted." Maggie brightened. "But she's not alone anymore, is she. Now she has little Jessica Margaret."

Cary laughed. "You don't really intend to call her that, do you? That's quite a mouthful for such a little thing."

"No, I guess not." Maggie sighed. "But I can't help reminding anyone who'll listen that Susan named her after

Grandmam Jessica and me. It's an honor, Cary, it really
is. Don't you think so, Amelia?"

"Yes, I suppose." Amelia knew she was having a hard
time coping with the birth of Susan's baby. It made her
feel old, so old. . . . And Cary was taking this birth with
such rejoicing. Did he want a child of his own? At forty-
two, he certainly was young enough to become a father
for the first time. But who'd give him that child? She
certainly couldn't. No, it would have to be someone young,
someone like Eileen.

Maggie was still jabbering. "I can't wait to shop for
the baby. Lacy dresses, frilly bonnets. They make such
beautiful toys these days—creative and progressive. Oh,
and she must have an English coach carriage. You know,
Amelia, like the ones those English nannies push around
Hyde Park on sunny afternoons. The ones with the huge
wheels. I'm going to telephone Harrod's first thing and
have them send one over," she said happily. She couldn't
help wondering, though, why the baby hadn't been placed
in a bassinet beside the other infants after the viewing.
The masked nurse had whisked little Jessie away as soon
as the oohs and aahs were over.

The phone was ringing when Maggie and Amelia entered
the house. Maggie caught it just before Martha. "Suse!
What are you doing calling? Couldn't wait to hear the
compliments over little Jessie? You should be resting."

She listened, her face going absolutely blank.

"What's wrong?" Cary asked, his arm going around
Maggie for support.

"I've never heard of spina bifida. Operating on her
when she was just born!" Maggie listened intently. "Suse,
I'm coming back to the hospital to be with you. Yes, yes,
I want to." She replaced the receiver and sat down on
the bottom step of the staircase.

"Don't keep us in suspense, Maggie. What's wrong?"
Amelia demanded.

"It's the baby. She was born with something wrong
with her spine, a hole or something. Suse doesn't quite

understand it yet. They're going to operate within the next few hours."

Amelia shook her head. "Will it never stop? Always one crisis after another. And Susan all alone except for us. She should have a husband by her side." Her eyes narrowed. "It's all Jerome's fault! If there's anything wrong with that child, he's to blame. Working Susan the way he did, fitting her into corsets so her pregnancy wouldn't show—"

"Amelia," Maggie implored wearily, "please don't go on this way. I know Jerome was hard on Suse, but I'm certain none of this was his doing, or Susan's, either. It just happened. Little Jessie will be fine; she has to be. Whatever you do, don't repeat any of this to Susan. She has enough to contend with. Do you understand?"

"Yes, of course we do, Maggie," Cary interjected. "You won't say any of this to Susan, will you, Amelia?" He spoke sternly, tightening his grasp on his wife's arm. "We'll all be very careful of what we say."

"All right, Cary!" Amelia pulled her arm away. "You don't have to speak to me as though I were some kind of witch ready to pounce on Susan." She flew up the stairs, brushing past Maggie, her slim-heeled Bally shoes noiseless on the thickly padded carpet runner.

"Now, what the hell has gotten into her?" Cary asked. "She's so damn irritable lately; everything I say seems to come out wrong. I didn't mean to be rough on her, but there's no telling what she'll do these days. I didn't want to take the chance that she'd face Susan with all sorts of accusations that wouldn't help the situation."

I know, Cary," Maggie said quietly. "But remember that Amelia practically raised Susan, and she's never really liked Jerome. She's worried and so am I. I'm leaving again for the hospital. Do you think you'll be here to eat dinner with the boys? You could tell them about the baby and reassure them that everything will be all right. At least I pray it'll be all right."

Susan lay propped up in bed. The peach-colored bed

jacket seemed out of place against the starched white sheets. The room was bare of flowers and cards. Tomorrow it would be full.

"Here, blow," Maggie said, holding out a white handkerchief.

Susan blew her nose obligingly and dabbed at her eyes. "They're operating on her right now. The doctors assure me it's standard procedure for spina bifida. I didn't even know what it was till they told me. It originates in the first month of pregnancy. The vertebrae of the spinal cord are not formed correctly. That's why they have to operate right away. It's my fault. I knew I should have taken better care of myself. I shouldn't have let Jerome bully me the way he did."

"Suse, it's not your fault and the doctor will tell you so. Children are born all the time with defects. They're operating, so that will make it right, won't it?"

"There could be fluid in the brain. The doctor said they can treat and monitor the children and possibly they can grow into independent adults living full lives. But I know it won't happen. Why should I be one of the lucky ones?"

"You can't think like that," Maggie said sternly. "Your thoughts have to be positive. Your baby is alive and being taken care of. Other mothers aren't that lucky. Count your blessings."

"I am. I'm fortunate that the pediatrician recognized the disease and acted on it. This is one of the few hospitals that can treat it. I was listening, but he was talking so fast, I think I only caught half of it, and I was a little groggy. He said something about incontinence of bowel and bladder, paralysis of leg muscles, and lack of sensation. That's all I know."

"We'll find out all there is to know tomorrow," Maggie promised. "When the doctor comes back, you'll have to talk to him yourself and ask every question you can think of. It's going to be all right, Susan. Be glad you're here with your family. We'll all do what we can."

Susan held on to Maggie's hand until she dozed off.

An hour later the doctor entered the room. He was a tall man, dressed in operating green. He looked, Maggie thought, like a man who didn't smile enough. He was smiling now, though. How awesome, she thought, to hold the power of life and death in your hands. She looked at his long, slender fingers. What must he have thought when he sliced into that tiny back? She had to know, had to ask. "Please, Doctor, tell me, what did you think about when you started to operate?"

"I wasn't thinking. I was praying. I always pray when my scalpel makes the first incision. The baby came through just fine. She's sleeping now and will get some glucose in a little while. It's too early for me to say anything else at this time. So, for now I'd say the baby is resting." He smiled again, a smile that would warm any mother's heart.

Four hours later Susan woke, a look of alarm on her face. Maggie reached up to smooth the hair back from her brow. "Jessie came through the operation just fine. She's sleeping and probably getting glucose right now."

"He came in, the doctor, I mean?"

"Hours ago. I didn't want to wake you. He said he'll be in to see you tomorrow. I checked with the night nurse a while ago, and she said when you woke they'd wheel you down to see her. Suse, he said he prayed when he made the first incision. I thought you might want to know that."

"Thanks, Maggie. I couldn't have gotten through this without you."

"After you see the baby, try to get some sleep. It's what you need now." Maggie kissed Susan lightly and tasted the salt of her tears. "You can handle it," she whispered.

"Yes, I will. It's late. Go home. Call Mam."

"I already did, but I'll give her another call. See you tomorrow."

Cary felt as though he were tiptoeing around the bedroom when he was really making more noise than usual.

He knew Amelia was antsy, waiting for him to ask what was bothering her. Had she understood about his trip to New York? Damn, it couldn't have come at a worse time. Just last week she'd told him that in the next few days the carpet and draperies were going to be installed in the house and she'd have to be there. She was bound to think he'd planned this trip deliberately so she wouldn't be able to go with him.

Amelia had been acting strange these past few weeks. She'd taken the news of Sawyer's illness very badly. And tonight she'd curled into a ball on her side of the king-size bed. He'd had to be extra gentle with her, cajoling her into telling him what was wrong. She'd gulped and cried that suddenly, for the first time, she was aware of her own mortality. Think of little Jessie; think of Sawyer. It could happen to anyone—it could easily happen to her. Look how much older she was. He'd tried everything he knew to shake her out of it, but she'd been inconsolable. Now he had no choice but to go to sleep. He *had* to get up in the morning. It wouldn't make a difference if Amelia was late getting to her house.

When Cary woke the following morning, more tired than when he'd gone to bed, he saw Amelia lying on her back, staring at the ceiling. He knew she hadn't slept at all. He felt annoyed with her and then with himself that she could upset him like this. God knows he'd done his best. He'd shared every aspect of his life with her, and there weren't many men who did that.

Cary lay quietly for a few moments listening to Amelia's light breathing. God, he loved her. Of all the women he'd slept with in his life, she was the one he wanted to wake up next to. She always smiled and reached out to him. He knew he'd be grouchy and irritable all day if he didn't make the first move. He reached out, a sleepy smile on his face. "C'mere."

Amelia obligingly snuggled closer to him. She sighed deeply. This was where she belonged. "I'm sorry I was so..."

"Bitchy?"

Cary could feel the smile against his shoulder. "Yes, bitchy. I don't expect you to understand about this family. All I can do is tell you the way it is. Susan's baby . . ."

"Amelia, listen to me. I do understand. It gnaws at my gut about Sawyer. She hasn't even begun to taste what life has to offer. But neither of us can change things. If it was something simple like an organ transplant, I'd donate one of mine if it would make you happy. Susan's baby is alive. It could be worse, much worse. None of it is your fault. You can't shoulder it all."

"I'm not trying to. I'm trying to come to terms with it. Oh, Cary, I'm so afraid to die."

"Don't you think everyone feels like that? I do. Just the thought of leaving this earth and not having you with me makes me sick to my stomach. Now, I know men aren't supposed to say such things, but that's how I feel. You're my life, Amelia. I wouldn't be here now doing what I'm doing if it wasn't for you."

Amelia rolled over petulantly. "I don't want you to be grateful to me."

"Goddammit, Amelia. I am grateful. That's only a small part of it. Why are you fighting me? We never had a problem till we came back here. Maybe it was a mistake. Maybe I wasn't cut out to take on this project. I did it for you. For us."

Amelia stubbornly closed her ears to Cary's explanations. She'd heard it all before. Why wasn't he talking about Eileen? Eileen was what was bothering her. Couldn't he see it? If he understood her as well as he said he did, he should know what was bothering her.

"When are you leaving for New York?"

"Tomorrow morning." Cary sighed. He couldn't dally any longer or he'd be late for the office.

Amelia made no effort to get out of bed. So what if she was late? The contractor had a key to the house; he could let the workmen in. Cary was upset with her. She was upset with Cary. Where did they go from here?

She swung her legs over the bed, slipped into a lime-green robe and matching mules, then fluffed at her hair. "How busy are you going to be in New York?" she called through the open bathroom door.

"Pretty busy. My evenings should be free, though. At least part of them. Want to change your mind and hit Fifth Avenue?"

"No. I was thinking maybe I'd make the trip with you and go on to Vermont and see Billie. I guess I can delay things at the house. I could join you the last day and we could see a play or something. I don't want to interfere with your business." Warily she watched him to see his reaction. He appeared to be delighted.

"That's a great idea. Call Billie and tell her before I leave so I know you'll be happy today. You'll have to make a reservation, though. I can have Eileen do it for you."

"I'll do it. Yes, I think it's a great idea myself. I need a break. We could take Sawyer and Adam out to dinner if she's up to it. I'll pack your evening clothes."

"Good girl. Hey, maybe we could stay an extra day and make it a sort of fourth honeymoon."

Amelia giggled. Maybe they could get back on track.

On the way down the hall, both Amelia and Cary stopped at the nursery. Susan was cradling the baby, a dreamy look on her face. "She falls asleep and doesn't want to burp. I have to take her into the doctor's today. She's gorgeous. Don't you think so?"

Amelia blinked. All newborn babies looked like creatures from the unknown to her. Baby Jessica *was* different, though. She looked pink and perfect, her tiny lips puckered as though expecting more. The soft, downy fuzz on her head was standing on end. Cary laughed as he tried to smooth it down. "Porcupine hair."

"Have you had breakfast yet?" Amelia asked.

"Good heavens, no. Jessie comes first. I had to change her from the skin out. When she's ready to eat, she's ready. She's a slow eater and she takes forever to burp.

You go on. I'll be down in a little while."

Cary, who was by now quite late, gulped a quick cup of coffee and left. Amelia picked at some scrambled eggs and watched as Maggie devoured a stack of pancakes. "How can you eat like that and not gain an ounce?" she grumbled.

"I rarely eat lunch. Breakfast is the most important meal of the day. I gain; don't kid yourself. How's the house coming?"

"It's almost finished. Cary is going to New York tomorrow on business. I'm going to make the trip with him and go on up to Vermont to see your mother for a few days. I'll spend a few days with him on the return trip and do some shopping. I thought we'd take Sawyer out to dinner if she's up to it."

"That's a great idea. Mam is going to love having you. I think you're her best friend."

Amelia waited for some mention of Sawyer. When Maggie returned to her pancakes, Amelia set her coffee cup down. "Look, I know I'm out of line, but I have to know how you can be so . . . so completely—I don't even know what word to use—in regard to Sawyer."

Maggie pushed her plate away, the pancakes half-eaten. "Callous is probably the word you're looking for. You are out of line, but it's okay. We're family. I suppose I do appear that way to you. From long habit I've had to cover up my feelings. But I do have them—feelings, I mean. Right now I'm trying to figure out what I can do, if anything.

"There's something else I suppose I should tell you. I wrote to Rand and told him I made a mistake in sending him home. I love him, Amelia, and he loves me. Mam made me see that I have to reach out for whatever happiness I can get. And by God, I'm going to. Now, if you want to condemn me for that, it's okay. I understand."

Amelia mashed the egg on her plate. When she finally looked up at Maggie, her eyes were full of tears. "Your mother was right. You should be happy. I'm sorry if I indicated anything else. If I had my way, everyone in the world would be in love and happy as Billie and Thad. And Cary and me," she added as an afterthought.

"Sawyer?" Maggie hadn't meant her voice to be so hoarse, so whispery.

"I think I know Rand better than anyone on this earth. I know he wouldn't play you against Sawyer. His mind was made up long ago—last spring, in fact. I suppose we all thought . . . we all wanted the two of them to get married. But that wasn't what Rand wanted. Who are we to sit and judge? Every person walking this earth deserves to be happy."

"But you still don't approve of me, do you?"

Amelia buttered a piece of toast she had no intention of eating. "You remind me so much of myself in my younger days. Those days are behind me and they should be behind you, too. What I didn't approve of was your indifference to your mother. And your indifference to Sawyer now. My own mother died before I could make it up to her, all those awful, rebellious years. You at least had a chance to mend fences with Billie. What you do or don't do for Sawyer is something you're going to have to live with. No one can help you but yourself."

Maggie smiled. "That's honest, all right. I'm glad we had this little talk. I was beginning to wonder if you were avoiding me."

"In a way I was. I don't like to think about those long-ago days. I hate confrontations because I had so many of them in my life. There comes a time when you have to look everything square in the face and deal with it. Soul-searching is not for the weak."

"Tell me about it." Maggie smiled. "What do you think of little Jessie? Isn't she gorgeous? I love rocking her and giving her a water bottle."

"Another one. Between you and Susan, you're going to have one spoiled child on your hands."

"Susan is taking it all very well. The doctors have mapped out a routine for her, and she's to take Jessie in for treatment. I managed to get together some material for her to read. She's tough, Amelia. I didn't know that about Susan. And she means it when she says no one but her is going to take care of this baby. She wrote to Jerome, you know, right after the baby was born. She sent the letter in care of their old business manager. She said he had a right to know, and of course he does, but I'm a little concerned about what he might try to do."

"If you think Jerome is going to be interested in a baby with a birth defect, forget it. The divorce will go through and we'll never see Jerome again." It was brave talk and Amelia knew it for the lie it was. Sooner or later Jerome would show up and cause trouble. She could feel it in her bones.

Maggie sat at the table for a long time after Amelia had left. She herself had a busy schedule, but she couldn't seem to get herself together this morning, couldn't seem to stop thinking. Amelia and Cary, Cranston and Cole, Sawyer . . . Rand.

Why hadn't Rand called or written? Certainly enough time had gone by. On an impulse she pulled the phone to the table from the sideboard and placed a call to England. The phone rang fifteen times before she replaced the receiver.

Cary was so cheerful, Amelia could feel her teeth grind together. She wasn't looking forward to the plane ride or the layover at Kennedy Airport before she could get a flight to Vermont.

"Amelia, if you don't hurry, we're going to miss the plane. What's the problem?"

"My hair," Amelia said shortly. "I should have gotten it cut, but I didn't have the time."

"You look beautiful. Let's go. Eileen just pulled up in front of the house."

"Eileen?" Amelia's hairbrush paused in midair.

"Yes, Eileen. She's going to leave her car at the airport. Come on, we really have to hurry. I have your coat, and the bags are downstairs."

"Why is Eileen taking us to the airport?"

"Because she's going with us. Sherman thought it would be simpler if she came along and I didn't have to scrounge around for a temporary girl to take notes and then wait for the papers to be sent back here. Eileen's on top of things. I thought I told you."

Amelia seethed as she followed her husband down the stairs. She was going on to Vermont, and Cary was staying in New York. With Eileen! Her head started to pound, and she could feel the perspiration breaking out on her forehead.

The ride was filled with Eileen's gay chatter. She'd never been to New York, and there was so much she wanted to see, so many things she wanted to buy.

"I thought you were going along to work," Amelia said coolly.

"I am, but I get a lunch hour, and some of the stores are open in the evening. Cary promised me Saturday off."

Cary could feel the chill emanating from his wife. Jesus, surely she didn't. . . . That was exactly what she thought! Was that how much she trusted him? First he felt annoyed, and then angry. He'd asked her to come with him in the beginning, but the house was more important. Then it was going on to see Billie. Women! Well, let her stew for a while; it would do her good. Maybe then she'd realize how ridiculous she was being.

"Why don't you drop me off at the door," Amelia said. "I have to pick up my ticket. If you give me yours, Cary, I can check both of you in."

"Eileen, do you have the tickets?"

"In my bag. That's nice of you, Mrs. Assante. I might not be lucky in finding a parking spot and end up taking the shuttle. We're cutting it close. I was on time," she added apologetically.

"No one's blaming you. Amelia is at fault here," Cary said in a gruff voice.

"You didn't tell me we were being picked up. In fact, you didn't tell me a lot of things. I thought we were taking the limo to the airport. When Martin drives us, we don't have to worry about a parking space. You stay with Miss

Farrell. In case you don't make this flight, you can be together for the next one. If that happens, I'll leave your tickets with the reservation clerk. This is fine. Let me out here."

Cary hopped out of the car and ran around to open the door for Amelia. The look she gave him froze him in his tracks. Out of the corner of his eye he could see Eileen rummaging in her purse for something. She was smiling.

Amelia waited patiently in line till it was her turn. She handed over Cary and Eileen's tickets and waited for her own. "There seems to be a mistake here," the young girl said hesitantly. "Miss Farrell and Mr. Assante are sitting together. Preseating," she said by way of explanation. "You requested a seat in smoking. Do you want me to change the seats?"

"Absolutely not. Is the flight on time?"

"The plane's at the gate. In fact, they're boarding now. You don't have much time."

Amelia felt like kicking something. She looked around for some sign of her husband. "I don't think they're going to make it," she said tightly.

"You'll miss it if you don't hurry. The next flight is booked solid. I recommend you board and leave the other two tickets with the desk."

Amelia was the last passenger to board the plane. Behind her dark glasses, she cried all the way to New York. She was still crying when she boarded her flight to Vermont.

Cary and Eileen gathered up all their papers, stuffing them haphazardly into briefcases. Cary was in a hurry to get back to the hotel so he could make arrangements for an intimate in-room dinner with Amelia. They'd spend the evening together and tomorrow take in the Big Apple. He was as excited as a college kid on his second date.

Christ, he'd missed Amelia! He'd felt like a louse when they'd missed the plane. His phone calls to her over the next few days had been made on the run or when he was too exhausted to think straight. He didn't know why he'd bothered except that he couldn't let her think the worst. But she did; he could tell by her voice.

"I think I have everything, Cary," Eileen said hoarsely.

"We're going to get you back to the hotel and call a doctor. I can tell just by looking at you that you're running a fever. You should have stayed in bed today. All you're doing is sneezing and coughing. I wouldn't be surprised if you had pneumonia."

"Bronchitis maybe, but not pneumonia. I'll take some aspirin and I'll be fine. I hate it when you fuss over me," she said. Fuss, fuss, hold me! she wanted to shout. Tell me you'll take care of me.

"Someone has to take care of you. What the hell kind of employer would I be if I didn't? We're in a strange city. Make sure you take a good hot bath before you settle in. Amelia says that's a cure-all for colds."

"Amelia should know. Amelia is really knowledgeable, isn't she?"

"She certainly is. She knows something about everything. She can hold her own in any situation."

In the warm taxi Eileen managed to sit closer to Cary than necessary, pleading the chills. "Do you know what I want more than anything right now?"

"What? Don't tell me you want a company credit card." Cary laughed.

"That, too. No, I want a good hot toddy. I haven't had one in years. You know, the kind your mother makes for you when you're really sick. Not that I'm really sick."

"You're wrong. I can feel the heat from your body. You do have a fever and I'm calling the doctor. I have to make sure you're all right before I can enjoy my evening with Amelia. When I tell her how sick you are, she'll say I did the right thing."

"I wouldn't bet on it," Eileen muttered under her breath.

Eileen got out of the taxi on wobbly legs. She realized for the first time that she really was sick. Maybe a doctor wouldn't be such a bad idea. At least he'd give her an antibiotic, and she'd have the weekend to recuperate before the return flight on Monday. She wished there was someone who cared enough for her to sit and hold her hand. It was a hell of a way to spend time in New York.

Cary grabbed both briefcases and helped Eileen through the lobby to the elevator. "I'm taking you right to your suite. I'm not leaving till the doctor is on his way and you're in bed."

"Thanks, Cary. Your wife is one lucky lady."

"I keep telling her that, but she doesn't listen." Covertly his eyes dropped to his watch. Amelia's plane would get in in another thirty minutes. He would have to hurry to make all the arrangements in time. "Get in bed and I'll start making calls."

The desk clerk assured him a doctor would check on Miss Farrell in half an hour. He called room service for a hot toddy for Eileen and dinner for himself and Amelia for nine o'clock. Then he made two calls to Texas and one to the airport to check that Amelia's plane was on time. It was. At this time of day it would take a taxi about forty-five minutes to make it into the city; he might as well hang around and wait for the doctor. His last call was to the hotel florist. Roses and daisies would be delivered in abundance to room 1012. Amelia's favorite flowers.

When room service arrived, Cary tipped the waiter and carried the tray into Eileen's room. As she was taking her first sip, there was another knock on the door.

Cary ushered the doctor into Eileen's room and quietly withdrew to the sitting room. He was sipping at a Scotch and water when the phone rang. He picked it up on the third ring. "Hello." There was no response, and after a moment he hung up.

The doctor emerged ten minutes later. He was a round, pudgy man with a no-nonsense demeanor. "The young lady has a good case of bronchitis. I gave her a shot and left some antibiotics. She'll be asleep in a few minutes. I'd like you to get her a small vaporizer from the pharmacy; it will help her to breathe easier. She's to take the

capsules four times a day. She'll be fine in a few days.
I'll leave my bill at the desk. If you like, I can stop at the
pharmacy and have them send up the vaporizer."

"I'd appreciate that," Cary said.

Cary waited around for another thirty minutes until the
vaporizer arrived. He hooked it up on the dresser, checked
Eileen again to be sure she was all right. He turned the
lights off, leaving only the bathroom light on in case she
woke and was disoriented. He made sure the water pitcher
was full and placed a glass on the night table next to the
packet of pills.

Now it was time for his wife. He could hardly wait.

Amelia ended her all-too-short visit to Billie after the
second day and arrived at Kennedy International Airport
late in the afternoon. She entered a cocktail lounge, trying
to make up her mind whether to join Cary at the Hyatt
Hotel or take the five-o'clock flight back to Texas. She
knew she was being stubborn, even stupid. She trusted
Cary; she really did. It was Eileen she didn't trust. Eileen
would have to go before she would ever feel safe again.

"And what happens to all the Eileens after that?" Billie
had asked her. "You can't insulate him from women,
Amelia. If—and this is a big if, because I don't think Cary
would ever stray—but if it does happen, you won't have
anyone to blame but yourself. You'll be the one who drove
him to it."

Billie was right, Amelia thought as she sipped at her
brandy Alexander. But Billie hadn't seen Eileen Farrell.
Even Thad's head would turn for a second look. Now,
Thad was one man who would never stray; he might look,
but he'd never touch. She hadn't known Cary for a lifetime the way Billie knew Thad.

Amelia ordered a second drink, glancing at the departure monitor from her seat at the bar. She had twenty
minutes to make her flight to Austin, if that was what she
wanted to do. She had the rest of the day to hail a taxi
that would take her to the Hyatt. She gulped her drink,

paid the check, and hurried to the check-in counter, where she was told there would be a ten-minute delay. Just enough time to call the Hyatt and leave a message for Cary. Let him eat his heart out.

Information gave her the number. She dropped coins into the slot, got the Hyatt, and asked for Cary Assante. The phone rang and rang. Finally she hung up and dialed the Hyatt a second time, this time asking for Eileen Farrell's room. The phone was picked up on the third ring, and she heard her husband say hello. Her gloved fingers felt numb when she replaced the receiver.

Her change purse yielded enough coins to make a third call. The message she left was brief: Mrs. Assante is returning to Austin.

Cary looked around at the beautiful flowers. His watch told him Amelia was two hours late. Somehow, in his gut, he knew she wouldn't be here. Suddenly he thought to call the desk and ask if there were any messages.

"Yes, sir, there is a message. The boy is on his way up to your room right now. We've been terribly busy, and couldn't get to it before now; I'm sorry."

Cary opened the door, tipped the bellhop, and read his message before he closed the door. It had been Amelia on Eileen's phone. He felt like crying.

At nine o'clock room service knocked on the door, and Cary didn't have the nerve to tell the man to take the food away. He watched as everything was carried in. How Amelia would have loved this, he thought. He reached for the magnum of champagne in its silver bucket. Why the hell not? Who cared?

Amelia Coleman Nelson Assante slept on the floor of her mother's house that night, wrapped in her sable coat. It was a deep, soundless sleep of defeat.

{{{{{{{{ CHAPTER TWENTY-TWO }}}}}}}}

Sunbridge took on an air of strain when Cary returned from New York. Amelia was civil as she listened to his account of the trip, didn't bat an eyelash when she heard how sick Eileen was— so sick, said Cary, that he wanted her to fill in at the office if she could find the time. Secretly, Amelia was pleased, and she agreed to help out until Eileen was able to return to work.

"All you have to do, darling, is answer the phone. Eileen can catch up on the other stuff when she's back on her feet."

Cary looked to miserable, so worn, that Amelia took pity on him . . . for the moment. Maybe he was telling the truth. Time would tell. But she had no intention of going upstairs and making love with him as if nothing had happened. She still felt too raw and bruised for that.

Forcing a smile to her lips, she said cheerfully, "Go to bed, darling. You look tired. I have some papers and bills to go over. After all, I was away for three days. And I promised Susan we'd have a talk. She wants some input from me on little Jessie. I think she's considering forming some kind of organization or starting a little club for parents of children with spina bifida."

Cary nodded like a schoolboy who was being punished for something he didn't understand. He went upstairs without another word.

Damn, she thought petulantly, he might have coaxed

340

her a little! How quick she was to accept her reasons why she wasn't ready for bed. The truth of the matter was she herself was so tired and strung out, she couldn't see straight. If ever there was a time for a drink and a joint, this was it. The den would be dark and as welcome as her thoughts; she could hang out there till morning with no one the wiser.

She couldn't ever remember feeling so awful, so alone. This was her first serious rift with Cary since they'd been married. Maybe she should tell him *exactly* how she felt. Her fears might be foolish and unfounded, but they were damaging her relationship nevertheless Wouldn't it be better to get everything out in the open?

Amelia lit the marijuana cigarette she'd purchased from one of the young workmen.

Good weed, the young man had said. Pure Colombian. Amelia dragged deeply on the joint and leaned back. She could feel the tension leave her body almost immediately. She felt almost giddy. . . . She giggled and wondered vaguely if she had shut the study door, not that it mattered. She was somewhere else now and enjoying every minute of it.

It was five o'clock when Amelia came down off her cloud. The room reeked of pot. She gulped her watered-down drink and opened the window a good two inches. Then she closed the door behind her and climbed the steps. A shower and fresh clothes would make her feel better. Today she was replacing Eileen Farrell.

Cary waited till after three for his wife to come to bed. He'd refused to seek her out and beg for her favors, how ever—they were married, for Christ's sake! When he finally heard her come into the room, he cracked one eye open to look at the clock on the night stand. Jesus, it was practically dawn. She went immediately into the shower. Then, just as he'd decided to join her, he heard the snick of the lock.

Two minutes after the alarm was turned off, Amelia opened the bathroom door. Cary noticed that her makeup was fresh but her eyes were lusterless. He felt rotten. They were going to be in real trouble if something wasn't done soon.

"Morning, babe," he said softly. "I missed you last night."

"I slept downstairs. I guess I dozed off. When I did wake, I thought I would disturb you, if I came up, so I finished out the night on the sofa."

"Alone?"

"In a manner of speaking. I smoked a joint and had a couple of drinks." Defiantly, she added, "I needed it."

"What about Susan and the work you had to do?"

Amelia turned to face her husband. "I changed my mind. I decided I wanted to be alone. Surely you can understand that. I'm going to have some breakfast, so anytime you're ready to leave, I'll be ready."

Cary blinked as the door closed behind his wife. By God, he thought, she's declared war! This room is the front, and I'm going to get caught in the cross fire if I don't take charge damn quick.

His shower was the shortest on record, the spray barely touching his body before he hopped out and dressed. Twice he nicked himself shaving and plastered bits of tissue over the bleeding spots. Now he not only felt like a war casualty; he looked like one, too.

Most mornings, Amelia filled his plate from the sideboard and buttered his toast. This morning, however, she remained seated, reading the *Crystal City Times* while she munched on an English muffin.

"What's new in Crystal City?" he asked heartily as he dug into his eggs.

"Not much. We're supposed to have a wet spring this year. The Cattleman's Association is meeting next week on some land bid. The Canterbury Club is sponsoring a St. Patrick's Day Dance. The tickets are a hundred dollars each."

"Buy a block of them."

"Why?" Amelia asked as she folded the paper in two. She passed it over to Cary, who ignored it.

"I'll give them to some of the workers. Don't you think it's a good idea?"

"No," Amelia said shortly. "Your workers won't be welcome at the Canterbury Club. You don't want to embarrass them, do you?"

"You just said the tickets were on sale for a hundred dollars each. Don't they want to sell them?"

"Of course they want to sell them, but to the right people. They don't want riffraff. I don't make the rules; I'm just telling you the way it is."

Cary put down his fork. "What you're telling me is some hardworking stiff who puts in fourteen hours a day to take care of his family and has dirt under his fingernails isn't going to be permitted to attend even if he has one of those expensive tickets." Cary's face was grim, his eyes cold and hard. "Will they be turned away at the door?"

"Of course not. They'll feel ill at ease. I seriously doubt if any of your men would even take the tickets, much less attend."

"Well, if that's the case, count me out. If some man who is out there busting his ass for me isn't good enough to go where I go, then I don't belong there, either. You make up your own mind, Amelia. I've had enough breakfast. I'm ready to leave."

"You're just being stubborn. You know how they do things here. I've certainly told you enough times. You even laughed."

"That was before I got involved. The next thing you'll be telling me is they burn crosses on lawns and go around in white sheets. Just because I married you doesn't make me one of you. I'm no different than those guys out there slogging away day after day. I've never asked anyone to do anything for me I wouldn't do myself. You knew that when you married me. I don't want to be a Coleman. You aren't a Coleman anymore, either."

Amelia bristled as she buttoned her coat. "Right now you're feeling guilty, so don't take it out on me, okay? If you don't want to go to the dance, don't go. I'll buy myself a ticket. I am on the board, after all. If you want to argue, let's argue about the issues. Don't go throwing some stupid dance into the ring to divert me. We're a little too old to play games."

"Guilty? Me? Come off it, Amelia. I told you the truth and I'm not going to go through that scene again. What you see is what you got. I've never lied to you, nor have I ever been unfaithful. And in your heart you know it. Whatever the hell your problem is, I hope you solve it before you bust up this marriage. Get the hell in the car, because I'm leaving."

Amelia's back stiffened. "Don't talk to me like I'm one of your workers. I'm your wife. I won't stand for it, Cary."

"If you're my wife, I wish to hell you'd act like it. I'm sick and tired of dancing around you, worrying about saying the right thing at the right time. You're the one who's screwing things up."

They rode to the construction site in silence. Cary glowered all the way. Amelia sat in a pitiful huddle, angry with herself and with Cary.

Cary's face lost none of its grimness as he set about turning on the heaters and the lights. He waved his arm vaguely in the direction of the coffee machine. "It'll warm up soon. Make some coffee. Some of the men come in from time to time and may want something to warm them up. Keep it filled. Do you know how to work the phone system?"

"I know how it works." She watched as his eyes looked up toward the fluorescent lights and then down at her hair. She felt a moment of panic. What was he seeing? She longed suddenly for the pale light bulbs in their bedroom. Go, her mind shrieked, so I can see what this is doing to me. God, go!

"I'll try to make it back for lunch," Cary told her. "Order something around one o'clock."

"I'll do that. Have a good day."

He hesitated a moment. "You have a good day, too. I'll see you later."

"I'll be here."

The second the door closed behind him, Amelia had her compact open. She angled it this way and that, hoping to see whatever it was Cary had seen. Damn, it was too small. She removed the huge square bathroom mirror and carried it out to her desk, then sat down and inspected herself.

She looked awful. Her makeup was garish; her dark hair cast unflattering shadows on her face, the roots showing at the part line. All she needed was a red nose and she could pass for a clown.

Wobbling on the swivel chair, Amelia reached up to lift the ceiling block. She unscrewed not one but two of the bright lights. Immediately she felt better. Now that the glare was gone, she might be able to get through the day. She looked into the mirror again. It was better now, but she'd lost something in those few minutes under the glaring light. She was getting old and it was eating her alive.

By mid-morning Amelia was bored to tears. She called her house, spoke to the workmen, and was assured that everything was progressing on schedule. She went over her paperwork, made a few calls, rescheduled delivery of the upstairs carpeting, and watered Eileen's plants. She read two chapters of a Herman Wouk novel, got bored, and put it back in her bag.

One o'clock came and went. She ordered hamburgers and French fries from a diner down the road. The smell made her nauseous. At two o'clock she poked through the files to see what kind of system Eileen used,

An hour later, Amelia Assante's world crumbled around her. She sat in stunned disbelief, staring at the papers in her hand. One was the deed to a co-op apartment in Eileen Farrell's name; the other was the certificate of ownership for a new Ford Mustang. When the phone rang, she answered it automatically. She even managed to record messages.

Her movements were awkward and clumsy as she

searched through the cabinets a second time. When she found what she was looking for, she sat down and fought her tears. The co-op had actually been purchased by Cary Assante, but a copy of a quitclaim deed said Cary had deeded the apartment to Eileen Farrell for the princely sum of one hundred dollars. The Mustang had been purchased outright; a photostat of the registration and bill of sale carried Cary's name.

At three-forty-five Amelia took the phone off the receiver and left the trailer. She drove home, packed her husband's bags, and brought them back to the office, placing them neatly by the door. She left the incriminating papers on the blue desk blotter. The receiver was still off the hook, pinging noisily. She replaced it and the light bulbs overhead.

She didn't look back. There were some things a person didn't need to see more than once.

Susan sat across the desk from Jessica's pediatrician. The metal plate on his desk read Ferris Armstrong, M.D. She liked him and the way he treated Jessie. He didn't mince words—he warned her what she was up against and what the future might hold for Jessie and herself. But he was always hopeful.

Now his cornflower-blue eyes twinkled when Jessie belched loudly. Susan flushed. "She hasn't learned her manners yet."

He laughed, stretched backward on his swivel chair, and propped his foot up on the desk. In the time Susan had been bringing Jessie to him, he'd come to like her and had learned he could drop his professional demeanor after the baby's examination and relax. He enjoyed talking with her. Lacing his long fingers behind his head, he studied the tips of his shoes down the length of his long legs. "Do you plan to stay here in Texas or return to England?" he asked.

"I'll be staying on. I'm living at Sunbridge with my sister, as I've told you, but I'm planning to find my own place. Actually, I own a house that was given to me years ago, but it's being rented. I might consider moving there. I want a yard for Jessie and room for her to grow. She will grow, won't she?"

"I've told you everything there is to know, and I've given you pamphlets and books and articles to read. You know I'm not holding anything back. What you must understand is that spina bifida affects each child differently. The prognosis for Jessie is excellent. Why would you think I was holding back? I know how precious Jessie is to you; I want what's best for her as well as you."

Susan sighed and relaxed in her chair. Jessie cuddled on her mother's shoulder. "I have no reason to think you're holding anything back. I just feel so lost sometimes, as though Jessie were the only baby in the world with this defect. My family tries to help, but they can't really share it with me."

Ferris Armstrong looked at Susan compassionately. She had told him of the breakup of her marriage, and without even knowing the details, he had developed a strong dislike for Jerome de Moray. Jessie needed a father and Susan needed a husband, someone to share her worries and help with the burden of raising a child.

"I've been in touch with some of the names you gave me, Dr. Armstrong—you know, other parents of spina bifida children. We're forming a group to help each other. You know, to seek out information, hold little gatherings, and just talk. It's already helped me and, I hope, some of the others. I want to start an organization here in this area."

Ferris smiled. "I approve. How far have you gotten?"

"Not very far. Just some ideas I've been kicking around. Jessie is only an infant, but you know the needs of other children, older children, like her. I was hoping you'd have some suggestions."

"You're taking on a handful. Once begun, it wouldn't be fair to drop such a thing midstream. Be careful; you could pull the rug out from under a lot of people who are already in a painful situation. An undertaking like this would require a strong commitment."

"I know. And that's why I've been doing a lot of thinking. I've consulted my sister and she's agreed to deed me a piece of land on Sunbridge property where I could build a camp. That seems to be what's needed. According to other parents I've talked with, our special children have little or no opportunity to experience things that normal children do because there aren't any facilities for them. But it's all in the thinking stage at this point. The only thing I'm certain of is that I want Jessie to live as full a life as possible and to be with other children. If I can help others while I'm helping her, so much the better."

"It's commendable," Ferris heard the excitement in his own voice. "It would take a good deal of money."

Susan frowned. "Unfortunately, that could be a problem. Do you have any kind of ballpark figure in mind?"

"Nothing under a hundred thousand, and that would just get it off the ground. But if you're campaigning, I'd be more than glad to make a donation when you're ready."

Susan was struck by his wide smile and realized that whenever she was with him she watched for it, allowed herself to be warmed by it. Ferris Armstrong loved his work and he loved the children; she could tell by the way he handled little Jessie. His hands were incredibly large, with long, sensitive fingers; he could hold Jessie's bottom in one palm. His blue eyes could be compassionate one second and stern the next and merry the second after that. She gauged him to be somewhere in his early forties, and once when she'd mentioned his family, he'd told her he didn't have one.

Single, attractive, and sensitive. The thought pleased Susan, and she felt herself flush. "I like you, Ferris Armstrong, M.D.," she blurted.

His eyes met hers, and for an instant there was a sense of tension and indecision between them. Then Jessie belched again and they both laughed.

"Raising money for your foundation shouldn't be much

of a problem," Ferris said after a moment, dropping his feet from the desk and fixing his gaze intently on Susan. "I heard you play when I was in Los Angeles three years ago. You were magnificent. I shouted with the rest of the audience at the end of the concert. Why don't you think about playing here? You certainly are a celebrity, and all of Texas would turn out to hear you, especially if they were spending tax-deductible dollars to do so. Give the proceeds to your foundation." He held up a hand. "Don't say no too quickly. A talent like yours shouldn't be hidden. Jessie might need a lot of things, but so does her mother. Think about it."

"I don't know if I have the time to spend practicing," Susan said doubtfully. "Hours and hours at the piano, hours Jessie will need me. But yes, of course, I'll think about it."

"Good. Now, I want to see Jessie next week. I'll give you a call over the weekend to let you know what I've come up with in the way of the suggestions you want. First, I want to talk to several physicians in the area and see what they think about an outdoor camp for children with special needs. Getting their input from the beginning would help to ensure their participation later. Get me?" He winked.

Susan found herself laughing again. "Gotcha! But I've got a better idea than having you call. Why don't you come to dinner on Saturday night? If you've no other plans," she added hastily. "I can show you the piece of land my sister is turning over to me."

Ferris quickly ran a mental check of his plans for Saturday. "I'm free as the breeze," he said cheerfully. "What time?"

"Early, while it's still daylight. If you come in the afternoon and the weather is nice, we can ride out on horseback."

"You've got a date." He made a few illegible squiggles on a notepad—for Susan's benefit; he knew he wasn't going to forget.

"I'll see you on Saturday, then. Thank you, Dr. Armstrong."

"Why don't you call me Ferris? I'll call you Susie."

"My family calls me Suse."

"I like Susie better."

Susan's heart fluttered all the way to the car. She'd never felt like this. Not even Jerome had made her heart flutter. Wait till she told Maggie.

"Sounds like a date to me," Maggie said, smiling. "Is he good-looking? Not that it matters, but it's the first thing women think about."

"Not terribly good-looking, but he has these incredible eyelashes. I like him, Maggie. I can't believe I had the nerve to ask him to dinner, though. I hope you don't mind. He's coming over early in the afternoon. Do you think you could watch Jessie while we go horseback riding?"

"Of course I don't mind, and of course I'll watch Jessie. I can't wait to see this man who can turn my sister into a weak-kneed mass of jelly! What shall we have for dinner? What do you think he likes?"

"Maggie, I hardly know him. But when in doubt, always go with prime rib and some fancy dessert, right? . . . Maybe I'm making too much of this. Here we are thinking this is actually a date, and it isn't. He's just coming to lend his expertise so Jessie can have a better life. It's true that I asked him because he interested me, if you know what I mean. But that doesn't mean he's reciprocating my feelings."

"Little Suse, listen to your sister Maggie. Men, especially doctors, don't go out of their way unless they're interested. Doctors simply don't have the time, and what time they do have they guard very jealously. That's my expert opinion."

"That's good enough for me. Oh, Maggie, I can't tell you what it means to be here! There was a time when I thought we were lost to each other."

"Yeah. Me, too," Maggie said softly.

Susan wrapped her arms around her sister. "Have you heard from Rand?"

"No," Maggie whispered. "I screwed up, Suse. Maybe someday I'll learn."

Susan could hear the hint of tears in Maggie's voice. "No, I refuse to believe that. I'm sure there's an explanation. Rand is always on the go; he might be traveling. You did send him away. He probably went off to the country to lick his wounds. He never has mail forwarded; it just piles up, sometimes for as long as two months. You could call him, you know."

"I've tried. No luck. Actually, I don't know which is worse—the fear that he will answer or the fear that he won't. No, a letter is best. I'll just have to wait it out. I still can't believe Mam told me to go for it. Does that surprise you?"

Susan thought about it. "No, not really. All Mam ever wanted was for us to be happy, to be a family. She made her mistakes just like we did—and she learned from them the way we're going to have to. Mam's one wise lady, Maggie. Her seal of approval can make you happy. So that's exactly what she gave you."

"I wish I called her before I sent Rand away. I didn't know. I expected her to choose up sides."

"You dope. She did. She picked you, if that's the way you want to think of it. You have to get it out of your head that it's you versus Sawyer. That's not the way it is."

"Go take care of your baby. I hear her crying," Maggie said, not unkindly. "I'll think about what you just said while I prepare a gastronomical delight for Saturday."

"I'm partial to peach cobbler, if that makes a difference."

"Cole likes it, too. Peach cobbler it is."

Peacefully nursing little Jessie in the old nursery, Susan had a clear view of the corridor. She watched in stunned amazement as her aunt Amelia stalked into the room she shared with Cary. She continued to watch and puzzle over her aunt's actions, when, approximately five minutes later, two huge traveling bags were pushed into the hall by Amelia's foot. An oversize plastic bag, the kind bowlers and athletes used, was pitched down the hall ahead of the suitcases. There was anger in Amelia's straight back, and strange sounds seemed to be coming from her mouth.

Something was wrong. Susan could feel herself start to tremble. She'd played out a scene much like this once herself. Cary was leaving, Amelia was leaving, or they were both leaving. Where were Maggie and the boys? She looked at her watch: four o'clock, too early for the boys to be home from school. Maggie was probably in the study or out riding.

It was five-fifteen when Amelia once again stalked down the hall to her room. This time Susan had a clear view of her aunt's face. It looked old, beaten, and drawn. So, she thought, it was Cary who was leaving. Did he even know?

Susan willed the small bundle in her arms to burp. It took a while, but Jessie finally complied, and Susan sighed with relief. She kissed the downy head, felt the baby's diaper, and then laid her down to sleep. She rocked the cradle a few times just for the pleasure of doing it, and then closed the door halfway.

To knock or not to knock on Amelia's door. Susan put her ear to the wood and heard the sound of hard, deep sobbing. Maggie. She had to find Maggie.

Maggie was just coming up the steps, boots and riding crop in her hand. When she saw Susan's wild eyes and trembling lips she drew her sister into her room. "What is it, Suse? What's wrong? It isn't Jessie, is it?" Maggie asked in alarm.

"No, it's Amelia." Quickly, Susan recounted the scene she'd seen played out for her. "She's in her room now, sobbing."

"Do you think we should interfere? Amelia might want to be alone. I mean, this is between her and Cary. She's been real touchy lately. I knew something was wrong when she came back from New York. Mam would know."

"Mam isn't here," Susan said curtly. "She's really hurting, Maggie."

Maggie licked her lips. "Okay, but I don't think she's going to appreciate this." She rapped softly on Amelia's door and then turned the knob. Amelia was lying on the bed, sobbing into her pillow, great hulking sobs that shook her slim shoulders. Susan and Maggie looked at each other helplessly for a moment. Then Susan climbed on the bed from the right side, Maggie from the left. It was Maggie who gently drew Amelia to her. She was stunned at how thin the woman was. "What can we do, Amelia?" Maggie asked soothingly.

"Nothing. I already did it. It's over. I've been such a fool. How all of you must have laughed at me."

"No one has ever laughed at you, Amelia. What did you do? If you've done something foolish, you're entitled. We're all fools at one time or another. Talk to us, Amelia. Perhaps we can help."

Amelia started slowly, haltingly. Then the words began to speed up, and soon she was like a runaway car down a steep hill.

Susan looked at Maggie and then at her aunt. She knew they were both thinking the same thing. "When we fuck up, we really fuck up."

Maggie burst into hysterical laughter. She'd never heard Susan say so much as "damn." "We sure do!" Amelia nodded miserably.

"Maybe you should talk to Cary one more time," Susan said softly, ever the peacemaker.

Amelia sat bolt upright on the bed. "Why? So I can listen to more lies? No, thanks. Tell me, what would you have done? When you'd had enough, didn't you leave Jerome? Maggie, when Cranston got to you, didn't you leave? What makes me different?"

"He'll come back; you know that," Maggie told her.

"I took his keys off his ring before I left. Don't let him in, Maggie. Promise me."

"I promise, if that's what you want. Look at us. We're all in the same boat and not a paddle among us." She hesitated. "What are you going to do, Amelia?"

"I'm going back to England on the first available plane. Susan, will you call and make me a reservation on the Concorde? Book me a flight to New York. I'll sit in the airport. This place," Amelia said, looking around, "has caused me nothing but grief my whole life. Why I thought it would be different now is beyond me. Maggie, you'll help me pack, won't you?"

"Of course, if that's what you really want. But what about your house? You've done so much work on it." She struggled for just the right words. "Sometimes, Amelia, when you do things in haste or hatred, they can't ever be made right. Do you know what I'm talking about?"

"I'm not an idiot, Maggie, just a fool. I know exactly what you're saying. You're even thinking of all the mistakes you made with Sawyer. But this is different. Cary was my life—I made him my life. I didn't leave room for anything else."

Maggie felt as if she'd been slapped in the face. She forced herself to speak calmly. "It's not too late. You could go back and talk to Cary. I mean really talk. This time listen to what he says. Don't just hear him, listen, Amelia."

"Is that what you'd do, Maggie?" Amelia asked tearfully as she threw her clothes into an open suitcase.

It took Maggie so long to answer that both Amelia and Susan stopped what they were doing to wait for her reply. "If I loved him with all my heart, yes. I wouldn't give up without a fight."

"Will you please *look* at me?" Amelia cried. "Do I look like I have any fight left? I'm an old woman. Eileen Farrell is just a name. There will always be Eileen Farrells. And each one will be younger as I get older."

Maggie bit down on her tongue. When she tasted her own blood, she grabbed Amelia by the arm. "You aren't running away from Cary or Eileen. You're running away from yourself. Admit it, Amelia. You're a Coleman and you're copping out. For shame. I thought you were tougher than that. We're all that's left. Fall back and regroup! Go talk to a shrink and get it all in perspective, but make sure you know the reason. It's you, Amelia."

"We're all that's left! You fool, we're all there ever was. Your mother wasn't a Coleman, only by marriage. We didn't have a choice. Maybe you are right." Amelia turned to look at Susan, who had just gotten off the phone. "What's the verdict, Suse?"

"There's a ten-o'clock flight to New York. You can pick up your ticket at the airport. I told them you would American Express it. You have a seat on tomorrow's Concorde flight."

Maggie's shoulders slumped. "How about some coffee? A sandwich or something."

"I'll take the coffee and a chicken sandwich." Amelia looked at herself in the dresser mirror. "I'm going to have to wear dark glasses," she muttered.

Maggie turned to stare at her aunt. "You only have to wear dark glasses if you want to wear them. The choice is yours. You have nothing to hide, Amelia."

"My age," Amelia whimpered. "I have to hide my age."

Susan crossed the room in three strides. Maggie held up her hand to stop her sister. "Then hide it. If you want to hide behind dark glasses to keep the boogeyman away, then you do it. I'll get the coffee." She made a motion for Susan to follow her. When the door closed behind her, Maggie sagged against it.

"You were a little hard on her, don't you think?"

"Maybe I wasn't hard enough. When you give up the fight, it's all over. You exist. But this is as much as we're going to interfere. Do you agree?" Susan nodded. "If Cary comes here, we don't know anything. Let's see what kind of man he really is. If he's what I think he is, he's going to sweat it out. He won't go after her the way she wants. And that's when we'll know who Amelia Coleman Nelson Assante really is."

"I feel so sorry for her. I never thought of her as old. For me she's never changed. I don't understand how that could be so important to her. So many things in life that are more important, yet she's only worried about her age."

"That house of her mother's was important to her. She actually used to light up a room when she came in at the end of the day. Cary was so proud of her. Where did that go? I can't believe that he got mixed up with that little snot Eileen. If he did, she engineered it. She had her claws out for Rand, too."

"I think, if you want my honest gut opinion, that Cary is a victim. I think there's an explanation for everything. He loved Amelia."

"Past tense?" Maggie asked.

"I haven't been as close to the situation as you. I've been busy with Jessie—and coming to terms with her disability. But I've accepted it now, so I can go on and do the best I can. No one can ask more of you than your best."

"Good girl, Suse. Come on, help me with the coffee. I don't think any of us are going to be hungry this evening. Didja ever notice how good we all are at stirring our food around the plates?"

"Yeah, I noticed.... She's going to be all right, isn't she, Maggie?"

"I don't know. It's going to hit her hard once she's back in England. If Cary is a no-show, I can't even imagine what she'll do. All we can do is be supportive. I'll call Mam after she leaves and give her the facts. I hate to burden her, though. It's time we left her alone. But I'm glad they're coming for the christening. Have you heard from Sawyer?"

"Not yet. I was going to call her this weekend. She'll come through."

Sawyer didn't come through. It was Maggie who held Jessica Margaret in her arms for the christening.

It was a private ceremony with just the family. Cole, dressed in a new suit, stood quietly next to his mother, watching the proceeding with narrowed eyes. Billie, Thad, and Riley sat at the front of the church. Ferris Armstrong stood in the back next to Cary Assante. Both men left quietly before the family started the walk back down the long center aisle.

Billie and Thad stayed for mid-afternoon dinner and caught an early-evening flight to New York.

There was no mention of Sawyer.

{{{{{{{{{ CHAPTER TWENTY-THREE }}}}}}}}}

Rand Nelson waved to his mother as she took off down the lane on her bicycle. The sight of her maneuvering the old one-speed made him smile, as usual. He still couldn't get used to having her here, with him. He'd been shocked and surprised a month ago when he'd received the call to pick her up at Heathrow Airport. She'd done little talking on the way back to the house, but what she had told him was enough to make him angry. Not with Cary, but with her. He'd tried to talk sense to her, and she'd listened politely, but he knew she hadn't really heard a word he'd said.

But she'd changed a great deal since then. She'd put on some weight. She was letting her hair color fade out. Her artificial nails and phony eyelashes were gone. She made no effort to coat her eyes with the makeup she used to buy by the pound; they looked wistful now, but alive. She was quite beautiful, possibly the prettiest woman he'd ever known.

For the first few weeks Amelia hovered close to the

phone and was outside, rain or shine, when the postman arrived. Eventually she'd given that up; these days she forgot to pick up the mail unless he reminded her. Once she'd had her old bicycle fixed, she'd begun to take long rides on the country lanes, sometimes asking him to join her. He could do more than relate to Amelia now: he could actually understand.

There'd been no phone calls from Texas for him, only that short letter from Maggie after the holidays. His guilt was so overpowering, he couldn't make himself pick up a pen or the telephone to make things right. In her own way Amelia was handling things better than he.

The only regular mail that arrived from Texas to Ribbonmaker Lane was from Susan. She wrote faithfully, every ten days or so. Rand never answered, and from Susan's letters, he learned that Amelia didn't respond, either. Once again he read the letter that had arrived today, enjoying the chatty, breezy tone.

Dear Amelia and Rand,
Spring has finally come to Texas. It's almost as beautiful as Jessie. Sometimes I put her out on the patio in her carriage for hours at a time. I've actually gotten Cole and Riley to baby-sit if I go out. Of course, they don't do it together. Some things never change!

Did you know the boys were taking Sawyer and Adam Jarvis to Hawaii for a summer vacation? They're going to be staying someplace high in the hills, at the house Mam stayed in when Pap was stationed at Pearl Harbor. It's where I was conceived! They're leaving in June and staying for about six weeks. Maggie is going in April to ready the house for them. No one knows that, so please don't mention it. It seems the place has been closed for years and years. I don't know how long she'll be there.

Sawyer didn't make it for the christening. Maggie took her place. She's so wonderful with the baby. I've enclosed some snapshots the boys took. Jessie's hair is starting to curl now into little ringlets. Cute, huh?

My attorney informed me yesterday that Jerome will

be here the early part of April. I'm dreading that. I suppose he can make all kinds of trouble, but I won't allow it. I don't even want him to see Jessie, but I suppose I have to let him. Of course he'll blame me for her disability.

I saw Cary in town one day last week. He looked so tired and drawn. He asked about you, Rand, said that he received your check and where the hell is your body? They could use you. That's a direct quote. Why don't you give him a call?

Cary tells me the progress they're making on his inner city is phenomenal. Some of the structures are actually up. I plan to take a look the next time I'm there. Ferris is impressed. Ferris is Ferris Armstrong, Jessie's doctor. I've been seeing him a little on a social basis. He's helping me organize a small group of parents with children like Jessie. He's very nice.

Well, that's my news for now. It would be nice to hear some news from England. I miss you both.

I send my love and Jessie's, too,

Susan

Rand watched Amelia pedal her bike up the lane. He waved the letter as she drew near. "Susan," he called loudly so he wouldn't have to see the disappointment on her face.

She hopped off the bike and adjusted the kickstand. "Be back in a minute," she told him. "I want to put this fish in the fridge."

It was a long time before Amelia joined him. Long enough to read the letter three more times. Maggie was going to Hawaii soon.

Amelia read the letter, folded it, and replaced it in the envelope with the bright red border. "Would you like rice or noodles with your fish?"

"Rice. What did you think of the baby's pictures?"

"She's adorable. She looks like Susan, thank God. One of us should write to her."

"Yes, one of us should," Rand said thoughtfully.

"I'm not much of a letter writer," Amelia said, sipping her tea.

"I'm worse."

"Then one of us should call," Amelia said tightly.

"Yes, I suppose you're right. One of these days."

"Yes, one of these days," Amelia said. They were like an old shoe and an old sock, she thought sourly. "We're having an early dinner this evening. I'm playing back-gammon with the Goodwins. Would you like to join us?"

"No, thanks. Do you want me to drop you off?"

"I'm quite capable of driving myself, but I'm going to bike it. Since you put that light on my bike, I can use it in the evening. Don't worry about me, Rand."

"It's that bike I'm worried about. It's prewar."

"Almost as old as me. It's holding up very well. Most things do over the long haul. Do you get my drift?"

Rand laughed. "I sure do. Do you?"

"You bet. Dinner in an hour. Is that all right with you?"

"Yes," Rand responded absently. Maggie in Hawaii.

Amelia pedaled her bike down the lane at five minutes of six. At five minutes past six Rand placed a call to Vermont. He talked to Billie for well over an hour. Actually, he did more listening than talking. Why was it, he wondered, that some people had the ability to make others feel wonderful and always, always, had the right words?

That night Rand slept deeply, peacefully, for the first time since he'd returned to England. It was only when he woke to a new day that he realized he hadn't needed half a bottle of whiskey to sleep. He felt like singing.

Her name was Valentine Mitchell and she was Maggie's attorney. She was thirtyish and tall, almost six feet. Crisp and neat in a gray flannel suit with a white silk blouse. There was a Mark Cross bag over her shoulder and she carried a Gucci briefcase in her hand. Her hair was short and wavy, complementing a sharp, suntanned face. Her eyes, Maggie noticed, were the color of bright new spring leaves just coming into bud.

"I know you must be surprised to see me here, but Mr. Abramson said he thought I was the best one to handle this case. I used to practice in New York before joining this firm. I was one of the legion of assistants to the Manhattan district attorney. I watched your husband in court many times. I've done nothing but work on this case for the past month. I think we can beat him."

"Think? That isn't good enough, Miss Mitchell. He's clever and he's hateful."

"Yes, think. A good lawyer never says he knows anything for certain. Trust me. Yes, Cranston is clever, and yes, he can be hateful. I've seen him when he lost a case. I never even knew he was married till Dudley told me."

Maggie giggled. "I never heard anyone call Mr. Abramson Dudley before. I always thought of him as being born old and everyone bowing down to him."

"Dudley likes young women. I'm his right hand, or so he says." The bright green eyes were bitter when she added, "And that hand has been very busy indeed."

"I see. I'm sorry."

"Don't be. I was one of these young women who believed Gloria Steinem when she said, 'Be a lawyer, don't marry one.' I bought it. I'd like to talk to your son. I want to hear exactly what it is you're prepared to give up and what you want to keep. I want to hear from the boy where he stands. I'm good with kids. I want you to trust me with your son, and I don't want you to interfere. Your case comes up in two weeks, so we don't have a lot of time."

Maggie looked into the leaf-green eyes. Something she saw there made her nod. "Whatever you want. Stay for dinner and you can talk to Cole afterward. My time is yours now."

"Good." The Gucci briefcase snapped open. Legal papers crackled.

Maggie's eyes dropped to Valentine's feet. Ferragamo shoes at three hundred dollars a pair. This was going to be one expensive divorce. "Shoot," Maggie said happily.

* * *

Dinner was more than pleasant. Maggie enjoyed every minute of it. Val, as she preferred to be called, regaled them with tales of her stint in the Manhattan prosecutor's office. The boys, in turn, talked about baseball and archery. Riley surprised his aunt and Cole, too, by bragging that Cole was the number-one archer on the school team. Cole could do no less than supply all of them with Riley's batting average. "His RBI is the best the school's ever had."

Maggie beamed.

They had coffee in the living room, after the boys had excused themselves to do homework.

"Cole, don't go anywhere. I need to talk to you. When do you think you'll finish your homework?" Val asked.

Cole's eyes swiveled to his mother and then returned to Val. "Forty-five minutes."

"Good, I'll be up then."

Maggie sipped at her coffee. "Just how well did you know my husband?"

Val grinned. "Very well. But I didn't go to bed with him. I know somebody who did, though. His name was Evan Lantzy."

Maggie sputtered her coffee all over the front of her blouse. "*What?*"

"Feel better about this case now?"

"My God! I never. . . . Who would . . ."

"Isn't it great? Once in a while I love to play dirty. Just tell me what you want, Maggie, and it's yours."

"Cole. That's all I want. Forget the rest. Are . . . are . . ."

"Yes. He has to know. Dudley and I discussed it. Regardless of what that old bird is, he does know law and he knows Cranston. We did a run-through on his past cases. Hey, he could destroy you in two minutes without Evan's affidavit. He's got enough on you to. . . . You know what I'm saying. You were married to him, so you know how dirty he can be. It's a game. All lawyers play games and make deals."

Maggie was still in shock. 'I don't know if Cole can

handle this. Are you sure he has to know?"

"Yes. That's why I'm going to be the one doing the telling and not you. As far as you're concerned, you never heard what I said. That kid can handle anything. I watched him during dinner. I told you; I'm good with kids, especially kids in trouble. I worked with them a lot in New York. Do you want to see Evan's affidavit?"

"No. God, no."

"It wasn't a one-night stand. It lasted quite a while. According to Evan, he was devastated. Right now, the man of the hour is a buyer for Saks Fifth Avenue. He buys children's outerwear. His name is Wade Holder."

Maggie shook her head. "It's so hard to believe. He told me he's getting married."

"He is. To a very nice woman, I might add. Dumb, but nice. She bakes cookies, is a hospital volunteer, and quite rich. We ran a check on her, too."

"Do you ever get sick of what you're doing?" Maggie asked curiously.

The bitterness was back in Val's voice. "Every day of my life."

"Why do you stay with it?"

"Because I bought the bullshit line that I could do it on my own. They told me I didn't need someone to take care of me; that I could do it myself. They're right. I can. I suppose it's a case of wanting versus needing. Men do business like this every day of the week. Everyone has to work in the gutter once in a while. You go home at night and take a bath. Some of it washes away."

"What happens when you can't wash it away anymore?"

Val laughed. "Then I'll get married and scrub my husband's back. Dirt doesn't seem to stick to a man like it does to a woman.

"While we're waiting for Cole to finish his homework, I have a pile of papers for you to sign. You won't even have to appear in court. I'll personally deliver your divorce papers."

It was nine-thirty when Valentine Mitchell walked out

of Cole's room and came down the wide circular staircase. The leaf-green eyes had tears in them.

"Remember what I told you before," she said to Maggie. "Don't ever let Cole know you know. If you do, you'll destroy him. He came through it. He'll be all right. Trust me."

Maggie did.

Maggie lay in her bag bed staring at the dark ceiling. A clap of thunder overhead made her jump. She must have been dozing a little. She was about to get up and close the window when she noticed her door opening.

"Mother?" It was a hoarse whisper from Cole.

"Yes. Are you sick, Cole?" Of course he was sick. Sick in his heart and sick in his soul.

"No. I can't sleep. I want to talk to you about something."

"Sure. Do you want to go downstairs and have some cocoa?"

"Yeah. Let's do that. I want some bright light. Did I wake you?"

"No. The thunder did," Maggie replied truthfully.

Sitting in the brightly lit kitchen, sipping cocoa, Maggie watched her son struggle for the right words. She wanted to help him, but remained silent.

"Do lawyers lie? I know Dad's a lawyer, but do they ever say things that... that... you know, they make up so their case is better than the other lawyer's?"

"That's pretty hard to do, Cole. They could get disbarred if anyone found out. Perjury is a very serious offense. Why are you asking? Are you worried about your father?"

"Father? No. What about that lady that was here tonight? The one who talked to me."

"What about her?"

"Would she lie?"

"She works for the biggest and best law firm in Austin.

They've been this family's attorneys since before I was born. No, I don't think she would lie. Why? What's the matter?"

"Everything they put down on those legal papers... They have to have real proof, right?"

"Yes, they do." God, she was sick to her stomach. How must her son feel?

"That's what I thought. I guess I'll be staying on here until it's time to go to college. Dad doesn't need me."

"I'm sorry. It's his loss, Cole. You have to believe that."

"I wanted him to like me. I wanted us to go to ball games and do things."

"I know. I used to want those things myself. My pap never had time for me, either. Mam tried, but I didn't give her a chance. I regret that now. I think your father loves you as much as he's capable of loving anyone."

"He hates me. He only tried to use me to get what he wants."

"No, Cole, you're wrong. It's me he hates. Not you. He used you and you used him. You have to accept that."

"He was going to use Sawyer, too, and make me use her. I hate that!" Cole cried, rubbing at his eyes with the back of his hand. "Sawyer's going to die and I can't do anything."

"That's not true. You're doing one hell of a thing by planning the trip to Hawaii. Mam was impressed when she told me all about it. I wish you had told me, Cole."

"I thought you wouldn't let me do it. I didn't care; I was going to do it anyway. But you said she was off-limits."

"We all say things when we're angry. I regretted it the moment I said it."

"Then I can go?"

"Of course you can go. I'll be cheering you every step of the way. You make this the best, the very best time of Sawyer's life."

"How sick is Sawyer going to get?"

"I don't know. Maybe God will be merciful and won't make her suffer."

"What are you going to do about her?"

Maggie sighed. "It's all I think about, Cole. I'm going to . . . I'm going to try and make things right between us. I don't know if it will work, but I'm going to . . . to go to New York. . . . I have to give her some time to adjust to this crisis in her life. I'll go before you leave for Hawaii."

"I want to know about Rand."

"Yes, I guess you do. It's very simple. I love him. I sent him away because I thought no one would understand. I didn't steal him or snatch him away from Sawyer. It just happened. When he came here for the Fourth of July, he told Sawyer that he wanted to break off their relationship. He felt he was too old for her. . . . He's a fine man. I'm sorry he let me send him away. After it was too late, after he was gone, Mam told me I made a mistake. Cole . . . wait here. I want to show you something. Make some more cocoa till I get back."

Maggie raced up the stairs in her bare feet, her night-gown crunched above her knees. She pushed the small button in her desk and a secret door popped out. Her father's last letter lay there ready to be snatched up by her eager fingers. She slammed the drawer shut and loped down the hall, then took the steps two at a time. By the time she came back into the kitchen, she was breathless. If ever she was to get Cole, this was the time. She handed her father's letter to her son, and watched his eyes as he read. She could see his hands trembling much as hers were. When he finished, she folded it and put it back in the envelope.

"Keeping you here was the sunshine. Do you understand? Rand was going to make me happy. That's what it's all about."

"You let him go. You sent him away. Yet, you'd fight for me. Why?"

"You're my son. My flesh and blood. I had to fight for you, for myself as well as you. The love, the feeling, I have for Rand is different. I could send him away because it was best. I'm sorry. I'd give anything to undo some of the things I've done in my life, but some things can never be made right."

"I want to know about Sawyer."

"Cole, it's four o'clock in the morning."

"I want to know."

"All right."

They talked and talked and talked. When Martha walked into the kitchen at six o'clock, Maggie waved her away. At seven o'clock Maggie took Cole by the hand and led him upstairs. She settled him in the bright rust-colored chair in her room. "You aren't going to school today. I'll tell Riley not to wait for you. You're going to read these," she said, handing him her box of diaries. "It's time for you to know who I am. Don't come downstairs till you finish. I'm going riding now. I'll see you later."

Cole drew away from the box. "Mother, I don't think I want to read these."

"I don't want you to read them, either, but you have to if we're ever to be mother and son. I'll send up some breakfast."

Maggie slipped from Lotus's back and tethered her. She crept up to the grassy knoll, her face full of hope. "I think I'm on the way, Pap," she said, crunching down. "I couldn't have done it without you and your letter. In a little while we're going to know how much Coleman is in my son. I took a big chance, and I don't really know if my gamble is going to pay off. Maybe I blew it. Rest easy, Pap, I'll be back."

Lotus nickered softly and danced around in a circle, sensing her mistress's uneasiness. "Let's ride, Lotus." Maggie leaned low, crouched against the horse's silky mane. The animal's hooves pounding the ground sounded like thunder in Maggie's ears. She gave the horse her head.

Riley peered from the school bus window at the lone

rider thundering across the fields. He knew it was his aunt Maggie. He also knew something was going on. Cole was staying home . . . and not because he was sick.

It was one o'clock when Maggie climbed the stairs to the second floor. Her heart hammered in her chest. What would she see in her son's eyes? What would he say to her? She opened the door and entered the room.

It was empty. The diaries were piled neatly in their respective boxes. For a moment she thought she was going to faint. She hadn't allowed herself to think, even for a moment, that Cole would cut and run. He was her son; he wouldn't do that. She ran into the hallway shouting his name.

"Psst, shhh!" Cole hissed loudly, almost as loudly as his mother was shouting.

"Cole!" Maggie leaned against the door frame, her face drained of all color. Cole was sitting in the rocking chair giving Jessie a bottle of water.

"Jeez, I just got her to sleep."

Maggie literally slid down the door frame till she was sitting on the floor. She waited.

Cole watched his mother for a few seconds. He knew she was waiting for him to say something. "You're one hell of a lady, Mam."

Maggie rolled her eyes back in her head. "Don't swear in front of Jessie."

Cole grinned. "So, you're one heck of a lady. I was trying to emphasize a point. Did you get it?"

"Yeahhh," Maggie drawled.

"Where'd you go?"

"Up on the knoll."

"Didja get any answers?"

"No. I just talk it out up there. The answers have to come down here. Welcome to Sunbridge, Cole."

"You want to take this kid? She just wet my pants. Aunt Susan said I didn't have to worry about her nappies. That's her pants, right?"

"Yeah. Diapers. In England they call them nappies. Here, I'll take her."

Cole smiled. Maggie smiled back.

"I'm going to school," he said, heading out the door. "I have archery practice, and the coach kicks us off if we miss. I'll take the the the moped. See you at supper."

"Shoot one for me," Maggie called.

"Shoot one what?"

"Arrow, you ninny. Go, go already."

Jessie's diaper secure, Maggie laid her on her stomach. Her fist went immediately to her mouth. God, she thought, I have a son. I have my son.

She walked to the window. The sun shining down on Sunbridge was warm and golden.

She watched from the window as Cole rolled his moped out to the driveway. She saw him look up and around. He, too, was noticing for the first time how bright it was. Sunbridge.

A dusty pickup truck rattled down the road, its bed overloading the springs until the rear license plate was only inches from the ground. It bumped to a halt and the driver, Ben Simms, rolled down the window and peered up at the wooden arch proclaiming the name Sunbridge. Callused hands jammed his worn straw hat farther down onto his grizzled head. He turned to the young girl sitting beside him. "Looks like this is it. Mind your manners now, gal. We need this job."

She wanted to die, just die. At the last crossroads a ranch truck filled with workers had hooted and hollered as the Simms truck strained past them. And no wonder—they looked like a rerun of the *Beverly Hillbillies*. The only thing missing was Old Granny in her rocking chair.

"Luana, you hear me? We need this job and you well know it. Just sit there like the proper little lady you are and let me do the talkin'. When the missus talks to you, just smile and let her know you're willin' to work. Got that?"

"Yes, Pa."

Ben forced the truck in gear and turned into the drive. He glanced at his daughter and was satisfied when he saw her running a comb through her long, sandy-colored hair. Sprucing up, just like her ma. Spittin' image of her ma, too. Luana dropped her comb and sat with her hands in her lap just the way he liked. She was a good girl, he thought, not like her ma. Trixie had been a wild one till the day he'd married her, and then she'd settled down some. But when Luana was six years old she'd cut and run with a farmhand, and he hadn't seen or heard from her since.

"I think we'll like it here, don't you, Luana?" he said enthusiastically. "Look out there at those fields. Hear tell they raise a good strain of cattle out this way. You seen it, ain'tcha? The sun with the single bar? Stands for Sunbridge."

He squinted through the bug-spattered windshield, his wind-roughened features and square bristly chin strong and still beneath the brim of his hat. His caramel-colored eyes narrowed as they rode past outbuildings and stables and miles of white cross-fencing.

"This is some spread, ain't it, Luana?"

"Yes, Pa."

"That all you got to say? Yes, Pa; yes, Pa. You sound like a broken record."

"Yes, Pa." There was an insolent tone in the soft, girlish voice that drew Ben's attention. Saucerlike brown eyes, a color deeper and brighter than his own, continued staring out through the windshield. When she felt him looking at her, she dropped her thick, sooty lashes demurely.

"You know I don't like you wearing them short skirts," he growled, more for her lack of interest and insolence than for the skirt. He eyed her legs and the generous expanse of thigh. "What's these people gonna think, you dressed like that? Ain't no call for you to dress like some tramp. You sit in the truck while I talk business. Don't get out, you hear?"

"Pa, this skirt's the only one I got. Miz Halpern give it to me. You said it was all right; you said! There ain't no hem to let down."

Looked like her ma and had a mouth like her, too. Trixie always had an answer. In another year or two he was going to have his hands full if he didn't come down hard on her now. "Then you should've worn long pants. Sinful. It's a sin to show so much of yourself."

Luana snorted. She stared at her father, her eyes half-closed in the bright early-spring sunshine. She'd been practicing this expression from the cover of *True Confession's* magazine for weeks now; she couldn't wait to try it out on some real men. Pa was always saying this was trampy, that was trashy. Hell, yes. Pa was the tramp and she was the trash. But all that would change when she turned sixteen and got herself away from him and his preachin'. She'd head for the big city, and the first thing she'd buy was the brightest dress she could find and high-heeled shoes to match. She'd get fancy combs and do her hair up like in the magazines, and then she'd buy a whole bagful of Maybelline and go to town on her face. Big gold earrings and some bracelets, maybe even one for her ankle.

"You wearin' a brazzere, gal?" Ben said abruptly; breaking into her thoughts. "You know I don't like it when you're bouncin' around under your shirt. You're a good girl, and I want you to stay that way. You ain't gonna turn out like your ma."

"Yes, Pa. I'm wearin' one. Only it ain't my fault it's all stretched out. I need new duds. You keep sayin' you're gonna get me some, only you don't," Luana complained petulantly.

"We ain't been in one place long enough to put money aside for extras. We're clean and that's what counts, a lot more than fancy duds do. If the folks in town were right about them needin' help out here, we just might have that extra money right soon."

Luana rolled her eyes and slipped on her sunglasses. It was the same tired old story, all the same excuses. This place wasn't going to be any different from all the others.

They'd live in a shack for a few weeks and then they'd move on, mostly because Pa would run up bills and drink all his wages. But Pa was a good worker. Some of the time it wasn't even his drinking—it was when the women got a look at her that they were sent packing. But Pa never got mad about that. He'd say in his best Sunday preacher voice that God gave her her beauty, and she had to bear it and so did he. Then they'd read from Scripture. Every day it was the same thing. Maybe if they stayed here, she could go back to school. She was so far behind now, she didn't know if she could ever catch up. But she was a fast learner, and usually there was some boy who'd offer to help her as long as he could look down the front of her blouse.

Luana had learned early that boys wanted to look real bad. If you let them touch you, they'd give you just about anything you wanted. She'd managed to get three dollars off one boy just for letting him stick his hand down her blouse. She'd bought black mascara and a bag of M&M's from the dime store. She would've had ten dollars from that hunk who hung out by the trailer court in Pineville if his girlfriend hadn't come along. Maybe she was like her ma, she thought defiantly. So what? Pa couldn't give her the things she wanted; she had to find a way to get them for herself.

Luana squirmed in the cracked leather seat. Just thinking about all those things the boys wanted to do to her made her feel funny. She wondered what it would be like to really "do it." She'd had enough offers, but she was holding out. Being a virgin had its good points. She knew she was what men called a tease; boys called her that, too. Her breasts were big, full and ripe. She wanted to look like Dolly Parton. Her waist was tiny and her legs were long and slender. If she just had the right clothes, she knew she'd be a knockout.

The pickup bounced over the road. Ben could see his daughter's breasts jiggle with each bump. His lips tightened. Maybe it *was* time the girl had some new clothes—

clothes that fit. Other things, too. Living like gypsies, from pillar to post, wasn't good for Luana. His pretty little girl deserved better than he was giving her.

"I'll drive around the back," he said as he maneuvered the truck around the circular drive. "You stay inside. Keep the windows rolled up and don't go talkin' to no one."

"Good luck, Pa," Luana said softly, looking around her. Maybe her pa could get work here. The people in town had said something about putting up some cabins for crippled children. It might be fun to live in a nice place like this for a while.

Maggie and Susan talked to Ben Simms for a long time. Susan showed him the sketches of the buildings that were to go up. He looked at them carefully. "I can do it. I do good work, missus. You'll find no fault with anything I do."

"We plan to erect modular units, constructed at the factory and brought out here to the site. It would save a good deal of time. You'd be responsible for helping to lay in the foundations for the buildings and for building fences. I need a kind of jack-of-all-trades, Mr. Simms. Think you can fill the bill?" Susan had already decided to hire him. He looked capable and eager. The work she was offering was menial and the pay low. Most of the skilled laborers and construction workers in this area had already been snapped up by Cary.

"Yes, ma'am," he replied eagerly. "But I'll have to find a place to live. I have a daughter to take care of. She's fourteen and needs to go to school."

Maggie met Susan's gaze. Maggie nodded. "There's a small apartment all furnished over the garage. You could stay there. The school bus stops at the end of the road. Our boys take it."

"Boys! You got boys here? My girl is only fourteen. How old are your boys?" he asked anxiously.

"Sixteen. They're good boys, Mr. Simms," Maggie assured him. "You don't have anything to worry about."

"Boys that age are full of juices. I speak my mind,

missus. I'm a God-fearin' man who reads Scripture, and so does my daughter. If you say they're good boys, I'll take your word for it. About that apartment, now. If I take it, I'll work Saturdays for nothing. Is that fair?"

Susan and Maggie nodded. "When can you start?" Susan asked.

"All I got is out there in that truck. My daughter and our belongings. We can move right in. I can start to work this afternoon."

"That's just fine, Mr. Simms. Why don't you drive around to the garage. The door leading to the upstairs is open. It's probably dusty. I can send our housekeeper over to clean it up for you."

"No need for that. Luana is a good little housekeeper. Just like her ma used to be."

"After you're moved in, you come back here and we'll go into town and order your supplies," Susan told him. "Everything's been staked out."

"If we're going to town, do you think I could register my daughter for school?"

"Of course."

As they followed Ben Simms outside; Maggie and Susan smiled gleefully at each other. "God does work in mysterious ways, doesn't he?" Susan whispered, and both women giggled. Then they saw Luana Simms get out of the truck to help her father carry the cartons and bags up the stairs.

"That's Luana?" Maggie gaspped, gripping Susan's arm. "Didn't he say she was fourteen?"

"That's what he said," Susan said in awe. "More like fourteen going on thirty-four!"

"I never looked like that at fourteen." Maggie giggled. "I was pregnant, though. This smells like trouble to me, Susan. My God, wait till the boys see her at the bus stop tomorrow." She groaned. "You don't think she'd wear that skirt, do you?"

"God, I don't know."

"Maybe I'll wander over there after you two go to

town. You know, offer my help or something."

"Why do I have this feeling I've made a mistake?" Susan muttered.

"I'll give you my expert opinion a little later. If you're going into town with Mr. Simms, I'll have Martha stay with Jessie while I talk to the child."

"That one is no child. Trust me. I like Mr. Simms, though. I bet he gives me a good job." She shrugged. "And if it doesn't work out, we'll ask him to move on."

Maggie's face wore a dubious look. She'd never known Susan to make such a quick judgment before. Normally, she thought about things until you wanted to scream at her to make a decision. She didn't realize her fingers were crossed till one of them started to ache.

When Susan and Ben Simms left for town, Maggie knocked softly on the door of the garage apartment. A muffled voice told her to come in. Maggie drew in her breath and walked inside, not knowing quite what to expect.

Neither did Luana, it appeared. She'd been wiping the kitchen floor and stood up abruptly at the sight of Maggie, stopping only to put the soapy rag back in the bucket. She looked around for a towel; finding none, she wiped her hands on her short denim skirt. "Are you Miz Tanner?" she asked shyly.

"Yes. You must be Luana. I hope you and your father like this place. It's kind of small, but it does have two bedrooms."

"Ma'am, this is the grandest place. The grandest. We ain't never had anything this fine before. I don't know how to thank you."

Maggie stared at the girl, feeling as if she'd just been run over with a tractor by her vehemence.

Luana's chest heaved as she continued to talk at breakneck speed. "We ain't white trash, Miz Tanner. We're poor, but we're good folks. My ma, she run off when I was six. My pa says she was trash, but I don't believe that. She wanted fun and bright-colored clothes and perfume. Pa couldn't give it to her."

"Yes . . . well . . . I'm sure everything will be fine. Your father is going to be working for my sister. . . ."

"You must be happy living in this swell place. I don't think I ever saw such a beautiful house." She pronounced it bee-yoo-tee-ful.

Maggie laughed. "Yes, I am happy here. Look, your father was concerned about the school. The bus stops right at the end of the road. It picks up my son and my nephew at seven-fifteen and gets back here around four in the afternoon. I think your father is going to register you this afternoon. . . . Is there anything you want to ask me?"

Luana tilted her head, and Maggie groaned inwardly. The ripe little mouth seemed to pout as the girl thought about what she'd just been asked. "No, I don't think so. I don't want you to worry about me breaking these nice dishes or making a mess. I know how to keep house and cook. I'll keep this place just spotless. You can come here anytime and check it over. How old is your son and nephew?"

Maggie was still working on the house check. "Sixteen," she said without thinking. Whoaaa, she thought. "Are you interested in boys?" she asked carefully.

Luana's voice was soft, without guile, almost shy. "No, not really. Boys seem to like me, though. Pa keeps a tight rein on me. I'm too young to date. I was just wondering how much older they were than me because they might not know where to direct me at school tomorrow."

"They'll know. Trust me," Maggie said flatly.

"What do the kids wear? Is it a fancy school?"

As compared to what? Maggie wanted to ask. She supposed it was fancy or would appear so to someone like Luana. "Neatness counts," she said.

"I'm clean and I'm neat. I don't have much, only hand-me-downs from people Pa worked for."

Maggie almost choked. Honey, she wanted to say, there

isn't going to be anyone looking at your clothes. "Well, if there's nothing more I can do, I'll be going back to the house. If you think of something, let me know. By the way, there's a washer and dryer in the back of the garage. Feel free to use them."

"Ma'am, do you mean that? Do you really mean that?"

"Of course I mean it. Why do you sound so surprised?"

"We ain't never lived anywhere where there was such fine things. I do the wash in the bathtub unless there's a Laundromat, but that's so expensive."

On the walk back to the house, Maggie couldn't make up her mind if her leg had been pulled or not. She puzzled over it all evening. When the boys left the table after dinner she casually mentioned Luana and asked both boys to watch out for her.

"Eighth grade! Mother!" Cole grimaced. "How's it going to look with us squiring an eighth-grade baby around?"

Riley grinned. "You're asking a lot, Aunt Maggie. We've got our images to consider."

"Nevertheless, you'll do as I ask, won't you?" Maggie said pointedly.

"Yes, ma'am, only we're not going to like it."

When the boys left the room, Maggie smiled at Susan. "Wait until they see this eighth-grade baby. At least it's only for one day, and I suppose that won't kill them."

The next morning Cole and Riley were crossing the yard to the garage, where they kept their mopeds. If they'd forgotten their promise to Maggie to look after the daughter of the hired help, they soon remembered. Luana Mae Simms had just stepped out of the long, deep early-morning shadows into the sunshine. The boys stopped in their tracks. Cole had seen girls like this in New York; Riley hadn't even known they existed.

The early-morning sunlight caught the sandy blond of Luana's hair and made it glint with gold. The breeze caught the ends and blew them about her face—not a pretty face, especially, but one that was still softly rounded with youth. Her mouth was full, her lips pouting and ripe, and her

thickly lashed eyes were dark and smiling as though she
alone knew a delicious secret. She wore faded jeans that
hugged her thighs and delineated the globes of her back-
side. Her blouse was of simple oxford cloth and the first
three buttons were open, revealing a suggestion of cleav-
age between her high round breasts. She walked across
the driveway, the heels of her boots tapping on the concrete.

"Are you gonna take me to school?" she asked, looking
at the mopeds and then back at the boys. "I ain't never
rode on one of those."

"Yeah . . . well, you're supposed to take the school bus,"
Riley said. "If you need to know anything at school, just
ask one of us." With sinking heart, he thought of Kelly
Jensen. She wasn't going to like this one bit.

Luana stood in their path, her lower lip jutting out
stubbornly. "But I don't know nobody on the school bus.
Miz Tanner said you'd look out for me. Can't I ride with
one of you?" Her speech was slow, almost indolent, and
the boys found themselves waiting almost breathlessly for
the next syllable.

Riley shook his head. "I don't think it's a good idea.
It can get pretty cold riding on the back of a moped, and
that little windbreaker you're carrying won't keep you
warm."

"I won't mind," she insisted, turning her attention to
Cole, who was standing there as though carved from gran-
ite. "You must be Miz Tanner's boy. Your mama said you
were nice. I'm Luana. Luana Mae Simms."

Riley, watching Cole, thought he'd never seen such a
sappy expression on anyone's face. He felt sort of stupid
himself and almost dropped his books when Luana hooked
her thumb into the waistline of her jeans and swung her
windbreaker over her shoulder, one hip jutting forward,
the thin fabric of her blouse straining over her breasts.

"Yes, I'm Mrs. Tanner's boy . . . er, son—I mean, I'm
Cole."

"Nice te meetcha, Cole." She smiled, her full lips parting to reveal nice white teeth with very even edges. Her lips were pink, but Cole couldn't see any traces of lipstick.

"Are you from China?" Luana asked Riley.

"No, Japan. Look, Cole, we better get a move on. Luana, you'd better get down to the road or you'll miss the bus."

"I won't mind. Then maybe Cole here would take me to school on his motorbike."

"Moped," Cole corrected. "I'll ride you to the road so you don't miss the bus. Wait till I get 'er started and then hop on."

The mopeds rattled and sputtered to life. Luana straddled the seat behind Cole, her arms clamped around his waist, her full breasts pressing into his back, her strong thighs gripping his bottom. She lowered her head and buried it against his back as protection from the wind. He heard her giggle with delight as they sped down the drive, Riley close behind. When Cole turned out of the drive, the school bus was just coming up the road, but he spun out ahead of it and carried Luana all the way to school.

Riley didn't have to wonder why. Just the sight of Luana's neat little bottom bouncing and swaying on the back of Cole's moped gave him all the answers he'd ever need.

CHAPTER TWENTY-FOUR

Spring settled over Sunbridge like a bright green cloak.
Maggie always thought it was her favorite time of year
...until she saw the golden foliage of autumn. For now,
the brilliant spring flowers in their neat, trim beds nodded
sociably to one another. New growth on the lush shrubbery gleamed like emeralds in the bright sunlight. Maggie
just *knew* the sun was brighter.

She walked onto the patio, letting the sun's warmth
caress her from the top of her head to the tip of her toes.
Her world was wonderful. Cole was back in her life. He
knew who she was and he still loved her. His gentleness
had stunned her. Her son.

The only thing missing in this perfect setting was Rand.
Twice more she'd tried to call him in the London apartment because Susan had said there was no phone in the
country house. Her shoulders twitched. She was going to
have to accept this rejection the way she had so many
others. A letter, three attempts to call, told her all she
need to know. Too much, too little, too late Maggie.

She should be thinking about going to New York to
see Sawyer. In fact, she should make a reservation today
and go next week. Spring in New York was almost as
wonderful as spring in Texas.

It was such a beautiful morning, she hated to go indoors.
The decision was taken out of her hands momentarily
when she heard a shrill argument wafting from the garage

apartment. Shamelessly she pushed her chair closer to
the patio railing so she could hear. Her eyes widened.

"I won't have you acting like a slut. I told you, I warned
you, what I'd do if I caught you hanky-pankin' with those
boys. Now you bend over and take your punishment.
Then we'll read Scripture."

Maggie didn't know which was louder, the sound of
the belt whacking through the air or Luana's screams.
"Pa, I didn't do nothin'! The boys was just bein' nice.
Paaaaa," she wailed. "I was bein' polite because Miz Tanner is bein' so good to us."

"Your nice Miz Tanner is goin' to fire me if you keep
on actin' like a slut. I ain't about to let that happen. You
ain't goin' to turn out like your ma. You hear me, Luana?"

Maggie cringed. She could almost imagine the red welts
on that round, voluptuous bottom. But this was none of
her business. How Ben Simms raised his daughter had
nothing to do with her. She realized suddenly that she
was angry. Angry at Ben Simms for abusing his daughter
because of his hatred for his wife.

She was worried about the boys and their open admi-
ration for Luana. These days she could see and feel the
tension between them. Just last night Riley had told her
he'd asked Luana to go on a picnic with him. Luana, of
course, had declined. Cole had smirked, but there'd been
a look in his eye Maggie had recognized. He meant to
ace his cousin out, if he could.

Maggie had made it her business to observe the girl
for over a week now. As far as she could tell, Luana was
a little snip, playing one boy against the other. She'd go
to archery practice and watch Cole; then she'd go to the
baseball diamond and cheer Riley on. In bad weather she
rode the bus home. When it was nice outside, she'd hang
around school, allowing herself just enough time to walk
the three miles or hitch a ride. She'd careen into the yard,
and before long the smell of frying onions or garlic would
sift through the kitchen screen door. Maggie often heard
the faint rattle of dishes. Inside twenty minutes, the girl

would have the beds made, the breakfast dishes done, laundry going in the machine, and dinner in the oven or on the stove. Then she'd take another few minutes to change her clothes and put on skimpy shorts or the denim miniskirt. By the time Cole and Riley rode their mopeds up the drive at five-thirty, she'd be sitting on the steps reading one of her schoolbooks—at least Maggie had thought it was a schoolbook at first. Cole had told her Luana kept a copy of *True Confessions* magazine folded up inside her schoolbook. At the time Maggie had grinned; she used to devour the pulps by the pound herself. The boys, of course, would head immediately for the garage and talk with Luana until the timer pinged from the kitchen window. Ben Simms walked up those steps promptly at five minutes past six. By that time, the boys were safely in their rooms doing their homework or washing up for dinner. The girl had it down to a science.

Luana's sobs were now shrieks of pain. "All right, Pa, I won't talk to them no more! You tell Miz Tanner they ain't good enough for me. Go ahead, you go and tell her! There goes your job and this swell place. Sometimes I hate you, Pa. Go ahead, hit me some more. I don't care no more! You keep telling me you want me to get book learning, but we move around so much I forget from place to place. Cole and Riley said they'd help me. What's wrong with that?"

Whack. Maggie flinched.

"Get the Good Book and we'll read."

Maggie listened as Ben Simms's voice droned on and on. Once in a while she could hear Luana as she responded to her father.

The following week Maggie made plans to go to New York. She also made it her business to cancel most of her charity work in order to hang around the house. She didn't know why until Wednesday, when she just happened to see Riley skirt the main road and roar across the field on his moped. He had a rider on the back, whom Maggie knew instantly was Luana.

Riley never cut school. And he certainly never cut baseball practice. She looked at her watch,—1:15. Where were they going?

For hours she paced Sunbridge like an expectant father. Finally, at five-fifteen, Maggie heard the roar of Riley's moped. She sighed heavily. Time for both of them to get back—Riley to his room, Luana to her frying onions.

On Friday, Luana left for school in a new dress, a brilliant red silky thing, and matching high-heeled shoes.

On Saturday, Maggie canceled her trip to New York and rescheduled it for the following week.

On Monday afternoon it was Cole who cut across the field with Luana on the back of his moped. On Wednesday, when Luana left for school, she was wearing Calvin Klein jeans and a LaCoste pullover.

That morning, as Maggie was brooding over what she'd seen, Susan joined her on the patio, a cup of coffee in hand. "What happened to good deeds lately? Why are you so antsy? What's going on you haven't told me?"

Maggie filled her in.

"You mean that little bitch is peddling her ass?" Susan asked outraged.

"It looks that way," Maggie said morosely. "I know one thing, though. Both boys think they're 'it' as far as Luana goes. I shudder to think what's going to happen when they find out they're at opposite ends of the rope."

"Does her father . . . Of course not. She'd be black and blue if he did. Maybe I should talk to him."

"No, Suse, don't do that." Maggie told her about the beating Luana had gotten from Ben Simms.

Susan sipped her coffee, nearly scalding her tongue. "Maggie, that man is an absolute powerhouse. He's already laid two foundations for the modular buildings, and his work is exact. Ferris is very impressed. Because of Ben Simms, we can expect to have the modules ready by Labor Day."

Labor day. That was five months away. A lot could happen in five months. Then Maggie remembered that the boys were leaving for Hawaii in June. Still, even two-and-a-half months was a long time. A girl could get pregnant in two-and-a-half months. Maybe she should have a talk with Luana.

At four o'clock on Saturday afternoon, Ben Simms knocked at the back door and asked for Susan.

"Missus, I have to go to town. I need to order some more supplies. I want to bring back a keg of nails so I have them first thing Monday morning. I'll be owing you two hours of time, but I'll make them up Monday. I need to buy some groceries at the supermarket, too. Luana tells me it's open till ten o'clock."

"That's fine, Mr. Simms. Have the lumberyard send me the bill. You can take off early whenever you want. Here's your pay, cash like you asked for."

Ben thanked her, tipped his hat. "I wonder if you'd give Miz Tanner a message for me."

"Surely, Mr. Simms."

"Tell her I was wrong with the boys. They're very respectful of Luana. I don't cotton to that one with the slanted eyes, but Luana says he's real good with numbers and she needs help. If the boys still have a mind to help her, they can come over after supper and work at the kitchen table. I'll be right there."

Luana watched her father as he headed for the bathroom. He'd told her to make a grocery list, and she had—a nice long one.

She hummed to herself as she stirred the onions in the pan. Pa would do just like he said—he'd get his keg of nails, the groceries, and load everything in the back of the truck. But after that, he'd stop at the roadside cafe and wouldn't be home till past midnight or maybe not till morning, if he found a woman. So she had six hours she could definitely count on, perhaps the entire night.

Her mind raced as she fried the last of the hamburger meat. She smiled, remembering the set of lacy black underwear she'd bought in Austin on Friday. Maybe she'd wear it tonight. . . .

The minute supper was over, Luana leaped up to do the dishes. She'd just finished wiping the last one dry when Ben stuck her grocery list into his pocket. "You be a good girl while I'm gone. Keep the door locked. Study your homework and read your Scripture because I'm going to ask you questions in the morning."

"Yes, Pa," Luana answered obediently. She was stunned when Ben handed her a twenty-dollar bill.

"Next week you buy yourself some new duds."

"Thanks, Pa." She perched on tiptoe and kissed Ben's cheek.

He reddened with pleasure. "Trixie'd always do that when I give her something," Ben said and patted her cheek awkwardly. "You're all I got, gal."

"I know, Pa. Don't you go worryin' about me. Both of us is going to be all right from here on out. When words gets around what a good worker you are, jobs will be lining up from here to kingdom come. You watch. Maybe Miz Tanner will let us rent this place permanently."

"You like it here, do you, gal?"

"I really do, Pa. This is the first place that seems like home since Ma left. I keep it nice, don't I?"

"You do. You make me proud."

Luana kissed him again and obediently locked the door behind him. She didn't move till she heard the pickup truck drive out of the courtyard. Then she stripped and showered and powdered herself all over with talcum from the dime store. "Djer Kiss." It smelled nice and she liked the name because it had the word kiss in it.

Her fingers itched to touch the lacy black underwear. After she slipped it on, she looked into the big, round mirror over the chest of drawers. She had to hop on the bed for a full look. The silky black made her skin look whiter, and the bra pushed her breasts up and together, making them fuller. The little black bikini pants barely covered her where they should, but they made her legs look longer and slimmer.

She wobbled on the lumpy mattress and fell into a heap,

laughing, delighted with herself and her purchase. She pulled on the Calvin jeans and rummaged for a dark plaid blouse, worn but ironed. She didn't want the lacy bra to show through. The blouse was primly buttoned to the neck; her long, almost flaxen hair was pulled into a high ponytail. She tugged at a few loose ends near her ears and did the same with a light fringe of bangs. Her face was shiny clean—better not wear makeup around Miz Tanner. But she did curl her eyelashes.

Five minutes later Luana knocked timidly at the back door, waiting for Martha to answer. She wondered what time it was. Maybe by this time next week she'd have a watch.

"I'm here to see Riley and Cole, ma'am," she said politely when Martha answered the door. "I'll wait out here on the porch."

"Mrs. Tanner," Martha said into the intercom, "that little girl from across the way is here to see Riley and Cole."

"I'll be right down, Martha.

"Is something wrong, Luana?" Maggie asked when she reached the service porch.

"No, ma'am. Cole said maybe he'd help me with homework tonight if he wasn't doing anything."

Maggie stared at the girl, trying to see beneath the surface innocence. But when she remembered the way Ben Simms had whipped his daughter, sympathy overrode her suspicions. She knew it shouldn't, especially since both Riley and Cole were involved, but she felt she should take up the issue with them and not Luana.

Luana met Maggie's gaze, her eyes level and innocent. "Would you call Cole, Miz Tanner?" She asked gently. "Can I see how you used that gadget on the wall? They have something like that in school. Is it the same thing?"

"The intercom? Yes, I suppose so, but on a much smaller scale." Before Maggie realized what she was doing, she'd called Cole on the intercom. Within seconds, she heard his feet down the stairs.

"Hi, Cole. I came to see if you'd help me with my

homework," Luana cooed, her big brown eyes flashing, just the hint of a smile touching her full, youthful mouth.

Cole was staring at Luana as though she were Christie Brinkley, and it irritated Maggie. She wanted to shake him till his teeth rattled.

"It's okay with me," he agreed readily. "I wasn't doing anything tonight. Wait for me. I have to go get a book. I'll be right down."

Cole sprinted up the stairs. He could feel his Jockey shorts filling out. It had gotten to the point lately where he couldn't even think of Luana without a feeling of tension in his loins. She hadn't ever let him go all the way, but she'd taught him things he'd never learned from *Playboy*. Quickly he calculated the amount of money he had in his wallet, money he'd been saving for his trip to Hawaii with Sawyer. Fifty dollars ready cash. He wondered exactly what Luana would give him for fifty dollars.

Maggie watched Cole and Luana cross the courtyard to the apartment over the garage. She wanted to call her son back. Instead, she comforted herself with the knowledge that Ben Simms would be there; nothing would happen under his watchful eye.

"Gee, Cole, for a minute I thought your ma wasn't goin' to let you help me with my homework." Luana laughed. "There was sparks shootin' from her eyes like the Fourth of July. Does she always get jealous when her baby boy is gonna be with a girl?"

Cole bristled. "Cut it out. You don't have a mother, so you don't know how they are. And I'm not her baby boy."

"Are you a man, then, Cole?" They'd reached the door to the apartment on the far side of the garage. In the shadows Luana turned and pushed herself against him, looking up into his face. "Are you, Cole? Are you a man yet?"

"What do you think?" he growled, wrapping an arm around her waist and pulling her hard against him so she could feel his erection.

"I think you're impatient, that's what." She giggled,

sliding through the doorway and racing up the stairs.

Cole followed her neat Calvined bottom, reaching for her when she stopped at the top landing.

"Now, you be a good boy, hear?" she said coyly. "I don't want you gettin' all mad at me the way you did day before yesterday. It wasn't nice to leave me out there by my lonesome. I had to walk all the way home."

"I went back for you, but you'd already left. I didn't know which way you went."

Luana raised her brows, giving him the wide-eyed innocent expression that Cole knew was just another way of teasing him. There was nothing innocent about Luana.

"Well, never mind," she told him. "I managed to get back on my own. That's what matters, ain't it? I don't suppose I'm mad at you anymore."

She led him into the kitchen and saw him wrinkle his nose. The smell of fried onions lingered in the air. "It's my pa," she said quickly. "He likes them stinky old onions. Sometimes I think I'll never get the smell off me. Did I?" She pushed her palm under his nose, knowing that it held traces of "Djer Kiss." "Is it in my hair?" she asked, sliding up close and laying her head against his chest. She could feel his heart pounding as though it were going to burst.

"You smell good to me," he muttered.

"Well, I don't like how this kitchen smells, anyway. Let's go into my room; I want to show you this story I've been readin'. The boy in the picture looks just like you, Cole; that's why I bought the magazine."

He followed her into the sparsely furnished bedroom. On the narrow iron bedstead were several pairs of socks and the new pink blouse she'd worn to school the other day. Scattered about were schoolbooks and papers, and on the dresser was her hairbrush and a large bottle of shampoo.

Quickly, she reached beneath the mattress and brought out several magazines: *True Confessions, Secret Love, Intimate*. "My pa don't like me readin' these. He says they're dirty." She giggled. "Maybe they are, a little." She riffled through the pages. "Here, this is what I wanted to show you."

Cole sat down on the edge of her bed. He didn't want to look in magazines; he wanted to look under Luana's blouse. She stuck the picture under his nose.

"See, don't he have nice light hair like you? And don't he look a little like you around the mouth? And don't the girl look like me, even a little?"

Cole wasn't sure the boy in the photograph looked like him, although the girl did look something like Luana: long blond hair, full petulant lips, eyes half-closed. But it was what they were doing in the picture that quickened his pulses. The boy was leaning over the girl; he was shirtless, his bare back glistening with sweat. And the girl was lying on her back, one leg lifted to rest on the boy's shoulder, the other wrapped around his waist. Her panties were white, and it looked as though the boy were about to pull them down to see the origin of the darker shadow between her legs.

"Don't you think we look like these two? Don't you." Luana was saying. "Let's see if we do. I could tilt that mirror and we could see ourselves. Take your shirt off, Cole. I want to see." She stood and kicked off her sneakers and pulled down her Calvins. She watched for Cole's reaction to her lacy black underpants and was satisfied when she saw him staring at them. "I'll just tilt the mirror this way. . . ." She flopped down on the bed and looked toward the wall. "Yes, that's right. I can see myself. Can you see, Cole?"

He had stripped to the waist; the room air felt chilly against his skin. In order to look into the mirror, he had to lean over Luana, his face very close to her breasts. He saw the playful look in her eyes and took his cue. "Your blouse has to be opened, like the girl in the picture." He undid the buttons, revealing her flesh inch by little inch.

"Cole! That girl don't have her blouse open all the way!"

"But you do. Here, put your leg up like she does. Is this the way?"

"Cole, don't you be naughty. We're only seein' if we look like the picture."

"You're prettier than the girl in the picture, Luana. And you have prettier underpants."

"You think so? Me, too. I got these underpants and bra for you, Cole, with the money you gave me last time. I like having nice things to wear for you."

"I like when you wear nice things, Luana." He felt himself become breathless. He was watching her small rounded belly as it moved with each breath. She was getting that look in her eyes that said she wouldn't mind if he touched her.

"Don't we look like the picture? Don't we, though? Look, Cole, look in the mirror!"

He dragged his gaze away from her to the glass on the wall. He found it strangely exciting to see himself there with Luana as though he were only an interested observer. He watched his hands graze over her skin, saw her wriggle beneath his touch. He pulled her bra straps over her shoulder and exposed her breasts. Still watching himself in the mirror, he touched her, seeing the palms of his hands graze over the stiff little nubs of her pink nipples. He saw her watching him, her eyes directed also to the mirror.

"Oooh. It's like being in the movies, ain't it?" She sighed.

This was like no movie Cole had ever seen. He'd only heard about them from the other boys at school. But this had to be better. This was Luana and her beautiful body, lying here with him. It was his own hands touching her, feeling her. He rolled her over onto her side and undid the hooks of her bra, freeing her breasts of their confinements. In the old barn Luana had allowed him to do this, but she'd never let him take all her clothes off. If he stripped her of her panties, she insisted on wearing her bra and blouse. And if it was her breasts she allowed him, then her jeans remained firmly in place. But tonight would be different.

"Cole! What are you doin'! That's not how it is in the picture!"

"You should see some of the pictures in my magazines, Luana. You're a whole lot prettier than any of the girls in those books, too. And they don't wear anything, nothing at all."

"Nothing! When are you gonna show me? I want to see those pictures."

"I'll show you, right now. Just keep looking in the mirror."

Luana turned her head toward the wall, watching him through the mirror. She lifted her hips to allow him to take off her underpants. When he lifted one of her legs and rubbed a knuckle against her, she squirmed and sighed. She liked it when Cole played with her. He wasn't afraid to see what was between a girl's legs, the way Riley was. Riley only wanted to play with her breasts, and sometimes he bored her. Other times he left her, nerves jangling and strung out tight, and she never felt better until she'd had a nice hot bath.

Cole was different. He let her see how much he liked to look at her. And he knew where to touch her, like now. He was making her feel all funny inside, and there was a heat growing at her center. She wanted to press herself against his hand, and she wanted him to kiss her nipples the way he liked to do at the old barn. But she was afraid she was losing control, and that would never do. She liked the power she held over Cole, and if she gave too much too soon, the money and pretty gifts would stop.

"Do I look like the girls in your magazines?" she asked, her voice hardly more than a whisper.

"Better than the girls in the magazines," Cole's voice was choked. He was mesmerized by the sight of her, by the excitement of being with a girl who was naked. He imagined Luana pressing herself against his hand, allowing him to open her with his fingers. The tension in his loins was becoming unbearable; his jeans were too tight, squeezing him. He explored her sweet pink-lined cleft, feeling her grow wet and warm. He found the place he knew she liked to be touched and then watched the reflection in the glass. Luana's hips began to move, rotating, her legs stretching out, spreading, hiding nothing from his touch or his view. Suddenly, she clamped her thighs shut, imprisoning his hand, squeezing it against her with contractions of her muscles. When the moment had passed, she looked up at him, her eyes languorous and glazed. "You do such nice things, Cole. Such nice things for Luana."

"Now do something nice for me," Cole said hoarsely. The rigidness in his loins was unbearable. He grasped her hand and drew it toward him, already anticipating relief.

"No, I can't!" She pulled her hand away as though it had been scorched. "I don't know what time it is!"

"I do. It's early, it's early." He searched again for her hand.

"No! I have to know exactly what time it is! My pa might come home. I'm always worried about the time, Cole, always!"

Cole glanced at his watch, a handsome gold Piaget. "It's not even nine o'clock."

"If I had a nice watch, I'd know what time it was." Luana smiled. "And I could be nice like you want me to be."

Cole got the message. He dug into his hip pocket. "Here's fifty dollars. Now you can be nice, can't you?"

She stuck the money under her pillow and reached for the belt on Cole's jeans. As her hand searched to free his sex from his jeans, she leaned over him and whispered, "I know how to be nice, Cole. Just you wait. I know how to be very, very nice."

Ben Simms was almost sober when he drove his pickup onto Sunbridge land. It would be light in another twenty minutes or so. Dawn. Sunday morning. He'd have to sleep an hour or so and go heavy on Scripture to cleanse himself of his animal lust. He was disgusted with himself for doing all the things a man does when he hasn't been with a woman for a couple of months. If a man ever does anything like that to Luana, he thought darkly, I'll kill him with my bare hands and ask questions later.

His stomach felt sour and his mouth tasted the way mouse fur smelled. For a moment he wondered guiltily if Luana realized he hadn't come home last night.

Then he told himself defensively that every man needed to go on a rip every so often. It might be sinful, but it proved he was a man.

He cut the engine of his truck and glided down the little rise leading to the garage. He stumbled out and tried the front door. Good, he nodded in satisfaction. Luana had locked it. He fished around for his key, jiggled it a little, and finally got the door open.

The place looked the same as when he'd left. The dishes from supper had been put away. Luana's schoolbooks, pencils, and notebooks were stacked neatly on the kitchen table. The small living room was neat and the television was off. He walked around the corner and peeked into Luana's room.

She was lying almost spread-eagle, the sheet and light blanket half-on and half-off. She looked like an angel in sleep, he thought. Then he saw black lace panties and a black shoulder strap, and his eyes widened. He walked boldly into the room, staring down at his daughter in her fancy underwear. One lone, shapely leg with a light feathering of pubic hair showing at the panty line made him draw in his breath. Suddenly Luana rolled over, her buttocks exposed, the sheet falling away from her breasts. Anger spilled out of him when one pink-tipped breast escaped its lacy prison.

Ben leaned over, reached for a hank of Luana's hair, and pulled her off the bed. All he saw was pink flesh. "Where did you get those sinful things?" he demanded.

"What sinful things?" Luana asked cursing inwardly for having been dumb enough to put the set back on after Cole had left. "What's wrong, Pa?"

"That underwear," Ben said through clenched teeth. "You cover yourself back up before I turn your flesh as black as what you're wearin'."

Luana hastily complied. "Miz Tanner give it to me,

Pa. She said it was just to sleep in. She said it cost sixty dollars but don't fit her no more. It's just to sleep in, Pa," Luana whined. "I wouldn't never wear this under clothes. Never, Pa, I swear it."

Ben looked down at his daughter's frightened eyes. Luana never lied to him. If she said Miz Tanner give it to her, then she did. Just for sleeping.

"I don't want to see you in that outfit ever again. You ain't old enough for the likes of that. That's something your ma would have worn. Under her clothes," he said tightly.

"Well, I ain't like Ma. I just wore it to sleep like Miz Tanner said. You see for yourself, Pa." She smiled up at him, a sweet, innocent smile. "You want I should make you some breakfast, Pa?" she asked.

Sleep was out of the question—he was wide awake now. "Yeah, might as well. Make up a kettle of grits and some bacon and eggs. I'm gonna take a shower. The groceries are in the back of the truck. You can bring them up."

"Okay, Pa. I'll have it ready by the time you're done shaving. Are we going to church?"

"Not this Sunday. We'll read the Bible. It's just as good as going to church and neither one of us has Sunday clothes."

Luana sighed with relief. Every Sunday she asked the same question, and every Sunday she got the same answer. She knew her pa.

The bacon was fried just the way her father liked it, light brown and crisp. The eggs were scrambled in butter, not bacon grease. The kettle with the grits was sitting in the middle of the table on a pot holder. She'd even folded up a paper towel for a napkin and placed it under the fork. When she heard the bathroom door open, she knew she had a few seconds to run downstairs and snatch a few flowers from Miz Tanner's garden. She set them on the table in a water glass.

Ben walked into the kitchen and stood there a moment,

taking in the scene. No doubt about it, his daughter was one a man could be proud of. He felt more of a man today than he'd felt in a long time. Clean clothes, a shower, and a good meal made by someone who loved him.

Luana ate with her eyes downcast. From time to time she'd steal a look at her pa. He wasn't a bad-looking man. In fact, he was kind of handsome in a craggy sort of way. She wished he wasn't so God-fearing and straitlaced, but he'd always tried to provide for her.

Sunday brunch at Sunbridge was usually pleasant and drawn out, an opportunity for Riley and Cole to regale Maggie and Susan with the week's activities—sports, school events, what parties were coming up, school dances, and the eternal question, When are we going to get cars of our own?

This Sunday was different. There was an added dimension to the hostility between Riley and Cole, and Maggie knew it had to do with their competition for Luana. She felt responsible; she knew she should have intervened before this. But she'd been afraid her interference would somehow rock the wonderful new relationship she had with Cole.

Now she listened uneasily as Cole mentioned that he'd been with Luana, helping her with her homework. Riley, she noticed, nearly gagged on his food, his deep olive complexion reddening alarmingly. Another mouthful of milk and his fork clattered on his plate. "Last night? You didn't say anything about helping Luana before I left to go out with Kelly," he said angrily. "I've got to hand it to you, cuz; you really know how to get the jump on somebody."

Susan fidgeted and leaned over to check little Jessie, who lay in the bassinet beside her chair. She didn't like it when the boys argued, and she blamed herself for hiring Ben Simms and bringing Luana onto Sunbridge.

"How are her studies going?" Maggie asked Riley, trying to speak calmly.

"Okay," he said sullenly. "She's behind in her math and it isn't easy to catch up."

"Does she understand the basics—addition, subtraction?"

"More or less," Riley answered evasively. He knew he wasn't a very good liar. He hadn't spent fifteen minutes helping Luana with math. If there was anything to be taught, it was Luana doing the teaching.

"Cole, how's her English coming?" Maggie prodded.

"Fair. She still has a long way to go." He glanced at Riley and knew they were having much the same thoughts. But he was one up on his cousin, he thought with satisfaction. Last night had been something else. Luana had never let him go so far before, and every time he thought about how they'd looked together in the mirror over her dresser, he could feel the heat build in his body.

Maggie set her cup down. "I think it might be a good idea for Luana to have a certified tutor. In fact, I'll insist on it when I speak to her father."

"But then they'll have to pay, and they don't have the money," Riley said, a note of desperation in his voice.

Cole looked trapped. "Tutors are expensive. They don't have that kind of money."

Maggie looked from one boy to the other, disgusted. "How much money have you given Luana?" she asked sharply. "And why did you give it to her? Do you both think I'm blind? How much longer did you think you'd get away with it before Mr. Simms noticed the way you look at his daughter? And all those new clothes she's wearing. The man's not stupid." She took a deep breath. "I've seen *both* of you take her back to the old barn. I know you've been cutting school."

As if at some unheard signal, the boys pushed back their chairs and faced each other. Cole's arm shot out, but Riley blocked the blow.

"You stupid son of a bitch!" Cole hissed. "I knew you'd get caught. And you squealed to get the edge on me. I knew you Japs couldn't be trusted."

Maggie gasped and stood up. Susan quickly moved the baby's bassinet out of the way. Little Jessie began to cry.

Riley suddenly swiveled, striking a karate pose, one arm extended, the other held close to his chest. The sound that came from his throat was menacing and frightening. He straight-armed Cole and then spun around, catching his cousin's midsection with the heel of his foot. "I told you to lay off me and I mean it! You ever call me that again and I'll kill you!"

Suddenly Maggie looked up from the boys and saw a figure standing in the doorway. Ben Simms. How much had he heard?

As Cole rolled on the floor, Riley stood over him, daring his cousin to retaliate.

Simms crossed the room and reached for Riley. Sensing movement behind, Riley spun around, one arm stiff, the fingers splayed. Maggie thought he looked carved from stone. Deadly. Capable of killing. Something in his eyes stopped Ben Simms, and they stood facing each other, two figures frozen in time.

It was Maggie who finally moved, going to Cole and helping him to his feet. She sat him down in his chair, then spoke to Riley. "That's enough. Sit down. You boys are too rough on each other, and I won't have you fighting at the table." She hoped she was conveying to Simms that this was a family dispute, plain and simple.

"You wanted to talk to us, Mr. Simms?" she asked, turning to him with a gracious smile.

"Yes'm. I come over here to thank you for them clothes you gave my daughter and to ask you not to give her any more. Some of them things ain't suitable for a gal her age, especially some of them nightclothes."

Maggie stiffened. Then, after a long moment, she said, "All right, Mr. Simms, I won't give Luana any of my clothes."

"And I'd be real obliged if you'd keep these two boys away from her. Especially that one." He jerked his thumb in Riley's direction. "And I'm sad to say I don't think you own boy is any better. Luana's young, real young, and she ain't wise when it comes to boys. You know what I'm saying, Miz Tanner?"

She smiled grimly. "Yes, Mr. Simms. I know."

"I'm takin' you on your word, Miz Tanner. When I went into town last night, I didn't know a minute's peace leavin' Luana all by herself at home. If you don't bring those boys into line, Luana and me will have to move on."

Silence lay heavy in the room long after Ben Simms left. Then Maggie's anger erupted.

"I hope you're both satisfied. And I hope that poor man doesn't really know what's been going on here, or I feel sorry for Luana." She told the boys of the time she'd heard Ben beating his daughter. "I should have stopped it, I know, but it's hard to know where to draw the line. It isn't easy interfering between a father and daughter. Now I'm afraid for the girl and there's no one to blame but you. She's not blameless, but you both know the difference between right and wrong. From now on that girl is off-limits to both of you. Understand? Off-limits!"

She stalked out of the dining room, her thoughts rioting with images of Luana and Riley and Cole. She felt sorry for Luana, even sympathized with her. At Luana's age she hadn't been much different, a little girl searching for something. But sympathy only went so far—looking out for herself and the boys took precedence. And they're was no getting around it: Luana was a scavenger.

The thought made Maggie's blood run cold.

{{{{{{{{ CHAPTER TWENTY-FIVE }}}}}}}}

The first day of May was all an early spring day should be. The new grass was a tender green, the windswept sky a vital blue, and the air fragrant with Grandmam Jessica's early roses.

It was a perfect day for traveling. Maggie's bags were packed and ready to be put in the car. Cole joked that it looked like a mountain of Louis Vuitton. Despite her high spirits, however, Maggie dreaded her stopover in New York. Eight hours to see and talk to Sawyer before she went to Hawaii. Eight hours to try to set things right when a lifetime hadn't been enough.

She checked her purse. Airline tickets, travelers' checks, a full line of credit from the bank in case the cost of refurbishing the house was more than she anticipated. Car rental reservation, a map of the island, directions to the Kamali house. She had everything she needed. Everything except Rand. He came to mind suddenly, as he always did, when some foolish thing or word reminded her of him. She'd sent him away and hadn't returned. She couldn't even find it in her heart to blame him. How could he know, how could he trust, that she knew her own mind and now had the courage to follow her heart?

Maggie snapped her handbag shut and turned to Cole and Riley. "I'm not going to lecture you or beg you to behave while I'm gone. I trust you. Both of you. If you know what's right, you can't do wrong. Remember that. Don't bring shame on Sunbridge."

She embraced both boys, lingering a moment longer with Cole, looking deeply into his eyes. She smiled at what was reflected there and gave his shoulder a gentle squeeze. "I'll call after I see Sawyer. So stick around, okay?" She looked around at the gentle slope rising behind the house, at the fair expanse of lawn and the miles of white fencing creeping off into the distance. "I hate leaving here. I love it so."

"You'll be back before you know it," Susan said cheerfully. "Good luck, Maggie. But don't expect too much. Some things can never change."

Maggie smiled at her sister, then leaned in close. "C'mon, Jessie, give Aunt Maggie a big buss." The infant gurgled happily in Susan's arms. "Take care of things, Suse. So long, guys."

Cole watched the big limousine take his mother down the drive. She seemed to be taking something with her.

It was Susan who noticed Cole squinting up at the sky. "You still don't get it, do you? Maggie is the sunshine. She just took a little bit of it with her."

Adam Jarvis sprinted down the stairs to answer the bell. He looked through the peephole. "Oh, Jesus!" It was Maggie. He recognized her at once from the pictures Sawyer used to carry in her wallet. That had been many years ago, but there was no mistaking the shining dark hair and summer blue eyes, or the striking resemblance to Sawyer. He sighed deeply and opened the door. "Mrs. Tanner. I'm Adam Jarvis."

"Hello, Adam. I was hoping to see Sawyer. Is she at home?"

Adam hesitated. "Yes, she's up there. I was just on my way out to jog." He wavered as a thought struck him. "Mrs. Tanner . . . before you go up, could we go down to the corner and have a cup of coffee? There's something you should know."

Maggie walked beside Adam to the coffee shop, in reality a Jewish delicatessen complete with the tantalizing aromas of cured meats and garlic pickles. Adam found them a table and held the chair for her. Maggie was quite taken with him, aside from knowing how much Billie liked this young man. He was near Sawyer's age and she knew, already quite successful. Tall, broad-shouldered, good-looking, and with such an expression of tenderness in his eyes that she wondered how Sawyer was able to resist him. He loved Sawyer; Billie had said so, and now Maggie could see it for herself.

"I don't want to be there when you see Sawyer," Adam said abruptly after he'd ordered two coffees. "Okay, so I'm a coward, but she's been putting me through hell and I don't know how much more I can take." Those broad shoulders seemed to slump, his chin lowered to his chest. "I guess I'll take whatever she wants to dish out, won't I? It's no secret. I'm crazy about her."

Maggie stretched her hand over the table and touched Adam's. "Yes, it's pretty evident how you feel. Adam, I'm so sorry."

"I didn't drag you down here to get your sympathy, Mrs. Tanner."

"Maggie, please."

"Maggie, there's something you must know. Sawyer's going to be livid when she finds out I've told anyone, but that's a chance I have to take. She's had tests, more tests. We went to the Sloan-Kettering Institute, where they do a lot of experimental work. The group of doctors there have reached the conclusion that Sawyer's tumor might be operable. They give her a twenty percent chance of success."

Maggie's eyes brightened with joy and relief. "That's hope, real hope!"

"Not according to Sawyer. She refuses to have the surgery."

"Why? I can't believe—"

"I don't know why, and I don't much give a damn what her reasons are!" he exploded. All the worry and concern, all the defeat, everything he felt was there on his face, in the agonized tone of his voice. "She swore me to secrecy, but I had to tell someone. We've been arguing for days."

"This is stupid. I'll have to call her grandmother. If anyone can talk some sense into her, Mam can. When do they want to operate?"

"As soon as Sawyer will allow it. Fortunately, that thing in her head is growing slowly, but there's no doubt it will be fatal if she doesn't do something."

"You want me to talk to her?"

Adam nodded, his eyes glazing with tears. "I love her, Maggie. But she's so filled with resentments and hates, she wants to punish the world. It's almost as if she wants to die to get even with everyone who's ever hurt her. Does that make sense?"

"No," Maggie told him sadly. "But these things never do. C'mon, walk me back to the loft. Then you can go for your jog. I think I should see Sawyer alone."

Lugging the carry-on bag over her shoulder, Maggie climbed the stairs and let herself into the apartment. It was a beautiful loft. A loving place. She could feel it.

She walked around slowly until she found the dining area. Sawyer was at the table having coffee, dressed in a lavender sweat shirt and jeans. It was impossible to believe she wasn't in the best of health. Her golden hair was shining, her skin clear and luminescent in the sunlight streaming through the windows. She registered no surprise when she looked up and saw her mother.

"Slumming?"

"Hardly. This is a beautiful home you've made here with Adam."

"Why are you here? What do you want? Whatever it is, I'm all tapped out."

"Sawyer, I want to talk, about us."

"You're a little late, Mother." Sawyer was trembling so inside, she had to use both hands to hold her coffee cup.

"You aren't going to help me, are you?"

"You're right about that. I told you, it's too late."

"It's never too late. Look, Sawyer, I won't beg you. All I can do is ask that you *try* to understand. I'm sorry—"

"Sorry!" Sawyer laughed, a bitter sound that sent chills down Maggie's back. "Who's that supposed to make feel better? Me? You? Go get absolution somewhere else."

"Look, Sawyer, I can't undo what's past, but I want to try to . . . to at least have an understanding with you. The past is gone; the future isn't here yet—all we have is the present. Why can't we work on that?"

"For some reason that doesn't make me feel better. I'm going to die. I won't be in your life anymore. That shouldn't bother you. It never bothered you before. I hate you," Sawyer cried vehemently. "Don't you understand that?

"And you know something else? I'd have worked my butt off to get Cole away from you. You won that round, too. You always win, Maggie. You're a bitch—a living, breathing bitch. If someone has to die, it should be you."

Maggie flinched at the hatred in Sawyer's eyes and the venom dripping from her tongue. But she didn't turn away. "I thought the same thing," she said quietly. "That I should be the one to go. I did make life miserable for everyone. If you'd let me try to explain . . . maybe you could . . ."

"Forgive you? Never. I don't know a lot about motherhood, but I know this: either you're a mother or you aren't. You never even bothered to pretend."

"Everything you've said is true. Maybe I am a bitch. But as long as you want to fight in the gutter, let's tell it like it is, okay? I did hate you, but it was a crazy kind of hate all mixed up with love I didn't understand. For God's sake, I was only a child myself. What did I know about babies? You got it all. You got to live at Sunbridge; I was sent away. You had everything that should have been mine. You had Mam. You helped bring Pap's dream to life. I couldn't share any of that. You were loved, doted on. I was the outcast. Everything that should have been mine was given to you."

Sawyer's voice was filled with ice. "No good, Maggie. It's all bullshit. The only thing I ever wanted was you. You couldn't be bothered. What was your excuse when you were finally on your own?"

Maggie spread her hands. "It was too late. Mam filled my shoes. I had to live with that. There wasn't a day that I didn't think of you. Most of them I spent hating you; I admit that. I fed off that hatred for a long time, just the way you're doing now. I understand. Maybe, in some small way, I can help."

"I don't want your help. I don't want anything from you except to be left alone. You have it all now. Grand, Sunbridge, Rand, Cole. Even Riley thinks you're the best thing since peanut butter. They just don't know you. You said I was a thief, that I stole your life from you. What about you? You just walked in and took over. Man-eater Maggie. Get out of here and don't ever come back."

Maggie stood her ground. "If you're referring to Rand, let's get one thing straight right now. I didn't snatch him from you. If you want to be crude about it, he dumped you. And he had his own reasons for doing it, Sawyer— Rand and I were nothing more than friends at the time. Later on . . . yes. I did go to bed with him. Several times, as a matter of fact. The first time was out of anger, anger with you. I had your man, the one who dumped you. At the time I thought you had your whole life ahead of you, that one rejection wasn't going to kill you. I was still hating, you see, even then. But he made me take a good long look at my feelings. And when I did, I saw that I cared for him. But I didn't want the wrath of God coming down on me, so I sent him away. And that's the truth.

"You say you want honesty. You want truth, right? Okay. Well, now I'm going to give you some more. Mam said if Rand made me happy, I should go after him. She told me I deserved to be happy. I couldn't believe it at first. I love that man, Sawyer, but I sent him away because of you. Everything is always because of you. I'd cut off my right arm to keep you alive if I could. Rand loves me;

honest-to-God loves me. But I was willing to give him up. Hell, I did give him up. I wrote to him afterward, but he hasn't answered. That should make you happy. He doesn't want me either now. *I did not steal him from you.*"

"I loved him, too," Sawyer said through clenched teeth.

"Sometimes that isn't enough. Rand loved you, but in a different way. I tried to be jealous of that, but I understood. The commitment two people make has to be strong, unshakable. I never had it—and I flubbed up just when it was within my grasp." She smiled bitterly. "I always fail. Surely you've noticed that. Whatever I touch seems to wither and die. I couldn't be a mother to you because I knew I'd fail you. And that's the best, most honest explanation I can give you. Now that my guts are hanging out to dry, I have something I want to leave with you." Maggie tossed her carry-on bag across the floor to Sawyer.

"Whatever it is, I don't want it," Sawyer said flatly. "I don't want your garbage invading the place I live."

Maggie's eyes brimmed. "I can't say as I blame you. But don't be too quick to discard what's in that bag. It's my life. Up until last evening. You can make today's entry, any way you want. I have a plane to catch. If there's anything you need or want, call me."

"I'd die before I called you." The realization of what she'd just said made Sawyer bite down on her lip. She tasted her own blood. She could barely see Maggie through her tears, but she heard her voice before the door closed behind her.

"A twenty percent chance is better than no chance at all. You're a quitter. I used to be like that. You don't like me, don't want to be like me, yet you're doing just what I used to do—give up, don't fight. Blame everything on someone else. I said it before, and I'll say it again: You have no guts. You *say* you care about Cole; you *say* you care about Mam, but it's a lie. If you did care, you'd fight.

"Twenty percent. Some people don't even get that. I can't believe you'd use your own life to get back at me.

That's sick. You're trying to make us all guilty. Well, it won't work with me. If you need my help, you know where I am. Call me."

Sawyer screamed, "Didn't you hear me? I said I'd rather die than call you!"

"Then you probably will," Maggie said evenly.

"You bitch!" Sawyer screamed again. "You can't fix this. You can't go back and make it right!"

"It's taken me all my life to realize that. I'm glad you finally do. Good-bye, Sawyer."

"Go to hell!" Sawyer yelled. "Go to hell, goddamn you!"

"I'm already there," Maggie whispered to herself as she made her way down the narrow steps.

Sawyer paced the apartment, wishing Adam were there. Marble followed her, her tail swishing furiously as she tried to rub against Sawyer's leg.

The nerve, the gall, the unmitigated gall of Maggie. How dare she come here and . . . and . . . Why had she come? To offer help, to pity her. To tell her Rand didn't want her, either. Was that supposed to make them friends?

No guts. It was true; she had no guts. A fifteen to twenty percent chance for success. Why bother? An accident on the operating table wasn't her idea of the best way to end her life. Even worse, what if she lived through the operation but came out a vegetable? It could happen. Still, if the operation was a success, she might live to see Cole grow to manhood. Riley, too. Maybe someday she could fall in love again. She might even get the chance to dance on old Maggie's grave.

"Get away from me, cat. I'm trying to think, and I have enough trouble without you crawling up my—" Sawyer broke off as she saw the bag. She bent down to pick it up, surprised at the weight. She unzipped the nylon bag and looked inside. Diaries. Old Maggie was really pulling out all the stops now. Well, wasn't she going to be surprised when she found out they'd been burned.

Breathing heavily, Sawyer hefted the bag and carried

it to the fireplace. She was shaking the little books from the bag when Adam walked in.

"What are you doing?" he asked curiously.

"Burning Maggie's life. She must be out of her mind to think I'd want to read about her trashy life! Where are the matches?"

"We ran out," Adam lied. "Don't do it, Sawyer. If you don't want to read them, okay, but don't destroy them. I'll pack them up and mail them back."

Sawyer's foot kicked out, scattering the different-colored journals. She was pleased to see a fine dark ash settle all over them. "Go ahead. I have to leave now. I have an appointment with Nick."

Adam looked up at Sawyer from his crouched position, one of the coffee-colored books in his hand. Sawyer noticed his thumb tracing the word "Diary" on the cover. "I didn't know you were seeing Nick," he said softly. "I'm glad."

"I'll probably stop after this visit. I don't like opening old wounds. I'm going to die, so what's the point?"

"You have a choice. Twenty percent isn't great odds, but—"

"Fifteen to twenty percent is what the doctor said. No guarantees. I could end up a slobbering idiot. Will you let me live here then? Will you wipe the spittle from my chin? Will you spoon-feed me? Will you put diapers on me if I wet my pants? Will you be able to look in my eyes and see nothing? . . . Well?" Sawyer demanded cruelly. "Answer me, Adam."

"Yes."

"You're lying," she said, but she knew in her heart he wasn't. He would do all those things.

"Keep feeding on your hatred, Sawyer," he said. "Just don't direct it at me. Direct it where it belongs, at yourself. Go on, see Nick, try to fool him. Or try to help yourself if you have the guts."

"You sound just like my mother. What do any of you know about guts? Neither of you ever had a death sentence."

"That's true," Adam said, zipping the carry-on bag.

"But you're copping out. You have a choice, and I'm going to jam that choice down your throat every chance I get. There's a lot of things I don't like in this world, but the one thing I cannot stand, cannot tolerate, is a quitter. You've got all of us plugging for you. The best doctors, the best medical care, the best goddamn support system in the world. But you—you're in a cold secret place full of hate and darkness. This is your ultimate end: get Maggie where it hurts. Die. Make her pay. Make her live with it every day after you're gone. But there's a kicker here. If everything you say about Maggie is true, she really doesn't give a shit, does she? She wins, but what does she win, Sawyer? She has it all now. So you won't really be getting back at her, will you?" He turned away, dismissing her. "Now get out of here before I really get mad. Nick charges for missed appointments."

Adam picked up the phone when he heard the downstairs door slam shut. He was breathing as if he'd just run five miles.

"Nick? Adam. Listen..."

All the way to Hawaii, Maggie brooded about her meeting with Sawyer. By the time she disembarked from the L1011, she was a bundle of nerves, exhausted and drained of all emotion.

A rented Chevy station wagon was waiting for her, and she wasted no time settling herself behind the wheel. She turned on the engine and listened. It sounded tinny, kind of like a Ford sounded in the States. She tested the windshield wipers and horn, checked to see that the lights were where they were supposed to be. Automatic transmission. Everything seemed to be just fine.

According to the map, she should head for the north shore. She drove carefully, following the turnoff for a route through Kunia. The narrow road made her uneasy. It was very close to the Waianae Mountains and ran through endless fields of what looked like pineapple and sugarcane fields.

She was feeling more confident when she led the car through Haleiwa. She ignored the bridge to the north and turned left, past the harbor to the shore.

Maggie gasped in pure delight at her first glimpse of Hawaii's famous surf. The ocean was so blue it looked like a giant jewel. The waves were breaking clean, eight to ten feet high. Native Hawaiians were scattered all along the shore, stretching out fishing nets. Children were gathering shells, their honey-colored skin shimmering in the bright sunlight. It was so beautiful she wanted never to leave, but she had at least an hour's drive ahead of her.

She almost missed the turnoff. Lush hibiscus and a monstrous banyan tree, like a giant umbrella, shrouded the timeworn iron gates at the entrance to Ester Kamali's estate. The snakelike drive eventually widened and became circular, edged on both sides by regal palms standing sentinel. The house itself was long, low, and sprawling, and much in need of paint. But the sparkling Pacific was exquisite, a perfect backdrop. Maggie felt her breath hiss between her teeth.

She stopped the car and glanced down. The grass looked like dark green fur, recently trimmed. Impulsively, she kicked off her shoes and walked up to the house. She knocked on the door and then laughed, remembering no one lived here. She tripped back across the emerald meadow to get her purse, savoring the scent of plumeria.

Maggie slid the key in the lock, then panicked for a moment when it didn't turn. She tugged furiously, perspiration dotting her brow. When she heard the cooperative snick of rusty tumblers, she leaned against the wall in relief.

The hilltop house opened its arms to Maggie. It was large, yet not overlarge, and it gave her a cozy feeling of coolness and light. She worked busily, ripping off dust covers and dropping them in a heap in the middle of the floor. Every door opened to the outside. The French doors leading to the patio were sheltered from the sun and rain by the sloping overhang of a tiled roof. Beautiful gardens were part of every view and seemed to come indoors to blend with the light bamboo furniture and the vivid greens and whites of the walls. Graceful paddle fans were centered on every ceiling, creating a pleasant breeze. And the tang of the sea far below seemed to fill each room.

Maggie toured the house, removing dust covers as she went along. She felt refreshed by the scented sea breeze that billowed the sheer curtains when she opened the doors. The carpet in the bedroom was eggshell white, bringing into relief the dark tones of the native mahogany furnishings. The bed, headboard, and upholstered chairs were covered with a fabric of pale blue flowers scattered over a background of deeper blue. Here, too, a paddle fan beat the air in a slow, hypnotic rhythm.

She crossed to the bathroom to find a tiled bath complete with tub, shower, and expanse of mirrors. Dusty towels of the palest blue hung from the racks.

Everything was so beautiful. She tried the water faucet. Good, the water had been turned on.

As she made her way back to the car to drive it up to the garage, Maggie wondered how it was possible to have two such beautiful homes in a lifetime. She tugged at the garage door, but it wouldn't budge. It didn't matter, she decided; the car could stay in the driveway.

She carried in her bags and headed for the kitchen. In the refrigerator she found juice, eggs, a loaf of untouched bread, bacon, and a bowl of mangos. She wondered who her unknown benefactor was—probably the same person who had turned on the utilities and manicured the lawn.

She poured herself a glass of orange juice and toured the rooms again, this time paying careful attention to what had been done. All the rooms would have to be painted, draperies and carpets cleaned. Everything had to be washed and polished, and the outside would have to be scraped and painted. So many things would have to be supplied or replaced—cookware, bedding, appliances... Maggie sighed. Not today, though. Today was for savoring this paradise. A pity she wasn't going to be able to share it with Sawyer. But at least she'd be making everything perfect for her daughter. And then maybe, just maybe, Sawyer would rethink her decision. How could a person give up things like this in life? Perhaps the island would work some magic. She prayed it would.

Maggie fixed herself a light supper and spent the rest of the evening on the back lanai, drinking in the scent of the rich flowers. Jet lag claimed her at nine-thirty and she headed for bed.

She slept deeply and awoke at seven o'clock. She padded barefoot to the kitchen and made a cup of instant coffee, carrying it out to the back terrace to watch the graceful swell of the waves on the shoreline. In her whole life she'd never seen anything so beautiful. She could almost picture her mother and father here. How happy they must have been! And Thad—Thad was part of all this, too. Now she could talk to Mam about that time in her life.

When she'd had her fill of the Pacific jewel, Maggie reluctantly returned to the kitchen. Phone. She couldn't do anything without a phone. She picked up the white receiver and was rewarded with the buzz of the dial tone. Thank God. Now she could begin.

Twenty-one days later, the house was finished, inside and out. Maggie looked in her checkbook. She'd shelled out twenty-eight thousand dollars. But she didn't care; she would have spent three times that much.

The pantry was loaded with every staple available, the deep freeze filled with a side of beef. Maggie washed the crystal and dishes herself, piece by piece, then dried it all the same way. The only thing left for her to do was engage a housekeeper for the time the children would be here. One of the cleaning girls had said her aunt would be glad to take on the job.

Maggie walked through the rooms, delight written all over her face. Cole, Riley, Adam, and Sawyer were going to love this place. She opened a fresh bottle of wine and poured some into one of the fine crystal wineglasses she'd just bought. She toasted her efforts. Then she called Susan.

"It's done, Suse. I took pictures. Now I'm feeling at loose ends with nothing to do and I'm beginning to worry about the boys." Susan's silence alarmed Maggie.

"What's doing with Ben and Luana?" Maggie asked, testing the waters.

"Everything's going fine," Susan said, satisfied she could report truthfully. "The boys are behaving themselves—sort of an armed truce, if you know what I mean. I haven't seen much of Luana, thank the Lord. I'd really hate to lose Ben Simms at this stage of the game. Those modular units that Ferris and I ordered are going to be delivered by the end of the summer when all the foundation work is done. A representative from the company came down to check on the work. He told me how lucky I was to have such a conscientious man working for me. Everything that should be level is level, and all the corners are square."

"That's nice, Suse." Maggie hoped her voice conveyed some kind of enthusiasm. "About Luana, though. Do you know if Mr. Simms hired a tutor for her?"

"No," Susan confessed, "but he's joined the church, and Luana goes to Bible class on Sunday. They both attend services, of course. He . . . he asked if we'd rent out the apartment to him when his work is done, but I told him there would always be work at the camp as long as he wanted it." Susan hesitated. "I hope that's okay, Maggie. I really do need him. You know our funds are limited."

"I know, I know," Maggie said wearily. She was getting a headache. "As long as Luana stays away from the boys and they stay away from her."

"Trust me," Susan said.

"I do, but I get all queasy whenever I think about the situation. I guess I'm not as much of a freethinker as I thought."

"You're Maggie." Susan laughed. "I got a letter from Aunt Amelia the other day. She says she's well and coming to terms with things, whatever that means. And didn't

I tell you Rand was in the country with her? That's where you should have mailed your letter, Maggs. Amelia said Rand was working too hard and holding long telephone conferences with his bankers and lawyers. Something about dissolving his interests in several companies without causing a run on the stock. I didn't understand what she meant. No other mention, Maggie. I'm sorry."

A long silence. Maggie squeezed her eyes shut to prevent the tears.

"Cary stopped by last week wanting to know if we'd heard from Amelia. Of course, I hadn't received her letter yet. He looked awful. I don't think he eats or sleeps. I can't believe Amelia is behaving so childishly, and I'm going to tell her that when I write."

"We all do what we have to," Maggie said softly.

"When do you plan to come home?"

"I think I'm going to stay on here another week or so and enjoy this place. Suse, it's so beautiful, it takes your breath away. First I'm just going to hang out on the beach. And then I might visit Diamond Head and take in Waikiki. I may even consider a side trip to Maui. I'll call you before I leave."

"I wish you weren't alone. I don't like being alone. That's why I'm so glad Ferris is in my life." Susan hesitated, then said shyly, "Maggie, he's asked me to marry him once I'm divorced."

"Oh, Suse! If it's what you want, I'm happy for you," Maggie said sincerely. "Any news on Jerome?"

"Nothing. But I really haven't tried. I guess I'm afraid to confront him. Remember how Rand used to say that I'd avoid nastiness and ugliness at any cost? Well, I suppose he's right."

"But what if it means losing Ferris? Are you willing to pay that kind of price?"

"No. But I don't have the stomach for making hundreds of calls to Europe to track him down. And our agent doesn't want to cooperate with me. He's a greedy bugger, and since I'm not making money for him, he has no use for me."

"You could always try Valentine Mitchell. She could set some bloodhounds on Jerome's trail. She's got the knack, all right."

"I suppose that would solve my problem. But I'm still worried about you, Maggie. Are you sure you don't mind being alone?"

"Suse, I've been alone most of my life. Sometimes you can be alone with yourself without being lonely." Before Susan could reply, Maggie said, "Kiss Jessie for me and tell the boys I love them and am counting on them."

"I will. Enjoy."

Maggie hung up the phone and stared morosely out the window. She ached to hear Rand's voice; her fingers itched to reach out and touch him. She pulled the phone closer and placed a call to England.

The phone rang and rang. There were tears in her eyes when she replaced the receiver. The tears stayed with her until she fell asleep in the blue bedroom.

Rand sat across from Amelia in the sunny breakfast nook. Outside the open window the daffodils and tulips were making a grand show against the verdant lawn. The rosebushes were in bud, their droopy little heads hinting at the color that would soon arrive if this dazzling May sunshine continued. The hedgerow bordering the path was already in need of a second trim, and the birds splashed in the puddles left by Amelia's early-morning watering.

Rand smiled at his mother. "I haven't seen you look this well in a long time. I'm trying to decide what you've done to yourself. I know you've put on some weight, but that's not what it is, exactly. Would you care to satisfy my curiosity?"

Amelia leaned across the table. "I think it's called coming to terms with oneself. You look rather well yourself. Maybe we're kidding ourselves, and it's really this clean fresh air and sleeping with the windows wide open."

"I'm leaving this afternoon," he said abruptly. "I'll drive to London and then take the Concorde to New York."

"I know. I'm glad for you, Rand."

"What about you, Mother? Are you ready to go back with me?"

"Do you want an answer this second?"

"Before noon; that's when I'm leaving. Be certain, though." Amelia nodded. "I'll clean up the dishes," he said. "Why don't you take a walk, do some thinking? I know you could be packed in ten minutes."

"Yes, I could, but it isn't time for me to go back. You do what's right for you. Are you going to Sunbridge?"

"No, Hawaii." Quickly, he filled Amelia in on his plans. "I don't know if she'll have me, but I'm going to give it another try. It feels right."

"Go for it," Amelia said forcefully.

"You know, I could set down in Austin and see Cary."

"No. I have to work out my own problems. I don't need or want you to run interference for me."

"Okay. I hope you know what you're doing."

"I hope so, too. You go along and have a good trip. Give Maggie my love."

"Before or after I give her mine?" Rand chuckled.

"Before. She won't be interested later."

For all her bright, savvy attitude, Rand knew Amelia had been hurting for a long time. When Cary hadn't followed her to England, some of the heart had gone out of her. She looked now, though, as if that heart were making a comeback. Her face smoothed out somehow, lost its tight, nervous look. She moved calmly, gracefully, as though she were seeing things from a new perspective. Out of the rat race, she was the Amelia he had loved since he was a toddler.

Long after Rand left, Amelia sat on the country porch, surrounded by early spring blooms. She'd lugged the crocks from the quarry and filled them herself with bright petunias, daisies, and pansies. From the high ceiling she'd hung clay pots filled with luxuriant ferns and grape-ivy. She sipped at her tea, her thoughts on Cary.

She'd been so sure he would come after her. For all of two weeks she'd been sure. Then, when she'd finally realized he wasn't going to follow her, she'd done some hard soul-searching. And in those first weeks without him, as she'd cleaned the country house and started her garden, she'd come to understand something that had evaded her all of her life: she didn't belong to anyone but herself. She realized she'd slavishly embraced all Cary's hopes and dreams as if they were hers, never bothering to find out what it was *she* wanted. The house she'd been renovating was one of her biggest, costliest mistakes. It was a decoy, something to make her feel needed, important. Something for her to suck on, like a pacifier, while her life line was otherwise occupied.

How was it possible for one person to be so unhappy, so unsatisfied, so filled with low self-esteem? She thought of all the surgery she'd had done to retain an illusion of youth. To compete. Now she knew she'd only been fooling herself.

Once she'd reconciled herself to the fact that Cary wasn't coming after her, she'd felt better. And she realized now that if he had, she might never have learned anything about herself. Billie had told her at their last meeting that she had to have faith in herself and who she was, or no one else would. "It comes from within," Billie had whispered. "You have to dig down, way down, and get rid of all the clutter and garbage. Do it, Amelia."

Amelia was almost ready now to go back and set her various houses in order. First she'd finish decorating her mother's house. It was a symbol of the past, and she should never have bought it—but she had, and this was one project she was going to complete. Then she'd move from Sunbridge; she had never been happy there. Why she'd thought Cary would make a difference was something she was still trying to come to terms with.

She'd loved him with her heart and soul. He'd loved her, too—she'd had enough love affairs in her life to know the difference between love and lust and passion.

Cary had seen into her soul, something she'd never allowed herself to do. She'd opened up, given of herself, because she loved him. And he hadn't abused that generosity. *She* was the one who'd destroyed it. She'd let

Cary see her soul, then hadn't trusted him to nurture it.

But things were different now. She'd changed. She felt rested for the first time in her life. The cares and pressures she'd imposed on herself had dropped away shortly after she'd arrived here, in this peaceful place. She'd learned she had no one to account to but herself. She was sleeping, thank God, although every night Cary made a guest appearance in her dreams. She welcomed her pillow at night and the familiarity with her subconscious. She was on the mend. Soon, another week or so, and she'd be ready to go back to Texas. And knew now, hoped really, that if she went back to Sunbridge, Cary wouldn't see the ten pounds—or was it twelve?—she'd put on or the fine networking of wrinkles that were coming back. He wouldn't see the natural gray streaks in her hair or the fact that she wasn't hiding behind a mask of makeup.

Amelia smiled, a genuine expression of contentment came from deep within. Even her eyes smiled. Her right index finger caressed the wide gold band on her finger, loving symbol of her marriage to a wonderful man. Now maybe she could make it work.

She looked at her watch. Rand should be in London by now. In four hours he'd touch down in New York, and then his life would really take on meaning. There was no envy in her. Rand deserved happiness, and if Maggie was the one to give it to him, so much the better. Soon it would be her turn.

If it wasn't too late.

{{{{{{{{{ CHAPTER TWENTY-SIX }}}}}}}}}

This time Rand felt as though Kennedy Airport were welcoming him on this, the first leg of his journey. Even the expected delay, circling before they could land, didn't annoy him. What did a few moments matter when he had an entire lifetime ahead of him?

He took a taxi to town and got out on the corner of Forty-first and Third. He paid the driver and turned around to get his bearings. He couldn't believe his luck when a block later he saw Sawyer swinging toward him. He stopped in the middle of the sidewalk as people jostled and cursed at him. Sawyer, too, stopped in her tracks, a look of confusion on her face. She advanced a step as though she intended to go by without acknowledging him; then she stopped. "Hello, Rand," she said, her voice cool, indifferent.

"Hello, Sawyer. I was heading for your apartment. Where are you going?"

"To the market. Why were you looking for me?"

"To talk to you."

Sawyer stared at this man, whom she loved. Who once claimed he loved her. How long ago that seemed now! All the words had been said. What did he want—absolution like Maggie? "We can get a cup of coffee over there." Sawyer pointed across the street to a sign that claimed Mike served the best coffee in the state of New York. It was a lie, of course; the coffee was rancid and tasted as though the pot had never been cleaned. But neither of them noticed.

Rand removed his sunglasses. Sawyer kept hers on. Looking at him through the brown glass somehow made it bearable.

"I wanted to talk to you, face-to-face," he said. "I have something to tell you, and I wanted you to hear it from me."

"That's assuming I want to hear what you have to say. Obviously, you have me confused with someone who gives a damn."

Rand blinked. She sounded like she was talking about the weather or making casual conversation with one of her friends. "What I want you to know is I'm going to ask Maggie to marry me. I'm hoping she'll say yes."

"Why wouldn't she? She wins—the whole ball of wax. Why tell me? That's your business and Maggie's."

Rand wished he could see behind the dark glasses. He didn't want to hurt her. God, he'd never do that, not intentionally. He struggled to find the right words, knowing it was impossible. "Maggie sent me away. She said it was best. I was angry . . . much the way you were, I suppose. I know how much I must have hurt you. Sawyer, I'd do anything for you. You know that. And I do love you, but it isn't the same. Your feelings for me—"

"Were wasted time on my part. It should be obvious to you, as it is to me, that I lowered my standards. You fit right in there with the love of your life."

"Don't, Sawyer. Please don't . . ."

"Don't what, Rand? Why is everyone so concerned about how I feel? Breathing down my back, saying love is love and you and Maggie deserve to be happy. Now that I'm going to die, no one knows quite what to say. They all dance around it, trying to appease Maggie and me at the same time. My grandmother gave her seal of approval to your affair, and that's all that was needed. So you see, you really came here to make *you* feel better. Only I'm not interested in how *you* feel or how *Maggie* feels or how my *grandmother* feels. I have nothing to give any of you."

"I don't want anything, Sawyer. I just wanted you to hear it from me."

"Well, don't bother to invite me to the wedding. I might not be around."

Anger sparked in Rand's eyes. "I'm not going to pretend I don't know about your illness. I'm disappointed, though. I thought you had more guts than that. Maggie said you didn't, but I didn't believe her. Billie told Amelia about the operation you refuse to risk. How can you . . . just give up? Any kind of chance is better than none. Reach for the brass ring! You have nothing to lose and your whole life to gain." He reached across the table and removed the polished sunglasses. Then, speaking very slowly, deliberately, he said, "You're a taker, Sawyer. You don't know how to give."

It was almost dusk when Rand drove past the big banyan tree on Ester Kamali's estate. It was beautiful, breathtaking. The rental car took the last rise to the end of the drive. He felt himself trembling as he removed the keys from the ignition. The thought he'd been trying to avoid throughout the entire trip would no longer be denied. What if Maggie didn't want him? He hadn't heard from her since he'd left Sunbridge just after the first of the year. His nerves were jangling, spidery tingles creeping close to the surface of his skin. He walked across the soft green fur carpet to the house and rang the bell. When there was no answer, he tried the back of the house. On the terrace he saw a beach towel. He let his eyes travel down the path to the shimmering Pacific, where the huge ball of sun silhouetted a slim female figure scampering from the surf.

Maggie looked up, droplets of seawater dripping from her eyelashes and clouding her vision. Standing on the back lanai was a man. She hesitated, frightened. She rubbed her eyes. It couldn't be. Not here, not all this way.

Her throat closed; her heart leaped.

Rand stood mesmerized by the sight of Maggie, a sea nymph, a gift from the sea. She'd seen him. He waited.

Rand. Her eyes must be playing tricks on her. Rand. Her life. Her future. The figure moved. She took a step forward. "Rand!"

She flew into his arms, finding her happiness, her safety. "How, when?!.. I thought I'd never..."

"Shhh, I'm here."

"You've always been here," Maggie whispered. "I brought you with me, here." She pointed to her heart. "I take you everywhere I go."

"That's because I belong here, with you, and you belong here." He tapped his own chest.

"You came halfway around the world to find me?"

"I'll always find you, Maggie, I'll never let you go. I'll never let you send me away again." As if to make his words true, he slipped his arms around her waist, pulling her tighter against him.

"Let's go inside so I can change. We have so much to talk about."

"Yes, we do, Maggie, my Maggie."

The sound of his voice warmed her heart. They walked inside, Rand's arms still around her, holding her close. He said all the appropriate things about the house and prowled around until Maggie came out in a pair of cotton shorts and a T-shirt. Arm in arm they walked back to the lanai overlooking the sea. She fixed them drinks and took her place beside Rand on the glider. It creaked slightly as she nestled herself into the crook of his arm.

"Now let's talk," she said.

By the time Maggie and Rand finished talking, the early-morning sun had slanted over the island and glistened on the water like fairy dust. The air was already warm, with hardly a breeze, and the Pacific swelled and ebbed, foaming the shoreline. After a leisurely breakfast on the back lanai, they took a stroll along the sun-warmed beach.

"How do you feel about skinny-dipping?" Maggie teased.

"The same way you do." Rand laughed, already out of his shirt and working on his belt.

She was about to plunge into the surf when he seized her hand, pulling her tightly against him. He loved the feel of her, the delicate framework of her bones, her satiny-smooth skin that invited his touch and the caress of his lips. "Not yet, Maggie, not yet. First I want to show you how I love you."

She looked into his eyes, and it was like peering into his heart. Dark eyes that told her how much he wanted her, loved her, needed her in his life.

"I like beginning the day with you, Rand," she said softly. "Welcome home, welcome. I've missed you."

"And I've missed you, Maggie, my Maggie."

She could barely catch her breath; she was mesmerized by his eyes, drugged by the meaning she found in them. Her blood was racing through her veins, her flesh tingling and eager for his touch.

Rand traced her mouth with a delicate concentration, teasing the fullness of her lower lip with his tongue and claiming his kiss while his hands caressed the long, slender ridge of her spine and the swell of her bottom. Her knees lost their strength and he gently lowered her onto the pile of their discarded clothing. She opened her arms to him, holding him close, sighing with the simple pleasure of being with the man she loved. His hands possessed her, finding those places that intrigued his imagination, discovering those places that made her cry out with delight. She loved having his lean, warm body pressed against the length of hers once again. She realized the hollow ache that had plagued her since he left her, since she'd so foolishly sent him away. His hands covered her; his mouth moved slowly from her throat to the valley between her breasts and lower until he groaned, "Maggie, Maggie, I want you now!"

"Take me, Rand. I want you to take me," she whispered, her consciousness floating above waves of undulating heat as she took him into her ready flesh.

He held himself above her, supporting himself on his arms, his hips pressed hard against hers. He was fighting himself, denying his needs, holding himself back, struggling for self-control. He wanted it to be good for her; he wanted to satisfy her. But Maggie would not be still. She captured his buttocks, pulling him closer, deeper within her. Her legs lifted, her body opening to his.

"I love you, Maggie," he cried hoarsely, surrendering to the strokings of her sheath that surrounded and rippled around him. He saw her smile, joyous, victorious, the smile of a woman who knows she's bringing herself to the man she loves. He looked into her eyes, summer-blue, and he found himself drowning in her, reaching for her, finding her, and touching her. They joined, their hearts caressed, their souls met, and together they chorused their joy.

Sawyer greeted Amelia with outstretched arms. When her aunt had phoned from Kennedy Airport, she couldn't have been more surprised. Even more unexpected, however, was this change in her appearance. When Sawyer cried, "You look wonderful!" she meant it sincerely. There was a softer look about Amelia, as though someone had smoothed the hard edges. Her hair, salt-and-pepper now that she had let it grow in, was more flattering to her skin tones than the sable-brown that had come from a bottle; and she seemed to have fleshed out. More than anything, though, Amelia looked happy. Still stylish, still perfectly groomed, but happy.

"How was England? What made you decide to come back?" Sawyer asked, leading her aunt over to the comfortable sofa that faced the long, unadorned windows. Sawyer had removed the curtains and blinds in her desperate desire for light. Her eyesight was failing her, and she was determined to see everything as clearly as she could for as long as she could.

Amelia turned sideways to avoid the glaring brightness streaming through the windows. "I decided," she said firmly, "to fight. But first, if it isn't too late, I'm going to apologize. Your grandmother tells me it's never too late."

"Sometimes it is," Sawyer said somberly.

"Never," Amelia declared. "Look, darling, I want to talk to you, but I don't know what to say. I've made such a mess of my own life, I have no right to intrude on yours. . . . You—you look well." Then, remembering her new resolution, she said abruptly, "That's a lie; you don't look well at all. You look ill."

"That's because I am ill, Aunt Amelia. I can talk about it."

"I can't. I can't understand why you won't at least consider the operation. If it's because of Rand, let me tell you, no man is worth giving up your life for. I almost made that mistake. You can't give up. One chance in a million is better than no chance at all!"

"You look wonderful," Sawyer interrupted. "Really wonderful."

Amelia sniffed. "I thought you said your eyesight was failing."

"It is, but you're six inches away from me. I can see you clearly. You remind me of Grand now. I don't know, you look . . . womanly. Not so brittle. I don't mean that to sound unkind, but you were so thin and . . ."

"Hard-looking is what you're trying to say. I wanted to look like you. I wanted to be like you. The impossible dream. Or is that the American dream?"

Sawyer laughed hollowly. "No, I just saw on television the other day that the American dream was a Gold American Express Card, a Mercedes, and a Kirby vacuum cleaner."

Amelia laughed. "Where's Adam?" she asked. "And what is that!" She pointed to Marble, who was contentedly washing her face. "I hate cats. They slink and stare and see things the human eye can't see."

It was Sawyer's turn to laugh. "Adam went to the post

office," she said. "Marble's been a great companion. I talk to her and she doesn't ask questions or make demands."

"I told you the cat was an idiot. So are you if you don't give it your best shot. That's what life is. I know. Either you go for it or you don't. Either you win or lose. I can't get any plainer than that. I never thought of you as a loser, Sawyer."

Sawyer grimaced. "I've been called a lot of things lately. A quitter, no guts . . . Cole says I'm burned-out or a burn-out, something like that. There were other names, too, but no one has called me a loser yet."

"So make them eat their words," Amelia said bluntly. "That includes me, too. Don't let this awful thing beat you. You're a Coleman, and by God, it's time you started acting like one!"

"I'm so scared," Sawyer whimpered against Amelia's cheek. "I've been seeing a shrink. A friend of Adam's. In fact, I have an appointment in a little while. Adam usually walks me over there. To make sure I go."

"Is it helping?" Amelia asked, stroking Sawyer's hair.

"I suppose so. I talk. He listens. He doesn't make judgments. Today is the day I talk about Rand's visit. He met me on the street two weeks ago, if you can believe that. He was coming here to talk to me. He said a lot of things, too, things I didn't want to hear. Things I don't want to think about. I will today, though."

"Sawyer, look at me. Listen to what I say. There is every possibility the operation will be a success. *Think.* For God's sake, use that wonderful brain you have to see what's out there for you. Reach out. Fight with everything you have. How can you not want to see the first buds of spring or the first snowflakes of winter? I don't understand it. When it's time for me to go, I plan to kick and scratch all the way. How can you give up Cole and Riley? They love you. Your grandmother is eating herself alive because you won't fight. And what about Adam? That young man loves you. *Loves you*, Sawyer."

"It's my life," Sawyer said defensively.

"You belong to all of us. Even Maggie and Rand. Once you touch someone's life, they have a claim on you. Has Maggie been here?" Amelia asked suddenly.

"Yes. She dumped her garbage on me." At Amelia's perplexed look, she explained, "Her diaries. Seems she kept them from the time she was ten years old. Just the way I did. In fact, she gave me my first one. It's probably the only thing we have in common. We both write in diaries."

Amelia was dumbfounded. "Maggie actually gave you her diaries! I can't believe it."

"Well, she did. I threw them in the fireplace. I was going to burn them, but Adam rescued them. I don't know if he mailed them back or not."

Amelia found herself at a loss for words. She felt awe, relief, and something like pride that Maggie would bare her soul to her daughter. "Sawyer...do you have any idea, any idea at all, what it cost your mother to bring those diaries to you? Do yourself a favor and read them."

"I can't. I don't want her in my life. I don't want to be in hers. Rand told me he was on his way to ask her to marry him—said he wanted me to hear it from him. He told me that in some greasy restaurant. Then he left."

"How did you feel?"

"Numb. It was a terrible experience. I made it through, though. It took a lot of courage for him to tell me; I know that now. Nick—that's the shrink—made me . . . What he did was help me see that you can't make someone love you. It's like Adam and me. He loves me. I love him, too, but not the way he loves me. Maybe someday. Rand couldn't wait for someday."

"Why should he wait, Sawyer? Life is too short. Surely you can see that. Don't begrudge his happiness or Maggie's. Don't hate."

"It's what I feed on now," Sawyer said honestly. "It's what keeps me going."

"Then you're lost. I'm just wasting my time. And I

don't have all that much left, so I have to put it to good use. Go to your shrink and play games. Wait till it's too late and blame everyone but yourself because you're going to die. I'm sorry if that hurts you, Sawyer, but that's the way it is." Amelia stood up. "I was going to stay overnight, but I don't think I will. You depress me. I need sunshine in my life and I'm going back to get it. You stay here with that crazy cat and wallow in your misery. I'm glad your grandmother can't see you. Good-bye, Sawyer."

Adam found her crying at the dining room table, Marble purring softly in her lap. "What happened?"

"Amelia stopped here on her way to Sunbridge. She let me have it with both barrels. It's closing in on me, Adam. They're all saying the same thing: that I'm a quitter, a loser, that I have no guts. Rand said I was a taker, that I don't know how to give. They're all disgusted with me. Instead of being supportive like you are, they come here to jab at me and leave. Fight, they tell me. What the hell am I fighting?" she cried suddenly. "Do you think I want to die? I don't. Honest to God, I don't. I'm scared out of my wits. I don't want to die on an operating table. I don't know what to do."

"For starters, you're going to wash your face and comb your hair. Then we're going to see Nick. You're going to talk this out if I have to force him to cancel all his other appointments. Go on now; do as I say."

While Sawyer was in the bathroom, Adam called Nick. "I'll pay. I want you to stick with her till she can't talk anymore. I don't care how long it takes."

"Be glad to do it. Do you think she's coming around?" Nick asked hopefully.

"I'm afraid to think. I'm hoping."

"I'm waiting for her now, so get moving."

Nick settled his soccer-ball body comfortably in an easy chair across from Sawyer. "Take off your sunglasses. I want to be able to look at you when we talk."

"The mirror of one's soul, is that it?"

"More or less. So, tell me what's been going on. You haven't been here for two weeks."

Sawyer spoke haltingly at first, and then she sped up, like a child on a downhill slide. Soon there was no stopping her. At one point she jumped up angrily and lashed out, "They have no right, no right at all!"

"Do you feel like smashing something, putting your foot through the wall?" Nick asked complacently.

"Huh?"

"Don't play games. You heard me. If that's what you want to do, do it. I told you, when you come to this office you can do whatever you want. If you want to cry, cry. If you want to scream and yell, do it. You want to smash something, be my guest. You will, however, clean up and replace when you're finished. Go ahead. I'm not stopping you."

"That's stupid," Sawyer said in disgust.

"Don't you think it's more stupid to hold the anger in and direct it at people who don't deserve it?"

"Of course. You're saying that's what I'm doing?"

"No. I asked you a question. You assumed that's what I meant. You already know the answer. I told you, Sawyer, no games are played here. Now, tell me about Rand."

Nick listened carefully to Sawyer's wild babblings, all the while sifting, collating, making neat little summaries in his head. In the beginning he'd made notes, but his scribbling seemed to bother Sawyer, so he'd opted for this "sit and chat" area, as he called it. She'd relaxed almost immediately.

"What, in particular, didn't you like about the meeting?"

"I didn't like his nerve. I don't owe him anything, even conversation. He assumed he could 'get through to me' where the others failed."

"Did he?"

"He hit some nerves. Yes. He made me think."

"Do you still hate him?"

"Hate Rand? Oh, no!" Sawyer cried passionately.

"You said he's going to marry your mother. Does that bother you?"

"Of course it bothers me! It's tearing me up inside. She tricked him."

"Does even one small part of you believe he could really love her? You told me he didn't love you enough to make that final commitment. Yet now he's ready to make that commitment to your mother. How do you explain that?"

Sawyer hedged. "He might care for her . . . a little. I told you, Maggie is a man-eater. She mesmerized him."

"But you said she sent him away. Sometimes people do that when they love too much because they can't handle it."

"Maggie can handle anything," Sawyer said bitterly.

"Even your illness? Is she handling that?"

"Of course. She came to see me, dumped her trash on me, and left." She hesitated a moment, then burst out defiantly, "It's *her* fault—all of this is her fault!"

Nick lit a cigarette, his third of the day. "You told me you didn't want to read her diaries, that Adam packed them up. You said her life was trash. Actually, I believe you used the word garbage."

"So what if I did? It's how I feel," Sawyer cried. "Why should I waste my time reading about *her* life?"

"You tell me. Why would it be a waste? Are you afraid of what you might see in those diaries?"

"Of course not," Sawyer blustered.

"If I asked you to read them, would you?"

"Probably not."

Nick stubbed out his cigarette. "I have to assume you're afraid."

"I'm not afraid. I'm petrified," Sawyer whispered.

"Tell me what you're petrified of."

Sawyer lit a cigarette with trembling hands. "There might be something in them that would . . . that I might not like. Maggie always comes out on top. She wouldn't have given me those diaries if they were going to hurt her. She wants to hurt me. That's why she gave them to me."

"That thing you think might be in those books, would it absolve Maggie?"

"Of course. It would make me take the rap. I told you, Maggie always wins. Didn't she finally get Sunbridge? She got Rand. Amelia and Susan are living there. My grandmother gave her permission, *gave her permission*," Sawyer shouted, "*to take Rand!*"

"If you read those diaries and your worst imaginings are true, then you won't have anyone to blame. That's what you're saying."

Sawyer pondered Nick's words. "I suppose ... in a manner of speaking, you're right."

"So now, at the most crucial time of your life, you need someone to blame. Your illness is the biggest crisis you've ever had to deal with. But you aren't dealing with it, are you?"

"I'm trying."

"Then why won't you go for the operation?"

"I told you, I'm petrified."

"I don't believe you."

"I really don't care. You all expect too much of me. I'm only human."

"Ah, you're only human. What does that make the rest of us, inhuman?"

"I didn't mean that."

"Then what the hell did you mean?"

"People are choosing up sides. When you do that, there's a winner and a loser."

"Which are you?"

Sawyer laughed hysterically. "I'm going to die and you ask me a stupid question like that! Of course I'm the loser."

"How did that happen, that you're the loser?"

"Maggie."

"Maggie has nothing to do with your illness. You lose

when you don't fight. If you decide to go ahead and have the operation and it's successful, what will happen then?"

"I don't know. Look, I don't want to talk about this anymore."

"I know you don't, but we're going to talk anyway. Now answer the question."

"Life will go on."

"Maggie and Rand will live happily ever after. Your grandmother and her husband will live happily ever after. Your aunt Amelia is going back to Texas to reconcile with her husband, and they'll live happily ever after. Your aunt Susan is going to get married again, and she and her new husband will live happily ever after. Cole and Riley are going off to college, two handsome studs with girls dropping at their feet. Who does that leave who isn't going to be happy?"

"Me," Sawyer cried. "Damn you, me! What about me? When do I get to be happy?"

"When you open yourself to it. You can't buy it; it isn't a commodity. You want to know something else I found out? You have to earn it. Take my old buddy Adam. He's unhappy—miserable, as a matter of fact. He'd die for you if it would make you happy. You know that, don't you?"

"Yes."

"Let's talk about something here for a minute." Nick handed her a piece of paper and a pencil. "I want you to list all the things in order of importance—now that's crucial—all the things you'll never see or do again if you don't go for this operation. I'm going out to the other office to call some of my patients who think I'm the greatest thing since sliced bread."

"You must be kidding."

"Do I look like I'm kidding?" He nodded as Sawyer reluctantly picked up the pencil. "When you're finished with that list, I want you to make another one on the back of it. Things you can do and will do; things you *want* to do if the operation is a success."

Nick closed the door behind him and immediately called Adam. "Look, I'm not promising anything. I think I have her on the run, though. Christ, for a minute there I thought she was going to wreck my office. I actually gave her permission, knowing you'd pay the bill." He grinned at the hysterical squawking on the other end of the line.

"I think the best thing for Sawyer was having Rand and Amelia talk to her. She's thinking, and that's the first step. I'm hopeful. Don't worry about her getting home. I'll put her in a cab. Just be there for her."

Nick waddled to the men's room and back to his secretary's desk, where he made several more phone calls. When he returned to his office, Sawyer was sitting with her feet propped up on the round table in the chat area. There were tear streaks on her cheeks, which he pretended not to see. He scanned both sides of the paper in front of him. "Good," he said briskly. He lit another cigarette and held the light for Sawyer.

"Is that it for today?" Sawyer asked through a perfect smoke ring.

"Not quite. Let's touch on the operation." He held up his hand to ward off her objection. "My talking about it isn't going to change anything. I want you to talk about it. I do understand more now, though. I called your doctor because I wanted to make sure I could explain anything in case you had some questions. You gave me permission, so wipe that look off your face.... Well?"

"Twenty percent odds aren't very good," she said in a tight voice. "Actually, the neurosurgeon said it was more like fifteen."

"When you buy it in a car accident, there aren't any odds at all. You live in one of the biggest cities in the world, with one of the highest crime rates. You could get killed in a grocery store. There aren't any odds there, either. Don't look at the numbers."

"You sound like the rest of them. It's easy for you to say, easy for you to be objective. It isn't easy for me. It's my life."

"I'm trying to give you perspective. I do know one thing, though. Your chances are better right now than they would be six months from now. The bottom line is, it has to be what you want, what you're willing to do. The reasons have to be the right ones. What your grandmother or I think isn't important. The right reasons, Sawyer. For you. For these," he said, waving the papers under her nose. "Do you want me to make a copy of them for you?"

"No," she replied, so faintly that Nick had to strain to hear her.

"What say I take you over to Jim McMullen's for a brew?"

"How about a rain check? I just want to go home and put my feet up. I have another one of those nasty headaches. I'd appreciate you flagging a cab for me, though."

Nick locked up the office, and they rode the elevator in silence. Outside, he hailed a checker and helped Sawyer climb in.

"The truth," she said hesitantly. "How did today go?"

Nick grinned. Sawyer thought he looked like a cherub. Or a munchkin. "You tell me. You know we shrinks don't answer questions. See you next week."

"Good night, Nick."

Sawyer leaned back for the ride downtown. She didn't know if she felt better or worse. But she did know one thing: she had a lot of thinking to do.

CHAPTER TWENTY-SEVEN

Amelia fought her way to the baggage area in the airport terminal. She'd never seen such crowds before. She engaged a redcap, who got her a taxi. Amelia tipped him, gave the driver the address of the Hilton Hotel, and leaned back. God, she was exhausted.

Forty minutes later she checked into the Hilton and accepted a copy of the *Crystal City Times*. All she wanted was a long, hot bath and some sleep. It would be bliss to hear or see Cary, but not now. One thing at a time.

The following day, as Amelia dried her hair in front of the hotel mirror, she wondered if she was doing the right thing by not going to Sunbridge. She planned to go to her house first and follow through with her renovations, actually sleep there until the project was completed. It was time to see something through to the end. Then, and only then, would she call Cary.

It was noon when Amelia checked out of the Hilton Hotel. A uniformed doorman tipped his hat to her, smiled, and crooked his finger at a bellboy, who was standing at attention. "Put the lady's bag in the cab." He smiled again at Amelia, approvingly, and tipped his hat a second time. Amelia smiled in return. Usually, she didn't notice hotel personnel. She'd been too busy comparing herself to the other guests. And another thing: She usually hired a limousine. Now she felt she didn't have to impress anyone but herself. Anything with wheels would get her to where she wanted to go.

As the taxi driver pulled into the driveway, Amelia noticed it had been paved in her absence. The wide, circular front porch was finished, gleaming in the noon sunshine. The inside must be done, too, for she heard no hammering.

A little thrill coursed through her when she slipped the key into the new oiled lock and the solid oak door swished open. Slowly she walked from room to room. All the carpentry work was finished. The bathroom was remodeled, the carpeting laid. All she had to do was clean everything up, arrange the various *objets d'art*, and outfit the bedrooms. The furniture she'd ordered months ago was being held, as were the drapes. She'd made calls this morning to arrange delivery for tomorrow and the following day.

Amelia climbed the stairs a second time to change into her coveralls. Then she set to work with a vengeance, scrubbing and polishing till late in the evening.

A long, soothing bath made her feel drowsy. She spread her sable coat on the clean floor and slept like a newborn infant, her hand tucked under her cheek. When she woke in the morning, she couldn't remember if she'd dreamed or not.

At nine o'clock the rental car she'd ordered arrived, and Amelia immediately drove to a deli in Crystal City. Hot coffee in three containers and a bacon-and-egg sandwich to go would hold her till later. She also picked up a copy of the morning issue of the *Crystal City Times*. Back at the house, she ate breakfast and read her paper from cover to cover, rereading the local business page. There was a brief mention of Cary and his associates and the remarkable progress they'd made. But there were no pictures. Amelia looked longingly at the yellow wall phone. Not yet. Not till she was finished.

By three-thirty every window in the house was draped. By six o'clock all the downstairs furniture was in place.

She had only to dust, arrange her art objects, hang the pictures that were in the hall closet, vacuum. At eight o'clock everything was done. Amelia called the deli and had them deliver a pastrami on rye and two cups of coffee.

She bathed early, ate dinner, and slept, wrapped in her sable coat in the middle of the furnished living room.

Every night before he returned to his empty apartment, Cary drove through the silent streets trying to relax. And somehow—like tonight—he always found himself driving to Amelia's house. Why? he wondered. Why did he keep punishing himself? What was it he expected to find?

As usual, he slowed his car once he rounded the curve of the road. There it was, all by itself on thirty acres of ground. He pulled up to the curb and cut the engine. The house was dark and silent, as always. He sat for over twenty minutes staring at it. For some strange reason, he felt closer to Amelia than ever before. If only . . . if only . . .

He didn't notice the car in the driveway when he slipped the car into gear and drove away.

It rained the next day, great buckets that slapped at the newly draped windows. Amelia turned on the heat to chase away the chilly dampness. The upstairs furniture arrived at eleven-thirty. At twelve-thirty she backed the Mustang out of the driveway and headed for Crystal City's poshest department store. She bought bedding, towels, soap dishes, mattress covers, sheets, blankets, spreads. The last things she purchased were bathroom mats and drinking glasses for the four bathrooms. The trunk and backseat of the car were so full, she had to use her side-view mirror to drive. She stopped at the deli for more sandwiches, then continued on to the house.

She spent the next three hours dressing the beds and manicuring the bathrooms. She vacuumed a second time for lint, then replaced the sweeper in the upstairs closet.

It was done. All of it. She felt absolutely giddy with relief. She'd started from scratch and seen the whole thing through to the end.

Amelia ate a corned beef sandwich and munched on the deli pickle as if she were eating pheasant under glass. The coffee tasted good, so she opened the second Styrofoam cup and drank that, too. Then she wadded up her trash and carried it to a container in the garage.

Everything smelled so new. All the place needed was someone to move in. Amelia smiled when she sat back down at the kitchen table with her work papers in front of her. She used a purse minicalculator and worked for close to an hour. She'd spent a quarter of a million dollars renovating this house that had been her mother's. Added to that was the original cost of the house and land: 1.6 million dollars. Before leaving England, she'd instructed her bank to pay off the mortgage company in Austin. So she was now full owner of a house worth roughly 1.85 million dollars. She'd done the work, paid for it with her own money. It was all hers.

An hour later Amelia walked out onto the back porch. It was still raining, and she shivered inside her fuzzy robe. She secured the dead bolt on the door, then turned off the lights as she made her way to the living room, where she would again sleep wrapped in the sable coat. No way was she going to disturb the newly made beds upstairs. She was sound asleep when Cary drove past the house at eleven-fifteen.

Amelia stayed in the house for four more days, waiting for what she called perfect weather. She was getting sick of deli sandwiches and pickles, but she had no other choice. When she woke on the fifth day, she could feel that it was right. She checked outside: it was airless; not a leaf in the garden moved. All she had to do now was wait. She sat on the back porch eating her sandwiches, drinking her coffee, and reading snatches from a lusty romance novel that set her teeth on edge.

At twenty minutes before noon Amelia walked into the Liberman Insurance Agency and presented her homeowner's policy. "Cancel it and issue me a credit. I'll wait." The scurrying around amused her. When a Coleman canceled a policy of any kind, the whole town would know.

That was all right; she didn't care. When she left the office with the huge red CANCELED stamped across the face of the policy, she felt pleased. As of 12:01 she was uninsured.

She laughed as she got into her car. God, she felt good! To celebrate, she stopped at a steak house on the highway and ordered a T-bone, rare, a large country salad, a baked potato with butter and sour cream. Then she finished off her meal with blueberry cheesecake and coffee, left a generous tip, and returned to the house that was now hers—and uninsured.

Amelia sat on the back porch with coffee she'd heated in the microwave. It tasted awful, but she sipped at it complacently as she leafed through the romantic novel.

At seven o'clock, just as dusk was settling in, she took the gardening shears and walked across her perfect lawn to her perfect flower beds and neatly clipped exquisite perfect flowers, which she arranged in a perfectly cut crystal vase. She set them in the foyer on a cherrywood table that was a genuine, perfect antique. She returned the shears to the potting shed in the yard and resumed her seat on the back porch. The evening hadn't gotten cooler; it was still hot and airless. Deathly still.

It was ten-thirty when Amelia left her chair on the back porch. She entered the house, closed and locked the back door. She walked through the rooms, admiring her hand-iwork. Her mother would have been pleased. She walked upstairs, going from room to room. Everything was perfect. She parted the draperies in the master bedroom and looked outside. She pulled the drapes in the bedroom, then did the same in the rest of the bedrooms. She didn't turn her head for a second look. On the landing of the stairway she turned off the night-light. She walked through the downstairs, turning on the magnificent chandelier for a better look. She loved it.

She picked up her sable coat, then debated a second. People would think she was crazy, carrying around a sable coat in this weather. She folded it neatly and laid it on the back of a beautiful morris chair she'd had custom-made. The chandelier twinkled and glistened before she turned it off. The only remaining light was in the foyer.

Amelia left the front door slightly ajar when she went out to the rental car. She threw her purse into the backseat and backed the car down the driveway with only the parking lights on. She opened the trunk and removed a filled kerosene can, stuffing the car keys into the pocket of her slacks so she could use both hands to carry the can. Inside the beautiful house, she hurried up the stairs, sprinkling the kerosene as she went. Then she turned and did the same thing downstairs until the can was empty. She placed it outside the front door and went back upstairs, digging in her pockets for matches. She lit little fires that blazed into big fires. The steps were burning behind her as she rushed down to light still more fires.

The house was blazing when she closed the door for the last time. With the kerosene can in one hand, four unused matches in the other, she walked down the drive. It would be a while before anyone noticed. The fire department would come . . . maybe. She'd stand right where she was in case they did come. She'd tell them to let it burn . . . to the ground.

It was almost midnight. She was free. The past was gone. Tomorrow would be a new day. Only the future remained. What she did with it would be up to her.

Amelia stood in the darkness and watched her house burn. She was officially broke now, by Coleman standards a pauper. She laughed, enjoying the feeling.

Damn, a car was coming down the road. Well, when the driver slowed and finally got out, she'd tell him the same thing. Let it burn to the ground.

Cary slowed his car and stared. Amelia's house was lit up like a Christmas tree. When he slammed the car into park, he realized the whole damn thing was blazing, a bright red-and-yellow conflagration against the dark Texas sky. "Holy Jesus!" he groaned, about to get back into the car to go for help.

A figure emerged from the shadows. "Let it burn."

"Amelia! Amelia, is that you?"

"Cary? Cary darling, what are you doing here?"

"I can't believe it's you." The house, the fire, everything was forgotten in that one instant as Cary reached out. Amelia. How good she felt. "My God, how I missed you. I thought you were never coming back. I prayed. Amelia, I prayed."

"Shhh. So did I. I'm free now. Look at me, Cary."

"You're the most beautiful creature on earth," he said as he gazed into her loving eyes. "Look at me! I've lost sixteen pounds and I look like hell. Life was hell, without you."

Amelia laughed, a young, girlish sound. "I guess beauty is in the eye of the beholder."

"In this beholder's eyes, anyway." Cary squeezed her tightly. He was never going to let her out of his sight again. Never. "Amelia, your house. What happened?"

"I finished it. I came back from England and finished it. I've never really finished anything I've started until tonight." Tears glazed her eyes, but they were not tears of regret. "I was using that house just like my mother did. As an escape, a place to hide. I made myself so busy trying to regain the past that I couldn't look ahead to the future, and I cheated myself and everyone else of the happiness of the present. I burned it down, Cary. It's an effigy to the ghosts of the past, and I don't need it anymore."

"We don't need anything, Amelia, only each other."

Someone had alerted the Crystal City Fire Department; Amelia heard the distant whine of sirens. Quickly, she explained about the insurance and paying off the house. "Don't let them fight it, Cary. I don't want anyone hurt, and there's nothing in there worth saving. Let it burn."

Dawn broke when the last engine pulled away from the ashes of what had once been Amelia's house. The firemen hadn't fought the fire but had stood in readiness to keep it from spreading.

"Let's go home," Cary said, nuzzling Amelia's hair.

"Hey, you did something different to yourself," he said in surprise. "I don't know what it is, exactly, but you look great. Fatten me up, okay? My clothes don't fit anymore."

Amelia laughed, a joyous sound that rivaled the music of the early-morning birds.

She was finally free. Free of the past, of the ghosts that had haunted her, of fear of the future. She was Amelia Assante now. She'd be Amelia Assante until the day she died.

When the intercom in the nursery buzzed, Susan leaned over and listened. "Miss Susan, Mr. de Moray is here. Will you see him?"

Susan's heart skipped a beat. Her eyes flew to the crib where Jessie was sleeping. "Did you let him in?"

"No, ma'am. He's standing on the porch."

"Good, let him stand there. Tell him I'll be down in a few minutes." She immediately called Valentine Mitchell, who chuckled when Susan explained the situation.

"Don't panic. I'll be right there. This saves us a lot of time and bother. Invite him in, by all means. Offer him a drink; be cordial. It'll be the last time he ever enjoys Sunbridge's hospitality."

Susan's heart refused to return to its natural beat. Her eyes were drawn again and again to the sleeping baby as she threw the infant's laundry back into a basket. Should she call Ferris or not? She decided to deal with it herself, with Valentine's help.

Susan opened the door and motioned for Jerome to enter. She led the way to the living room and offered him a drink. Jerome asked for a gin with a twist of lemon. With surprise, she realized she'd forgotten this was her husband's favorite drink.

"This is as hospitable as I'll get. Now, what do you want? Why did you come here?"

Jerome's eyes widened. "For you, of course. Now that you've had the baby, maybe we can get on with our lives."

Susan laughed hysterically. "You must be out of your

mind! I haven't heard from you in almost a year. You steal all my money, don't call or write, and suddenly you show up and expect me to welcome you back. Didn't you get my letters? Didn't you get the divorce papers?"

"No. I don't know what you're talking about."

Susan knew he was lying, and Jerome knew she knew; still he persisted. "I managed to get us a South American tour. The money is fabulous. Now that you have this motherhood thing out of your system, we can pick up where we left off."

Susan hooted. "You are out of your mind! I don't want anything to do with you. Do you realize you haven't even asked about our daughter? By the way, her name is Jessica Margaret."

Jerome blanched. He should have known he'd have to go through the baby to get to Susan. "I didn't forget; it was just that the pleasure of seeing you again drove it from my mind. Of course I want to see her. Our agent said she's crippled or something."

"Or something," Susan said coldly. "I noticed you mentioned a tour before Jessie, too. Well, forget it. I'm not interested. All I want is to be rid of you. Did you go through all the money you stole from me?"

"It was *our* money."

"Wrong, Jerome, most of it was *my* money, left to me by my father. It's all gone, right? That's why you're here. All I want from you is a divorce."

Jerome changed his tactics. "Look, Susan. I need you. If you want to bring the baby, that's okay. Get a nurse or something. We can take on the world, be really famous the way we were in Europe. You liked it—the applause and the recognition and the money. Admit it!"

"That was light-years ago. The only playing I do now is for charity to help our daughter. As a matter of fact, I'm giving a recital next week. This might surprise you, but we sold seven hundred and fifty tickets for one hundred dollars each. All of the monies will go to the spina bifida organization I've started here."

Jerome's eyes almost popped out of his head. Susan was talking about seventy-five thousand dollars! "You're giving it away to some ... some ..."

"Say it, Jerome. Spina bifida. Yes, I'm giving it away. In the fall I'm giving another recital in Austin. And another thing. I want you to hear this from me and not someone else: As soon as my divorce is final, I'm remarrying."

"Susan, please reconsider. I can't make it without you. I want us to stay married."

Susan's heart was beating normally now. She looked at the man she'd been married to for so long and felt only relief that she wouldn't ever have to see him again after today. "I have a baby now," she said calmly. "I have to put her first. Music will always be a part of my life, but it won't *be* my life. Jessie is. I'm sorry you won't be around to enjoy her. I can't believe you're not interested in your own child."

"She's crippled," Jerome said as if that explained everything. "But I love you," he said, grappling for something to say.

"That's really funny, Jerome. See how I'm laughing," Susan said coldly.

"You'll be sorry. I'll never give you a divorce. I can even sue for custody of that kid. Now what do you have to say?"

"She isn't going to say anything," Valentine Mitchell said as she laid her briefcase on a mahogany table. "I'm Valentine Mitchell, Susan's lawyer.'

A woman lawyer. It figured. "Well, Valentine Mitchell, Susan's lawyer," he said mockingly, "maybe you better tell *my wife* what my rights are."

"I suppose I could do that, but why don't I show you a few things I have in my briefcase. Maybe you'll want to rethink what you just said."

Jerome's eyes narrowed. Susan was folding and pleating the folds of her dress nervously. The only sound in the room was the lock of the Gucci briefcase snapping open.

"What we have here are signed affidavits from two banks. In this hand are canceled checks and bank drafts. In this third pile here are your joint accounts, which you had every legal right to use. This fourth pile, the long papers, are the divorce agreements."

"If you think I'm signing anything, you're crazy," he said contemptuously.

Valentine smiled, showing a perfect set of even white teeth. She looks like a barracuda, Jerome thought, suddenly afraid.

"I think you will," she replied. "Now, as I said, it was all right for you to withdraw the seven thousand eight hundred sixty-five dollars in your joint checking and savings. Also the stocks and bonds in both your names. I'm not concerned with those. But the authorities take a very dim view of forgery, both in England and here in the States. And you forged your wife's name on monies that were sent to her from her trust. You also requested some rather large advances, forged your wife's name to the letters and then to the drafts." She smiled at him. "You could get five to ten for that.

"Now here are the divorce papers," she continued, "and this other legal-looking sheaf of papers is also waiting for your signature. It says, in layman's terms, that you are giving Susan sole custody of Jessica Margaret de Moray. No alimony or child support is requested. I will give you—" Valentine looked at her watch "—exactly three minutes. At the end of those three minutes I'll call the sheriff, who, by the way, is my granddaddy." Valentine uncapped her silver pen and handed it to Jerome.

"You're railroading me!"

"I suppose you could say that. It's your choice. Prison life doesn't agree with anyone."

Jerome signed his name in a mean, narrow scrawl. He was seething with anger when he stared at Susan.

Valentine looked up from the papers. "What was that you just whispered? A threat? Tell me that wasn't a threat."

Jerome stalked to the door . . . then stopped and came back. Susan stared at him as he spoke, not believing a man could actually force words past tight lips and clenched teeth. "I don't have enough money to get back to England."

"I thought of that," Valentine said coolly. "Check into the airport. There's a People's Express leaving tomorrow. I prepaid a ticket for you. Good-bye, Mr. De Moray."

When the door closed behind him, Susan broke down and cried. "He didn't even want to see Jessie. He called her a cripple. How could I have loved such a person?"

"Everyone's entitled to one mistake. What did he say to you?"

"He said... he said... he made it sound like Jessie wasn't worth loving because of her handicap. *He's* the cripple, not her. She's different, and I love that little girl more than life itself!" Susan cried vehemently.

"Then that's all that's important. I understand you'll be getting married when the divorce is final. I hope you'll invite me to the wedding."

Susan smiled. "Of course. But it won't be right away. I want to be sure I'm doing the right thing. I don't want to make any more mistakes."

"Honey, Ferris Armstrong is no mistake. He's as good a person on the inside as he looks on the outside. You snagged yourself a real hunk this time. You Coleman ladies seem to have a knack for picking winners."

"Only after we go through hell with the losers. Thanks, Valentine."

"My pleasure. Listen, there aren't any more of you, are there?"

"No, I'm it. What do you think will happen to Jerome?"

"He'll go back to England and scout around for some nice lady who is musically inclined, and then go on from there. The Jeromes of this world always keep going. I'll get this on the court calendar, and you should be a free woman in thirty days."

Free. What a wonderful word. Just her and Jessie. Ferris too, if she wanted him.

And she was beginning to think that she wanted.

{{{{{{{{ CHAPTER TWENTY-EIGHT }}}}}}}}

Maggie and Rand returned to Sunbridge over the Memorial Day weekend. They were greeted with enthusiasm and hoots of pleasure, and Maggie basked in her family's joy at seeing her. It was Rand who announced that they would marry at the end of summer when the boys returned from Hawaii.

"We'll have just enough time to take you guys shopping for new clothes. Do you still want to stay in New York a few days before leaving?"

"Adam said it might be a good idea," Cole said. "The plane leaves New York on the twelfth of June."

"Has anyone heard from Sawyer or Mam?" Maggie asked anxiously.

"Not a word," Susan said. "I'm sorry, Maggie."

In the middle of her unpacking Maggie stopped, picked up the phone, and called Sawyer. "It's Maggie, Sawyer. How are you?"

"What difference does it make? Is there something you want?"

"Yes. I want to know how you are."

"I'm still alive. I'll be able to make the trip. Does that make you feel better or worse?"

"It doesn't make me feel anything. I'm numb. I want to know if you've changed your mind about the surgery."

"No. I haven't changed my mind."

"You're a fool."

"Like mother, like daughter. Right, *Mam*? So why don't you just get off my back?"

Maggie hesitated, trying to think of things to say. At least Sawyer wasn't hanging up on her. It was almost as though she wanted her to stay on, to bait her, to keep the verbal exchange going. "I wish I could, but I can't."

"It's too late. You're always too late, Maggie."

"I know," Maggie said, and Sawyer could hear the pain in her voice. "Nothing can ever be the same again. We aren't the same people we were back then. But I think we're wiser now. Why can't we come to terms, try to work things out? I'm willing."

"You should be. After all, it's easy to be forgiving when you're the one who screwed up. I'm the result of your screwup. You want me to forgive you; well, I can't. So why don't you just hang up and let me alone?"

"Why don't you hang up?"

"You called me, remember?" Sawyer said through clenched teeth.

"I want to see you before you leave for Hawaii. I'll come to New York with the boys. I won't stay. I just want to see you."

"Why?"

"Because I care how you're doing. Because I want to see you with my eyes."

"You want to play ghoul so you'll feel better is more like it. Well, I don't look so great, so save yourself the trouble," Sawyer said, her voice cracking.

"I'll be there with the boys. You can always tell me to leave. Will you let the boys see you act like that?"

"They know my feelings."

"I suppose they do, but they don't understand them. Not anymore. I don't think you have either of them mesmerized anymore. They know you're being selfish and acting like a fool."

"Let them tell me that."

Maggie sighed. "Sawyer, regardless of what you *think*,

you know I care. I want to help you if you'll let me."

"Don't you mean you want to help yourself? You can't help me. No one can help me."

"That's a damn lie!" Maggie screamed. Rand came running, and so did the boys. They stood helplessly in the doorway while Maggie ranted into the mouthpiece. "You're being stupid! Everyone wants to help you. Mam, Adam, Rand, all of us. Dr. Marlow is the best surgeon Sloan-Kettering has to offer and he will do his best for you. His best. Do you *hear*? Goddamn you, Sawyer, use your head and stop blaming everyone! You're really getting off on this phone call, aren't you? You like making us sweat. Admit it!" Maggie cried. "You like playing martyr. It must have been a real comedown for you after being pampered and coddled all those years. You're getting all the attention again, just like before. Let's all pity Sawyer. Look how noble she's being. She's going to die. Rally 'round, everyone. Coax Sawyer, plead with her, tell her how much she's loved and cared for. You make me sick. If I were Adam, I'd have booted your tail out of there a long time ago. You must make him sick, too."

"Get off this phone and don't call me again!" Sawyer screamed.

"No!" Maggie screamed back.

"Go to *hell*!

"I've been there and back. It's not a nice place. Think about that. God will punish you for giving up. You're a Coleman."

"Shit on the Colemans!"

"We're only good enough when it's convenient for you. Is that it?"

"Hang up! Damn you, hang up!"

"No. You hang up on me." When Maggie heard the sound of crying at the other end of the line, she gently replaced the receiver. Tears streamed down her face, but she was smiling when she turned to face the trio at the door. "It isn't what you think. She wouldn't break the connection. She's starting to reach out."

"Mother, is she all right?" Cole asked fearfully.

"She's on the way. She's thinking, considering the odds. I don't know which way she'll go. Pray—that's my best advice."

While Maggie, Rand, and the boys shopped and packed, Sawyer took long walks in the park and saw Nick Deitrick every day. She paid two visits to the Sloan-Kettering Institute. She called her grandmother, and the gentle sorrow in Billie's voice was almost more than she could bear. Why didn't she rail her out the way Maggie and the others had done? "I want to come up there to talk with you, Grand," she begged.

"No, I'm sorry. You can't come here. I can't make decisions for you. It's not the operation anymore. It's Maggie. Don't confuse the two. I can't help you, darling. Only Maggie can help you. Don't be afraid. Make the first move . . . and call me again if I can help."

"She thinks I've forsaken her for Maggie," Billie said sadly after she'd hung up. "She really believes it, Thad."

"No she doesn't. She's just floundering. She has to struggle before she can accept what she needs most. You did the right thing. Poor darling, your heart is breaking. It'll be all right. I have a good feeling about it."

"If you told me it was light outside and I knew it was midnight, I'd believe you." Billie smiled wanly. "Let's go for a walk."

"With the dogs?"

Billie laughed. "All ten of them." She whistled, and they came from every corner, slipping and sliding on the kitchen tile, then lined up with unbelievable precision at the door.

"This is the way we're going to do it, gang," Thad told them. "I go first because I'm an admiral, and Billie goes next because she's an admiral's wife. You follow one at a time. There will be no cheating."

Billie looked over her shoulder at the dogs, who trotted in single file till they were on the road. Then Thad clapped his hands. "Disss-misssed!" The dogs scattered.

"We should take pictures of that. No one would believe it."

"It's just a question of authority. It's the tone, the rank, and my straight back."

"And the gumdrops you'll feed them when we get home."

Thad sniffed. "That's just a small part of it."

"So I'm Sawyer's authority figure. Is that it?"

"I knew I married you because you were bright."

"What about beautiful and charming?"

"That, too."

"You always make me feel better. It will be all right, won't it, Thad?"

"Yes, darling. Like I said, I have a feeling about it. But let's pray that someone up there is going to help us out."

On one of the shopping expeditions into Austin, Cole and Riley both picked out a gift for Luana—unbeknownst to each other, of course. Riley chose an exquisite bottle of perfume called Joy. Cole, more daring, bought a Gucci shoulder bag.

Cole didn't know what was worse: being with Luana for a few minutes of furtive kissing and hugging, or worshiping her from a distance. He'd obeyed the rules because he didn't want to see Luana get hurt. But he knew he was in love and wondered how he was going to get through the summer without seeing her. He imagined all the things he would buy her—native jewelry, a muumuu, a flower lei. He knew she liked him best, even though she hadn't said so. She'd cried when he'd told her he was going away for the summer. Then she'd asked offhandedly if Riley was going, too. He wished she weren't so nice to everyone. It gnawed at his gut.

Right now she was angry with him because he wouldn't risk going over to her apartment. But tonight was Saturday, date night. He was going to hang around the back porch like some ninny, hoping Luana would come out and sit with him on the steps. Maybe, just maybe, he'd take a chance, and if Ben Simms did go into town, he might . . .

When dinner was over, Riley left the table to get dressed for his date in town. "A cool chick," he told Rand, laughing. "She knows all about sports, and baseball is her favorite. She knows all about ground balls and sliders, and she says my curveball is the best she's ever seen."

"As compared to what?" Rand teased.

"As compared to an older brother who plays ball in the minors. I don't think I'll be too late, Aunt Maggie."

Maggie and Rand were going to the country club. Susan had a date with Ferris, and Ferris's mother had a date with Jessica. Cole was on his own.

In his room he could hear Riley whistling. He hated the sound. They'd both been fighting long and hard for Luana's affections, but Riley, not content to put all his eggs in one basket, kept dating—one girl after another. Evidently Riley wasn't as lovesick as he was. Cole hated what the feeling was doing to him. He *wanted* her. The other girls, even the ones who chased him—something he thought would never happen—didn't appeal to him at all. He knew the guys talked about Luana. Tease, trash, slut—they'd whispered all the worst names, and he'd heard them. But he knew in his gut that Luana was a virgin. Besides, she'd told him she was. And she was different with him. She didn't pretend the way she did in school. He knew how hard it was for her there. He hadn't belonged in the beginning, either.

Ever since he and Riley had gotten their own cars, though, things had changed. Luana seemed to prefer his Cougar convertible to Riley's Berlinetta. His mind raced as he tried to figure out a way to take Luana for a spin this evening. If he just happened to be out on the road leaving Sunbridge, and she just happened to be out there, too, he could pick her up. He could christen the Cougar. Jesus. He almost fainted with the thrill of excitement that rushed through him.

Riley had given up whistling; now the Oak Ridge Boys

were singing. Cole grimaced and stuck a Lionel Richie tape in his player, turning up the volume. Luana liked Lionel and Michael Jackson.

It was just starting to get dark when Cole heard the Berlinetta roar out of the driveway. He looked out his bedroom window and saw Luana sitting outside the apartment door, an open book on her lap. He craned his neck to see if her father's truck was in the yard. It wasn't.

Quickly he finished dressing. Preppy tonight—a white polo shirt, gray slacks, a navy-blue blazer, and topsiders. He doused himself with Brut after-shave, then slicked his hair back with both hands. He was ready. This was going to be *the* night; he could feel it.

In the circular driveway Cole pretended not to see Luana. He made sure, though, that she saw the way he was dressed. Susan had just secured Jessica into her travel seat and was about to climb behind the wheel. He walked over nonchalantly and leaned in the car window.

"Wow!" Susan said, whistling. "Don't you look nice. And you smell terrific." She grinned. "Big date?"

Cole knew their voices would carry to Luana. "Yeah," he drawled. "There's a party in town."

"You're going to have to fight the girls off with a stick, looking the way you do. Remember now, don't drink and drive."

"I won't, Aunt Susan. Did Mother and Rand leave yet?"

"About five minutes ago. You have a good time. I'll see you tomorrow."

Cole backed away from the car and stuffed his hands into his pants pockets. That's what movie stars did to show nonchalance. He was going to turn in a second now and walk to his car, at which point he would notice Luana for the first time. He turned, a look of pleased surprise fixed on his face.

The look turned sour when he saw Luana was gone. He sprinted upstairs and grabbed the big white gift box with the red-and-green stripes, then raced down the back steps, across the yard, and up the stairs to the apartment above the garage.

It was empty.

Cole tossed the Gucci box on the kitchen table next to Luana's books. Where the hell was she? She'd been here just minutes ago. He'd be dead meat if Ben Simms found him here. Maybe she'd gone for a walk. His pulses pounded in his ears on the way down the steps. By the time he climbed into the red sports car, he was in a near frenzy. He slammed it into reverse, then first, and was already in third when he tooled out of the yard onto the long stretch that would lead him to the main road.

Just outside the arch, Cole flicked on the high beams and screeched to a stop, his hand working fast as his left foot stomped on the clutch. There she was. He let the car idle as he pulled to the side of the road. The window slid down with a press of his index finger. "Want a lift?" he asked coolly.

"Where y'all goin'?"

"Party in town. Want to go?"

"I wasn't invited and I'm not dressed for a party," Luana said, pointing to her jeans and faded T-shirt. "If you have time, I could go to MacAllister's for a Coke."

"Sure, why not. Those parties never start to move till after ten anyway. Hop in."

"I do love this car, Cole," Luana cooed breathlessly as she hooked on her seat belt. Cole felt like groaning when he saw the way it mashed her breasts. He wanted to reach over and slide it between her breasts instead of over them.

"By the way," he said casually, "I left a present for you on your kitchen table. One minute you were there and the next you were gone."

"I didn't want to see you leave. Everyone from the big house was going out. I saw Riley leave. I felt jealous, so I decided to work it off by going for a walk. You didn't have to get me a present. It was nice of you, though. What is it?"

"When I drive you back home, you'll see it." Cole knew Luana was smiling in the darkness.

"I'm going to miss you guys when you leave. Just a few more days," she said softly.

"I'll send you a postcard, or I could write you a letter."

"That would be nice." She noticed there was a Michael Jackson tape playing, although it was hard to hear with the wind roaring in her ears.

"What are you going to do this summer?"

"Summer school, and I got a part-time job as a mother's helper for some six-year-old runt. The guidance counselor got it for me. The pay is three fifty an hour. I can use the money for school clothes in the fall."

"Too bad I won't be here to see them," Cole said morosely. "Your clothes, I mean. I'm leaving the end of August for prep school for my senior year, and then it's college."

"Riley, too?" Luana asked conversationally.

"Riley's going to Yale."

"You sound pleased. Are you going to Yale?"

"No, Notre Dame. Riley almost had a perfect SAT score. Fifteen ninety. I only scored thirteen hundred. Riley is Yale material." He wasn't going to tell her he actually felt proud of his cousin, even if he didn't like him.

"What are you going to do tonight?" he asked as one of McAllister's carhops brought them their Cokes.

"Read *The Red Badge of Courage* for a book report. It has to be in on Monday."

"You want to use mine? I got an A on it. I think I have it in my old papers from school."

"That'd be cheating," Luana said virtuously.

"Hey, I just asked. You don't have to use it. I thought maybe instead of going to the party, I could take you for a drive somewhere. Unless your father is coming home early," he added anxiously.

"No, he's out for the night. Okay, I'll use the report. Where do you want to go?"

"Hell, I don't know. We can't go to your place." He slapped at his head as though he just remembered something. "Hey, I know! There's an old line shack at the end of the north acreage. It's got an old couch, a stove, and some chairs, I think. And a hurricane lamp. No electricity or bathroom, though." He could feel his heart pounding.

"What'll we do there?" Luana asked innocently.

Cole grinned. "What do you think?"

"All the way?" Luana gasped.

"I have some rubbers. Come on, Luana, you're driving me crazy. You said you would when the time was right."

"My pa would kill me. You, too, if he ever found out."

"How's he gonna find out? I sure as hell won't tell him. That leaves you."

"He might be able to tell. My pa watches me like an eagle."

"Hawk," Cole corrected. He could almost feel her full, round breasts in his hands. "There's no way he'd be able to tell. Make up your mind; the girl's coming to take the tray."

Luana considered. "What am I gonna get out of this? The first time is supposed to hurt, and I'll have messy underwear. I've been saving myself. I know guys like you think that's corny, but I don't care. You're going away pretty soon. What am I supposed to do till you come back?"

"Wait for me. I won't hurt you. Maybe a little, but you'll forget it in a hurry. I have about two hundred dollars. Will that help you make up your mind?"

"Two hundred dollars! Well, sure, but there's something not right about taking money for . . . for . . ."

"You don't have to take it."

"I didn't say I wouldn't take it. I sure could use it. . . ." She thought it over for a few moments. "Okay, let's go to the line shack."

Cole's gut churned as he backed the Cougar out of the parking lot.

Forty-five minutes later Cole sat in the line shack staring at Luana. He handed her the two hundred dollars and she quickly slipped it into her hip pocket. Then he watched, fascinated, as she pulled her T-shirt over her head. He sucked in his breath. She was wearing a pink lacy bra that barely contained her breasts. A moment later the faded jeans slipped to the floor.

As Luana put her hands behind her back to unhook her bra, the strangest thing happened to Cole. First, his whole life flashed before him. Then a vision of his future crowded out his past. When he could see clearly again, the half-naked girl who stood before him no longer interested him. He wanted to tell her so, but the words wouldn't come.

Her breasts were free now, large and pink-tipped. There was no hunger on his lips to taste them. He continued to watch her as the bikini slid down. She was beautiful. She beckoned him with her eyes as she lowered herself to the old leather couch; her movements slow, sensual. Suddenly she squirmed and yelped as the sharp strips of aged leather cut into her skin. She jumped up, twisting and turning.

Even in the dim light from the hurricane lamp, Cole could see the thin slashes of blood. He walked over, bent down to feel the cracked leather. It cut his finger like a knife. He drew in his breath sharply and straightened up, cursing. "This was the worst idea I ever had. Get dressed," he said, sucking the blood from his finger. "I'll wait outside. Blow out the lamp before you leave."

Oh, shit, now he was going to want the two hundred dollars back. Just her damn luck. If her pa ever saw the marks on her back and ass, she was going to have some real tall explaining to do.

"Do you want the money back?" she said when she climbed into the car.

"No. You were willing. We made a deal."

"Why'd you change your mind?"

"Is it important for you to know?" Cole asked through clenched teeth.

"Well, sure it is. I thought you liked me. You been after me for a long time, and when I finally say yes, you tell me to put my clothes back on. You must be nuts, givin' me two hundred bucks for nothin'. Well, not for nothin', exactly. I did strip for you. But why'd you change your mind?"

Cole pressed his foot to the gas pedal. There were a lot of things he could tell her, but he decided to spare her. "I couldn't get it up," he said coolly, hoping she could hear him over the rush of the wind.

When Luana had absorbed what he'd said, she laughed. At Sunbridge she got out of the car, leaned over, and said quietly, "I know a lie when I hear one. You decided I wasn't good enough for you. I *saw* it in your eyes."

Cole looked away. "You better put something on those scratches," he said quietly. Luana backed away from the car, and he spun out, burning rubber.

She watched till she couldn't see the taillights any longer, then sprinted up the stairs and tore open Cole's present. A real Gucci bag! Excitedly, she fished for her two hundred dollars and put it inside. Then, slinging the brown strap over her shoulder, she walked about the kitchen, feeling like the richest woman in Texas. She forgot about putting something on her cuts. After she'd tucked her gift safely away, cut the Gucci box into small pieces and carried them down to the trash, she settled down to read *The Red Badge of Courage*.

It was after one in the morning when the high-beam headlights of the Berlinetta swooped around the circular drive, shining upward to Martha's room. On her way to the bathroom, the housekeeper stopped to look out the window, a habit of many years. She watched Riley climb from the car and noticed that the bright red Cougar was parked alongside. He was headed toward the house when she saw him turn.

Martha drew back a little into the darkness of her room and watched as Luana raced across the driveway. She nodded in satisfaction when she saw Riley shake his head and motion to the house. Luana took his arm and tried to pull him toward the garage. Riley resisted but allowed himself to be pulled as far as his car. Then he jerked free and leaned back against it, his hands jammed in his pockets. Martha strained to hear their conversation, but finally had to give up. Whispers didn't carry to the second floor.

The digital clock on her nightstand read 1:23 when she climbed into bed. If she'd had her way, she would have sent Ben Simms and his daughter packing five minutes after they'd arrived. She was almost asleep when she heard a door close. Riley. She opened one eye to look at the clock: 1:44. Two minutes later, she was asleep.

Cole, too, had seen the Berlinetta's lights sweep into the yard. Must have been a good party, he thought as he got up to go to the bathroom. On his way back to bed, he looked down into the courtyard, just in time to see Luana run across and grab Riley's arm. He stood by the window a long time, watching them. He felt pleased when Riley turned and went into the house. A few minutes later his cousin passed by, and he heard the sound of a door closing.

Cole nodded in satisfaction. They'd both obeyed the rules. Neither of them would bring shame on Sunbridge or the Coleman name.

Ben Simms climbed the stairs to the apartment, his arms loaded with the weekly groceries. The stove light was on, casting dim shadows over the neat kitchen. He put the groceries away, folded the bags neatly, and stuck them between the refrigerator and stove.

He walked wearily to his room. He'd had a few drinks, shot some pool, played some poker. The woman he'd been seeing, he was told, had gone to Maine to see a sick sister. There'd been no point in hanging around at two-thirty in the morning, and as a rule he didn't like dingy bars anyway. So he'd taken his bag of meat the bartender had kept in the refrigerator, slapped it in the back of the pickup, and driven home.

He tiptoed to the bathroom, relieved himself, washed and dried his face and hands. He opened the laundry hamper and was about to throw his clothes in when he noticed Luana's faded yellow shirt and threadbare jeans. He pulled them out and held them up to the bathroom light. They seemed to be crisscrossed with lines of blood. He stared at them for a long time, then, his teeth clamped together, he strode down the hall to his daughter's room. He threw open the door and turned on the light switch. Luana was lying naked on the bed but hastily pulled the covers over herself when the overhead light came on.

"What's the meaning of this, girl?" he demanded harshly, shoving the blood-streaked clothes close to her face. Half-asleep, Luana could only stare guiltily at the soiled clothing. "You better give me some quick answers."

"Pa, I didn't do nothin'. I swear I didn't."

"Git up, right now!" Ben thundered.

"Paaaa, I ain't got no clothes on."

"That's right; I'm yer pa. Now, get up and let me look at you."

Having Cole see her naked was fun. She'd wanted to see him stare bug-eyed at her bare breasts, wanted to see him swallow hard when he saw her without a stitch of clothes. Having her pa see her was sinful; she felt ashamed as she slipped out of bed. There was a look on his face, in his eyes, that made her feel sick. He reached for her, turning her around. "How'd you get those marks?"

"I don't know, Pa. I swear I don't!" Luana cried.

"Ye're lyin' to me, girl. I kin see it in yer face." He pulled her to him till he could feel her breasts against his own bare chest. "Ye're jest like yer ma," he said softly. "Jest like her."

Luana struggled. She didn't want to have him touch her, but suddenly his hands were all over her. The more she struggled, the more intense her father became. She found herself being dragged to the bed. She wanted to scream, to make someone hear what was going on, but she couldn't. Shame ripped through her at what she knew was about to happen.

Exactly eight hours after Riley entered the kitchen the night before, his life changed. It was 9:14 when four sheriff's cars roared into the Coleman driveway. Martha blessed herself and used the intercom to tell Maggie she was wanted downstairs right away.

"Rape!" Rand shouted, staring at Ben Simms in stunned disbelief. He was still in his robe and pajamas, his hair tousled from sleep. Maggie stood beside him, clutching his arm.

"Who was raped?" she asked hoarsely.

"My little gal, that's who," Simms said sharply. "If you want, you can go to the hospital and see for yourself."

"Who raped her? Who'd do such a thing?" Maggie tried to organize her thoughts. "Why is she in the hospital?"

"She was found wandering the main highway, Mrs. Tanner," said one of the sheriff's men. "Pretty badly beaten. The first aid squad was called and they took her straight to the hospital. She *said* she was raped, but there's no conclusive evidence yet, ma'am. They're doing tests on her now." He looked pointedly at Ben Simms.

Maggie felt Cole standing beside her. "Will she be all right?" she asked.

"Yes, ma'am. She's been roughed up, but she'll recover."

Cole's heart was thundering in his chest. He saw Riley, his face almost white, standing beside Rand.

"You got some gall askin' if my little gal will be all right!" Ben Simms cried. "She'll never be all right again! But she was able to talk to me when I got to the hospital. Wouldn't talk to nobody else, neither, not my gal. She knows her pa's the only one to help her. And she told me who did it to her. Told me clear and loud. It was that Jap kid, that's who it was!" Simms lunged for Riley. Two of the officers pulled him back.

"You're lying!" Maggie cried, and turned to Rand. "For God's sake, do something!"

"Deputy Pierson, ma'am," a tall young officer said politely. "Stand back, Mr. Simms. I'll handle this."

"Tell us what happened, Deputy," Rand said quietly. "But first I'd appreciate it if you'd remove Mr. Simms from this kitchen."

When Ben had been escorted away, Deputy Pierson turned back to Rand and Maggie. "Mrs. Tanner," he said soberly, "Luana Mae Simms has accused your nephew of beating and raping her."

"But it isn't true! Riley wouldn't do such a thing."

"Mr. Simms says the boy is violent. Is it true that Riley Coleman attacked him in your dining room when he tried to break up a fight between your son and your nephew?"

"No, Riley didn't attack him; he just didn't want the man to touch him...."

"That's not what Mr. Simms says. Have there been any other acts of violence between your nephew and your son, Mrs. Tanner?"

"What does that have to do with Luana?" Maggie asked, wringing her hands.

Riley sagged against Rand. "I didn't touch her. I didn't do it. I swear I didn't. I talked to her for a couple of minutes when I got home, but I didn't touch her!"

"That's true, what the boy says," Martha interjected. The deputy took notes as she explained about being awakened by Riley's headlights. "I heard him come in. I heard the door close."

"Thank God, Martha. Thank God you heard."

Cole stepped forward. "I saw him come in. I heard him, too. I also saw Luana go back up the steps. I was watching from my window."

Cole moved back until he was standing next to Riley. Maggie saw her son's hand touch Riley's shoulder. Any other time she would have been pleased; now she was frightened out of her wits.

"I want to call our lawyer," she said, trying to speak calmly. "None of us will say one more word until she gets here."

"Please have your lawyer meet us at the Crystal City Sheriff's Office. I'm sorry, Mrs. Tanner, but we have to take the boy in for questioning."

Rand stepped forward. "Deputy Pierson, do you have to take Riley immediately? Why not let the lawyer come here? It would be much less disruptive to the family. How would you like a cup of coffee?" He turned to Martha without waiting for an answer. "Martha, how about some of that delicious coffee of yours. And would it be too much trouble to cook up some breakfast? We're all starving, and I'm sure the deputy and his men haven't eaten for hours."

Martha hurried to the stove. "Yes sir, Mr. Nelson, a nice mess of grits and ham with eggs on the side. How's that sound?"

Maggie smiled weakly as she headed for the study to call Valentine Mitchell. They'd take Riley to the sheriff's office eventually, but not before they gorged on Martha's biscuits and ham.

Two uniformed officers stood outside the kitchen door, their hands on their holsters. Everyone else was seated at the table in the breakfast nook waiting for Valentine Mitchell when Maggie excused herself again and returned to the study. This time she called Amelia.

"I need you and Cary," she said, then tersely explained what was going on.

As soon as she'd hung up, she called Ferris Armstrong. "Send Susan, please, Ferris. I want the family here."

Her last call was to Billie. Thad answered and when Maggie explained, Thad was comforting. "Has anyone thought about calling the boy's grandfather?"

"I thought about it, but I don't want to alarm him. He's elderly and not well. Will you do it, Thad?"

"Of course, as soon as I hang up. Stand tough, Maggie. Don't let some smooth-talking pickup jockey railroad the boy."

The ensuing hours were a nightmare.

When Valentine arrived, the police led Riley away. Cole watched in silence until the police car was out of sight; then he turned and kicked out at the kitchen chair, overturning it. Swearing savagely, he raced upstairs, nursing his injured foot. He ran straight to the bathroom and was violently sick. After he'd cleaned up and brushed his teeth, he went to his room and called Sawyer, explaining the situation in jerky sentences.

"I think you should come here," he said harshly. "Grand is on her way. We need everyone. I'm the next one they're going to haul in."

"Of course I'll come. I'll bring Adam with me. I don't know when we can get a flight, though."

"Charter one! If ever there was a time to use all that Coleman money everyone brags about, this is it."

"I'll be there, little brother," Sawyer promised. "Just hang on."

Cole hung up and made a second trip to the bathroom, retching till his stomach muscles ached.

It was after two when Luana was brought back to the house. The ambulance driver handed Deputy Pierson an envelope. He handed it to Maggie, who read what was inside and then passed it to Rand.

From her seat in the breakfast nook, Maggie could see the ambulance drivers helping Luana up the steps. She'd been raped; it was on paper now, a fact, not something Ben Simms made up.

By three o'clock the Cougar and the Berlinetta were impounded. Riley and Valentine were still at the sheriff's office. Maggie chewed off three of her fingernails.

{{{{{{{{{{ CHAPTER TWENTY-NINE }}}}}}}}}}

Thad and Billie arrived at four-thirty that afternoon, Sawyer and Adam shortly after. The sheriff's deputies arrived at six with a warrant for Cole's arrest. Cole's face was grim and frightened when he kissed his mother and then Sawyer. "I didn't do anything and neither did Riley. You've got to believe us!"

"We do!" Maggie and Sawyer cried in unison, then watched helplessly as he was led away.

Just after midnight Shadaharu Hasegawa arrived in a limousine. He embraced Billie and Thad and bowed low to the others. "Now, tell me."

The old Japanese gentleman listened as Thad explained the situation. "My grandson would not bring dishonor on his family," he said calmly. "And I do not believe my good friends' other grandson would do such a thing. There is a truth here beyond what we see. We must find it."

At around twelve-thirty Valentine Mitchell called with a status report. Riley and Cole were to be brought into court for arraignment in the morning.

"What's an arraignment?" Maggie asked Rand, who had taken Valentine's call.

"She says it's to go before the court to see if there's enough evidence to set bail and put the wheels in motion for a trial. Valentine says not to worry; the boys will be released to our custody. They're to appear in court at nine o'clock tomorrow morning."

* * *

Appearing before the judge was a sobering experience for Riley and Cole. Up until then, everything that happened the day before had seemed like a bad dream. Now it was a reality. They had been accused; the grounds of suspicion had been weighed and found substantial. Both boys had been implicated, but only Riley had been charged with rape. Cole, they believed due to evidence found in his car, had aided and abetted the crime.

Riley was still dazed from his appearance before the judge when he entered the anteroom outside the court. The first person he saw was his grandfather. Tears sprang to his eyes. "Old One, I did nothing to disgrace our family."

Cole, who had entered the anteroom behind his cousin, felt a lump in his throat. His mother was crying; they were all crying except Thad and Rand. The old Japanese gentleman reached out his arms, and Riley, two heads taller, walked into them. Words were unnecessary.

"Where do we go from here, Valentine?" Rand asked in a muted voice.

"We wait," she answered, stuffing papers into her briefcase. "I want you to take the boys into Austin General Hospital for semen sampling. It would be easier on them if you didn't bring Maggie. We're waiting for the results of the slides made from cervical smears taken from Luana Simms. If we're lucky, the two tests won't compare and Riley and Cole will be off the hook. I'm not taking any chances, though; the test work will be done by two independent laboratories as well as the hospital. Tell Maggie that was Dudley's quick thinking, and thanks to the Coleman sway, we managed to get the D.A.'s office to agree."

"We'll leave in a while," Rand assured Valentine. He turned in time to see Cole walk out the front door, Riley following behind.

"Where're you going, Cole?" Riley asked.

Something in his tone caught Cole's curiosity. "What's it to ya?"

"Because I want to talk to you."

"So talk."

"Not here. Out back."

Cole shrugged and walked around to the back, Riley dogging his steps. From the way Riley was acting, Cole sensed there was going to be trouble. He wasn't surprised when Riley's arm shot out and turned him roughly around.

"You bastard," Riley hissed. "It was you who attacked Luana, because I know it wasn't me. You were the one, and you're going to let me take the rap! I heard the evidence this morning, and if no one else is asking you questions, I am. How did Luana's fingerprints get all over your car? How did her blood get there? She wouldn't let you into her pants, so you roughed her up and then raped her!"

"Hold it, Riley. That's not the whole story; you don't know what happened!"

"Don't I? I sure as hell do, and I'm not going down with you. Damned if I am!" The anger Riley had been struggling to control since early that morning erupted. Cole never saw the blow coming and took it full on the chin. Another kick from Riley's foot hit him square in the gut, bending him over double.

"Fight! Stand up and fight!" Riley shouted, already bracing himself against attack.

Cole lashed out, his knuckles grazing Riley's cheeks and then returning for a closer aim at his nose.

"Rand! Thad!" Billie shouted. "Stop them! Stop them!" They had all followed behind Rand when he'd hurried out after the boys. He'd sensed trouble coming, seen it in the bearing of Riley's shoulders, in the clenching of his fists as he'd followed Cole out the door.

Rand held Riley back; Thad kept Cole's arms pinned behind him. Blood was dripping from Riley's nose; Cole's lip was split and swelling.

"Let me go!" Cole struggled. "Let me go. I've gotta tell him something."

"Not now," Maggie said. "Just be quiet. There's been enough damage done." She reached into Riley's pocket for a handkerchief to wipe his nose.

"Let him speak," Mr. Hasegawa said firmly. "It's time we all knew what they know. Let us all hear, Cole. Riley, only a fool refuses to hear."

"Riley," Cole began, sputtering through his swollen mouth, "it isn't what you think. I didn't touch her. I met her on the road; she was hitching a ride." He looked guiltily at his mother. "Anyways, you know how it is with Luana. One thing led to another and I took her to that old line shack. But nothing happened! I didn't touch her. I told her to get dressed. I saw that her back was bleeding from the crackly split leather on that old couch in the line shack. *That's* how her blood got in my car. *That's* why her fingerprints were all over the place!"

Riley's shoulders relaxed. Rand felt the tension leave the boy's body.

"Believe me, Riley. I'm no more guilty than you are."

"I do believe you," Riley muttered. "And I know what it cost you to tell me all this in front of the family. I'm sorry, Cole."

"So it is East meets West," Mr. Hasegawa said sagely.

"Sir." Cole smiled shyly. "Just for once, could we make that West meets East? It'd be nice to get top billing."

Riley laughed, the first joyful sound they had heard in what seemed an eternity.

The following days were an agony of waiting. The tests had been taken on both boys. Ben Simms had packed up his daughter and their belongings and moved into town. What had happened to Luana was no secret, and Ben aired his hatred of the Colemans at every opportunity.

It was the old Japanese gentleman who put the man's actions into perspective. "There is no prouder man in the world than the man who can claim an injustice. Mr. Simms is pleased with the attention he is receiving, even for these few days, by being the center of a community's sympathy. And the more he cries and grieves his daughter's lost virtue, the more praise he will receive and the purer she is thought to have been. And for his grief, Mr. Simms receives praise from his neighbors for being the perfect father."

Sunbridge seethed with hostility, directed and misdirected. As Maggie tried to describe it to her mother, "It's like we're an accident waiting to happen. Everyone's temper is short. Everyone has an idea, but no one knows what to do about it."

"Darling, the 'accident' already happened," Billie said. "Thad and I both believe it's a question of money. Has Miss Mitchell come up with anything from the private detectives the firm hired?"

"Only that Simms is exactly what he is—a drifter who does handyman work and who goes to church, when he's in the mood, and who can recite the Bible from one end to the other. They've never, ever been in trouble. He has no record anywhere. Not so much as a traffic or parking ticket. The girl is behind in school, but that's because they move around so much. She's pretty big on reciting the Bible herself." She hesitated. "Valentine tells me the psychologist who is treating Luana told her, or sent her a report—I don't remember which—that said Cole forced Luana to have sex with him. But they aren't classifying Cole's actions as rape. Because"—Maggie drew in a deep breath—"he gave her things and money in return for . . . for her favors. But she's sticking to the rape story."

Billie sighed. "There isn't anything we can do, then?"

"Nothing. If we could just get to the girl, I think one of us could talk some sense into her. The last I heard, and that was in the *Crystal City Times* yesterday, was that Luana is being watched by some woman, a friend of Simms. I don't know if she's a housekeeper or what her function is, exactly," Maggie said dejectedly. "If only those tests would come in; I know the boys would be cleared."

"The press has been very unkind. If Seth were alive, this wouldn't have gotten off the ground."

"In those days *we* were the good guys. Today it's a whole new ball game. They're raking up all that old stuff on me. I just want to sit down and cry my eyes out. But I have to be strong and take everything they throw at us. I'm dreading the day the other side comes up with the dirt Valentine dug up on Cranston. If she has it, it's a matter of public record."

"No it isn't. Those records are sealed. That's one good thing about being a Coleman. Seth always had that agreement with the law firm. He paid handsomely to whoever it was in charge. I know that for a fact, Maggie," Billie added quietly.

"They're really out to get us, Mam. You must have noticed the phone hasn't rung once since you've been here for anything but crank calls. We're off everyone's list. It's hitting Cary hard. Some of the men actually walked off the job. The real big investors are nervous. If they decide to pull out, he loses everything."

"I know just the person to step in and help out." Billie grinned. "Riley's grandfather. He helped us once before; he'll do it again. Don't even think about it. As far as the workers go, all Cary has to do is up the wages and other men will come running from out-of-state." Billie hesitated, then asked, "Where is . . . everyone?"

Maggie knew who she meant. "Sawyer's down at the barn with the boys." She smiled. "Adam is over in your old studio, working up a storm. He decided to take on the state of Texas. The muckrakers may be getting in their shots, but he's retaliating. And the papers are printing his stuff. He's made quite a name for himself, and he does have some powerful friends in the media. And he's from Texas, a native son, so they have to pay attention. For now, it's our only plus. You went to bed early last night, so you didn't see the eleven-o'clock news. We made it— the wire services, the whole bit. We're news, Mam." She shook her head. "I can't believe this is happening to us."

"I can. The Colemans have always been news."

"Let's talk about something else," Maggie said. "More coffee?"

"Half a cup. I'm jittery enough without caffeine."

"How do you think Sawyer looks?"

"Like she's held together with spit and glue. Dry spit and old glue," Billie said sadly.

"We've had some fairly civil conversations," Maggie told her. "Of course, they had to do with the boys. It was a little awkward at first with Rand being here, and Adam and all. But I think we've managed to put those feelings aside for now. Maybe some good will come of all this."

"What do the three of them *do* down in the barn?" Billie asked curiously.

"Talk, I guess. I really don't know."

"They're up to something. Sawyer always was a planner, a master one at that."

"Maybe that's what we need, a plan. Action. This sitting around is driving me insane. We should be doing something."

"There's nothing to do. Drink your coffee, Maggie. I think I'm going to take a walk."

"To the cemetery?"

"Yes. Would you like to join me?"

"Yes. Yes, I would."

Sawyer stared at the boys. They stared back. Her head pounded, but she did her best to ignore the pain. From where she was sitting on a bale of hay, she could see them clearly. They looked so hopeful, so expectant. "Okay," she said, "let's go over it one more time. I know you've said it three hundred times. Humor me. Once more." She listened carefully. When they were finished, the only thing it seemed they were in agreement on was that Luana had been a virgin.

"If she was a virgin when you left her at home around ten, Cole, and when Riley left her at one-forty-five or so, that gives us some time to play with. Simms says he got home at three. That gives us one hour and fifteen minutes. Whoever it was had to have raped the girl in that span of time. Simms says—and this is just his word—that he didn't find out about Luana until the deputies came to take him to see Luana at the hospital. But he's lying; we all know that. We also know why. Big bucks. Right now, the only thing you have going for you is the hospital test. So, what we have here is one hour and fifteen minutes or five hours, give or take a few minutes."

"The cops have gone all over this," Cole muttered. "So have the lawyers."

"We're it, Sawyer," Riley groaned. "We can't prove we didn't do it. It looks like they can prove we did."

"Unless..." Sawyer let the word hang in the air. Both faces were so hopeful, she wanted to cry. "Unless, in that hour and fifteen minutes, or in that five hours, give or take a few minutes, Ben Simms raped his own daughter."

Cole's mouth dropped open. Riley's jaw dropped just as far as Cole's.

"Her own father!" Cole gasped.

"That's... that's..."

"The word you're looking for is incest," Sawyer said coldly. "Think about it. In all the years I lived at Sunbridge, we never, ever had anyone come on this land who didn't belong. Not up to the house, anyway. Somebody would have heard. The barn dogs would have barked. Strangers just don't pop up, even for a girl like Luana. She might have jerked your strings, but she'd never take the chance and invite someone from the outside here. There'd be a car, a moped, at the very least a bicycle, and I think we have to rule that out. We live twenty-five miles from town. Does either of you think she'd ask someone here?" At their negative nod, Sawyer continued, "That leaves Ben Simms committing the ultimate sin."

"It makes sense, but why didn't Miss Mitchell say something?"

"Think about it, Cole. Incest. You can't accuse a man of something like that. You can't even dance around it. Look, I'm not pretending to be a wizard or anything like that. I'm sure it's occurred to everyone, but no one wants to put it into words. If we did that, we'd open ourselves to the biggest lawsuit this state has ever seen. I think we should talk to Adam. I'm kind of tired, so why don't you guys go get him and bring him here. I'm going to flop down on that straw and see if this headache will go away."

The boys glanced at each other. "You stay with her, Cole, and I'll get him," Riley offered.

Cole nodded and lowered himself to the sweet-smelling straw. "It's worse, isn't it?" he asked Sawyer when Riley had left.

"Yeah. I don't think I would have made it to Hawaii. I was going to give it a hell of a try, though."

"You're nuts," Cole said, not unkindly. "What's happening to us can't even compare to what you're going through. You have to do something."

"Wave your magic wand and make me better," Sawyer said nastily.

"That's bullshit. Tell your surgeon to wave his magic scalpel and take your chances. That's what I would do."

"Well, you aren't me, little brother, so keep your opinions to yourself. If you're worried about me being around for the final verdict, forget it. I'll be here."

"I don't care about that. If I have to lose you, I want it to be the right way. I want to know you gave it everything you had."

Sawyer leaned up on one elbow, piercing Cole with her gaze. "And if I don't make it?"

Cole swallowed hard. "Like Miss Mitchell says, there aren't any guarantees. Not for me or Riley, and not for you. You aren't a gutless wonder, so stop acting like one."

Sawyer groaned. "I'm supposed to be in charge here."

"Well, shit, if you're in charge, act like it. Not just for Riley and me, but for yourself. You must be driving Adam fucking crazy."

Sawyer burst out laughing. "Where'd you learn to talk like that? Maggie would put soap in your mouth." Cole laughed, too, and then fell back into the hay. They were both laughing and throwing straw at each other when Riley and Adam walked into the barn.

"I wish you'd tell us what's so damn funny. We could

sure use a laugh or two," Adam said, smiling.

Sawyer leaned up on both elbows, straw sticking out of her hair and ears. When she spoke, her voice was solemn. "My brother here, this pip-squeak, says he'll put flowers on my grave if I die. He said he'd pray for me. This guy," she said, pointing to Riley, "said yesterday he'd stay with me through the entire operation. He has one small fear: he's paranoid about the sight of blood. I have decided to go ahead and have the operation. As soon as this is all wrapped up."

"No. Now," Cole said forcefully.

"Wrong. It's my decision. When this is over."

"I take it all back," Cole said coldly. "Now or forget it. We can hang on till this is over. You don't have the time."

"I'll think about it," Sawyer blustered.

Riley grimaced. "That's something I'd say. Tell us now, in front of Adam, so he can make the arrangements."

Sawyer struggled to get to her feet. It was getting worse; who was she kidding? How many more days could she take like the last few? "Okay," she said, swaying dizzily.

"You get a free ride for this one," Adam said, scooping her into his arms. Cole noticed that his eyes were wet. Shit, he didn't care. He felt like he'd just climbed the tallest mountain in the world.

"Did they tell you what I came up with?" Sawyer asked sleepily.

"Don't think about that now."

"Don't tell me what to do, Adam. I can still think for myself. While you're making the arrangements, I want to talk to this family. Get them all together around the dining room table."

"You're a real pain, you know that?"

"Yeah, I know. Just humor me and then I'm all yours."

"Do you mean that?"

"For God's sake, of course I mean it! When we get to the house, get me one of those green pills and a shot of brandy. C'mon," she squawked, "what's the delay here?"

"Just shut up and enjoy the ride," Adam said. Cole grinned. Riley punched him playfully on the shoulder in return.

Maggie and Billie ran out to the driveway as they saw Adam carrying Sawyer up the walk. "What's the matter?" Maggie gasped. Billie immediately put her hand on Sawyer's forehead.

"She wants a meeting," Adam said. "You boys explain while I get the pill and the brandy. She wants Cary and Amelia here, too."

Ninety minutes later the entire Coleman family was assembled at the dining room table. "You're on, Sarah," Adam called to Sawyer, who was in the kitchen. "This better be a performance worthy of Bernhardt."

"I have something to say to all of you," Sawyer announced." She paused a moment to marshal her strength. "We find ourselves involved in not one but two crises. I'm the first, Cole and Riley the second. Each is equally important. I could literally die. Their lives could be ruined. In my eyes, that's the same thing." Again she paused, this time for effect. "I've agreed to have the operation. At the insistence of Cole and Riley, I'm leaving this afternoon for Sloan-Kettering. Now, if I'm willing to put my head on the block, I want all of your necks on the same block. I want you—us—to accuse Ben Simms of raping his daughter. I think we all know that's exactly what happened. So put it on the line, just like I am. If I can do it, so can you." She looked around fuzzily, blinked to regain her vision. But it wasn't working; the faces were still blurry. Her heart fluttered wildly as she gripped the edge of the table and spoke. "Maggie? Grand? Amelia? Susan? I want an answer." She thought she was seeing horror, dismay, fear, when actually all the faces held something she couldn't see—pride.

"Good girl," Cary said loudly. "I'm with you and so is Amelia."

"Me, too. And include Jessie in my vote," Susan said happily.

"I agree and so does Thad," Billie said, rushing up to Sawyer. "I'm so glad."

It was Maggie's turn. She looked around wildly, tears sliding down her cheeks. Rand reached out to her. Riley handed her his handkerchief. "So, you do know how to fight. You have my vote."

"One more thing," Sawyer told them. "If I don't make it, I want you all to know that . . . I . . ." She swayed dizzily, then her knees crumpled as she started to slip to the floor. Rand was there first, his arms outstretched. Adam came around the side of the table a second too late. He bent down, his eyes locking with Rand's. What he saw there made him nod and stand up. It was Rand who carried Sawyer to the waiting ambulance.

Cole stood next to Riley in the driveway. "This is big shit, you know," he said. "They're putting everything on the line for us." He sat down on the garage steps where Luana always sat. "I think we just grew up."

"My grandfather will assist in whatever way he can. I wish he hadn't come here though. I see the way he looks at me. I've caused him trouble."

"I saw him look at you, too. He doesn't believe you did it, and no one else thinks so, either. He's . . ." Cole groped for the right word. "Sad."

"Do you think Sawyer'll make it?"

"Hell, I don't know. She did real good in there, didn't she?"

"She sure did. Maybe we can still go to Hawaii when she's better."

"Yeah, maybe," Cole said glumly.

"I was thinking about something," Riley said uneasily. "If I ask your opinion, will you give me a truthful answer?"

"Sure."

"I was thinking about getting my eyes fixed, Westernized. What do you think?" He held his breath, waiting for Cole to answer.

Cole turned to stare at his cousin, looking at him closely from different angles. Finally he said, "Why the hell would you want to do a dumb thing like that?"

Riley laughed. "You mean it?"

"Hell, yes. You can't do that to the old man in there. He'd lay down and die. You're who you are and I'm who I am."

"I'd look more like a Coleman," Riley said defensively.

"Man, being a Coleman is being one. It doesn't matter how you look. I'm only half, too. When push comes to shove, that's when you know who you are. I hated your guts in the beginning. Guess you know that."

"Yeah. Well, I wasn't too fond of you, either. I thought you were a real jerk."

"I thought you were a real fag myself. You had it all. At least I thought you did. You didn't have it so easy, either, did you?"

"No," Riley replied. He wasn't about to tell his cousin he'd had a wonderful life till he came here. They were even now, starting from square one.

"We're it, you know. The last of the Colemans. Little Jessie doesn't count, because she's . . . she's different. I don't think Susan will have any more children. She might adopt. And we don't know about Sawyer. So, cousin, we're it."

"Yeah, look where we are."

"I have a gut feeling we're gonna make it," Cole said with more confidence than he felt. "With a family like this, how can we lose? Your grandfather is okay, too," Cole added generously. "Maybe that's what set me off about you. He bailed out the Colemans when the going got tough."

"Don't you think your family would have done the same thing?" Riley asked curiously.

"Back then, when you first got here, I probably would have said no. Now I know differently." He leaned back, resting on his elbows.

"How do you think you're going to like Yale?"

"Probably the same as you're going to like Notre Dame. I'll think of you doing all that praying."

"Ah, shit." Cole grinned.

"How fast does that Cougar go?"

"Just as fast as that Berlinetta. Do you drink and drive?" Cole asked curiously.

"No way, man, do you?"

"Nope. You ever score with a chick?" Cole asked slyly.

"Nope. Did you?"

"No. Guess we do have a lot in common."

"You wanna keep in touch when we go off to college?" Riley asked.

"Sure. Maybe we can even visit each other. I think it's time we started spending some of this Coleman money. Did anyone say anything to you about allowances?"

"Don't worry. What's mine is yours," Riley said generously.

Cole stuck out his hand. Riley gripped it. Both boys grinned.

While the boys were coming to terms with each other, the remaining Colemans sat around the dining room table, waiting as Valentine Mitchell opened her briefcase and took out a legal pad, then fished for a pen. "Okay, let's hear it."

Two minutes later she got up, looked around, and said, "You want to do *what*?"

"You heard right," Maggie said firmly. "We're all in agreement. And we're prepared for anything. You do your job, and we'll handle the rest."

Valentine sat down heavily. "I guess I don't have to tell you—"

"No, you don't. We know. Now, who's going to the newspapers, you or us?" Valentine read the determination in Maggie's expression.

"I'll do it." The leaf-green eyes looked around the table. "You have guts; I'll say that for you. Procedure is that I go to Simms's attorney."

"We aren't interested in procedure. You go for the jugular," Maggie said coldly.

"What if they want to make a deal; what if—"

"No deals. Not a penny. We want the press. We want our lives back."

The Gucci briefcase snapped shut. Maggie thought it looked a little more worn since she'd seen it last.

The following morning every newspaper in the state of Texas carried the banner headline: COLEMAN FAMILY FIGHTS BACK. Maggie winced several times when she read the printed words to the family over breakfast.

The phone had to be taken off the hook shortly after the story broke. Three ranch hands, armed with rifles, stood guard at the entrance to Sunbridge. The Colemans were prisoners in their own home.

Maggie packed her bag carefully, putting in enough clothes for at least a week. If she needed more, she could buy them. She was New York bound. There was nothing more she could do here, and she needed to go to Sawyer.

"You understand," she said to Shadaharu Hasegawa, "why I have to go to New York."

The old Japanese bowed and nodded. "But of course, Mrs. Tanner. We will handle everything in your absence."

"I know that. If you need them, there are two other phones in the study. Both private lines." She embraced the old man and looked deeply into his dark eyes. "Riley will come out of this just fine. Trust us. My daughter wouldn't have asked us to do what we did otherwise."

"You will please give her my best wishes for a speedy recovery."

"I'll do that, Mr. Hasegawa," Maggie said in a choked voice.

Martin, the chauffeur, blew the horn in front of the house. "Mam, you should be the one going, not me," Maggie said.

"No. It's you Sawyer needs."

Maggie kissed them all and hugged Jessie. "I'm not deserting you, boys. It's just that Sawyer needs me more. Or I need her. Rand, take care of my boys," she said, kissing him lightly on the cheek.

"My best to Sawyer."

"Our love," everyone chorused.

A few minutes later the Mercedes 300 SD roared down the road to the arched gate. The guards moved back, and the car shot through as though jet-propelled. The reporters standing guard hopped in their cars and followed. Forty-five minutes later, Maggie climbed aboard a Coleman Lear jet and was airborne in less than ten minutes.

When she landed at Kennedy Airport, she went straight to Adam's apartment. He answered the door. "I wasn't sure you'd be here," she said nervously. "How is she?"

"Holding her own. They're running tests. I'm going to the hospital later. They want her a little stronger before they operate, my guess would be at least five days. What are we standing here for? Come on up."

"I can stay someplace else if—"

"No way. You're staying here. I even think we have clean towels."

"The price sounds right," Maggie said quietly.

"I heard the news. How's it going?"

Maggie shrugged. "It's only been a day and a half. I wanted to be here; they can all ... The boys ... There's Mr. ..."

"I understand. Coffee?"

"Yes, I could use a cup. How are you?" Maggie asked, noticing the dark circles under his eyes.

"Hey, I'm t-u-f-f! I'm from Texas."

"Sometimes I wish I'd never heard of the state," Maggie said wearily, then grimaced. "This coffee is terrible! How old is it?"

Adam shrugged. "Yesterday, I guess. Let me make some fresh. It'll give me something to do."

"Have you spoken to the doctors?"

"No. I thought maybe this evening I'd get a chance. Sawyer is comfortable. They're medicating her and she isn't in too much pain. She's drowsy most of the time."

"I want to go with you this evening."

"Good," Adam said as he measured coffee into the wire basket. "I think you should talk to the doctor, too."

"How upset do you think Sawyer is going to be when she sees that I'm here?"

"I don't know. She isn't exactly with it, if you know what I mean."

While the situation in Texas brewed and simmered, Maggie made daily treks to the hospital. Most of the time Sawyer was sleeping, but she'd stay and try to read. Once Sawyer woke and stared across at Maggie. "You remind me of a vulture, just waiting to descend," Sawyer said through clenched teeth. "If I had any strength, I'd tell them to throw you out."

"Not a vulture, Sawyer. How about a mother hen? I wouldn't let them throw me out."

"Vulture."

"Mother hen."

"Damn you."

"Why are you damning me?"

"For never being there when I needed you," Sawyer said, tears slipping through her lashes.

"I can't change that time in our lives. I'm here now."

"It's too late."

"Do you want me to grovel? I will. Do you want me to kiss your feet? I will. If you want me to leave, I won't."

"You left the boys, knowing what was going on," Sawyer said, mustering all the anger she could.

"It was a question of priorities. The boys will be fine. I believe that, and I know you do, too. If you hadn't had the guts to do this, we'd all still be sucking our thumbs. You're my daughter and I'm proud of you."

"Is this where we kiss and make up, and I say I'm proud to have you for my mother?"

"Only if you want to. I don't expect anything from you, Sawyer. I just want you to understand. If only you'd try, we might be able to go on from there."

"Just me and you. And Rand."

"Don't bring Rand into this. It's just you and me, kid."

"Go home, Maggie. I can't give you what you want."

"What is it you think I want?"

"You know what you want," Sawyer said uncertainly.

"No, you tell me. Tell me what it is you think I want. I want to hear it from you."

"Go away. Nurse," she called weakly.

"What is it I want, Sawyer?"

"To pretend you're my mother. To pretend you are. You want me to believe that. Well, I don't. You never cared. You never even tried."

"That was then and this is now. Give me a chance. Please, Sawyer."

When Sawyer didn't respond, Maggie panicked and called the nurse. "What happened? Is anything wrong?" She asked anxiously.

"No, Mrs. Tanner. She does that. Just slips into a deep sleep for a while. Why don't you go home and get some rest."

"I guess I will. You'll call if . . ."

"Of course we will," the nurse said compassionately.

"How do you do it?" Maggie whispered. "How can you take care of dying patients day after day?"

"I like to think I make their days a little better. I do my best; we all do here. There are some days when I say I'm not coming back tomorrow, and then someone like your daughter comes in who has a fighting chance, and I want to be sure she gets it. I guess that's it."

"Bless you," Maggie said hoarsely. "Take care of her."

"We will."

Adam looked up from his worktable as Maggie let herself into the loft. "Not a good evening, huh?" he said sympathetically.

"I might have been too hard on her. She fought me. Then she slipped off to sleep. The nurse told me to come home."

"At least you're obedient. Want a sandwich?"

"I suppose so. How old is the coffee?"

"Fresh."

"Adam, where are my diaries?"

"In the hall closet in the bag you brought them in. I wouldn't let her burn them."

"Thank you for that. I think maybe I'm spinning my

wheels trying to talk to her. I can never convince her that I . . . Oh, what's the use?"

Adam nodded to show he understood as he slapped mustard on some tired-looking bologna. Maggie ate her sandwich mechanically, not tasting anything. She drank cup after cup of coffee. "How's your work going?"

"Okay, I guess. Actually, my editor told me it's some of my best yet. I can't figure that out. The stuff I turned out in Texas really had grit in it."

"You're telling me. I think it helped, though. You really love her, don't you?"

"Body and soul. I think she cares for me, too. Not a dependent kind of caring, either. Hell, I know the difference. If she'd just let go, we might have a shot at something really good. If only we had more time."

Maggie snorted. "Time. It's everyone's enemy." She stood up wearily. "I guess I should call home."

"Oh, hell, I almost forgot. Billie called while you were at the hospital. You made the headlines. The newspapers said you cut and ran. Deserted the kiddies and are seeking sanctuary here, in the city where millions can get lost. A whole bunch of bullshit, if you'll excuse the expression."

"What's going on?" she asked sourly.

"Just what you'd expect. Ben Simms was interviewed on the morning news, the noon news, the six-o'clock news, and the evening news. The Colemans are standing fast and speaking only through their attorneys. By tomorrow everyone'll know why you're here. There are some decent reporters out there. If and when you want to make a statement, I'd appreciate it if you'd do it through a buddy of mine. It'll be printed just the way you give it to him. He's an ace."

"When it's time. I'm tired now. I think I'll turn in if you don't mind."

At five-thirty the following morning, the phone rang. Adam got it on the first ring and craned his neck. Good, it hadn't wakened Maggie.

It was Sloan-Kettering. Sawyer wanted to see him. He

dressed hurriedly, fishing his running clothes from the closet. His eyes fell upon the bag with Maggie's diaries and he grabbed it on impulse.

Sawyer was wide awake when he arrived, more coherent than she'd been in days. "They want to operate this afternoon. One o'clock, they said." Adam nodded. He felt a lump in his throat. "I said okay." Adam nodded. The lump was getting bigger. "Maybe I do love you. You're so goofy, who could help but love you? That cat has to go, though." He couldn't swallow past the lump, nodded, and wondered if he was drooling. "What's in the bag? The diaries?" Another nod. "Okay, read them to me."

"You want me to read them?" Adam asked, startled into speech.

"I can barely see, so who else is there?"

Adam opened the first little journal and began to read. He felt terrible, as if he were prying into Maggie Coleman's life. He knew she hadn't intended the diaries for anyone's eyes but her daughter's. Somehow, though, he didn't think she would mind. He read on, finishing one and picking up another. Sawyer lay still, her eyes closed. One time he looked up, thinking she was asleep. "Keep going. Don't stop," she said weakly.

He read on, from time to time noticing a tear roll down her cheeks. When he'd finished the last page and closed the journal, Sawyer opened her eyes. "What time is it?" she asked.

"Eleven o'clock. Why? Are you going somewhere?"

"They'll be coming in to give me a shot soon. And they have to shave my hair. Will you do something for me?"

"Name it."

"Call my mother. Tell her I want to see her."

"Okay, sure." God, there was so little time left. He might never see her again. They might never be able to banter back and forth. He might not be able to yell at her to wash the towels. They now had eighty-four of them.

"Adam, what are you thinking?"

Adam told her.

"I'm glad you didn't lie to me. We have eighty-four

towels, though." They both laughed. "Will you hold my hand a minute? You know, I can hardly see you."

"Why would you want to look at me?" he asked huskily as he squeezed her hand.

Sawyer didn't answer. "Will you wait? It's going to be a long operation."

"I'll read a book, maybe one of those trashy romances you read."

"Okay. Are you going to call Ma—my mother?"

"As soon as you let go of my hand. You know I love you, right?"

"Yeah, I know. Tell the boys . . . You know what to tell them. You know, in case . . . And Adam . . ."

"Yes?"

"Sometimes first loves aren't what they're cracked up to be. Sometimes it's the last love that counts."

Shit, he was crying. It was a good thing she couldn't see him. He bent down to kiss her cheek and was surprised when she turned so his lips would find hers. It was a long kiss, and by the time it was over, the blood was roaring through his veins.

Sawyer heard the door close behind him. "Good-bye, Adam," she said softly.

The nurse came in, her starched uniform crackling busily. She readied a hypodermic. Another nurse came in with a covered tray to shave her head. She prayed silently.

Maggie picked up the phone and listened to Adam. "She said *what*?"

"She said, call my mother. In fact, she said it twice. Not Maggie, 'my mother.' Hurry up. I don't know what the shot will do to her."

Maggie was out of the apartment and down the stairs within minutes. She ran up the street and across and out onto the road. She flagged a cab and told him where she wanted to go. The driver took one look at her face and sped away. When he pulled to the curb minutes later, Maggie handed him some crumpled bills. She had no idea if it was too much or too little—she couldn't even read the meter.

"Good luck, ma'am."

"Thank you," Maggie whispered. "Thank you very much." She was breathless when she got out of the elevator. The first person she saw was Adam. Part of her registered that he was carrying the flight bag that contained her diaries. Quickly he told her what he'd done.

Outside Sawyer's room, she stopped long enough to take several deep breaths, then went inside.

She thought she could feel death in the room. So close. She wanted to shout, to scream, "Not yet!" She walked over to the bed where Sawyer lay so still. There was a puckered cap on her head. She'd never really noticed before how long and thick Sawyer's lashes were. It was hard to tell now where they started, with the sooty smudges under her eyes. "Sawyer, are you awake?" she whispered.

Sawyer heard the words and tried to make her tongue work. She felt as if there were cotton balls in her mouth. She tried again. Her arms flailed at the air around her.

Maggie, sensing what was wrong, reached for her hand and clasped it tightly in both of hers. "I'm here." Sawyer squeezed slightly. Maggie tried to find her own voice and had to clear her throat twice. "Adam told me he read you the diaries. All I want, Sawyer, is for you to tell me you understand. Later, we'll work on the rest. Blink, baby, if you understand." Sawyer's eyelashes fluttered faintly.

Maggie's head bowed. All the years slipped behind her, the weight suddenly lifted from her shoulders. Almost home free. Almost.

"You'll have to leave now, Mrs. Tanner," said the nurse. "Mr. Jarvis is waiting for you at the end of the hall. Dr. Marlow will be out shortly to speak with you."

Sawyer summoned every ounce of strength left in her. She was so groggy, she just wanted to sleep, but she had to do something, say something. No one else would have understood the mangled word that came out through her dry mouth.

"M-mam."

Maggie heard. She thought she could hear a choir of angels singing when she walked down the hall to join Adam. Taking him by the arm, she asked, "Do you hear them, the angels singing?"

Adam stared at her, bewildered. He realized she was deadly serious. "No, I don't," he said slowly, "but if you do, that's okay with me. That's a plus for our side."

Maggie walked around the waiting room, her gaze sweeping the ceiling. Adam shivered when she said, "It could mean they're getting ready to take her."

"Don't talk like that," he said sharply.

When the surgeon arrived Maggie and Adam listened to him. When he left, they looked at each other. "Do you know what he said?" Maggie asked crazily. Adam shook his head.

"Seven hours. Then, if she comes through it, it'll take another seventy-two till they know if it was a success."

They waited. The minutes ticked by; the hours crawled. Twice Maggie called Sunbridge just to hear her mother's voice. "I really do have two children, Mam," she cried before she hung up.

"Be strong, Maggie."

"I am."

"Call me later."

"Mam . . . I heard angels sing. I really heard them. I know Adam thinks I'm crazy, but I did hear them; I know I did. Say you believe me," Maggie pleaded.

"Darling, if you say you heard them, then I believe you. I, for one, still believe in miracles."

"What if . . . what if it means they're getting ready to take her?" Maggie cried.

"Then, baby, you have to let them take her."

Maggie cried, great huge sobs that ripped at her insides. Adam found her in the phone booth and led her back to the waiting room.

More minutes and hours crawled by. They smoked and drank coffee. Adam scrounged in his pockets for some stale M&M's, which he offered to share with Maggie. She refused. "How long has it been?" she asked hoarsely.

"Six hours."

"One more to go. It must be going all right, or we would have heard by now. Don't you think so?" Maggie asked, looking at him imploringly.

"I think so." Jesus, one more hour. Sixty minutes. Three thousand six hundred seconds. A lifetime.

Forty-five minutes later the surgeon entered the waiting room, a cup of coffee in his hands. He ripped off his green skullcap, his mask dangling around his neck. He looked tired, Maggie thought. She waited for him to speak.

He took a long swallow of the horrible coffee. "She came through it, and she's in recovery now. We'll know in seventy-two hours. I'd say her chances are better than I first thought. I've seen people that should be dead still living because they will it. When she first came to me, Sawyer had given up. I was dumbfounded when you called and said she wanted the operation," he said to Adam. "Something happened to that girl along the way. I'm confident she'll fight now. I would have liked her to be a little stronger, but we simply couldn't wait to build her up. She's got round-the-clock nurses. I can be back here within fifteen minutes at any time. One of my associates is staying the night. Is there anything you want to ask me?"

Maggie's mind was full of questions, but she couldn't voice them. She looked at Adam, who was just as mute. Both of them shook their heads. Then, when he saw Maggie glance up, Adam closed his eyes.

"Do you hear them?" she asked, smiling at the doctor.

"Who?" he asked tiredly.

"The choir of angels. This is the second time I've heard them today."

The doctor smiled, his eyes warm and gentle. "I hear them every day. I'd say they're a little louder than usual, though. A good sign." He held out his hand, first to Adam and then to Maggie. "Go home now and get some rest. You both look like I feel."

Adam and Maggie linked arms and walked to the elevator. In the main lobby they stopped to call Sunbridge.

Maggie reported happily that Sawyer had come through the operation. She could hear Billie repeat the news to the others. "The next seventy-two hours are crucial. Pray, Mam. I heard the angels again. Even Dr. Marlow says he hears them. The surgeon—he said they were louder than usual. A good sign. Mam, I'm not crazy."

"I know you aren't. Take care, Maggie. Go home and get some rest."

"Anything new?"

"Not a thing. When Sawyer comes to, give her our love."

"I will. Good night."

In the taxi Adam stewed and fretted. "Why didn't I hear them? What does it mean?"

"I wish I could explain it to you, but I can't. Perhaps it has something to do with life and death. I gave Sawyer life. The doctor deals in life and death all the time. It's the best I can do."

"Damn, I wish I'd heard them. I'd feel so much better."

"Maybe you don't need an angel to sing for you. Maybe you're supposed to do your own singing. I don't know. . . . I'm so tired, I can't think. Can we discuss this tomorrow?" Adam nodded.

Billie called a family meeting. "Things are on hold here. How would all of you like to go to New York and be there when they pronounce Sawyer's operation a success? I'll call Valentine and see if she can get permission for Cole and Riley to go. Amelia, you know Judge Bellows, don't you?" At her nod, Billie said, "See what you can do. Make it easy for Valentine. Tell him we'll be back in forty-eight hours."

Twenty-four hours after Sawyer's operation, the Coleman jet took off with all the Colemans aboard. They camped out in the hospital waiting room, returning to Adam's to freshen up, then going immediately back to the hospital to watch the sleeping girl through the glass in the intensive care unit.

It was Maggie who kept vigil across from the clock.

In just four hours the time limit would be up. How still Sawyer looked, how pale and wan. She wished she could hear the angels again. She was so tired, she could barely keep her eyes open.

Suddenly she caught a movement out of the corner of her eye and looked through the glass. Sawyer's hand fluttered, but the thumbs-up salute was unmistakable. Maggie's own thumb went up in response.

Sobbing, Maggie ran back to the others and fell into Rand's arms. "She's okay! She just did this." She demonstrated the cocky salute that had been a favorite of her father's. Adam collapsed on the sofa. Cole and Riley took off and pressed their faces up against the glass. Both boys shot their fists into the air. Sawyer again stuck her thumb up.

"You hear something?" Cole asked.

"Yeah, a radio. I didn't think you could play radios in this unit."

"That's no radio. It sounds like the choir at school."

"Yeah, it does," Riley agreed. He shrugged it off as they made their way back to the others.

"She's got a long road ahead of her, but I'm confident she'll make it," Dr. Finley said heartily. "Now, I think all of you should go home and let our patient begin her recovery. She knows you've all been here; I told her. I also told her I was sending you home. She understands. I want all of you to get at least eight hours of sleep, and that's an order.... Damn, they're at it again," he muttered as he left the room. Maggie smiled happily.

Kisses and hugs were the order of the day in the lobby. "Tell Sawyer I'll be back, Adam," Maggie said. "I have business at home. And take good care of her."

"I still didn't hear them," he whispered.

"Don't worry. Sawyer will sing a song for you. Just for you. Call us."

"Will do."

{{{{{{{{ CHAPTER THIRTY }}}}}}}}

It was almost midnight when the Coleman jet touched ground. The tired but happy clan climbed into the waiting cars that would take them back to Sunbridge. Amelia immediately placed a call to Judge Bellows, informing him the boys were back in Texas and would soon be asleep in their own beds. She also reported on Sawyer's progress and hung up feeling better than she had in days. Maybe that little talk she'd had with Sawyer had helped.

That night they slept, all of them. If their sleep was invaded by demons in the shape of Ben and Luana Simms, no one ever knew.

It was two-thirty the following afternoon when Maggie sent Rand out to invite the reporters and news media to the house. Valentine Mitchell was in attendance. Maggie read a statement and then waited for questions.

"Are you serious, Mrs. Tanner? You really want a face-to-face confrontation with Luana Simms? What if her lawyers won't go for it?"

"We have nothing to hide. If they have nothing to hide and the girl is telling the truth, why wouldn't they? Unless, of course, this is all for money."

"You said you'd offer ten thousand dollars to anyone who would come forward and tell what they know about that night. You mean only if it clears Cole and Riley. Is that right?"

"Absolutely right," Maggie said tightly.

"Does that include Luana herself?"

"It includes anyone who can clear Riley and Cole," Valentine said clearly.

"How's your daughter, Mrs. Tanner?" asked a young woman.

"On this side of the angels. Thank you for asking."

"Then that's it, ladies and gentlemen," Valentine said, dismissing the reporters. "We'll be here at the same time tomorrow. Hopefully, the Simmses will be here, too."

When the door closed behind them, Valentine put her hands on her hips, glowering. "That's probably the dumbest, the stupidest, thing I've ever done in my life. That goes for you, too. If you think for one minute that the Simmses' attorneys are going to let them come out here, you're all out of your minds."

"You're probably right," Maggie said ruefully. "What I'm hoping for is that Luana will come forward. Ten thousand dollars will get her away from here. If she tells the truth, Social Services will take her from Simms, where she'll be safe. When she's of age, she'll have ten thousand dollars plus the interest it gathers." She shrugged. "It was worth a shot. I saw that child after one of her father's beatings, and it's something I'll never forget. We have absolutely nothing to lose." The others nodded.

Valentine left the ranch shaking her head. It was so damn dumb, it just might work. She couldn't allow herself to think beyond this time tomorrow.

"Cole, take the pickup, and you and Riley go to the line shack and bring that old couch back here. Put it in the garage and cover it up."

Ben Simms watched the six-o'clock news with his daughter, his face dark and full of rage. Luana cowered in her chair. "Don't you go gettin' no funny ideas, you hear, girl?" he snapped. "I'm going out to call our lawyer. You stay right here with Louise."

Sullenly, Luana looked at the woman sitting across from her. They'd been staying with Louise since they'd moved from the dirty apartment they were in. This place was clean and Louise was a good cook. But she was mean, just like Pa—watching her every move as though she were some kind of thief.

Luana stared moodily at the TV. Nothing was working right. The lady she was supposed to work for had canceled her, summer school had never materialized, and she'd been cooped up here like a prisoner. All because of her pa and what he'd done to her. If there was only some way she could get out of here, she'd go to the police and tell the truth. She often thought of Cole and Riley and wondered if they hated her. They sure had a right to.

Ben Simms came back in, a look of joviality on his face. "Our lawyers said them Colemans are just grabbin' at straws because they know we got 'em cornered. He said we could expect more tricks like this one." Luana didn't say anything. She hadn't been able to look her father in the eye since that night. She didn't even want to be in the same room with him. "He said we ain't goin' out there tomorrow, so don't go thinkin' we are, girl."

"Yes, Pa," she said obediently, keeping her eyes on the TV. If she could just get to the Coleman ranch...

That night, Luana lay awake in her bed for a long time, listening to the sounds coming from the room next to hers. When the bedsprings finally stopped groaning, she waited another fifteen minutes, then stole out of bed and threw on a pair of jeans, a T-shirt, and sneakers. Then she crept into the other bedroom, pocketed two quarters from Louise's purse, and quietly let herself out the front door.

Once outside, she ran, tears flowing down her cheeks. She ran till she came to Bill's Sunoco Station, which was brightly lit but closed. She went right to the phone booth and called information to get the number for Maggie Coleman Tanner of Sunbridge. She repeated it aloud five or six times, then dropped the returned quarter back into the slot. Her hands were shaking so badly, she could barely punch out the numbers.

The phone was picked up on the tenth ring. "Miz Tanner? This is Luana," she said, her voice trembling. "Can you come get me? I'm at Bill's Sunoco Station on the highway. Please, Miz Tanner."

"I'll be right there. Are you all right?"

"I will be soon as I tell the truth. I can't stay out here in the light. I'll be across the road in the dark. You stop, and if I see it's you, I'll come out. My pa might find me gone, and he knows the first place I'd go is to you."

"It'll take us about twenty minutes. Just stay there."

"Was that who I think it was?" Rand demanded when she'd hung up.

"It certainly was. We have to get dressed. Do you think we should call a doctor or a nurse or somebody?"

"Or somebody. I think you should call Valentine and let her pick Luana up. Simms might accuse you of kidnapping her. Christ only knows what that bastard will do."

Maggie shook her head. "Luana will think it's some kind of trick. I promised her I'd be there. I think she trusts me; otherwise she wouldn't have called."

"Maybe it was the ten thousand dollars," Rand said sourly.

"That was bait. It made her move, didn't it? It must have taken some of the fear out of her. I don't care about the money. I can't imagine what it must be like to be raped by your own father."

"Are we going by car or horseback?"

"Horseback. Luana can ride with me. I don't dare drive through the gate. Let them figure it out in the morning. Be quiet, though. Voices carry when it's quiet like this."

They saddled their horses silently and led them on foot for a good quarter of a mile. Then they mounted and raced off. Lotus whickered softly as her mistress urged her on.

Five minutes later, Maggie reined in her horse. "We have to cross the highway. Bill's station is about a quarter of a mile down the road," Maggie whispered softly. "Wait until there's no sign of a car and then go for it."

Luana gasped when Maggie called out to her from behind. "Over here, Luana. We're on horseback. Hurry. There're cars coming and we have to get on the other side of the highway."

They'd no sooner crossed the road and were in the

shadows than they saw two police cars race by, sirens blaring.

"I knew it. I knew it. Pa heard me sneak out. Don't send me back. God, Mrs. Tanner, don't send me back."

"No one is sending you anywhere. Hang on. You're going to find out what it's like to ride with the wind. I think we can make it back to the ranch before they get there." Maggie gave Lotus her head and the horse galloped off.

Soon they were walking back from the barn, keeping well in the shadows. The flashing lights could be seen from the driveway. "Shhh," said Maggie, laying a finger against her lips. "I told you voices carry."

Rand grimaced. Luana shivered against Maggie. They all listened.

"Any cars come or go out of here in the past two hours?"

There was a chorus of nos. "What's up?" a brash reporter shouted.

"The Simms girl split. Her father thinks the Colemans snatched her. You sure no one came or left here?"

"Would we be standing here if there was any action going on?" the same voice demanded.

"Back to the barn," Maggie ordered quietly. "We're going to have to sleep out here. The others will think we went out for a while and just aren't back yet. It's better if we don't have to lie to the police."

Rand unsaddled the horses while Maggie and Luana watched from one of the barn windows. The flashing red and blue lights lit up the entire driveway. A few minutes later, lights came on in Sunbridge. Then someone was at the back door; the porch light went on. Mam.

Fifteen minutes later the porch light went out. The police cars backed up, their blue and red lights twirling like batons.

"What we've just done is probably illegal," Maggie whispered to Rand. Luana was asleep in the straw, her cheek resting on her hands. Rand stared at her for a long time before answering.

"I suppose it is. As soon as the Social Service Office—
or whoever is in charge of things like this—opens, get on
the phone. I don't think it would hurt to . . . what is it you
Texans say?—call in a few favors. That judge Amelia was
talking to: call him again, too. And for God's sake, make
sure Valentine is here. The police will be back as soon as
it gets light." He cradled Maggie's head against his chest.
"Sleep, Maggie. I'll keep watch." He stroked her hair
gently and thought he could hear her purr. For one crazy
second he felt as though he were back in the RAF.

Rand shook Maggie gently. "It's going to be light in a
few minutes. Go back to the house. I'll stay here with
Luana. Send somebody out with some food when you
can."

Maggie dusted off the straw. "You're being a real brick.
Are you sorry you got tangled up with this crew and all
our problems?"

"No way. We're seeing daylight now. By this time
tomorrow things should be settled with the boys. Sawyer
is on the mend. This isn't exactly the time to say this,
but how would you like to honeymoon back in Hawaii?"

"I'd love it!" She kissed Rand soundly. "Now, keep
your eye on that little girl in case her feet turn cold." With
that, Maggie raced back to the house. She let herself in
quietly and watched as Martha eyed her up and down.

"I think I'll have breakfast now. Everything. Flapjacks,
eggs, ham, toast, and coffee. Make enough for three."

"Three?"

"Three," Maggie repeated.

Maggie ate and waited while Martha carried a steaming
tray to the barn. Shortly after seven the police arrived.
Maggie listened to Deputy Pierson's explanations. "You're
welcome to search the house, Deputy," she said cour-
teously, "but I must ask you to be quiet. Martha and I
are the only ones awake."

"Where were you last night, Mrs. Tanner?"

"At what time?"

"All evening. My men were here after midnight, and

your mother said you must have gone out. Your room was empty."

"Well, I was here till around eleven or so. Then I went riding. I do that when I can't sleep."

"Did you ride alone?"

"No, as a matter of fact, Rand Nelson was with me."

"Would you get him for me, or is he asleep, too?"

Maggie could feel her neck start to prickle. "As a matter of fact, he's in the barn rubbing down the horses. I'll call him for you."

Her heart fluttering, Maggie walked out to the back porch, onto the driveway, and cupped her hands to her mouth. "Rand . . . will you come here, please?" She almost fainted with relief when Rand walked out of the barn with a curry brush in his hand.

He sauntered over to Maggie as though he had all the time in the world. "What's wrong?"

Maggie motioned to the kitchen and said, "The police want to talk to you." They walked inside.

"Where were you last night, Mr. Nelson?" asked Deputy Pierson.

"With the others right here in the house till after eleven. Mrs. Tanner wanted to go riding, and I didn't think she should go alone, so I joined her. I was rubbing down the horses."

"Is Luana Simms here?"

"Look," Maggie interrupted, "I told you you could search the house if you wanted."

"No," Rand said coldly. "He only searches if he has a warrant."

"I can get one in an hour."

"Then get one. Maggie, I'd like some breakfast."

Martha was already whipping eggs in a bowl. She saw Deputy Pierson glance at the open dishwasher and the frying pans on the stove. "I always eat before the family," she said, eyeing him coldly.

Pierson knew he was being conned, but there wasn't anything he could do. "Enjoy your breakfast," he said coolly, and left.

"I thought he was going to click his heels there for a minute," Rand muttered.

"He's only doing his job," Maggie said. "I almost feel sorry for him." She looked out the window at the departing police car. "Where's Luana?"

"Don't worry about her. She's so petrified, she isn't moving a muscle. We had a long talk after you went into the house. She'll come through for you and the boys. She wanted to know what was going to happen to her. I told her you'd make sure she was well taken care of. So, as far as she's concerned, you're the white knight now, or is that knightess?"

"She's a minor. We snatched her," Maggie said fretfully.

"We didn't snatch her—we picked her up. She called us. There will be a record of that from the phone booth. Under the circumstances, her being a minor will work in your favor if she tells the truth. She shouldn't be allowed to stay with a father who abused her sexually."

"I'm frightened, Rand."

"So am I," Rand said, laying his cheek on Maggie's dark hair. "I have to get back to the barn before Luana gets itchy. Don't forget to make those calls."

Maggie looked at the clock: 7:50 A.M. She climbed the stairs and walked into Susan's room, shaking her awake gently. "Shhh, it isn't Jessie. I need your help." She explained what had happened. "Call Ferris. He must know someone in Social Services we can trust. Do it now, okay?"

Susan was already dialing when Maggie closed the door behind her. She walked on down the hall into the nursery, smiling as she bent over the crib. Jessie was sucking her thumb, her blanket clutched in her hand. "Nothing is ever going to hurt you, little one. Not while I'm around, anyway. Sleep," she crooned.

Next she stopped at Amelia's door and knocked softly. Cary opened it and stood aside. Amelia was slipping into a robe. Again Maggie explained the situation.

"Grandpap would say it's time to palaver a little. This family is owed a lot of favors, and it's time to call them in. Seth kept a book on who owed who; it's still in his desk. Will you do the honors?"

Amelia grinned. "Could you fortify me with some coffee while I'm doing it?"

"I'll get it for you, honey," Cary said. "You go down to the study and do what you do best. I love that word 'palaver'." He laughed. "What can I do?"

Maggie opened the door. "After you get her the coffee, stand around and listen to how the Colemans have survived all these years. You're going to need the experience if you plan to stay in Texas. Your wife is a pro."

Maggie tripped down the steps, her mind clicking. Maybe she was playing by different rules, Coleman rules, but two boys' futures were at stake. Fair was fair. Sometimes you had to pull out all the stops. Money couldn't buy happiness, but maybe it could buy truth. And that was all she wanted—the truth. They would all be seven-day wonders for a while, but they'd all survive.

"I think we're going to have guests for lunch, Martha. A buffet. I can help you or we can have it sent it. What do you think?"

"I think I can handle it. I have a lot in the freezer. About a ton of fried chicken." She laughed. "Those boys of yours can eat two at a time. I'll just pop it all in the oven, make a mess o' salads, and order some fresh cold cuts from Ferdie's. You do whatever you have to do, ma'am; I'll take care of this. And ma'am, I'm real happy about Miss Sawyer. I like her young man."

"Thank you, Martha. Yes, Adam is a fine young man. We all like him."

"This is all going to be all right, isn't it, ma'am?"

"I hope so, Martha. We've had our little family problems with the boys, but they don't deserve this; none of us do. The Simmses just marched into our lives and are trying to ruin us. Making a very good job of it, too."

Martha snorted. "And him pretending to be so virtuous, reading the Bible and all. Always preaching to the girl. She's not what we're used to around here. I knew

they were trouble the minute I saw them. You can preach—
if you practice what you preach."

Maggie backed out of the kitchen, hoping Martha had
finished her monologue. She was right, though. Loyal
Martha. If anyone knew the Colemans, she did.

At one o'clock Valentine Mitchell arrived, Dudley
Abramson shuffling alongside her. Maggie noticed with
amusement that he carried not only his own briefcase but
hers as well. Later that afternoon, Amelia personally welcomed the lieutenant governor and poured him a drink.
They chatted like old friends. The police chief shook Billie's hand and kissed her lightly on the cheek. Maggie
could hear them discuss Thad's indecision about running
for Congress. Susan introduced everyone to Rita Introne,
the head of Social Services, Juvenile Division. Maggie
watched out of the corner of her eye. As soon as Rita's
introductions were over and the small talk had trailed off,
Rita followed Susan to the kitchen. From there, Maggie
knew, they would go to the barn. Luana would be in good
hands.

Maggie remembered her promise to Adam and greeted
Steve Axelrod at the kitchen door. She showed him into
the study and offered to keep one of the private lines open
for his newspaper. Then she talked. Steve made squiggles
on his notepad. He listened. He wrote. He showed neither
approval nor disapproval.

"May I talk to the boys?" he asked. "I'd like to get
their views."

Maggie hesitated. "I'll ask them. It's their decision."
She summoned the boys and explained the situation.

"Okay," Cole said.

"Why not. Maybe it's time we got to say something,"
Riley said agreeably.

Steve leaned back in Seth's chair. He was so skinny,
he looked almost lost in it. Riley grinned. Cole smirked.
It would take one hell of a man to fill that chair, and he
said so to Steve.

"Hell, I'm just resting my butt. I've heard tales of Seth

Coleman all my life. You're right; there's no one around here who could fit that chair. Give me a break, huh, and let me sit here. You guys into baseball?"

"I am," Riley said shyly. "Cole here is an expert archer. He's also an expert marksman," he added generously.

"You trying to warm us up or something?" Cole asked suspiciously.

"Yeah, as a matter of fact, I am. I'm a good friend— and by good I mean grade school, high school, and college—of Adam Jarvis. Does that help?"

Cole grinned. "Shit, why didn't you say so?" He pulled up two chairs and both boys sat, each rotating his chair to straddle the seat.

"So talk. Tell me what it's like to see your life shot to hell. Tell me what you thought, what you felt. Tell me what it's like to be a Coleman with all this money. There's all kinds of people out there on your terrace that I only read about in the paper. Powerful people. They're here for you. Tell me about Luana Simms. Tell me what you know about Ben Simms. Tell me about your dreams, your ambitions. I want it all."

They gave it to him.

Steve hooked a gadget to the phone and played the tape to an associate on the other end of the line. He shook their hands. They weren't kids; they were young men. Colemans, true; but they were something else. The future. From the Texas panhandle to Yale and Notre Dame. East and West.

The Colemans gathered together at exactly two-thirty. Sid Jackson, the anchorman for the six-o'clock news, held out a microphone. Maggie stepped forward. She spoke haltingly at first, and then the words flowed. Out of the corner of her eye she could see both boys, Shadaharu Hasegawa behind them.

"Luana Simms called me last night and asked for my help. I brought her here. Rita Introne from Social Services is with her. They're coming now."

They were like a gaggle of geese, firing questions like machine-gun bullets. Cameras clicked and the news stations fought for clear shots. Luana licked her dry lips. She searched the crowd for Riley and Cole, then broke free from Rita's grasp and walked over to them.

Her conversation, because it was brief and no one expected it, was not overheard. "I couldn't spoil your chances to go to Yale and Notre Dame. I bet you thought I was so dumb, I didn't know they were the best Ivy League schools going. I'm sorry. Real sorry."

"Just tell the truth, Luana," Cole said softly. "Don't worry about us."

"You'll be okay. That lady with you, she'll make sure nothing happens to you," Riley whispered.

Cole thought the girl's back was a little straighter as she returned to Rita Introne. They listened as she told her story, trying to keep the horror from their faces. When it was all over and Luana was taken to the children's shelter, Riley bowed low to his grandfather. "I have regained our honor, have I not, Grandfather?" he asked anxiously.

"There is no one who walks this earth who could ever convince me otherwise. Come. I think we must eat some ... fried chicken." He made a slight grimace. "I wonder if it is as bad as Yankee bean soup."

Cole smiled. "Sir, my mother made something special for you. You won't have to eat fried chicken."

"My boy, you have just saved my life," the Japanese said heartily.

"Will you stay on, Grandfather, just for a little while? I must remember to return the money to you for the trip."

"I will go to New York and see Sawyer. I want to see with my own eyes this miracle that was performed. I have seen that you are fine. I came only to show support." Both boys beamed when he kissed them. "Come. I can't wait to see what Mrs. Tanner has prepared for me."

When the last car left the driveway, Cole and Riley stood alone, one dark, one fair. Neither could see the family watching them from the terrace. "We almost lost all of this," Cole said softly as he waved his arm about.

Riley reached into his back pocket and pulled out his baseball cap. He settled it carefully on his head. "Now it feels right." He bent down and reached inside the Berlinetta and pulled out a cap. He shoved it at Cole.

Cole looked at the yellow letters. Notre Dame. Son of a gun. He clapped it on his head. "It's not so bad being a Coleman."

"Not bad at all." Riley grinned.

States. In two world wars the British helped destroy German ambitions to become the dominant world power. But instead of Britain's power being preserved, that of the United States was established.

Many historians and strategists have commented on the ferocity with which the British contested German claims, but the tameness with which they conceded American. One of Britain's main war aims in 1914 had been to preserve its naval superiority against that of Germany and all other states. At the Disarmament Conference after the war Britain was warned by America that maintaining such superiority would no longer be tolerated. Britain conceded.[31]

Such episodes underline how supinely the British governing class reacted to the rise of the United States. The British position was surrendered without a fight. The Germans always found this hard to understand. Although there were circles in both Germany and England before 1914, and again in the 1930s, that worked for an Anglo-German understanding and an Anglo-German alliance, it never happened, although its real possibility, even in 1940, has tended to be obscured.[32] Many reasons can be advanced for this. They do not detract from the central point – that Britain chose to fight Germany, and to ally with the United States, and furthermore that Britain sought a total victory over Germany rather than an early negotiated peace in either war. As a result Britain was itself an agent in liquidating its own power and surrendering its world role to the Americans.

One of the decisive factors in this outcome was a fundamental loss of will in British ruling circles. The strategic dilemma at the beginning of the century was certainly acute. It was summed up in the assessment made by the Admiralty in 1902: Britain could not simultaneously fight a war against Germany and America. America, potentially, was a greater oceanic power than Britain and either had to be crushed or had to be made an ally. British dependence on the world economy for the very survival of its metropolitan base meant that there was no alternative but to ensure (as a minimum) American neutrality. Such neutrality depended, however, on making concessions to American interests. So long as the preservation of the capitalist world economy was considered Britain's pre-eminent interest, the Americans appeared both as a power that had to be appeased and a power that was more likely than any other to contribute to preserving it. Germany had quite different strategic aims. The rulers of Germany wanted to consolidate a land empire, securing control of a continental market by establishing a customs union pro-tected by a common tariff extending from the Baltic, through Austria and the Balkans, to the Middle East and Persia. This would ensure the dominance of Germany over France and give parity with England. At the same time Germany sought to expand in Africa and extend its colonial empire there.[33]

The Germans had less interest in the wider world economy than in securing exclusive markets. They used tariffs as a weapon in their commercial struggle with England, and so helped undermine the free flow of goods and capital on which British prosperity had been founded, and on which British survival depended. The tariff refor-mers greatly admired German organisation and their policy of industrial development in a unified continental market protected by high tariffs. Their failure to move British policy in that direction was closely linked to the failure to reach an understanding with Germany and the increasing recognition that it was necessary to ally with the United States. A protectionist Greater Britain Federation might conceivably have so reduced British dependence on the world economy, and so eased the constraints which that dependence imposed on British policy, as to prevent an armed clash with Germany. It would, however, have made eventual war with the United States much more likely as American capital sought to break into these protected spheres. The significance of the defeat of tariff reform was not just that Britain did not abandon free trade, but that out of its two main industrial rivals and challengers, Britain fought Germany rather than America.

Not that the tariff reformers were reluctant to fight

Germany. On the contrary, they were among the foremost prosecutors of the war – one of their most prominent adherents, Lord Milner, was a leading member of Lloyd George's War Cabinet. But one of the results was that the tariff reformers themselves came to realise the extent of Britain's strategic weakness and America's growing power.

This produced two different reactions. One wing of the tariff reformers continued to fight tenaciously for an independent British imperial strategy. The other concluded that Britain could neither organise its own wider federation nor match American power and resources, so the best course was to seek an Anglo-American alliance in which America would gradually take over the British role of dominant power in the world economy. This current was to merge with that sector of liberal opinion which was forced to accept in the 1920s and 1930s that Britain could not maintain the international monetary system alone, that sterling was no longer strong enough to be the leading world currency, and that American co-operation was indispensable if an open capitalist world economy was to survive.

Decisive strategic choices were thus made in the first two decades of this century affecting the future development of the British state. The result of the two wars disrupted a pattern that went back centuries. British weakness was exposed and the total British reliance on sea power suddenly became outmoded. Just as air power changed the strategic balance, so the failure to consolidate the British Empire as a world state brought the end of British world power. It was still not certain in 1918 but there was no question by 1945. Sea power, industrial power, financial power, passed decisively and irrevocably to the United States. Henceforward the British Empire, the pound sterling, and the very survival of Britain, depended on American sufferance. The tariff reformers had enjoyed a belated triumph in the 1930s when the world economy fragmented into currency and trading blocs following the Great Depression. But the opportunity was already gone of turning the Empire from a strategic and economic burden into a source of British strength. The British state now began to acquire a very different relationship to the world economy it had once dominated and done so much to develop.

The military underpinning of the British state's traditional commercial policy had been sea power. Sea power had permitted the commercial alliances, the trade wars, the seizure of territory, the protection of shipping, the flow of slaves, settlers, plunder, and commodities which made Britain the greatest commercial nation in the world by 1815, enjoying control over more colonies than any other state. But even at the moment that this policy was being so triumphantly successful it was giving way to a new set of commercial opportunities, which relied much less on British naval power and protection and much more on the lead established by British industry. A new informal empire began to grow up alongside the formal one, an empire which prospered and grew through free trade and a more specialised division of labour. By exploiting commercial advantages to the full, Britain abandoned first self-sufficiency, and then protection, for the unprecedented wealth created by modern industry. As Alexis de Tocqueville wrote of Manchester in the 1840s:

> From this foul drain the greatest stream of human industry flows out to fertilise the whole world. From this filthy sewer pure gold flows. Here humanity attains its most complete development and its most brutish; here civilisation works its miracles, and civilised man is turned back almost into a savage.[34]

The spread of industry in the world economy created new commercial and military rivals by the 1880s, and made formal empire valuable once more as security against the designs of the rising powers. But in the struggle that opened between rival imperialisms it became clear that much of the British Empire was a burden rather than an asset. To become effective it needed to be organised and co-ordinated in the manner of the great land empires of the United States, Germany, and Russia. The British state became caught between two strategies – securing its future by attempting to transform its loose and far-flung empire into a disciplined protectionist bloc in the world market, the equal of both Germany and the United States; and accepting the wider responsibilities for maintaining a liberal world economy that the success of commercial expansion and the adoption of free trade had imposed on Britain. What slowly became clear was that Britain was losing the strength and the capacity to fulfil these responsibilities. But the dependence on the continued existence of this liberal world economy did not diminish.

3

The unfinished revolution

In the course of the nineteenth century England adopted peacefully and without violent shocks almost all the basic civil and political reforms that France paid so heavily to achieve through the great Revolution. Undeniably, the great advantage of England lay in the greater energy, the greater practical wisdom, the better political training, that her ruling class possessed down to the very end of the past century.

Gaetano Mosca[1]

Sitting at your ease on the corpse of Ireland . . . be good enough to tell us: did your revolution of interests not cost more blood than our revolution of ideas?

Jules Michelet

The success of the policy of expansion was greatly aided by the organisation of a centralised and efficient public power controlling the whole of the land area of the British Isles. But it was. also made possible by the English revolution in the seventeenth century, which cut short the development of royal absolutism in England and converted the centralised bureaucratic military and legal apparatus, which the English kings had created, into an instrument for the security and progress of the civil society which developed alongside it. The interrelation between successful overseas expansion, the creation of a strong centralised multinational state in the British Isles, and the subordination of the state power to the interests and needs of a dynamic and assertive civil society, are the necessary historical ground for exploring the next major problem that arises from a study of Britain's hundred years' decline: why has Britain alone amongst major states experienced such an exceptional degree of institutional continuity, such a gradual evolution in its political arrangements?

3.1 The state and civil society

The British state has not suffered a major break in the pattern of its development since the civil war in the seventeenth century, which ended in the execution of the King and the establishment of a republican government. Changes there certainly have been. The basis of representation has several times been widened to embrace new social groups and interests; the major institutions of the state have frequently been remodelled and the pattern of recruitment to them altered. But all this has been done within the same constitutional framework. The central role of Parliament and its executive, and the supporting role of the Crown, have been preserved throughout.

All this has occurred during three centuries in which Britain has experienced not calm and stability, but profound social, economic and cultural change, the crossing of the watershed from an agricultural to an industrial society, the rise of an urban civilisation. Such changes elsewhere have been accompanied by major political upheavals and social revolutions. Political continuity has generally been the first thing to snap. Industrialisation has been accompanied by revolutions, counter revolutions, civil wars, military coups, new republics, new empires – the form of political regimes has been regularly shifting. When compared with the political history of France or Germany, Italy or Spain, China or Japan, the degree to which continuity has been preserved in Britain is remarkable. The early organisation of a strong state commanding the whole territory of the British Isles, and the consequent ability to resist foreign invasion and occupation, go a long way to explain it. External military defeats have so often accelerated internal revolution. Nevertheless, by itself the external success of the British state would not have been sufficient to preserve it from internal overthrow, had it not been for the relationship that was early established between the state and civil society.

This relationship was the lasting result of the English civil war, the Great Rebellion as it was known to contemporaries. It was fought between two sections of the landed gentry with varying degrees of popular support enlisted on each side. The major issues were what powers and prerogatives the King could rightfully claim, particularly in relation to taxation, the liberties of the subject, the toleration of religious belief, and the organisation of the church. Protestantism with its radical, individualist doctrines was a major driving force in enlisting support for the Parliament and against the King. There was no direct conflict of economic interests, although the forces ranged against royal power, and most anxious to repudiate royal authority, were strongest in the commercial centres and the more prosperous and advanced agricultural regions. The King's strongholds lay in the more backward North and West.[2]

The war was won by the New Model Army which Cromwell and Ireton created, but the demands which then ensued for much more radical social and political change were resisted and eventually contained. The programmes of Levellers, Diggers, and militant puritans were all defeated. This prepared the way for the Restoration of the monarchy after Cromwell's death, a move that by then commanded the support of the great majority of the landowners. The dispossessed royalists received back their lands, the Anglican state church was re-established, and Parliament reverted to its former composition. Little seemed to have changed. Cromwell's Commonwealth appeared a brief interlude, a short suspension of traditional political arrangements.

Nevertheless a fundamental breach had occurred; the British state had been set on a new course. The importance of the civil war was not so much in what it achieved as in what it prevented. It reduced royal power permanently. Charles II chafed under restrictions that never troubled his cousin, Louis XIV, and although he managed to regain some of the initiative, his brother James was swiftly deposed when he appeared to threaten one of the crucial aspects of the Restoration settlement – that England should remain a Protestant country.

James II's deposition in 1688 was proclaimed the Glorious Revolution, and though long regarded as more important than the Great Rebellion forty years before, in fact consolidated the gains of that period by demonstrating that the balance between King and Parliament had permanently shifted. The direction of the state and the centre of its authority had passed to Parliament. For the first time a state had been created whose policies and activities were shaped in response to the needs and movement of civil society. The state of the Tudor and Stuart Kings had been strong enough and legitimate enough to maintain social order, enforce its laws, protect property and guarantee a medium of exchange, and under it considerable progress was made towards the creation of a national market, as well as the establishment of a growing commerce in simple manufactures and primary products. This emerging network of economic relations was decisively strengthened by the political upheavals of the seventeenth century, for from that time onward it became inconceivable that the central public power would be used against the system of free exchange, against the vital interests of the civil society. On the contrary, its task became the active removal of obstacles to the widening of the sphere of exchange and the accumulation of wealth, both internally and abroad.

The idea that state policy should be governed by the private interests individuals acquired as members of civil society was a novel one, but it became the essence of the English way. What it specifically ruled out was the attempt made by many of the absolutist regimes in Europe in the eighteenth century to reimpose or reinforce the system of legal privileges for different estates of the realm as the basis of their authority. The legal codes they promulgated attempted to freeze these patterns of social relationships in

their societies by ensuring a permanently privileged position for the aristocracy and for landed property. Such codes
helped multiply the obstacles to the development of an
independent civil society and an economic system based on
equality, mobility and free exchange.

In England the position was different and increasingly
came to be recognised as different during the eighteenth
century when England first received wide acknowledgement
as the 'land of liberty'. From the seventeeth century
onwards the principle and the idea of legal equality, so
essential to a market economy, was gaining ground.
England remained laden with social privileges, yet these
were not in general buttressed by legal privileges and
English civil society, for all its inequalities of wealth and
property and for all its accumulation of ranks and titles, was
more flexible and open to change, and its property-owning
class more unified than any other society in Europe.[3]

A civil society emerged in England whose property
owners were generally more concerned with enlarging their
wealth than with preserving their status, and with preserving their liberties than with increasing the power of the
state. All wealth, however diverse its forms, came to be
viewed as having a common origin in human labour, whilst
the source of its expansion was found to lie in the widening
of exchange. For Adam Smith, in a society conducted on
correct economic principles 'every man . . . lives by
exchanging or becomes in some measure a merchant, and
the society itself grows to be what is properly a commercial
society'.[4] The importance the English attached to trade and
exchange became notorious. England became widely
regarded as a new Carthage, a great commercial power,
preying parasitically on the great land empires of the
continent. 'A nation of shopkeepers', Napolean scornfully
remarked, whilst the German economist Friedrich List
fulminated against the English assumption that the world
was an 'indivisible republic of merchants'. The English
appetite for commercial opportunities, buying cheap and
selling dear, and the evident aim of their state to promote
the commercial interests of its subjects were widely noted.
Yet despite the expansion overseas and the beginnings of

industry at home in the eighteenth century, the property-owning class in England particularly that section with most influence over the state, belonged overwhelmingly to the landed interest. What made the difference between the landed aristocracy in Britain, and the landed aristocracy in many other states, was that in Britain the rapidly developing network of exchange in British civil society, and the growing hold of British interests over the world economy, provided a range of opportunities for property owners to consolidate and extend their wealth in agriculture, in trade, in colonies; and by the end of the eighteenth century another avenue for the creation and appropriation of wealth was emerging – industry.

The most important long-term result of the English civil war was the clear separation between the state and an independent sphere of private interests and private exchange, and the subordination of the former to the latter. This independence and importance of a realm of private individuals was proclaimed by numerous political writers, and became expressed in practical terms by doctrines of political and civil liberties, which defined the rights of all individuals, not just property owners, against the arbitrary exercise of state power. It was not just freedom of economic interests but freedom of private interests, including a degree of freedom of religious belief and worship.

English liberties and freedom from arbitrary government were sufficiently unusual to attract considerable attention, and became the basis for the Whig interpretation of history.[5] This laid great emphasis upon the uniqueness of English history, which becomes the unfolding of liberty, the story of liberties once held, then lost, then gradually regained. It is a history of progress and enlightenment, of the genius of the island race. The liberties once enjoyed by the Anglo-Saxons were taken away after the Norman Conquest, which brought a time of suffering only relieved by victories such as Magna Carta, the first step in challenging royal power and reasserting traditional liberties and throwing off the Norman yoke. The growing resistance of the people to tyranny and absolute power eventually erupted during the civil war, which only succeeded however in replacing one tyranny with another. It required the settlement of 1688 to inaugurate the new age of English liberty. It created a constitution which balanced the powers of the monarchy (the Crown), the titled aristocracy (the Lords), and the landed gentry (the Commons), so safeguarding many vital rights and providing important checks to arbitrary government. It provided the stable framework within which progress was possible. New interests could be accommodated, new social forces represented, new rights recognised. The forum for the balancing and harmonising of interests was the British Parliament, whose legitimacy was paramount and whose independence was unquestioned. Broadening the basis of representation, acknowledging and creating the rights of citizens to equal opportunities and certain standards of provision, all could proceed within the framework established in 1688.

Like all interpretations of history the Whig interpretation contains much myth. But it remains the most potent of all the interpretations of Britain's internal political evolution. What was real was the sphere of liberty that did emerge during the eighteenth century.[6] The idea that every Englishman was 'born free', and enjoyed certain inherited liberties as rights, was important. It meant widespread suspicion of government power and constant pressures to limit it. It encouraged the principles that the power to levy taxes should reside in the hands of Parliament, not the Crown or the executive, that the standing army should be as small as possible, that the judiciary should be independent of the government. The English claimed the right to revolt against tyranny, the right to freedom from arbitrary arrest and arbitrary search, the principle of equality before the law and the right to trial by jury. When to these were added a limited degree of freedom of publication, speech, and conscience, and a much wider freedom to travel and to trade, there was a body of rights which, although often abused and infringed, provided a distinct sphere of legal equality, the basis of a bourgeois order.

These rights were justified as the traditional liberties once enjoyed by Englishmen, rather than asserted as the natural and inherent rights of man. But they were no less real for that.

3.2 The English governing class

What emerged from the civil war and the consolidation of its gains in the eighteenth century was a relationship between state and economy which influenced the whole subsequent history of industrialisation. The extent of legal equality and personal liberty that were established tended to unify the different sections of property owners by making all forms of property commensurable. An aristocracy of wealth was more evident in Britain than in any other country in Europe. This made the constant widening of the ruling social bloc much easier to accomplish. Social privileges and distinctions were numerous, but they did not create insuperable obstacles to the assimilation of new groups. Most important of all was the accommodation reached in the 1830s and 1840s between the representatives of landed property and the representatives of industry.[7]

The ease with which new interests were accommodated, new groups absorbed, and the continuity and ethos of British institutions preserved, was in marked contrast to the often bitter struggles and political upheavals that accompanied similar changes in other states. The evident skill and flexibility of the British governing class was much admired. Joseph Schumpeter spoke of:

> the unrivalled integrity of the English politician and the presence of a ruling class that is uniquely able and civilised make many things easy that would be impossible elsewhere. In particular this ruling group unites in the most workable proportions adherence to formal tradition with extreme adaptability to new principles, situations and persons. It wants to rule but it is quite ready to rule on behalf of changing interests. It manages industrial England as well as it managed agrarian England, protectionist England as well as free trade England. And it possesses an altogether unrivalled talent for appropriating not only the programmes of oppositions but also their brains.[8]

This skill and adaptability was not very evident in the seventeenth century, nor has it been in the years since 1945. If the British governing class and its politicians were really so able, why has the halting of Britain's economic decline proved so difficult? Why did its capacity begin to fail so visibly and so dramatically, so that even the central institutional symbol of legitimacy, Parliament itself, came under increasing attack?

One answer lies in the dominant pattern of relationships between the state and the economy, which have been modified but never fundamentally altered.[9] The early development of a market order, and the redefining of public interest to mean the safeguarding of private interests and the liberation of private energies, all meant that the efforts of the agencies of the British state were concentrated to a high degree on enlarging commercial opportunities for its citizens. This strategy proved successful, not because of any innate qualities enjoyed by the English aristocracy, but because it aided colonial expansion abroad, and first agrarian and then industrial expansion at home. The wealth and power which the policy brought to Britain was so enormous that a policy of conceding to the demands of new interests and then absorbing them was not too painful. The Whig perspective triumphed. If the object of the state was to preserve liberty and promote the conditions in which civil society would flourish, then the private realm had to be respected and its major interests, whatever they were, had to be recognised as the legitimate interest of the state.

Every particular concession was the occasion for sharp conflicts within the ruling groups, and those advocating flexibility did not always win immediately. The sphere of private liberties was exceedingly frail and always in danger of being encroached upon. The corruption of the eighteenth-century state was notorious. Yet the growing strength of a bourgeois civil society, a market order based upon the legal equality of all who participated in it, ensured that the state, despite its deformations, continued to respond to the movements and interests and pressures of civil society rather than seeking to lead it or dominate it.

The relations between state and economy in Britain were shaped by this pattern. Manufacturing, like overseas trade and agriculture production for the market before it, was seen primarily as another branch of commercial opportunity, another avenue to the creation of wealth and the enlargement of fortunes. The aristocracy were active in promoting it from the start. There was no fundamental issue of principle at stake. There were conflicts, but they were far from being irreconcilable.[10] The interests and the new classes that industrial capitalism created, and the wholesale transformation of British society that it necessitated, were accommodated within the existing state system. The price of admitting the industrialists into the groups that ruled England was reform of all the major state institutions, and acceptance (in 1832) of the principle of Members of Parliament representing individual voters rather than corporate interests. But although the state became more efficient and less corrupt in the course of the nineteenth century, as a result of the indefatigable efforts of utilitarian reformers and the pressure of a bourgeois public opinion and a bourgeois electorate, the guiding principle of its actions and its interventions remained the preservation and safeguarding of the system of free exchange. The success of this state depended on the continuing dynamism and expansion of the civil society which it served. It proved much less capable of intervening successfully to remedy some of the deficiencies of that civil society, which began to appear once other nations began to industrialise and to compete with Britain. The permissive orientation of the state to the market order, the tradition of suspicion towards the government and its initiatives, have constantly hampered the development of an interventionist state in the past hundred years. They have not prevented it from arising, but they have prevented it from being as successful as its protagonists hoped.

The greatest success and the greatest failure of all has been the attempt to incorporate the working class. The owners and agents of industrial capital themselves posed few problems.[11] They accepted the aristocratic panoply of the landowners' state with its titles and traditional flummery. They abandoned dreams of a republic and an egalitarian social order; they sent their sons to be educated in the new public schools which sprang up to provide an education for gentlemen and a training for service in the empire and the state;[12] they accepted the dense and secretive web of the British governing class and its internal rituals, whilst pressing successfully for the reform of its more obvious abuses, such as the sale of army commissions. But this accommodation within the ranks of property, which was worked out in the course of the nineteenth century and which was to give the British governing class so formidable and so impenetrable an appearance, and give the culture and outlook of the upper middle class such coherence and strength, had its costs. The most important was that the other great class which industrial capitalism had created was never fully incorporated as a constituent part of British society. The working class in Britain has always remained to some extent outside – in it but not of it.

3.3   The resistance of the working class

The success of the traditional governing class in avoiding overthrow during the period of industrialisation, either by a radical industrial bourgeoisie or by a revolutionary working class, permanently shaped civil society and state in Britain. The degree of social conservatism amongst all classes, the tenacity of antiquated institutions, the secrecy surrounding central processes in government and the major institutions of civil society, the enduring liberal perception of the state's role in the market order – all these are easily recognised features of twentieth-century Britain, and they stem directly from the exceptional continuity which British institutions have enjoyed.[13]

The most important legacy of all which the bourgeois order of Britain's ascendancy bequeathed to a Britain in decline was the problem of the working class. From the outset it was a class of which much was expected and much feared, a class which came relatively early to occupy an important position in British society and which developed a unified and expanding trade-union movement and only one major political party. Yet despite all its advantages and all its social and political weight, it seemed to lose its early radicalism and be progressively incorporated within the British state as one more element of its constitution.

The result is often hailed as a triumph of Whig politics. If the bourgeois order could absorb and integrate a class as powerful and as alien as this, then it must be invulnerable. But as with the much simpler integration of the owners of the new industries themselves, the relatively smooth integration of the working class was only achieved at the cost of an accumulation of institutional and social weaknesses. In the hundred years' decline, weaknesses stemming from the international orientation of British policy and the external dependence of the economy have reinforced weaknesses stemming from the obstacles to more rapid capitalist rationalisation and reorganisation. These were sustained most obviously by the liberal bias of the state, the social conservatism and inertia of so many British institutions, and the organised political and industrial resistance of the Labour movement.

Industrialisation began in England in the eighteenth century. The overseas explorations and conquests had brought into the country significant hoards of capital, available for any profitable investment;[14] more important, they had permitted the organisation of wide markets and trading networks which could supply raw materials like cotton to the new industries. In the domestic economy, agricultural production for the market was flourishing, and the population was abundant and beginning to expand. The enclosing of the common land did not force an exodus of labour from the land, but it did mean that in many areas the choice of employment came to be between wage labour on the land or wage labour in the new industries. The scope for economic independence, whether as smallholder or artisan, steadily narrowed as capital accumulation got under way. A class of labourers began to be created who were free to sell their labour power on the market, but were also free from ownership of means of production that alone could ensure their independence.

From its beginnings the process of industrialisation was marked by repeated conflict between the owners of capital and the owners of labour power. Its history reveals little of the continuity, the harmony, and the gradualism so often paraded as the moving spirit of British development. Industries have risen and declined, traditional skills and whole communities have been displaced, culture and patterns of living have been radically transformed, and the economy has developed in spurts punctuated by major crises, heavy unemployment and widespread distress. The working class were both agents and victims of this most productive and destructive of all economic systems, and around their experiences of it resistance began to organise and to grow.

The struggle against capital centred on the process of production itself: the determination of the length of the working day and the intensity of work during it; and the conditions under which new machines were introduced to raise productivity.[15] The state which had emerged from the upheavals of the seventeenth century was concerned with the sanctity of contracts and the security of property. This meant the placing of its armed power at the disposal of the industrialists in any conflict with their workers. The early class struggles often took the form of machine breaking and riots.[16] So frequently did such conflicts occur, and on so large a scale, that the state gradually had to become involved in regulating not just the system of market exchange and the circulation of money, but also the production process itself. Governments were forced to acknowledge by their interventions that however free, equal, and unforced the contract between employer and worker might be, the antagonism between labour and capital in the production process made necessary external regulation of hours and conditions of work in the factories if social disorder and industrial conflict were to be kept within tolerable bounds. The early factory legislation and the Ten Hours Bill of 1847 were major working-class victories, which forced the public power to take note of the new interests and demands of the industrial proletariat.[17]

Working-class resistance to the conditions of work and the new labour discipline of the factories challenged the freedom of capital and its agents to control the labour process, and was broadened into a general attack on the existing basis of the state. Political agitation to extend civil and political rights to workers, particularly the right to form trade unions and the right to vote, grew rapidly. The struggle for socialism and the struggle for democracy were closely intertwined, not least in the minds of many of the representatives of the new bloc of property interests, who viewed with horror the rise of political movements like Chartism in the 1840s[18] and the growing numbers of the industrial proletariat in the vast new urban centres. If full citizenship rights were extended to the whole nation, the passing of power from the propertied to the propertyless, and an open attack upon property, seemed inevitable. How could democratic governments avoid plundering the rich and redistributing wealth? If state power remained securely in the hands of representatives of property, then challenges to the rights of property could be suppressed, as they had been so forcibly during the wars against revolutionary France. If, however, the franchise were to be broadened and an attempt made to give the working class full citizenship, what guarantee was there that the state power would any longer be used for the defence of property? Karl Marx expressed the fears of many in the British ruling class when he wrote:

Universal suffrage is the equivalent of political power for the working classes of England, where the proletariat forms the large majority of the population, where, in a long, though underground civil war, it has gained a clear consciousness of itself as a class, and where even the rural districts know no longer any peasants, but only landlords, industrial capitalists [farmers] and hired labourers. The carrying of Universal Suffrage in England would, therefore, be a far more socialistic measure than anything which has been honoured with that name on the Continent. Its inevitable result here is the political supremacy of the working class.[19]

3.4 The response to the working class

The franchise was widened during the nineteenth century, if only slowly. In 1832 the grosser abuses of the old system were removed by the Reform Bill, and the basis of parliamentary representation broadened to include all the property-owning classes.[20] This reform was bitterly resisted by a section of the landowners and it almost precipitated revolution; its passing allowed the institutional order to survive but it also meant that further extensions were ultimately necessary. The state was already deeply involved as a constituent element of the market order by maintaining a framework of law in which free and equal individuals could make exchanges and pursue their interests. The equal rights under the law guaranteed by every bourgeois legal order were always in sharp contrast to the actual social and economic inequalities that resulted from market exchange. Maintaining the legitimacy of the market order has always been difficult, since the equal legal status of all individuals implies that all should have an equal voice in determining the national interest, yet the inequality of their social condition implies that the majority may vote for measures which will infringe the principles of the market order on which the security of a private realm depends.

The problem was particularly acute in England because of the great numbers and the urban concentration of its proletariat.[21] All capitalist states have had eventually to face the tension between the economic liberty of the capitalist market order and the popular sovereignty of the democratic political order, but none faced it so early as Britain, for nowhere else was the working class so quickly in a majority. No class of peasants, no smallholders, no backward regions existed in Britain to provide the social basis for a democracy organised against the interest of the working class. The franchise was extended in 1867 and again in 1885 when male manual workers first constituted a majority of the electorate. Full universal suffrage came in 1928.[22] The preponderance of the working class in the electorate has since that time been overwhelming; the urban character of Britain has become more, not less marked, and several generations have now experienced working-class life in an urban industrial society.[23]

From the standpoint of industrial capital there were two main ways in which working-class demands for greater control over the production process, and greater participation in the state, might have been met. The power and strength of the workers' movement could have been harnessed in an alliance to fight for a fundamental reconstruction of the state and the civil society aimed at the abolition of social privilege and exclusiveness and the inauguration of a genuine democratic republic of equal citizens, a more egalitarian bourgeois order, a more energetic and mobile civil society. The six points of the Charter were a programme for such a democratic republic.[24] It called for universal male suffrage, equal electoral districts, annual parliaments, the payment of members, a secret ballot and no property qualifications for MPs. These demands could not have been met in the 1840s when they were made, except by breaking the still powerful hold of the landed interest on the state and on civil society, and unleasing a much wider process of social change.

The danger of such an alliance lay in the radicalisation inherent in any revolutionary upheaval, with consequences witnessed in France after 1789 and 1848. So long as those sections of the bourgeoisie still outside the British governing class were not forced into revolution, it was almost certain that it would prefer a different path, the path of accommodation with landed property and its political arm, gradual reform of the state to make it more effective in protecting the market order and aiding capital accumulation within it, and gradual concessions to working-class demands. A radical break in British institutions might have placed property itself at risk. As it was, once the landed interest had divided and given way first in 1832 and then in 1846, the industrialists and the bourgeois radicals found they could achieve all they wanted.

What they gave up, apart from a democratic republic free of the aristocratic ethos and rituals which continued to shroud most national institutions, was the chance to forestall the working class organising itself industrially and politically as a class. Only the creation of a new order in which all individual workers could participate as full members – free sellers of labour power, sovereign consumers, and potential capitalists – might have prevented the independent political organisation of the working class as a class conscious of its common interests against capital. Liberalism offered instead the opportunity to rise as compensation for the inequalities of the market. As Napoleon put it, 'Every French soldier carries in his cartridge-pouch the baton of a Marshal of France.'

The bourgeois radicals did not believe in the existence of a working *class*; a market order contained only individuals – individuals who worked, individuals who consumed, individuals who competed equally under a common framework of rules, which provided benefits for everyone, though in differing proportions. The bourgeois radicals correctly recognised that their ideal of a classless individualist market order required resistance to trade unions and all associations that sought to interfere with the workings of the free market, and resistance also to any state interventions in relations between individual workers and individual employers. No one has expressed such ideas better than Richard Cobden:

> I yield to no man in the world (be he ever so stout an advocate of the Ten Hours' Bill) in a hearty goodwill towards the great body of the working class; but my sympathy is not of the morbid kind which would lead me to despond over their future prospects. Nor do I partake of the spurious humanity which would indulge in an unreasonable kind of philanthropy at the expense of the great bulk of the community. Mine is that masculine species of charity which would lead me to instil in the minds of the labouring classes the love of independence, the privilege of self-respect, the disdain of being patronised or petted, the desire to accumulate and the ambition to rise.[25]

The second strategy for dealing with the problem of the working class, which gradually became dominant, also sought on occasion to attempt to stifle the class as a class. But it did not in general seek to do so by trying to win the consent of workers to the rule of capital through their participation as individual citizens and producers in an expanding bourgeois order, although this element was never absent. Instead, occasional repression was combined with a gradual recognition of the right of the working class to exist as a class and to organise as a class. The working class came to be treated as an estate of the realm, a privileged caste, a corporate body which required exceptional privileges and dispensations. Working-class demands and pressures were met by making concessions which eased the pressures, at the same time disturbing as little as possible the overarching order of the British state. The effect of this strategy was to preserve the social privileges, the wealth and the aristocratic culture of the upper classes, while greatly increasing the corporate power of the working class and blunting any tendency for it to develop in the direction of revolution.[26] A place was found for it in the British state.

Every specific concession, whether over political rights, or trade-union rights, or social rights, still had to be fought for by the working class and often created sharp divisions in the British ruling class. There was never a single coherent strategy for handling the Labour movement. Nevertheless, out of the balance of forces in the British state and its priorities arose a pattern of response to Labour and its demands which helped establish the Labour movement as a powerful and privileged estate by 1914, a world of Labour with its own culture, its own organisations, its own ideology and preoccupations.

So although the rise of Labour was bitterly resisted, ways were gradually found of accommodating this unwelcome class. The development of British capitalism was as a result significantly unlike either the United States or Germany. Britain lacked the egalitarian, open, and mobile bourgeois society of the United States, where the 'desire to accumulate' and the 'ambition to rise' did not encounter so many social obstacles. But it also lacked the nationalist drive to political modernisation, the building of national strength and national organisation, which in Germany established a very close partnership between government and business. Britain failed to move strongly in either direction and it was this failure which was a prime cause of the relative economic decline.

It follows that it was not Britain's early start that was the cause of the failure to keep up with later competitors, but the very social relations that made that early start possible, and which remained intact and strengthened by the success of that start. British dominance and British industrialisation belonged to an earlier phase in the development of the world economy. The domination of that world economy by industrial capitalism and the new assertive nation-states it helped create only started to come about in the 1870s and 1880s with the beginnings of industrialisation in Germany and the United States. From the standpoint of world economy, what went before was a preliminary – the creation of the conditions for 'full capitalism', for capital accumulation on a world scale.

Such a view is reinforced when the character of industrialisation in Britain is examined. The superiority of British industry over all competitors in the first half of the nineteenth century, and the huge wealth it created for the propertied classes, was due less to an overwhelming lead in technology, or to the mechanisation of the production process, but rather to a fuller development of production for the market in all spheres. Even the most mechanised sectors of British industry in the middle of the nineteenth century still relied upon a vast array of manual skills and sweated labour. Labour power was in abundant supply and most production methods remained highly labour-intensive and often highly skilled.[27] Capital accumulation was able to proceed at such a rapid pace because a vast labour force was available to be drawn into employment when demand was booming, and expelled when it slackened. The existence on one side of a large surplus population which could find no employment or tenure on the land, and the possibility of feeding such a population by imports of cheap food through the established network of trade and colonies, created the particular character of Victorian capitalism – an unparalleled accumulation of capital and an enormous industrial proletariat.

Britain's subsequent failure to maintain its lead reflected the slowness with which British ruling opinion grasped that industrialisation as it unfolded had created new conditions for successful accumulation, in particular the continual raising of productivity not by individual skill, or by numbers, but through the constant revolutionising of techniques and the reorganisation of production. In Britain, the security of Empire, and the stability of its domestic institutions, prevented changes occurring rapidly enough, which alone could have met the long-term peril. The response to competition that did occur – the retreat into trade and finance, the preference for traditional methods and traditional technologies – has been well documented.[28] The very success of the market order in Britain, and its extension overseas, geared commerce and industry and government to the maximisation of short-term profits, the exploitation of every existing opportunity to the full. The more difficult task, the planning for future growth and the anticipation of the long-term needs of capital accumulation, was provided for neither by British civil society, whose social conservatism continued to grow in line with its wealth, nor by the British state, which remained wedded to the liberal conception of its role in the national economy.

3.5 Mass democracy and the imperial state

The 1880s are a decisive watershed in the development of a world capitalist economy, not only as the period which saw industrialisation accelerating in several major states, but also because, as the scale of capital accumulation grew, so the conditions for maintaining it became increasingly onerous and the resistance to it more organised. The interventionist role of every national state expanded to promote the conditions, both in production and circulation, that would sustain accumulation and offset the tendency for profitability to decline; and also to meet and incorporate all those political pressures from nation-states, from the working class, and from oppressed national groups, which threatened the survival of the state and the viability of national capital. The result was a considerable expansion of both the administrative and the military agencies of the state and their links with the leading business sectors; at the same time the basis of representation was broadened, and national assemblies and parliaments gradually became institutions not for the direct representation of property interests, but for the conferring of national legitimacy upon the executive which now presided over the enlarged and expanding permanent apparatus of the state. This was accompanied by rising public expenditure and a broadening of the tax base until it embraced the whole community.[29]

Such developments were common to all the major states, although the exact pace of development and the eventual balance established varied according to local circumstances. Every major capitalist state saw a steady expansion of military and police expenditures and of welfare expenditures, as well as more overt intervention at many levels of the economy. In Britain the political system, through which the new pressures and problems of mass democracy were channelled, still centred upon Parliament. This had been reformed but very gradually. The franchise had been widened, and after 1885 the manual working class for the first time was in a majority. The ballot had also become secret. But the procedures of Parliament, the hereditary basis of the House of Lords, and the bizarre and arbitrary electoral system with its random relationship between votes cast and seats won, still remained.[30]

The rise and containment of the Labour movement has dominated the hundred years of British mass democracy. That this has coincided with the hundred years of British decline is not thought coincidental by many on the Right. Yet it is parties of the Right which have dominated British government since the advent of mass democracy, particularly before 1945. Whilst the Right emphasises the *rise* of Labour and the spread of collectivism throughout British society, the Left laments the containment of Labour and the blunting of its socialist purpose.

The parties that initially contested the space which mass

democracy created, the Liberals and Conservatives, were both developed out of the fairly loose factional groupings and personal cliques that dominated the unreformed Parliament. As the franchise was extended, so the party leaders began to perceive new realities that faced them, and the urgent need to create a party organisation outside Parliament if they were to compete effectively. The Liberals led the way, the Conservatives followed.[31] What each leadership also came to recognise was that the effect of mass democracy, and the expansion of the state administrative and military machine to cope with the new responsibilities and range of interventions that were required, brought a sharp separation between the roles politicians traditionally had to perform – organising support and exercising power. The task of managing the new electorate, the mass parties, and the party in parliament, became tasks which were related to, but by no means identical with, the tasks of directing the government and presiding over the permanent agencies of the state. Each group of party leaders became involved in an elaborate balancing act, because the open debate on policies, ideologies and values which took place in the political arena produced a conception of national interest which then had to be reconciled with the national interest as it was perceived by its more permanent guardians, those who staffed the agencies of the state.

The party debate conferred legitimacy on the executive through the idea that the party winning the election could employ the sovereign power to carry through its policies. But such an arrangement, such open competition between parties, the 'parts' of the political nation, was only stable so long as certain conventions were observed. In some states these were enshrined in formal constitutions. In Britain they were understood as unwritten rules and conventions. They included the notions that no party should implement a policy to which another was fundamentally opposed, that election defeats should be accepted, and that a new government should not attempt to reverse measures passed by its predecessor. Most important of all, however, was the idea that governments should attempt to govern according to realities and circumstances, which generally meant as these were perceived and interpreted by their military, financial and administrative advisers. They had to pursue policies which, by falling within a range accepted as politically practicable, would not create such opposition that they could not be implemented.

Democracy in capitalist states has always been marked by the open and pluralist nature of its electoral arena, and the narrow bounds of the consensus within which state policy moves. The harnessing of the two is performed by politicians, often imperfectly. For such a feat to be possible, the party system has continually to uphold the constitutional legitimacy of the government and the social organisation of the economy. Parties which seriously question either have to be excluded from government, or the political system will be in danger of collapse.

The history of British democracy reveals these problems well. In the period up to 1916 the competition for votes was dominated by the Liberals and the Conservatives. Both parties had established party caucuses, but although fears were expressed that Parliament might come to be dominated by the party caucuses, what actually happened was that both the party caucus and the parliamentary parties came to be dominated by the party leaderships. The competition between the parties centred upon foreign policy, education and church reform. Both parties in government accepted a policy consensus which covered the Empire, the gold standard, free trade, and the principles of sound finance, as well as taking for granted the capitalist organisation of the economy. A major conflict developed over free trade and tariff reform but the determination of the Conservatives to implement the latter was not tested before 1914. The other major conflict which came closest of all to a breakdown of the political system was over Home Rule for Ireland, but this was averted.

The undercurrent throughout this first period of mass democracy was the steadily growing influence of the working class. In electoral terms they were now dominant. The exceptional uniformity of the social structure in Britain gave little scope for regional ethnic or religious parties, and forced all parties to present themselves as national parties appealing on a national base, putting forward programmes and policies in the national interest, claiming to speak for the whole national community. It also forced them to compete for the votes of the working class, and gradually made the concerns of the working class the central concerns of domestic politics. Every party seeking to be a party of government in Britain has been obliged to be a working-class party – in electoral terms at least.

3.6   The Labour party and the Constitution

When the Labour party first appeared, in 1906, it was from the start a very different party from the two principal established parties. First, it did not originate in Parliament but out of an alliance between the trade unions and three socialist societies. Its mass organisation preceded its entry into Parliament. Second, it had no need to make a national appeal since it aspired to be the party of the working class. It was the only party which could afford to be openly sectional in its appeal to the electorate. Third, its aims at first were decidedly limited. It did not aspire to form governments. The aim of the Labour Representation Committee was 'to organise and maintain in Parliament and the country a political Labour party'. Its purpose was not to supplant either the Liberals or the Conservatives but to help defend trade-union rights. These had been seriously undermined by the legal judgement in the Taff Vale case in 1901, and this had persuaded the unions to modify their electoral alliance with the Liberals by sponsoring a party directly under their control which could put their case in the Imperial Parliament.[32]

The formation of the Labour party at first made little impact, but the situation was transformed by the First World War, which was the occasion for the first of the two major and lasting shifts that have so far occurred in the hundred years of mass democracy (the other was the Second World War). The disintegration of the Liberals, the considerable strengthening of the trade unions, and the shockwaves of the Russian Revolution all helped catapult

Labour from the modest 30 seats it had won in 1906 to being the major opposition party after 1918.[33] Once that happened, a central question of domestic politics came to be how Labour was to be handled. How was the governing class to adjust to the prospect of Labour becoming the second party in the two-party system, and therefore the alternative party of government? Labour was no longer the voice of a sectional interest but a party which had adopted in 1918 a new constitution whose goals included public ownership and industrial democracy, and proclaimed its readiness to make those goals the basis for a government programme.[34]

The task of handling Labour devolved upon the Conservative party, which had emerged after 1918 as the undisputed party both of property and of the state machine. Formerly it had been the party of landed interests and sections of industry, as well as the party of the Establishment. It was the party of the established Church, the Law, the Crown, the Universities, the Armed Forces. It was the party more mindful of England's institutional continuity than any other. It had become before 1914 the party of the Union, the party of the Empire, and the party of Tariff Reform.

In 1918 this party entered the period of its greatest electoral dominance. Between 1916 and 1945 the Conservatives were out of office for only three years. Yet throughout this period the party remained on the defensive. Although overwhelmingly dominant in Parliament, it entered coalitions on three occasions (on two the Prime Minister came from another party). Although committed on paper to overturning free trade, the party continued throughout the 1920s to pursue the orthodoxy of free trade and sound finance.[35] Only in 1931 when the gold standard had to be abandoned did the party partially implement its protectionist programme. Similarly, and despite the existence of contrary views within the party, the Conservatives moved cautiously in confronting Labour.[36] Conservative tactics helped to contain and delay Labour's advance but they did not prevent it, and they helped to prepare the ground for Labour's electoral triumph in the 1940s.

The party was divided in the 1920s between the advocates of three strategies. There were those who wanted to treat the Labour party as the advance guard of Bolshevism, and to use every opportunity to smash the Labour movement both politically and industrially. There were those who believed class war was the greatest danger facing the country, and that the way to avert it was to implement the programme of Social Imperialism which Joseph Chamberlain and Lord Milner had evolved before 1914, and create a national movement that transcended class divisions.[37] Finally there were those who believed that the primary task must be to incorporate the Labour movement within the state by winning its leaders both in Parliament and in the trade unions to constitutional methods, to an acceptance of the existing state and the need to govern within its constraints.[38]

All three strategies involved risks and costs, but the third was most in accord with the past pattern of British development. Its triumph is most visible, perhaps paradoxically, during the General Strike – the most serious confrontation between organised Labour and the state this century. This was a strike deliberately provoked by the government, which had made meticulous preparations and calculated the balance of forces with precision.[39] The more serious period of unrest immediately after the war had been ended by a slump and rising unemployment after 1920. By 1926 trade-union membership and industrial militancy were already falling. The government had no need openly to confront the industrial power of the working class. In 1919 Lloyd George had pledged that the National government was 'determined to fight Prussianism in the industrial world as they have fought it on the Continent of Europe, with the whole might of the nation'. But there was no longer anything very Prussian about the stance of organised labour in 1926.

The reason the government provoked the strike was that it needed to force through a general reduction of wage costs in British industry, following the decision to return to the gold standard in 1925 at the pre-war parity of $4.86. Otherwise British exports would be uncompetitive. As

Baldwin expressed it, 'all the workers in this country have got to take reductions to help put industry on its feet'. The coal industry was a leading exporter and began making heavy losses following the return to gold, and so the mineowners demanded a lengthening of hours and a cut in pay, to make exporting profitable again. The miners' refusal was backed by the TUC which threatened a general strike in their support. The government postponed the strike for six months, during which it made its preparations, then it precipitated it, arbitrarily breaking off negotiations with the TUC.

On the government side there were many who wanted to use the strike as the opportunity to deal a mortal blow to the Labour movement. The *Daily Mail* articulated such views with its customary vigour. It denounced the TUC as a 'barely disguised Soviet' and it declared 'Two Governments cannot exist in the same capital. One must destroy the other or surrender to the other.' In an editorial on 5 May, the day before the strike began, the *Daily Mail* told its readers:

> In Italy . . . the Government, which had been placed in power by lawful and constitutional means, failed to do its duty. It did not organise the essential services. It did not protect the nation against a truculent and lawless minority and the immediate consequence was that, after a period of intense suffering, society in Italy organised itself in the Fascist Movement to defend its existence.

Several government ministers, including Churchill, and Joynson Hicks, the Home Secretary, were closely associated with this perspective. Churchill, placed in charge of the *British Gazette*, the Government newspaper, was responsible for many of its inflammatory statements[40] and was reportedly in favour of sending troops and tanks into working-class districts.

The other face of government strategy was represented by Baldwin. He had no illusions as to the nature of the TUC challenge. From the start the TUC defined the strike as a large sympathy stoppage with limited aims, to bring pressure to bear on the government and the mineowners to prevent the cuts in the miners' standard of living. There was no thought of seeking the overthrow of the government. Baldwin also knew that many of the Labour party leaders feared a victory for the strikers far more than they feared a victory for the government. As Jimmy Thomas put it so memorably in the House of Commons: 'I have never disguised that in a challenge to the Constitution God help us unless the Government won'. The government, by defining the strike from the outset as a challenge to the Constitution and therefore refusing to negotiate on any of the strikers' demands, ensured that the leaders of the Labour movement would quickly be faced by the alternative of either challenging the Constitution and organising to overthrow the government, or surrendering. After nine days they surrendered, leaving the miners to fight on alone to eventual defeat.[41]

The complete victory won by the government helped consolidate the strategy of ensuring that the TUC and the Labour leadership would always act within the existing Constitution, and would not seek to use industrial power to obtain political ends. Subsequent political developments, notably the collapse of the Labour government in 1931, and the muted resistance of organised labour to the slump and the depression, fully justified Baldwin's decision against arresting the TUC leaders in 1926 and attempting to crush the strike militarily. He recognised that an important factor in containing and blocking the advance of Labour was the nature of its leaders and their political perspectives. In this sense the General Strike and its outcome represented an important stage in the accommodation of Labour's interests and the incorporation of its leadership.

Yet the policy had its drawbacks. For although the Conservatives remained overwhelmingly dominant electorally, they were now compelled to fight on a different terrain. By helping to define the basic party division in Britain as between Conservative and Labour, they helped make class the basis of party politics. Class identity became for fifty years the most important factor in electoral choice. This placed the Conservatives in a highly vulnerable position, since it threatened to place them in a permanent minority, should a high proportion of the working-class electorate ever identify with the party of the working class. Since the 1920s the Conservatives have been obliged to compete in a class-based two-party system by maintaining an appeal to working-class voters across the class divide.

Conservatives were confident that they could do so because of their deep understanding of the nature of class in Britain. They saw that much class voting was a passive affirmation of a particular status rather than a class interest, and that that particular status was not a universal experience or aspiration throughout the working class; many workers could be detached and won for Conservatism by identifying the party with the authority and hierarchy of the traditional state, and by appealing to the patriotism of the working class, and to the desire of many workers for social mobility or for economic independence. This electoral perspective proved highly successful. The national issues the Conservatives have espoused have kept the Labour party from the position of natural dominance of the electoral system, which a class-based politics would appear to ensure for it.[42]

But for such a class-based party system to function smoothly both party leaderships had tacitly to agree to govern within the constraints of the Constitution and the state. The price of ensuring that the Labour movement would observe those constraints was confirmation of the special role and privileges of its organisations. This helps account for the strange aftermath of the General Strike. Before the strike began the *Financial Times* wrote:

> The strike will be the biggest bull point that the Stock Exchange has had for years if it should be settled in favour of authority. For investment and speculation alike have been overcast these many years by Labour threats, fears, strikes. Victory of the Government in this greatest strike of all would mean the loss by the trade unions of so much prestige and money as would cause wholesale defections from their ranks amongst the men of whom great numbers are none too loyal Trade Unionists as it is.

It would also have the moral effect of showing the nation is strong enough to defeat the poisonous doctrines chewed by foreign-bred firebrands. Once a permanent peace becomes assured, finance will find its feet firmly fixed upon a basis more secure than it has obtained this century.[43]

The strike was indeed settled in favour of authority but the British economy remained stagnant and unemployment high. Part of this was due to the difficulties in the world economy, but part was because an employers' offensive did not materialise. There were many sackings and victimisation of strikers in some industries in 1926 but there was no general reduction of wages. The government, urged on by its backbenchers, passed a Trades Dispute Act in 1927 which limited trade-union privileges, but it did not remove those that had been granted in 1906.[44] The Conservatives failed to press home either their victory over the Labour movement in 1926 or the political victory in 1931, and this was not because of the great strength of trade unionism, which was declining, but because of the paramount importance attached by the Conservative leadership to encouraging the emergence of a responsible leadership in control of the Labour party.

The story has often been told of how the British Labour movement lost its revolutionary will after the collapse of Chartism and became increasingly integrated within British capitalism, how a defensive trade-union movement, organised initially around skilled craftsmen, fought for extremely limited material gains and the defence of trade-union rights; how the close involvement of the trade unions with the Labour party committed that party to the defensive and corporate perspectives of the unions, and nourished the growth of a leadership that was prepared to meet basic trade-union interests whilst managing the state in a traditional and orthodox manner. But the other side of that process is just as important. The party never succeeded in being entirely a party of managers, nor in severing completely its links with the union leaders, and socialist activists in the constituencies.[45]

The two-party system where parties are expected to alternate in government depends much more than do multi-party systems upon a consensus on fundamentals. The Labour party's adherence to that consensus has been real but it has also been insecure. The insecurity derives from the way the party is organised, and has periodically threatened the ability of the party leadership to assert its control not only in the parliamentary party but over the party organisation outside Parliament. The ability of the leadership to dominate the party has always rested heavily on the support of major trade-union leaders whose block votes can dwarf constituency party votes. Whenever that support has been lost or split the party leadership has been in trouble. The party originated as the political arm of the Labour movement, a mass organisation outside Parliament. Its internal structure has been more democratic than other parties for that reason, and its debates have been less about how support can be organised for the government policies that are deemed to be necessary for the state, than about which policies will most advance the interest of organised labour and the construction of socialism. Given the political goals and ideologies of the Labour rank and file and the close links with organised labour, the Labour party despite all the efforts of its leaders has never succeeded in ridding itself of its class character. Although it became an alternative party of government, particularly between 1940 and 1980, it never entirely lost its identity as a political movement. The constitutional question posed by the rise of Labour was not fully settled in that period because the Labour party never completely accepted capitalism ideologically and never severed its connection with the trade unions.

The way in which the working class was eventually incorporated preserved property and preserved the existing state; it averted social revolution but it also put major obstacles in the path of a successful capitalism. It prevented a consensus ever being extended to include the overriding importance of a successful and competitive industrial economy. Instead, the economy became the main battle-ground between the parties, with continued disputes over the rival merits of private and public enterprise and over the system of taxation. The consensus on foreign policy, on Britain's relations with the world economy and alliance with the United States, as well as the consensus on the formal constitution of the state, was complete. What was lacking was a consensus on the means for industrial modernisation.

PART III

STRATEGY

4
Managing social democracy

The question is whether we are prepared to move out of the nineteenth century *laissez-faire* into an era of liberal socialism, by which I mean a system where we can act as an organised community for common purposes . . . while respecting and protecting the individual – his freedom of choice, his faith, his mind and its expression, his enterprise and his property.

J. M. Keynes[1]

When we came in we were told that there weren't sufficient inducements to invest. So we provided the inducements. Then we were told people were scared of balance of payments difficulties leading to stop–go. So we floated the pound. Then we were told of fears of inflation: and now we're dealing with that. And still you aren't investing enough!

Edward Heath (speech to the Institute of Directors, 1973)

The history of external expansion and internal compromise examined in Chapters 2 and 3 left important legacies and allowed the accumulation of specific internal weaknesses. The legacies were the patterns of external dependence of the British economy and the international orientation of the British state and British business. The weaknesses were the institutional organisation of the principal classes and interests, and their relations to the state. In the social democratic era that opened in 1940 the interaction of these two elements established the constraints within which government operated.

Britain's dilemmas in the post-war world stemmed from an inability of its leaders to make clear strategic choices about the relative importance of the traditional world role, as against the modernisation of the society and the economy. The fatal persistence in the belief that no choice was necessary gravely undermined the modernisation strategy of the 1960s and wrecked many of the reforms which it launched. This chapter considers the background to that modernisation strategy and outlines its main features.

4.1   The triumph of social democracy

1940 was a major watershed in British politics. It also opened a new phase in the hundred years' decline. The war emergency meant not only the organisation of a war economy but the establishment of a national coalition between the Conservative government, now led by Churchill, and the Labour party. Participation in the National government completed the incorporation of the parliamentary and trade-union leadership of the Labour party into the service of the state. As a result the second war against Germany was fought, to a greater extent than in 1914–18, in the name of goals that commanded popular support: the defeat of Fascism, the defence of democracy, and the promise of reforms after the war that would eliminate unemployment and create a more egalitarian society. The military struggle and the plans for reconstruction were closely related in the overall war effort.

The war established social democracy in Britain. The patient strategy of containment of the Labour movement pursued by the Conservatives finally broke down as German tanks poured into France. Labour's leaders henceforward were to be generally accepted into the policy-making élites, and major concessions were made to the long-standing demands and interests of the Labour movement. But important though this internal accommodation was, both for the degree of resilience and unity with which Britain fought and for the development of British politics after the war, it was greatly overshadowed by the effect of the war on the world balance of power and the organisation of the world economy.

Britain's decision to fight Germany a second time brought a sudden end to Britain's world dominance. Between 1939 and 1945 Britain was not only forced to liquidate a great part of the foreign assets accumulated before 1914 and then rebuilt after 1918; it also amassed sizeable debts. Sterling liabilities were now three times as great as British gold and foreign currency reserves, whereas before 1939 they had been roughly in balance.[2] This was seriously to undermine the continued operation of sterling as an international currency. In order to prosecute the war against Germany and Japan, and still more to win, Britain was forced to rely on United States aid.

In military terms the war not only established the ascendancy of the United States and the Soviet Union; it also exposed the weakness of the British Empire. British naval power was clearly no longer sufficient to protect it, and parts of the Empire, particularly India, could not be retained for very long against the wishes of the two leading world powers and rising nationalist opposition. The course and outcome of the war made eventual withdrawal from the Empire certain. It ended for ever the traditional military strategy which had aided British expansion and secured British dominance.

The war also brought about what years of peace had not accomplished, a new world economic order. Its basis was the now immense productive and military power of the United States. Britain's forlorn attempt in the 1920s to rebuild a stable international system and free trade had finally foundered in 1931, when the gathering Depression forced even Britain off the gold standard and into adoption of protectionist policies. There was to be no repeat attempt after 1945. British financial and industrial weakness, in relation to the United States, had become such that Britain was quite unable to continue to play the leading role in maintaining the institutional order of world capitalism.

The rebuilding of the world economy around the United States, which at first was intended to embrace but later excluded the Soviet bloc, formed the framework in which Britain's experiment in social democracy went forward. The political basis of the British war effort substantially increased the support of the Labour party so that it became an equal contender with the Conservatives, and it also weakened the resolve of the Conservative leadership to resist the consolidation and extension of new state functions and responsibilities which had been developing since the beginning of the century.[3]

Labour's victory in 1945 was decisive in parliamentary terms (a majority of 146), although this was still less than half of the poll.[4] The new government began carrying through the plans for reconstruction which had been agreed by the Coalition. The war marked a sudden alteration in Britain's world status and the balance of its internal politics, but there was no similar discontinuity in the formal organisation of the state itself. The general character of British institutions was little changed. Whereas some of the defeated powers had their institutions entirely remodelled, few such changes occurred in Britain or were proposed by the Labour party. The fundamentals of the education system, the electoral system, the House of Lords, and the civil service all remained – although all had been major targets for reform in the past.[5]

The changes Labour did introduce, and which became the basis for the internal policy consensus of the post-war years, owed a great deal to the ideas and plans of Keynes and Beveridge. Their acceptance was most clearly signalled during the war with the publication of the White Paper on Full Employment (1944), which committed governments to maintain a high level of activity and employment in the economy; and by the Beveridge Report (1942), which laid out plans for a comprehensive scheme of social security. To these were added Labour's plans for a national health service and the nationalisation of major public utilities including gas and electricity, as well as the railways and the mines.[6]

The implementation of all these plans meant a permanent enlargement of the public sector, more detailed public regulation of the economy, and a higher level of public spending.[7] This required a further major extension of the tax base; direct taxes on the whole working population were to be the major source of revenue for the social democratic state.[8] Apart from the measures of nationalisation, which were mostly confined to loss-making industries and public utilities,[9] the status and organisation of private business were not questioned, but confirmed. What had changed was the relative weight of the Labour movement. The trade unions recovered the privileges they had lost in 1927 and won the commitment to full employment, concessions which were expected to increase their membership and improve their bargaining position.[10] The working class as a whole now exerted more pressure on government, because the new levels of public expenditure that were established made issues of collective consumption, as well as economic prosperity, central to the competition between the parties.[11]

4.2   Reconstruction

The economic policy of the Labour government was naturally dominated by the problems of reconstruction. The loss of exports and of overseas investment income during the war meant a huge structural deficit on the balance of payments.[12] Essential imports could not be financed. The difficulty of quickly switching the economy back to peacetime production, the backlog of demand built up during the war, and the continuance of public spending at a high level, mainly because of the new welfare plans, all added to the pressure of demand and the risk of a very rapid inflation. These difficulties, however, were overcome with assistance from the United States, exports were expanded enormously and the export gap closed.[13] Manufacturing output recovered.[14] Strikes remained illegal under wartime regulations, rationing and many physical controls stayed in force to restrain consumption and direct investment, interest rates were kept at 2 per cent, the trade unions accepted wage restraint and the electorate accepted austerity.[15] Inflation was not entirely avoided but fairly successfully suppressed, until the decision to rearm in 1951.[16]

A measure of the success of reconstruction was the fact that Britain still accounted for 25 per cent of exports of world manufactures in 1951. At the beginning of that decade the British economy looked strong. The slump in the world economy which had been widely expected after the post-war reconstruction boom had not occurred and Britain seemed certain to benefit from any expansion in the world economy that now took place. Britain's industrial structure had been substantially transformed in the inter-war period, particularly during the 1930s when both domestic and imperial markets were protected by tariffs. The new high technology and mass production industries – electrical engineering, cars, chemicals – which had been so slow to develop in Britain before 1914, were all now well established.[17] Britain still possessed a powerful financial sector with unrivalled and long-established banking, commercial, insurance and shipping businesses. The Americans, who had always been one of the most protectionist nations in the world economy, were now eager to reduce trade barriers. Britain had also emerged once more from a major conflict still formally undefeated, still free from invasion, its institutions still intact, and having apparently increased its cohesion and its unity by completing the successful incorporation of the Labour movement within the state, and establishing a new social democratic consensus, guaranteeing civil, political, and now social rights to every citizen.[18]

How could such a state fail? Yet fail it did. It was during the decades of the long boom, as the tables in Chapter 1 clearly indicate, that Britain's decline began in earnest. For Britain to fall behind the leading world powers with their continent-sized economies was unsurprising; it had been inevitable from the time Britain committed itself to remain inside the liberal world order and decisively cast aside any attempt to develop its empire as a protected sphere. What is more surprising is why despite all the initial advantages it appeared to enjoy in 1945, Britain has consistently performed worse than other states with similar populations, resources, and industrial, and social structures.

The obstinate refusal of the economy to respond to the national consensus for growth and modernisation has produced sweeping searches for sinister sectional interests which have dared frustrate the national will. Gladstone once remarked, 'The interests are always awake, while the country often slumbers and sleeps.' Scapegoats for Britain's ills have included the civil service, the trade unions, the City of London, the managers of industry and, more generally, Britain's 'anti-enterprise' or 'anti-business' culture.[19]

Certainly Britain had accumulated many internal weaknesses during the years of power and success, affecting the performance of all sections of society. But, in themselves, these weaknesses could have been identified and might have been overcome. What preserved them and made their effect ultimately so damaging was the world role of the British state in the post-war period.

4.3 The American connection

The real linchpin of the post-war consensus is the one least often discussed – the alliance with the United States. It was the policy which all governments maintained and, though occasionally questioned, it never looked remotely like being overthrown or seriously challenged. That was because it was no ordinary alliance. It was a 'special relationship', more special for the British than for the Americans, because it was the means by which the British world role was preserved – by being transferred to the Americans. Britain accepted American leadership in the new world economic and political order and became prepared to act as a junior partner of the Americans, subordinating its interests to the United States, but maintaining those roles and commitments which the Americans found useful. Britain reduced its commitment to police this world economy and no longer provided its principal medium of exchange, but still maintained extensive military commitments in certain parts of the world – including Greece, Palestine and the Middle East, Singapore and Malaysia; and sterling was restored as an international currency, not as powerful or important as the dollar, or as eagerly sought, but an international medium of exchange none the less.[20]

Why were the British prepared to undertake such heavy commitments to assist the Americans in the new global role as the dominant capitalist power? Two interlinked considerations were crucial: first, the dependence of the British economy on an open liberal trading network; and second, the need to ensure the security of the capitalist world against the Soviet Union.

The terms of the special relationship after 1945 meant the prolongation, not the termination, of Britain's traditional world role. The Americans came to appreciate the advantages of sharing the burdens of leadership in the world economy, so long as Britain remained subordinate to overall American interests and strategy. Earlier antagonism between the two powers had been much more intense. The Americans were strongly opposed to the British Empire, particularly in the 1930s, when it formed a protectionist bloc which discriminated against American goods.[21] As American productivity rose so the Americans became articulate advocates of the need for free trade and open national economies, and American industries emerged from behind the protectionist walls that had nurtured their early development.

American hostility to Britain was still marked at the end of the Second World War. One American General objected to weapons purchased under Lend–Lease being used to recapture Hong Kong and so restore part of the Empire to British control. As one Congressman attacking further loans for Britain put it, aid would merely promote 'too much damned socialism at home, and too much damned Imperialism abroad'.[22] The existence of the British Empire and the colonial empires of other European states was viewed as inimical to American interests, and Britain was still regarded as a major commercial rival. As soon as the war was over the United States dismayed its principal ally by abruptly ending Lend–Lease. The American view was that British imperialism only deserved aid when it was fighting on behalf of the United States. This ruthless decision reflected how much the British war effort had depended on American aid and the British naturally felt they were being treated as one of the defeated powers. They were forced to apply to the Americans for a new loan to pay for the imports they desperately needed while the economy was reconstructed.

The loan that was finally negotiated – the Washington Loan Agreements (1946) – spelled out fairly clearly the new balance between Britain and America. The conditions of the loan were that Britain should not seek to reintroduce imperial preference and discriminate against American goods in Empire markets; and that sterling should be made convertible at the earliest opportunity.[23]

Strong opposition was mounted in Britain to the terms of the loan by the imperialist wing of the Conservative party and by the Left of the Labour party. The former stressed the loss of British independence of action, the latter argued that a 'socialist' Britain should not ally with a capitalist America. Many in America likewise questioned whether a capitalist America should grant loans to countries that were planning to nationalise industries and take other steps hostile to capitalism. That the terms of the loan had to be accepted, however, was never in doubt in Britain, partly because of the serious consequences if the loan were withheld, partly because the makers of British foreign policy were anxious that nothing should be done to jeopardise the willingness of the United States to use its dominant military and industrial power to create a new world political and economic order. The shape of such an order was already appearing with the Bretton Woods Agreement of 1944, which resulted in decisions to set up the IMF (the International Monetary Fund), and a World Bank; to establish the dollar as the leading world currency; and to work for more open and unrestricted trade in the hope of avoiding any return to the protectionist and fragmented world economy of the 1930s.[24]

The bitterness over the terms of the Washington Loan Agreements was soon forgotten once the Cold War began. As soon as the other capitalist powers – former allies like Britain, or occupied enemies like Germany – were no longer seen primarily as potential or actual industrial and military rivals, but as territories that might be penetrated and incorporated into an expanding Soviet Empire, American attitudes to loans for its allies abruptly changed. The plan to dismantle German factories and plough over their sites was shelved. The Marshall Aid programme poured in funds to help rebuild the economies of the capitalist world, both to provide long-term markets and investments for American companies and to stave off either internal social revolution or external Russian intervention.[25]

The British played a major part in this change of direction of American policy. A crucial moment in the evolution of the new strategy was the speech by Churchill at Fulton, Missouri, in 1946 when he declared that an Iron Curtain had descended across Europe. Churchill's speech continued the policy over which he had presided when Prime Minister, and reflected the Foreign Office view of the Soviet Union and its intentions. In the latter stages of the war British strategic thinking became preoccupied with containment of Soviet power. In this perspective the utter defeat of Germany would make Russia the supreme continental power in Europe, a power which not only strove to be autarkic like Germany, but had also abolished capitalist relations of production, and proclaimed an ideology of world revolution which disguised the pursuit of its national interests.

It was a major triumph for British policy after 1945 when the Americans endorsed the idea that the Russians must be contained and isolated at all costs, for the security of the world order. The moral and crusading bent of American foreign policy soon made the Cold War assume extravagant dimensions.[26] Its lasting result was to launch the Americans irrevocably on their career of world power and responsibility. The British loyally supported them. The role of principal ally proved more rewarding than the role of principal commercial rival.

The change in direction in American policy was a fundamental one. Their hostility to colonial empires remained, but pressure on Britain to withdraw immediately from its colonies was eased. Similarly the failure of the attempt to restore convertibility for sterling in 1947 was accepted calmly. Sterling did not in fact become fully convertible until 1958. More important to the Americans became the fact that the British were active and willing members of all the military alliances the Americans set up – NATO, SEATO and CENTO; that they were prepared to rearm, and to maintain armed forces in Germany and in a network of bases around the world; that they fully accepted the new economic and financial institutions, in particular the IMF and GATT (General Agreement on Trade and Tariffs) and the programme of financial stability and more open trade.

In return the Americans were prepared to underwrite aspects of the British world role. Sterling was allowed to remain an international currency. Britain was allowed to retain a colonial Empire that was still sizeable, even after the granting of independence to India and Pakistan in 1947. It was not simply an illusion after 1945 that Britain still had a world role and could still act in part as a world power. The special relationship with America permitted it. The Foreign Office view of Britain's place in the world prevailed.

4.4 The burden of the world role

An influential school of writing on British decline has long argued that the effort to sustain a world role helped cripple Britain in the post-war world.[27] It postponed the acknowledgement that British world power was finally at an end; at the same time it imposed quite exceptional burdens on the British economy. Britain emerged as one of the two states bearing the costs of maintaining an international economic and political order, yet it no longer had the industrial base to support such costs. Military spending was higher in Britain than in any country of the western alliance other than the United States itself.[28] More important, overseas military spending was high,[29] much higher in real terms than it had been in the heyday of the Empire, when British forces had been kept to a minimum and the cost of forces stationed overseas had largely been met by local taxation. Government policy placed a heavy extra burden on the British balance of payments.

This meant that Britain had a very different relationship with the reorganised world economy from that of Germany, Japan or even France. The level of military spending and overseas military involvement, the special status of sterling, and the scope for the international expansion of British business, all marked out Britain from the others. It helps to account for one of the great paradoxes of British decline – why an economy performing so poorly should nevertheless have produced more transnational companies than any country apart from the United States. The opportunities that Britain's imperial trading and financial connections provided led to the development after 1950 of some large and very successful international businesses. In 1970, although Britain was considerably poorer than Germany, eleven of the world's one hundred largest businesses were British, compared with eighteen for the rest of the EEC. Among the 200 largest non-American companies, fifty-three were British, forty-three Japanese, twenty-five German and twenty-three French. Throughout the period of the long boom foreign investment and overseas sales were both much greater by British companies than by German, Japanese or French. By 1971 the value of foreign production by British business was more than double the value of visible export trade, whereas it was less than 40 per cent for Germany and Japan. The number of British firms operating six or more foreign subsidiaries had expanded from one-fifth in 1950 to one-half in 1970, and all the top hundred British manufacturing companies had become multinational by 1970. Furthermore, investment overseas as a percentage of investment in domestic manufacturing was never less than 17 per cent in the 1970s and in some years was above 30 per cent.[30]

As a result, Britain's relationship to the world economy after 1945 was more like that of the United States than like that of France, Germany and Japan. Britain achieved a growth rate similar to that of the United States, but the productivity gap between the two economies remained immense. The result of the renewal of Britain's traditional liberal orientation to the world economy was that a serious conflict began to develop between the international priorities of British policy and the needs of the domestic economy. This was sometimes presented as a new clash between manufacturing industry and the financial sector. But the real clash was between the new and often combined international operations of British industry and British finance, and the requirements of domestic expansion.[31]

The conflict was expressed in the repeated balance of payments crises of the 1950s and 1960s. The margin of failure was always small. British trade had improved dramatically compared with the position before 1939. After 1945 exports of goods were seldom less than 95 per cent of imports in value. Before 1939 they had generally covered only 75 per cent. The 5 per cent shortfall was more than made up by the regular surplus on invisible trade. Therefore, taken on its own, the British balance of *trade* would have ensured balance of payments surpluses in every year up to 1973, with the possible exception of 1964.[32] The immediate cause of the sterling crises in 1947, 1949, 1951, 1955, 1957, 1961, and between 1963 and 1967 was generally, though not invariably, a deficit on the balance of payments. These occurred not because exports were too low but because government spending overseas and private investment overseas were too high.

The argument of the Treasury, the traditional custodian of Britain's liberal external policy, was that such spending was essential to maintain political stability and an open world trading system, and to develop new supplies of food and raw materials. The Treasury calculated in the middle of the 1950s that an annual surplus of £200 to £300 million was required on the balance of payments to finance the level of overseas spending that was considered desirable.[33] If such a surplus however were not forthcoming there was rarely any suggestion that overseas spending should be cut or drastically restricted. The burden of adjustment was placed instead on the domestic economy. If demand were reduced sufficiently in the economy imports would fall and external balance would be restored.

The external balance had to be corrected because of the effect on sterling if it was not. Sterling was used as an international currency not because it was any longer the currency of the capitalist economy which enjoyed the highest productivity in the world economy, but partly because it was the international medium of exchange for the sterling area, and partly because of its use in international trade.[34] This latter function was closely linked to the financial, shipping, and insurance services provided by the City. The willingness of foreign holders of sterling to continue to hold it and use it depended on them remaining confident that the value of sterling would be maintained at its fixed parity of $2.80. The surest trigger of a sterling crisis was the announcement of a heavy balance of payments deficit. Restoring confidence was achieved by raising interest rates, squeezing credit and increasing taxes, in order to lower the level of demand in the economy. Such measures caused a stop–go cycle, and alternating periods of expansion and stagnation, and this cycle can be identified as a leading cause of Britain's slower rate of growth of productivity and output, especially since the periods of 'go' got shorter, whilst the periods of 'stop' got longer.[35]

The fluctuations in demand appear to have been of relatively little importance in themselves. Other countries suffered as great fluctuations without any apparent adverse effects on investment.[36] One reason was that their industrial structure was different. Japanese and German firms were nationally based and nationally directed. In Britain a significant section of its leading businesses was already internationally oriented. Erratic growth of demand in Britain appears to have accelerated the tendency for firms to diversify and expand abroad. The virtuous circle between high growth of output, high investment and high productivity was not realised within Britain, in part because of the opportunities many British firms already had, and others sought to acquire, of expanding outside the British economy. The result was that the leading sector of British capital retained its competitiveness and its strength by operating internationally, rather than by building outwards from its base in the domestic economy, and this was an important reason why exports, productivity and investment were all lower than in the more successful economies.

4.5 The growing awareness of decline

The return to Britain's traditional liberal, outward-looking policy after 1945 was revealed principally in the priority given to sterling and also by the relatively few restrictions placed on the export of capital. These policies were not the only cause of Britain's slow growth rate, but they made it much more difficult to tackle the internal weaknesses of the economy, and with each successive sterling crisis the prospect for escape from the straitjacket grew smaller. After the special circumstances of reconstruction, government energies were never so concentrated again on renewing and reorganising domestic industry for the industrial challenge that now faced it.

The difficulties the British economy encountered during the long boom were not those of an underdeveloped economy lacking in successful businesses. On the contrary it had a very successful business sector. The problem was that this sector often found it easier to accumulate capital by expanding abroad than by investing in the domestic economy. This had been true of the City before 1911 when the greatest outflow of capital of all took place. But that movement reflected the fact that the absolute level of British productivity was still considerably higher than productivity in most other countries, and that the rate of return on loans, even at 5 per cent, was generally higher than could be obtained by investing in Britain, where technological advance was only proceeding slowly. British industry was not starved of funds by the City – it was merely that domestic investment did not appear profitable enough.

The situation was apparently very different during the long boom. The technological lead established by American industry was now colossal, and America was far better organised than Britain had ever been to develop new technologies. The overseas expansion of American goods and American capital now became a flood, as American companies strove to expand their markets and their overseas production by exploiting their technological and organisational advantages over their competitors in the rest of the world. International companies became the major agent of capital accumulation and an ever-extending division of labour. The older pattern of foreign investment of capital loans raised in one country and employed by local entrepreneurs in another was superseded. Britain had been the centre of the old kind of *rentier* investment, but its assets had been severely depleted by the cost of the two world wars. What was surprising was that British companies should be second only to American in expanding overseas after 1945, when British productivity lagged so far behind. What might have been expected was that the 'best-practice' techniques developed by the Americans would have spread to British industry, either through direct American investment by American companies, or through the sales of patents and licences and the reorganisation of British industry by its own efforts. In this way innovations would have been diffused and absorbed, investment and productivity raised throughout the world economy, and the technological lead of the Americans steadily reduced.

This kind of process is precisely what did happen to many developed economies during the long boom, and was a major factor in the economic 'miracles' and the exceptional rates of growth that some countries achieved. It was certainly a factor in the improved rate of growth of output and productivity that Britain experienced. But by the end of the boom the gap between British and American productivity was still virtually as wide as at the beginning.

The problem that began to preoccupy policy-makers was why this should be so; why countries like Germany and Japan were able to grow continuously at such higher rates than Britain and to adjust to new industries and new techniques so much more rapidly. One major factor that was isolated was the growing division between the profitable and expanding international businesses of the City and the leading manufacturing companies in Britain on one side, and the rest of British industry on the other. It was argued that much of British industry had been uncompetitive for far too long, shielded by first informal and then formal protection in Empire markets, and protection in the 1930s in the home market. With government encouragement aimed at reducing the numbers of closures and bankruptcies during the Depression, the formation of cartels, price-fixing and production-sharing agreements had grown apace in the 1930s.[37] Allied to the social conservatism of British institutions, the comparatively low status of industry in relation to the professions and public service, the lack of technical and business education, the proliferation of small family businesses, and the resulting poor quality of many British managers, what British industry clearly required after 1945 was a wholesale clear-out and reorganisation, and the patient building of new practices in technology and organisation that the most successful industrial capitalism in the world was employing.

No such new beginning was made. The pace of adjustment to the demands of competition in the world economy was leisurely, and this was partly because of two major factors from Britain's past development – the liberal ethos of the state which had always characterised government – industry relations, and the relations between the state and the working class. The first was most clearly evident in the general reluctance governments had long displayed in enforcing greater competition in the domestic economy except through the external sanction of free trade. This reluctance showed itself most clearly in the unwillingness to tackle the uncompetitive, status-ridden institutions of British society, which helped maintain the cohesion of the ruling class but also diverted energies into the service of the Empire, and the state, and encouraged conservative attitudes which impeded industrial rationalisation. A traditional British lament was that expressed by the *Westminster Gazette* in 1900:

The problem if we are considering civilised life and not merely what is called commercial supremacy, is to find

the mean between this American disease and the complacency which is fully convinced that old ways are best
because they are old.[38]

That mean was not easily found, that complacency not
easily dispelled.

Alongside the failure of the state to create greater
competition in the past and to ensure a more dynamic and
expanding civil society, growing dissatisfaction began to be
voiced at the inadequacies of the traditional non-
interventionist role of the state in the economy. As with so
many other things the Attlee government had left much of
this untouched. The state was spending more in the 1950s
and was involved more in ensuring the success and viability
of the economy. Governments were expected to find
remedies for economic problems rather than declaring in
the traditional manner that it was nothing to do with them.
They organised their economic policy around the achievement of full employment, stable prices, a surplus on the
balance of payments and economic growth.

What is remarkable in retrospect is the scale of the goals
governments sought to achieve, and the paucity of the
means with which they equipped themselves for achieving
them. The bulk of industry was still in private hands and
industry retained its traditional suspicion of the state.[39]
The far-reaching controls of the war economy were all
dismantled and nothing was put in their place. No effort
was made to forge the close institutional links between
government, industry, and the banks that existed in many
other countries and formed the basis for their national
industrial and commercial strategies. The Keynesian
'revolution' in Britain, although it marked a stage in the
extension of government involvement in the economy, was
also fully in accord with the liberal tradition of economic
policy. As understood and practised by the Treasury,
Keynesianism meant a policy of manipulating the total level
of demand to correct the tendency that markets had, if left
to themselves, to produce unemployment and stagnation.
Beyond such 'fine tuning' no interference with individual
decisions on investment, prices or output was contempla-

ted. So long as the government maintained through its monetary and fiscal policies a correct balance between effective demand and the productive potential of the economy, the market could be allowed to work freely to create prosperity and rising output and living standards.[40]

The failure of such indirect manipulations of the economy to produce a rate of growth or a level of investment that matched Germany and Japan created great pressure in favour of more active government involvement in the economy, more planning, more spending on infrastructure and on research, more attention to the questions of supply rather than the questions of demand which dominated government policy in the 1950s. It was all to bear fruit of a sort in the 1960s.

The other great problem which began to receive attention in the search for explanations of Britain's poor growth performance was the working class. The very high levels of employment that were achieved in the 1950s were taken as a sign of a shortage of labour and as a factor in increasing the bargaining power of organised labour. Other countries during the boom were able to draw on supplies of labour from their undeveloped countryside or from abroad. In Britain reserves of labour were small, although the employment of women began to expand greatly. Immigration from the New Commonwealth provided extra workers, but increasing restrictions were placed upon it after 1961 because of internal political pressures.[41] The only other source of labour was from industry itself, and this could only be realised by drastically reducing manning levels and eliminating restrictive practices. Any such programme needed the co-operation of the trade unions, whose legal position had never been stronger, but who remained split in a variety of craft, industrial, and general unions. The defensive strength and conservatism of the unions meshed with the conservatism and international orientation of large sections of British capital, and greatly reduced the scope for increasing productivity.

The unions were undoubtedly partly responsible for the low rate of increase in productivity, for as shown in Chapter 1, not just the quantity of investment but its efficiency was

much lower than in many other countries. Low investment
was however the key problem, and it was the failure of
British companies and British governments to create the
kind of climate for large-scale investment and rapid
increases in productivity that was most striking. Few British
industries adopted the kind of organisational practices
which were developed by their competitors to overcome
restrictive practices on the shop floor and make investment
pay. The failure was more a failure of management than of
the work-force. By the end of the 1950s it was apparent that
any successful strategy for growth had to find a way of
winning and keeping the co-operation of organised labour.
But it was not to prove an easy task.

4.6   The attempt at modernisation

On the surface, the 1950s were a period of great prosperity
in Britain. The pace and duration of the long boom brought
the end of austerity and all controls on consumption. With
only minor exceptions, all four targets of government
economic policy – full employment, sustained growth, low
inflation, and a balance of payments surplus – were broadly
met.[42] The Conservative government elected in 1951, and
its successors, proved quite ready to govern within the
constraints of the new political consensus established in the
1940s. Projecting itself as the party that could best ensure
prosperity while maintaining welfare provision, the Conservative party succeeded in winning three elections in a row in
the 1950s. The Conservatives went on to govern for thirteen
years, a longer period on their own than any other party had
managed this century before the election of the Thatcher
Government.

Yet the 1950s for all their outward success were also the
years when the decisive slide in Britain's relative economic
position began. Much of the British governing class was
more concerned with the rather more precipitate decline in
Britain's status as a great power, of which the events at Suez
in 1956 were a painful reminder, and with the task of
organising an orderly withdrawal from the Empire. But

many were becoming aware that despite its success the British economy was being outperformed by its European rivals and still more so by Japan. This realisation and the anxiety it caused erupted in a flood of self-criticism spiced with denigration of the British Establishment in the early 1960s,[43] and helped to prepare the way for a major change in the direction of policy after the 1959 election victory.

The change did not disturb the fundamentals of the consensus that had been established after the war. What was now agreed was that the rate of growth was too low, and that demand management policies were no longer enough. Government needed to intervene more actively to create a general climate for growth and to remedy deficiencies on the supply side of the economy. The new policies were initiated by the Conservatives but taken up and continued enthusiastically by the Labour party. The 1964 election was fought on the question of which party was more likely to modernise Britain faster, and enable the British economy to break out of the cycle of stop–go and emulate the rates of growth of the most successful national capitalisms. The Labour administration it brought to office, headed by Harold Wilson, promised the creation of a New Britain.[44]

The new policies intended to create the British economic miracle were diverse. There was a more effective competition policy initiated in 1956 with the Restrictive Practices Act and continued with the abolition of Resale Price Maintenance in 1964 and the Monopoly and Mergers Act of 1965. There were concerted attempts made to revive the co-operation between labour and capital that had existed during the war, by creating the kind of institutionalised, tripartite links between government, industry and unions which many other countries had developed so successfully, and to experiment with the planning of incomes and output. The National Economic Development Council (NEDC) and the National Incomes Commission (NIC) were followed after 1964 by an attempt to draw up a National Plan, and by the establishment of a Prices and Incomes board to oversee a permanent incomes policy. In addition Labour established new ministries, the Department of Economic Affairs (DEA) and the Ministry of Technology, which were intended to represent the interests of the national economy. From them flowed programmes of subsidies, investment incentives, and rationalisation. The Industrial Reorganisation Corporation (IRC) was established to assist in the rationalisation of British industry and the creation of industrial enterprises that could compete successfully in world markets. Finally, public expenditure was greatly increased with the intention of modernising the infrastructure of the British economy, its communications network, its educational system and its health service, so as to assist in the task of creating a dynamic and fully adaptable industrial economy.[45]

Such an array of virtuous policies, accepted by both parties and implemented with such vigour, could surely not fail. But in general they did. The judgement of Francis Cripps writing at the end of the 1970s has been echoed by many others:

> After two decades at least of government attempts to improve the non-price competitiveness of UK exports none of the policy instruments tried so far seems to have had any measurable effect.[46]

The explanations from Right and Left as to why it failed are examined in the next two chapters. The failure greatly undermined the consensus and brought a new political turbulence and the rise of new political forces. The immediate reason for the failure is not hard to grasp. Neither the Labour government between 1964 and 1970, nor the Conservative government before it, was either able or willing to defy the international orientation of British economic policy and break the stop–go cycle. The whole strategy of expansion and modernisation depended upon financing increased public expenditure from growth, and winning the co-operation of the trade unions to temporary pay restraint in exchange for the prospect of faster growth in living standards. But both policies depended in the short term on governments finding some way to expand the economy that would not lead straight to a balance of payments crisis and a sterling crisis, or if it did, on finding a way to handle them without resorting to the deflation of home demand. This entailed decisions on the exchange rate, on the future of sterling as an international currency, on the scale of British commitments abroad, and on the freedom of its leading firms to expand abroad. Without such decisions, expanding the economy meant certain balance of payments and sterling crises followed by the familiar deflationary package to restore confidence. Yet for all their intellectual recognition of this dilemma successive governments proved quite incapable of escaping it in practice – the Wilson government least of all.[47] But the spending programme of modernisation was not curtailed, and this meant a rapid increase in public expenditure and in taxation against a background of a stagnant economy and collapsing profits. Much of the burden of adjustment was thrown upon the working class through heavy increases in taxes and increasingly draconian pay restraint. Since inflation was accelerating, such measures led eventually to a pay explosion.[48]

4.7 The Heath government

The Conservatives won the general election in 1970 against a sombre background: the industrial and social turmoil of the late 1960s, the evident failure of the strategy of modernisation on which such hopes had been placed to reverse decline, and growing difficulties both in financing public expenditure and in containing the pressure for pay increases to match the rate of inflation. Although the Conservatives had initiated the modernisation strategy, dissatisfaction with Labour policies had grown, and the Conservative leadership had been subject to intense pressures from its own supporters to promise a major change of direction in economic policy. The Heath government saw its own election as marking a major break with the consensus, both in the nature of its policies and in the vigour with which it attempted to implement them. But in the context of the record of the government as a whole, the Heath government's 'quiet revolution' to 'change the course of history of this nation' not only turned out to be an extremely noisy one, but also a final attempt to create an expanding economy within the limits of the social democratic state. The highest priority was given to the achievement of sustained economic growth; at first free market policies were attempted, but when these failed to work quickly they were replaced or supplemented by interventionist policies which went beyond anything tried in the previous decade.

The strategy of the Heath government was the most radical attempted by any government since the war. It had been planned in much greater detail than was usual for Oppositions. It attempted to break out of the vicious circle of low investment, low productivity and higher costs by seeking to reduce the short-term constraints on government economic management.[49]

The setting of the Heath strategy was the determination to make Britain a member of the EC, a decision which involved a major reassessment of British policy and Britain's role in the world. The first application to join the EC made in 1961 was already a tacit recognition that the history of external expansion was over, and that British economic security was best served by joining a regional economic bloc within the wider world economy.[50] The costs, including the abandonment of cheap food, were to be weighed against the benefits of free access to the European market. Many supporters of the decision to enter the EC, which had been so strongly resisted after 1945 and in 1956, hoped that the community would evolve into a federal or a unitary state capable of protecting European economic interests, and bargaining on equal terms with the United States and Japan.

The European policy that was launched in the 1960s therefore implied a fundamental re-evaluation of the American connection and the long subordination of British interests to American. It implied that Britain was ready to shed the last vestiges of its world role – the pretence of an independent nuclear deterrent, the overseas military bases, the international currency role of sterling – and to approach world political and economic problems from a European rather than an Atlantic perspective. It was because he seriously doubted whether such a change in outlook had genuinely occurred that de Gaulle vetoed Britain's application twice during the 1960s, fearing that Britain would be merely a Trojan horse for the United States inside the Community.

Heath's success in securing entry in the 1970s depended upon convincing the French that Britain now had a political leadership which was firmly European in its outlook, and which accepted that Europe was to be the focus of British energies and political ambitions; that the independent world role was over, that British interests could no longer be protected by the British state alone, and that a strong Europe was more likely to protect them than was America. But there was a further problem remaining. For Britain to play a leading role in the EC, British economic decline had to be reversed and a strong national economy built, able to compete on equal terms with Germany and France.

The Heath government hoped to create such an economy by attempting to remove some of the major constraints on economic management. Its competition policy, for example, aimed to eliminate subsidies and incentives which had proliferated under Labour, axeing all the agencies of detailed intervention, and reducing public expenditure and taxation. The intention was to force industry to solve its own problems and become more efficient and competitive, so restoring profitability, boosting investment, and preparing the way for a rapid expansion of output and productivity. The trade-union policy was aimed at reducing obstacles in the labour market and in the labour movement to expansion and modernisation. The government reformed trade-union law with its Industrial Relations Act[51] and renounced a formal incomes policy, hoping that between them the new laws and the more competitive climate in industry would restrain wage costs.

The aim of both sets of policies was to prepare the way for a new experiment in sustained expansion. In its first two years in office the Heath government inherited the huge balance of payments surplus which was the main fruit of Labour's economic policies over the previous six years.[52] In 1971, with the disintegration of the Bretton Woods interna-

tional monetary system the government seized its opportunity and in 1972 floated the pound.[53] It was determined
that once the economy began expanding again the expansion would not be cut short by a balance of payments crisis.

The priority which the government gave to achieving
growth was shown by the lengths it was prepared to go to
ensure it. All its free market policies had run into difficulty
by 1972. The Industrial Relations Act which had been
intended as an extension of the successful Restrictive
Practices legislation of 1956 and 1964 suffered from a fatal
ambiguity of purpose, and still more from the intense
opposition it aroused from the trade-union movement. The
attempt partially to withdraw from pay determination led to
a series of major strikes and courts of enquiry, some
victories and some defeats for the government, but little
noticeable reduction in the level of pay increases and an
explosion, not a diminution, of industrial militancy.[54]
Government efforts to reduce public expenditure were
singularly unsuccessful although it did carry through some
major tax reforms including the introduction of VAT.
Unsuccessful also were attempts to create a more competitive climate in industry. Aid to a few major firms like Upper
Clyde shipbuilders was cut off, causing still more industrial
unrest, but most state funding of industry continued and in
the case of firms like Rolls-Royce, which suddenly became
bankrupt in 1971, it had to be extended.

The failure of pay settlements to come down, the high
rate of inflation, the high unemployment in 1971, and above
all the slowness of industry to begin investing on an
appropriate scale, prompted a major revision of policies
during 1972. The level of industrial unrest which the
policies had created and the growing electoral unpopularity
of the government were also important in persuading the
government to seek alternative means of reaching its
objectives.[55] Membership of the EC was now within its
grasp, and it appeared anxious that the British economy
should be in a condition to prosper in the Community as
soon as entry was formally achieved at the beginning of
1973. It had been an axiom of Conservative electoral
strategy since the war that the party could not afford to be

identified with a negative and restrictionist policy, but should be ready to encourage more rapid rates of growth, if necessary by using public agencies to prod capital to invest more and to produce more.

In 1972 the Conservative Chancellor of the Exchequer, Anthony Barber, collected what became known as the Barber boom. In some respects it was a continuation of the Maudling plan of 1963–4. Maudling, appointed Chancellor of the Exchequer by Harold Macmillan in 1962, had believed that Britain could break out of the stop–go cycle and achieve its own 'economic miracle' so long as overseas borrowing could be arranged to cover any temporary deficit that arose on the balance of payments. In this way there would be no interruption to the expansion of demand. If the policy of expansion was persevered with, then in time investment would start rising, so would productivity, and so would output.

This plan was never tested because the deficit did not arise until after the general election: Labour having inherited the deficit proceeded to precipitate the crisis and gave first priority to defending the exchange rate. In 1972–3 the Heath government, urged on by most commentators at the time, showed that it was quite prepared to risk inflation in order to boost growth. Public spending was greatly increased, and the money supply was allowed to soar so as to raise the level of demand in the economy. The government reversed its industrial policy and with the passage of the new Industry Act appeared prepared to intervene on a considerable scale.[56] Major new prestige projects like the Channel Tunnel and Maplin airport were announced, and at the end of 1972, having failed narrowly to reach agreement with the TUC and the CBI, the government introduced the most comprehensive statutory prices and incomes policy since the war.

For a short period it looked as thought the policy might succeed. The entire capitalist world economy began to expand strongly in 1973 and for once the British economy was expanding as fast as its rivals. Its rate of growth in 1973 was 5 per cent which equalled Germany's.[57] The counter-inflation policy proved very successful in its first two stages, and looked like moderating the upward movement of prices and pay.[58]

The whole strategy suffered a spectacular shipwreck at the end of 1973, partly because of the internal crisis over pay caused by the miners' overtime ban and subsequent strike, partly by the loss of control of monetary policy, but mainly because of the abrupt termination of the world boom by the quadrupling of oil prices by OPEC, which was the trigger for the commencement of a generalised recession and plunged Britain into a balance of payments deficit which dwarfed all previous experience. Once again the attempt to break out of the constraints which for so long had governed British economic management had failed, and the economy was left in an extremely weak position to face the full force of the recession. It was to become clear that the old priorities of the social democratic consensus could be maintained no longer and that a new political terrain and new political possibilities were emerging. This was reflected in increasing polarisation between elements of the two major parties, and the canvassing of much more radical political solutions to Britain's problems than had appeared for a long time. But the key strategic question of the continuing debate about how to reverse the decline of British capitalism in the new context of world recession remained in keeping with Britain's past: not the issue of internal organisation, of individualism versus collectivism, or the free market versus planning, but the relationship Britain should have to the world economy and to the other capitalist powers, now that the long boom had ended and the recession had begun.

5

The sovereign market

The visible signs of Britain's unique course – as it slides from the affluent Western World towards the threadbare economies of the communist bloc – are obvious enough. We have a demotivating tax system, increasing nationalisation, compressed differentials, low and stagnant productivity, high unemployment, many failing public services and inexorably growing central government expenditure; an obsession with equality and with pay, price and dividend controls; a unique set of legal privileges and immunities for trade unions; and finally, since 1974, top of the Western league for inflation, bottom of the league for growth.

Sir Keith Joseph (1979)[1]

Two new strategies emerged in the 1970s to challenge the priorities of the established social democratic consensus: the free economy strategy of the New Right and the alternative economic strategy of the Labour Left. Both arose because of the apparent inability of either major party to secure the full co-operation of the organised working class and of business, in modernising the economy. The failure to secure and extend social democracy gave the opportunity for unravelling the post-war settlement and exploring new ways of ordering British capitalism and making it legitimate. This opportunity was seized in the great revival of economic liberalism which started at the end of the 1960s and began to make powerful inroads into the Conservative party. The ideological and political roots

of this strategy, which so strongly influenced the policies of
the Thatcher government, is the subject of this chapter.

5.1   Free trade and sound finance

Of the many possible standpoints within political economy
from which the problems of capitalist development and
economic policy can be assessed and analysed, two have
been particularly important in the economic policy debates
on British decline. They are liberal political economy, the
standpoint of the market, and national political economy,
the standpoint of the national economy. Both take for
granted the existence of the modern state, and its separation as a public realm from the economy, but they clash over
the principles for regulating and managing modern economies and determining the boundaries of state activities.

Liberal political economy has always been the stronger
ideological tradition in Britain, and its ascendancy became
firmly established in Britain during the movement to free
trade in the first half of the nineteenth century. It was
always associated with Liberals, Radicals and Utilitarians
and the analytical refinements undertaken by Ricardo gave
it a solidity and a certainty as a doctrine which made it a
formidable weapon in ideological debate. By the middle of
the nineteenth century liberal political economy had
become orthodoxy for British governments, because it
seemed to express so well the national interest of the British
state, and the logic of its commercial policy, clothing both
with the dignity of universal principles.

The virtues of liberal political economy as an ideological
doctrine would not have given it such ascendancy, however,
had it not also found continual reinforcement in some
important features of the organisation of the British state
and the British economy. British economic policy and
British business have long been dominated by perspectives
originating in banking and trade rather than in industry.[2]
This has given both an international orientation, which
liberal political economy with its emphasis on the world

market perfectly expresses. It has been strengthened in numerous institutional ways. The wide-spread use of sterling as an international currency, and the importance of London in the operation of the gold standard in the nineteenth century, encouraged expansion of the banking, insurance and shipping services provided by businesses in the City. The size and importance of the financial sector was enhanced because the British government depended on it to fund the National Debt and to control the money supply. The Bank of England, established in 1694 expressly for this purpose, grew to be the main channel for articulating the City's view of the national interest in economic policy.[3] Within the government two of the oldest Departments, the Treasury and the Board of Trade, have always tended to share this perspective on British national problems and therefore have endorsed the assumptions of liberal political economy. But the most important factor has been the external dependence of the British economy on the world economy, which the policy of free trade helped create in the first place. This basic reality of Britain's position has enormously reinforced the tendency to view Britain's economic problems from the standpoint of the world market. The external links of the British economy with the world economy have generally been presumed to be beyond dispute; any attempt to reduce them or limit them has been condemned as wrong in principle and damaging in practice; and national policy has been conceived as finding ways to adjust the national economy as smoothly as possible to world economic conditions, so uniting external and internal economic management.

In the nineteenth century this unity was achieved in the programme of free trade, sound finance, and *laissez-faire*. All three principles supported one another. The ideal state was a minimal state, which was parsimonious in its expenditures and undertook only those functions that were necessary to permit the widest possible sphere for free association and free exchange. The extravagance of the military establishment, and the expenses of administering colonies were prime targets for attack, because such state expenditures supported an idle and unproductive aristocracy and were financed by taxes on those directing the creation of wealth. A policy of sound finance meant subordinating government policy to the overriding need to maintain a stable medium of exchange, while the policy of *laissez-faire* meant that the budget should be balanced at the lowest level of expenditure that was compatible with maintaining the conditions for free and expanding markets. Stable money was also assured not only by governments concentrating on those functions that the market could not perform, but by the severe discipline of the gold standard. By tying domestic currency to gold reserves, limits were placed on domestic currency expansion, since all issue of paper money had to be backed by gold. At the same time deficits on trade had to be paid in gold, so any persistent imbalance in trade resulted in a loss of gold reserves which required automatically a contraction of the amount of money in domestic circulation, hence a fall in prices and a general deflation, until costs had been lowered and balance restored.

Before the nineteenth century economic doctrines played only a small part in shaping economic policies and economic strategies, but since that time they have become much more important. No system of political economy has ever been applied in isolation. Intellectual strategies have always had to wrestle with the multitude of immediate pressures arising from the interplay of institutions, interests, and circumstances. But the different systems of political economy have been increasingly employed to isolate causes, define goals, and suggest ways of reaching them.

So firmly embedded, however, did liberal political economy become that it has rarely appeared a crusading doctrine in England, but generally as an orthodoxy emanating from the bowels of the state. Only in the early nineteenth century and in the 1960s has it appeared as an outsider creed. Its rise to orthodoxy was consolidated during the struggle over the Corn Laws, the final bastion held against free trade. Their repeal in 1846 signalled the complete triumph of the free trade cause. The landowners who opposed repeal were defeated mainly because so substantial a measure of free trade had already been conceded that by the 1840s the balance of the economy decisively favoured the new financial, commercial, and industrial interests. If the final move to complete free trade had been blocked, not only would it have meant a decisive turn from the established commercial policy of expansion, but it would have directly threatened political stability, and might have led to the violent overthrow of the landowners' state. Cheap food was needed to sustain both the standard of living of the urban proletariat and the profits of the manufacturers.

Repeal in 1846 signalled that the state policy would conform to the new interests and new classes that had become dominant within the market order. The course Britain pursued after 1846 was consistent with the policy of the past 200 years, a hard-headed assessment and exploitation of commercial opportunities. Nevertheless it was to be a course without historical parallel. The balance between industry and agriculture was deliberately allowed to disappear as the law of comparative advantage suggested it should. The law stated that if all nations specialised in producing for the world market those things they could provide more cheaply than anyone else and relied on exchange to obtain whatever other goods they needed, then all nations would be better off. Yet even in states devoted to free trade principles, agriculture has normally been excepted from this remorseless logic and protected against foreign competition, because of its importance to the existence and independence of a national economy. The lack of protection afforded British agriculture between 1846 and 1916 is a major exception.[4] But the policy worked. It aided the expansion of the cities as well as an urban proletariat and contributed to an enormous enrichment of the whole British propertied class.

What made such boldness conceivable was not just the doctrine of free trade and the faith it inspired in the law of comparative advantage, but the fact that comparative advantage in producing manufactures was reinforced by a comparative advantage in naval and colonial possessions. These gave the British state the effective power to take on state functions for the world economy it dominated – policing the free movement of goods and capital and labour along the major trade routes, coercing recalcitrant and militarily inferior states into opening their markets to western trade, and increasingly guaranteeing a stable medium of exchange throughout the world economy.

A great challenge to free trade imperialism arose once the expansion of the world economy had brought the beginnings of industrialisation in states too strong to be coerced by Britain militarily. Once the world economy moved into a period of depression after 1873 and markets contracted, these states, Germany and the United States in particular, protected their industries against British competition by extremely high tariffs, and built up their productive capacity behind them. From the 1890s onwards when markets began to revive, many British industries began to face increasing competition both in the British domestic market and in world markets, yet still found themselves effectively shut out from the German and American markets by high tariffs. Such tariffs were increasingly used as weapons for waging trade war, since they maintained domestic producers' control of their own home market, and enabled them to sell their surplus production on world markets at prices that competitors could not match. In the face of the rising commercial and naval challenge of Germany and, to a lesser extent, of the United States, Britain's adherence to unilateral free trade brought the first major domestic clash over the priorities and direction of British economic policy since the struggle over the Corn Laws.

By the end of the century the landed interest as such had become relatively insignificant in domestic politics,[5] so the battleground over tariff reform was drawn within urban and industrial Britain, and expressed divisions among the leaders of industry and finance and their political representatives and allies. Both sides actively sought the support of the working class, whose electoral weight had become much greater since 1885. Apart from Irish Home Rule no other issue proved so divisive before 1914. The programme of Social Imperialism which the tariff reformers advanced is discussed in the next chapter. What is remarkable is that, despite all its apparent advantages, it was successfully resisted until 1916. Only total war forced the British government to abandon free trade.

The ascendancy of the Liberal party before 1914 preserved free trade. It was based on a number of factors. The bulk of British capital appears to have continued to favour free trade. No bankers are known to have supported or been associated with the campaign for tariff reform, and although industries like iron and steel, chemicals, glass and building wanted protection, all the leading export industries, including coal, cotton and shipbuilding, remained tied to free trade. The years of the tariff reform campaign were also years of booming world trade and a recovery by the old established industries of their former prosperity. The concrete advantages of the network of trade and finance which Britain had established, which the British state guaranteed, and which liberal political economy had consecrated as embodying not just a national and sectional advantage but the advantage of all nations, remained more attractive than the more speculative benefits of an imperial policy. Even when it came under challenge the informal commercial empire which Britain maintained over the whole world was still thought superior to a formal political empire over only one-quarter of it.

Tariff reform might still have triumphed, however, had not the Liberals preserved their electoral dominance. They did so partly through their parliamentary alliance with the Irish Nationalists after 1910, but mainly because they won the battle for working-class support. They constantly emphasised that tariff reform would mean dearer food, and that large sections of the working class were employed in industries which had grown to their present size because of free trade.[6] The Conservatives had hoped to prise the working class from its alliance with Liberalism by presenting tariff reform as a programme that would guarantee high employment and fair wages, and would provide revenues for social reforms and higher welfare spending.

The Liberals, however, now showed themselves quite prepared to legislate to give the trade unions crucial

immunities from certain provisions in Common Law.[7] The
Liberals proved more skilful in adapting to the pressures of
the new working-class electorate, and recognised the more
general need for the state to expand its role and assume new
tasks. They sacrificed and compromised important principles of the traditional individualist doctrine of liberal
political economy, to take account of the emerging needs of
a developed industrial economy and the demands of an
already overwhelming working-class electorate. Social
Imperialism could not be rooted in the working class on a
scale sufficient to tip the electoral balance. A large reservoir
of peasants and smallholders would have been needed to
provide the necessary political support; but if that had
existed, the policy of free trade might never have been
established in the first place.

The Great War of 1914–18 marks the beginning of the
collapse of British military, financial and industrial power.
Though the British ruling class was divided over free trade
before 1914, and over whether Ireland should be allowed its
own Parliament, it was much more united over the need to
prevent Germany establishing a mastery over Europe,
which could overshadow and undermine Britain's world
interests. The war was fought with strategic and political
and economic objectives that were closely intertwined. One
major British interest was to force Germany to abandon its
policy of capturing world markets from a protected home
base and to accept the disciplines of the liberal free trade
order Britain had constructed.

Yet from the outset British leaders knew how much
Britain stood to lose from a protracted war, and serious
attempts were made to limit the disruption as much as
possible. Only later when the struggle became prolonged
did Britain's leaders accept the need to abandon hopes of
maintaining the international credit and trading system
intact, and to wage total war. The war economies that were
established after 1916 and after 1940 brought lasting
changes to the British economy. They expanded the role of
the state more successfully than in any time of peace.[8] They
are major landmarks in the progress of collectivism in
Britain. They inspired policies to plan investment, to direct

labour, to channel consumption, to fix interest rates, to increase direct taxation, to control prices, wages and rents, to improve education, to stimulate research and to mobilise all unused resources.

After neither war did the state revert to its former size or former role. The war economies helped to move internal economic policy away from the individualist principles and *laissez-faire* principles of nineteenth-century liberalism.

They had much smaller impact, however, in relation to external policy. In 1918 and in 1945 the British state emerged quite determined to restore a liberal world trading and financial order as quickly as possible. After 1918 it was assumed that Britain would quickly resume its former role; in 1945 leadership and initiative had plainly passed to the Americans. Nevertheless on both occasions it was accepted almost without dissent that the reactivation of Britain's traditional international policy was a priority. The decision was particularly odd in 1918, since the difficulties in its path were enormous, and because the Conservatives, the bitter enemies of free trade, now dominated the government. The Liberals were losing ground as a major party, to Labour. Yet it was Conservative government in the 1920s who removed almost all the protective tariffs imposed during the war[9] and who took the major decision to restore Britain to the gold standard in 1925 at the pre war parity of $4.86.[10] The main argument for the return was that only if the old trading and financial networks were reconstituted would prosperity return to the industries whose markets had been so disrupted and diminished during the war. Despite the deflation this policy imposed on the British economy, despite the evident inability of the British state to carry it through, and despite the industrial confrontation it directly created, the policy was little challenged either intellectually or politically. The Conservatives in government accepted without reservation the orthodox external policy. The political will to fashion something different had passed.

The only period apart from the two war economies when liberal orthodoxy has been overthrown was during the 1930s. But once again the abandonment of the gold standard and the turn to protection were policies forced on

the National government by the severity of the world slump.
The National government was explicitly formed in order to
prevent the collapse of the gold standard. The organisation of
the sterling area and imperial preference was a response to
the fragmentation of the world economy, stagnant world
trade and output, and the absence of any power strong
enough to rebuild an international order. The new policies
sank no lasting roots, and once a power appeared after 1945
ready and able to undertake the rebuilding of the capitalist
world order, the traditional international policy of the
British state re-emerged to flourish once again.

What stands out in British economic policy is not simply
the dominance of liberal political economy, and the failure
of any political party successfully to challenge free trade,
the international status of sterling and the free movement of
capital, but the precise nature of this dominance. British
policy pursued open markets for British industries, but as
important for Britain's rulers became the state functions the
British state performed for the world economy. This
became the heart of the liberal orthodoxy. At home the core
of the policy was sound finance, which meant after 1918
continual attempts to retrench government expenditure
and balance the budget at a level of taxes that was thought
politically practicable. Persistence with this orthodoxy in
the face of the slump after 1929 brought the financial crisis
of 1931, because paying dole to the rapidly growing
numbers of unemployed unbalanced the budget.[11] Rather
than raise taxes, the leaders of the minority Labour
government preferred to follow the advice of the May
Committee and cut the dole. The government fell when
nine members of the Cabinet refused to support such
measures[12] and they had to be implemented by the National
government which Ramsay Macdonald proceeded to form.

The policy of sound finance was tied remarkably closely
to the policy of maintaining sterling on the gold standard.
The chief reason why an unbalanced budget was so much
feared was that it might cause a run on the pound. Sound
finance always had both an internal and an external
dimension. But strong as this liberal orthodoxy was, it was
consistent with other internal policies that had long been

undermining the basis of the individualist market order in Britain. The National government did not go back on retrenchment in the 1930s but it did permit a significant weakening of internal competition. Liberal political economy had always prescribed open markets as the best means for ensuring domestic competition, but in Britain this traditional external policy had not been accompanied by measures aimed at improving the workings of markets by creating the conditions for a more aggressive and dynamic capitalism. Instead the market order was allowed progressively to silt up. The wealth and power from long years of formal and informal Empire helped to ossify not just British industry but liberal orthodoxy as well. That was why the revival of liberal political economy in the 1960s was to have such impact.

5.2   The New Right

After 1945 the principles and perspectives of liberal political economy once more governed Britain's external policy, but internally Keynesianism triumphed. Nevertheless, although Keynesianism justified a much larger role for the state in the economy, and broke decisively with the orthodox notion that the government should not concern itself with the overall performance of the economy, it remained compatible with the goals of liberal political economy, because it proposed no interference with the detailed workings of markets and individual decision-making, only with aggregate demand, aggregate investment and *national* income. The automatic link between internal and external policy was dropped, but the priority given to sterling and to increasing the openness of the British economy meant the effective subordination of internal Keynesian demand management to the traditional liberal concerns of Britain's external policy.

Although Keynesianism originated as a variant of liberal political economy and many attempts were made to assimilate it theoretically to the main corpus of liberal

economics,[13] in practice it took the standpoint of the state
and the national economy, and so was particularly suited to
social democracy because it justified interventionist
policies.[14] The modernisation strategy of the 1960s did not
flow directly from Keynesian principles, from which could
be deduced only the indirect manipulation of demand, but
it did fit with the general Keynesian presumption that if the
market economy were not functioning satisfactorily, ways
should be found through public agencies of correcting its
outcomes. Keynesianism never shared the assumption of
liberal political economy that if markets were not working
there must be some obstacle which should be identified and
removed.

During the 1960s a fierce onslaught on Keynesianism
began which developed into a major revival of liberal
political economy. The main thrust of the attack was over
the policy of demand management and it crystallised in the
doctrine of monetarism. The dispute between Keynesians
and monetarists over the causes of inflation might have
remained merely a technical dispute, a development of the
earlier dispute between adherents of demand-pull and cost-
push theories of inflation.[15] But monetarism proved to be
only part of a much broader ideological and political attack
upon government intervention and upon social democracy.

The political force behind the revival of liberal political
economy was the rise of a New Right in the Conservative
party. The promulgation of the doctrines of economic
liberalism and the principles of a market order became
linked by New Right Conservatives to positions on issues
like immigration, law and order, strikes, social security
abuse, and permissiveness. A general offensive was initiated
upon many of the positions and values and assumptions of
social democracy by a great variety of right-wing pressure
groups, which from the late 1960s onwards began germinat-
ing like dragons' teeth.[16]

The main target of the New Right has been social
democracy; not merely the party and trade unions of
organised labour but also the willingness of Conservative
governments since the war to accept social democratic
policies and goals, and to work within social democratic

constraints. A constant complaint was that since 1945 the Conservative leadership had constantly betrayed Conservative principles by acquiescing in the steady consolidation of the power of organised Labour and the social democratic state, and had never 'put the clock back a single second'. Collectivism had steadily increased, economic liberty had been undermined, the economy as a result had declined and political freedom itself placed in jeopardy.

After 1968, and still more after 1974, the refurbished doctrines of liberal political economy made rapid progress. Keynesianism was in considerable disarray; the monetarist doctrines on the control of inflation became increasingly influential; and state expenditure, state intervention, and state enterprise all came under considerable attack.

It might seem surprising that the agency in Britain of this world-wide swing back to liberal political economy should be the Conservative party. which had always distanced itself from economic liberalism. It had often chosen to present itself as the party of the national economy and the state, the party of the community rather than the market, the party of protection and social imperialism, intervention and paternalism rather than the party of free trade, cosmopolitanism, self-help, and *laissez-faire*.

It was not inconsistent with its traditions that this party with its instinct for changing realities of power should have accepted Keynesianism and social democracy after 1940. The party had always had an individualist wing, but in the era of mass democracy its collectivist paternalist wing was more often in the ascendancy. Party historians were able to show how hostile the party had been to the doctrines of economic liberalism and to the policy of *laissez-faire* and free trade, and how often in the past Conservatives had condemned economic liberalism as doctrinaire and inflexible.[17]

One major reason for earlier Conservative hostility to economic liberalism was that it promoted individualism, questioned the authority of established institutions, and encouraged selfishness and competition between individuals and social classes. The Conservatives tended to think that preserving the social order was more important than preserving a market order. This attitude survived the disintegration of the Liberal party after 1916 and the entry of numerous 'doctrinaire' Liberals into the party, whose presence was resented by its imperialist and protectionist wing. But although these elements may have helped dilute the enthusiasm of the party for abandoning free trade, throughout the 1920s the Conservative leadership showed hardly any signs of even attempting to move outside the traditional liberal consensus on the role of sterling and the importance to Britain of the liberal world trading order. In their domestic policies the Conservatives pursued financial retrenchment. Neither policy involved a crusading commitment to the principles of economic liberalism, merely the acceptance of policies that had become orthodoxies for the British state. The substantial erosion of competition which took place in the 1930s worried the Conservatives not at all. On the contrary they encouraged it.[18]

The steady growing ascendancy of the doctrines of economic liberalism within the Conservative party can be traced back to the 1950s, but it acquired much greater significance once it became joined in the late 1960s to the forces and spokesmen of the New Right. The calls for greater competition and more economic freedom, which both the Conservative Bow Group[19] and the Institute of Economic Affairs.[20] had begun making in the late 1950s, acquired quite a different meaning in the general groundswell of New Right opinion. By the late 1960s a substantial section of the Conservative party was openly critical of the social democratic state and much of the record of post-war Conservative governments. In this context liberal political economy was used to challenge the assumptions and the priorities of economic management that social democracy and Keynesian economics had established.

The considerable advance made by the New Right within the Conservative party and the increasing pressure it was able to exert on the leadership, particularly when the party was out of office, was the result of the linking of the principles of a free market with more congenial Conservative emphases on a stronger state in the fields of defence, and law and order, and a strengthened family. It made the liberal political economy of the New Right in the Conservative party very different from the liberal political economy of Cobden and Bright.

The growth of popular discontent with so many of the institutions and policies of social democracy created a major problem of internal political management for the Conservatives, whose leaders remained committed to governing within the limits of the social democratic consensus. If the Conservatives had been unable to contain these new ideological forces they might have spilled outside into new parties and organisations. The danger was all the greater since the Conservative party has no formal democratic structure, and the leadership is more effectively insulated than the Labour party from the demands and pressures of its members.[21] To some extent a movement outside the party did begin to arise, but it was limited by an important shift within the Conservative leadership itself towards acceptance of the programme of the New Right.

Enoch Powell prepared the ground for this, although it was Margaret Thatcher who ultimately benefited, and it was Thatcherism not Powellism that captured the party and gave its name to the new strategy. Powell's importance initially was that he became an articulate exponent of the principles of liberal political economy from the 1950s onwards, and was regarded as highly eccentric and old-fashioned for doing so. But then in the 1960s, as a response to the failures of the modernisation strategy and the increasing disarray of social democracy, he broadened the focus of his political concerns and began to denounce not merely inflationary economic policies and the evils of high government spending and intervention, but also the permanent settlement of West Indian and Asian immigrants in Britain. Combined with his later attacks upon the EC, and his defence of the Ulster Protestants and the need to maintain the Union, he developed a major new political programme in which economic liberalism and political nationalism were skilfully and explicitly combined.

Powell attracted considerable support, bursting through the log-jam of political alignments and interests.[22] Ejected from the Conservative Shadow Cabinet he nevertheless became a power within the party that the Conservative leadership could not ignore. He acted as a focus for New Right opinion, and he demonstrated the popularity of a political programme that declared itself against the state and openly expressed popular frustrations and grievances. Powell won a big following in the working class for his nationalist position on immigration, but he chose not to consolidate it by establishing a new party. He preferred to continue to remain inside the Conservative party, and there became an isolated and ineffective critic of the Heath government and of the last desperate bid to achieve expansion within the constraints of social democracy.[23]

Nevertheless, after the Heath government's strategy had collapsed and the Conservatives had once again lost office, the alternative strategy Powell had staked out in his criticisms of the policies of the government became a rallying point for many in the party. The dismay in the party at the government's defeat in 1974, and the retrospective gloom which that threw over the whole record of the Heath government allowed Margaret Thatcher to seize her chance and to win the leadership. Powell had disqualified himself from contention by refusing to fight as a Conservative in 1974, but more importantly because his positions on Europe and immigration were not policies the party leadership was prepared to accept. Nevertheless, with the election of Thatcher to the leadership, the New Right, although not dominant within the party, was stronger than ever before.[24] The leadership in particular was extremely divided, and this was reflected both in the balance of the Shadow Cabinet and in the character of the policy documents that were issued.[25]

Unlike Powellism, Thatcherism has not been an anti-state movement. Thatcher owed her elevation to the normal procedures of the Conservative party, not to any popular pressure; nor did she encourage any movement outside the institutions of the established political system. She always operated as an insider. Whereas Powell did attempt to change British politics by establishing a populist and nationalist platform from which he strongly attacked many Establishment institutions and policies, Thatcher's style was to translate the themes of the new economic liberalism into slogans and ideas that tapped popular discontent with many aspects of the existing state, such as the arbitrariness of bureaucracy, the inefficiency of nationalised industry, the burden of taxation, the 'privileges' enjoyed by immigrants, the damage caused by strikes, the lawlessness of demonstrations and the undermining of the independence and moral responsibility of families. The key to the translation was the posing of central questions of government policy as problems of individual responsibility and individual choice. This ideology of self-help preached the right to be unequal, the need for self-reliance, and the need for everyone to take full responsibility for themselves and their families. It was closely allied to the call for stronger measures to discipline and control all social elements and minorities that threatened social order.

After 1974 Thatcherism emerged as the leading ideological force within the party and helped to revitalise Conservatism. It sought the creation of a new national consensus, through the breaking of the chains of collectivism, the revival of a liberal economy and the liberal society, and the restoration of Britain's national economic fortunes. An end to decline was what the New Right promised, and an end also to social democracy. The core of the strategy was derived from liberal political economy, but its especial strength and its popular appeal rested on rather different foundations, an atavistic emphasis on nation and family of the kind that have always nourished political movements of the right.

5.3 The free economy

The development of a strategy based on the principles of liberal political economy for halting economic decline already began from a position of considerable strength. Throughout the long night of Keynesianism and social democracy the liberal orientation of British external policy and the openness of the British economy were not threatened, they were restored. In the 1950s sterling was made convertible again, the specialised commodity markets of the City of London were reopened, trade barriers began to come down, the export of capital was resumed. But internally Keynesian demand management policies were pursued, public spending and taxation were high, and the government attempted to reconcile stable prices with unemployment, economic growth and a surplus on the balance of payments.

The key to the free economy strategy as it emerged in the 1970s was that it attempted to bring the internal policy once more into line with the external. Such a correspondence existed under the gold standard, when the internal money supply and level of activity was directly affected by any change in the external balance, because the money supply was tied directly to the gold reserves, and the gold reserves were used to settle debts. Governments could not interfere with the mechanism of adjustment, whatever the short-term effects on prices and employment. Expansions and contractions of the money supply and domestic activity were determined by changes in the trading balance, and the shipments of gold which these made necessary. The ideal of an international monetary system that was 'politician-proof' inspired Montagu Norman, the Governor of the Bank of England, in his efforts to rebuild the international monetary system during the 1920s.[26] It is remarkable how strong the faith remained. Even in the 1950s, during the height of Keynesianism, a plan was drawn up, although never implemented, by the Treasury, 'Operation Robot', for reuniting internal and external management once more, making many key economic policy decisions automatic, and therefore binding on the Chancellor, rather than a matter for his discretion.[27]

The heart of the free economy strategy was a search for just such a robot which could be entrusted with the management of the economy. For economic liberals the modern economy is not truly an economy at all, in the sense of a household which is centrally controlled and planned because it seeks to balance income and expenditure. Rather, it is a market order, a complicated network of individual exchanges organised through many different markets. This network of markets is not controlled by anyone, and so long as its basic rules are guaranteed, offers unparalleled opportunities and freedom for individuals to choose how to make the most of their talents, how to satisfy their wants, and how to live in the way they choose. A market order is a fragile and artificial creation which is threatened both by anarchy and by tyranny. To avoid anarchy a public power must be instituted to keep the self-interest of individuals within bounds, to protect property and persons, to enforce contracts and to guarantee a medium of exchange. A market order is necessarily an order governed by general rules which apply equally to all. Such rules create a sphere of individual liberty – the market. But the difficulty arises as to how the public power that is instituted to maintain the market order can be prevented from going beyond the establishment and enforcement of general rules, and intervening in the detailed choices and outcomes of the market.

From the perspective of liberal political economy such interference must be arbitrary and discretionary. It has nothing to do with law, understood as a system of general rules. A liberal government would be one which confined itself to its primary functions and sought to keep its expenditure at the minimum required to do so effectively. The problem with which all modern liberal thought has wrestled is that the greatest threat to the market order, the greatest urge to expand discretionary intervention and bureaucratic administration, to plan and organise ever greater parts of society collectively, to increase public spending and the taxes that have to be levied to finance it, have all been associated with the rise of democracy. The assertion of equal political and social rights, alongside equal legal rights and the development of collective organisations and mass parties to press for them, has created a continual tension between the ideal of a market order and the ideal of a social democracy. It is hard for the modern state to be both, and it has become increasingly difficult to find a democratic basis for a market order. That is why most economic liberals put liberty first and democracy some way behind.[28]

From the standpoint of the new economic liberalism, the cause of Britain's economic decline and the steady withering of Britain's industrial base is the wholesale perversion of the market order that has occurred in Britain since the turn of the century. It involved the supplanting of individualism by collectivism and it led, so it is argued, to the proliferation of obstacles to the workings of free markets throughout British society, so that Britain was rather rapidly transformed from a country with some of the most sensible and efficient social and political arrangements from a liberal point of view, to a sink of collectivism, bureaucracy and inefficiency.[29]

In foreign economic policy there had been a partial retreat from the principles of free trade and openness to the world economy with the introduction of protectionist measures during the 1930s. Market liberals wanted a return to free trade principles and an end to all controls on capital movements and on trade.

There was disagreement over the best kind of international monetary system. The impossibility of maintaining sterling's traditional international role was acknowledged, but opinion tended to be split over whether floating exchange rates or a new gold standard were the best solution for creating the kind of international financial stability that international capitalism has lacked since 1971. The problem with floating exchange rates is that they impose no automatic constraint on the domestic expansion of the money supply in individual nation-states, and can therefore permit and even encourage accelerating inflation. They do not force countries to adjust to external price shocks. They leave them the option of inflating. On the other hand floating exchange rates do avoid the problems of fixed rates. There is no longer any need for periodic realignments of currencies, whilst the need for either international political agreement or the unchallenged dominance of one state in order to preserve international financial stability is reduced.

Another problem in Britain's external relations with the capitalist world was disagreement over the EC. Many economic liberals denounced the EC because one of its key programmes, the Common Agricultural Policy, was protectionist and inefficient. It subsidised the weakest producers. Those like Powell who were British nationalists opposed also any moves towards tighter federation and to economic and monetary union because they would have involved the loss of the freedom of each nation to determine its own taxes and expenditure and to be responsible for its own money supply and exchange rate.[30] Some economic liberals support the EC because of the progress it represents to freer and wider markets, but do not accept that Britain's sovereignty must eventually be merged in a wider European sovereignty.

But whatever the disagreements, the priority accorded to maintaining Britain's traditional liberal orientation was never questioned. No course other than complete integration in the world economy was contemplated. The thrust of the free economy strategy was aimed at identifying and removing those obstacles in Britain's internal policies and arrangements that prevented a more rapid and flexible adjustment of the British economy to the requirements of international capitalist competition.

5.4 Monetarism

Four areas were singled out by the free economy strategy for major changes. They were Keynesian economic management, the interventionist role of government in the economy, the power and privileges of the trade unions, and the demands for high public spending which arise in democracies. All created obstacles to the workings of free markets; and together they provided the core policies of social democracy.

The significance of monetarist doctrine for liberal political economy is that stable money is one of the indispensable conditions for a market order.[31] Inflation attacks the basis of the market order, since not only is it a tax that no one has voted for, but it threatens to disrupt the elaborate mechanism of exchange between individuals and therefore calls into question the legitimacy of the market order itself.

The starting point for all free market thinking was that the chief aim of government economic policy should be maintaining price stability by firmly controlling the money supply. Monetarism revived the traditional orthodoxy on monetary questions. Inflation is always and everywhere a monetary phenomenon; it can be halted if the growth of the money supply is curtailed; and control of the money supply is one of the few things that governments can control in a capitalist economy, provided they are determined enough.[32] They must aim to balance their budgets, or at least borrow in a way that does not increase money supply. This means they must either raise their taxes or reduce their spending. They must also set firm monetary targets, preferably several years ahead, in order to keep control of the volume of private credit. The recommendation for monetary targets appeared to have special force in a world of floating exchange rates, since only if internal monetary discipline is observed can internal inflation be mastered and external inflationary shocks, such as a sudden rise in the price of oil, be accommodated. In this way the policy of openness to the world economy was reconciled to domestic stability.

Monetarist doctrine made stable money and the control of inflation not just the main goal but the only legitimate goal of government policy. Money is an essential condition for a market order, so must be guaranteed by a central authority.[33] But while money can and must be an object of government policy, and general rules should be pursued in regulating its supply, monetarists argued that no such general rules can cover growth, employment and the balance of payments. From the monetarist standpoint this is not to compare like with like. Growth, employment and the balance of payments are all regarded as the outcomes of a multitude of individual decisions in which no government should be directly interfering. The delicate trade-offs of Keynesian economic management, the careful adjustment of the fine tuners, were to be no more. To trade unemployment against inflation was to sacrifice one of the fundamentals of a free market and opened the way to ever greater discretionary intervention in pursuit of a national economic interest.

Inflation had to be mastered if the market order was to be preserved, and demand policies that raised the rate of inflation only ensure that the cutback which would eventually be necessary to restore stable money would be more painful and involve higher unemployment and a deeper recession. Salvation either lay in the market or it did not exist at all.[34]

5.5   State intervention

Sound money is compatible with many different levels of government activity. In market doctrine, however, only a minimal state will ensure that sound money is maintained, and that it has the beneficial effects on the economy that are intended. The attacks made by nineteenth-century liberals on the expenses of the military establishment and the administration of the colonies as an unproductive burden upon industry have been refurbished; only this time the target is rarely the enormous defence establishment, but the social and welfare programmes of advanced capitalism when these are financed collectively through the state.

In Britain, this part of the public sector, which has been steadily expanding since the turn of the century, and was significantly enlarged after 1940, was treated by market strategists as a major obstacle to greater internal competition and a major unproductive burden on the 'wealth-creating' sector and on taxpayers. It was regarded as 'unproductive' because only individual producers could create 'wealth' by producing commodities and exchanging them on the market. The government was only a producer in its role as manager of the nationalised industries. In all its other roles it was necessarily a parasite dependent on raising taxes from individual commodity producers and property owners.[35]

Only the private sector can create wealth, only the public sector can guarantee the right framework for its operation. In so far as the state carries out those functions it is legitimate and has a duty to raise taxes because it is enforcing what is a true general interest – the preservation of the market order. But once it begins increasing its expenditures and interventions, then it undermines the workings of the market order by reducing the incentives for individuals to work and compete, and to take responsibility for themselves and their families. It also distorts the pattern of choices and activities that would have spontaneously emerged if state intervention had been absent.

Cutting back public expenditure from the levels it had attained in Britain was a central part of the free economy strategy for reversing decline, not just to assist in the control of inflation, but to inject greater dynamism and incentives into the economy by making market forces more effective and lowering taxation. The society would not only then be morally improved but more efficient too. If government spending is too high and the government is forced to borrow money, then either it borrows from the banks, which directly increases the money supply and eventually the rate of inflation, or it must raise the money from the financial markets, paying whatever rate of interest is required to elicit funds. Since the government has compulsory powers of taxation, it can normally afford whatever interest rates are needed, but in the process it 'crowds out' the borrowing of private individuals and companies who cannot afford credit at the going interest rate.[36]

Both sound money and a free, competitive market require major reductions in the size of the public sector, and the confinement of government to a 'neutral policy stance' eliminating detailed interference in markets. Again the principle is quite clear. Apart from the maintenance of the general conditions without which a market order could not exist at all, governments composed of fallible politicians and bureaucrats are regarded as quite unsuitable to be trusted with decisions which could be left to markets. This is because governments do not have to calculate risks in the same way as private individuals and companies, because they are protected from the consequences of failure. Their interventions lead necessarily to privileges being granted to particular individuals and interests in the market and denied to others. Subsidies, special incentives, special prohibitions have all to be financed out of general taxation. Instead of taxes being used only to provide 'public goods'[37] which cannot be provided by individuals, they are used to give some individuals special advantages over others.

The main targets were public spending on welfare, and subsidies to industry, including nationalised industries. Welfare spending came under such attack because most of the services, including health, education and housing, could be provided almost entirely through the market. Individuals would have to pay for all the services they used and to insure themselves; but the great reduction in public spending that would result would allow genuine reductions in taxation – not just a rearrangement of the balance but actual reduction of the burden. The immediate aim would be to cut back state spending sufficiently to reduce income tax by one-third to one-half. Ending all subsidies to industry and returning all nationalised industries to private ownership would force much more rapid contraction and reorganisation on industries like shipbuilding, steel and cars – all of which had previously been given government aid to ease their steady run-down. A free economy strategy could provide large redundancy payments (although even this would be to give the workers involved 'privileges'), but every firm would have to survive in the world market entirely on its own. Market forces alone would be relied upon to force restructuring of industry, the raising of productivity and the creation of conditions in which profitable enterprises could once more emerge.

5.6   Trade-union power

The major obstacle to the rule of the market once the state had been rolled back was the resistance of the trade unions. Britain had long been regarded as possessing an especially powerful trade-union movement. From a New Right point of view trade unions are voluntary associations which have a legitimate purpose in providing insurance and welfare for their members. When, however, they seek to interfere in contracts in the labour market, and to influence the attitudes and behaviour of employees at work, they cease to be voluntary associations and become coercive groups and private monopolies. As such they are by far the most important obstacle to the workings of a market order. Monopolies enjoyed by firms are regarded not only as rarer but as a much more minor problem. There are no suggestions amongst market theorists that existing concentrations of capital should be broken up, or that attempts should be made to create competitive markets made up of a multitude of small individual producers. From the social market standpoint the activities of even the most gigantic economic 'individual' like General Motors are still regulated by the world market and by international competition. Trade unions, however, stop markets from functioning at all.

Their ability to do this in Britain is regarded as resting upon three special privileges which they enjoy – Enoch Powell listed them in 1968 as 'the freedom to intimidate' (peaceful picketing), 'the freedom to impose costs on others with impunity', and 'the immunity of trade unions from action of tort'.[38] These three privileges do represent a major part of the concessions won by trade unions in their long battle for recognition and for greater bargaining power. They are the essential privileges protecting and making effective the right to strike. Granted in 1906, they were not revoked even in 1927, and had been confirmed or extended by parliamentary legislation whenever threatened by new legal interpretations based on the Common Law. It is these privileges that the free economy strategy would revoke in order to create a much more 'flexible' labour market and a much more co-operative work-force.

Trade unions were seen as the organisations which must either be destroyed or drastically reduced in their importance and power if a social market economy is to arise. This is because although they are absolved from direct responsibility for the rate of inflation, they are considered responsible for most of the other ills that afflict the economy. They are blamed for whatever level of unemployment exists, because by resisting cuts in real wages they prevent competitive downward bidding among the unemployed for the available jobs.[39] They are blamed also for stagnation and low productivity, by insisting on levels of manning, and rules covering the safety, the speed and the intensity of work, which impose significantly higher costs on firms and prevent more rapid rationalisation and modernisation. Instead of firms being co-operative ventures between management and workers, trade unions often make them a battleground for opposing interests and limit managerial authority.

Ways of tackling union power varied. The simple monetarist line was that once sound money is restored trade unions lose their power, because they can no longer influence government policy and because they cannot indefinitely resist market forces. They can create unemployment by pricing their members out of work, but they cannot cause inflation itself (since they cannot directly print money). Rising unemployment is expected eventually to break the militancy and weaken the organisation of the unions by reducing the numbers enrolled, as it did in the 1920s and 1930s. Other advocates of the strategy, however, argued that high unemployment in the past weakened but did not destroy or reform the trade unions. They feared the consequences of prolonged high unemployment on the electorate, on social order and on the finances of the state, so they called for more direct measures; not outright abolition of the right to strike, but certainly the organisation of powerful strike-breaking forces and the rescinding of the legal privileges trade unions had enjoyed. A minimal state does not mean a weak state. On the contrary the state had to be strong to ensure the conditions in which a free economy could work. That meant confronting and transforming all those institutions and interests which currently stood in the way.[40]

5.7 Democracy

The problem of trade unions merges into the problem of

democracy itself. Free economy strategists are acutely aware of the short span of time available between elections to introduce changes, and how much longer on average are the time spans of the policies themselves. They place more importance on the presence of a public power that is able to guarantee a market order and therefore a realm of individual liberty, than on how that public power is established and to whom it is answerable. It makes them unenthusiastic democrats. They have never accepted that temporary democratic majorities have the right to interfere with the workings of the market order or to threaten individual economic liberty. Since the fundamental principles and conditions of economic freedom are already known they may be endorsed but cannot be discovered through the democratic process. It has always seemed safer to economic liberals to devise ways in which economic policy can be placed above politics, and made a matter of expert administration within unalterable constraints.[41] Some states have experimented by writing certain precepts of economic liberalism into their constitutions, so taking a range of important economic decisions and options out of the hand of politicians. There has been some support for such constitutional devices in Britain.[42]

The chief problem with democracy for the social market strategy is that it tends to generate pressures and demands that are not compatible with a market order. In Britain the problem was regarded as especially serious, because the trade unions were not only a major obstacle to the working of the market order, but are also closely associated with one of the two leading political parties. The Labour party, in which the trade unions are a major force and the main source of funds, has been a vehicle both for the preservation and consolidation of trade union privileges, and also for the extension of bureaucratic intervention in the economy, for expanding public enterprise, and for expanding public expenditure and taxation. As a result of post-war electoral competition between the two main parties for the votes of the working class, free economy theorists argued that the balance of the economy had swung away from the market order towards collectivism. Governments had steadily expanded universal welfare provision and adopted numerous policies, for example in housing, which enlarged the scope for arbitrary administrative decision-making and weakened the flexibility and the universality of the market.[43] At the same time the electorate was encouraged to expect that governments, using their new technical ability to control the economy, could achieve goals like prosperity, growth, and full employment. So anxious did governments become to fulfil them that they expanded the money supply and raised demand whenever there were temporary setbacks to growth or slight rises in unemployment. In this way the sphere of bureaucracy expanded and the sphere of law declined, and the economy became riddled with distortions, inefficiencies and accelerating inflation. Prosperity was maintained but at an increasing cost.

The problem of how to prevent democratic electorates voting for policies that damage the market order and lead to economic ruin was one of the central problems for free economy strategy. In Britain it appeared to require either the destruction or the transformation of the Labour party, or the severing of the links between organised labour and any political party. Otherwise any revocation of legal privileges might not endure. Some Conservatives as a result became convinced of the need for a radical overhaul of the British political system, including the introduction of proportional representation.[44]

The free economy strategy was an ambitious attempt to realign Britain's external and internal policies of economic management, to recreate a free economy and to make the state strong enough to establish and police it, and to attack social democracy at its roots. It identified the main causes of British decline as the abandonment of the domestic commitment to sound money, the growth of state spending and state intervention, and the power of trade unions. All these have come about and consolidated one another as the result of the workings of British democracy over the past hundred years. As a result Britain has become progressively enfeebled, less and less able to compete internationally.

Since Britain's integration in the capitalist world market

was taken as the starting point for the strategy, the whole burden of adjustment to the demands of international competition falls on internal institutions and practices. The strategy therefore envisaged a prolonged struggle to force through the necessary changes in attitudes and behaviour. Its advocates were always more adept at setting out the general principles of their doctrine than at specifying exactly how the political and social conditions necessary for its implementation could be created.

6
The enterprise state

The post-war consensus, built upon full employment and the welfare state, failed to command the support of people because they have seen first that it did not contain within it any element whatsoever of transformation, and secondly, that even by its own criteria it failed. That policy could not bring about growth, it could not extend freedom, it could not even maintain let alone develop welfare and it could not sustain full employment.

Tony Benn[1]

The second strategy to be discussed is the alternative economic strategy of the Left in the Labour movement. Like the free economy strategy this was not a single strategy. Many variants existed and many different groups on the Left contributed to it. There is considerable ambiguity surrounding the alternative economic strategy because it drew on two different traditions of political economy – national political economy and the socialist critique of political economy. The free economy strategy fits into a tradition of liberal political economy that stretches back through the nineteenth century. But the immediate precursors of the alternative economic strategy with its concern for the national economy and making the state an 'enterprise state', devoted to raising industrial output and social wealth, were the alternative strategies of Joseph Chamberlain and the Social Imperialists, and Oswald Mosley and the Fascists. Neither movement at the time attracted significant support from the organised Labour movement. But just as the programme of Margaret Thatcher is not that of Richard Cobden, so the alternative economic strategy is different from these predecessors. What they have in common is the perception that it is the external policy which must be challenged and the external relations which must be transformed to reverse decline, whereas liberal political economy has always started from the assumption that it is individual attitudes and behaviour within Britain that must be adjusted to world market forces.

Many socialists became supporters of the alternative economic strategy and argued that the objective of seeking to establish control over a national economy was a socialist objective, because the world economy had moved into a new phase. The rise of nation companies and economic interpenetration had destroyed the world of competitive national capitalisms of the period before 1914 and during the 1930s. The bourgeoisie had become international, and the appropriate response for every national working class was to seek to win control of each national economy and in this way lay the foundations for a socialist world economy. Such arguments, with their often explicit relationship to Marxist theory, shared many of the central preoccupations of national political economy.

6.1   Social Imperialism

Liberal political economy became a doctrine of compelling force in the nineteenth century but it did not go unchallenged. Standpoints other than the market arose for viewing and assessing the development of capitalism. One of the most important of these was national political economy. Its standpoint is not the market and the individual, but the national economy and the state, an approach rooted in the fragmentation of the capitalist world market into a large number of rival political authorities, the nation-states.

The distinctive doctrines of national political economy were never strong in England because national economic policy early embraced the doctrine of free trade and identified the British national interest with the furthest possible expansion of the world market. Those who argued for a different external policy and a more cautious development of industry were cast aside.[2] National political economy developed at first in other countries, notably Germany and the United States.

From the outset it was directed against some of the key doctrines of liberal political economy, particularly free trade. It never had the intellectual coherence of economic liberalism but it increasingly exercised great practical influence. This was because it offered explanations for the shortcomings of markets, and remedies, which did not involve submitting to the internal restorative powers of markets themselves. As capitalism developed so there were more and more things which liberal political economy seemed unable to explain: economic backwardness and the problems of industrialisation; economic power and military power; the rise of bureaucracy and large-scale enterprise; the increasingly collective basis of the industrialisation process and the need for greater state intervention; the independent industrial and political organisations of labour movements; crises of overproduction and the collapse of investment and demand; and amidst all this growing difficulties in maintaining the legitimacy of the market order on which capitalist relations and capitalist production depended. All these trends which accompanied the development of capitalism as the first world system of production and accumulation continually created the need for national economic policies that protected nations and groups within the nation, against the effects of markets.

National political economy as a rather disparate collection of doctrines draws its fundamental strength from viewing capitalism as more than a series of markets connecting the economic activities of individuals. It places the emphasis instead on capitalism as a system of organised and increasingly collective and interdependent production. The aim of policy accordingly is not to give first priority to fostering commercial opportunity and the widest possible system of exchange, but to building up and safeguarding productive capacity and securing collaboration between the major classes and interests involved in industry.

Such an emphasis was already present when national political economy first took shape as a protest against Britain's industrial monopoly and the way in which free trade consolidated it. The most vociferous advocates of protection against British competition were in Germany and the United States, the two countries with the greatest prospects of effectively challenging it. Friedrich List[3] quite readily accepted the superiority of liberal economic theory but denied that the political conditions – a single world state – existed for a liberal order to be practicable. Rivalry between nation-states provided the framework within which all economic development had to proceed. To elevate the principles of liberal political economy from a distant goal into a set of maxims for policy favoured the interests of the strongest states against the weaker.

National political economy originated as a protest against the inequalities and injustices of free trade, and this has remained one of its central features. But as industrialisation developed and the character of the new processes of production became better understood, so national political economy became broadened into a concern with production rather than with the market and with the role of public agencies in making good deficiencies in markets. This rarely meant a wholesale rejection of markets but it did entail going beyond the liberal rationale for state involvement – creating the conditions for markets to function effectively. The basis of national political economy in all its forms has been to recognise not how smoothly the market economy adjusts to shocks and disturbances, but how discontinuities and crises and instability are inherent in the working of the capitalist production process. The remedy as far as national political economy is concerned is not the removal of obstacles to the workings of markets but the removal of obstacles to the development of production.

Viewing capitalism as primarily a system of production rather than a system of markets flows naturally from the assumption that it is not individuals who compete in the world market, but nation-states. Economic policy must have the aim not merely of realising the interest of individual producers and consumers, but of increasing the power and maintaining the security of the state. From the standpoint of national political economy, free trade is a tactical policy that may at certain times be in the interests of a state to adopt. List admitted that if he were an Englishman he would be a free trader.[4]

In the nineteenth century liberal political economy and national political economy came to offer alternative conceptions of national interest, and become associated with different social bases and political forces. National political economy became the perspective of all those groups entrenched in the apparatuses of the state and practised in defining and formulating the national interest. It supplied the economic principles for nationalist and right-wing political forces, but because its bias was collectivist rather than individualist it also proved increasingly attractive to those liberals and social democrats who wished to use public agencies to reform and restructure social institutions.

What marks national political economy so clearly is its tendency to treat the nation as a single strategic commercial and industrial enterprise, competing with other similar enterprises in the world economy. Liberal political economy treats the nation as an association of individuals pursuing their own separate purposes within a framework of law. The nation has no purpose other than the purposes of the individuals who compose it. If these purposes demand exchanges with foreigners, the government must not obstruct but facilitate them. For national political economy there is a national interest beyond the purposes of individuals, which it is the task of the permanent agencies of the state to identify, formulate and secure.

Once British industry began to lose ground in world markets, because of the very high tariffs erected against British goods, and subsequently because of direct competition from the industries that developed behind them, the free trade policy began to be re-examined. New forces on the Right in Britain began to clamour for a policy of imperial protection and national efficiency to meet the growing challenge from foreign rivals, and safeguard Britain's future prosperity. A struggle erupted between the adherents of a policy of free trade and the adherents of tariff reform. A national policy was inescapable. The dispute was over whether it should aim to maximise the opportunities and the returns for British companies, banks, and workers by maintaining the greatest possible degree of openness to the world economy, or whether it should be subordinated by public agencies to a national assessment of British interests, British welfare and British security.

This battle was on a much grander scale than the battle over the Corn Laws, where the pleas for protection were so much more clearly the pleas of a sectional interest. What was new about the tariff reform debate sixty years later was that in the meantime industrial capitalism had completed the transformation of British society and the organisation of a world economy, and the urgent questions of policy concerned not whether industrial advance should be reined back, but how it was to be sustained and the gains from the past consolidated and extended.[5]

The Social Imperialist movement at the turn of the century was the first major political response to the problem of British decline, the first major attempt to change the course of British policy. The Social Imperialists proposed to meet the threats to Britain's strategic position and commercial superiority by consolidating a political empire within the world economy, which could make Britain self-sufficient. For the Social Imperialists the tariff reform programme was not merely a means of maintaining and extending British prosperity, but also of meeting the military and strategic challenge of other states. The dream of Greater Britain, of a federation of Anglo-Saxon settlers states, organised as a bloc within the world economy and strong enough to maintain its independence and prosperity, is a dream that has faded. It was a major alternative geopolitical strategy, but it was not pursued, and the opportunity for it disappeared. Its rationale was to preserve Britain's great power status, and to secure permanent world markets for British industry, but once that status was no more, protectionism rapidly lost its practicality and its appeal for most of the Right. The American alliance, and a junior role in helping to maintain the open trading and financial system of the world economy, became the new framework for Conservative thinking after 1945.[6]

National political economy was regarded as inescapable for states that desired independence to pursue ambitions and to order their own internal affairs as they saw fit. Milner declared, 'This country must remain a Great Power or she will become a poor country' and all the Social Imperialists constantly stessed the links between military strategy and commercial strategy. The Boer War (1899–1902) was regarded as one of the greatest successes of the new Social Imperialism. Julian Amery has described it as:

> a masterstroke of policy. Few victories in British history have done more to increase Britain's economic or military power. After the peace of Vereeniging British settlers and British capital poured into the country. Today it has become Britain's second most important market in the world and the ground where well over £1000 million of British capital are profitably invested.[7]

The Social Imperialists were successful in getting Britain to adopt a more aggressive and conscious policy of imperialist expansion. Liberal as well as Conservative governments were equally committed to the principle of a strong navy and the maintenance of the colonial possessions, even though there was disagreement between the parties over specific acts of imperial policy. But the real conflict came over whether Britain should seek to make its dominant position permanent by an economic and political policy aimed at converting the Empire into a single world state. The rationale was always that Britain could only hope to solve the problems of her economy within a much wider framework of trade and payments than the British national economy permitted, and only a Greater British state could guarantee that Britain remained dominant within such a framework.

The Social Imperialists believed that Britain could only preserve its power and its wealth if its leaders realised the dangers into which the policy of expansion had led the nation. Chamberlain emphasised this point again and again in his speeches:

> Why do the people not realise that Germany is making
> war upon us, that her economic attack is just as surely an
> act of aggression as if she had declared hostilities? She
> will never rest until she dominates the world . . . Tariff
> Reform is our defence. It is just as vital as the navy. We
> must arm if we are not to be beaten without striking a
> blow.

> Workers cannot live off investments in a foreign country.
> If that labour is taken from you, you have no recourse
> except perhaps to learn French or German . . . you cannot
> go on forever watching with indifference the disappear-
> ance of your principal industries.[8]

But the Social Imperialists never did succeed in wresting
Britain from its traditional liberal policy. Protection was
always resisted and only triumphed briefly, during the First
World War after 1916, and again after 1932. In both cases
the liberal order in the world economy had first to be
destroyed.

Social Imperialism also involved an internal strategy for
winning the support of the working class and increasing
industrial efficiency. The reason for Britain's decline was
ascribed directly to the long period of *laissez-faire* policies,
the pursuit of short-term commercial gains leading to the
neglect of military preparedness, and the shameful
exploitation of the working class. Social Imperialism set out
to win the mass support for imperialist policy of the kind
which Chamberlain had long enjoyed in Birmingham. It
sought mobilisation of the population behind collective
national goals and recognised as a result that concessions
were necessary to secure loyalty. The leading Social
Imperialists despised the ineffectiveness of national policy
and the lack of strong leadership which parliamentary
politics produced. Germany was feared but also much
admired by them. It had abandoned a liberal economic
policy and it had never had to endure liberal political
institutions.

The result was a concerted attempt to put forward a programme and build a movement that could overcome the grievances of the working class and dramatically increase national power. The Social Imperialists regarded class conflict as one of the most serious elements weakening the nation in its competition with other nations. Free trade policy might provide cheap food but it also provided slums, low wages, unemployment, illiteracy, and malnutrition. The physical condition of the English workers was regarded as so poor by many Social Imperialists that they doubted whether an efficient army could be formed.[9] The Social Imperialists proposed social reforms that would be paid for out of the revenue from tariffs and could heal the rift between capital and labour, and establish a new spirit of class harmony and class collaboration.

The failure of the external programme of the Social Imperialists did not prevent the steady realisation of the internal programme, as pressure from the working class was increasingly exerted and as the scale of the needs that were not being met through markets became more appreciated. This part of Social Imperialism, increasing public expenditure to bear the costs of free market competition in the interests of social stability and greater economic efficiency, became part of the general political consensus and was appropriated by other political forces fully committed to maintaining free trade, especially the 'New Liberals' and social democrats who came increasingly to dominate the policy discussions of the Labour movement.[10]

6.2 Fascism and the slump

Under Chamberlain, Social Imperialism had captured the Unionist party, but the Unionist party failed to oust the Liberals from office. In the aftermath of war, revolution abroad and the rise of Labour at home, the new dominant Conservative party in the 1920s remained trapped within liberal orthodoxy and failed to implement the programme of Social Imperialism. The rejection of tariffs, the return to gold, and the General Strike, were all viewed by many Social

Imperialists as a fatal policy of negative anti-Socialism, holding the line for property and defending Britain's traditional world interests. They saw it as a policy doomed to eventual defeat, since it could delay but not avert the steady decline of British world power and the advance of Labour.[11]

It was under these circumstances that Oswald Mosley launched his New Party in 1931 to overthrow the 'old gangs' of politics and forge an entirely new course. The links with the strategy of Social Imperialism are obvious, although Mosley went further than Chamberlain in several respects. He attempted to create a mass movement outside the existing party system, he advocated much greater state direction of the economy, and he was much more explicit in identifying the City of London as one of the chief obstacles to implementing an economic policy that preserved the interests and future of the national economy.

Mosley was strongly influenced by Keynes in his economic thinking, particularly in his approach to the problem of unemployment, but he also shared the strategic and geopolitical perspectives of the Social Imperialists.[12] He argued that the breakdown of the liberal world economy, and the sharp reduction of Britain's major export markets as a result of the war, made a change in Britain's external policy still more urgent. The orthodox liberal policy of patiently rebuilding the international monetary system, restoring the liberal trading network, encouraging rationalisation of domestic industry, and waiting for a revival of the four leading industrial sectors – textiles; iron, steel and engineering; coal; and shipbuilding – had to be rejected. It condemned the British economy to perpetual stagnation and high unemployment. It would benefit finance because it would maintain the unlimited mobility of capital but it would seriously weaken domestic industry. Mosley argued that experience of the 1920s and the world slump proved that Britain's position of dominance in the world economy had been irretrievably lost. Other countries had developed their own local manufactures, new powerful industrial competitors had arisen to challenge Britain's hold on many markets, and British industry could not match the low costs of some foreign producers and had to face the dumping of their surplus production on the British market. At the same time, the progress of technology and mass production meant that modern industries throughout the world had a far greater capacity than ever before. The world economy was gripped by a general crisis of overproduction and Britain no longer had either the industrial or the military power to regain its control over world markets.[13]

Mosley's solutions were set out in the Memorandum on unemployment he submitted to the Prime Minister in 1930 when he was a junior minister, and in *The Greater Britain*, a founding document of the British Union of Fascists in 1932. He came to advocate a policy of economic self-sufficiency. Britain should tackle its unemployment problem by ruthlessly protecting its home market (using quotas rather than tariffs), developing trade links with the self-governing Dominions and controlling all colonial markets. He advocated, for example, the closing of the Indian market to Japanese competition and a new suppression of the local Indian textile industry, to maximise the demand for British products. In this way Britain could guarantee sufficient markets for its own industries. The chimera of a new world ascendancy for British capital would give place to the more attainable objective of a strong world empire, able to rival all other states.[14]

Such a policy meant confronting the City of London and subordinating finance to the objectives of national policy. The currency would be managed, and internal money supply and credit creation would be determined, by the need to secure full employment of resources and the development of productive capacity, rather than by the need to achieve an external trade balance and to maintain confidence in sterling. Mosley wanted to sweep away the minimal state and to concentrate the whole energies of government on finding a solution to the unemployment problem. He proposed establishing a small War Cabinet with its own civil service by passing the Treasury and the Board of Trade. This powerful executive would carry through measures to alleviate unemployment by whatever programme of public works proved necessary. It would seek controls over credit and investment, establishing new public agencies to achieve this, and would carry through major rationalisations of industry and agriculture. Such rationalisations would succeed, Mosley thought, because the government would ensure that markets were available and would not rely on market forces to carry them through. The greatly increased capacity of modern industry, which was causing the great shortfall in markets, could be handled if the state undertook to maintain effective demand at a high enough level through its spending and credit policies. Full employment of manpower and productive capacity, rather than stable money, was to be the priority of state policy.

Some of Mosley's ideas were acted on in the 1930s once the gold standard had finally collapsed. Protected home and imperial markets did bring a substantial recovery of British industry and the advance of many of the science-based mass production industries. But the drastic overhaul of the state machine which Mosley wanted, and the ambitious prog-ramme of state intervention which he proposed, were resisted. Mosley's Fascist movement failed to break through and the bases of liberal orthodoxy were not touched.[15]

6.3 Labour and the national economy

The failure of first Social Imperialism and then Fascism in Britain to change the liberal world orientation of the British state made the subordination of Britain to the United States inevitable after 1945. Since that time support for protection on the Right has noticeably dwindled, and within the Conservative party the tradition founded by Chamberlain has few heirs. Only the National Front on the Right has openly advocated protection.[16] Although some Conserva-tives were opposed to entry into the EC, they rarely did so as advocates of protection. The new nationalism of Enoch Powell, while rejecting the Common Market, was joined to the most uncompromising statement of the principles of liberal political economy.[17]

The weakness of national political economy in Britain

reflects the loss of military power and the new stage of the world economy. The fusion that took place after 1945 between industrial and banking capital, the spread of production overseas by companies based in Britain, the revival of world trade and the growing interpenetration of the markets of the developed world, all weakened the attractiveness and the practicality of a protectionist strategy.

The cause of protection and the national economy migrated to the Left. This was a fairly new development, since formerly the Labour movement had never wholeheartedly embraced national political economy. Social Imperialism had generally been resisted and the early Labour leaders – Philip Snowden in particular, who was Chancellor of the Exchequer in 1924 and 1929 – were often strict adherents of liberal political economy. Churchill, himself a free trader, wrote of Snowden that 'the Snowden mind and the Treasury mind embraced one another with the enthusiasm of two long-separated kindred lizards'. Snowden pursued orthodox financial policies, eventually resigning from the National government in 1932 when it introduced protection.[18] Mosley failed to carry any significant part of the Labour leadership with him in his plans to fight unemployment.[19] Labour leaders continued to hold liberal conceptions of Britain's external policy and world role, and shared the belief in free trade and cosmopolitanism which it proclaimed. At the time when an autarkic policy was most practicable Labour's leaders refused to contemplate it. They sought to defend the interests and rights of the working class but they had no conception of using the state power even to achieve modest shifts in the priorities of state policy, still less to attempt to influence the general balance of class forces in civil society.

There did exist perspectives in the Labour movement other than accommodation to the prevailing orthodoxy. Most important were the various socialist critiques of political economy, including Marxism, whose standpoint was the interest of the working class.[20] These critiques furnished arguments against the continued rule of capital, and generally emphasised either the inequitable distribution of the social product and the harshness and waste of market forces, or the exploitation and subordination of the worker in the production process. Ideals of greater equality of distribution and co-operative ownership were central to the idea of a socialist commonwealth as an alternative to capitalism as a way of organising industrial society. The critiques of political economy were divided in their attitude towards the state, and how capitalism might best be replaced. Many socialists believed that the existing state had to be destroyed because it was necessarily subordinate to the market order and therefore to the needs of capital. A new democratic state subordinate to the working class had to be established. But other socialists argued that the nature of the state as a public realm gave it an independence which a socialist movement could use to push through reforms that would permit gradual movement towards the building of socialism.[21]

This latter perspective was to become increasingly dominant in the party, and allowed the spread of the perspective of national political economy in the Labour movement with its emphasis upon the national economy and productive capacity. National political economy has always been relatively weak in Britain – there has never, for example, been a permanent government department to speak for and represent the interests of the national economy and national industry. Mosley's remodelled executive was rejected, Labour's Ministry of Economic Affairs (1947) and Department of Economic Affairs (1964) did not survive.[22] Nevertheless, the national economy could not be ignored, and a perspective based upon it continually reappeared because of the size of the state sector and the organised influence of the working class and national capital, as well as the pressures of the national electorate.

In the 1930s after the meagre achievements of its first two administrations, the Labour party began to develop a serious programme of policies for reforming the worst abuses of capitalism and creating high employment and prosperity. Public ownership, higher public spending, and planned trade were all among them.[23] Several of the party's new leaders became strongly influenced by Keynes and the idea that the chronic unemployment and stagnation which had been experienced in the 1920s and 1930s could be overcome by a rational state policy to control the level of demand.[24] The view that capitalist crises were essentially crises of insufficient demand suggested that if the political weight of social democracy were strong enough, the political barriers in the path of higher government spending could be removed, and an expanding economy created in which resources could be redistributed and new forms of public enterprise and welfare provision established.

Keynesianism was of enormous assistance after 1945 in legitimating the expanded role of the state over which Conservative and Labour governments presided. But the external policy remained unchanged and the internal policy of demand management permitted redistribution without reorganisation. The idea of an enterprise state remained anathema. Nevertheless, the deteriorating economic position of the British economy began to revive interest in strategies that could arrest the decline and safeguard those achievements of social democracy already secured.[25] In the process both national political economy and the socialist critiques of political economy began a major resurgence within the Labour movement.

6.4 The Left challenge

The revival of interest in strategies for socialism in the Labour movement dates from the failure of the modernisation strategy in the 1960s. After the prolonged battles within the party over unilateral nuclear disarmament and the proposals to end the party's commitment to public ownership, Harold Wilson skilfully united the party behind the programme for a 'New Britain'.[26] This envisaged a far-reaching modernisation of industry and the successful pursuit of economic expansion, accompanied by and financing major social reforms and large increases in public expenditure. For this new national economic policy Labour built wide national support. But by 1968 the whole strategy was in ruins and the extent of disenchantment and disillusion throughout the Labour movement was intense.[27] Not only had the government sacrificed all its plans for expansion to the need to maintain the confidence of the financial markets and bring the balance of payments back into surplus, but it had diluted all the measures that had some socialist content and was pursuing policies that held down wages and raised taxes on the working class, culminating in an attempt to impose legal curbs on union power.[28]

The late 1960s saw the development of many new radical movements and increasingly these developed outside the Labour party.[29] There was also a considerable growth in a socialist political culture, the revival of the Marxist critique of political economy being particularly pronounced.[30] When the Labour party lost office in 1970 a major review and discussion of its record took place. It was only the second period of majority Labour government Britain had ever experienced and it was inevitably compared unfavourably with 1945. Very little in the way of positive socialist achievement could be pointed to in the record of the Wilson government.

The evident failure of the attempt to modernise the British economy and to alter patterns of distribution revived interest in socialism and gave new impetus to the Left. One result was the drawing up of *Labour's Programme 1973*, the most left-wing statement the party had adopted since 1945.[31] The reason why the Left was once again making itself heard in the party was partly due to the leftward shift of several of the large unions in response to the increasing attacks by governments on union power.[32] But it also reflected increasing political tensions. The new programme emerged against a background of the industrial and political crises of the Heath government[33] and growing signs of weakness in the world economy.

The intellectual emphasis behind the new strategic thinking was provided by Labour party intellectuals like Michael Barratt Brown, John Hughes, Ken Coates, and Stuart Holland,[34] while political leadership was provided by Tony Benn who emerged as a leading advocate of a socialist strategy.[35] The increasingly severe plight of the national economy acted as a spur. The key to the new thinking was the idea that the way to a further socialist advance in Britain was by adopting a programme to restore health to the national economy through measures that increased state control and the power of the organised Labour movement, and would extend social rights and increase democratic participation, so breaking the stalemate between capital and labour that had lasted since the war. If Britain remained tied to the world economy, no such advance was possible, so dependent on world trade, so penetrated by international capital, so vulnerable to international financial pressures had Britain become. Another starting point was opposition to Britain's membership of the EC. The EC was increasingly opposed by the bulk of the Labour party, partly because it threatened to link the British economy still more firmly with the economies of the developed capitalist world, and partly because it was feared that British governments would progressively lose the power to introduce socialist policies, and plan the national economy as they wanted. To the extent that the EC was able to extend its co-operation from agricultural policy to monetary policy and industrial policy, the British national economy would become part of a much wider European national economy and the British state merely a regional arm of a European state.

Withdrawing from the EC was a major part of Labour's new programme from the outset. When Labour returned to office in 1974 the leadership compromised by attempting to 'renegotiate' the terms of entry. This elaborate exercise ended in a national referendum on the new terms, which were backed by a majority of the Labour Cabinet, but opposed by the Labour party.[36] The winning of the referendum was the signal for the removal of Tony Benn from the Department of Industry, where he had begun to implement the party's new industrial policies. These were abruptly curtailed, and the government drifted steadily towards orthodox policies to cope with the world recession. It introduced the first package of monetarist measures, including cash limits, monetary targets and round after round of spending cuts. It also organised, with the help of the trade unions, a new incomes policy. The slide into defensive orthodoxy intensified when the pound collapsed in 1976, and the government negotiated a loan from the IMF. Moderation was further consolidated after the government lost its small majority in the House of Commons in 1977 and was forced to conclude a pact with the Liberals.[37]

Amidst this familiar record of the Labour party in government, one thing was different. The Left in the party and in the Cabinet possessed in the 1973 *Programme* an 'alternative economic strategy', which was employed to criticise the direction of government policy. Just as a free economy strategy arose on the right so an alternative economic strategy arose on the left. Both were more than just technical economic policies; both represented major attempts to map our new political courses to overcome Britain's decline and transform British institutions and British society.

6.5   Regaining national economic sovereignty

The main condition for the implementation of the alternative economic strategy was the substantial severing of the ties that bound the British economy to the world economy. Only then could full economic sovereignty be regained, only then could the British state plan the national economy, only then would the measures not be undermined by foreign pressures. From the Labour Left's standpoint a social democracy could only be created if the British state regained control over the national economy.

The social democracy which the Labour Left aimed at was not the same as the social democracy advocated by Crosland and others in the 1950s. Crosland's ideal of social democracy was a dynamic and rapidly expanding private sector, which would provide the basis for high taxation and high government spending aimed at redistributing income and resources between classes and between generations, so as to ensure equality of opportunity and a high level of effective demand.[38] Such a goal, however, was not seen as conflicting with the integration of the British economy in the world capitalist economy.

The record of the Labour government after 1964, and again after 1974, as well as the experience of membership of the EC, persuaded a wide band of Labour opinion that the social democracy sought by Crosland was unobtainable, so long as the links which Britain maintained with the world economy remained unchanged. If those links were challenged, then the scope for internal reorganisation of the economy became much greater also. Integration in the world economy was seen to impose a market order and a liberal orientation on British policy whatever democratically elected governments in Westminster decided. There was always a potential clash between the national democratic state and the international market order.[39] The alternative economic strategy sought to abolish the tension by transforming Britain's links with the world economy.

The alternative economic strategy aimed to use political power to rebuild economic strength and extend civil, political and social rights to the fullest possible extent. The strategy was often caricatured as seeking the extension of bureaucracy and the centralised power of the state. But what all the theorists of the alternative economic strategy emphasised was the need to combine measures that socialised and collectivised the economy, with measures that gave greater civil, political, and social rights, and which encouraged democratic participation, not just in government but in all social institutions, including schools, factories, hospitals, and housing estates. The underlying idea was that full participation as a citizen in all social decisions was more fulfilling and satisfying for the individual than the pursuit of private interests within a market order. For full participation to be possible every individual had to enjoy equal rights, not just the equal rights they needed to be property owners and commodity producers, but the political and social rights they needed to be citizens – freedom of speech and publication, free elections, freedom of association and freedom of information, equal opportunities in education and health care, and social security against sickness, injury, handicap, and old age.[40]

Movement towards the granting of such rights has meant some movement beyond the provision of legal rights, in an attempt to reduce some of the social and economic inequalities that legal rights do not touch. Social democracy is an egalitarian ideal, whilst in a market order much greater emphasis is laid upon *individual* liberty. Freedom in a social democracy is enjoyed and experienced as a collective possession that belongs to the whole community and is consciously created by it. To the extent that social democracy is realised the state acquires a democratic and egalitarian basis. The guaranteeing of these rights becomes the foundation of its legitimacy.

Most capitalist states have become social democracies by creating universal suffrage and greatly expanding public spending. But while the deep and enduring problem of the legitimacy of the distribution of power and property in capitalist society has been eased by extending the public realm and accommodating new interests, neither the sphere of market exchange, nor the organisation of the production process, have altered fundamentally, and the degree of social and political inequality has only been marginally reduced.[41] Democracy and capitalism coexist at times uneasily, and social democratic policies must not encroach too far if the tension between them is to remain manageable. In Britain the welfare policies, the tax structure and the bargaining position, legal privileges and political influence of the trade unions, were widely regarded on both Left and Right as being policies which even if they had not changed the pattern of distribution very much, still laid burdens on British capital that other national capitals did not suffer, and contributed to slow growth during the boom. When the economy could no longer sustain them, repeated attacks began to be made on public expenditure and on trade-union rights.[42] An era of greater political turbulence and more open class confrontation began.

The Labour Left argued that since British capitalism could no longer tolerate either high public spending or strong trade unions, and was even becoming unenthusiastic about democratic government, the basis for the social democracy of Crosland and others had disappeared. The effective choice was between a thoroughgoing capitalist rationalisation, in which many of the gains and conquests of the Labour movement since 1940 were reversed, or a strategy to transform capitalism in a socialist direction. Only by tackling the inequalities that continually arose from the private ownership and private direction of the economic process could a basis be created for further advance towards social democracy.

The centrepiece of the alternative economic strategy was therefore seen to be 'breaking the chains of the world economy'. Because of its unique history of expansion and decline, the sovereignty of the British state was more penetrated and compromised than any other capitalist state outside the Third World. A socialist government would plan to introduce most stringent controls on foreign trade and on the export of capital. Trade would be planned through the imposition not of tariffs but of quotas, which might not reduce the existing volume of imports, and could even allow for the growth of some imports. Capital control would be imposed to end the vulnerability of sterling to sudden outflows of capital. Sterling would cease to be an international currency and would no longer be freely convertible; foreign holdings in sterling would be frozen. The exchange rate would then be controlled in line with British trade and industrial policy rather than determined through the foreign exchange markets.

These measures would be undertaken to safeguard the national economy. Import controls would be intended to halt 'de-industrialisation' – the remorseless rise in import penetration achieved by foreign manufacturers especially since the 1974–5 recession, which had threatened the survival of large parts of British industry and had contributed to steadily mounting unemployment.[43] Foreign exchange controls would be intended to halt not only runs on the pound and the panic deflations they so often produced in the past, but also to prevent so many British firms expanding abroad rather than in the domestic economy.

Both policies could only be accomplished if Britain had already left the EC or was prepared to leave it. Any import quotas or foreign exchange controls which could be negotiated with the rest of the EC would be unlikely to be effective enough to achieve their purpose. Such controls would also cause major problems with transnationals. Advocates of the alternative economic strategy regarded the advent of the transnational corporations, and the new world division they had organised, as not only one of the crucial contemporary features of the world economy, but one of the main causes of Britain's specific problems. The number of British firms that had become transnational, and the number of foreign transnationals operating in Britain, meant that any British government determined to take control of the British economy would have to confront the power of transnational companies. Foreign exchange controls and import controls would only go so far. Multinationals, it was argued, would find ways of evading the controls and would use their power to undermine government policies. One suggestion was that all the assets belonging to foreign transnational companies should be nationalised as well as the assets of most of the leading British transnational companies. To minimise retaliation from foreign governments, the assets of foreign transnationals would be paid for at full market value, by first requisitioning and then selling British overseas portfolio investments (as was done during both wars).[44]

In these ways a transformation would be wrought in Britain's external relations with the world economy. The international role of sterling would finally disappear, many of the activities of the City would be ended or drastically curtailed, and though foreign trade would not cease (no government could achieve that), it would become strictly monitored and regulated in line with the needs of the domestic economy as the government defined them. There would be many more bilateral trade agreements, particularly with Third World countries. The international orientation of the leading sector of British business would be ended and the penetration of the British economy by foreign transnationals would be reversed. The British economy would remain a major trading economy still dependent for supplies of food and raw materials, but no longer burdened by an international currency, a deteriorating balance of payments on visible trade, and an internationally oriented financial and business sector. If carried through this would indeed make possible a major change of direction in external policy. It was more radical than anything envisaged by Joseph Chamberlain or Oswald Mosley.

6.6 The regeneration of British industry

The loosening of Britain's ties with the market order of world capitalism would permit the pursuit of different internal policies. Safeguarded by import quotas from balance of payment problems the government would make the creation of full employment and economic growth its top priorities. It would try to do this by expanding demand, until all unused resources in the economy had been brought into play. This would be an orthodox Keynesian policy and would restore the priority given after the war to full employment and growth. Once full employment had been achieved by stimulating demand, the problem of inflation, whether caused by excess demand or the bargaining power of different groups in the economy, would be met by wide-ranging price and wages controls. A permanent prices and incomes policy that succeeded in at least suppressing inflation would be an essential part of the alternative economic strategy.

Demand-management policies, however, would be supplemented by measures aimed at improving British industrial performance, and which would involve a major expansion of state intervention. A national enterprise board, similar to the ill-fated IRC of the late 1960s and the NEB established after 1974,[45] though with greater powers and greater funds, would become the chief public instrument for directly raising the rate of investment in British manufacturing industry, establishing new companies alongside existing private firms or venturing into entirely new fields. To give the state overall control of productive investment, twenty-five of the largest manufacturing companies together with the banking system would be nationalised. Those large companies that remained privately owned would be expected to sign planning agreements, detailing their objectives on investment, output, and employment.

The aim of all these measures would be to remedy the comparatively low rates of investment in the British economy achieved since the war, so rebuilding British industrial capacity and raising productivity in British industry to world levels. Interest rates would be held at very low levels (as they were in the 1940s),[46] while demand would be maintained at high levels. Increasing public spending on investment and welfare would be the chief instruments used for raising demand. Although defence spending would be greatly reduced there would be little scope for any reductions in taxes. Control of the banking system and low interest rates would permit an expansive credit policy, although the areas of the economy where credit went would remain strictly controlled.

In all these ways a greater degree of central planning and central co-ordination would replace the more haphazard planning and co-ordination emerging through the interaction of the state and the private companies which dominate the economy. Government responsibilities would be greatly enlarged, beyond simply guaranteeing the conditions of the market order, or attempting to manipulate the economy indirectly from the centre to attain specified national objectives. The bulk of the economy would still be in private hands, but the state would be the dominant agent and no longer subordinate to the market order.

The role of the trade unions in this new regime was a major question. As organisations they grew up within market orders, but also challenged the attempt to enforce a separation between the political realm and the economic realm. A permanent incomes policy would remove many of their functions, while state direction of investment would establish a public and a national interest overriding all local and sectional demands. Trade unions would have to be fully incorporated into the national planning system, surrendering their privileges and powers as independent organisations in return for participation in the making and implementation of economic policy. Whether such a transition would be an easy one was another matter.

Accompanying the new policies on internal economic management and the new expanded role for the state would be a wide range of measures to extend and consolidate democracy. Many of the social privileges and antiquated institutions of Britain would disappear. The House of Lords would be abolished, the civil service remodelled to fit it for its new tasks in administering a much larger public sector, private schools and private health care would disappear, more open government as well as more open media would be introduced. They would be accompanied by egalitarian welfare measures that would extend the welfare state and force through a much greater redistribution of wealth than any so far achieved in Britain. At the same time ideas for workers' control in factories, subordinating management to new forms of industrial democracy, and popular administration of services like education, health and housing would be implemented.

6.7 The political problem

These were the policies which would be relied upon to win popular support while the economy was being reorganised and the foundations laid for a prosperous and expanding economy. The strategy was a response to the problem of British decline and the failings of its industry and the growing unemployment and social distress which were occurring. It was a strategy which had deep roots in Labour movement tradition and was seen as the best means both for securing the gains that the movement had won in the past and preparing the way for a transition to socialism.[47]

It inevitably attracted wide criticism. Opponents on the right saw it as a recipe for a siege economy, and a totalitarian state with a standard of living sinking to that of Eastern Europe. On the left criticisms came from two sides. There were those who thought it too bold, and those who thought it not nearly bold enough.[48] It was accepted that many of the proposed measures might prove indispensable for remedying the backwardness and inefficiencies of British capitalism. What was questioned was whether such measures, even if they could be introduced, would strengthen the position of the Left, or assist in the construction of socialism. The belief that they would rested on the assumption that the new social democratic consensus of the 1940s was achieved by a decisive change in the balance of class forces, through the organisation of a broad popular democratic alliance, which overcame resistance to the imposition of new policies and new priorities. With this consensus under attack and weakening, the time was considered right for the construction of a new popular democratic alliance, which could win national support by demonstrating that the most pressing national problem, economic decline, could only be overcome by adopting policies that extended the role of the state, redistributed wealth, made state and society more democratic, and broke the dominant pattern of relationships with the world economy that had evolved over 300 years.

Those who argued the strategy was too bold pointed to the enormous dislocations its implementation would bring. Import quotas would not only restrict choice but raise prices; if they were effective, retaliation by other countries could not be avoided. While trade was being reorganised shortages of many commodities would be inevitable. The external policies alone would therefore imperil popular support for the government. Extrication from so complex a trading network would necessarily be slow and painful. If Britain could easily revert to self-sufficiency it might be different, but as it could not, these critics doubted whether the foundation of the alternative economic strategy was sound: could Britain stand alone? Was Britain any longer powerful enough to sustain an independent economic policy against the political opposition of the leading capitalist states? Some suggested that a surer strategy for socialist advance was for Britain to remain within the EC, combining with other socialist movements on an international basis, and accepting and endorsing the moves to greater integration in the belief that this could create a new terrain on which an international socialist movement could be built.

For such critics the alternative economic strategy was flawed, chiefly because it treated the United Kingdom as though it were an underdeveloped economy seeking a path of industrialisation. Once its role as one of the leading metropolitan centres of world capitalism was recognised, then it was difficult to avoid the conclusion that its links with the world economy could not be broken to create the basis for a policy of re-industrialisation without causing quite major short-term dislocations in trade, employment and living standards which would require the government to enjoy very broad-based popular support as well as considerable support from business if it were to cope with them successfully, for external disruption would be accompanied by internal disruption. The government would face herculean political tasks: securing the co-operation of the existing civil service to implement a programme that ended Britain's traditional external policy; securing the co-operation or acquiescence of the military establishment in policies that took Britain out of NATO and drastically cut defence spending; securing the quiescence of the judiciary in the face of new legislation that overrode provisions of the Common Law in many new areas; securing the co-operation of business in a programme which nationalised a large section of its assets and gave the state major new powers; securing the neutrality of the media.

To overcome the combined opposition of the bulk of the British ruling class to the implementation of the alternative economic strategy would require far more than an electoral victory under the unrepresentative and antiquated electoral rules of the British Parliament. It would need more than the abolition of the House of Lords and the passing of a Freedom of Information Act. It would require a crisis of far greater magnitude than any so far experienced in Britain, which would divide the ruling class on the measures that should be taken; and it would also require united trade-union and broad popular support.

Critics of the alternative economic strategy doubted whether the Labour movement was in any position to implement its programme as a solution to such a crisis. Bringing back prosperity, full employment and economic growth were all popular aims. What was in doubt was not the goals but the sacrifices and hardships that might well be needed in the attempt to realise them. Could such a government find sufficient support not just for the ends of its policies but for the means as well? The free economy strategy faced the same problem but in a less acute form. If the alternative economic strategy were attempted against united ruling-class opposition and with only slender support for socialist change, internal conflict and dislocation could become enormous. The hopes for increased investment and productivity would prove illusory and the government could be faced by investment strikes and tax strikes, which if not quickly averted would plunge it into a major fiscal crisis.

Many advocates of the alternative economic strategy were fully aware of all this. They never proposed it just as a technical policy for overcoming decline.[49] What they argued was that an attempt to implement such a strategy inevitably polarises class forces and itself creates the new bases of working-class and popular support that can carry the government through. The argument therefore turns on the class capacity and class consciousness of the British working class, and whether despite all its ideological and organisation rifts, despite its continuing high vote for the Conservative party, despite the ideological perspectives of so many of its leaders, it would nevertheless burst into new life and rally effectively to support a socialist government that was implementing the alternative economic strategy.

Critics of the strategy who thought it not bold enough did not disagree that the obstacles to the successful implementation of the strategy were formidable. But they argued that this pointed to the essential weakness of the strategy. It was a strategy for socialism that was to be implemented by the existing state. Instead of organising to overthrow this state and constructing a new state to oversee the construction of socialism, the alternative economic strategy would depend upon securing the goodwill or neutrality of the existing civil service, the existing military, the existing judiciary, the media and large sections of the capitalist class, as well as the neutrality of the major external capitalist powers.

These critics from the left argued that any attempt to implement socialist policies had to involve an immediate and direct challenge to the sources of class power in society and, in particular, the class character of the existing state.[50] A government attempting to implement the alternative economic strategy, which was not prepared to organise and base itself on a mass movement outside Parliament to mount such a challenge, would go one of two ways. Either it would follow the road of previous Labour governments with its leaders forced to submit to the prevailing realities of power, and therefore to policy orthodoxies not of their own choosing, or it would collapse or be toppled by the weight of resistance and sabotage from the capitalist class and the state machine, like Allende's Popular Unity government in Chile.[51]

The disagreements over the alternative economic strategy reflected differences about the nature of the crisis that faced world capitalism in the 1970s, and the significance of the changes which increasing state regulation and the advances made by labour movements had brought. There was no agreement on the Left about whether the recession and the slowdown in the rate of capital accumulation was a sign of a deep-seated crisis of profitability, or a less intractable deficiency of demand which had arisen from a number of contingent causes. Had the achievements of social democracy so altered the state as to permit a strategy of intervention that used the agencies of state power to create openings to the Left? Could a broad national coalition be assembled within the mass democracy that could sustain a government which implemented policies aimed at transforming the basic network of capitalist power and shifting the political balance in favour of the working class and towards socialism? Similarly, there was no agreement on the nature of the modern state. The alternative economic strategy was enmeshed in these debates. It was the first clear sign for a generation that serious strategic thinking about socialism had re-emerged on the British Left.

7
The end of decline?

Remember the conventional wisdom of the day. The British people were 'ungovernable'. We were in the grip of an incurable 'British disease'. Britain was heading for 'irreversible decline'.

Well, the people were *not* ungovernable, the disease was *not* incurable, the decline *has* been reversed.

Conservative Election Manifesto 1987

7.1 The Thatcherite project

The free economy strategy and the alternative economic strategy were responses to the deep political and economic crisis which gripped Britain in the 1970s. Their success in influencing policy was very different. The alternative economic strategy won much support in the Labour movement, but only a mild version of it was ever adopted as party policy. That was in 1983 when the party suffered its heaviest post-war electoral defeat.

The free economy strategy captured large sections of Conservative opinion after Margaret Thatcher became Leader in 1975. The Conservatives won the general elections in 1979, 1983, 1987 and 1992. Their success permitted an extended trial of their ideas for creating a free economy and breaking free of the chains of corporatism and social democracy. At the 1979 general election the Conservatives made decline one of their central themes. They refused to accept that decline was inevitable, and they pledged themselves to reverse it.

In 1980 and 1981 the economy plunged into a severe recession. Output and investment slumped and unemployment soared. Sterling moved up sharply as did interest rates, and inflation accelerated. When riots erupted in several cities during 1981 some feared that Britain was locked into a spiral of decline which was leading to a breakdown of public order. The slump threatened not just the future of the Conservative party but the stability of the state.

During 1981, however, the bottom of the recession was reached and also the nadir of the government's political fortunes. In 1982, even before the Falklands War, both the economy and the government's popularity began to improve. After receiving such a battering in the previous two years government ministers were quick to seize on every sign of recovery. The Prime Minister began claiming that there had been a dramatic improvement in productivity and that the economy had turned the corner.

In the 1981 budget the government had chosen to increase taxation and risk further deflation of demand although unemployment had reached three million and was still rising. Several cabinet ministers had come close to resigning over it. This budget quickly became an important landmark for the Thatcherite project. Supporters of the Treasury declared that this was the budget that had turned the tide, because it had convinced the financial markets that the government was serious about financial discipline, and had sent a signal to trade unions, employers and bankers that sound money was the government's top priority.[1]

As the economy continued to improve during 1983 the tone of government proclamations became steadily more triumphant. The theme of the Conservative manifesto at the 1983 general election was that national recovery had begun:

> When we came to office in May 1979, our country was suffering both from an economic crisis and a crisis of morale. British industry was uncompetitive, over-taxed, over-regulated, and over-manned . . . This country was drifting further behind its neighbours. Defeatism was in the air.[2]

But the manifesto remained cautious. There were still many obstacles that remained to be overcome:

> In the last four years, many British firms have made splendid progress in improving their competitiveness and profitability. But there is some way to go yet before this country has regained that self-renewing capacity for growth which once made her a great economic power, and will make her great again.[3]

The recovery at this stage was fairly modest. The main achievement was the substantial fall in the rate of inflation from over 20 per cent at its peak to single figures. Unemployment stopped climbing but it did not fall. Output had begun rising again but was far below its 1979 level, and although productivity had sharply increased, many observers attributed it to a once-for-all increase reflecting the huge shedding of labour in 1979–81.

By 1987, however, and its third election triumph the government could claim that the economic recovery had lasted six years and appeared to be gathering pace. Inflation had not been eliminated but it had been kept generally below 5 per cent. Unemployment had at last begun to fall, and manufacturing output was almost back to its 1979 level. Profits had risen sharply and productivity was increasing steadily. Falling interest rates and two tax-cutting budgets in 1986 and 1987 were used to promote a vigorous consumer boom and a rise in living standards just before the election. Rarely had a government managed to align the economic cycle with the election cycle to such good effect.

The Conservative manifesto at the 1987 general election was euphoric about the state of the economy. It boasted that 'the British economy has never been stronger or more productive.' A vast change it suggested separated the Britain of 1987 from the Britain of the late 1970s:

> Is it really only such a short time ago that inflation rose to an annual rate of 27 per cent? That the leader of the Transport and General Workers Union was widely seen as the most powerful man in the land? That a minority

Labour government, staggering from crisis to crisis on borrowed money, was nonetheless maintained in power by the Liberal party . . . ? And that Labour's much-vaunted pay pact with the unions collapsed in the industrial anarchy of the 'winter of discontent', in which the dead went unburied, rubbish piled up in the streets, and the country was gripped by a creeping paralysis which Labour was powerless to cure?

It seems in retrospect to be the history of another country.[4]

The manifesto went on to make specific claims about the British revival:

1. Britain was in the seventh successive year of economic growth and had moved from the bottom to the top of the league for output growth among major European economies, and from the bottom to the top of the productivity league among major world economies.
2. Inflation had reached its lowest level for twenty years, and unemployment had fallen in every month since July 1986.
3. The number of strikes had dropped to their lowest levels for fifty years.
4. Overseas assets had been built up to their highest level since the Second World War, worth over £100 billion, second only to those of Japan.
5. Living standards were higher than ever before in British history, a 21 per cent increase in real terms for the takehome pay of the average family with two children.
6. Profitability of industrial companies had risen to the highest level for over twenty years.

In addition the manifesto spoke of a new climate of enterprise in the country, born of the confidence that Britain was internationally competitive again.

Many of these claims were contested, but in 1987 many observers acknowledged that the weight of evidence was impressive. Something significant had happened to the British economy, and the Conservative claims could not be dismissed simply as political hype. British decline might just be a thing of the past. *Fortune* and *Newsweek* in the United States ran cover stories on the theme 'Britain is Back', reflecting the substantial confidence which the overseas business and financial communities now had in the British economy, and specifically in the policies and leaders of the Conservative government.

The bubble burst almost as quickly as it had formed. The rapid expansion of demand in 1987–8 fuelled by tax cuts, credit, and public spending reintroduced rising inflation in 1989–90. Thatcher entered office and left office with inflation rising. Thatcher's long rearguard action against membership of the Exchange Rate Mechanism (ERM) was partly to blame. Those states which were members of the ERM experienced no upsurge in inflation in 1989–90. Britain's inflation was entirely due to monetary mismanagement at home.

It precipitated a recession which lasted until 1993. Unemployment and bankruptcies began to climb sharply again, which put pressure on public spending. By 1990 public spending as a proportion of gross domestic product had returned to the levels the Government had inherited. But the reduction of the fiscal base during the years of growth had left the Government with less flexibility, and led to a very rapid rise in public borrowing as the only means of bridging the gap between expenditure and revenue and preserving the image of the Conservative party as a low tax party. The Government was forced to raise taxes sharply after the 1992 election in order to reduce the borrowing which had risen to £50 billion.

Another aspect of the recession was the widening trade gap. With the declining value of North Sea Oil and the continuing appetite for the British economy for imported manufactures the balance of payments surplus was transformed into a large deficit. It represented a serious obstacle to any early reflation of the British economy, and indicated that Britain would suffer a long period of slow growth until the financial imbalances created by the Lawson boom had been corrected.

The recession at the end of the 1980s punctured the extravagant hopes of some monetarists that Britan's new financial framework would ensure economic growth that was proof against inflation and recession. The 1980s boom ended in a crisis of an all too familiar kind, and raised questions as to how much had really changed.

In a longer perspective how will the Thatcher decade of the 1980s come to be judged? Will it be seen as the moment, notwithstanding the recession, when a lasting recovery began and decline ceased to be a problem in British politics? Will it be recorded as another failed attempt to break out of the cycle of decline? Or will it perhaps be looked on as a period of transition in which the nature of the problem which decline represents was redefined? In the new period in the development of the world economy which has been inaugurated by the collapse of communism, the trends towards globalisation of production and finance, and regionalisation of economic regulation may make the debates of the rise and fall of nations that flourished during the national-protectionist era obsolete.

The Thatcher project for reversing British decline was a product of the national-protectionist era and drew significantly upon a rhetoric of national revival and national effort. The claims and counter-claims about Britain's economic performance during the Thatcher decade raise important issues for all theories of decline. If a trend apparently so well established as Britain's relative economic decline can be reversed by a combination of political determination and the adoption of a particular set of policies, then either the obstacles to modernisation were less substantial than previously supposed, or the general context had changed in such a way as to make the earlier obstacles less important. This second possibility will be discussed in the final section of this chapter. But first it is necessary to look more closely at Conservative policies and at what they did and did not achieve.

7.2 The market cure

After its two general election defeats in 1974 and a change of leadership the Conservative party became firmly identified with a version of the free economy strategy for reversing British decline. It was unclear however how far the Conservative government elected in 1979 would go in implementing it, particularly since the party leadership and the new Cabinet were deeply divided over aspects of the strategy.[5] Some party opponents of the strategy predicted that the monetarist experiment would last no more than six months.

The role of the Prime Minister in ensuring that market principles influenced the framework for policy formulation was crucial. Her personal commitment to the market approach was strong. Only supporters of the strategy were appointed to the key economic ministries, in particular the Treasury. Those who were opposed to the strategy or who grew sceptical were isolated and many of them were eventually dismissed. Those that survived learnt to become supporters of the new policies. Three consecutive general election victories gave the party leadership unchallenged legitimacy, and seemed to justify its claim that there was no alternative to its policies.

It would be very misleading to suppose, however, that the Thatcher government had an economic strategy which it proceeded to implement in detail as soon as it entered office. What actually occurred was very much more complex than this. Events and circumstances were often more important determinants of policies and decisions than the ideas and principles of the market strategy. Although the 1987 manifesto presented the evolution of policy as a smooth and coherent progression, the reality was very different. Like all governments there was considerable improvisation and opportunism.

Policy under the Thatcher government during the 1980s passed through three distinct phases: 1979–82, 1982–7, and 1987–90. The first was dominated by the second oil price rise and the world recession; the second by the sustained recovery in the world economy led by the United States; and the third by the stock market crash of October 1987 which was triggered by fears over the enormous trade and financial imbalances which were emerging in the world economy and signalled a new recession.

The British economy fared differently in each phase. In the first phase the British recession was earlier and deeper than in most other countries. By contrast the British recovery in the second phase was longer and more rapid (see Table 7.1). In the third phase the British economy at first continued to accelerate but the boom was unsustainable and once again

Table 7.1 Comparative economic performance of major OECD countries 1979–92

	USA	Japan	Germany	France	UK	OECD
Growth of real GDP (percentage changes)						
1979	2.5	5.5	4.1	3.2	2.8	3.6
1980	−0.5	3.6	1.1	1.6	−1.9	1.2
1981	1.8	3.6	0.2	1.2	−1.0	1.6
1982	−2.2	3.2	−0.9	2.5	1.5	0.0
1983	3.9	2.7	1.6	0.7	3.5	2.7
1984	6.2	4.3	2.8	1.3	2.3	4.4
1985	3.2	5.0	1.9	1.9	3.8	3.3
1986	2.9	2.6	2.2	2.5	4.1	2.8
1987	3.1	4.1	1.4	2.3	4.8	3.2
1988	3.9	6.2	3.7	4.5	4.4	4.4
1989	2.5	4.7	3.4	4.3	2.1	3.3
1990	0.8	4.8	5.1	2.5	0.5	2.4
1991	−1.2	4.0	3.7	0.7	−2.2	0.7
1992	2.1	1.3	2.0	1.3	−0.6	1.5
Standardised unemployment rates (percentage of total labour force)						
1979	5.8	2.1	3.2	5.9	5.0	5.1
1980	7.0	2.0	2.9	6.3	6.4	5.8
1981	7.5	2.2	4.2	7.4	9.8	6.6
1982	9.5	2.4	5.9	8.1	11.3	8.1
1983	9.5	2.6	7.7	8.3	12.4	8.5
1984	7.4	2.7	7.1	9.7	11.7	8.0
1985	7.1	2.6	7.1	10.2	11.2	7.8
1986	6.9	2.8	6.4	10.4	11.2	7.7
1987	6.1	2.8	6.2	10.5	10.3	7.3
1988	5.4	2.5	6.2	10.0	8.6	6.7
1989	5.2	2.3	5.6	9.4	7.2	6.2
1990	5.4	2.1	4.9	8.9	6.8	6.1
1991	6.6	2.1	4.4	9.4	8.7	6.8
1992	7.3	2.2	4.8	10.2	9.9	7.5
Current balances (percentage of GDP)						
1979	0.0	−0.9	−0.7	0.9	−0.2	−0.4
1980	0.1	−1.0	−1.7	−0.6	1.2	−0.9
1981	0.2	0.4	−0.5	−0.8	2.6	−0.3
1982	−0.4	0.6	0.8	−2.2	1.7	−0.4
1983	−1.3	1.8	0.8	−0.9	1.2	−0.3
1984	−2.6	2.8	1.6	−0.2	0.6	−0.7
1985	−3.0	3.7	2.7	−0.1	0.8	−0.7
1986	−3.5	4.3	4.5	0.3	0.0	−0.3
1987	−3.6	3.6	4.1	−0.6	−1.1	−0.5
1988	−2.6	2.7	4.2	−0.5	−3.4	−0.4
1989	−1.9	2.0	4.9	−0.6	−4.1	−0.5
1990	−1.6	1.2	3.2	−1.3	−3.1	−0.7
1991	−0.1	2.2	−1.2	−0.5	−1.1	−0.2
1992	−1.0	3.2	−1.3	0.2	−2.0	−0.2

Source: OECD, *Economic Outlook*, 53, June 1993.

Britain was the first major OECD economy to move into recession.

The government's claim to have produced if not an economic miracle at least a significant reversal in the trend of decline rested on its monetary cure for inflation and its supply-side policies for making the British economy more competitive and enterprising.

The monetary cure had a high profile during the first phase of policy. But it was less of a break in policy than supporters and critics have sometimes claimed. One of the great advantages enjoyed by the new government was that it could pursue its monetarist experiment in a political climate in which opinion had already shifted decisively towards monetarism as the necessary framework for controlling the impact of the recession.[6]

The Thatcher government did not need to abandon Keynesian demand management policies. That had already been done by Labour. It was the Labour government that had presided over a doubling of unemployment between 1975 and 1977 without resorting to prescribed Keynesian remedies. It was the Labour government that had introduced cash limits in 1975 to exert stricter control over public expenditure. It was the Labour government during the sterling crisis of 1976 that had accepted a formal commitment to observe monetary targets and pledged itself to contain and reduce the burden of public expenditure in order to reassure the international financial markets about the direction of government policy and ministers' intentions.

The main contribution made by the Thatcher government was to consolidate the new policy regime by the fierceness of its ideological commitment to it. Monetarism was justified not on pragmatic but on doctrinal grounds. Not even token endorsements of previous social democratic objectives such as full employment were given. The control of inflation was proclaimed from the outset as the central objective of the government's economic policy.

The one major innovation introduced by the government was the Medium Term Financial Strategy, announced in the 1980 budget, which set targets for the growth of money supply over a period of four years ahead, as well as indicating desired levels for public borrowing.[7] The government seems to have expected that a strict financial policy would gradually restore sound money and squeeze inflationary expectations out of the economy. The cost would be a small rise in unemployment, but this would only be transitional, and the economy would quickly bounce back, helped by major cuts in public spending and taxes to stimulate private initiative and investment. Falling inflation and slightly higher unemployment would promote faster growth, and growth prospects would be further enhanced by measures to remove obstacles to free markets. Public spending would be reduced and trade-union power curbed.

The actual course of events was spectacularly different. The government found itself presiding over the worst economic collapse since the Great Depression. The high interest rates which the monetarist strategy prescribed to reduce inflation assisted the rapid appreciation of sterling following the oil price rise. British companies suffered a sudden loss in competitiveness of 20 per cent.

The consequence was a major contraction of manufacturing industry. Company liquidations soared, reaching 12 000 in 1982, the highest ever. Unemployment doubled, rising to over three million. It did not begin to fall until 1986. The output of manufacturing industry fell by 14.5 per cent and investment in manufacturing by 36 per cent.

One of the most telling statistics, however, was the further rise in import penetration which the recession brought. In 1983 more manufactured goods were imported than were exported – the first time ever. A surplus on trade in manufactures of £5 billion in 1980 had become a deficit of £4 billion by 1985. In some major sectors like electrical engineering, textiles, and clothing there was a jump in import penetration of 25 per cent. By 1988 the deficit on manufactures was £14.4 billion.

Many service industries continued to expand and there was a sharp increase in the flow of capital abroad, assisted by the removal of all exchange controls in 1979. Between 1979 and 1983 £35.4 billion was exported, a net outflow of £18.8 billion. By the time of the stock market crash in 1987 Britain's overseas assets were worth more than £100 billion.

The scale of the recession meant that public spending on social security and industrial subsidies increased while revenues were reduced. The government managed selective cuts in taxes and in public spending programmes, but these were outweighed by the increases it was forced to make. By the end of the first phase the burden of both direct and indirect taxation was higher than under the previous Labour government, and public expenditure as a proportion of GDP had increased (see Table 7.2). Inflation having accelerated to over 20 per cent in 1980 fell back very quickly under the impact of the recession to less than 5 per cent in 1983. It was the government's one clear success, achieved at a very high cost.

Such a record would have sunk most governments and it almost wrecked that of Margaret Thatcher. But ideological convictions helped keep it afloat. Having broken from the spell of the post-war consensus the Thatcher government was able to turn even mass unemployment to its advantage. The slump was blamed partly on the world recession, for which the government disclaimed any responsibility, but also on the weaknesses, mistakes, and extravagances which had accumulated during thirty-five years of social democracy. The recession became proof of what the new Conservative leadership had been saying all along. The nation had been living on borrowed time and it needed a sharp shock to bring it to its senses.

The government made relatively little progress in this first phase towards some of its key objectives. It suffered many reverses and encountered major obstacles. But the ideological thrust of its programme and its strategic understanding of what needed to be done remained firm. During the second phase of the government, 1982–7, the nature of the strategy became much clearer.

At its centre was Britain's relationship to the world economy. The government insisted that there could be no salvation outside the world market; only those goods and services which were internationally competitive should be produced. Although for short-term tactical reasons the government continued to subsidise many sectors of British manufacturing industry in addition to traditionally protected

Table 7.2 Changes in government spending and taxation in major OECD countries
1979–92

	USA	Japan	Germany	France	UK	OECD
Government receipts (percentage of nominal GDP)						
1979	30.3	26.3	44.6	44.1	37.7	33.7
1980	30.5	27.6	45.0	46.1	39.5	34.6
1981	31.1	29.0	45.0	46.7	41.5	35.5
1982	30.5	29.4	45.7	47.6	42.1	35.7
1983	29.9	29.6	45.3	48.2	41.4	35.7
1984	29.7	30.2	45.5	49.2	41.2	35.8
1985	30.1	30.8	45.8	49.3	41.2	36.3
1986	30.2	31.0	45.0	48.6	40.1	36.3
1987	31.0	32.6	44.8	49.0	39.4	36.9
1988	30.5	33.1	44.1	48.3	39.0	36.7
1989	30.9	33.4	44.9	47.8	38.5	37.0
1990	30.9	34.6	43.2	48.3	38.6	37.3
1991	30.8	34.4	45.6	48.5	37.9	37.5
1992	30.7	34.0	46.6	48.1	37.4	37.5
Government outlays (percentage of nominal GDP)						
1979	29.9	31.1	47.2	45.0	40.9	36.0
1980	31.8	32.0	47.9	46.1	42.9	37.3
1981	32.1	32.8	48.7	48.6	44.2	38.5
1982	33.9	33.0	49.0	50.3	44.5	39.8
1983	33.9	33.3	47.8	51.4	44.7	40.0
1984	32.6	32.3	47.4	51.9	45.2	39.3
1985	33.2	31.6	47.0	52.1	44.0	39.5
1986	33.7	32.0	46.4	51.3	42.5	39.5
1987	33.4	32.2	46.7	50.9	40.7	39.2
1988	32.5	31.6	46.3	50.0	38.0	38.4
1989	32.4	30.9	44.8	49.1	37.6	38.0
1990	33.3	31.7	45.2	49.8	39.9	39.0
1991	34.2	31.4	48.7	50.6	40.8	40.0
1992	35.4	32.2	49.4	52.0	44.1	41.2
Government financial balances (percentage of nominal GDP)						
1979	+0.4	−4.7	−2.6	−0.8	−3.2	−2.3
1980	−1.3	−4.4	−2.9	0.0	−3.4	−2.7
1981	−1.0	−3.8	−3.7	−1.9	−2.6	−3.0
1982	−3.4	−3.6	−3.3	−2.8	−2.5	−4.1
1983	−4.1	−3.6	−2.6	−3.2	−3.3	−4.4
1984	−2.9	−2.1	−1.9	−2.8	−3.9	−3.5
1985	−3.1	−0.8	−1.2	−2.9	−2.9	−3.3
1986	−3.4	−0.9	−1.3	−2.7	−2.4	−3.2
1987	−2.5	+0.5	−1.9	−1.9	−1.3	−2.3
1988	−2.0	+1.5	−2.2	−1.7	+1.0	−1.7
1989	−1.5	−2.5	+0.1	−1.3	+0.9	−1.0
1990	−2.5	+2.9	−2.0	−1.5	−1.3	−1.8
1991	−3.4	+3.0	−3.2	−2.1	−2.9	−2.6
1992	−4.7	+1.8	−2.8	−3.9	−6.7	−3.7

Source: OECD, *Economic Outlook*, 53, June 1993.

areas such as agriculture and defence, it went further than any previous post-war government in accepting the logic of Britain's position in the international division of labour, even when this involved a substantial contraction of the manufacturing base of the economy.

The government disclaimed responsibility for preserving prosperity and employment throughout the national economy. It pinned its hopes for future prosperity on the continuing success of those sectors of the British economy already internationally competitive, on the development of new small businesses, and on the growth of internationally traded services.

The role of the financial policy within this wider economic strategy was crucial. It was seen as the best help that could be given by government to reconstruct the economy and assist recovery. High levels of unemployment and bankruptcies were justified as necessary to purge economy of wrong attitudes and misallocated resources, and to lay the foundations for profitable investment and production. Unemployment was desirable also for shifting the balance between labour and capital, and introducing a new realism to industrial relations. Managements would have the opportunity and the need to reduce their workforce and to increase efficiency.

Financial discipline was only the first stage, however, in the market strategy for national recovery. It had to be reinforced by a major cut in public spending and taxation, made possible by a significant contraction in public activities. The aim was not just to facilitate tax cuts but to remove as much economic decision-making as possible from the political process.

The severity of the slump meant, however, that the government was obliged to increase both spending and taxes. Financial stabilisation required social stabilisation. Spending on the police and armed forces increased, the employment programmes of the Manpower Services Commission were greatly enlarged, and the budgets for social security, unemployment pay, and industry were allowed to expand.

Some of the government's strongest supporters were dismayed at the slow pace of change, particularly in the field of welfare expenditure. Many of the government's measures, such as council house sales, higher prescription charges, and higher fees for overseas students, while welcome to the market lobby, were marginal to the main spending programmes. Hopes during the first two phases of the Thatcher government that ministers might introduce private health insurance or educational vouchers were dashed.

Many market lobbyists advised much more drastic action to cope with unprofitable nationalised industries and the trade unions. Propping up loss-makers in steel, coal, cars and shipbuilding only converted their managements into civil servants administering subsidies, increased public spending, and hindered reconstruction through market forces.

There was some disappointment too about changes in trade-union law. In June 1980 Hayek warned that the unions should be quickly confronted and stripped of their power, if the market strategy was to have any prospect of success.[8] If the confrontation was prolonged the ability of the unions to resist market forces might entail a level of unemployment and a degree of stagnation in the economy that could make the government so unpopular as to endanger the changes of a Conservative victory at the next election. To break the union veto he proposed the holding of a national referendum to seek approval for the immediate abolition of all legal privileges granted to the trade unions since 1906. Trade unions could once again become liable for damages suffered by an employer from strike action.

The government had wider political objectives in view, however, and preferred to move cautiously, taking on opponents one at a time, seizing opportunities as they presented themselves.[9] Trade-union law was reformed in stages in three bills, in 1980, 1982 and 1984, and major confrontation with the whole trade-union movement was avoided. The government gave full support to employers in a succession of major disputes, in steel, printing, and mining. The defeats suffered by unions that fought against the restructuring being imposed on their industries, coupled with the effects of the new legislation and high unemployment, helped transform the climate of industrial relations and the perception of union power.

The other key aspects of the supply-side policies as they

unfolded during the second and third phases were privatisation, cuts in direct taxation, and training policy. Having discovered that privatisation was feasible, and contributed useful sums to the Exchequer, privatisation became the flagship of the Thatcher government's supply-side revolution.[10] Privatisation, however, was more successful in the denationalisation of state-owned industries than it was in moving many public services into the private sector. Nevertheless by the end of the decade the 'new public management' had become firmly established, and was reshaping the character of all public sector institution, with the introduction of devices such as internal markets, tendering, and contracting out. The Next Steps Report proposed splitting the civil service into policy-making agencies at the centre and delivery agencies which would be responsible for implementing the policies, and which could in principle be privatised.[11]

Another revolution which gathered pace during the 1980s were the new training programmes, associated with the Manpower Service Commission, which survived the massacre of the quangos at the beginning of the decade, mainly because of the pressing practical need to respond to rapidly rising unemployment. Training provision was gradually shifted from a tripartite regime which involved unions, government, and employers to a new neo-liberal regime from which trade unions were virtually excluded. The Manpower Services Commission had been abolished by the end of the decade and the supervision of training programmes transferred to the new Training and Enterprise Councils (TECs) which were dominated by local employers, and aimed primarily at rectifying short-term skills shortages.[12]

Many of the supply-side changes did not change the size of the state, but they did restructure it in important ways. The symbolism of the shift in the boundaries of the public and private sectors was important politically. This was true also of the assault on the principle of progressive taxation. Overall the tax burden had not been significantly altered after ten years of Conservative government. But for those on high incomes the changes had been substantial, and were justified as part of the process of creating an enterprise and incentive economy.

The scope for tax cuts came partly from the proceeds of privatisation sales and oil revenues, but mainly from the sustained growth during the second policy phase (1982–7) and the government's ability if not to reduce public spending, at least to contain its growth. The determination to resist pressure from special interest lobbies for sharply increased spending strengthened rather than weakened during the government's term of office.

The strategists of the government believed that if the recovery could be sustained and the public sector contained, there would be a relatively painless expansion of private sector activity and provision financed through tax cuts and rising incomes. The political problem was how to win the political argument for keeping public expenditure constrained in key areas such as health and education and pensions, and how to regain control over those areas of public expenditure in the hands of autonomous public bodies or locally elected councils outside direct central control. The realisation that more needed to be done here if the momentum of the move away from the state was to be maintained prompted the announcement of the new radical programme on which the Conservatives fought and won the election in 1987.

The government calculated that keeping inflation low, containing public spending and funding direct tax cuts would help it retain the electoral support that was necessary for the longer-term supply-side changes to be implemented and to take effect. Institutional reforms designed to remove as many obstacles to free markets as possible and to weaken political opposition to Conservatism still depended on the growth of the second phase being sustained.

7.3 The debate on recovery

The success or failure of the Thatcher economic experiment has been fiercely debated. Like many of the debates on British decline the conclusions that are reached often depend on the starting point. Decline has always been a contested concept, and recovery is equally so.

The government's case that the economic recovery is real

and lasting has received considerable support from economists. The tone of the OECD reports on the British economy became steadily more favourable through the 1980s. Until 1989 the British government was perceived by the international community as having pursued a consistent and increasingly successful set of policies which were permitting the British economy to make up lost ground.

In its 1987 report the OECD declared that recent developments compared favourably with the long-term performance of the UK. The performance was less impressive when economic performance was measured from the previous cyclical peak in 1979 (see Table 7.3). But even when account was taken of the slump between 1979 and 1981 GDP growth now appeared in line with the average of the European Community countries rather than lagging behind it. The output losses in the initial years of the medium-term financial strategy were subsequently made up. Following that period, the OECD concluded, the strategy was implemented more flexibly, but the basic framework remained intact.

The 1988 report was even more positive, despite the stock market crash and gathering economic problems. The UK performance was still judged to compare favourably with other OECD states, especially the growth of output. The report concluded:

> Notwithstanding the risks attached to the short-term outlook it is already now clear that the 1980s will stand out as a decade of impressive improvement in economic performance, reversing a long-term trend of decline relative to other countries.[13]

It singled out what it called a new flexibility in the labour market and the new trends in productivity. It argued that the evidence that was now accumulating suggested that there was a change in trend rather than simply a transitory cyclical development as many observers had initially suggested. Productivity was rising because of changes in work organisation rather than because of capital investment. The scope for further increases was present as British companies caught up with the performance of their international rivals. Only

Japan, the OECD noted, had recorded higher productivity growth rates than the UK in the 1980s.

The OECD report then asked whether the improved performance meant that the British disease had been overcome, as the government had claimed. On the positive side it noted that the old stop–go cycle which had plagued British post-war economic management appeared to have been overcome; productivity growth had accelerated markedly; there had been a substantial reduction in government intervention in the economy, with markets being given much greater freedom to determine resource allocation; Britain had enjoyed the benefits of North Sea oil, and the British economy had become further integrated into the world economy.

But the OECD also cautioned that too much should not be read into the recovery since 1981: 'as the improved performance has coincided with a cyclical recovery there is uncertainty as to the extent to which these changes are permanent'.[14]

The improvement in productivity performance was the key, although the OECD estimated that in 1986 output per employed person in the UK still fell short of productivity levels in the USA by one-third and in the European Community by one-quarter. But the OECD believed that the government's supply-side policies were gradually transforming Britain's economic performance.

These supply-side policies included the abolition of exchange controls; the reorientation of the objectives of the nationalised industries; legislation on trade unions; reduction in personal tax rates; deregulation; privatisation; and reforms in education, housing, and regional and urban policies. The effect of this supply-side strategy, the OECD report argued, had forced the private sector to take more responsibility for adjusting to the changing economic environment. Both management and unions had had to reassess their attitudes.

This positive judgement of the achievements of the Conservative government in the 1980s has been echoed and amplified by others. Supporters of the market cure argue that in order to assess properly the record of the Thatcher government it should be compared with that of the 1974–9 Labour government. One common view is that the policies pursued after 1979 represented a return to economic reality.[15]

The era of corporatism and government intervention had steadily moved large sectors of the economy away from profitability and responsibility towards subsidy and dependence. Britain was becoming ungovernable because of a weak state and an assertive trade-union movement.

The economic recovery of the 1980s therefore is a recovery of the basic rules and attitudes necessary for success and efficiency in a market order. It is a political triumph before anything else. As Nigel Lawson put it:

> the British experiment . . . consists of seeking, within an explicit medium-term context, to provide increasing freedom for markets to work within a framework of firm monetary and fiscal discipline . . . the true British experiment is a political experiment. It is the demonstration that trade union power *can* be curbed within a free society, and that inflation *can* be eradicated within a democracy.[16]

There remains a difficulty, however, as to how this political triumph, if such it is, is to be explained. The New Right analysis of the political process is noted for its pessimism. Democracy encourages the political parties to outbid one another in their campaign promises, which encourages the electorate to have excessive expectations about the capacity of governments to deliver the costless benefits. Democratic institutions also encourage the proliferation of organised interests, all pressing their own special interest on government in the guise of the public interest. All groups seek to gain the maximum benefits from the political process by loading the costs onto other less well organised and protected groups. In Mancur Olson's account the longer established a democratic political system the more tenacious and wide-ranging will be its special interests, and the greater the political interference in the workings of free markets.[17]

If the causes of decline are structural in the way Olson suggests they cannot be overcome by changes in the culture of a country or in the political will of its leaders. The logic of collective action will always reassert itself. Organised distributional coalitions will always be more effective in the political process than the unorganised majority. The political process will always lack the kind of constraints which in economic markets are provided by prices and competition. Some market enthusiasts therefore dream of abolishing politics altogether. But only through a political process can a market order be established and maintained.

If the iron laws of political economy do not bend before the good intentions of politicians and the soundness of their ideological credentials, it follows that the Conservative government's claims to have launched a genuine recovery depend on its having discovered some way of breaking the grip of the special interests which paralysed government before.

One solution is to argue that the institutional sclerosis created by a long-established democracy can be broken by an external shock, typically war or invasion. Such a shock allows a political system to be reorganised, and its distributional coalitions dispersed. Geoffrey Maynard, among others, claims that the Thatcher government benefited from just such an external shock – the shock created by the slump of 1979 81, which temporarily destroyed the power of the special interests, and allowed the Thatcher government to reassert the rules and institutions of the free, competitive market economy as the overriding public interest.[18]

On this view the economic recovery of the 1980s was a real recovery and made possible by the sharp break with the previous social democratic era which the 1979–81 slump permitted. The most obvious casualty among the special interests was the trade-union movement. It was systematically excluded from national policy-making, it suffered a considerable drop in membership and a decline in its bargaining position as a result of the slump, and a general deterioration in its political influence due to the decline of the Labour party and the contraction of the public sector.

The main grounds therefore for believing that the improved economic performance of the 1980s signals a lasting economic recovery are firstly the improvement in productivity, and secondly the decline in the bargaining strength and political influence of the Labour movement.

Those who question the extent of the recovery argue that the improvement between 1981 and 1987 must be placed in the context of Britain's past economic performance and of its continuing structural problems. As the OECD pointed out, the UK economic performance is only markedly better than other economies when the period 1979–81 is excluded from the figures. When entire economic cycles are compared, the figures show that in the 1979–87 cycle Britain performed as well as the average. This was an improvement on previous cycles when it had performed less well than the average. It is also true however that UK performance, although better relatively, fell short of its performance in the 1950s and 1960s (see Table 7.3).

The least that can be said of Britain's economic performance in the 1980s is that the decline was halted. But only the next cycle will show whether this better performance has become permanent. As reflected in the OECD statistics Britain would need to maintain the above-average growth rates it achieved in 1986–8 for a considerable period to make further inroads into unemployment and to catch up the performance of its main rivals.

Critics of the government's policies argued that the structural foundations of the recovery remained very weak. Particular concern was expressed about the position of manufacturing industry which suffered such severe contraction in 1979–81 and did not regain its 1973 level until 1989.

This concern was forcibly expressed in the report from the House of Lords Select Committee on Overseas Trade, published in 1985. The Select Committee was set up to

Table 7.3 Productivity in major OECD countries

	Total factor productivity			Labour productivity		
	1960–73	1973–79	1979–91	1960–73	1973–79	1979–91
USA	1.6	−0.4	0.2	2.2	0.0	0.7
Japan	5.8	1.3	1.9	8.6	2.9	3.0
Germany	2.7	1.8	0.8	4.5	3.0	1.4
France	4.0	1.7	1.4	5.4	3.0	2.3
UK	2.3	0.6	1.3	3.6	1.6	1.9
OECD	3.1	0.6	0.9	4.5	1.6	1.6

Source: OECD, *Economic Outlook*, 53, June 1993.

consider the causes and implications of the deficit in the United Kingdom's balance of trade in manufactures.

The Committee noted that between 1963 and 1983 the UK had run a surplus of between £1.5 billion and £6 billion every year on manufactures. In 1984 the surplus had become a deficit of £4 billion. They attributed this change to the fall in manufacturing output of 14.5 per cent in 1980 and 1981. As a percentage of GDP manufacturing output decline in the UK fell from 28 per cent in 1972 to 21 per cent in 1983. Among similar economies only the UK suffered a sustained absolute fall in manufacturing in this period. Yet manufacturing remained very important to the UK economy because although it represented only one-fifth of all activity in the UK it provided 40 per cent of overseas earnings.

Britain had only been able to survive the contraction of manufacturing because of the contribution made by North Sea oil. Some economists argued that the contraction in manufacturing was made necessary by the existence of oil.[19] But no one disputed that in the long term Britain needed to retain and extend its manufacturing base. What concerned the House of Lords was that the contraction of manufacturing might make this much more difficult in future. Britain's share of exports of world manufactures which had stopped falling in the 1970s resumed its downward drift in the 1980s. In most major sectors import penetration was becoming more marked, and in some sectors previous trade surpluses were being turned into deficits.

The arguments presented by the Treasury to the Committee were summarised in its report. The Treasury took view that Britain was suffering a long-term decline in manufacturing both as a share of GDP and in the balance of trade in manufactures. In addition the impact of North Sea oil on the balance of payments made a further deterioration in the balance of trade in manufactured goods necessary. Otherwise Britain would have run very large current account surpluses. It was right that manufacturing rather than any other sector should contract to make way for oil because the comparative advantage of the UK in most sectors of manufacturing was weak.

The Treasury agreed that the recovery since 1981 had

produced an upturn in imports and a further deterioriation in the trade balance, but argued that the trade deficit in manufactures was not as important a measure of economic performance as output. Moreover, once the contribution of oil to the balance of payments began to decline there would be 'compensating adjustments'. Income from overseas assets built up during the oil years would increase and manufacturing would recover. New industries and new businesses would emerge. The task for government was not to plan in detail the future shape of the British economy, but to pursue macro-economic policies which favoured competitiveness and growth in all sectors, and did not attempt to give priority to any one.

The evenhandedness of the Treasury was entirely rejected by the House of Lords Select Committee. They argued that a sustainable growth in GDP was not possible without a favourable trade balance in manufactures. Many services were not tradable and could not fill the gap left by manufacturing. Many service industries were also highly dependent on manufacturing. Twenty per cent of all service industry output had manufacturing industry as its main customer.

The Committee rejected the idea that there was anything inevitable or automatic about the decline of manufacturing as a result of the windfall of North Sea oil. It was a deliberate policy choice to use the oil wealth to increase overseas investments, maintain a high pound, and run down manufacturing. The Committee believed this policy to be a mistake. There was no guarantee that there could be a spontaneous rebirth of manufacturing at some point in the future. The costs of re-entry might be prohibitive once overseas markets were lost and an integrated manufacturing base was destroyed. There was no guarantee either that Britain could suddenly become competitive in new industries. The Committee pointed to the example of the information technology sector which was expected to be in substantial deficit by 1990.

The Committee's conclusion was stark and pessimistic about the future:

> The Committee's view is that the continuing deficit in the balance of trade in manufactures is a symptom of the

decline in Britain's manufacturing capacity on the one hand and of the poor competitiveness of important areas of manufacturing on the other. Unless the climate is changed so that the manufacturing base is enlarged and steps are taken to ensure that import penetration is combatted and that manufactured exports are stimulated, as the oil revenues diminish the country will experience adverse effects which will worsen with time. These will include

i. a contraction of manufacturing to the point where the successful continuation of much of manufacturing activity is put at risk

ii. an irreplaceable loss of GDP

iii. an adverse balance of payments of such proportions that severely deflationary measures will be needed

iv. lower tax revenue for public spending on welfare, defence and other areas

v. higher unemployment with little prospect of reducing it

vi. the economy stagnating and inflation rising driven up by a falling exchange rate.[20]

Given this grim litany it hardly came as a surprise that the Committee should warn that if these dangers were not recognised and tackled there could be 'a devastating effect on the future economic and political stability of the nation'.

The government refused to recognise that there were such dangers. The fears of the Committee it thought were entirely illusory.

Many economists, however, broadly shared the Committee's view. Most Keynesians had believed the British economy would not recover spontaneously from the slump of 1979–81. The sustained economic recovery after 1982 caught many by surprise and appeared to vindicate the monetarist claim that sustainable non-inflationary growth was possible if monetarist prescriptions were followed. With the difficulties which the boom ran into after 1987, however, the Keynesian critics came back into their own.

In the 1970s Wynne Godley and the Cambridge Economic Policy Group had argued that Britain's economic problem was a structural one and could only be cured by structural means.[21] The heart of the problem was an economy whose industrial base was so weak that whenever demand expanded beyond a certain point it could not be satisfied by domestic production and led to a sharply increased deficit. Governments had repeatedly dealt with this problem by financial means, deflating the economy to reduce demand, which also had the effect of weakening business confidence and reducing investment.

From this perspective the recovery of the 1980s appears a re-run on a larger scale of the policy cycle and mistakes of the 1960s. An expansion driven by consumer demand and fuelled by a massive credit expansion and substantial tax cuts produced faster rates of growth than were achieved even during the Barber boom of 1972–3, but resulted in a record balance of payments deficit of £15 billion in 1988, coupled with the re-emergence of inflationary pressures and a resurgence of labour unrest. The basic cause of the problem according to the Cambridge analysis was that the British economy was simply not productive enough. It could not generate sufficient exports to ensure continuous economic growth, full employment of resources, and a broad balance in its trade. Every economic expansion was brought to a halt by a deterioration in the trade balance.

The supply-side policies of the Conservatives did little to remedy this problem. By encouraging indifference to the fate of manufacturing they helped to make the problem more acute. The level of investment in manufacturing in the 1980s was below even the level achieved in the 1970s. The problem was hidden for a while when the economy was growing smoothly, but it reappeared larger than even at the end of the 1980s.[22] The Thatcher government had presided over a doubling of imports while exports had risen by only 50 per cent.

This analysis has been given its most precise formulation by two other Cambridge economists, Bob Rowthorn and John Wells.[23] They analyse three scenarios for a return to full employment by the year 2025; a green scenario, and a supergrowth scenario.

In the green scenario, GDP is only 26 per cent higher in 2025 than in 1985. Productivity growth of 1.4 per cent per annum has been used almost entirely to reduce hours worked rather than to boost output and consumption.

In the growth scenario, the economy expands at the rate achieved by the UK economy between 1950 and 1973. With productivity increasing at 2 per cent per annum, GDP would be 178 per cent above the 1985 level.

In the supergrowth scenario, the economy grows at 4 per cent a year. By 2025 GDP is 450 per cent above its 1985 level and productivity is 350 per cent higher.

Each of these scenarios has different consequences for the balance of payments. The green scenario has only modest consequences for the balance of payments, but is the least likely to be realised because of its radical implications for the way the economy is organised. In the growth and supergrowth scenarios imports would increase rapidly and could only be financed if there were a large increase in exports of manufactures. For the growth scenario the UK would need a surplus in its trade on manufactures of £3 billion per annum by 2005 and £8 billion per annum by 2025. For the supergrowth scenario the surplus required would be £6 billion and £13 billion per annum.

The inescapable conclusion which Rowthorn and Wells draw from their analysis is that Britain needs a large and growing surplus in its trade on manufactures if it is to sustain an expanding economy at full employment. They note that the most likely scenario, the growth scenario, is not predicting an economic miracle; it merely reproduces the UK performance of the 1960s. But even this fairly modest ambition is seen to require a very large improvement in the present ability of the manufacturing sector to earn a surplus on its trade.

From this perspective the 1980s recovery appears to have very shallow roots, because it is unsustainable. It has been associated with a sharp deterioration in the manufacturing trade balance, not an improvement. The scrapping of so much manufacturing capacity during the 1980s may have created a more efficient manufacturing sector, but one that is perilously small for the role it needs to perform for the UK economy.

To remedy this situation would require a major programme of investment to increase industrial capacity, diverting scarce resources from other potential uses, notably consumption and social investment. Such austerity policies would be politically unpalatable, since they would involve not just a short sharp shock but a prolonged period of reconstruction. The Thatcher government may have weakened the trade unions and other producer interests for a time. But it did little to challenge the tax privileges and consumption expections of major consumer interests. It protected their privileges and fuelled their expectations, and was richly rewarded electorally. Despite its rhetoric it did not face the majority of the population with hard choices, still less with hard times. Those who bore the brunt of the policies and suffered poverty and unemployment were a minority, and could safely be ignored.

Scepticism about the claims made for the economic recovery is often rooted in a view of how the economy works which places much less faith in the spontaneous powers of the market to regenerate the British economy. The poor performance of the British economy is seen as an institutional failure, the failure to develop the kind of 'regulative intelligence' for the economy which other countries have achieved through the forging of close relationships between the state, finance, industry and labour.[24] The nature of those relationships in Britain have prevented the emergence of a viable corporatism and have led consistently to the subordination of an independent manufacturing interest to the dominant financial interest of the City and British transnational companies.

From this standpoint the Thatcher decade of the 1980s represented no revolution, and only a partial break with what went before. It was, rather, one further triumph for the financial and commercial strategy to which the British state has always been wedded. What the Thatcher years achieved was the dismantling of many of the collectivist institutions of the Fordist era in Britain. But nothing was put in their place.

The economic recovery in the 1980s did very little to remedy the deficiencies in investment, in training, and in research that had long hindered the performance of the manufacturing sector in Britain. As a result many economists concluded that there was only likely to be a marginal improvement in Britain's relative economic performance as a result of the supply-side reforms of the 1980s. This judgement was confirmed by the sudden deterioration of the trade

Table 7.4 Inflation: consumer prices percentage changes at average annual rate

	Average 1971–80	1980–9	1990	1991	1992
United States	8.2	4.6	5.4	4.2	3.0
Japan	9.3	1.9	3.1	3.3	1.7
Germany	5.1	2.6	2.7	3.5	4.0
France	10.1	6.6	3.4	3.2	2.4
UK	14.2	6.2	9.5	5.9	3.7
OECD	9.8	5.7	5.8	5.2	4.0

Source: OECD, *Economic Outlook*, 53, June 1993.

balance in 1988 and 1989, the rise of inflation (see Table 7.4) and the renewed plunge into recession in 1990. The oil wealth had been spent, but there were few signs of a lasting improvement in the competitiveness of Britain's leading economic sectors.[25]

7.4 The criteria for success

The record of the Thatcher government in the 1980s can also be analysed in terms of the three strategic political economy perspectives on decline outlined in Chapter 1. How far have the policies of the Thatcher government succeeded in tackling the problems identified in the four theses of decline?

As might be expected the Conservative record appears best when evaluated in the light of the market perspective. The government moved some way to increasing the openness of the British economy through its abolition of exchange controls, its hostility to many forms of industrial protectionism and subsidy, and the encouragement it gave to inward investment by transnational companies. Its economic strategy was directed to providing the most favourable environment possible in terms of labour costs, local taxes, and state aid in order to make Britain a more attractive site for transnational investment than comparable economies in the European Community.

The exposure of the British economy to greater international competition was one of the most important successes of government policy in the 1980s. Substantial protection continued initially for sectors such as defence, agriculture and even coal. But by the end of the decade even these sectors were being market tested. The doubts some ministers retained about the wisdom of allowing all production decisions to be decided by comparative advantage had largely disappeared. The Major Government continued and extended the principle, most notably in the rapid rundown of the coal industry announced in 1992, the defence cuts, and the government's support for the reduction of agricultural subsidies in the 1993 GATT agreement.

Internally the supply-side policies made market disciplines more important throughout the economy by dismantling corporatist structures, weakening trade unions, and containing public spending. Industrial conflict declined and the quality of management improved. The government made efforts to promote an enterprise culture through a mixture of exhortation, tax cuts and institutional reform.

From the market standpoint many of the changes were limited and tentative. They did not launch any great cultural revolution. The gains were piecemeal and cumulative. Some saw this as a virtue and as part of the process whereby the whole framework within which people made choices and formed attitudes would be transformed. Others worried that too little would be achieved before a swing of the political pendulum brought a return to collectivist policies.

Least change of all was registered in the organisation of the political system itself. The government displaced some distributional coalitions but it reinforced others. It showed no interest in constitutional reform to impose permanent limits on government. It made full use of the powers of the British state to push through many measures which lacked popular support. It turned out to be a government which rolled the state back in some areas and rolled it forward in others. It deomonstrated how few obstacles the old constitutional state in Britain placed in the way of a government determined to exercise its powers to the full and push through controversial legislation.

So long as these powers were in the hands of those who

sought to extend the role of markets they might seem tolerable, but there was no guarantee either that the Conservatives could continue to win elections indefinitely, or that the free market wing would continue to dominate the party as it had done under Margaret Thatcher's leadership.

From the state and class perspectives on British decline the assessment of the Thatcher record is much less favourable. It appears far more as continuity with the past than a radical break with it, liquidating some of the manifestations of Britain's backwardness but either failing to tackle many of the structural reasons for Britain's decline, or in some cases reinforcing them.

On each of the four theses on decline the Thatcher record is found to have major deficiencies as a strategy for modernisation. Far from using the opportunity of the 1980s and the opportunities for European co-operation as a means for finally ridding Britain of the imperial legacy of its world role, the Thatcher government chose to reaffirm that the Atlantic relationship with the United States remained the lynchpin of Britain's foreign policy. By the end of the 1980s there were still many areas where Britain appeared to be clinging to aspects of its former world role and was reluctant to accept the reality of its position in the post-imperial world order. The troubled relationship with the European Community was the clearest example, but so too was the continuing level of British defence spending, and the resulting bias of spending on research and development towards military projects.

In a powerful polemic against what he calls the 'declinist' literature[26] David Edgerton has argued that Britain always was a developmental state, and always did attach a high importance to technological and industrial development, only that its energies and priorities were aimed primarily at building a strong military-industrial complex to service the needs of Britain's imperial state and its world role. His view is an important corrective to that of Corelli Barnett, whose gloom about Britain's industrial performance is so unrelieved that it is sometimes difficult to understand how Britain managed to fight two world wars at all, still less to emerge on the winning side. But Edgerton exaggerates his own case. The key point in understanding British decline as a historical process is that the decline in competitiveness and the decline in world power were interlinked. It was precisely because the British state spent so much of its energies on defence industries like military aircraft that the needs of domestic industrial reconstruction were given a lower priority. It never was the case that all British industry was equally backward. Some sectors including the defence industries have always been world leaders. The argument about decline from the developmental state perspective was about the balance of the economy. The Thatcher Government did little to change that balance, and in important respects because of its renewed commitment to what remained of the world role of the imperial state it reinforced it.

No less serious from a state perspective was the failure of the Conservative government to tackle the supply-side problems that had prevented effective modernisation of the economy in the past.[27] The liberal ethos of British institutions which had so hindered the emergence of a developmental state was not shattered but further strengthened. The government turned away from the experiments with greater co-operation between the key institutional sectors of the economy. It gave no attention to forging new links between the financial sector and manufacturing. It abandoned attempts to build consensus around an industrial strategy and its industrial relations reforms were confined to a one-sided attempt to weaken the trade unions through new union laws. It did little to tackle the long-term structural problem of industrial relations in Britain – the low level of co-operation between management and shopfloor.

The cultural revolution which the government promoted was also limited. It proved more hostile to established British institutions than previous Conservative governments, but from a state perspective on Britain's decline what was require above all was a determined assault to raise the importance of manufacturing the production relative to finance and consumption.

In political matters the government was at its most conservative. It centralised power still further, withdrawing powers and legitimacy from local government and other public agencies to which power had been devolved. It resisted calls for constitutional reform except for a limited increase in the powers of parliamentary Select Committees. Political modernisation was thwarted.

From the class perspective also the apparent radicalism and the novelty of the Thatcher government's policies masked deeper continuities. The government remained tied to the logic of Britain's traditional foreign economic policy. The City's role was unquestioned; manufacturing again was sacrificed without scruple. The reconstruction of the British economy was guided by the priorities of the bloc of class interests that had for so long dominated Britain's metropolitan heartland and the policy of the British state. The accommodation with organised labour and all the institutions and policies which that had spawned over eighty years were stripped away to reveal once again the old constitutional state and the old commercial policy.[28]

Seen in this way, the Thatcherite project proposed only a limited modernisation. Some of the gains of the labour movement were rolled back, but the kind of class confrontation which a decisive restructuring of British capitalism would have required was avoided. Instead manufacturing industry was downgraded still further. It was found that profitability could be restored by opening the British economy and taking full advantage of the rentier and financial opportunities which the world market afforded. The special nature of British capitalism's relationship to the world economy was reinforced. The industrial power of the British working class was contained and its political influence marginalised, but little was done to remedy the cycle of low pay, low skill, low investment and low productivity in which many sectors had become caught.[29]

What the Thatcher government assailed most vigorously were the institutions and traditions of Labourism – which for long had been British Conservatism's ritual foe but at the same time one of its most dependable supports. The curtailment of the powers and responsibilities of local councils, the abolition of the metropolitan councils, the legislation to weaken unions, the (unsuccessful) attempt to stop the unions making financial contributions to the Labour party, the privatisation of public companies and services, and the denigration of public sector workers, all fit into this pattern.

Many Conservatives came to believe during the 1980s that socialism and the Labour movement could be permanently marginalised in British politics, particularly following the split in Labour's ranks in 1981 and the formation of the SDP. The fear that had mesmerised Conservatives since the 1920s that the next general election might produce a Labour government was lifted. The need to accommodate Labour and the interest of the Labour movement was openly repudiated. For many Conservatives the secret of Britain's recovery was simply this – the removal of Labour's veto.

7.5 The future of decline

The euphoria over Britain's economic recovery and Labour's continuing political eclipse at the time of the 1987 election soon faded. Familiar problems returned to trouble policy-makers: balance of payments deficits, inflation, industrial militancy, and pressure on sterling. As many government critics pointed out, an economy which so rapidly overheated, running up a record balance of payments deficit and generating inflation considerably above the OECD average when unemployment was still close to two million, could hardly be described as fundamentally sound. The ensuing recession confirmed that view.

The 1980s increasingly appears the end of an era rather than the beginning of a new one. Margaret Thatcher's resignation as Prime Minister in 1990 marked the end of the heroic period of Thatcherism and the end of perhaps the last political attempt to solve the problem of British 'decline'. At the same time the disintegration of the Soviet Union and the collapse of communism signalled the beginning of a new era for the world economy.

Yet some things did change irreversibly during the 1980s. During the decade a watershed was crossed and some important political questions resolved. The national protectionist option was pushed once more to the margins of British politics, perhaps permanently. Three general election victories for the Conservatives over a divided and increasingly demoralised Labour party ensured that it was the free market strategy which determined the agenda. By the time support for the Labour party began to revive in 1988–9 the party had abandoned all versions of the alternative economic strategy.[30] In its 1989 policy review it returned to its social democratic tradition and embraced economic policies which accepted capitalism, the profit motive, the role of markets, and the importance of competition and the consumer.

The key departure, however, was that the Labour leadership now accepted that the internationalisation of the British economy was irreversible. Labour conceded that economic management would have to proceed within the constraints imposed by Britain's membership of a regional grouping, the European Union, and by its wider involvement in the free movement of capital and goods in the world economy. If Britain was to prosper it would be as an integrated part of the world capitalist economy.

The plans devised at different times by both left and right for Britain to regain economic sovereignty within the world economy had depended on particular political structures – the British Empire and the British Labour movement. By the end of the 1980s the empire had disappeared and the Labour movement was a declining force. The basis for an independent and self-sufficient national economy within a capitalist world order had collapsed. By the end of the 1980s no substantial section of right or left opinion any longer supported generalised protection for the British economy.

The Thatcherite project was one particular strategy, whose origins lay in the 1970s, but which was powerfully re-shaped by the events and experiences of the 1980s. The objective of restoring the Conservatives' political hegemony was achieved, and so complete was Conservative dominance of British politics for a time that discussion of alternatives seemed unnecessary. But the Thatcherite project did not exhaust the options for modernising the British economy and making it competitive within the constraints of the world economy. It appeared more dominant than it really was because the main party of opposition remained divided over the merits of the alternative economic strategy and withdrawal from the European Community. But it was very important as a catalyst for change, not least for the change in the Labour party itself. It helped clear the ground by dismantling many established institutions and practices and by challenging entrenched attitudes.

Keith Middlemas has argued that one of the most important changes of the Thatcher years was that it moved decisively away from the tradition of the previous seventy-five years during which the state had acted as a broker between the three great economic submarkets – labour, industry and finance. The state was reorganised to achieve a smaller number of essential tasks, at less cost, with less conflict or disruption, and more under the control of party politicians.[31] The rules of the political game were rewritten, as the balance shifted to marginalise labour, and to prioritise the interest of finance and some sectors of industry. Middlemas' judgement is that after the Thatcher decade the state is closer to being effective as well as efficient although in relation to a narrower range of objectives.

The 1990s had a different agenda from the 1980s. It was centred around the shape of the new world economy, and the balance between regionalisation and globalisation, evident in the arguments over the future of the European Union and the North American Free Trade Association (NAFTA), over migration, over sovereignty and national identity, over new forms of democracy, and over the protection of the environment.

Within such a context the debate on decline became a debate about how a post-imperial and post-Labourist Britain can best survive within the capitalist world economy. By the end of the 1980s the two leading parties of the state offered alternative capitalist futures, less qualified than either had offered before. They differed on the degree of state involvement that was necessary to ensure the smoothest adaptation of the economy to international competition, to regulate markets, and to provide for the disadvantaged.

Among political parties with any prospects of commanding substantial electoral support only the Scottish Nationalists and the Green party articulated an alternative. The Greens offered a new version of the ideal of a socialist commonwealth, a transformed industrial society, a politics of moral absolutes and ultimate ends, which brought together elements of the peace movement, community activists, environmental groups, the anti-nuclear lobby, as well as many libertarian socialists.

By the end of the 1980s the crisis of the 1970s had been resolved through the imposition of the solutions favoured by the Thatcher government. Its success suggested that the long-term effects of the decline would continue to be manageable. The kingdom would not break up. The country would not become ungovernable. The reasons for its success also suggested, however, that the time was past when Britain might plausibly emerge once more as one of the leading capitalist industrial powers. The defeat of the national protectionist option in the 1980s implied that Britain was now relegated permanently to a secondary status within the hierarchy of capitalist states.

The national protectionist option might not have succeeded. There are many reasons for thinking that it would not. But it was perhaps the last attempt to forge a political will in Britain to overturn the political and ideological dominance of the financial/commercial interest, for so long the dominant bloc of capitalist interests in the British state. With the failure of the challenge certain consequences followed. Both parties sought to ensure that Britain would retain a continuing important role as a leading financial and trading centre. As an industrial centre activity would depend increasingly on Britain's ability to attract inward investment and production facilites from transnational companies. Neither party had a strategy for using state power to restore an integrated manufacturing sector in the United Kingdom.

Since the end of the 1940s the scope for national economic management has become more restricted, although it has certainly not vanished entirely.[32] But the acceleration of the pace of internationalisation in the 1970s and 1980s has a further implication. As economies became more interdependent so the measurement of the performance of national economies becomes less meaningful and the concept of a national decline more elusive.[33] As Britain becomes more integrated into the European Union the final end of Britain's long post-imperial era will approach, and with it the end of the era of decline.

In any scenarios of Britain's future the way in which the European Union develops is crucial. Two main possibilities are envisaged. In the first scenario the momentum towards greater European political and economic integration is maintained through the 1990s. The completion of the single market in 1992 is only the start of more far-reaching changes – economic and monetary union, the implementation of the social charter, and the emergence of more accountable and more powerful European state agencies.

The second scenario envisages little further economic integration beyond the completion of the internal market as the limit in the extent of European integration. Nation-states and national economies remain, and national governments still have substantial economic sovereignty to pursue whatever policies they deem appropriate. No new federal structures or executive state agencies are established. Europe remains decentralised. There is a set of unified markets but fragmented state authority.

Which of these two scenarios is more likely to be realised and which is the more desirable had already become fiercely contested within British politics by the time of the 1989 European elections and fuelled and debates on the Maastricht Treaty in 1993.[34] The veteran anti-Europeans of Left and Right are greatly diminished in number, but during the 1980s they received some new recruits, particularly from the New Right. Many market liberals had come to fear that economic and monetary union and the European social charter would introduce regulation and corporatist institutions across Europe. The result would be a much more tightly regulated and inflexible economy than was desirable. The survival of Britain's market experiment would be at risk.

What is at stake is the institutional character of European capitalism in the 1980s: whether it should be a free trade area with substantial economic sovereignty remaining with the national governments, or whether it should acquire the character of a developmental state, able to protect Europe's economic independence. British capital appears ambivalent. The leading transnationals and the leading financial houses want to reap the advantages of the single market. The City wants to be the major financial centre for the European Union after 1992. At the same time they do not want to be confined to operating within the EU. They want to retain their global reach. The City wants to be within Europe and outside it at the same time, just as it has for so long been inside yet outside the British economy. It does not want to be subservient to the needs of European industry. In this way many of the arguments that were once deployed at the national level look set to re-emerge at the European level.

In this contest the market solutions of the free economy strategy look more likely to dominate because of the rudimentary character of European state institutions and organisation. Unless this is remedied the European Union will be predominantly a large single market, a battleground for the world economy's leading transnational companies. Europe may enter the same path of development as Britain, ceding its economic independence and its ability to retain leading sectors in world economic development.

The Thatcher and Major governments vigorously urged their European partners to copy their policies of deregulation, privatisation, and free trade. Only the Thatcherite model, because it would open the European Union to full international competition, could assure Europe's prosperity. Such a policy if pursued would guarantee that Europe while remaining rich would evolve into a subordinate part of the world economy dominated by Japanese and American transnational companies. Only the German model with its emphasis on long-term investment, a highly skilled work-force and high social spending offers an alternative route. It has its supporters in Britain, in all parties.[35] But it faces formidable obstacles, in particular the absence of a European state.

Whichever model is realised it may become increasingly difficult to distinguish the economic performance of the British economy as a separate unit within the European Union. More and more of the parameters and the policies which determine economic performance will be decided at a European level. There will be substantial regional disparities and comparisons but these are unlikely to correspond to the boundaries of nation-states.

Many areas of Britain remain poorly equipped to compete within this new European economic space, but assistance is more likely to come in the future from action by European agencies or from other regional agencies than directly from national governments. A prospect is emerging in which the national level of policy-making may become less important, while the European level and the local level become more important. The Thatcher government tried to weaken the local level and block moves towards a stronger European level. But it is only likely to have delayed the process.

The possible emergence of new state structures at both regional and European level offer opportunities to Britain and the British left. The history of the decline and the shake-out imposed on manufacturing industry in the last two decades leaves Britain with more declining industrial regions than most other member states. Considerable scope exists for local economic strategies and partnerships between the public and private sectors to assist these regions.

Britain will also have some very rich regions and prosperous sectors. While the Westminster Parliament remains the central focus of British politics, the imbalance in Britain's territorial politics will be a source of instability. The Thatcher government handled the growing divisions between regions in the country by directing its appeal to groups which were employed and regions which were prosperous. It became increasingly remote from those areas of the country which had to endure the painful process of adjusting to the loss of major industries. The gulf between rich and poor widened under the Thatcher government, so did the gulf between regions. Electorally, however, the government was able to win sufficient seats in its electoral heartland in the South East to be able to ignore the loss of support in areas like Scotland and the declining industrial areas of the North.[36]

This kind of political management, rewarding the two-thirds of the electorate in secure jobs, at the expense of the one-third of unemployed and casual workers, was not unique to Britain's Conservative government. Governments of Right and Left throughout Europe practised it in the 1980s. Constructing an alternative electoral coalition that would bring forward a different set of economic and social priorities is no easy task.

The basis for a new radical politics exists in the new groups, identities and life-styles that have emerged in the last twenty years. The green movement is one sign of it. It has already had some success in shifting the policy argument about the relative merits of market and interventionist solutions in favour of more intervention and regulation in the environmental field. But it will be difficult for greens and socialists outside Labour's coalition to build an electoral coalition strong enough to interrupt the narrowly focused debate on policy between the two major parties.

The scope for radical politics of both left and right derives from the opportunities in Britain for political and cultural as well as economic modernisation. There has been growing awareness that Britain is viewed by many in Europe not just as economically backward, but politically and culturally backward also. The assumptions of superiority bred in the imperial era have been slow to weaken. But European integration is hastening the process.

If Britain's integration into Europe does progress, the pressure for institutional reform will intensify. Britain may emerge as a more typical European state, shedding in the process some of the burdens that have delayed its adaption in the past. Membership of the European Union might finally enable Britain to modernise successfully and lose the stigma of decline. If this happened it would be because Britain had successfully integrated itself within a regional economy whose main centre of gravity is elsewhere, not because Britain had once again re-emerged as a major economic and political power.[37]

Whatever its remaining problems Britain will still be part of one of the richest regional economies in the world. The imbalances within the European Union are negligible compared with the imbalances between the rich and poor regions of the world economy. The task of finding solutions to these imbalances and to the ecological problems associated with the present organisation of industrial activities will dominate politics in the 1990s and into the next century.

Notes and references

The purpose of these notes is partly to indicate the main sources used in writing this book, and partly to give a guide to further reading on its major themes.

Introduction

1. Carlo Cipolla (ed.), *The Economic Decline of Empires* (London: Methuen, 1971) p. 14.
2. Spoken by Ray Gunter, Minister of Labour, 1964–8.
3. W. A. P. Manser gives a scathing account of the obsession with the balance of payments in *Britain in Balance* (Harmondsworth: Penguin, 1973).
4. A phrase used by Roy Jenkins in 1975. The plural society he claimed was endangered because public spending had reached 60 per cent of GNP. Joel Barnett who was Chief Secretary to the Treasury at the time commented: 'It was a typically elegant phrase, if rendered more meaningless than might normally have been the case when in the following year we changed the definition of public expenditure, so as to reduce the percentage substantially.' Joel Barnett, *Inside the Treasury* (London: Deutsch, 1982) p. 80.
5. Striking examples of it may be found in Paul Einzig's book, *Decline and Fall* (London: Macmillan, 1967), and Robert Moss, *The Death of Democracy* (London: Abacus, 1975).
6. In a speech in 1979 subsequently published as a Centre for Policy Studies pamphlet.
7. See, for example, C. Barnett, *The Collapse of British Power* (London: Methuen, 1972); G. C. Allen, *The British Disease* (London: IEA, 1976); M. Wiener, *English Culture and the Decline of the Industrial Spirit, 1850–1980* (Cambridge University Press, 1981); C. Barnett, *The Audit of War* (London: Macmillan, 1986).

226

8. David Edgerton, *England and the Aeroplane* (London: Macmillan 1991); David Edgerton, 'Liberal Militarism and the British State', *New Left Review 185* January/February 1991, 138–69. Corelli Barnett's reply is contained in *New Left Review 187* May/June 1991, 143–4.
9. Between 1800 and 1970 world population tripled, and the quantity of manufacturing production rose 1730 times. See W W. Rostow, *The World Economy* (London: Macmillan 1978).
10. Charles Feinstein, 'The Benefits of Backwardness and the Costs of Continuity' in A. Graham (ed.), *Government and Economies in the Post-War World* (London: Routledge 1990) p. 291. When Britain actually began to fall behind continues to be disputed by historians. See Sidney Pollard, *Britain's Prime and Britain's Decline: the British Economy 1870–1914* (London: Arnold, 1989).
11. Joseph Chamberlain, *Imperial Union and Tariff Reform* (London: Grant Richards, 1903) p. 59.
12. For world system approaches see I. Wallerstein, *The Modern World System* (New York: Academic Press, 1974); S. Gill & D. Law, *The Global Political Economy* (Brighton: Harvester Wheatsheaf, 1988); Robert Cox, *Production, Power, and World Order* (New York: Columbia University Press, 1987). The approach taken in this book is discussed further in 'The Decline of Britain', *Contemporary Record*, 2:5 (Spring 1989) 18–23; 'From Empire to De-industrialisation: the problem of British development' in U. Ostergard (ed.), *Culture & History 9/10* (Copenhagen: Academic Press 1991) 85–104; 'Britain's Decline: Some Theoretical Issues', in M. Mann (ed.), *The Rise and Decline of the Nation-State* (Oxford: Blackwell 1990) 71–90.

Chapter 1: The hundred years' decline

1. Resignation speech in the House of Commons, 28 May 1930.
2. By 1960; two-thirds of the import trade of the industrialised countries were goods exchanged amongst themselves. By 1971 these were three-quarters. See A. Shonfield *et al.*, *Politics and Trade* (Oxford University Press, 1976) p. 103.
3. See S. Hymer, *The Multinational Corporation* (Cambridge University Press, 1979), and C. Tugendhat, *The Multinationals* (London: Eyre & Spottiswoode, 1971).
4. See P. Deane and W. A. Cole, *British Economic Growth* (Cambridge University Press, 1967), and W. W. Rostow, *The World Economy* (London: Macmillan, 1978) ch. 28.

5. The main issues between those emphasising temporary deficiencies in supply or demand and those emphasising more fundamental social and political obstacles to accumulation are well brought out in a debate between Bill Warren and Ernest Mandel, 'Recession and its Consequences', *New Left Review*, 87–88, September–December 1974, pp. 114–24. Most of Mandel's expectations were borne out by subsequent events.

6. E. Mandel, *The Second Slump* (London: New Left Books, 1978).

7. In the nineteenth century every boom terminated in a slump which enforced a restructuring of capital through bankruptcies and unemployment (often as much as 25 per cent of the labour force), and by a general fall in prices (sometimes as much as one-third), which in time made investment and expansion profitable once more. As the scale and complexity of capitalist production grew, so markets proved too unstable and too inflexible to create all the conditions necessary for profitable accumulation, and increasing reliance was placed on the state to provide them.

8. The nature of the long boom and the forces which undermined it are explored from different standpoints in E. Mandel, *Late Capitalism* (London: New Left Books, 1975), P. Sweezy and H. Magdoff, *The Dynamics of the Capitalist Economy* (New York: MR Press, 1972), and Rostow, *The World Economy*.

9. See Paul Mattick, *Marx and Keynes* (London: Merlin, 1969).

10. See M. Barratt-Brown, *The Economies of Imperialism* (Harmondsworth: Penguin, 1972).

11. United States policy after 1945 can be studied in D. Horowitz, *From Yalta to Vietnam* (Harmondsworth: Penguin, 1967), and R. Gardner, *Sterling Dollar Diplomacy* (Oxford University Press, 1956). See also B. Johnson, *The Politics of Money* (London: Murray, 1970).

12. The downfall of the dollar is analysed by R. Segal, *The Decline and Fall of the American Dollar* (New York: Bantam, 1974).

13. See the discussion in Paul Bullock and David Yaffe, 'Inflation, the Crisis and the Post-war Boom', *Revolutionary Communist*, nos 3–4, November 1975, pp. 1–45; and in Andrew Gamble and Paul Walton, *Capitalism in Crisis* (London: Macmillan, 1976).

14. This is discussed by Tom Nairn in 'Marxism and the Modern Janus', in *The Breakup of Britain* (London: New Left Books, 1977). See also A. Gerschenkron, *Economic Backwardness in Historical Perspective* (Harvard University Press, 1966).

15. There are two detailed studies of the reaction to the challenge: R. Heindel, *The American Impact on Great Britain, 1898–1914* (New York: Octagon, 1968), and R. J. S. Hoffmann, *Great Britain and*

the German Trade Rivalry, 1875–1914 (New York: Russell, 1964).

16. *Daily Mail*, 5 May 1901.
17. M. Wiener, *English Culture and the Decline of the Industrial Spirit, 1850–1980* (Cambridge University Press, 1981).
18. Sidney Pollard, *The Wasting of the British Economy* (London: Croom Helm, 1982).
19. Another symbolic expression of the declining importance of Britain in the world economy was the demotion of Britain from second to fifth in the order in which member countries are listed and surveyed in OECD statistics and reports.
20. For the calculations see *Labour Research*, January 1983, vol. 72, no. 1.
21. Prest and Coppock, *The UK Economy*, table 1.14, p. 50.
22. In *Saint Joan*.
23. A considerable anti-growth literature emerged in the 1970s. See, for example, Bernard Nossiter, *The Future that Works* (London: Deutsch, 1978), and E. Mishan, *The Costs of Economic Growth* (Harmondsworth: Penguin, 1969). The methodological problems of comparing the growth paths of different countries are examined in P. O'Brien and C. Keyder, *Economic Growth in Britain and France, 1780–1914* (London: Allen & Unwin, 1978).
24. See S. Gomulka, 'Britain's Slow Industrial Growth', in W. Beckerman (ed.), *Slow Growth in Britain* (Oxford University Press, 1979) pp. 166–93.
25. See D. McKie and C. Cook, *Election Guide* (London: Quartet, 1978) pp. 57–8.
26. F. Blackaby, *De-Industrialisation* (London: Heinemann, 1978) p. 243.
27. See R. Caves and L. B. Krause (eds), *Britain's Economic Performance* (Washington, DC: Brookings Institution) p. 136.
28. Central Policy Review Staff, *The Future of the British Car Industry* (London: CPRS, 1975).
29. C. F. Pratten, *Labour Productivity Differentials Within International Companies* (Department of Applied Economics, Cambridge University, 1976) pp. 5, 6.
30. F. E. Jones, 'Our Manufacturing Industry: The Missing £100 000 Million', *National Westminster Bank Review*, May 1978, pp. 8–17.
31. Second to the United States, which overtook Britain after 1945. See Rostow, *The World Economy*, ch. 7.
32. See index compiled by *Labour Research*, and published monthly in that journal. In June 1980 the index had only risen to 107 (1974 = 100).
33. The discrepancy between élite and popular perceptions of

decline has become a standard theme in the literature. See James Alt, *The Politics of Economic Decline* (Cambridge University Press, 1979).

34. Particularly important have been Andrew Shonfield, *British Economic Policy Since the War* (Harmondsworth: Penguin, 1958); W. A. P. Manser, *Britain in Balance* (Harmondsworth: Penguin 1971); and Stephen Blank, 'The Politics of Foreign Economic Policy', *International Organization*, vol. 31, no. 4, 1977, pp. 673–722.

35. R. C. O. Matthews, 'Why has Britain had Full Employment Since the War?' *Economic Journal*, vol. 78, Sept. 1968.

36. Manser, *Britain in Balance*.

37. W. Beckerman, *The Labour Government's Economic Record* (London: Duckworth, 1972). R. Caves *et al.*, *Britain's Economic Prospects* (London: Allen & Unwin, 1968).

38. M. Holmes, *Political Pressure and Economic Policy* (London: Butterworth, 1982).

39. This is most associated with the Cambridge Economic Policy Group. See also B. Gould *et al.*, *Monetarism or Prosperity* (London: Macmillan, 1981).

40. Jones, 'Our Manufacturing Industry – The Missing £100 000 Million', pp. 8–17.

41. An excellent survey of monetarism is provided by N. Bosanquet, *After the New Right* (London: Heinemann, 1983).

42. One variant of the unproductive public expenditure thesis is R. Bacon and W. Eltis, *Britain's Economic Problem: Too Few Producers* (London: Macmillan, 1978).

43. See, for example, F. Blackaby (ed.), *Demand Management* (Cambridge University Press, 1978) ch. 9.

44. S. Brittan and P. Lilley, *The Delusion of Incomes Policy* (London: Temple Smith, 1977).

45. S. Holland, *The Socialist Challenge* (London: Quartet, 1975).

46. B. Semmel, *Imperialism and Social Reform* (London: Allen & Unwin, 1960); G. R. Searle, *The Quest for National Efficiency* (Oxford University Press, 1971).

47. See the further discussion in Chapters 2 and 6. The way in which decline was perceived by the political élite before 1914 is the subject of an important study by Aaron Friedberg, *The Weary Titan* (Princeton University Press, 1988).

48. D. Cameron Watt, *Succeeding John Bull* (Cambridge University Press, 1984).

49. Stuart Hall and Bill Schwarz, 'State and Society, 1880–1930', in M. Langan and Bill Schwarz (eds), *Crises in the British State* (London: Hutchinson, 1985).

50. For an excellent analysis of the concept of Fordism, see Henk Overbeek, *Global Capitalism and Britain's Decline* (London: Unwin Hyman, 1989).
51. One of the influential accounts of the development of policy is Keith Middlemass, *Politics in Industrial Society* (London: Deutsch, 1979) The best short survey of the literature on decline is Alan Sked, *Britain's Decline* (Oxford: Blackwell, 1987).
52. For the crisis of the 1970s see especially Colin Leys, *Politics in Britain* (London: Verso, 1989); and David Coates and John Hillard (eds), *The Economic Decline of Modern Britain* (Brighton: Harvester, 1986).
53. W. A. P. Manser, *Britain in Balance* (Harmondsworth: Penguin, 1981).
54. R. Bacon and W. Eltis, *Britain's Economic Problem: Too few Producers* (London: Macmillan, 1978); IEA, *The Dilemmas of Government Expenditure* (London, IEA, 1976).
55. F. A. Hayek, *A Tiger by the Tail* (London: IEA, 1972).
56. Keith Joseph, *Stranded on the Middle Ground* (London: CPS, 1976).
57. M Olson, *The Rise and Decline of Nations* (Yale University Press, 1982).
58. S. Brittan, *The Economic Consequences of Democracy* (London: Temple Smith, 1977).
59. See Joseph, *Stranded on the Middle Ground*; and Corelli Barnett, *The Audit of War* (London: Macmillan, 1986).
60. Paul Kennedy, *The Rise and Fall of the Great Powers* (London: Unwin Hyman, 1988); Joel Krieger, *Reagan, Thatcher, and the Politics of Decline* (Cambridge: Polity, 1986).
61. Stephen Blank, 'The Politics of Foreign Economic Policy', *International Organisation*, vol. 31, no. 4, 1977, pp. 673–722; Andrew Shonfield, *British Economic Policy Since the War* (Harmondsworth: Penguin, 1958).
62. David Marquand, *The Unprincipled Society* (London: Cape, 1987); Andrew Schonfield, *Modern Capitalism* (Oxford University Press, 1964); Peter Hall, *Governing the Economy* (Cambridge: Polity, 1986); S. Pollard, *The Wasting of the British Economy* (London: Croom Helm, 1982).
63. D. Ashford, *Policy and Politics in Britain* (Oxford: Blackwell, 1981); S. E. Finer, *Adversary Politics and Electoral Reform* (London: Wigram, 1979); S. Beer, *Britain Against Itself* (New York: Norton, 1982).
64. D. Marquand, *The Unprincipled Society*.
65. M. Wiener, *English Culture and the Decline of the Industrial Spirit* (Cambridge University Press, 1981).

232   *Notes and references*

66. G. K. Ingham, *Capitalism Divided* (London: Macmillan, 1984); Colin Leys, 'Thatcherism and British Manufacturing: A Question of Hegemony', *New Left Review*, 151, 1985, pp. 5–25; Perry Anderson, 'The Figures of Descent', *New Left Review*, 161, 1987, pp. 20–77; Michael Barratt Brown, 'Away With All the Great Arches', *New Left Review*, 167, 1988, pp. 22–52; G. K. Ingham, 'Commercial Capital and British Development', *New Left Review*, 172, 1988, pp. 45–66.
67. Henk Overbeek, *Global Capitalism and Britain's Decline*; Ben Fine and Laurence Harris, *The Peculiarities of the British Economy* (London: Lawrence & Wishart, 1985).
68. Andrew Glyn and Bob Sutcliffe, *Workers, British Capitalism, and the Profits Squeeze* (Harmondsworth: Penguin, 1972); Andrew Glyn and John Harrison, *The British Economic Disaster* (London: Pluto, 1980); Coates and Hillard (eds), *The Economic Decline of Modern Britain*; T. Nichols, *The British Worker Question* (London: Routledge, 1986).
69. Tom Nairn, *The Breakup of Britain* (London: NLB, 1977).
70. Hall and Schwarz, 'State and Society, 1880–1930'.
71. Bob Jessop, 'The Dual Crisis of the State', in *Essays in the Theory of the State* (Cambridge: Polity, 1989).
72. Nairn, *The Breakup of Britain*.
73. Caves and Krause (eds), *Britain's Economic Performance*.

Chapter 2: The world island

1. *The Testament of Adolf Hitler* (London: Cassell, 1961) p. 34.
2. Wales was incorporated in England in 1536. Scotland and England were united by the Act of Union in 1701, so forming Great Britain. The United Kingdom was created in 1801 when the formal independence of the Irish Parliament was abolished, although Ireland had long been an English dependency.
3. This was certainly true for Scotland and England, though less true for Wales. Wales did have heavy industry, but has been described (by Eric Hobsbawm) as a 'mining annexe' of the British economy with its own distinctive class structure. Nevertheless it was still very different again from Ireland.
4. A very good and concise survey of Irish history is given by Liam de Paor, *Divided Ulster* (Harmondsworth: Penguin, 1971).
5. Four million emigrated from Ireland during the nineteenth century. Irish labour was employed in England particularly in building and railway construction.

6. The most important was the split in the Liberal party in 1886 over Gladstone's Home Rule Bill. Joseph Chamberlain led the breakaway Liberal Unionists into alliance with the Conservatives. The Union was to be a central political issue for the next twenty years, the Conservatives even adopting a new name, the Unionists, to emphasise its overriding importance. For Chamberlain's career see D. Judd, *Radical Joe* (London: Hamish Hamilton, 1977).

7. See A. T. Q. Stewart, *Ulster Crisis* (London: Faber, 1967).

8. The history and dynamics of this world economy have been explored in the major study by Immanuel Wallerstein, *The Modern World System* (New York: Academic Press, 1974).

9. This strategy is set out by Halford Mackinder (Geographer, Imperialist, Director of LSE, Unionist MP, Commissioner to the White forces during the Russian Civil War) in *Democratic Ideals and Reality* (London: Constable, 1919).

10. A judgement made by the Cambridge historian J. R. Seeley in his highly influential work *The Expansion of England* (London: Macmillan, 1909). The growth of this trade was not uniform and its expansion was generally interrupted by wars. There was a peace party in England which disliked the expense of the commercial policy because of the wars it involved. Nevertheless, it was the successful prosecution of the wars that laid the foundation for the periods of greatest expansion of trade. Some historians seem curiously blind to this. W. E. Minchinton in his Introduction to *The Growth of English Overseas Trade in the Seventeenth and Eighteenth Centuries* (London: Methuen, 1969) notes how trade always expanded fastest in times of peace and concludes that the idea that the commercial expansion began with Cromwell is mistaken. At the same time he notes the crucial steps that were taken under Cromwell which made the great expansion from 1660 to 1685 possible – the Navigation Acts, the war with Holland, and the seizure of Jamaica from Spain.

11. See B. Semmel, *The Rise of Free Trade Imperialism* (Cambridge University Press, 1970), the outstanding study of the subject. In 1815 the Empire covered some two million square miles with a population of approximately 100 million.

12. The Anti-Corn Law League, in which Cobden and Bright were leading members, never became strong enough to force through repeal against the united resistance of the landed class. Repeal came because of a split within this class. See N. McCord, *The Anti-Corn Law League, 1838–1846* (London: Allen & Unwin, 1968).

13. By the 1840s 3.4 million Britons were fed on foreign wheat.
14. See E. Hobsbawm, *Industry and Empire* (Harmondsworth: Penguin, 1969) ch. 7.
15. The most notorious use of British naval power to open markets was the Opium war of 1839–41. The Chinese Emperor had attempted to halt all trade, especially the trade in opium. At the conclusion of the war Hong Kong was handed over to Britain and China opened to trade and western penetration.
16. Tariffs rose very steeply after 1870. The general American tariff was 57 per cent by 1897. Russia imposed protective tariffs in 1877. France in 1878, Germany in 1879.
17. There were many different protectionist programmes. Some wanted a uniform tariff imposed on all imports, others wanted it imposed only against those countries that discriminated against British goods. The latter principle was often acceptable to pragmatic free traders, but it was the former that marked out the true tariff reformers, since the object was not primarily retaliation against those states that had themselves imposed tariffs, but a permanent protection of trade. Ideally they wanted the Empire to be a single free trade economic bloc protected by an external tariff barrier. Imperial preference was a second-best solution whereby every self-governing state of the Empire would impose its own external tariff but admit goods from other imperial countries at preferential rates. Protectionist sentiment began to stir in the 1880s, and the Tariff Reform League, established in 1903, was preceded by the Campaign for Fair Trade in the 1880s and such organisations as the United Empire Trade League.
18. The Free Trade doctrine is set out with great clarity in Richard Cobden's *Political Writings*, 2 vols (London: Ridgeway, 1867), and also in the *Sophismes Économiques* of Frederic Bastiat, which the Cobden Club (motto: Free Trade, Peace, Goodwill among Nations) reprinted at the height of the controversy on tariff reform under the title *Fallacies of Protection* (London: Cassell, 1909).
19. Jingoism was so named after the popular music hall song.
    We don't want to fight but by Jingo if we do,
    We've got the ships, we've got the men, we've got the money too.
20. A point emphasised by D. K. Fieldhouse, *Economics and Empire* (London: Weidenfeld & Nicolson, 1973).
21. Charles Dilke, the radical liberal politician, wrote a very influential book, *Greater Britain* (London: Macmillan, 1868), which set out these ideas. See also the earlier theories and

practical enterprises of Edward Gibbon Wakefield for middle-class settlement of the Empire, described in Semmel, *The Rise of Free Trade Imperialism.*

22. For the very varied ideology of imperialism see A. P. Thornton, *The Imperial Idea and its enemies* (London: Macmillan, 1957).

23. Before the Tariff Reform League was established this was already made embarrassingly clear at the Congress of the Chambers of Commerce of the Empire in 1896. The Dominions feared that any scheme of imperial free trade would be mainly to the advantage of British manufacturers. They wanted protection against British competition so as to establish their own industries. The Social Imperialists were forced to recognise this reluctance, but believed that if a strong enough political initiative were taken by Britain, all parts of the Empire would be prepared to make sacrifices for the sake of greater unity.

24. Although free trade triumphed over protection, the Liberals remained committed to the Empire and to a policy of free trade imperialism safeguarding Britain's colonial possessions while maintaining the openness of the world economy to British goods.

25. The Empire, though vast, was extremely undeveloped. Only Malaya was a significant source of supply of raw materials for the British economy, and even by 1914 the bulk of British investment still continued to flow to the more developed parts of the world economy. See S. Pollard, *The Development of the British Economy* (London: Arnold, 1969) pp. 19–23. The British empire was always very unlike the continental empires which America and Russia already had, and to which Germany aspired.

26. See A. Imlah, *Economic Elements in the Pax Britannica* (New York: Russell, 1958). The total foreign investments of Germany, France and Italy combined were £5500 million in 1914.

27. H. Mackinder, *Britain and the British Seas* (London: Heinemann, 1902) p. 343.

28. The British battle fleet had to be superior to the two next largest navies in the world combined. The arms race before 1914 was begun by the German decision to build a fleet. The German bourgeoisie, not the German aristocracy, was the class that pressed for this, with the explicit aim of challenging England. See David Calleo, *The German Problem Re-Considered* (Cambridge University Press, 1978) chs 3, 4.

29. Mackinder's strategic ideas had most influence not in Britain, but in Germany, on Haushofer. One of Haushofer's research assistants in the early 1920s was Rudolf Hess, shortly to spend some time in a prison cell with Adolph Hitler. In this way

Mackinder's ideas helped to shape the geopolitical thinking of Hitler.

30. This is most strongly argued by Corelli Barnett in his book, *The Collapse of British Power* (London: Methuen, 1972). He goes so far as to state: 'The British and imperial armies which marched and conquered in the latter half of the war . . . were not manifestations of British imperial power at a new zenith, as the British believed at the time and long afterwards, but only the illusion of it. They were instead manifestations of *American* power – and of the decline of England into a warrior satellite of the United States' (p. 592). This is an exaggeration, but it is a correction to the view of Britain as an equal ally and equal power in the war.

31. See D. Watt, *Personalities and Policies* (London: Longman, 1965), especially 'America and the Elite, 1895–1956'.

32. Joseph Chamberlain, when Colonial Secretary in the 1890s, briefly favoured a German alliance. British ties with Germany were close, particularly through the royal family. When the Great War broke out the British royal family changed their surname from Saxe-Coburg to Windsor (in 1917).

33. German war aims are discussed by Fritz Fischer, *Germany's Aims in the First World War* (London: Chatto & Windus, 1967), and by David Calleo, *The German Problem Re-Considered*.

34. Alexis de Tocqueville, *Journeys to England and Ireland* (1835).

Chapter 3: The unfinished revolution

1. Gaetano Mosca, *The Ruling Class* (New York: McGraw-Hill, 1939), p. 119.

2. Christopher Hill's many books on the civil war are outstanding. See particularly his book on Cromwell, *God's Englishman* (Harmondsworth: Penguin, 1972). See also Barrington Moore Jr, *Social Origins of Dictatorship and Democracy* (Harmondsworth: Penguin, 1969) ch. 1.

3. See the discussion in R. R. Palmer, *The Age of the Democratic Revolution* (Princeton University Press, 1959).

4. Adam Smith, *The Wealth of Nations* (London: Methuen, 1961) p. 26.

5. Two of its most noted practitioners were Lord Macaulay and Lord Acton. One of its most stringent critics was Herbert

Butterfield, *The Whig Interpretation of History* (London: Bell, 1931).

6. See the discussion by E. P. Thompson in *The Making of the English Working Class* (Harmondsworth: Penguin, 1969) part I, especially chs 4, 5.

7. The two key changes were the widening of the franchise and the move to free trade, which were accompanied by major administrative and financial reforms, particularly the re-introduction of income tax in the 1840s, and the Bank Act of 1844.

8. Joseph Schumpeter, *Capitalism, Socialism and Democracy* (London: Allen & Unwin, 1949) p. 229.

9. This theme has been most thoroughly explored by Tom Nairn in 'The Twilight of the British State', *New Left Review*, 101–2, February–April 1977.

10. The struggle over the Corn Laws was bitter and intense but it did not lead to any armed conflict. The landed interest accepted its defeat. An important reason for this undoubtedly lay in the high rentier incomes which monetary stability provided for all owners of property. See B. Johnson, *The Politics of Money* (London: Murray, 1970) p. 40.

11. Quoted in B. Semmel, *The Rise of Free Trade Imperialism* (Cambridge University Press, 1970) p. 8.

12. See the analysis of the public schools in Corelli Barnett, *The Collapse of British Power* (London: Methuen, 1971) ch. 2. He writes, for instance; 'The qualities imparted to this future ruling class by their education – probity, orthodoxy, romantic idealism, a strong sense of public responsibility – admirably fitted them for running the British Empire as they saw it; an unchanging institution of charitable purpose and assured income. Such qualities were however ill-suited to leading the Empire, a great business and strategic enterprise, through drastic internal reorganisations and against ferocious and unscrupulous competition' (p. 43). The shortcomings and social divisiveness of the public school system have long been major themes in the writing on British decline. A recent example is G. C. Allen, *The British Disease* (London: IEA, 1979).

13. The classic analysis was provided by Perry Anderson and Tom Nairn in their essays in *New Left Review* in the 1960s. See especially, Perry Anderson, 'Origins of the Present Crisis', *New Left Review*, 23, January–February 1964, and Tom Nairn, *The Breakup of Britain* (London: New Left Books, 1977).

14. Whether they found their way directly into industrial investment is uncertain. Historians tend to regard accumulated savings of

the new industrialists themselves as more important. But there is little doubt about the later utilisation of these accumulated hoards once industry had become securely established.

15. This history is vividly described by Thompson, *The Making of the English Working Class*, and by Karl Marx, *Capital*, vol. 1 (Harmondsworth: Penguin, 1976), particularly his chapters on the working day (ch. 10), and on machinery (ch. 15).

16. See, for example, the account in Eric Hobsbawm and G. Rude, *Captain Swing* (London: Lawrence & Wishart, 1969), and Eric Hobsbawm, *Labouring Men* (London: Weidenfeld & Nicholson, 1964).

17. For a review of the growth and the extent of state involvement in the nineteenth century see J. Brebner, '*Laissez-faire* and State Intervention in Nineteenth Century Britain', in E. Carus-Wilson (ed.), *Essays in Economic History* (London: Arnold, 1962) pp. 252–62.

18. For Chartism see G. D. H. Cole and R. W. Postgate, *The Common People* (London: Methuen, 1961) section V.

19. Karl Marx, 'The Chartists', *New York Daily Tribune*, 25 August 1852, reprinted in *Surveys from Exile* (Harmondsworth: Penguin, 1973) p. 264.

20. The increase in the total electorate was tiny; it rose from 510 000 to 720 000, 2.1 per cent to 3.3 per cent of the population.

21. Over three-quarters were estimated to belong to the manual working class. See Eric Hobsbawm, *Industry and Empire* (Harmondsworth: Penguin, 1969) pp. 154, 157–8. By 1850 more lived in cities than in the country and by 1881 2 out of 5 lived in the six giant conurbations.

22. Universal suffrage was slow in coming. The electorate was doubled in 1867 and again in 1885, when it stood at five million, still only 16 per cent of the population. In 1918 full manhood suffrage was conceded and votes for women over thirty. Votes for all women came in 1928.

23. See J. H. Goldthorpe, 'The Current Inflation: Towards a Sociological Account', in F. Hirsch and J. H. Goldthorpe (eds), *The Political Economy of Inflation* (London: Martin Robertson, 1978) pp. 186–213.

24. See Cole and Postgate, *The Common People*.

25. Richard Cobden, *Political Writings*, 2 vols (London: Ridgeway, 1867).

26. The rise in real wages after 1850 was significant. Trade-union rights were gradually extended. The 1871 Criminal Law Amendment Act and the 1875 Conspiracy and Protection of Property Act legalised trade unions.

27. See Raphael Samuel, 'The Workshop of the World', *History Workshop*, no. 3, Spring 1977, pp. 6–72.
28. See Hobsbawm, *Industry and Empire*, ch. 9, and P. Mathias, *The First Industrial Nation* (London: Methuen, 1969) ch. 15. Recent research has challenged this interpretation.
29. Custom and excise were indirect taxes levied on consumption, but with the move to free trade went the reintroduction of an income tax to make good the shortfall in revenue. This was to grow into the Treasury's most dependable source of revenue.
30. There were attempts to reform all these in the early decades of this century but no radical changes emerged.
31. The Liberals established their caucus, the National Liberal Federation, in 1877. The Birmingham Liberal Association, which became Chamberlain's power base, was founded in 1865.
32. See Ross McKibbin, *The Evolution of the Labour Party 1910–1924* (Oxford University Press, 1974).
33. In 1918 the Labour party still had only sixty-three seats compared with forty-two in 1910, but, mainly as a result of contesting many more constituencies, its share of the vote rose from 7.1 per cent of 22.2 per cent, and it received over two million votes.
34. The most important socialist element of the new programme was contained in Clause IV of the new constitution. See R. Miliband, *Parliamentary Socialism* (London: Merlin, 1961) for a discussion of its significance.
35. The only concession of its protectionist views was the policy of Safeguarding. See note 9 to Chapter 5.
36. See Maurice Cowling, *The Impact of Labour* (Cambridge University Press, 1970) for a painstaking analysis.
37. See Chapter 6 (pp. 162–5).
38. The three positions were represented in the Conservative party by, for example, Lord Birkenhead, Leo Amery, and Stanley Baldwin. See Amery's own account in *My Political Life* (London: Hutchinson, 1953).
39. All recent histories of the strike agree on this. See Patrick Renshaw, *The General Strike* (London: Eyre Methuen, 1975), and Margaret Morris, *The General Strike* (Harmondsworth: Penguin, 1976).
40. The *British Gazette*, for instance, declared: 'There can be no compromise of any kind. Either the country will break the General Strike or the General Strike will break the country.' When the strike was over Churchill urged conciliation.
41. See R. P. Arnot, *The General Strike* (London: Labour Research Department, 1926), and E. Burns, *Trade Councils in Action*

(London: Labour Research Department, 1926). There is little
doubt that the solidarity of the strikers was growing; more
workers were in fact out on strike the day after it was called off
than during the strike itself.

42. This paradox has given rise to an enormous literature. See
especially R. T. McKenzie and A. Silver, *Angels in Marble*
(London: Heinemann, 1968), and F. Parkin, 'Working Class
Conservatives: a Theory of Political Deviance', *British Journal of
Sociology*, vol. 18, no. 3, 1967, pp. 278–90.

43. The *Financial Times*, 6 May 1926.

44. The Trade Disputes Act (1927) outlawed sympathy and
political strikes, it restricted picketing, and it forced trade
unionists wishing to pay the political levy to the Labour party to
contract in. Formerly those wishing to avoid paying the levy had
had to contract out.

45. See D. Coates, *The Labour Party and the Struggle for Socialism*
(Cambridge University Press, 1975); Miliband, *Parliamentary
Socialism*; and T. Nairn, 'Anatomy of the Labour Party',
reprinted in R. Blackburn (ed.), *Revolution and Class Struggle*
(London: Fontana, 1977) pp. 314–73.

Chapter 4: Managing social democracy

1. J. M. Keynes, quoted by Robert Skidelsky, in C. Crouch (ed.),
State and Economy in Contemporary Capitalism (London: Croom
Helm, 1979) p. 58.

2. Many of these assets were acquired cheaply by American
companies. By 1945 one-quarter of British overseas assets worth
£1118 million had been sold. Sterling liabilities had increased
from £476 million to £3355 million, and British exports needed
to be raised by 75 per cent over pre-war levels to pay for
imports.

3. I have explored this transformation of the Conservative party in
The Conservative Nation (London: Routledge & Kegan Paul,
1974).

4. Labour's vote in 1945 was 47.8 per cent of the poll.

5. Labour's constitutional reforms were marginal – the business
and university votes were abolished, and the power of the House
of Lords to delay legislation was reduced from two years to one
year. The paucity of Labour's constitutional reforms showed the
extent to which the Labour leadership had become reconciled to
the existing state.

6. One of the fullest studies of the emergence of the consensus is Paul Addison's *The Road to 1945* (London: Cape, 1975).

7. Public spending stabilised at 45 per cent of GNP after 1945 compared with a level of around 25 per cent in the inter-war years. See A. Peacock and D. Wiseman, *The Growth of Public Expenditure in the UK* (London: Allen & Unwin, 1966).

8. After 1945 the bulk of public revenue was derived from direct taxes levied on the whole population. Before 1913 direct taxes accounted for only one-third of public revenue; by 1975 they accounted for three-fifths. For further discussion see Ian Gough, *The Political Economy of Welfare State* (London: Macmillan, 1979).

9. The main industries nationalised were the Bank of England (1946); the coal mines (1946); electricity (1947); gas (1948); railways (1948). They joined the Post Office, the airlines and the BBC. Iron and Steel was nationalised in 1949 but was denationalised in 1953, then renationalised in 1966.

10. The commitment to full employment made in the 1944 White Paper on Employment Policy. See Addison, *The Road to 1945*, pp. 243–6.

11. See the influential analysis by Samuel Beer, *Modern British Politics* (London: Faber, 1965), especially ch. 12; and the new study by Keith Middlemas, *Politics in Industrial Society* (London: Deutsch, 1979).

12. Commodity exports had fallen by one-third, and invisible exports and rentier incomes had greatly diminished.

13. Exports increased 77 per cent between 1946 and 1950. See S. Pollard, *The Development of the British Economy* (London: Arnold, 1969) p. 362.

14. Ibid, p. 376ff. Real output per head between 1937 and 1950 rose 25 per cent.

15. The period of pay restraint between 1948 and 1950 was the most successful incomes policy ever operated in Britain. Links between the unions and the Labour party were still close and the memories of wartime collaboration still strong.

16. The decision to rearm was announced in January 1951. The Labour government committed Britain to a £4700 million rearmament programme. This necessitated immediate increases in taxes, including health service charges, in the 1951 budget. The programme was scaled down by the Conservatives when they came into office.

17. Despite the damage to the market order the 1930s did see a considerable economic expansion. The part played in this by the protectionist policies is disputed. The high unemployment was concentrated in the older industries and older industrial areas.

The extent of the recovery should not, however, be overstated. For contrasting views see B. W. E. Alford, *Depression and Recovery: British Economic Growth 1918–1939* (London: Macmillan, 1972), and D. H. Aldcroft, 'Economic Growth in the InterWar Years: A Reassessment', *Economic History Review*, vol. XX, 1967.

18. See T. H. Marshall, *Citizenship and Social Class* (Cambridge University Press, 1950).

19. The literature on these themes has been unending since the end of the 1950s. Among the more significant are Anthony Sampson, *The Anatomy of Britain* (London: Hodder, 1961); M. Shanks, *The Stagnant Society* (Harmondsworth: Penguin, 1961); and more recently, G. C. Allen, *The British Disease* (London: IEA, 1976).

20. See Susan Strange, *Sterling and British Policy* (Oxford University Press, 1971).

21. Cordell Hull described the Ottawa agreements of 1932 as 'the greatest injury in a commercial way that has been inflicted on this country since I have been in public life'. Quoted by Julian Amery, *Joseph Chamberlain and the Tariff Reform Campaign* (London: Macmillan, 1969) p. 1034.

22. Quoted by D. Watt, *Personalities and Policies* (London: Longman, 1965) p. 61.

23. Convertibility meant that the pound should be convertible into other currencies, i.e., freely traded on the foreign exchange markets so giving maximum opportunity to American companies to sell their goods in England.

24. See R. N. Gardner, *Sterling-Dollar Diplomacy* (Oxford University Press, 1956) for a very full account of the negotiations. For an account which challenges conventional interpretations see Peter Burnham, *The Political Economy of Post-War Reconstruction* (London: Macmillan 1990).

25. The Marshall Aid programme scheduled $17 thousand million to finance European recovery.

26. See David Horowitz, *From Yalta to Vietnam* (Harmondsworth: Penguin, 1967).

27. Susan Strange, *Sterling and British Policy*; and Andrew Shonfield, *British Economic Policy Since the War* (Harmondsworth: Penguin, 1958).

28. In the 1960s British defence spending averaged 6 per cent of GNP, compared with 4.4 per cent in France, 3.6 per cent in Germany, 3.3 per cent in Italy, and 1.1 per cent in Japan. See Strange, *Strange and British Policy*, ch. 6.

29. Overseas military spending rose from £12 million in 1952 to £313 million in 1966.

30. Net overseas investment averaged £120 million in 1952–5, and £305 million in 1972–3.
31. W. B. Reddaway *et al.*, *Effects of UK Direct Investment Overseas* (Cambridge University Press, 1967).
32. W. A. P. Manser, *Britain in Balance* (Harmondsworth: Penguin, 1973).
33. See the discussion in Pollard, *The Development of the British Economy*, pp. 468ff
34. Susan Strange's analysis is the most detailed. See Strange, *Sterling and British Policy*. She distinguishes between top currency, master currency, and negotiated currency status for international currencies. Sterling had been a top currency before 1914; after 1945 it was still a master currency for the sterling area, but outside that, and even within part of the sterling area, it was becoming increasingly a negotiated currency, which meant that the terms of its use had to be negotiated between the holders and the British government.
35. See Pollard, *The Development of the British Economy*.
36. See, for example, R. Caves (ed.), *Britain's Economic Prospects* (London: Allen & Unwin, 1968) part I; and R. C. O. Matthews, 'Post-War Business Cycles in the UK', in M. Bronfenbrenner, *Is the Business Cycle Obsolete?* (New York: Wiley, 1969).
37. Cf. G. Turner, *Business in Britain* (London: Eyre & Spottiswoode, 1969) ch. 2.
38. Quoted by R. Heindel, *The American Impact on Great Britain, 1898–1914* (New York: Octagon, 1968) p. 215.
39. Only 20 per cent of assets were nationalised. See A. Rogow and P. Shore, *The Labour Government and British Industry* (Oxford: Blackwell, 1955).
40. A detailed review of this period is given by J. C. R. Dow, *The Management of the British Economy, 1945–60* (Cambridge University Press, 1964). See also, S. Brittan, *Steering the Economy* (Harmondsworth: Penguin, 1971); Alan Budd, *The Politics of Economic Planning* (London: Fontana, 1978); and J. Leruez, *Economic Planning and Policy in Britain* (London: Martin Robertson, 1975).
41. The scale of the immigration was smaller than the immigration into many other European economies. By 1961 there were 600 000 Commonwealth immigrants in the United Kingdom. By 1971 this had risen to 1.2 million. In 1962 the Commonwealth Immigration Act imposed the first set of restrictions on entry. These were tightened by further legislation in 1968, 1971 and 1979.
42. Governments were forced to attempt trade-offs between unemployment and inflation, and between growth and the balance

of payments, but the underlying trends were very favourable. Unemployment in particular was very low until after 1966.

43. The most obvious aspect was the satirical boom represented by television programmes like *That Was The Week That Was* and magazines like *Private Eye*. Of the great tide of ephemeral writing, the collection of essays edited by Arthur Koestler, *Suicide of a Nation* (London: Hutchinson, 1963), is representative. The economic problem over which some of its contributors agonised looks rather puny today.

44. The new enthusiasm for growth and supply-side management of the economy is traced by Samuel Brittan in *Steering the Economy*.

45. For the origins and fate of Labour's policies see W. Beckerman. *The Labour Government's Economic Record 1964–70* (London: Duckworth, 1972), and David Coates, *Labour in Power* (London: Longman, 1980) chs 4, 5.

46. F. Cripps, in F. Blackaby (ed.), *De-Industrialisation* (London: Heinemann, 1978) p. 170.

47. It is quite salutary now to read Harold Wilson's collection of speeches, *The New Britain* (Harmondsworth: Penguin, 1964), which was published as a Penguin Special in the run-up to the 1964 General Election, and to compare the plans with what actually transpired.

48. It began in 1969 and subsequently gave rise to the notion that pay rises were the chief factor driving inflation forward. But grave doubt was thrown on this by subsequent research. See D. Jackson *et al.*, *Do Trade Unions Cause Inflation?* (Cambridge University Press, 1971).

49. See Robin Blackburn, 'The Heath Government', *New Left Review*, vol. 70, 1971, pp. 3–26.

50. See David Calleo, *Britain's Future* (London: Hodder, 1968), for a survey of the arguments being used in the 1960s.

51. The main provisions of the act were specified legal rights for individuals; a concept of unfair industrial practices; a National Industrial Relations Court; registration of trade unions; and the granting of special powers to the Secretary of State for Employment to declare states of emergency and order ballots of the work-force in certain strikes.

52. The current account surplus was £437 million in 1969 and £631 million in 1970.

53. See B. Tew, *The Evolution of the International Monetary System 1945–77* (London: Hutchinson, 1977).

54. Between 1958 and 1967 the average annual loss of working days in the United Kingdom was 3 274 000. This rose to 10 136 000 between 1968 and 1977.

55. The level of unemployment that had been reached is generally regarded as the most important factor. See B. Sewill and R. Harris, *British Economic Policy 1970–74* (London: IEA, 1975).
56. The Industry Act (1972) increased the incentives for investment in all regions of the United Kingdom by offering free depreciation and an initial 50 per cent tax cut. It also made provision for grants to industry in exchange for state shareholdings.
57. See Samuel Brittan, *The Economic Consequences of Democracy* (London: Temple Smith, 1968). There was an orgy of speculation particularly amongst the fringe banks, but very little productive investment.
58. Heath's counter-inflation policy was extremely successful. Six million workers settled under Phase 3. Only the failure to accommodate the miners wrecked it.

Chapter 5: The sovereign market

1. Sir Keith Joseph, *Solving the Union Problem is the Key to Britain's Recovery* (London: Centre for Policy Studies, 1979), p. 5.
2. Grahame Thompson, 'The Relationship between the Financial and Industrial Sectors in the British Economy', *Economy and Society*, vol. 6, no 3, August 1977. It is emphasised by writers from many different schools, especially Andrew Shonfield, Susan Strange, Brian Johnson, Sidney Pollard and Tom Nairn.
3. It performed this role most notably when Montagu Norman was Governor, 1920–43. But the City has never needed a direct representative of its interests within Whitehall, in the manner of the CBI or TUC, partly because of the loose nature of the 'City', partly because the City outlook is so embedded in the Treasury and the Board of Trade, but mainly because the pressures brought to bear on governments by the decentralised workings of the financial markets have generally been quite sufficient to keep government policy within certain paths.
4. Repeal of the Corn Laws in 1846 did not spell immediate ruin for British agriculture. The 1850s and 1860s were a period of prosperity. The real decline came in the 1870s and 1880s when other sources of food made possible by the new railways and steamships began to be developed, particularly in North America. This coincided with the raising of protectionist barriers by many other states, leaving Britain by far the largest open market for surplus world food production. Acreage in

Britain under cultivation fell from 17.1 million in 1872 to 13.4 million in 1913. See A. Imlah, *Economic Elements in the Pax Britannica* (New York: Russell, 1958) p. 184.

5. Although the majority of MPs and still more of Cabinet Ministers continued to come from the landed aristocracy. See W. L. Guttsman, *The British Political Elite* (London: MacGibbon & Kee, 1963).

6. Support for free trade was strongest in the great export industries. The textile industry employed 1.5 million, coal 1 million, shipbuilding 1 million. There were 200 000 seamen. Only 100 000 by contrast were employed in the industry that was foremost in demanding protection, iron and steel. See B. Semmel, *Imperialism and Social Reform* (London: Allen & Unwin, 1960) ch. 7.

7. The most important measure was the Trade Disputes Act of 1906, which reversed several adverse legal judgements against trade unions, most notably the decision in the Taff Vale case of 1901. Henceforward unions were given crucial legal immunities which meant that they could not be held liable to employers or to third parties for damages which strikes necessarily caused.

8. Measured by the fairly crude yardstick of government expenditure as a proportion of GNP, state expenditure which had averaged approximately 12 per cent before 1914 and 25 per cent in the inter-war years rose during the Second World War to 60 per cent, falling back after 1945 to 45 per cent. It continued to fall during the 1950s until it reached 36 per cent in 1958, but then began rising again until it stabilised at around 50 per cent in the late 1960s and early 1970s. In 1975 with the impact of the recession it reached 57.9 per cent. For the overall growth of public expenditure see A. Peacock and J. Wiseman, *The Growth of Public Expenditure in the UK* (London: Allen & Unwin, 1966), and Ian Gough, *The Political Economy of the Welfare State* (London: Macmillan, 1979) ch. 5.

9. The government did retain a weakened form of protection known as Safeguarding, designed to protect British industries in their home markets from competition from protected industries abroad. But no duties were placed on food imports and the more ambitious schemes of imperial preference were not implemented, especially after Stanley Baldwin lost an election on the issue in 1923. In 1930 only 17 per cent of imports by value were dutiable, mostly by revenue duties. Protective duties only covered 2–3 per cent of imports. See S. Pollard, *The Development of the British Economy* (London: Arnold, 1969) p. 194.

10. What was most remarkable about the decision to return to the

gold standard in 1925 was the lack of coherent opposition to it, either from industrialists, the Labour movement, the civil service, politicians, or intellectuals. See S. Pollard, *The Gold Standard and Employment Policies between the Wars* (London: Methuen, 1970).

11. The May Committee was established in 1931 to advise the government on what economies it could find to balance the budget. Large increases in taxes were ruled out; so was an increase in government borrowing; so was a raid on the Sinking Fund; so the burden had to fall on spending. Because unemployment was rising so steeply the most obvious area for savings was the dole. The Committee proposed to cover the deficit of £120 million by increasing taxes by £24 million, and by making economies of £96 million, which included a cut in the dole of 20 per cent.

12. It split 9–11 and the nine opposed to the cuts made clear their intention to resign. The new National government implemented the May Report (although it only managed economies of £70 million), but it also cut the pay of all public employees including the armed forces. The resulting mutiny in the fleet at Invergordon caused the final avalanche of funds that pulled down sterling and the gold standard.

13. See, for instance Don Patinkin, *Money, Interest, and Prices* (New York: Harper & Row, 1965).

14. Social Democrats like Evan Durbin and Hugh Dalton were particularly attracted by Keynesian ideas, and it was the means by which many former Marxists, such as John Strachey, renewed their connection with the Labour party and adopted a perspective of a constitutional and peaceful transformation of capitalism into socialism. See especially John Strachey, *Contemporary Capitalism* (London: Gollancz, 1956).

15. Adherents of demand-pull blamed excess demand in product and labour markets for inflation. Adherents of cost-push pointed to the degree of monopoly exercised by companies and unions in determining prices and wage rates. For a general review see R. J. Ball (ed.), *Inflation* (Harmondsworth: Penguin, 1969).

16. For a general survey see Stuart Hall, 'The Great Moving Right Show', *Marxism Today*, January 1979.

17. Most recently the case against economic liberalism has been argued by Ian Gilmour, *Inside Right* (London: Hutchinson, 1977). But see also earlier arguments by Aubrey Jones, *The Pendulum of Politics* (London: Faber, 1946); and Quintin Hogg, *The Case for Conservatism* (Harmondsworth: Penguin, 1947).

18. See the detailed examination of Conservative policies by Nigel

Harris, *Competition and the Corporate Society* (London: Methuen, 1972).

19. For early history and a discussion of the role of the Bow Group in the Conservative party see Andrew Gamble, *The Conservative Nation* (London: Routledge & Kegan Paul, 1974) ch. 4.

20. The IEA was founded in 1957, since when it has published well over 250 papers, analysing questions of economic policy from a free market perspective. Its key figures are Ralph Harris and Arthur Seldon. I have briefly discussed its role and its main ideas in 'The Free Economy and the Strong State', *Socialist Register*, 1979.

21. See the analysis by Patrick Seyd, 'Factionalism in the 1970s', in Z. Layton Henry (ed.), *Conservative Party Politics* (London: Macmillan, 1980) pp. 231–43.

22. A detailed examination of the support he acquired is given by Douglas Schoen, *Enoch Powell and the Powellites* (London: Macmillan, 1977).

23. In the 1970–74 parliament he voted against the government on no fewer than 113 separate occasions. See Philip Norton, *Dissension in the House of Commons* (London: Macmillan, 1975).

24. For the circumstances of Thatcher's election see R. Behrens, *The Conservative Party From Heath to Thatcher* (Farnborough: Saxon House, 1980). Only two members of the Shadow Cabinet, apart from herself, are thought to have voted for her.

25. The division in the leadership which led to the issue of such vague and inconclusive policy documents was satirised by Peter Jay in 'All Things to All Tories', *The Times*, 7 October 1976.

26. Norman's career and attitudes are surveyed by Andrew Boyle, *Montagu Norman* (London: Cassell, 1967).

27. The intention of Operation Robot was to make sterling convertible to non-sterling holders at a floating exchange rate, while freezing certain sterling balances. See S. Brittan, *Steering the Economy* (Harmondsworth: Penguin, 1971) pp. 195–200.

28. I have discussed this at greater length in 'The Free Economy and the Strong State', *Socialist Register*, 1979. The most important statement of this position is to be found in F. A. Hayek, *The Constitution of Liberty* (London: Routledge & Kegan Paul, 1961).

29. The growth of public regulation in housing and the level of welfare benefits are particularly cited in addition to nationalisation. But the spread of trade unionist is blamed most of all.

30. Powell's views on the Common Market have been collected in *The Common Market: the Case Against* (Kingswood: Elliott Rightway Books, 1971).

31. For a clear exposition of the principles of monetarism see T. Congdon, *Monetarism* (London: Centre for Policy Studies, 1978), and Milton Friedman, *Inflation and Unemployment* (London: IEA, 1977).

32. Whether any such control of money supply is possible, and whether money supply can be exactly defined, has long been a matter of controversy. Grave doubts were expressed by the Radcliffe Committee in 1956. See R. S. Sayers, 'Monetary Thought and Monetary Policy in England', in H. G. Johnson (ed.), *Readings in British Monetary Economics* (Oxford University Press, 1972). The more coherent position in liberal political economy is to argue not for control of monetary aggregates, which have proved extremely hard to pin down and still involve a degree of macro-management of the economy, but to embrace the cause of sound money, as Enoch Powell does. Here the government does not need to worry about the wider money supply but merely has to concentrate upon balancing its own budget. But the commitment of modern monetarists to the principle of balanced budgets has always been rather less than wholehearted.

33. Hayek has suggested that even this power could be limited by making all national currencies legal tender, with the intention that good money would drive out bad and provide yet another means of subordinating government policy to the market order. See F. von Hayek, *The De-Nationalisation of Money* (London: IEA, 1976).

34. This is best expressed by F. A. Hayek, *A Tiger by the Tail* (London: IEA, 1972).

35. See R. Bacon and W. Eltis, *Britain's Economic Problem: Too Few Producers* (London: Macmillan, 1978) for this argument. But see also Gough, *The Political Economy of The Welfare State*, for an analysis of its limitations.

36. Crowding out became a fashionable doctrine in the late 1970s. See G. Pepper, *Too Much Money*, Hobart Paper no. 68 (London: IEA, 1976).

37. A 'public good' is a good whose consumption by one person does not diminish the amount available to others. Whether any 'public good' can be defined unambiguously and independently of individual preferences and perceptions without destroying the whole edifice of liberal economic theory is another question.

38. Enoch Powell, *Freedom and Reality* (Kingswood: Elliott Rightway Books, 1969) ch. 10.

39. This emerges in the doctrine of the national rate of unemployment which states that in any economy there is a level of unemployment

that cannot be reduced by expanding demand without at the same time increasing inflation. This natural rate exists partly because of the numbers of handicapped and 'unemployables', partly because of inefficiencies in the labour market which are caused by housing policies, trade union rules, government regulations on employment of women and children, minimum wage and maximum hour legislation. If pushed to its extreme the theory states that if workers were prepared to work for negative wages there would be no unemployment. For further clarification see J. Wood, *How Little Unemployment?*, Hobart Paper no. 65 (London: IEA, 1975).

40. This means that a market order cannot be sustained on the basis of the market itself. This leads to a double prescription – every state should be *laissez-faire* in relation to the exchanges and contracts between individuals, but interventionist when dealing with the conditions for making markets function.

41. Montagu Norman's hopes for the gold standard were one example. Recent speculation about a Currency Commission is another. This preference for fixed, eternal criteria to govern economic policy and reduce discretionary action has always been powerful. The monetary targets of the monetarists are only the latest example.

42. See Lord Hailsham, *The Dilemma of Democracy* (London: Collins, 1978), and Nevil Johnson, *In Search of the Constitution* (Oxford: Pergamon, 1977).

43. This conflict between the rationality of bureaucracy and the rationality of the market has been analysed by many as one of the chief strains in Western capitalist societies. See in particular Jürgen Habermas, *Legitimation Crisis* (London: Heinemann, 1977).

44. See the discussion of possible constitutional reforms in Samuel Brittan, *The Economic Consequences of Democracy* (London: Temple Smith, 1977).

Chapter 6: The enterprise state

1. Tony Benn, Interview with Eric Hobsbawm, *Marxism Today*, October 1980, p. 6.
2. Prominent among them was the economist, and intellectual opponent of Ricardo, Thomas Malthus. See B. Semmel, *The Rise of Free Trade Imperialism* (Cambridge University Press, 1970).
3. Friedrich List was born in Germany but spent many years in the

United States, and was also strongly influenced by the doctrines of the Saint-Simonians in France. His principal book was *The National System* (1856).

4. See M. E. Hirst, *Life of Friedrich List* (London: Smith, Elder, 1909).

5. The major study in B. Semmel, *Imperialism and Social Reform* (London: Allen & Unwin, 1960).

6. The last stand of the Social Imperialists, led by Leo Amery, was made at the Conservative Conference in the early 1950s. They were brushed aside. See Andrew Gamble, *The Conservative Nation* (London: Routledge & Kegan Paul, 1974) ch. 7.

7. Julian Amery, *Joseph Chamberlain and the Tariff Reform Campaign* (London: Macmillan, 1969) p. 998.

8. Joseph Chamberlain, quoted by Henry Page-Croft, *My Life of Strife* (London: Hutchinson 1948) p. 47. See also Chamberlain's series of speeches delivered in 1903, collected in *Imperial Union and Tariff Reform* (London: Grant Richards, 1903).

9. Their fears proved justified. When conscription was introduced in 1917, 10 per cent of young men were found to be totally unfit for service, 41.5 per cent had marked disabilities, 22 per cent had partial disabilities, and only one-third were completely fit. See E. Hobsbawm, *Industry and Empire* (Harmondsworth: Penguin, 1969) pp. 164–5.

10. What divided them from the Social Imperialists was not the need for greater state spending and collective provision, but how it was to be financed – out of progressive taxes on income or through regressive customs duties. There was a tension between the two principal parts of the Social Imperialist programme. They wanted tariffs to shut out foreign goods so that British industries could dominate both home and Empire markets; at the same time they were relying on revenue from the tariff to fund the measures that would promote collaboration between classes. This inevitably meant taxes on food. Even at the height of the free trade the imposition of tariffs for revenue purposes was accepted as quite legitimate by all parties, but with the increasing yield from income tax, and its obvious scope for extension, the importance of tariff revenues for funding the state had begun to diminish.

11. Leo Amery was particularly prominent in this group. See his account in *My Political Life, vol. I, England Before the Storm* (London: Hutchinson, 1953).

12. See Robert Skidelsky, *Oswald Mosley* (London: Macmillan, 1975) ch. 11.

13. The evidence of such overcapacity was striking. In the United

States in 1932 one-half of the total productive capacity of the economy was unused. See M. Flamant and J. Singer-Kerel, *Modern Economic Crises* (London: Barrie & Jenkins, 1968).

14. See *The Greater Britain* (London: British Union of Fascists, 1932) especially book 2.

15. The BUF failed to create a mass movement or to make any significant breakthrough, although Skidelsky has argued that it was the war not the British political culture that finally defeated it. 'Would British Fascism have done so disastrously at a general election in 1940 fought in the trough of a new depression?' Skidelsky, *Oswald Mosley*, p. 333.

16. Strong hostility to the Common Market was a major theme in the National Front's economic policies. See Martin Walker, 'The National Front', in H. M. Drucker (ed.), *Multi-party Britain* (London: Macmillan, 1979).

17. Powell's standpoint is shared by several committed economic liberals in the Conservative party. See, for example, John Biffen, *Political Office and Political Power* (London: Centre for Policy Studies, 1977).

18. Snowden threatened to resign when the government introduced the Import Duties Bill which imposed a general 10 per cent tariff, and he carried out his threat when the Ottawa agreements on imperial preference were negotiated.

19. See Skidelsky, *Oswald Mosley*, ch. 10, and his earlier study, *Politicians and the Slump* (Harmondsworth: Penguin, 1967). Mosley appealed for a time to a wide range of younger politicians from all parties, including John Strachey, Nye Bevan, Harold Macmillan and Robert Boothby. They were attracted by his new ideas and his personal dynamism. All abandoned their connections with him when his New party began to develop towards Fascism, which occurred once Mosley became convinced that he could not achieve what he sought through the existing party system.

20. Marxism had long been a formative influence on the Labour movement through, for example, William Morris and Eleanor Marx. It received enormous impetus from the Russian Revolution and from the formation of an independent Communist party in the 1920s. Some of the most important and widely read Marxist writings of the 1930s were the books of John Strachey. A British Marxist intellectual tradition began to form at this time.

21. The simple opposition between reform and revolution was never clear-cut. See Ralph Miliband, *Marxism and Politics* (Oxford University Press, 1977) for an examination of the problem.

22. Stafford Cripps became Minister of Economic Affairs in 1947,

but before a separate department could be established, Cripps became Chancellor of the Exchequer and his wider economic responsibilities were transferred with him to the Treasury. The Department of Economic Affairs, set up explicitly under George Brown to oversee the whole development of the national economy, including the work of the Treasury, was reduced to impotence after 1966, and abolished in 1969.

23. On trade, see, for example, the writings of one of the most influential intellectuals in the Labour Movement, G. D. H. Cole: for example, *Principles of Economic Planning* (London: Macmillan, 1935).

24. See E. Durbin, *The Politics of Democractic Socialism* (London: Routledge & Kegan Paul, 1940).

25. The most influential works were Anthony Crosland, *The Future of Socialism* (London: Cape, 1966), and John Strachey, *Contemporary Capitalism* (London: Gollancz, 1956).

26. The flavour of the programme is captured nowhere better than in the pages of Harold Wilson's *The New Britain* (Harmondsworth: Penguin, 1964).

27. By-election local government election losses were particularly severe. The government trailed the Conservatives by 24 percentage points in the Gallup poll in May 1968. Many Labour party activists had also been alienated by government support for the Americans in Vietnam, the tightening of immigration policy, and policies of pay-restraint and deflation.

28. The proposals were put forward in a White Paper (Cmnd 3888) *In Place of Strife* (London: HMSO, 1969). They were strongly opposed by the trade unions and by a considerable section of the Cabinet, and had to be withdrawn after the Whips had warned Wilson that the measure would split the party and might not pass the House of Commons.

29. Foremost among them were the women's movement, the campaign against the Vietnam War, and new tenants and community groups. The scope of the new movements are explored in Nigel Young, *An Infantile Disorder: Crisis and Decline of the New Left* (London: Routledge & Kegan Paul, 1977), and by David Widgery, *The Left in Britain* (Harmondsworth: Penguin, 1976). On the left-wing political parties see Peter Mair, in Drucker (ed.), *Multi-party Britain*.

30. An integral part of the New Left was not only the breaking down of old divisions and the birth of new movements, but the ending of the intellectual paralysis of Marxism which had been so marked a feature of the period of Stalinism and the Cold War. The renaissance of Marxism as a system of thought was shown

particularly clearly in Britain by the *New Left Review*, which established itself as a major international journal of Marxist theory, and by such new organisations as the Conference of Socialist Economists, which was established in 1970 and soon had more than 1000 members.

31. Its proposals which were based on the earlier 'social contract' between the trade unions and the Labour party included new legal safeguards for trade unions; price controls; a radical housing policy; the strengthening of public transport; a major redistribution of wealth; an end to prescription charges; an increase in pensions; industrial democracy; and the expansion of investment through the creation of a National Enterprise Board, controls on capital movements, and planning agreements.

32. The informal alliance between the TGWU headed by Jack Jones, and the AUEW headed by Hugh Scanlon, was the most notable expression of this shift.

33. During its 3½ years of office the Heath government declared five states of emergency: July 1970, national docks strike; December 1970, power station workers' strike; February 1972, miners' strike; August 1972, dockers' strike; November 1973, miners's strike.

34. Amongst their writings see particularly Michael Barratt Brown, *From Labourism to Socialism* (Nottingham: Spokesman, 1972), K. Coates and T. Topham, *The New Unionism* (London: Peter Owen, 1972), and Stuart Holland, *The Socialist Challenge* (London: Quartet, 1974).

35. Tony Benn's ideas are best studied in his collection of speeches, *Arguments for Socialism* (Harmondsworth: Penguin, 1980). See also his interview with Hobsbawm, *Marxism Today*, October 1980.

36. The Referendum campaign and results are analysed in David Butler and Uwe Kitzinger, *1975 Referendum* (London: Macmillan, 1976).

37. See David Coates, *Labour in Power* (London: Longman, 1980) for a full assessment.

38. See Crosland, *The Future of Socialism*.

39. In this sense the events of 1966 and 1976 reinforced the attitudes that had been shaped in 1931.

40. This wider conception of rights is most fully set out in T. H. Marshall, *Citizenship and Social Class* (Cambridge University Press, 1950).

41. See the evidence presented in John Westergaard and Henrietta Resler, *Class in a Capitalist Society* (Harmondsworth: Penguin, 1975); Peter Townsend, *Poverty in the UK* (Harmondsworth:

Penguin, 1979); and Frank Field *et al.*, *To Him Who Hath* (Harmondsworth: Penguin, 1977).

42. See, for example, the analysis put forward by Andrew Glyn and Bob Sutcliffe, *Workers, British Capitalism and the Profits Squeeze* (Harmondsworth: Penguin, 1972).

43. The most detailed advocacy of import controls has been made by the Cambridge Economic Policy Group. See their annual *Economic Policy Review* from 1975; also the summary of their position by Wynne Godley, 'Britain's Chronic Recession – Can Anything be Done?', in W. Beckerman, *Slow Growth in Britain* (London: Heinemann, 1978).

44. Ideas put forward most explicitly by the Cambridge Political Economy Group in their pamphlet *Britain's Economic Crisis* (Nottingham: Spokesman, 1975). See also the important study, *The Alternative Economic Strategy* by the CSE London Working Group (London: CSE, 1980).

45. The Industrial Reorganisation Corporation was set up by the Labour government in 1966 to encourage 'concentration and rationalisation and to promote the greater efficiency and international competitiveness of British industry'. It was abolished in 1971. The National Enterprise Board was established in 1974 but its power and funds were drastically reduced after the EEC Referendum in 1975, and its chief role became that of holding the government's shares in British Leyland and sponsoring a number of relatively small projects.

46. Interest rates had been held at 2 per cent during the 1930s, and despite the enormous pressure on demand they were held at that level in the 1940s so as to aid reconstruction.

47. Some of the more important statements on the Alternative Economic Strategy are The Cambridge Political Economy Group, *Britain's Economic Crisis*; CSE London Working Group, *The Alternative Economic Strategy*; Geoff Hodgson, *Socialist Economic Strategy*, Labour Party pamphlet, 1979, and Stuart Holland, *The Socialist Challenge*.

48. Among the critics are Andrew Glyn and John Harrison, *The British Economic Disaster* (London: Pluto, 1980); David Coates, *Labour in Power*; A. Cutler *et al.*, *Marx's 'Capital' and Capitalism Today*, vol. 2 (London: Routledge & Kegan Paul 1978) Conclusion; Alan Freeman, 'The Alternative Economic Strategy: A Critique', in CSE Conference Papers, 1980; and David Purdy's contribution to *Politics and Power 1* (London: Routledge and Kegan Paul, 1980).

49. Critics like Cutler *et al.*, *Marx's 'Capital'*, who assert this give a very selective account of the strategy.

50. See Glyn and Harrison, *The British Economic Disaster*, David Coates, *Labour in Power*; Alan Freeman, 'The Alternative Economic Strategy: A Critique'.
51. This line of argument is pursued particularly by Freeman, 'The Alternative Economic Strategy: A Critique'.

Chapter 7: The end of decline?

1. See Alan Walters, *Britain's Economic Renaissance* (Oxford University Press, 1986); Geoffrey Maynard, *The Economy Under Mrs Thatcher* (Oxford: Blackwell, 1988).
2. CUCO, *The Conservative Manifesto 1983*, p. 7.
3. Ibid, p. 18.
4. CUCO, *The Next Moves Forward* (1987) p. 4.
5. Hugo Young, *One of Us* (London: Macmillan, 1989) ch. 11. See also Ian Gilmour, *Britain Can Work* (Oxford: Martin Robertson, 1983).
6. See Paul Mosley, *The Making of Economic Policy* (Brighton: Harvester, 1984). The historical and theoretical significance of the shift from Keynesianism to monetarism is assessed by Simon Clarke in *Keynesianism, Monetarism, and the Crisis of the State* (Edward Elgar, 1988).
7. William Keegan, *Mrs Thatcher's Economic Experiment* (London: Allen Lane, 1984).
8. *The Times*, 13 June 1980.
9. For a more detailed analysis see Andrew Gamble, *The Free Economy and the Strong State* (London: Macmillan, 1988). See also, R. Jessop et al., *Thatcherism* (Cambridge: Polity Press, 1988).
10. Cento Veljanovski, *Selling the State* (London: Weidenfield, 1987); Andrew Gamble and Celia Wells (eds), *Thatcher's Law* (University of Wales Press, 1989); Cosmo Graham and Tony Prosser (eds), *Waiving the Rules* (Open University Press, 1988).
11. See Keith Dowding 'Government at the Centre' in Dunleavy P. et al. (eds), *Developments in British Politics 4* (London: Macmillan 1993) pp. 175–93.
12. Desmond King, 'The Conservatives and Training Policy 1979–1992; from a Tripartite to an Neo-Liberal Regime', *Political Studies* 41:2 1993, 214–35.
13. OECD, *Economic Survey 1987/88: UK* (OECD, July 1988) p. 8.
14. Ibid, p. 48.
15. Martin Holmes, *The First Thatcher Government* (Brighton: Wheatsheaf, 1985).

16. Nigel Lawson, *The British Experiment*, Fifth Mais Lecture, City University Business School, 18 June 1984.

17. Mancur Olson, *The Rise and Decline of Nations* (Yale University Press, 1982).

18. Geoffrey Maynard, *The Economy Under Mrs Thatcher.*

19. P. J. Forsyth and J. A. Kay, 'The Economic Implications of North Sea Oil Revenue,' *Fiscal Studies*, vol. 1, no. 3, July 1980, and 'Oil Revenues and Manufacturing Output', *Fiscal Studies*, vol. 2, no. 2, July 1981.

20. House of Lords, Select committee on Overseas Trade, Session 1984/5, Volume 1 Report (238–1), 30 July 1985, pp. 47–8.

21. See the Cambridge Economic Policy Group, *Economic Policy Review.*

22. Wynne Godley. 'The Mirage of Lawson's Supply-Side Miracle', *The Observer*, 2 April 1989. Godley pointed out that since 1982 imports of manufacturers had once again doubled while exports had risen by less than 50 per cent. He forecast that this would lead either to a sterling crisis or another severe bout of deflation. In either case the supply-side 'miracle' of 1982–7 would disappear. See also Ken Coutts and Wynne Godley, 'The British Economy Under Mrs Thatcher', *Political Quarterly*, vol. 60, no. 2, 1989, pp. 137–51. For an earlier negative verdict see C. F. Pratten, 'Mrs Thatcher's Economic Legacy', in K. Minogue and M. Biddiss (eds), *Thatcherism: Personality and Politics* (London: Macmillan, 1987).

23. R. Rowthorn and J. Wells, *De-industrialisation and Foreign Trade* (Cambridge University Press, 1987). See also the earlier collection of papers edited by Frank Blackaby, *De-industrialisation* (London: Heinemann, 1978), especially those by Ajit Singh and Alec Cairncross.

24. Perry Anderson, 'The Figures of Descent', *New Left Review*, 161, 1987, pp. 20–77.

25. Assessments of the economic policies of the Thatcher decade include Francis Green (ed.), *The Restructuring of the UK Economy* (London Harvester Wheatsheaf, 1989); Jonathan Michie (ed.), *The Economic Legacy 1979–1992* (London: Academic Press, 1992); Nigel Healey (ed.), *Britain's Economic Miracle: Myth or Reality* (London: Routledge, 1993); Stephen Wilks, 'Economic Policy', in P. Dunleavy *et al.* (eds.) *Developments in British Politics 4* (London: Macmillan, 1993) 221–45.

26. David Edgerton, *England and the Aeroplane* (London: Macmillan 1991); 'Liberal Militarism and the British State', *New Left Review 185* January–February 1991, 138–69.

27. Scott Newton and Dilwyn Porter, *Modernisation Frustrated*

(London: Unwin Hyman, 1988). See also David Marquand, *The Unprincipled Society* (London: Cape, 1987); Bernard Elbaum and William Lazonick (eds), *The Decline of the British Economy* (Oxford University Press, 1986), and Henrik Halkier, 'The Political Economy of Britain's Decline' in U. Ostergard (ed.), *Culture and History 9/10* (Copenhagen: Academic Press 1991) 105–36.

28. Perry Anderson, 'The Figures of Descent'.

29. Ben Fine and Laurence Harris, *The Peculiarities of the British Economy* (London: Lawrence & Wishart, 1985).

30. For different perspectives on Labour's evolution in the 1980s, see Paul Whiteley, *The Labour Party in Crisis* (London: Methuen, 1983); Barry Hindess, *Parliamentary Democracy and Socialist Politics* (London: Routledge, 1983); Geoff Hodgson, *Labour at the Crossroads* (London: Martin Robertson, 1981); Hilary Wainwright, *Labour: A Tale of Two Parties* (London: Hogarth, 1987); Eric Hobsbawm, *The Forward March of Labour Halted?* (London: Verso, 1981). See also Martin Smith and Jo Spear (eds), *The Changing Labour Party* (London: Routledge 1992).

31. Keith Middlemas, *Power, Competition, and the State: Vol. 3 The End of the post-war era: Britain since 1974* (London: Macmillan 1991).

32. Jim Tomlinson, *Can Governments Manage the Economy?*, Fabian Pamphlet 524 (London: Fabian Society, 1987).

33. Hugo Radice, 'The National Economy – a Keynesian Myth?', *Capital and Class*, 22, 1984, pp. 111–140.

34. David Baker, Andrew Gamble, and Steve Ludlam, 'Conservative Splits and European Integration', *Political Quarterly*, 64:4 (October–December 1993) 420–34.

35. Such a strategy is set out in Paul Hirst, *After Thatcher* (London: Collins, 1989).

36. Ron Martin and Peter Tyler, 'The Regional Legacy' in Jonathan Michie (ed.), *The Economic Legacy 1979–92*, 140–67.

37. John Grahl and Paul Teague, 'The Cost of Neo-Liberal Europe', *New Left Review*, 174, 1989, pp. 33–50.

Index